"In *Elusive Dawn*, author Gabriele Wills shows talent that is anything but elusive. Her skillfully crafted scenes populated by well-drawn characters will pull readers into the story and not let go until the very last page." - *Writer's Digest Magazine*

"*The Summer Before the Storm* by (written story that shows humanity f very wealthy to the poorest." – *Write*

"Both Muskoka Novels... are historic .... *Focus on Books – Gisela Kretzschmar*

"Gabriele Wills is as enterprising in the book world as she is adept in story-telling. A tribute to both these qualities is the fact that Muskoka Chautauqua selected *The Summer Before the Storm...* for its esteemed 2010 Reading Circle List." – *Dr. Patrick Boyer, QC, Muskoka Magazine*

"*The Summer Before the Storm* is a richly detailed, complex novel - one that will stay with you long after you've turned the last page." - *The Book Chick – Jonita Fex*

"Just like *The Summer Before the Storm*, *Elusive Dawn* had me riveted from the beginning. Once again Gabriele Wills has done an almost superhuman amount of research and has managed to combine her knowledge into an incredibly readable book about the horrors of war." - *The Book Chick – Jonita Fex*

"*The Summer Before the Storm* and *Elusive Dawn* are not only well written, suspenseful, and enjoyable, but also historically accurate." - *Arthur Bishop, WWII pilot and author, son of Billy Bishop, VC, Britain's top WWI Ace*

"Gabriele Wills' novels... all share one thing: they provide one of the best portraits of a particular era and the region in which they are set.... Small wonder that her many readers have exclaimed about each novel by this wonderful writer, 'I just couldn't put it down.'" - *Dr. R.B. Fleming, historian and biographer*

"You have created a masterpiece. I loved every moment..."

"I haven't been that emotionally invested in a story in many years."

"Once again, you have intertwined fact and fiction into a compelling story that educates and stirs emotion."

"I love your Muskoka novels. I attended the War Museum in Ottawa and with your characters in mind, I could see Chas flying high in his plane! Attaching a soul to the stories and pictures we looked at brought a whole new human meaning to me. It was no longer something we once learned about in school - it had a face, a life, a love and a tragedy."

"You have a way of drawing the reader into the lives and emotions of your characters.... I felt I was right there with them."

"I knew this novel was far above average when I found myself neglecting important business matters to sneak in another hour or two of reading."

"[*The Summer Before the Storm*] transports you into an era of privilege and decadence, which is depicted with such intimate detail and subtlety, I can't fathom how Wills achieved it short of having a secret time machine. The story is perfectly paced and beautifully told from the views of the wonderful characters, many of which I now consider cherished friends."

"What a masterpiece. What a talent. Yes, I cried.... It is truly great to read about our splendid history and you are a magnificent storyteller."

"When I read the Muskoka Novels I couldn't put the books down, and even though I've read them several times now I'm still unable to put them down. I am drawn into their world and I find myself still captivated by every detail."

"One of the things that really draws me to your novels is the rich social history that you have managed to incorporate."

"An exceptionally well-told story.... *A Place To Call Home* offers a delightful glimpse into Canada's past, told through characters who come to life and jump off the page." – *Writer's Digest Magazine*

"Once in a while a novel grabs the reader's attention from the opening pages to long after the final words have been savoured. Such is *A Place To Call Home*." - *Anne Forrest, NUACHT*

Under the Moon

Book 3 of "The Muskoka Novels"
by

Gabriele Wills

MIND
SHADOWS

Cover photos by Melanie Wills (DoubleHelixCreations.com)
Cover design by dubs & dash (d2-group.com)

Library and Archives Canada Cataloguing in Publication:

Wills, Gabriele, 1951-
    Under the moon / by Gabriele Wills.

(The Muskoka novels ; bk. 3)
ISBN 978-0-9732780-7-1

    I. Title. II. Series: Wills, Gabriele, 1951- . Muskoka novels ; bk. 3.

PS8595.I576U64 2012   C813'.6   C2012-903813-X

Comments are always appreciated at books@mindshadows.com

First Edition
Published by Mindshadows
Mindshadows.com

Foreword

Many thanks to the following generous people for research and other help: (Alphabetically) Kevin Austin (District Municipality of Muskoka); Harold Averill (University of Toronto Archives); Arthur Bishop (son of Billy Bishop); Dr. Patrick Boyer, QC; Sharon and Tim Butson (Butson Boats); Mary Beth Cavert (L.M Montgomery Literary Society); Cheryl, Louise, and Chris Cragg; Beverly Darville (Royal Canadian Yacht Club); Bill Dubs; Cathy Duck (Muskoka Lakes Public Library); Allen Flye (re: Harry Greening); Jeremy Fowler (Butson Boats); Marion Fry (archivist, Gravenhurst Public Library); Jeannette Gropp; Guelph Public Library; Andy Hughes; Jack Hutton and Linda Jackson-Hutton (Bala's Museum with Memories of Lucy Maud Montgomery); Kathleen James; Emily Lancaster (Archivist, Women's College Hospital); Laurie R. McLean; Tom McNiece; Derry Miller and family; Janice Palmer (Tiffany & Co.); Captain Randy Potts (Sunset Cruises); Bill Rathbun; Phil Simone; Tim Spence; Blair Stewart; Mary Storey (Director, Muskoka Steamship and Historical Society); Richard Tatley; Vic and Laurie Tavaszi; Robert Wills; the Reverend Fay Patterson-Willsie; Captain Ron Wolf (Palm Beach); Anne Wright. Thanks to "Perfessor" Bill Edwards for contributing a line to my lyrics for *Under the Moon.*

Special thanks to Amitav Dash of "dubs and dash" for creating the cover design, and for continued marketing and moral support.

I am deeply grateful to my family for believing in me, and for their enthusiastic support and unstinting help. This book would not be as rich without the thoughtful, creative input of my daughter and editor, Melanie Wills. She is my sounding board, who advises and guides me with wise as well as artistic suggestions. Once again, I'm delighted that one of her evocative photos graces the cover. My husband, John, as well as helping to edit, is my innovative e-guru - responsible for e-books, e-commerce, and e-marketing advice. Thanks, team!

This book is dedicated to my dear friend, the Reverend Fay Patterson-Willsie, and her family, at whose Mazengah Island cottage on Lake Rosseau I spent many delightful and memorable times during my youth, which inspired these Muskoka Novels.

The Islands

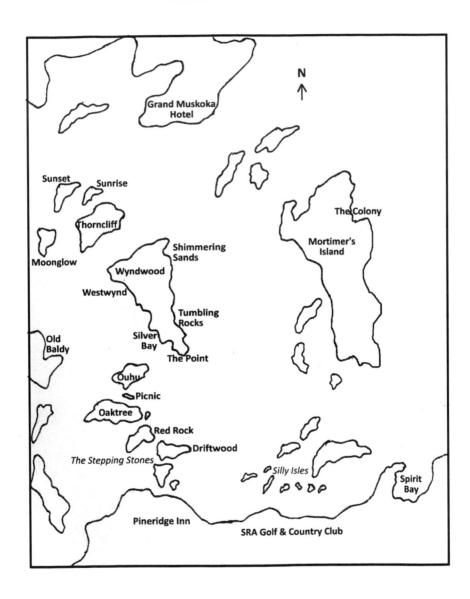

Cast of Characters
(ages in 1919 or when we first encounter them)

Wyndham Family: Wyndwood Island
The Point:
Ria (Victoria Wyndham) Thornton – 23
Chas (Charles) Thornton – 27 – her husband
Reggie Wyndham Thornton - their stillborn son
Sophie Thornton – 9 – their adopted daughter
Charlie Thornton – 3 – their adopted son
Alice Lambton – 17 – their ward
Augusta Wyndham – Ria's deceased grandmother
Johanna Verbruggen – nanny
Grayson – butler
Branwyn Grayson – housekeeper – Grayson's second wife
Gareth – Branwyn's son - gardener
Mrs. Hadley – cook
Tilda – maid, married to Patrick
Patrick – footman, married to Tilda

Silver Bay:
Richard Wyndham – Ria's uncle
Olivia Wyndham – Richard's wife
Zoë (Wyndham) Carlyle – 23 – their daughter – widow of Blake
  Carlyle
(Blake) Ethan Carlyle – 1 - Zoë and Blake's son
Max Wyndham – 23 – Zoë's twin
Lydia (Carrington) Wyndham – 23 – Max's wife
Esme Wyndham – 18 – Richard and Olivia's daughter
Rupert Wyndham – 15 – Richard and Olivia's son
Miles Wyndham – 13 - Richard and Olivia's son
Mrs. O'Rourke – cook

Westwynd:
James Wyndham – Ria's father
Helena (Parker) Wyndham – James's second wife
Cecilia Wyndham – 3 – their daughter
Jimmy Wyndham - 1 - their son

Tumbling Rocks:
Albert Wyndham – Ria's uncle
Irene (Partridge) Wyndham – Albert's second wife
Edgar Wyndham – 24 – Albert's son

Daphne (Carlyle) Wyndham – 21– Edgar's wife
Phoebe Wyndham – 21 – Albert's daughter
Henry Wyndham – 26 – Albert's son – in England
Dr. Lorna Partridge – Irene's daughter

Other Wyndhams:
Jack Wyndham – 26
Lizzie Wyndham – 22 – Jack's sister
Emily Wyndham Garrick – 20 - Jack's sister - married to Hugo
  Garrick
Claire Wyndham – 18 - Jack's sister
Marie Wyndham – their mother

Carlyle Family: Ouhu Island
Professor Thomas Carlyle - physicist
Hannah Carlyle – his wife - pharmacist
Dr. Ellie (Eleanor) Carlyle – 25 – their daughter
Derek Carlyle – 18 – their son - biologist
Dr. Blake Carlyle – their son – killed in France

Carrington Family: Red Rock Island
Justin Carrington – 26 - lawyer
Lady Antonia (Upton) Carrington – 25 – his wife
Lydia Carrington – his sister - married to Max Wyndham
Vivian Carrington – his sister - died on the *Lusitania*
Keir & Megan Shaughnessy – his grandparents

Delacourt Family: Thunderbird Island
Lyle Delacourt – 25 - industrialist
Blanche Delacourt – 22 – his sister
Belinda (Belle) Delacourt – 19 - his sister
Gregory Delacourt – 27 – his brother

Roland Family: Ravenshill
Howard Roland – Pittsburgh industrialist
Erika Roland – his wife
Troy Roland – 25 – their son - biochemist
Felix Roland – 24 - their son
Stu (Stuart) Roland – 20 - their son
Eugene Roland – 18 - their son
Kurt Roland – their son - killed in France

Seaford Family: Pineridge Inn
Stephen Seaford - 22 – mechanic and boat builder

Mac Seaford – 27 – his brother – boat builder
Jean Seaford – 29 - his sister
Nancy Seaford – 20 - his sister
Roy Seaford – his brother - killed at Passchendaele
Edith Seaford – their mother - innkeeper

Spencer Family: Driftwood Island
Freddie (Frederick) Spencer - 25 - architect
Martha (Randall) Spencer – Freddie's wife
Emma Spencer – 22 – his sister - lawyer
Arthur Spencer – 19 – his brother - journalist
Maud Spencer – 17 - his sister
Hazel Spencer – 14 - his sister
Archie Spencer – his brother - killed at Ypres
Senator Spencer – their father

Thornton Family: Thorncliff Island
Chas (Charles) Thornton – 27 - married to Ria Wyndham
Fliss (Felicity) Thornton – 20 – his sister
Rafe (Ralph) Thornton – 24 – his brother
Lady Sidonie (Dunston) Thornton – 25 – Rafe's wife
Marjorie Thornton – Chas's mother
J.D. Thornton - Chas's deceased father - financier

Other islanders:
Hugo Garrick – songwriter - married to Emily Wyndham
Martin Daventry - 20 - publisher
Esther Daventry – 24 - his sister
Lucy Daventry - 18 - his sister
Ted Lorimer – 21 – advertising executive
Adele Fremont - 22 – wealthy American
Marshal Fremont – 24 - wealthy American
Stanford Vandemeer – 23 - wealthy American
Frank Sheridan – 25 - wealthy American
Josiah Miller – foundry owner
Rosie Miller – his daughter
Bobby Miller – his deceased son
Luke Miller – illegitimate son of Bobby and Phoebe Wyndham

Port Darling:
Roderick Mayhew - caretaker
Sky Mayhew - his Ojibwa wife
Thomas Mayhew – 2 – their son
Audrey Carver - daughter of general store owner

Mercer – pharmacist
Trick (Patrick) Butcher – 21
Jake Butcher – his brother
Dr. Douglas McIvor

Others:
Silas Robbins – 25 - poet
Bertram (Bert) Cracknell - Chas's former RFC comrade
Colin Sutcliffe – patient at Sanatorium
William Kirkbride – poet
Mildred Kirkbride – his sister - teacher
Harry Bellinger – Ted Lorimer's friend
Dottie Bellinger – Harry's sister
Cliff Sinclair – Emma Spencer's fiancé - killed at the Somme
Laura Sinclair – his sister - lawyer working with Emma
Dr. Mainwaring - Medical Director of Lakeview Sanatorium
Anders Vandeburgh – NY photographer

England:
Lady Beatrice Kirkland - cousin of Ria's grandmother, Augusta
Major Lance Chadwick – wartime friend of Ria's
Christopher (Chris) Chadwick – his son – 16 in 1922
Philip Chadwick – his son – 14 in 1922

France:
Comte Étienne de Sauveterre – owns winery – 30 in 1922
Véronique de Sauveterre – his sister - French film star - 23 in 1922

Real People Mentioned or Appearing (Alphabetically):
Reverend Charles S. Applegath – founder of the Muskoka
    Assembly of the Canadian Chautauqua
William Barker, VC – Canada and the Commonwealth's most
    decorated war hero
Lord Max Beaverbrook - Canadian-born British press baron
Billy Bishop, VC – highest scoring British Ace with 72 victories –
    Canadian
Margaret (Burden) Bishop - his wife and John Eaton's cousin
George Boyer – newspaper publisher and one-time mayor of
    Bracebridge
Al Capone – American gangster
Bliss Carman - Canadian poet
Vernon & Irene Castle - ballroom dancers
Coco Chanel – French couturier

Winston Churchill – British politician
Cecil B. DeMille – Hollywood director
Herb Ditchburn - Muskoka boat-builder
Sir Arthur Conan Doyle – author of the Sherlock Holmes stories
Sir John Craig Eaton – son of the Eaton mercantile dynasty
Lady Flora Eaton – his wife
Edward, Prince of Wales – known as David to family and friends
F. Scott Fitzgerald – American author
Zelda Fitzgerald – his wife
Edsel Ford - President of the Ford Motor Company
Frank Jay Gould – wealthy American
Florence Gould – his third wife
Commodore Harry Greening – Canadian boat racer
Ernest Hemingway – American author
Hadley Hemingway – his first wife
Adolph Hitler – Nazi leader in Germany
A.Y. Jackson – Group of Seven painter
James Joyce – Irish author
Rudyard Kipling – British author
Charles Lindbergh – American aviator
Matisse – French artist
Wilson MacDonald – Canadian poet
Alan Arnett McLeod - one of Canada's three VC aviators
Bert Minett - Muskoka boat-builder
L.M. Montgomery (Mrs. Ewan Macdonald) – Canadian author
Molyneux – Parisian couturier
Oswald Mosley – British Fascist
Emily Murphy – first woman magistrate in the British Empire
Sara and Gerald Murphy - wealthy Americans
Sir Henry Pellatt – financier – built Casa Loma in Toronto
Picasso – Spanish artist
Cole Porter – American songwriter
Linda Porter – his wife
Ezra Pound – American poet
Sir Charles G.D. Roberts – Canadian poet
Norma Shearer – Canadian Hollywood star
Gertrude Stein – American ex-pat writer
Dr. Emily Stowe - Canada's first licensed female physician
Gloria Swanson – American actress
Tom Thomson – Canadian artist
Alice B. Toklas – partner of Gertrude Stein
Madeleine Vionnet – French fashion designer
Gar Wood – American boat racer

Muskoka
by Wilson MacDonald
(1880-1967)

(Excerpt)

In one forgotten cove on Tobin's shore
My frail canoe crawls up the crying sand;
And here I watch the lights of Windermere –
Strange lights the stars can never understand.
Here a forsaken dwelling evermore
Dreams of its kinder past,
While tides of moonbeams wash its broken doors;
And all its ancient order stands aghast
That any vagrant storm may enter here
Or any stranger wander on these floors.

Here once I came with one who softly leaned –
As softly as this moonlight – on my arm,
And we, together, climbed the groaning stair
In this old wreck of wood and felt alarm
When at our touch the slender flight careened;
And in the dark her hand
Came searching for my own, and I could feel
Her hair against my temples softly fanned.
And that was long ago: she still is fair,
But I am touched with wounds that cannot heal.

Part 1: 1919

Chapter 1

A barrage of thunder rolled down the lake and echoed menacingly in Ria's head. Startled out of the eerie twilight of nightmares, she was momentarily alarmed, but then realized she was safely at her beloved island home. It was only rain that clattered sharply on the cedar shingles overhead. Not lethal metal fragments from exploding bombs.

The hellish war was over, although it brutalized her dreams and was etched into her flesh.

They'd been at the summer cottage on Wyndwood for almost three weeks, but she wasn't yet accustomed to waking in her grandmother's old room rather than the girls' dorm she had shared with her cousins for the first eighteen years of her life. Unlike her cousin Phoebe, she didn't see or fear the ghost of Grandmother, and in fact, took some comfort from the vestiges of Augusta's life - even the chaise lounge where Grandmother had rested while Ria had been required to read to her as punishment for some misdemeanor. Sadly she recalled that they hadn't progressed far in the last book, Dickens' *Bleak House*, when Augusta had mysteriously fallen off a cliff to her death, that momentous summer of 1914.

Ria had been afraid that either mad Phoebe or ambitious Jack, their destitute, newfound cousin, had been responsible, but had dismissed both suspicions as ludicrous. Augusta had been tottery and stubborn, and should long ago have stopped walking the dangerously narrow path. Ria had been shocked to discover that her uncle Albert had dynamited that cliff face to protect Phoebe from a lunatic notion that she could fly from the ledge or be coerced by the menacing voices in her head to jump. A new path was now sandwiched between the sheer wall of granite and the lake where the murderous, ancient boulders lurked just beneath the surface. "Tumbling Rocks", Phoebe had christened the spot, and so her nearby family cottage had acquired that moniker.

Another blast of lightning was closer this time, and Ria rolled over to snuggle against Chas, thankful, as she was every morning, that he was beside her. But there was a moment of panic when she realized he wasn't. She sat up, trying to distinguish shapes that were just beginning to crystallize out of the smothering darkness.

The next brilliant flash of light caught and held him frozen for an instant before he melted again into obscurity. Ria slipped silently out of bed and joined him on their private screened porch. Because of the heat, they had left the French doors open and neither had bothered with night attire.

She slid her arm around him, glorying in his warmth and the smoothness of his firm muscles. "Are you in pain?" she asked as he embraced her. He was still recovering from the surgery that had fused his bullet-shattered knee. In a cast for four months, he had been out of it for only a few weeks. If this procedure didn't work, then there was no alternative but amputation.

"It's not so bad," he reassured her. It certainly wasn't like the pre-operative agony that had sometimes driven him to suicidal thoughts. The orthopaedic surgeon had said that there might be some nerve pain for a while, and that another surgery could probably fix it if it didn't subside. The doctor was confident that the fusion of the tibia and femur had been successful. But Chas now had to accustom himself to being a cripple, with his left leg an inch shorter and flexed at a slight angle to make sitting easier. But never again able to bend or straighten, much as his will might wish it.

They both tensed as a blinding flash split the darkness. "I once liked storms. Before the war," Ria said. "Perhaps I can understand why Phoebe is terrified of them." And always hid under the grand piano, shrieking, her head buried in her arms. Ria wondered if Phoebe's fear had mellowed at all in the four years that Ria had been away.

While the lightning stabbed some of the nearby islands, it also skittered across the dolorous clouds with a continuous growl, punctuated by more violent expletives. The constant flashing reminded them of the distant explosions in France - the millions of shells that both sides had hurled at each other with such ferocity.

How often Chas had flown over and through that bombardment! Ria clung tightly to him, recalling the paralyzing fear that had often gripped her, thankful that he had survived when so many of their friends hadn't.

She cared not a whit that he was disfigured, only that he might be relieved of pain. They sometimes jested about their battle honours - Ria's piratical scar across her forehead, a jagged one from knee to ankle, and a deeper wound in her left shoulder; Chas assaulted by bullets in each limb. The arm and shoulder wounds he had sustained last spring would heal in time, the doctors told him, although an old thigh wound from 1915 still troubled him occasionally. They rarely spoke about his burns.

"I expect the storm will wake the children," Ria said as it grumbled relentlessly.

"Let's hope they run to Johanna and not to us," Chas replied with a laugh. "We're not exactly dressed for company."

"Charlie and his bear will likely cuddle up with Johanna, and Sophie and Ace will climb into bed with Alice," Ria said with a smile as she thought of their adopted family.

For a moment, the remembrance that their stillborn son, Reggie, lay alone in a windswept grave on the far distant Irish coast caused Ria such a sharp pain that she choked on a sob. His red granite headstone read, "Reggie Wyndham Thornton, beloved infant son of Victoria and Chas. Innocent victim of the *Lusitania.*"

It was aboard that ill-fated ship that Ria had befriended Alice, then a child of thirteen. And it was Alice who had insisted that Ria was still alive when the sailors had pulled her seemingly lifeless body from the sea. So when Alice was orphaned because of the Spanish flu, Ria and Chas had convinced her English grandparents to allow them to become her legal guardians. Having grown up in Ottawa, and not really knowing her British relatives, Alice had been delighted to become part of her dearest friends' family.

"You're shivering," Chas said. "Are you cold, my darling?"

"No," Ria replied. The rain had not driven away the oppressive heat. Like her shell-shocked cousin Max, she started trembling when something triggered memories best forgotten.

Chas understood only too well. "You need some distraction," he said suggestively as he took her hand and led her back to bed. "I'll just make certain the door is locked."

•   •   •

Partway up the west side of Wyndwood Island, in the cottage at Silver Bay, Max was sweating as he tried to control his shaking. He didn't want to wake his wife, Lydia, but, despite all his willpower and concentration, he couldn't slow the manic thumping of his heart, which threatened to burst through his chest. He gasped for breath, certain that the air was too thick and liquid to breathe. His limbs tingled with encroaching numbness. It was at times like this that he was sure he would die.

Feeling the bed trembling when she woke, Lydia reached immediately for Max. "Sit up and I'll rub your back." She had discovered that there was little else that helped him with these attacks.

"Sorry," he wheezed as he rested his forehead on his knees.

"Don't be silly! This will pass. And the storm will give way to a beautiful day. We'll have a picnic. Go sailing." She laid her head on his shoulder. "Don't ever forget how much I love you, Max Wyndham. We're in this together."

He was unmanned by tears, but they dissolved the panic as Max wept.

In the room next door, Max's twin sister, Zoë, was also awake. The storm transported her back into the war and to memories of her beloved. Not that she didn't think of Blake almost constantly, wishing he could know his son, wanting to tell Blake something she had read, to discuss an idea, as they had so often, whether in person or through letters. They had been married eighteen months, but had shared less than two of those together. Endlessly she wondered why he had been so unlucky, one of two doctors to die in that air raid on the hospital. Dear God, why? He had been so brilliant, so vital.

A childhood friend with whom she'd had years of shared memories, Blake Carlyle had been her first and only love. She had imagined such a triumphant and happy future for them. Now lonely days loomed endlessly before her, brightened only by the son that Blake hadn't even known she was carrying.

The cacophony of the storm reminded her of the air raids over London and the French coast, where she had nursed. Where Blake had been only miles away from her, and now was too many miles away in a massive graveyard beside the uncaring sea.

Lying in his cot next to her bed, seven-month-old Ethan Blake didn't awaken to the raging storm or his mother's heartrending sobs.

•   •   •

The dawn was still smothered by mournful clouds when Ria and Chas awoke again at 7:00, although the rain had stopped. A loon cried forlornly, a haunting trill that truly made Ria feel she was home.

"I used to be out for my daily swim to Wyndwood at this time of morning. When I was young," Chas said, feeling more ancient than his twenty-seven years. His family's island, Thorncliff, was a quarter mile north of Wyndwood.

Ria, cradled in his arms, said flippantly, "And I used to meet my lover at the Shimmering Sands," referring to her favourite spot on the island, where a granite outcropping slid into the lake and crumbled into a sandy crescent of beach.

Chas chuckled as he recalled their passionate trysts. "Which is why I promised to build you a love nest there."

It had been his 21st birthday present to her, to buy ten acres at the north end of the island with a plan to build a boathouse with living quarters above, as a retreat.

From her grandmother, Ria had inherited this forty-year-old summer home, now known as the "Old Cottage", at the south point of Wyndwood, along with the outbuildings, wet and dry boathouses, and the surrounding five acres. The rest of the triangular sixty-acre island belonged equally to her father and two uncles, who had built their own cottages in the past four years. Things had certainly changed since Ria had gone off to war.

"I've been thinking about that," Ria said. "It's a delightfully romantic idea, and I adore owning the Shimmering Sands. But I don't want to change it in any way. It will always be our special place, and fifty years from now I want it to be just the same as when we first made love there."

"As you wish, my darling. But do assure me that we can at least have chairs there when we're in our dotage."

She laughed. "Have I ever told you that you are the most thoughtful and wonderful husband?" she asked.

"Yes. But I'm never averse to praise. Go on."

"Kind and caring..."

"Aha..."

"Witty, unpretentious, debonair. An heroic leader of men." Chas had come back with a chestful of medals, including a Victoria Cross. "The heartthrob of women."

"Now I know you're lying," he accused.

She raised herself on her elbow, and he turned away slightly so that she couldn't as easily see the scarred left side of his face. "You have the most beautiful blue eyes, and enviously long eyelashes, and temptingly sensuous lips," Ria said as she kissed them.

"I'm so attractive that my sister-in-law screamed and burst into tears when she saw me," he said sardonically.

Ria was stunned for a moment, and then realized about whom he was talking. "You mean that spoilt infant, Cecilia? Lord, I don't even think of her as my sister." Three-year-old Cecilia was the eldest child of Ria's father, James, and his ambitious young wife, Helena. Ria's rift with them had mended somewhat during her lengthy absence.

The burn on the left side of Chas's face had healed into mottled and waxy new skin, slightly crinkled, like old parchment. His left arm and hand were more puckered, but he had regained some dexterity and could once again play piano, although not with his former élan. If he was no longer blessed with the transcendent beauty of his youth, he was nevertheless a handsome man. "You still turn heads. And not because of your scars," Ria told him, as she gently stroked his damaged cheek.

Chas had always taken his astonishing good looks for granted, so it was difficult for him to examine his unnervingly dichotomous visage in the mirror. He was becoming accustomed to the reactions from others - the initial shock, and then either pity or morbid fascination.

Upon his homecoming, his mother had merely taken him into her arms and said, "Thank God you've come back to us, my darling boy."

His sister, Felicity, had remarked frankly, "I was so afraid you'd look much worse!" Tearfully she had hugged him as if she would never let him go. They had always been close, and she had missed him terribly.

Chas tried to believe his own words as he now said, "I only care what you think, my darling."

"Which is as it should be," Ria retorted with mock archness. "And I shall have to take my little sister in hand before she becomes overbearing and unbearable. I've told Charlie that he mustn't let her bully him." Their adopted son, Charlie, was only a few weeks older than Cecilia.

"I'm not sure that's wise. Technically, she *is* his aunt. Besides, boys are supposed to let girls have the upper hand," Chas said with a grin. "It's called chivalry."

"Applesauce! Cecilia is a little terror, and will just become worse if she always has her way." But Ria knew that she would never be allowed to discipline "Daddy's little princess," as Helena so pointedly called her.

Ria tried to suppress the surprising jealousy that had surfaced when she realized how much her father doted on Cecilia. He had only ever been distant and stern with Ria, since her birth had caused her mother's death. It would be difficult not to resent her half-sister. Baby Jimmy was much easier to like. But there were concerns about him since he didn't seem to be developing as quickly as he should. A difficult birth may have affected him profoundly.

Throwing on a satin negligee, Ria stepped into the hallway and poured two cups of steaming tea from the silver tray that Tilda, the maid, had already laid out on a sideboard. She added fresh strawberry jam to a couple of warm, buttered tea biscuits and took these on a smaller tray into their room. When she handed a cup to Chas, she said, "Do you know the only thing that's missing here?

An aeroplane. I'm sure that flying a seaplane is really no different from an Avro 504 or a BE2c." Both of which she had flown.

"It's more difficult. Tricky, landing and taking off from the water. No aeroplanes, Ria."

"But Chas..."

"I don't ever want to fly again." The only time he thought of doing so was to envision one last spectacular flight, up into the breath-snatchingly cold and thin air that would suck out his life and finally end his pain. "And I don't want you flying, my darling."

"But Chas, you said I was a good pilot. And there are no enemy scouts to worry about," she quipped, recalling her encounter with one in France, when she had caused a sensation by disguising herself as an RFC pilot.

"No, Ria."

"You can't tell me that you're no longer interested in aviation, since you bought shares in the Bishop-Barker Aeroplane Company." Billy Bishop and William Barker were two of Canada's other Victoria Cross aviators. The only other, Alan Arnett McLeod, had tragically died of influenza after barely surviving a remarkable and truly heroic air battle. Chas never felt that he deserved his VC after hearing what nineteen-year-old McLeod had done.

"Purchased because I know Bishop, and he's married to John Eaton's niece."

"And because you see potential in air travel and such."

"Perhaps. I only bought $10,000 in shares, because Jack talked me out of investing more. He doesn't think that high-scoring Aces have the right demeanor to be good businessmen. He says they're brash and cocky daredevils."

"Whereas he, being just a regular Ace, is modest and level-headed," Ria said wryly. Her cousin Jack had scored six victories, thus becoming an Ace, before being recruited by Lord Beaverbrook as a war artist.

"He's certainly thorough and shrewd. That was a brilliant idea of his to merge our bank with the Dominion Commerce. Now we don't have to worry about running it, but still have substantial shares and rather ridiculous income considering we don't have to do anything."

"And Jack made himself a pretty penny helping to broker that. I sense Beaverbrook behind that idea." Not about to let him change the subject, Ria said, "Chas, aren't you excited that Alcock and Brown just flew across the Atlantic? Remember when you and Jack talked about trying for that £10,000 *Daily Mail* prize?"

That summer of 1914, when he had still been whole. "Of course."

"I love flying, and I so wanted to see the lakes from above! And I promised everyone I'd take them for a flight!"

"When the aeroplane became a machine of destruction, one felt differently about it," Chas said seriously. "You are all that keeps me going, Ria. I couldn't bear for anything to happen to you."

"You'll feel better about things once you heal, Chas," Ria replied brightly, disturbed to her core whenever Chas even hinted at despair. He had always been so easygoing and cheerful, so confident and adventuresome, which was one of the reasons she had fallen in love with him. He was shell-shocked in his own way, so she would say no more on the subject. For the time being.

•   •   •

The pain was less severe today, Ellie Carlyle was certain. Hopeful. She had taken only Aspirins last night, afraid of becoming addicted to the veronal that allowed her to sleep undisturbed. Now she needed to fight the lethargy that still possessed her. But the thought of marshalling all the muscles in her disjointed body required an insurmountable effort. So she didn't even open her eyes, but lay heavily in bed listening to the sounds of morning.

Birds twittered gaily; water lapped softly against the shore. Her mother clattered about in the kitchen below, while the thump of oars being shipped meant that her father and brother, Derek, must be returning from a dawn fishing trip. Ones that she had always enjoyed.

The distant roar of a motorboat was a more common sound on the lake these days, a harsh intrusion into the wilderness solitude, yet oddly exciting. It spoke of life and energy and possibilities.

As had the ferocious storm that had awakened her in the night. She had savoured its thrilling intensity, which had allowed her to focus on something other than her misery. And now it promised to be yet another perfect summer day.

A shaft of sunlight streaming through her uncurtained window felt soothing, but also meant that it must be at least eight o'clock. A few straggling clouds were being shredded by the bristly tops of the pines that she could see through her window.

There would be no maid bringing breakfast in bed, as there had been while she had stayed with her sister-in-law, Zoë, these past months, there being no one at home to look after her. Her mother, Hannah, worked mostly full time as a pharmacist, and her professor father spent long days at the university, save for his generous summer holidays. Her younger brother, Derek, had been deep into his biology studies at the university, and hopeless in any domestic situation anyway.

But now that they had all come to the cottage - her mother for only a few weeks - Ellie had thought it best to be here, on Ouhu. Zoë and the Wyndhams had cosseted and spoiled her. She needed to find the strength to become independent once more. How could she marry Troy otherwise?

She looked at the engagement ring he had given her at Christmas - a simple but exquisite solitaire diamond, not ostentatiously large, since he knew that she wouldn't wear something that screamed wealth. It scattered the morning light in rainbow splinters. She felt tears of joy and sadness sting her eyes.

So it was time to gather all the disparate, leaden bits of herself and command their cooperation. Pull back the blankets. Roll onto her side. Push up. Swing her legs over the edge of the bed. Regain balance. Prepare for the searing, needle-sharp pain as her sensitive feet touched the bare wooden floor. Soon she would feel an uncomfortable tingling, like the pins-and-needles of a sleepy limb, and then the numbness that would get her through the day, even if somewhat unsteadily.

She fought the despair that gnawed and niggled. Her friend and colleague, Dr. Lorna Partridge, had told her that many people were suffering aftereffects from the virulent influenza that had ravaged the world last fall and left countless millions dead. Some survivors were much worse, suffering from paralysis, encephalitis, heart and lung problems, while others battled neurasthenia and depression. Richard Wyndham – Zoë's father - was still debilitated and melancholic, though he tried hard not to show it.

Lorna had assured Ellie that her neuropathy was improving and that with plenty of rest, judicious exercise, gentle leg massage - which Zoë was providing - and nutritious meals, she had every chance of healing completely.

Ellie was frustrated by her own weakness, and her enforced hiatus from work, which had cost her her job at the hospital. After all, the men were back now, so women doctors were no longer in such demand. What little doctoring she had done these past eight months was for friends and neighbours, many of whom merely wanted prescriptions for booze, which was only legally obtainable with a doctor's order.

"At least you haven't lost sensation in your hands," Lorna had said. "I have a patient who can't do up buttons or hold a fork easily. He's a carpenter." The implication being that even if the inflamed nerves in her feet never healed completely, she could at least still work and walk. Or rather, shuffle like a cripple.

But what kind of wife would she make if pain continued to be her nightly companion?

No self-pity! She admonished herself. *I'm alive. I will work again. I will marry Troy.*

Or should she?

Ellie couldn't contain her initial gasp as she stood up. She steadied herself against her bedside table and then hobbled to her washstand. After brushing her teeth, she carefully slipped out of her nightgown and into her swimsuit. In the water she felt once again the freedom of unrestricted movement. Like a mermaid, she thought with a chuckle - useless on land but elegant in the water. Getting down to the lake was a challenge.

She used crutches for support, since she couldn't properly feel the ground, and any impediments - sticks and stones - were likely to unbalance her. She would not marry Troy until she could dance at their wedding.

If he still wanted to marry her. She wouldn't let him do it out of pity. Why wasn't he at the cottage yet? She had expected him last week, but there hadn't even been one of his daily letters.

She treasured those, and eagerly awaited their arrival. After returning from the war, Troy had come directly to Toronto to see her. At first he had refused to leave her, but she had insisted that he resume his studies at Harvard. It wasn't until she had sworn she wouldn't marry him until he had finished his degree that he had reluctantly left.

The letters had begun to arrive immediately. No matter how tired he was or how late the day, he wrote her a few lines at the very least. And it seemed as if she were sharing his life and his fascinating research in the laboratory. "Soon I will be telling you all this in person, every evening, over dinner, in bed. How glorious that will be," he often reminded her.

"Breakfast in half an hour," her mother called as Ellie lumbered past the kitchen. "Fresh fish."

"Super!"

Ellie loved the touch of the sun-warmed, gritty granite and spongy mosses on her bare feet, but now that these clumsy appendages seemed to be encased in layers of wool, she felt nothing but the disconcerting numbness. She proceeded cautiously, mindful of the uneven, glacier-gouged rock and the pools of prickly pine needles, skirted the scrubby junipers that clung to pockets of soil, walked more easily across the bit of lawn, and stepped off the grassy ledge into the water. The lake bottom was sand, but there was no happy wriggling of toes as usual. Discarding her crutches on the dock, she held onto it as she waded in, and finally allowed herself to drop. The instant shock of the cool water was invigorating.

And she knew exactly what she would do - swim over to neighbouring Picnic Island, her favourite spot. Surely she was strong enough by now to manage that short distance.

But despite doing an easy breaststroke and sometimes flipping onto her back to rest, she was exhausted when she crawled onto the sandy beach of the tiny island. Her heart pounded alarmingly. She lay half-submerged in the shallow water and recalled longingly that momentous night, two summers ago, when she and Troy had swum over in the nude and made love under the stars.

She hadn't realized that she had fallen asleep until the hiss of a boat being beached woke her.

"Thank God!" Troy said as he hopped out of the canoe and rushed to her side. He fell onto his knees beside her and scooped her into a crushing embrace. "For a moment I was so afraid..."

"Am I dreaming or are you truly here?" she asked.

"Truly here and never leaving you again," he said joyfully. "Especially if you do foolish things like swim too far." He kissed her deeply, and she was grateful for the familiar stirrings of desire. At least some things still worked.

"I've missed you so much," she admitted. "Is it really possible that we can be together now?"

"As soon as you set the wedding date," he replied.

"Troy..."

He could tell from the hesitation in her voice what she would say. "Don't even think that I don't want to spend the rest of my life with you, Eleanor Carlyle. You will mend, but even if you're never back to your formidable self, I still want you. Let me take care of you," he pleaded as he laid her back down in the sand. He brushed a wet tendril from her cheek and said, "I'll even forgive you for cutting off all that beautiful hair."

She chuckled. "Not the compliment that I expected for my new do. I couldn't manage with long hair when I spend so much time lounging about. Besides, I thought I'd look sassy, like Ria."

He laughed. "Sassy and sexy and very seductive. But now we'd better get back to Ouhu. Your family's worried, but I knew exactly where you'd be. So I borrowed the canoe, since I couldn't beach my launch in these shallows."

Despite her protests he picked her up and carried her to the canoe. He was glad to see her looking better than when he had left her in early January, but still concerned at how frail she was. She began shivering, despite the heat, so he took off his shirt and draped it around her.

"You are forever lending me your clothes," she said, recalling that summer of 1916 when they had first realized a mutual attraction.

"I guess that truly makes you my girl," he quipped.

He was gladdened by the grin that brightened her face.

"As long as you remember that I am an independent woman, Mr. Roland."

"Of course, Dr. Carlyle... Roland."

"Hyphenated sounds rather pretentious."

"We can be the Drs. Roland. I've been accepted to do my doctoral studies in biochemistry and physiology at the University of Toronto."

"That's wonderful! But what about Harvard? Shouldn't you continue there?"

"Not if it means waiting any longer to marry you. I respect that your work is in Toronto, Ellie. I won't ask you to abandon everything to be my wife."

"If I weren't sitting in the middle of a tippy canoe, I would throw myself into your arms. Sometimes I don't think you *are* real, Troy."

"Just you wait until I have you to myself!"

"Mmm, what a delicious prospect. Especially since you're already temptingly half-naked."

He laughed. "You're definitely on the mend!"

Despite their efforts not to fuss over their children, the Carlyles were visibly relieved when Troy brought Ellie home. She hadn't intended to distress them, knowing how much they suffered from the loss of her brother Blake.

They had a delightful breakfast on the veranda, Troy already seeming like part of the family.

He told them, "Harvard gave me credit for the work I had done in France, so I was able to finish my Masters degree last week. It's why I didn't arrive sooner."

"You mean you don't have to go back at all?" Ellie asked.

"Not even home. I have nearly all my worldly goods in my boat. So, how long do you need to prepare for a wedding? Three weeks?"

They all laughed. "You're certainly an eager young man," the professor said.

"I have the entire summer free, and plan to nurse my wife back to the robust good health that will have her winning regattas by next summer."

"A noble endeavour indeed," Ellie's father, Thomas, replied. "Well, I'll leave that up to the women to decide."

Troy waylaid his departure, saying, "Professor, I wondered if I might purchase a corner of Ouhu so that I can build a small cottage? I do have some money, and would like to begin working on that right away. If you don't mind, I've brought a tent and hope to camp out there until the wedding."

"Purchase? Nonsense! The island is big enough for at least half a dozen cottages. Just tell me where you want to put it. We'll make that a part of the wedding gift."

Without hesitation, Troy replied, "There's a point right across from Picnic Island, with sheltered bays on either side."

So her favourite spot would be within a stone's throw, Ellie thought as she looked gratefully at Troy. She could already imagine herself admiring the champagne-coloured beach backed by windblown jack pines, all neatly framed by the sitting room windows.

"Splendid!" the professor said. "Go ahead and I'll ensure that you have legal title to... well, let's make it half the island. Derek will have this part and Daphne won't need a share, since she and Edgar will eventually inherit Albert's Wyndwood estate." Ellie's younger sister, Daphne, had married Ria and Zoë's cousin Edgar in 1916.

"That is most generous, Sir!"

"The land is cheap enough. It's building the cottage on all this rock that will cost you."

"But Dad, how wonderful!" Ellie enthused.

"As long as you never sell it," the professor said firmly. "I want my grandchildren and theirs to enjoy the lake."

"You need never worry about that," Troy assured him. "In fact, I'm wondering what kind of doctoring Ellie could do that would ensure we spend entire summers here."

"You intend to become a professor, do you?" she asked him. "With summers off?"

"Absolutely! And not about to leave you slaving away alone in the hot city. I think that you should set yourself up as the resort and cottage doctor."

"Ah, so I have to work all summer while you play tennis and golf with our idle friends."

"If that's the only way I can guarantee that you're here," he replied with a grin.

Ellie's mother, Hannah, interrupted the banter. "We really must discuss wedding plans if we're to have it soon."

"I'm not sure I'll be strong enough in a few weeks," Ellie admitted reluctantly. "I want to walk up the aisle without crutches."

"It doesn't need to be a long aisle," Troy said. "Do you want a church wedding?"

"Heavens, no! Although I'm not averse to a minister performing the ceremony if he has Theosophical leanings. I want to have it outside, under a canopy of blue sky."

"I'll order up the weather now, shall I? Troy teased.

"It still takes a lot of planning," Hannah said.

"It needn't be an elaborate affair, Mum. I just want our closest friends there. I'm sure Ria would allow us to have it at The Point so that we can use the pavilion if it rains. Just in case your order doesn't get through," she said to Troy with a smirk. "And I expect that Daphne would be delighted to oversee a small reception. A luncheon, perhaps." Despite her elevated position in society as a Wyndham, Daphne still enjoyed cooking the occasional meal, and relished planning dinner parties.

"What about your dress and trousseau?" her mother asked. "And where will you live? I suppose you can live with us for a time."

"I'll borrow something from Ria," Ellie said.

"When I stopped in Toronto, I had a quick look at properties close to the university and your home," Troy said. "I saw a couple of possibilities."

"Troy, are you that rich?" Ellie asked in awe. "I thought your parents were going to disown you if you married me."

"I shall leave you two to your discussions while I do dishes," Hannah said, obviously uncomfortable about the way the conversation was going.

"Let's canoe over to *our place* and I'll tell you how things stand," Troy said to Ellie.

As he paddled down the southeast shore of Ouhu toward the point and Picnic Island, the   previous evening's scene replayed in his head. He had arrived at his family's cottage on the late afternoon steamer, and not having seen them for months, knew that he couldn't leave right away to visit Ellie, much as he longed to. It was after dinner, when his younger brothers had left to attend a dance at the Country Club, that he had told his parents his plans.

His mother had said angrily, "You cannot still mean to marry that woman! I thought you would have come to your senses by now. Besides all else, I expect that she is a pagan."

"A Theosophist," Troy had corrected.

"A heathen! God-less! I will absolutely not countenance such a union."

"I'm sorry, Mom, but I love Ellie and *will* marry her."

"You are my son. Nothing will change that. But I will never consider her my daughter-in-law. You are welcome home any time, but she will never be." Erika Roland had visibly drawn herself up, her haughty look challenging him.

"I won't come without my wife," Troy had retorted, trying to remain calm. His father had shot him a look that appealed for concessions. Erika had been devastated by his brother Kurt's death, but Troy wondered why she was then prepared to risk losing him as well. "What about your grandchildren?" he'd challenged.

"Will she take time to have and to nurture your children? You must think with your head, Troy, and not your baser instincts. That woman has bewitched you, but you can break away from her spell. Think about your future!"

Troy had shaken his head in exasperation. "I don't understand your antipathy towards Ellie."

"She is a regrettably *modern* woman who has invaded the realm of men, and thinks to be their equal. She will put her career above all else, including you, my foolish boy. That is not the kind of wife or life I wanted for you. I've always maintained that a woman must be the moral backbone of the family. Dr. Carlyle knows men's bodies too intimately for a respectable woman - in more ways than one. You cannot deny that you have already had relations with her! And how many others were there before you?"

"That's enough, Mom."

"Don't you *dare* to tell me what I can say in my house!"

It had taken a great deal of restraint for Troy to reply calmly, "I'm sorry that you won't support my decision, Mom. I think it best if I leave in the morning and stay with friends. You'll be invited to the wedding nonetheless."

"Make the boy see sense, Howard!" she had snapped to her husband before sweeping from the room.

"You have wounded your mother deeply, Troy, and disappointed me as well. I hoped that you would now settle down to work with me in the business, but you tell us that you will do yet another degree, and in Toronto no less! Have you no ambition to take over the company that I worked damned hard to build up for you boys?" he asked, referring to his successful paint manufactory in Pittsburgh.

"Of course I appreciate what you've achieved, Dad, and I'm sure one of the others will be only too happy to take over from you when the time comes. Felix certainly has a head for business. But my vocation is in medical research. I've already made a difference with my contribution to blood chemistry. We saved thousands of lives during the war, including Ria Thornton's. I hope that you can be proud of that as well."

Howard Roland had pursed his lips and finally spat, "Well, damn it, of course I am! Come along to my office."

After the door had been firmly shut behind them, Howard pulled a bottle of cognac out of a locked cupboard, saying, "I expect your mother knows that I keep some on hand, although she has never let on. But you know that nothing escapes her." There had been a note of regret in that last statement. "Can I pour you one?"

"Thanks."

"Now look here, how are we going to ensure that you don't live like a pauper? How much are academics paid? Four or five thousand a year? You know the factory is worth millions, but I can't give you a share of that, or continue your allowance now that you have no intention of working there."

"I don't expect that, Dad. Ellie doesn't have extravagant tastes or needs. We'll manage with the money from the trust fund you set up for me, and what we'll earn." Troy hadn't used much of the income from his trust fund during the war, and had invested it wisely, so that he had enough for a modest house and cottage. And now that he was twenty-five, he had control of the $50,000 capital as well. He'd also be earning around $1000 a year during his doctoral studies.

"It may seem like a lot of money now, but it won't go far if you're living off it, especially once the children come. You do want children, don't you?"

"Sure I do. Not just yet, but in time."

Howard had nodded and taken another gulp of brandy. "Now look here, Troy. I have nothing against Eleanor. Damned good-looking girl. Plenty of spunk. And I expect she'll settle down once the kiddies come along." Troy didn't bother to argue. "I'll do what I can to bring your mother round. But I can't be seen going against her. Not right now. You don't know how much she suffers. You boys are her life and she misses Kurt terribly. It's heartbreaking to hear her weeping, which she does every morning when she wakes and realizes yet again that he is gone. Of course she doesn't let it show."

He had stopped for a moment to rein in his own emotions, and Troy had said, "I'm sorry, Dad. I don't mean to add to her distress or yours. But this is my life we're talking about."

After clearing his throat and quaffing more of his drink, Howard had said, "Quite so. Now look here, I haven't had the heart to do anything with Kurt's trust fund, so I'll transfer it to your children. And that's the last penny I can offer right now."

"That's very generous, Dad."

"You'll have control of it once the little ones come along. It's to make sure that they have the best schooling, and all that your family needs. But not a word to your mother!" He had poured himself another, more generous measure of cognac, and lit a cigar, in part, Troy knew, to disguise the smell of alcohol on his breath. "I love her dearly, but she has very high standards, which she will never compromise. I daresay she will soften when she meets her grandchildren." He'd attempted a smile. "Damn it, I'm going to miss you, son. Perhaps you can swallow your pride enough to visit us occasionally, even if Eleanor can't accompany you." His hopeful, almost pleading look had cut Troy to the quick.

"Of course I will, Dad."

"Good. Good. Wish I could be at the wedding, but I expect your mother won't sanction that. Your brothers will manage to be off somewhere that day, I'm sure." He'd given Troy a knowing glance.

Once Troy and Ellie were settled on the granite slab that dominated the point - *their* point - he gave her the highlights of these conversations, softening his mother's objections, although they still smarted.

"I'm sorry, Troy. I can appreciate how difficult this must be for you, splitting your loyalties." She squeezed his hand. "Of course you'll have to visit your family. God knows, I don't want them to have even more reason to hate me."

"They don't hate you, Ellie. My mother just has... certain expectations for me."

Ellie said wryly, "Like Millicent Madison?"

"God forbid! Millicent is swathed in money, and never lets anyone forget that."

"So I noticed last summer. But that's when I realized I had to rescue you from her and your mother's schemes. I shall be eternally grateful to Felix for alerting me to the dangers."

"As shall I," he said looking deeply into her eyes. "So now we have to consider what *we* want and need to do. Definitely a cottage, strategically placed here. A modest home in the Annex. I have my runabout, which I bought with my allowance in '15. I expect we'll need a car."

"Those are riches beyond what I want most of all. You."

Troy hugged her tightly. After a while he said, "So now tell me what you envision in a cottage."

The rock beneath them turned a humped back to the prevailing west winds, but on its east side, the lake had bitten out a large chunk, leaving a trail of sandy crumbs. On this narrow crescent of beach they had pulled up in the canoe. Just beyond it, granite fingers once again reached into the lake. Ellie was thrilled to think that this spot would be theirs.

"Just what my family has - a sitting and dining room overlooking the lake, a kitchen behind, three bedrooms above, and an encompassing veranda. With the addition of a screened sleeping porch, if possible. I like that at Zoë's cottage. It's so lovely on a stiflingly hot night."

"Done! And what about a lavatory?"

"OK, no outhouse then."

"And a shower."

"An extravagance indeed."

"Yes, well I don't like the thought of soaping up in the lake and then pumping that water into the house for drinking."

"But Troy, haven't you read the advertisements for all the Muskoka resorts about the healthful benefits of our pure, crystal clear water?"

He snorted. "Fortunately the SRA coerced the steamships into no longer dumping raw sewage into the lake." He was talking about the Summer Residents' Association to which most of the cottagers belonged. "But I certainly don't like the idea of drinking out of a gigantic bathtub - and worse. I don't think many people would be happy to see what their drinking water looks like under a microscope."

Ellie laughed. All her doubts about marrying Troy had vanished. His very presence gave her strength and hope.

•   •   •

"Freddie says he and Martha will be here by Dominion Day," Chas said as he closed up the letter. Freddie Spencer, a long-time cottage friend, was an architect. Already he had designed the cottages at Silver Bay for Ria's Uncle Richard and cousin Max. After the war, Freddie and his new wife had stayed on in Britain while she finished her VAD nursing work and he'd given some lectures for the Khaki University. Then they had embarked on a tour of Europe. "But he says he won't participate in the Stepping Stone Marathon, which is just as well. It's time for us old codgers to let the youngsters win." Freddie, too, was recovering from wounds.

Chas had won that swimming competition five years in a row before Jack had snatched the trophy from him in 1914. Ria had won the first ladies' race that summer, but she had no desire to defend her cup, and wondered if Jack would.

She realized that these milestones in their summers held such poignant memories that each would, in some way, be an ordeal to endure. But would it be fair on the younger crowd to change traditions that had been going on for decades?

The sun had chased away the last of the storm clouds as she and Chas had had their morning swim in the calm Back Bay on the leeward side of The Point. After a leisurely breakfast with Alice, Joanna, and the children on the screened east section of the veranda that encircled the substantial, two-storey cottage, Ria and Chas had settled into cushioned wicker chairs on the broad front porch to read the newspapers and mail. Except on bug-infested evenings and nippy days, they lived and entertained in these shady, breezy spaces on the very edge of the natural beauty that surrounded them.

Looking at the shimmering blue lake across the rugged expanse of rock bristling with blueberry bushes, feathery pines, and tenacious oaks, and softened by stands of ferns, Ria sighed contentedly. Gareth, the gardener, had already chopped out the saplings that tried to encroach on paths and obstruct the panoramic view, but Ria had noticed other changes during her five-year absence. And was eager now to put her own stamp on her domain.

As if reading her thoughts, Chas said, "I'm going to ask Freddie to design a massive new boathouse for us."

"Massive?"

"To house the sailboat, the new cruiser, the Dippy, and a racer." Chas had just bought a Disappearing Propeller Boat - Dippy - for guests to use, and a runabout for the staff. It was important for them to be mobile, so that supplies, mail, and visitors could be fetched, and the servants themselves have the opportunity to leave the island in their free time. With Chas and Ria's pre-war launches, *Windrunner* and *Dragonfly*, the current two-slip boathouse was already occupied.

"A racer?" she asked.

"Yes. I noticed Herb Ditchburn was building one for Harry Greening. He plans to compete in next year's Fisher-Allison Trophy in the States. So I thought I might give him a run for his money," Chas replied with a grin. He had gone to the Ditchburn factory in Gravenhurst yesterday to check on the progress of the day cruiser he had ordered in the winter. "I'm considering using an aeroplane engine. There's a surplus of those around."

Ria was intrigued. "And who will build your race boat? Obviously not Ditchburn."

"I've been mulling this over. I thought of Bert Minett, but then I realized that Mac Seaford has worked for both Herb and Bert, and just started his own boatworks and livery in Port Darling. I have great faith in his abilities." Mac's family had worked for the Thorntons in various capacities for two decades. His youngest brother, Stephen, was currently the head boatman at Thorncliff, and helped with the boatworks during the rest of the year. "I expect Mac could use an infusion of cash. And even if I don't win the Trophy, I still want the fastest boat on the lake," Chas declared.

"An 'infusion of cash' meaning you're going to become a boat builder?" Ria asked in surprise.

"I haven't talked to Mac about it yet. But why not, if he's interested?"

Ria could sense his excitement, and was glad that he had a potential hobby to occupy him, and hopefully bring him out of the depression that still sometimes gripped him. Gazing out at the tantalizing blue water, she could imagine the exhilaration of zipping across it, spray shooting up behind them. It would almost be like flying. "May I help?"

"Of course, my darling! I bow to your superior knowledge of engines."

Ria had not only leaned to tinker with an aeroplane engine when she took up flying in England, but had also been responsible for maintaining her Rolls Royce ambulance engine when she had worked in France with the WATS - Women's Ambulance Transport Service. "Applesauce! I'm an experienced mechanic, but any technical changes I could offer would all be based on woman's intuition." She flashed him one of her quick and enchanting smiles.

Chas laughed. "And who's to say that wouldn't be brilliant? Remember how we'd talked about building aeroplanes after the war, Ria? Well, think how much more exciting it will be to build boats. No one needs a plane, but everyone on the lakes needs at least one boat. And we can builder fast ones that will be beautiful works of art as well."

"I can just imagine that we'll have a stable full of boats, like Rafe has his horses," she said, referring to Chas's brother. "Where will we build the new boathouse?"

"I thought where the old one had been." That was at the base of the bluff on which the cottage sprawled. It had been consumed by a spectacular fire in 1914, which had seriously threatened the cottage. "The water's deep there, and it leaves a nice swath of beach open between it and the other one. And since the ice never took out the old boathouse, it must be a safe spot. We'll put guestrooms, a bathroom, and a sitting room on the second floor."

"So visitors won't even have to come up to the house, except for meals."

Chas replied, "We can have those sent down as well. Everyone appreciates a private place to which they can retreat for a while. Honestly, my darling, I don't understand how all your uncles, aunts, and cousins lived together harmoniously here every summer."

"Have you forgotten the rows? Especially after Grandmother died. I once thought that the cottage would be too quiet after everyone left, but I'm thankful that they all have their own places now." Especially her father. There would be nothing but trouble if James and Helena had stayed on, as Augusta's will had stipulated they could, both here and at Wyndholme, Ria's city mansion.

"Actually, I was thinking that the sitting room and facilities would be handy for us when we plan to be down at the beach," Chas said. "There'll be a long slide for the children from a second floor veranda into the water, and a diving board somewhere. You and I can lounge on the upper deck with friends and cocktails, and watch the antics."

"On the contrary, I shall be the first one down the slide! What a delightful idea, Chas. And I think we should put in an inclined lift to make it easy to get up and down from the cottage."

Chas looked at her askance. "I *can* walk, Ria. Don't baby me."

"It's for all of us, Chas. And I expect the staff would appreciate not having to haul the supplies and trunks the long way round." Which was a path rising more gently from the bay and arcing around the back of the cottage to the east. "You know that it's not that easy for Patrick to get around on the island, and Grayson isn't young anymore." Patrick, the footman, had lost a leg in the war, while Grayson, the butler, was well into his fifties. "We'll put in a stairway as well, of course. So you can choose."

The carefree clatter of footsteps announced the children before they rounded the corner of the west veranda and raced toward them.

"Daddy Chas, is it time to visit Granny?" nine-year-old Sophie asked as she flung herself into his outstretched good arm. She was a thoughtful, pretty child with maple syrup curls and sea-blue eyes no longer shadowed by tragedy.

"Granny's not expecting us until lunch, poppet," he replied as he drew her into a hug. "So what should we do if we go early?" he teased, knowing that she loved tennis, and looked for any excuse to go to Thorncliff.

"We could play tennis!"

"Hmm, I'm not sure I'm up to the challenge."

"Alice and Esme and Johanna are!" she retorted gleefully. The three girls agreed, and Sophie was practically bouncing. Sensing her excitement, her devoted beagle, Ace, looked expectantly at Chas and wagged his tail as if preparing for takeoff.

Chas laughed as he said, "It seems that Ace wants to come as well. Do you think you can keep him from scaring Granny's cats?"

"He barks because *he's* afraid of *them*! We'll make him fetch the balls." Which Ace did so exuberantly that he often chased a ball still in play.

Sophie had been six when Ria first met her in the flower shop in Calais where the child had helped her widowed mother. Ria would never forget the heartbreaking day of the air raid when she'd had to pull Sophie away from the rubble that buried her mother. Because Sophie had no relatives who cared to look after her, Ria and Chas had eventually adopted her.

Ironically, Chas had a less easy relationship with three-year-old Charlie, who had attached himself to Ria. She put her arm about him now as he leaned against her and sullenly watched Chas's banter with Sophie.

"We'll have a lesson while the girls are practicing," Chas said to the boy in French. Charlie had picked up a lot of English since they'd adopted him seven months ago, but Chas and Ria often spoke to the children in French, especially when they wanted to reassure them.

Johanna, the teenaged Belgian refugee who Ria's Cousin Beatrice had found in England to act as nanny, also spoke the language fluently, and Alice had been raised by a French-Canadian nanny, so everyone in the household, aside from the servants, was comfortable switching back and forth.

"D'accord?" Chas asked Charlie.

The child nodded and clutched his bear tighter. The thumb of his other hand flew immediately into his mouth. Chas tried not to show his annoyance at the infantile behaviour. Ria had pointed out that Charlie might not be used to having men about. Or had been unsettled by too many of them coming and going.

Esme, Ria's cousin and Zoë's younger sister, said, "Would it be alright if I came along? Mrs. Thornton's not expecting me to lunch."

"Absolutely," Chas assured her. "You know how Mumsy loves company."

"I'd best run home and tell Mama."

"I'll come!" Alice said.

Ria was glad to see that Alice and Esme had become such good friends, although Esme, already eighteen, was a year older. Alice had spent the winter term with Esme at the private school that Ria and Zoë had attended, and had done well enough to pass her university entrance exams.

Chas took a circuitous route to Thorncliff so that each of the younger children could drive the runabout - Ria's smaller *Dragonfly* - and then let Alice take over as they neared the island. He was teaching her to dock.

"Well done!" he said when she finally took her sweaty hands off the steering wheel. The boatman was there to catch the rope that Chas threw him, and pulled the launch in the extra yard to bring them hard up against the dock.

"Only because Stephen is here to reel us in," Alice said wryly.

"That was dandy, Miss," Stephen Seaford replied. "It takes practice to anticipate how the wind and waves will affect your approach." He was a strapping, friendly young man.

"You'll have lots of practice this summer, Alice," Chas said. "So relax and enjoy it. Even old hands like us have problems at times."

Stephen offered a strong arm to each as he helped them from the boat, including Chas, who found it awkward to manoeuvre with his stiff leg and hated using a cane, which he certainly needed at times. He still had lots of adjustments to make, each one a surprise, until he felt comfortable with his limitations.

"I see you've been expanding the Inn again," Chas said to Stephen. The vast rock and thin soil of Muskoka not being particularly conducive to farming, the Seafords had, for decades, been taking paying guests at their mainland farmhouse - now the Pineridge Inn - next to the SRA Golf and Country Club.

"People kept coming back, and we had to turn some away," Stephen replied. "So the new wing has given us a dozen more rooms. We bought the Ellis property next door, so we have another five hundred feet of waterfront, and have that cottage rented for the summer."

As the children raced toward the tennis court, Chas said to Stephen, "With all that going on, I'm glad to see that you managed to open the boatworks. So, I have a proposition to make to you and Mac. Would you be interested in building me a racing boat?"

Stephen's eyes gleamed. "You bet, Major!"

"Capital! But you'll have to stop calling me Major."

"Begging your pardon, Sir, but God knows you deserve it. People shouldn't be forgetting that men sacrificed so much, so it's a reminder and a bit of respect, Major."

Chas grinned. That was more or less what his footman/valet, Patrick, had said as well. "I heard you worked your way up to Corporal."

Stephen had been in the transport corps for the last two years of the war. "Because I'd learned so much by messing about with your engines all those summers." He'd been helping his older brother, Mac, tend to the Thorntons' boats since he was twelve.

"Well, Corporal, let me tell you about the boat that's going to set records."

Ria left the men to discuss details as she strolled up to the house across the manicured lawn punctuated by glacier-scrubbed rock. Although Ria admired the luxuriant and colourful formal gardens, she preferred to keep her own landscape more natural.

The white-trimmed beige cottage belied its massive size and was undoubtedly one of the most sumptuous on the lake, boasting a ballroom, music and billiard rooms, formal sitting and dining rooms, and numerous bedrooms, some with private baths. Rising up from the stone foundation, which itself seemed to grow out of the bedrock, rugged granite pillars supported the roof of the deep veranda and the airy balconies above. Ria walked past the main entrance along to the end, where French doors opened into the bright morning room, which dominated the southeast corner of the cottage. Two walls of tall windows overlooked the gardens and tennis pavilion to the lake beyond, with the north end of Wyndwood visible in the distance. Fans in the lofty ceiling spun languidly, fluttering the fronds of the palms that were scattered about the dining and sitting areas. Informal and family meals were served here, and it was where they preferred to lounge when there were no guests. Chas's mother, Marjorie, and sister, Felicity, greeted Ria warmly.

"Sophie was keen to play tennis, so we're terribly early," Ria explained.

"How lovely!" Marjorie replied. "Let's have some coffee sent down to the pavilion and watch."

"Have Sid and Rafe arrived yet?" Ria asked.

"Oh yes, they came yesterday. Rafe's taken Sid on a tour of the lake this morning," Fliss said. "I think she's jolly impressed with

Thorncliff, and even loved the storm last night, since it reminded her of England."

Lady Sidonie Dunston had married Rafe in a quick December ceremony before they had all left Britain. After the excitement of wartime London, which Sid had relished, she found staid and prudish Prohibitionist Toronto incredibly dull. Rafe had taken her to Florida for March, and they just returned from six weeks in New York and Atlantic City.

"I'll run ahead and see the others," Fliss said as Ria took Marjorie by the arm and followed more slowly. Marjorie tired easily and suffered inexplicable pains on exertion, but a variety of doctors here and in the States had found no disease to explain her condition. Neurasthenia was the resulting diagnosis, with plenty of rest, fresh air, and massage, the prescription. And, of course, the inference that it was an hysterical female indulgence reserved for the well-to-do.

"There are times when I crave the energy to play tennis again," Marjorie admitted. "I was quite accomplished once, and still recall how good it felt to race about the court and return impossible serves."

"Then it's little wonder that Chas and Fliss are so good."

"Rafe would be, too, if he applied himself as they do. But he seems to care most for riding."

"Which he doesn't have much time for these days, since he and Sid keep going away." Ria's horse, Calypso, and Sophie's Buttercup were boarded in Rafe's stables, as the city was encroaching on Ria's Rosedale domain. It was no longer the country estate it had once been. So she and the others had been spending more time at the stables than Rafe. Fortunately, he had good people managing them.

"I expect this is all such a drastic and upsetting change for Sidonie, poor dear. Hopefully she'll adjust," Marjorie said.

The long enclosed tennis pavilion matched the cottage in style and colour, with a cupola filtering in more light, and walls of screened French doors that gave onto broad verandas. From here, spectators could watch a match, or a croquet game on the other lawn, or just enjoy afternoon tea and pre-dinner cocktails. A fireplace at one end provided warmth and ambiance on cool evenings. Ria would never forget the romantic dinner that she and Chas had enjoyed here in 1914.

The maid arrived with coffee as Ria settled Marjorie into a wicker chair. Her mother-in-law had been pleasantly plump when Ria had left in '15, but her silent grief over the death of her husband, J.D., last fall had made her thin and wan, and the added wartime stress over Chas and Rafe had aged her considerably, though she was not yet fifty.

Fliss and Sophie were already playing a match against Alice and Esme, while Chas was helping Charlie hold his racquet and return the balls that Johanna lobbed at him on the croquet lawn.

After she had accepted a cup of coffee from Ria, Marjorie said, "It's uncanny how much Charlie resembles Chas." She looked shrewdly at her daughter-in-law.

Ria was not one to underestimate Marjorie, so she said resignedly, "Is it that obvious?"

"Perhaps only to a mother. I see my own little Charles when I look at the boy." She waited.

"Chas had a... liaison with a French girl," Ria explained, looking away from Marjorie, wincing at the stab of betrayal that still accompanied that thought.

Marjorie put her hand warmly over Ria's and with a little squeeze, said gently, "I know how much Chas loves you, my dear. And how lucky he is to have you. I expect that he has sown his wild oats. But how generous of you to adopt him."

"His mother died of the influenza. What choice did we have? But I've come to love him as my own. And we don't plan to tell Charlie that Chas is his father."

"I don't consider any child to be 'illegitimate'. It's like saying that he is somehow less than human, and deserving only of scorn. So I do see your reasons. As far as society is concerned, you adopted a French orphan. But one day you may have to tell him. And we shall see if he'll forgive you for keeping the truth from him. If he has brothers, he may well see himself in them."

Ria hesitated, but encouraged by Marjorie's sympathy, said tentatively, "I can't have any more children, Mumsy. I hope you won't think badly of me, but I need to tell you... Chas and I had a baby, but he was stillborn. He's buried in Ireland."

Marjorie looked momentarily shocked, but quickly filled in the details. "He died because of your ordeal on the *Lusitania?*"

Ria nodded, not trusting herself to speak. She pressed back tears when Marjorie said, "How tragic! Oh, my dear child, you should never be afraid to tell me anything. To think that you kept that worry to yourself all those months before you left to join Chas. If I'd known that he had compromised you, I would have insisted that you marry before he left!"

"We thought he would be home by Christmas. You mustn't blame him."

"Love can be very foolish and impetuous, but rarely sensible."

"If I had told Chas right away, I would have gone to England sooner, and Reggie and Vivian wouldn't have died, and I probably wouldn't be sterile," Ria sobbed. Vivian Carrington had travelled with Ria, but her body had never been recovered. "And Charlie might never have been conceived."

Marjorie stroked Ria's hair as if she were a small child. "We can't live with if-onlys, my dear. You and Chas have made yourselves a nice little family, and are obviously devoted to one another. I envy you that. Joseph never loved me as I did him. But he was a good husband, kind and thoughtful, generous and caring. His passion lay with his work."

And elsewhere, Ria thought, but Marjorie was too loyal to expose her late husband's infidelities if she knew about them.

"This explains much that I found puzzling," Marjorie admitted. "I wrote to Margaret Dunston to express my condolences on the deaths of her two daughters on the *Lusitania*, and then Percy at the Front. In her reply, she said that we had both been duped by our daughters-in-law. I didn't know Sidonie then, of course, but I couldn't imagine what fault she could possibly find with you."

"She was vitriolic in her condemnation of me when she discovered aboard the ship that I was eight months pregnant, but not yet married to Chas," Ria explained. "I was a social pariah."

Marjorie didn't tell Ria that Lady Dunston had gone on to say that if there was any divine justice, then her innocent daughters should have been spared, and scheming, immoral creatures like Ria should have been taken instead. She said, "I wrote back that I couldn't possibly imagine a better wife for Chas than you, and that we are overjoyed to have you in our family." She had added, *I trust, Margaret, that you won't again disparage our cherished daughter-in-law like that. I'm attributing this sudden rancour for Victoria as a result of blind grief - the loss of your children when others survived - and will thus forgive you for this uncharitable attitude. I shall be extremely distressed should I hear that your unfounded opinion ever becomes food for gossip.*

Because their husbands had conducted business together - J.D. lending huge sums to finance Sir Montague Dunston's Transatlantic Steamship Line - Marjorie and Margaret had been on amicable social terms, but that had obviously been abraded by this correspondence. When Rafe had married Sidonie, Percy Dunston's widow, his mother had written to Marjorie with malicious pleasure, *Thank God someone has relieved us of that promiscuous flapper, who has done immeasurable damage to the Dunston name. But how unfortunate for you that she now bears yours. Knowing Sidonie as I do, I am convinced that she will be nothing but trouble. Be assured that you have my complete sympathy in trying to keep control of your 'modern' daughters-in-law, especially without J.D. at your side.*

Ria said, "You can't know what it means to me to have not only Chas, but you and Fliss and Rafe as my family. Sid thinks the world of you as well. And is thankful that she no longer has to answer to 'the Dragon', as she calls Lady Dunston."

"Sidonie is a delightful young woman, and I do hope that she and Rafe will make a go of it."

"Are you skeptical?"

"I'm not convinced that they are well matched, and they're certainly not besotted by one another." In fact, it unsettled her to think that Sidonie might be more in love with Chas than Rafe. Although poised and worldly, Sid couldn't always suppress the truth from her expressive eyes. Her brother Quentin had been Chas's best friend at Oxford, so of course Marjorie had heard about the family, at whose Elizabethan country estate Chas had stayed on several occasions during his four years at university. So it wouldn't surprise her if he and Sid had had a long-ago fling. "Rafe can be... difficult. I'm afraid it could take a great deal of devotion and strength to keep him in line. That's harder when it's more a marriage of convenience than passion."

Ria, too, had wondered about Sid's motives in marrying Rafe. Having lost everything during the war - both of her beloved brothers, her adoring husband, and her cherished ancestral home - Sid had perhaps not wanted to be left behind in England with ghosts while her friends returned to Canada. Ria sensed that there had been a bond forged between Sid and Chas long ago, which wasn't easily severed. But God help Sid if she ever tried to cross the boundary of friendship with Chas!

As if their words had conjured her up, Sidonie breezed onto the veranda saying, "Darling Ria, how lovely to see you!" They touched cheeks, and Sid added, "I will admit that I'm utterly enchanted already. And here I thought all this blather about the beauties of Muskoka was just Colonial piffle or homesickness. I can certainly understand why you like to spend entire summers here. And I can't imagine anyone staying in Toronto, especially in this heat. We had coffee at The Grand, so I think a pre-lunch cocktail would be just the ticket, don't you, Rafe?"

The nearby Grand Muskoka Hotel was one of the most opulent summer resorts in Canada, and a popular spot for affluent cottagers to dine and dance. Before the SRA Golf and Country Club had been opened in '15, the Grand had been the centre of all

Summer Residents' Association activities, like the annual Regatta and Ball.

Rafe greeted Ria with a peck on the cheek, and said, "Absolutely!" before disappearing into the pavilion to mix some at the bar.

"Rafe is taking me golfing at the Country Club this afternoon," Sid informed them. "And he's going to teach me to drive the boat, although he admits that Chas is a better driver."

"I could teach you as well, if Rafe doesn't feel up to it," Ria said as he returned and passed around the tray of Manhattans, and a glass of sherry for his mother.

Chas joined them saying, "If Rafe isn't up to what?"

Sid jumped up and embraced him warmly. "Up to teaching me to drive the boat. You *do* look better, Chas! What a relief it must be to be out of that nasty cast. You'll be twirling us about the dance floor at the ball on Tuesday. Rafe was telling me all about your traditions, so I had a fabulous costume made in New York. It's so deliciously daring that I shall undoubtedly steal the show!" she said with a smirk as she placed a cigarette in a long holder and waited for one of the men to light it, which Rafe did.

"That's hardly a surprise," Chas quipped.

She gave him a mischievous grin.

Ria was always surprised at how quickly Sid could switch from being a supremely sophisticated modern woman to a fun-loving ingénue. But she realized that the more sincere and vulnerable side of Sidonie was only ever exposed to the closest of friends.

Ria was actually glad for Chas's sake that Sid still found him attractive, which was a boost to his battered ego. But much as she liked Sid, Ria didn't trust her.

Lady Sidonie had been touted as the most beautiful widow in England before she married Rafe. It wasn't only her seductive green eyes, flawless complexion, and sculpted black bob that defined her elegance, but also her free-spirited exuberance. Ria was used to Sid's outrageousness, but that had become even more pronounced since her brother Quentin's death last October. Jack, who'd had an affair with Sid in London, confided that she steeped herself in booze and cocaine. Ria didn't expect that to have changed now that she was Rafe's wife, since he himself was too fond of the bottle.

He poured Sid and himself another Manhattan, but Ria and Chas declined.

"Ria, you'll be interested to know that I'm racing a colt at Saratoga Springs in August," Rafe said. "It's one of the ones that Calypso sired before I took him over to England." Chas had bought the thoroughbred stallion, Calypso, from Rafe as a present for Ria. Rafe had then paid her handsomely for stud fees.

"How exciting!" Ria replied. "What's his name?"

"North Star. And he's a winner."

"Then you'll have put a wager on him for me."

"Sure. How much? I'm betting $50,000."

"Good Lord!" Chas exploded. "That's a lot to lose."

"But I'm not going to lose," Rafe assured him.

"I've heard that before," Chas retorted. Their father had more than once had to pay off Rafe's gambling debts.

"I'll bet $500," Ria decided.

"That's not very adventuresome," Sid chided her. "I paid that for a few frocks in New York."

"Which you can sell when Rafe gambles away his fortune," Chas told her.

She laughed. "Oh ye of little faith!"

"You're speculating on the stock market," Rafe said to Chas. "Is that really any different?"

"Damn right it is! Especially with Jack looking after the investments. He's a real whiz, which Pater realized as well."

Rafe snorted, never having taken to Jack.

"Jack's arriving today, and bringing Lizzie and Claire," Ria said, referring to two of Jack's sisters.

"We saw Emily on Broadway. She was brilliant!" Sid exclaimed. "We took her and Hugo out for supper afterwards." Emily was Jack's middle sister, an astonishing singer who had married composer Hugo Garrick. His hit musical, *Under the Moon*, had been inspired by his visit to Muskoka in 1914, when he had fallen for Emily.

"Jack said that Emily and Hugo want to buy an island, and will be up in August," Ria informed them. "Hugo maintains he can re-energize and create here. I'm sure we can persuade them to perform for us at a soiree."

"It's surprisingly *civilized* here," Sid declared as she unceremoniously sprawled in her chair, crossed her attractive ankles, and laid her head back, blowing a long stream of smoke into the rafters.

•   •   •

The lone figure sat with his arms resting on his drawn-up knees, his right hand gripping a cigarette, which moved regularly and rhythmically to his mouth. He sucked deeply on the smoke as if it were a life-giving breath.

Phoebe felt his infinite sadness. It radiated from him in muddy indigo waves. He seemed disengaged from his surroundings - the granite on which he perched, the towering trees that dwarfed him, the panorama of lake and islands that he looked straight through.

Phoebe thought of a caterpillar that curled protectively in on itself when disturbed.

"Uncle James doesn't like people smoking in the woods," she said coming up behind him. "He's afraid the island will catch on fire."

The young man jumped and spun around. "Good Lord, you gave me a start!"

"We had a fire once, when the boathouse burned down. That was scary." Phoebe hadn't forgotten the voices that had threatened her with hellfire. She shivered as she sat down beside him. "Last year Faery Island burned completely - the cottage and boathouse and trees. And all the poor little animals. Some of them tried to swim. I found a dead squirrel floating in our bay. His tail had been singed. I buried him," Phoebe said, re-living that sorrow. "Somebody had trespassed on the island and lit a campfire. They left without making sure it was completely doused and by the time the neighbouring islanders spotted the blaze, it was too late to do anything. I'm Phoebe Wyndham."

"And I'm a trespasser, I'm afraid. Silas Robbins." He stubbed out his cigarette carefully on the rock and tossed the butt as far as he could into the water.

"Why are you trespassing?"

"I spotted this cliff when I was canoeing by and wanted to see the view."

"Only you weren't looking out. More... inside."

He harrumphed. "Trying to see beyond... Never mind."

She looked at him assessingly, at the haunted dark eyes, the gentle and pleasing features that nevertheless seemed restless, the sensitive mouth that she would like to kiss. "Were you in the war?"

He reached for his cigarettes but pulled back and crushed his fingers with his left hand. "Reluctantly."

"Why did you go?"

"Because my mother's bookstore was losing clients. Women with husbands and sons at the Front didn't approve of a slacker working in the shop when every able-bodied man was needed as war fodder," he said bitterly. "But my mother has only me. My father died when I was a baby, and she's struggled to make a living for us. How could I abandon her, especially when the odds of coming back were stacked against me?"

"My cousin Max is shell-shocked, too," Phoebe said matter-of-factly. "He used to be so silly and happy and now he sometimes shakes and sweats, and suffers from terrible headaches, and jumps at the slightest noise."

"I see bodies. Or the dead rising up. Everywhere I look. Walking down a street in Toronto, I'll suddenly see one of my dead mates coming towards me. Sometimes with a gaping hole in his chest or half his face a grinning skull, reaching for me to help him. And sometimes just the way he was before we went into battle, joking and brash."

Phoebe pried his right hand out of his left and held it.

"I'm sorry," Silas stammered. "I don't know why I told you that. I haven't mentioned it before."

"I see dead people, too. Only others don't believe me. You have to make your peace with them and not let them disturb you. That's what Irene tells me. She's a nurse and my stepmother."

"Can you? Make peace with them?" Silas asked, not attempting to remove his hand from hers.

"In a way. They don't go away, but I try not to let them frighten me. Grandmother and Mama are so very stern, and never allowed me to be happy. My boyfriend died in the war, but I never see him."

"I'm sorry."

Phoebe shrugged. "He died of the flu. Lots of people died of the flu." What Phoebe didn't know was that Bobby Miller had been in a venereal disease hospital when he was struck down with the deadly Spanish Influenza.

"One of my friends who owned a cabin on Mortimer's Island, where I'm staying, died."

"You mean Edelina? At the Colony?"

"Yes. Did you know her?"

"I met her a few times, but she was a friend of my cousins."

"Of course! Zoë Wyndham. I was staying with Edelina just before Zoë left for England."

"Are you a painter or writer or just a Bohemian? Mama did not approve of the Colony."

Edelina, an accomplished artist and free spirit, had opened her island property to struggling artists and writers who set up camp and offered readings and lessons to any visitors. It became known on the lake as "The Colony", and either titillated or scandalized people when rumours of nudity and free love had swirled about.

"I'm a poet. But the words aren't pretty these days. They're gruesome and blood-soaked." He looked at Phoebe sharply. "I keep saying things to you that I wouldn't to anyone else. Are you real,

Phoebe, or are you a forest nymph who's come to lead me into some fantastical underworld?"

She giggled. "I've always felt that I live in a different world, like Alice."

"Through the looking-glass?"

"Oh yes."

"I lived in books, too, when I was young. I was Huck Finn and Robinson Crusoe and Oliver Twist. Mum was forever catching me reading when I should have been stocking the shelves, but I never could resist opening a book to see what wonderful words and magical lands lived beneath the cover." Silas stared at her in puzzlement again.

Phoebe smiled. She had a made a friend. Her very own. Heeding Irene's advice about not giving herself too freely and eagerly to men, as she had to Bobby Miller, she would spend every moment she could with him, to get to know him. It was surely propitious that he had a "bird" name like she did. Her stepmother, Irene, had been a Partridge, and look at how well she had turned out.

Becoming Phoebe Robbins would suit her very well indeed.

•   •   •

Jack stood at the railing of the stately steamship and gazed at the sparkling water with excitement. Although he had only spent one summer in Muskoka, he felt that he was coming home. How different from that initial journey five years ago when he, full of determination and bravado, had come to make a claim on his Wyndham family. Because his father had been disinherited for marrying an actress, Jack and his siblings had spent miserable and hungry years fighting to survive in the slums of Toronto. Needlessly, as it happened, for as soon as his Uncle Richard had found out, he had generously bought Jack's family a house, where his mother now felt that she lived in paradise.

How proud Jack was to see the Wyndham name emblazoned on the mills that whined and screeched in the busy and log-choked bay in Gravenhurst. And how glad that he had escaped working in one of them by going off to war.

As they steamed through the Bay, Jack noticed the imposing new tuberculosis sanatorium that dominated a spectacular rocky bluff. Already it was being expanded. Further along an older one, which had been the very first in Canada, could be mistaken for a sprawling summer resort were it not for the "guests" wandering about in dressing robes. They waved as the ship tooted throatily.

He couldn't help but wonder if his father would have survived his consumption had he had the wherewithal to be treated there. If only he'd asked his brother Richard for help!

But Jack wouldn't dwell on past mistakes. He couldn't suppress a triumphant chuckle when he realized how far he had come since being a waiter at the Grand Muskoka Hotel, where he had first confronted his formidable grandmother. Through his newfound connections, his cleverness, and hard work, he was already a wealthy man. And he had the war to thank for that.

He had gone overseas with Chas Thornton to join the Royal Flying Corps, and they had become best friends, flying together for half the war. Indeed, Chas had probably saved Jack's life, for which Chas had been awarded his first Distinguished Service Order medal. Patriarch J.D. Thornton, one of the richest men in Canada, had liked Jack's investment strategies, and had paid him handsomely for conducting some business on his behalf in England.

And there, through Chas's friend Lady Sidonie Dunston, Jack had met Canadian-born Sir Max Aitken, now Lord Beaverbrook, who had taken to Jack, and offered him cunning financial advice and a less dangerous post as a war artist. A self-made multimillionaire, Aitken had recognized a kindred spirit in Jack.

But Jack had also distinguished himself first as an Ace, winning a Military Cross, and then through his powerful paintings, which were part of Beaverbrook's collection for Canada.

After a rift with Ria, he had been able to support her at crucial times, and they had grown close. Yes, the war had been good to him.

The money that Jack had inherited from his grandmother in 1914 was being doled out to him over ten years, but he had invested wisely. His steel stocks were up over 1400% in just the past two years, and General Motors, up 940%. He'd made a huge sum for helping to broker a merger of the Thorntons' Canada Investment Bank with the Dominion Commerce Bank, thanks once again to advice from Beaverbrook. Expecting that certain stocks would decline in a post-war slump, Jack was buying up real estate in the city and land on the edge of it. Chas also entrusted most of his investments with him, and paid him a princely sum to administer them.

Now he was going to Wyndwood for his ultimate bid to secure his future.

"You look decidedly smug," his sister Lizzie said as she joined him. Their youngest sister, Claire, stayed under the shade of the upper deck, reading a book.

He exhaled an exuberant guffaw. "I was just imagining how this summer will play out."

"Counting your chickens already?"

"I have no doubt that Fliss will accept my proposal. We got to know each other through our wartime correspondence, and I've been a devoted friend during the past five months. Christ, she was sweet on me before I left."

"She wasn't even fifteen then! You vile seducer." Lizzie chuckled. "She's never had a chance since you spun your web, has she? Mind you, she's damned lucky to get you. If she weren't rolling in money, she'd never bag the handsomest of the Wyndham men. She's still a rather plain little thing, despite all my efforts to make her more glamorous. Unlike her brothers. Who may well not see you as a brother-in-law."

"I can't imagine Chas objecting. Rafe will, of course, but to hell with him."

Lizzie frowned and stared at the water frothing where the bow cleaved it. "How am I going to deal with him this summer?" she asked. "When I just want to kill him!"

"He's not good enough for you, Lizzie. You'll meet plenty of eligible men who'll be making fools of themselves over you. Remember your aristocratic roots, pour on the charm, and don't think about the past."

When Lizzie had heard that Rafe married Lady Sidonie Dunston, she'd torn off the gold locket that he had given her and hurled it against the wall, accompanied by a string of profanities. That had been followed by the framed portrait of him that she had taken in New York. When he had told her that she was "his girl". The glass had burst into a thousand tiny shards that Lizzie savagely ground into the photograph.

She'd grabbed the pile of letters he had written to her and was about to burn them in the fireplace when her mother had said calmly, "Those might be useful some day."

"It's time for you to indulge yourself, Sis," Jack said, interrupting her thoughts. "Take what you want out of life."

But she wanted Rafe. If he was somewhat dissipated, it only added to his charm. Life would never be dull with him.

"Are you planning to stay with Olivia, or take Ria up on her offer?" Jack asked.

"Definitely with Olivia. Claire wants to be with Esme, of course, and I'm used to being there as well. Anyway, I have no wish to be reminded of my days as Molly the maid," she added with a laugh. "I'm still afraid that Grayson might take a good look at me one day and recognize me. Like Phoebe did. Christ, that scared me!"

She knew that she had played the humble Irish maid to perfection that summer of 1914 when she had worked at Wyndwood, but still felt a tingle of apprehension whenever she visited Ria's cottage as a privileged guest.

"Yes, well no one believes Phoebe anyway, so you shouldn't worry. You look nothing like meek little Molly Jones now," Jack assured her. "Just think, Lizzie, once I'm married to Fliss, you can stay with us at Thorncliff until you have your own cottage."

J.D. had left Thorncliff Island to Felicity, with the proviso that her mother, Marjorie, could have the use of it during her lifetime. Chas and Rafe were each to have one of the neighbouring islands, but Chas didn't need a cottage. Rafe had inherited the Thornridge estate in the city, since Chas and Ria had Wyndholme, and Chas got the bank building in the heart of the city. Fliss and her mother each received two million, Marjorie's allotment being ten times the amount that she had brought into the marriage with the shrewd and ambitious upstart, Joseph Davenport Thornton. Other lands, shares, and monies were divided equally between Chas and Rafe, making them superbly wealthy. But Jack knew he could turn Fliss's millions into many more. He laughed again at this prize that was his for the taking.

When the steamship pulled up to the Wyndwood wharf four hours later, Jack felt once again that exhilaration of belonging on this family island. After all, he and his siblings had grown up on stories about it from their father, who had loved it so intensely that he'd painted endless pictures of it from memory. When there had been money for paints. Even the cottage had seemed familiar, like a misty memory.

Sophie came skipping down the path to the dock, shouting, "Cousin Jack! Will we make a book about the lake? We can have Mr. Toad drive a racing boat, like Daddy Chas!" Ria had written a story for Sophie in France, based on *The Wind in the Willows* characters, which Sophie and Jack had illustrated.

As Sophie threw herself into his outstretched arms, Jack said, "I'm happy to see such enthusiasm, ma minette! We should certainly have a boating adventure for Mr. Toad."

Ria laughed as she, Charlie, and Alice sauntered down more slowly. "Sophie already has a job for you, I see."

"An artistic endeavor, which is more fun than mere work, isn't it? Perhaps Alice would like to take over the writing, since she is already a renowned author and foreign correspondent." During the war, Alice had written pieces for the magazine *Home Fires*, and still submitted the occasional article.

She giggled. "I wouldn't want to usurp Ria's role as author."

"Oh, but you must! I shall become publisher," Ria stated firmly. "It's so good to have you all back at Wyndwood," she added to her cousins. "And I'm delighted that you can stay for the summer!"

"It's wonderful to be here and to escape the city heat," Lizzie said graciously. "It's become quite unbearable."

"Then you really must persuade your mother to visit as well," Ria stated.

"She certainly appreciated your invitation and may join us later in the summer," Lizzie explained. Jack had insisted that his mother no longer needed to take boarders, now that he was home, so she had no excuse for staying away. But she felt awkward and bitter around the Wyndhams, who had for so many years ignored them. "Jack had electric fans installed, so the house is relatively comfortable."

Chas greeted them on the veranda, where refreshments were set out on silver trays.

"Ria, do you mind if I skip tea?" Claire asked. "I can hardly wait to go for a swim! Will you come, Alice?"

"Grab scones and eat them on the way, if you like," Ria suggested.

Claire grinned and did just that as Alice ran to her room to fetch her swimsuit. Chattering like long-time friends, they headed down the path towards Silver Bay. Lizzie was itching to go along, but politely stayed.

"So what's this that Sophie's been telling me about Daddy Chas driving racing boats?" Jack asked his friend.

Chas was eager to catch him up on the news.

"And I expect to be the marine co-pilot or whatever you call it," Ria stated.

"Riding mechanic," Chas replied. "And I've already hired Stephen, my darling. So you will have to lead the cheering instead."

"Oh, very adventuresome!"

"I would have thought you'd had enough adventures to last a lifetime," Jack said.

"That shows how little you know me! But for now, I will be content to take the children for a swim. Are you happy with your old room above the boathouse, Jack, or would you prefer to be in the cottage?"

"In the boathouse I can set up my easel. It's perfect, Ria. You don't know how much that means to me."

For a brief moment, Ria recalled her initial infatuation with Jack, and how she had visited him in his room. It wouldn't have taken much for him to seduce her, and she now respected him for not trying. What she didn't know was that Lizzie, disguised as a maid, had been hiding there at the time.

"I shall be off to Silver Bay then," Lizzie said with relief.

"Aunt Olivia invited us all for dinner, so we'll see you later," Ria replied.

An entire summer at the cottage. What luxury, Jack thought as he stepped onto the generous balcony outside his room and gazed at the lake afloat with rugged, tree-tufted islands. The odd business deal would take him to the city for a day or two, but otherwise he was planning to indulge himself. And, of course, woo Fliss.

The only disturbing note was that Ouhu was so close, and he imagined Ellie too readily. How delicious she had been five years ago when they had been lovers, and he had painted a nude portrait of her. How he still loved her, longed for her. Worried about her.

But he needed to push that into the past. Greater things beckoned him.

Chapter 2

"Thought I'd find a seaplane docked here, Chase," the man in the rowboat said as he shipped his oars.

Chas had just emerged from the boathouse, and was surprised to hear himself addressed by the nickname he'd acquired in the Royal Flying Corps 2nd Squadron in '15. Squinting against the sun to see the rower, he said, "Good Lord, is that Crackers?"

Bertram Cracknell laughed. "One and the same! How are you, old chap? Heard about your amazing VC battle, of course."

"I'm doing well enough. And glad to see that you survived relatively unscathed. Do come ashore!"

Bertram tied up at one of the docks flanking the boathouse. Chas shook his hand vigorously. "Just in time for drinks. Come up to the house. How the devil did you find me?"

"Remembered you talking about Muskoka. Thought I'd come and have a look at it for myself. Staying in a hotel in Port Darling. Asked around and doesn't everyone know the famous Major Thornton! Surprised they don't have a banner up in the village announcing that you live on the lake. Chap at the boat livery couldn't sing your praises highly enough."

"You must have rented from Mac Seaford."

"Right-o."

"He's building some boats for me."

"No planes then?"

"I've had my fill of them. I don't believe you've met my wife."

Ria and Alice were teaching the children croquet on the only flat piece of land at The Point - in the narrow valley that lay between the two bays. The old caretaker's cabin - modified for Patrick, the footman, and his wife, Tilda, the parlour maid - and the new cottage for the Graysons sat huddled beside it, beneath the steep cliff that rose to the "Dragon's Back", as Ria and her cousins called it. On the other side squatted the laundry shed next to the herb garden and the icehouse.

"Ria, this is an old comrade, Bert Cracknell. Crackers we called him because he was a crazy daredevil."

"Even more than you?" she quipped.

Chas chuckled, and introduced his family, wondering why Charlie was eyeing Bert suspiciously. "We'll go and reminisce, and you can join us at your leisure," he added to Ria.

She was happy to leave them to their memories, knowing that it was important for wartime pals to talk.

"Lovely lady. You always knew how to pick 'em, Chase. She the fiancé who was on the *Lusitania*?"

"Yes." Chas said, not pleased with Bert's flippant remark about women. Of course many of the pilots in 2nd Squadron had seen him with Madeline at some point, despite his attempts at discretion. A beautiful young woman, she had occasioned plenty of ribald comments in the mess.

"Recall how you went berserk when you heard about the ship sinking. Thought you were going to fly your bus to Ireland." Chas had threatened to, and his Commanding Officer had taken pity on him and given him compassionate leave to find Ria. "Happy ending after all then. Damn shame, your injuries, though," Bert said as Chas hobbled up the path to the back veranda.

"I'm alive. How was the rest of your war?"

"Got a Blighty in the arm, and was on Home Defence for a while after that healed. Finally got back to the Front in '17 as Captain, where I was made a Flight Commander in 60 Squadron, and met Bishop. Bagged twenty-three Boche."

"Impressive. And a medal or two?" Chas asked as they walked along the breezeway between the kitchen and the cottage, and then the west veranda.

"An MC and a DFC."

French doors opened into the library, where Chas offered drinks from the trolley that sported a variety of liquor and a soda siphon. Two walls were lined with books, but the room had been used mainly as an office, offering deep leather chairs facing a large rosewood desk from which Grandmother Augusta Wyndham had conducted business - or chastised her offspring. The smell of stale tobacco and decades of smoke mingled with the mustiness of leather-bound tomes that froze in winter and swelled in the damp summer heat.

Bert savoured his cognac. "Very nice," he said, holding the crystal glass up to the light. "You always had class, Chase."

They reminisced about their adventures and comrades who had survived. "Ran into Gerry recently. Says he's not interested in flying any more and has gone into the family jewellery business."

"And what are you doing now?" Chas asked.

"Father's trying to get me to settle down in Peterborough. Take over the hardware store. Can you imagine how deadly that would be? Flying's in my blood. Told him I'll make a career of it. Bishop and Barker have taken me on for some jobs. Told me that you've invested in their company."

"We'll see how that goes," Chas said.

"That's where I see my future. Commercial aviation. Aerial photographs, barnstorming, flying businessmen about."

"Planning to compete against Bishop and Barker then?"

"No, no. It's a big country. Lots of scope. Thought I might try the prairies." He wiggled his empty glass as if he could conjure up some more of the amber elixir. Chas poured him another measure. "Just need a bit of capital to get me going. Planning to enter that air race to New York next month. $10,000 in prizes. Barker's going to fly one of the Fokker D. VIIs that the government got as war trophies." The Fokkers were German planes that had been piloted by aces like the Red Baron.

"Thought you might be willing to take a chance on me as well, Chase," Bert said, looking at Chas a bit shamefaced. "Could use a good bus."

Chas was thoughtful, realizing the true purpose of this visit. "I'll certainly consider it."

Bert nodded and took a large gulp. "Isn't that Madeline's boy? Your son, Charlie?"

Chas was surprised and wary. "What makes you think that?"

"She was looking for companionship after you left her. Had some good times together. Told me how rich and generous the kid's father was, and how she still loved him and expected he would come back to her." He looked pointedly at Chas, who winced inwardly at those words. He didn't need to be reminded of his dishonorable behaviour that had wounded Madeline as well as Ria. "Didn't take much imagination to realize she meant you, especially when she called the kid Charles. Saw them just a couple of months before the war ended. Heard she'd died. Wondered what had happened to him."

Which explained why Charlie had seemed to recognize Bert. "I trust you'll keep it under your hat," Chas stated. "We adopted a French orphan. That's all that anyone needs to know."

"Sure thing, Chase. What are friends for if not to help and stand by each other, eh?"

Chas sensed a subtle threat.

"Does your wife know?" Bert asked.

"Of course."

"Generous woman."

"She is indeed."

"Won't keep you. Staying at the Northern Lights Hotel. Let me know what you think. $2500 would buy me a surplus Curtiss Canuck. Give me a good start. Not so much for a chap like you, eh? Heard your old man left millions."

Chas noticed how tightly Bert held his glass, and realized that he was probably desperate. Although Chas felt sorry for him, he was annoyed and disturbed that Bert was privy to his secret. It would be devastating for Charlie as well as the Wyndhams and Thorntons if the boy's true parentage were revealed.

"I'll discuss it with my financial manager. You remember Jack Wyndham."

"Sure thing! Appreciate it, Chase."

"You'll excuse me if I don't walk down to the dock with you."

"Sure thing! Rest that leg."

But Chas stayed not because he couldn't walk back down to the bay, but because he didn't want to do it in Bert's company. Damnation! Would that brief affair with Madeline haunt him forever? He had been in a deep funk, certain that he was going to die, like so many of his friends already had. Madeline had been alone and frightened, so they'd consoled one another. If only he had taken better precautions, Charlie would never have been conceived, and Ria would never have found out. That had almost destroyed their marriage.

And yet, a part of him rejoiced in his son, since Ria had lost their baby and wasn't able to have more.

When Jack joined Chas a little while later, he said, "It was an exhilarating day to be out sailing! Almost like flying." He poured himself a scotch.

"Bert Cracknell was here."

"Old Crackers? What's he up to?"

Chas told him.

"So it's thinly disguised blackmail," Jack said with a frown. "So much for the integrity of old comrades in arms."

"I'll admit that he seemed embarrassed to be asking for money. It's damnable that the government's doing so little to help men readjust to civilian life. There's not even a Canadian air force that pilots could join, to make use of their skills. Is it any wonder that unemployed veterans joined the General Strike in Winnipeg?"

"And got shot by the Mounted Police!"

"It's shameful! Makes you wonder what we were fighting for. Christ, do you know that Barker's having problems getting the government to pay for another operation that he needs on his arm? They tell him that he was a member of the RAF when he was wounded, and so, not Canada's responsibility. What a disgraceful way to treat our wounded heroes!" Chas had paid for his own operation in the spring, but then he could afford the best doctors.

"I've decided that I will help Bert. But not because of his implied threat. In fact, that almost put me off. An interest-free loan for three years, and then he'll be charged the going rate if he hasn't repaid it. Is that reasonable?"

"Very generous."

"Perhaps you can handle it for me, Jack. I don't want to see him at the moment."

"Of course, Chas. And I'll let him know that his approach wasn't appreciated."

"As long as you're tactful."

"Oh, I will be."

•   •   •

"Of course I realize that the Ball is your responsibility now, as I suppose it *must* be held here again. But I had hoped that you would appreciate my involvement, since I did carry on the tradition for the past four years, despite the exigencies of the war," Helena grumbled.

Ria had promised herself that she would start afresh, forget the pre-war rift between herself and her stepmother. And her father. So she said calmly, "I am grateful for your suggestions, Helena, but adamant about not having fireworks."

"But that's part of the tradition! People not only expect them, but enjoy them."

"For those of us, the children especially, who lived through air raids and bombings, it would be disturbing." She could have said "terrifying", but Helena would have thought her overly dramatic.

"Nonsense! This is just innocent fun."

Ria tried to control her temper. After all, how could Helena or anyone else who wasn't there comprehend or even imagine? "Not for us. Please try to understand, Helena."

"I'm beginning to find it quite tedious that the war is still being used for so many excuses. It's time to move on."

"And ignore the ordeals of those who were there? Yes, I do see how the truth can be quite inconvenient for society."

"You needn't be sarcastic, Victoria. It doesn't become you now that you are a mother."

Ria didn't question this odd logic, but it did amuse her and break the tension. "There will be fireworks at the Country Club, so we'll have a good view of those, and don't need our own." And that was far enough away for them to enjoy the spectacle without too much of the attendant noise.

Helena looked at Ria imperiously. "You may find that your renowned Dominion Day Ball will lose its lustre."

"If only our loyal friends attend, then so be it. Things change," Ria said dismissively.

Sophie came out to the veranda and said, "Oh, Grandmother, would you like to see my costume for the Ball?"

Helena shot Ria a sharp glance. "Not now, dear. And we'll have to think of something else for you to call me. Perhaps Aunt Helena would be best. Do run along while I talk to your mother."

Sophie shrugged disappointedly and went back into the sitting room.

"You could have shown some interest, Helena," Ria said, trying to smother her anger at her stepmother's abruptness. "The children are so excited about the Ball."

"You can't mean to allow them to attend?"

"Of course they will! Wyndham children have always participated. You should bring Cecilia and she could play with Charlie."

"Don't be absurd!"

"Life is less formal on the lake, Helena. It's an easier way for children to learn their social graces. That was Grandmother's contention. Jimmy is, of course, too young, and I expect that you're right that Cecilia is also. Perhaps in a couple of years." Before Helena could become indignant at the implied slight against her daughter, Ria said, "Now, Helena, I am grateful for the loan of your staff, so shall we review the menu and duties?"

She was proud of herself for handling Helena with more maturity than she had five years ago when her father had surprised her with his intention to marry a woman young enough to be his daughter. A gold-digger, Ria's grandmother had called her.

When Helena had left for home, which was about half a mile along the shore path on the west side of the island, Ria joined Jack and the children in the sitting room. They were still making decorations for the Ball.

The ballroom-sized living room stretched across the entire front of the cottage, but didn't seem cavernous despite the lofty ceiling. A grand piano, sofas and chairs grouped around the two fireplaces, and polished tables ready for card and other games offered more intimate spaces. The pale basswood that panelled the walls and ceiling, and the numerous screened windows and French doors that opened onto three sides of the veranda brightened the dim interior. Ria had already removed the mangy mounted heads of deer and moose - Grandfather Wyndham's trophies - which had always glared at them accusingly. Phoebe claimed that they spoke to her and longed to be set free. Original paintings - some from Jack and Edelina - were now more welcoming.

For the "fairyland" theme, they had created dragonflies, butterflies, fairies, gnomes, and toadstools, the latter, gigantic and carved by Gareth out of balsa wood. Jack was helping them to paint the props. Ria had recruited the older girls to string together "vines" of white carnations and roses, which would adorn the eaves of the veranda and pavilion roofs, and drape from the lower branches of nearby trees. Lying to the east of the house, the pavilion was merely a large, roofed, open-sided wooden platform, where concerts and theatricals were also held on occasion.

Chas returned from Thorncliff in time for tea. Fliss had persuaded him that she needed his expert advice to prepare for the Stepping Stone Marathon. The race, held on Dominion Day, involved swimming from one "Stepping Stone" island to the next and, for the men, the last longer stretch to Wyndwood. Although it had been going on for over two decades, 1914 was the first time that the girls had participated. Cousin Beatrice, visiting from England at the time, had supplied the Countess of Kirkland's Ladies Cup, which Ria had won.

She asked, "How was the training, coach?"

Chas guffawed. "Gruelling! Fliss is determined to win."

"That doesn't surprise me, since she is very much your sister," Ria replied.

"Well, she won't go unchallenged," Esme stated. "I'm determined to keep the Cup in the Wyndham family."

"I sense a battle brewing," Alice said.

"Dead right!" Esme said. "Don't think that friendship comes into play at all. It's serious business. You should have seen Ria and Ellie battling at the finish last time. And Jack nearly killed himself to beat Chas."

"Then why did you convince me to participate?" Alice asked. "I'm not very good. I didn't even know *how* to swim until Ria taught me in England."

"Precisely! So you won't be any competition." Esme grinned at her. "But it is terribly good fun!"

"Well, you can count me out," Claire said. "I can barely swim across Silver Bay." She hadn't felt completely well since her bout with influenza last fall, but that wasn't unusual. Many people were taking time recovering, including her Uncle Richard, Esme's father. "I will save my energy for the ball."

"You're so wet!" Esme teased.

"May I race, too?" Sophie asked.

"Not this year, poppet," Chas replied. "But when you're a bit older. In the meantime, you can concentrate on your tennis. Which reminds me, Ria. I don't see why we shouldn't have a tennis tournament for the youngsters, say twelve and under. We could hold it the day before the regular one."

"That's a terrific idea, Chas!" Ria said. "We'll provide the Thornton Junior Cup."

Sophie was bouncing with excitement. She admired the wondrous engraved silver chalice that Ria had won for the Stepping Stone Marathon. And, indeed, all the other trophies lining the mantelpieces.

When they had finished tea, Grayson said to Ria, "Might I have a word, Mrs. Thornton?"

"Certainly! Shall we go to the library?"

Originally from England, Grayson had been the Wyndham butler for twenty-five years, but he had become more like a father to Ria during their shared wartime experiences.

When he had shut the door, he said, "I'm delighted to tell you that Branwyn is with child."

"Oh, Grayson, how marvellous!" She almost threw her arms about him. "I'm so happy for you!"

He was beaming. "I felt blessed to have a stepson, and doubly so now." Branwyn's son, Gareth, was nineteen, and deaf since he'd had childhood measles. He was a talented gardener, who had created an herb garden behind the cottage, and flowerbeds tucked strategically into rocky crevices and highlighting paths.

Ria knew that Grayson had always wanted a child, but he and his first wife had had no luck. At fifty-five, he surely thought he would never have his own. "When is it due?"

"In January, we think."

"We'll have Dr. Carlyle examine Branwyn to be sure that everything is as it should be." Branwyn was forty - not the easiest time to have a baby.

"I trust this won't cause any problems, Mrs. Thornton."

"Not at all! I'm glad that you have your own quarters, so that your family will have some privacy." She was building a small house for the Graysons in the grounds of Wyndholme, while Patrick and Tilda would take over their suite in the main house. Both Ria and Chas had come to realize how valuable good and loyal servants were.

"Might Chas and I be allowed to be Godparents?"

"That is most generous!" Grayson said with obvious delight.

This time it was he who seemed to want to embrace her. Ria thought it absurd that although they felt such obvious affection for one another and had shared so much, whether heartbreak or joy, they couldn't show it. One didn't hug one's butler, although she had at his wedding, and he had allowed himself to reciprocate.

"Not at all! It's entirely selfish. You know how I love children. Now I must go and congratulate Branwyn as well. Is she in the kitchen?" Although officially the housekeeper since her marriage, Branwyn also helped Mrs. Hadley, the cook.

"Yes."

The kitchen was separated from the main house by a breezeway - for obvious reasons. Ria was instantly struck by the heat from the woodstove that burned all summer to cook meals and boil water. With temperatures outside well into the 80's, it must be at least ten degrees hotter here.

"Are all the doors and windows open, Grayson? It's stifling."

"Yes they are, Mrs. Thornton. I believe the new bathroom has blocked the cross-breezes." But eliminated the need for an outhouse, for which the staff was grateful.

"Oh dear, then we shall have to see how to make it more bearable in here. Mrs. Grayson, how wonderful that you are going to increase our household! You must be sure to take time to rest, and please avail yourself of Dr. Carlyle's services at our expense."

"Thank you, Madam!"

Branwyn's port-wine stain made one side of her face livid and somewhat strawberry textured. Yet she was still an attractive woman, as the discolouration of her skin didn't detract significantly from good bone structure and pleasing features. Because superstitious people attributed this birthmark to the sign of the devil, and because she was knowledgeable about herbs, Branwyn had earned a reputation as a witch in her rural Hampshire community. Ria found her and her potions invaluable, especially during the influenza epidemic last autumn. It was while Branwyn, then the scullery maid at Ria's English house, Priory Manor, had been nursing Grayson through a life-threatening bout that he fell in love with her.

"I give you fair warning that I intend to take an active interest in my Godchild," Ria told her.

After her initial surprise, Branwyn smiled, but was forestalled from replying by Mrs. Hadley saying, "You've always wanted a houseful of children, haven't you?"

"What good is a large house if you can't fill it with children and laughter?" Ria asked.

"But here you are, hardly more than a child yourself, and already mother to a nine-year-old!" Mrs. Hadley shook her head. Ria had turned twenty-three just weeks earlier.

"I started young," she teased.

"Get away with you! What would people think if they heard such nonsense? I don't know!" But the cook was amused nonetheless.

"Didn't Grandmother always say I was incorrigible?"

"Didn't she just, God rest her soul. And didn't I hear all about it when you came to the kitchen to tell me your woes?" Mrs. Hadley had been good to Ria, often a lonely child, who had always been welcome in the kitchen at Wyndholme where special cookies or other treats awaited her.

"As usual, something smells delicious. Roast beef?"

"Didn't you just finish your tea?" the cook asked.

"And a very fine one it was. But we should consider setting up an outdoor fire pit with a grill, like the Carlyles have, for cook-outs on really hot days."

"Whatever next? I won't be trudging outside to do the cooking or to make a cup of tea! This has been my kitchen for almost forty summers, so you just leave everything to me, Mrs. Thornton, and let me know if something's not to your taste."

"Yes, Mrs. Hadley," Ria said obediently. "Although I don't think you'll ever hear me complain." Ria knew that she took great pride in her cooking, and rightly so. "There are officers, including Generals, in Britain who still sing your praises." The delectable jams and preserves and rich, rum-soaked Christmas cakes that Mrs. Hadley had sent to Ria and Chas during the war had been praised by all who had sampled them.

The cook smiled with satisfaction.

•   •   •

"My little sister, Sarah, died when I was six. I was terribly upset until God told me that He would look after her, and that she would still be able to talk to me," Phoebe said.

"Does she?" Silas asked.

"Oh yes."

They were once again perched on the cliff at the north end of Wyndwood. It had been two days since they first met, and Silas had agreed to return.

"I don't believe in God anymore," he admitted.

"Don't you?"

"Not after the hell I saw in France."

"You can't blame God if people won't listen to what He says."

"Do you know Edelina's friend, Paul, who runs the Colony now?"

"He once came to our masquerade ball dressed as a priest."

"He *was* a Catholic priest. But he was a stretcher-bearer in the war, and he's lost his faith."

"I expect he's just lost faith in the church and the way they want us to think about God. When you truly know God, you don't need someone else to tell you how to worship Him or that you should be afraid of Him or He won't want you in heaven. Mama was always telling me that, and that I was wicked. But Irene says that I was just naïve. Anyway, I feel God, and He is everything good. But He can't stop people from being bad or even dying." She almost told him about her poor baby, but she knew that Gloria must forever remain a secret because people would think that she *was* wicked and would shun her, and the rest of her family would be socially embarrassed.

"You're so confident," Silas said, somewhat awed. "And wise."

"Do you think so?" she asked in astonishment. "People tell me I'm crazy."

He grinned. "They tell me that too."

Phoebe giggled and put her arm through his. Leaning against him felt so good and *right*.

"So how *do* you see God?" Silas asked.

"Just by looking around. He is everywhere - in the earth, the sky, the water."

"You mean I just have to look at things differently?"

"You have to open your mind and heart and just... be at one with Him." She sat up and took his hand, putting it flat on the stone. Placing hers over it she guided his as she said, "Feel the rock. Don't think of anything but how hard and gritty and yet smooth it is. Now look at the colours - the flecks of black and pink in the granite, and the dazzling white seam of quartz. The different shades of green and turquoise of the lichen and mosses. Notice the ripples in it, the twists and hollows, as if it had once been as soft as toffee. Now look at the lake. See how the light bounces off as it were alive? Then look up at the treetops. See how they web the sky? And beyond them, the wisps of clouds look like beckoning fingers. All that is God."

Silas looked at her in amazement.

"Don't you feel surrounded and touched by something greater?" she asked.

"Yes! If only I could ignore or obliterate all those images of wanton destruction and cruel suffering."

"Or if you stop blaming God for them. Irene says that we have to take responsibility for our actions."

"It's not always possible. Not when your superiors order you to kill."

"Then you can't blame yourself either." Phoebe stroked his arm. She was tempted to invite him to the Ball, but was afraid that her family would order her to stay away from him, because she knew that she shouldn't be meeting him alone like this. Besides, she wanted him all to herself.

•   •   •

Ria loved the heat of the sun on her bare arms and face. She had spent too many days freezing in England and France during the past few years. So she was with the children in the sun-drenched west bay, rather than the shady, sheltered, and smaller Back Bay on the opposite side of the point, where the change house was. In the old days, as she thought of those pre-war years, they had always swum in the Back Bay, except for their forays around the point. But even then, Ria hadn't concerned herself with staying fashionably pale under large hats and parasols. It felt invigorating to be sun-bronzed.

Jack and Lizzie were practicing their tennis at the SRA Golf and Country Club, to which all the Wyndhams belonged. Chas was in Port Darling talking to Mac Seaford about boats. So she was teaching Charlie to swim, while Sophie was splashing about beside them in the crystal clear water. Alice, Esme, Claire, and Johanna were sitting on one of the docks that flanked the boathouse, dangling their feet in the water and chatting. Ria felt a generation older as she watched them.

She was glad to see that Johanna had befriended Esme and Claire as readily as she had Alice. Ria felt sorry for the Belgian refugee who had witnessed the brutality of invasion, and had lost her father and brother to the advancing Germans. She didn't want the girl to exist in the governess no-man's-land between upstairs and down, and so treated her more like a member of the family, albeit one who had duties to the children. Obviously she and Chas weren't the only ones impressed by Johanna's guilelessness and enthusiasm.

And she wasn't surprised that Johanna, who had no pretensions despite her status with the family, had been as easily accepted by the servants, and, indeed, had already established a friendship with Gareth in England. She had quickly picked up the sign language that he and his mother had concocted. Because her father, a teacher and intellectual, had taught his children as much by observation as from books, Johanna spent lots of time outside with the children, often persuading Gareth to share his knowledge of nature. Ria wondered if there was a romance blossoming.

Just now Gareth was cutting back the soil and grass and scrub vegetation to enlarge the depth of the beach. Then he would build a stone retaining wall where nature hadn't already sculpted the granite or deposited boulders, and reroute the path. He was also creating artistic pockets of flowerbeds with the excess soil.

Threads of golden sunlight undulated and chased each other across the hard, ribbed sand. The clear water was warm and shallow, shelving gradually so that it was a safe place for young or inexperienced swimmers.

Sophie shrieked, but Ria's concern dissolved into amusement as Sophie tired to shoo away a dragonfly that had landed in her hair. "It won't hurt you, ma petite," she assured the child as she held out her hand in invitation to the dragonfly, which immediately landed on her finger. The iridescent green insect was pulsing its transparent wings. "See how beautiful it is."

A mating pair of blue damsel flies also landed on Ria's hand, and Sophie said, "Oh, look! Two of them stuck together! What are they doing?"

Ria suppressed a giggle. "Just having fun."

She noticed a canoe approaching them from the Stepping Stone islands and realized that Justin Carrington and his wife, Toni, were coming to visit. She waved joyfully.

Ria had known the Carringtons most of her life, and Justin's sister Vivian had travelled with her on the *Lusitania*, but hadn't survived. Their younger sister, Lydia, was married to Ria's cousin Max, and Grandmother had intended - virtually decreed - that Ria would marry Justin.

Ria recalled her swooning infatuation with him the summer when she was fifteen and he, eighteen. How kind and indulgent he had been. So she'd been disconcerted that he'd eventually developed feelings for her while her romance with Chas had blossomed.

How delighted she was that he had fallen for her WATS friend, Lady Antonia Upton, the spirited daughter of an Earl. They had married in a fairytale Christmas ceremony at the family estate, Quincy Castle, in 1917, once Justin had recuperated from his near-fatal wounds.

"Tell me you're here for the entire summer!" Ria insisted as she greeted them. She had only seen them once in the month since they had returned from England, Justin having just finished his work at the War Office in London.

He grinned. "I figured we deserved an idle summer after these last years, so yes."

"And besides, it will take me that long to learn how to canoe," Toni added with a laugh as they pulled up to the boathouse dock.

"We'll have you fit to race in the Regatta by August," Ria said.

"Well, I shan't mind the practice. It's heavenly on the lake. Just as you always said, Ria."

To Justin, Ria said, "Isn't it wonderful when people appreciate what we adore? It endears me to them even more."

After an exuberant greeting from Sophie and Alice - who had herself been enthralled with the charming and handsome Justin - the guests followed Ria to the veranda for tea. Johanna was back on duty with the children, but the other girls stayed with them at the beach.

"Chas is in Port Darling setting himself up as a boat-builder," Ria said and went on to explain.

"I thought it would be aeroplanes," Justin said.

"As did I," Ria sighed. "But I think Chas has developed a fear of flying. Not that he will admit it."

"It's not surprising after what he went through. And still does, I expect."

"There's much less pain since the operation. And I'm hoping that rest and sunshine and his new hobby will restore his strength and vitality. Besides, I don't mind fast boats."

Justin laughed. "I wouldn't be at all surprised if you intended to be the first woman boat racer in Canada."

She flashed him a mischievous grin.

A launch sped towards the bay, turned a sharp curve to send waves skittering into the shallows, delighting the children, and abruptly throttled back to glide sedately into the boathouse.

After Chas had joined Ria and their guests and caught them up on his latest venture, Justin said, "We have some news. Will you be Godparents to our first child?" Justin hadn't known how to break this to Ria. He was one of the few people who knew about her baby, and how devastated she had been to find out that an infection had left her sterile.

Although this reminder of her own infertility sent an initial wave of sadness through her, Ria went over to hug Toni. It was inevitable that all her married friends would be having babies soon, and she would just have to harden herself to her disappointment. And feel blessed for the children she had. "Of course! How wonderful! When is it to be?"

"In December, around our anniversary," Toni said.

"A Christmas child, perhaps. It seems somehow fitting," Ria said. "Well, I plan to have dozens of Godchildren whom I can spoil. And I shall encourage them to come to me when their parents are being unreasonable," she added with a grin.

"My wretched sisters have been trying to coerce Mother into bringing them over for a visit this summer, but I've suggested that they wait until at least next year, and then they can see their niece or nephew," Toni said. "I need to establish a credible reputation with my new neighbours before my sisters are unleashed on them, or they will start whispering about inbred aristocracy, and disdaining upper class arrogance and entitlement."

They laughed, but Ria knew that Toni had a strained relationship with her sisters, aside from the youngest.

"Which brings me to our other news," Justin said. "We've bought a house in Launston Mills and are moving there in September."

"Not Guelph then?" Ria said with surprise, for she thought that Justin would help run the family businesses. The Carringtons made their fortune in woolen mills and with their prized carpets.

"My grandfather Keir is eighty-one. He's been profoundly affected by Vivian's death, and one of my cousins was killed at

Passchendaele. He's aged a lot since you last saw him, Ria. He needs help with the newspaper and bookbindery, which my cousin was supposed to have taken over from him and my uncle. Another grandson is now being groomed for the job, but can't do it on his own. And Grandfather thought that the town could 'use a good lawyer', so he asked us to consider moving there. Toni was more enchanted with my grandparents than the location, but says she'll undoubtedly get used to it. It's not much different from Guelph in any case - all of it being rather a culture shock for someone who grew up in a castle."

Toni laughed and said, "A draughty one, don't forget. Besides, I've always relished a challenge."

"You can take the reins of the newspaper and allow the old gentleman to retire completely," Ria said.

"Don't put ideas into her head," Justin pleaded.

"Don't forget that Toni was supposed to become Queen of England," Ria noted, for Toni's parents had indeed angled for a union with the Prince of Wales. "If she can potentially run an Empire, she can surely manage a small newspaper."

"Very droll!"

"Speaking of David," Chas said of the Prince, whom he had known at Oxford. "Did you hear that he's coming to Canada this summer? Ria was always inviting people to visit us."

"I didn't think he'd take me up on the offer! Good Lord, do you think we should formally invite him to Wyndwood?"

Chas shrugged. "If I recall, he said he was looking forward to seeing Muskoka. You made the offer, Ria," he said with a smirk. "In fact, we told him to bring his banjo for our musical evenings."

"Hell's bells! I have no idea of protocol. Toni, you'll have to help me!"

"For someone who drove sanguinely through air raids, you're getting into rather a dither about entertaining royalty," Chas teased. "I should be the one concerned, because I think he's rather sweet on you."

"He does seem to have a penchant for married women," Toni stated dismissively.

"So that's why he didn't snatch you up when he had the chance," Justin said.

"He was never in the running, as far as I was concerned," Toni replied with a tender smile at her husband.

Chas said, "I hate to intrude on your summer vacation, Justin, but I'd like you to draw up the agreement for my partnership with the Seafords. Excuse us, ladies, while we retire to the library."

When they had gone, Ria said, "*Will* you be happy in Launston Mills?"

"I'm happy to be wherever Justin needs to be. And the town itself is charming in many ways, even if the countryside is dismally flat and somewhat marshy."

"I don't think anything could compare to the pastoral rolling hills that surround Quincy Castle."

"Yes, but remember how deadly dull it was there?"

"Even Toronto will seem like a backwater after London."

"I don't need the excitement of a big city. At least not every day," Toni added with a grin. "And there is nothing that can compare to this, so I shall be quite content if we can spend summers here. Justin said we'll be building our own cottage once Freddie is back, so that's exciting. And the house in Launston Mills is lovely, and quite one of the largest, I realized. It's around the corner from Grandfather Keir's place."

"I'll expect you to come to visit me at Wyndholme as often as you can. It's probably only a couple of hours to Toronto by train."

"Oh, I shall!" Watching a white sailboat skimming across the water, Toni said, "I already love it here, Ria. I've always hated the formalities and restrictions of my life and the expectations of my role, with minimal education in everything except the social graces and conventions of polite society. Here I feel so... free! It's exhilarating!"

"Isn't it just! And if you want to feel really liberated, you can join us girls for a skinny dip some time," Ria said with a chuckle. "Which means that we swim naked under the stars."

"Oh, I say, that does sound indulgently scandalous!"

"So tell me about your cottage. Where will you build it?"

"Justin's father has given us the western half of the island. There's a lovely cove that faces south..."

"I know it. Perfect for the two of you to skinny dip."

They discussed the design, and Ria gave Toni a tour of the Old Cottage, suggesting some things that Toni might wish to incorporate in her own. "Be sure to have good cross-ventilation in the kitchen, since ours becomes unbearably hot. I'm going to ask Freddie to redesign it when he plans the billiard-room wing that Chas wants to add. And you might consider having electric generators, like the newer cottages at Silver Bay. We're still using acetylene gas for our lighting, and Chas talks about changing it, but I think he rather likes being old-fashioned. It reminds him of the pre-war years."

In the library, the men had concluded their business, so Chas poured them each a whiskey and added a squirt of seltzer water.

"I can't tell you how glad and grateful I am to be back here," Justin said as he accepted the drink. "I've had my fill of England, and feel sorry for the poor buggers still waiting to come home. Little wonder that there've been riots in the camps. Of course we had to hush up the mutiny at Kinmel Park in March. Damn shame that five of our lads got killed. And now a group of our men are on trial for killing a copper in Epsom. Sad state of affairs."

"Why can't they be demobbed faster?"

"Logistics. We don't have the ships, since the ones we commandeered during the war went back into service as passenger liners. And all the bloody strikes there don't make things easier, especially the coal miners'. The fuel shortage delays transportation even more, and exacerbates the food shortages. I can't blame the men for being impatient to get home and put their lives back on track."

Chas offered him a cigarette, but Justin declined. "Bad for my lungs." A chest wound had permanently damaged one of them.

"How *are* you doing?"

"Not up to swimming the Marathon and prone to bronchitis, but otherwise fine." He chuckled. "Except that pieces of shrapnel occasionally make their way out of my arm. It's the damnedest thing!"

"You'll have to make a collection of your war souvenirs."

"Best forgotten, I think."

"Can we forget?" Chas asked, looking somewhat haunted.

Justin suffered nightmares and flashbacks as well. "I expect the horror will fade, and once we're gone, the war will become dry facts in history books that will bore future generations. But for now, it still grips and sometimes crushes us."

"It certainly does. And there are other things that won't go away. Unfortunately. I had a visit from an old colleague yesterday." Chas told him about Bert Cracknell.

"Let me know if he makes any more demands," Justin said with concern. "Perhaps a word from your lawyer will put the wind up him. You say he's from Peterborough, which isn't far from Launston Mills, so I'll see what I can find out about him. He may have some skeletons in his own closet."

Chas chuckled. "So we fight blackmail with blackmail?"

"It's more like 'know thine enemy'."

"Another sad state when former pals become that," Chas bemoaned.

"Indeed."

When Justin and Toni had left, Chas said to Ria, "Come along, my darling. I have something to show you."

"What?"

"You'll see," he replied with a twinkle in his eyes, and led her down to the boat.

They zipped past the Stepping Stone and Silly Isles and rounded a promontory, just beyond the SRA Country Club, which curved like a sheltering hand around a large bay. At its end sprawled the Spirit Bay Inn - a two-storey clapboard house boasting a hexagonal tower at one end. They pulled up to the dock, which was next to a fine stretch of sandy beach.

"It doesn't look open," Ria said, puzzled as to why they were here. It was not the sort of resort that catered to cottagers by providing dances or other entertainments.

"It isn't. And I've just bought it."

After her initial astonishment, Ria said, "So we're going to run an inn now as well as build boats?"

"Not likely! We're going to expand that old boathouse," he said, gesturing toward one along the shore, next to a change house, "and have a place where we can leave the Rolls if we decide to drive up to Muskoka - there's a large barn out back. They're constantly improving the roads, and we're less than two miles from Port Darling. Stephen told me that Pineridge just had its first guest arrive by motorcar. I'm thinking of the future, Ria."

"I thought we were going to build a big boathouse on the island."

"We are. But it still won't be large enough to house all the boats we're going to own. This will just be a utilitarian one, with no second floor rooms or rooftop decks. And it's a perfect spot since the bay is so sheltered and private."

"More boats?"

"They're constantly being improved, so ours are already outdated, Ria, but I don't want to sell them. I've ordered a runabout and a launch as well as my race boat."

"So we will single-handedly keep the Seaford Boatworks in business," she jested.

"Until they can ramp up production to take more clients," Chas replied with a grin.

"Well, there's plenty of space in the bay for a seaplane as well."

Chas deftly ignored her comment as he tied up the boat. Helping her out, he said, "Watch out because some of the boards are rotten."

After they had safely reached land, Chas said, "Stephen told me about this place being for sale. His family was considering buying it, but then the Ellis cottage right next to their place became available, so they snapped it up instead."

"It looks neglected," Ria said as they sauntered up the overgrown path to the house.

The original L-shaped farmhouse had grown, but with no obvious guidance from an architect. The long wing had become longer, and then jutted out with a bay and second floor balcony. Another addition took it further from its humble beginnings to end in a three-storey tower. A capacious veranda rambled across the entire front and down one side. The inn's sunny yellow paint and white trim were flaking. A ghostly stand of pale birches hovered around the perimeter.

"The old couple haven't been able to manage since their son got fed up with inn-keeping a few years ago and moved out west to farm. So they've retired to Toronto to live with their daughter. Anyway, I bought it for the property."

"It just occurred to me that we could have stables here, and bring up our horses. I would love to be able to ride Calypso during the summer!"

"Good idea! I expect that Rafe would want to stable some here as well."

"But what will we do with the house, Chas?"

"Let your vast army of friends use it when they come to visit," he teased.

"That's certainly an option."

"I haven't even been inside, but I'm told it has electric lighting and good water from a well."

Chas unlocked the main entrance in the original section. It was surprisingly well appointed inside, with an oak reception desk and wainscotting. Shabby furniture still invited guests to sit by the stone fireplace, or to entertain at the upright piano in the spacious lounge. Wicker chairs and tables destined for the veranda were also piled in. Deer and moose heads scowled down from walls incongruously papered in cheerful but peeling floral wallpaper. There was a games room behind the dining room, and the hexagonal sunroom beyond provided easy chairs and small writing desks that still offered coloured picture postcards of the inn for patrons to send to friends.

"Does it come with all the furnishings?" Ria asked.

"Yes, including the linens, and half a dozen canoes and a couple of skiffs."

Upstairs were twenty airy bedrooms of varying sizes, with two or four beds and a sink in each. The grandest was set into the tower and boasted its own bathroom.

"It's eerie to see it just waiting for people who will never come," Ria said in a hushed voice, as if afraid to disturb ghosts of the past.

"We can always rent it. Or tear it down."

"We couldn't do that! It's charming, and I adore all these little nooks and crannies."

"Perhaps the Seafords would like to use it as an annex, if they need more space. There's only the Country Club between this and Pineridge."

"Ha! So we'll be innkeepers after all!"

Chas laughed.

The third floor tower lookout had a lofty view of the surrounding countryside. A small stream trickled over rocks and through a shady glade of hardwoods before tumbling into the lake. Hardy perennials had spread beyond the formal gardens, so phalanxes of phlox marched toward the house. "Oh, look, there's a tennis court!" Ria exclaimed.

"And a croquet lawn that also needs mowing and rolling."

"Won't Sophie be delighted!"

"I can see we'll be spending some time here."

"It certainly has a lovely view." Beyond the next headland lay the scattered islands that were mostly occupied by their American friends, so there were plenty of Stars and Stripes fluttering in the warm afternoon breeze.

The large kitchen wing projected out back, with the floor above obviously having been the family's domain. Only here were the rooms empty of furnishings.

They walked along a naked ridge of granite to the narrow point, where a tumbledown gazebo overlooked a much greater expanse of lake. From that height, they could even see Wyndwood over the treetops of nearby islands. There was a precipitous drop to the water on the west side, but at the tip and on the bay side, the rock cascaded in gradual steps until it just slipped into the water. Mosses and junipers and a few tenacious pines had taken hold in the shallow pockets of soil.

"What a perfect picnic spot!" Ria enthused. She would have scrambled down to the inviting shore and walked into the water, delighting in the granite underfoot, but the rugged path might prove too much for Chas. "So I know you're just itching to tell me how this became known as Spirit Bay."

"You know me too well, my darling," he admitted. "In the late 1860s when this area was being opened up with free land grants, Zachary Hardacre arrived from England and set about clearing the land and building a homestead. Apparently he was a large, tough, amiable chap with a soft heart and great fortitude. He soon began courting one of the Mortimer girls whose family farmed Mortimer's Island. Being a devoted lover, he went over to see her in all weathers, rowing his boat even through late autumn storms, and walking across the ice through nighttime blizzards. One spring day, when the ice was already too soft and thin, he broke through and drowned. Here, in the bay."

"And the locals have seen him wandering about ever since," Ria finished.

"Some of them."

"When they've had a good dose of spirits themselves?"

Chas laughed. "Undoubtedly then. But apparently some of the guests here have asked who the strange giant of a man is who lurks by this gazebo and gazes longingly across the lake. He always mysteriously disappears as people come closer."

Ria couldn't suppress a shiver. "So he'll guard the place for us then."

"I'm sure he'll become your devoted slave, my darling. As have I."

"Applesauce!" But she put her arm about his waist and kissed him. "How much of this will be ours?" she asked as they strolled back down to the dock.

"The point and the entire bay shoreline, which is almost half a mile, but only fifty acres, since the family sold the rest of the land to the SRA for the golf course."

"Super! Then I won't have to worry that you'll want us to begin farming as well."

He chuckled. "Well, do you approve?"

"We're going to have splendid parties here!" She flashed him a smile. "Oh, I just realized we could hold Ellie and Troy's wedding here! I must ask them. In any case, how could I resist being mistress of Spirit Bay? So what happened to the sweetheart on Mortimer's Island?"

"Hardacre willed the farm to her. She's the old lady who's selling this."

"Poor chump! Here he is still pining for her and she lived happily on his land with another man."

"People are more pragmatic than romantic, my darling. Except for us, of course."

"Which is why we're building yet another boathouse," she chaffed.

•   •   •

"Never! How dare you even suggest such a thing!" Edgar Wyndham bellowed, barely able to control his rage.

Josiah Miller looked weary as he sat opposite Edgar's father, Albert, in the study at Tumbling Rocks. Edgar had remained standing when the unwelcome guest had been ushered in, and now paced the room. He cautioned, "It would destroy Phoebe if she ever found out!"

"I guarantee you that she never will, Mr. Wyndham," Josiah said.

"Can you, indeed, assure us of that, Mr. Miller?" Edgar challenged scathingly. "It appears that your daughters are too fond of gossip and of disparaging others."

Josiah ignored the dig. "Mrs. Miller and I will be the only ones who know the truth. Others will be told that we are adopting a distant cousin's child." He appealed to Albert, "Mr. Wyndham, my wife is devastated by Robert's death, but if she were to have the care of his lovechild, she might be brought out of her melancholia."

"I sympathize with you, Mr. Miller, but I agree that it is too risky, and unfair to the boy and his adopted family. He is already two years old. Don't you think that it would be cruel to take him away from those whom he considers his parents?"

"Was it not cruel to give him away to strangers?" Josiah countered. "To make your daughter believe she delivered a stillborn child?"

Edgar clenched his fists. Of course it had grieved him to do that, and had preyed on his conscience ever since. And Phoebe had suffered terribly.

Josiah went on. "Would you not like to keep an eye on your grandchild, Mr. Wyndham, to assure that he is well cared for? Watch him grow up?"

Edgar could see his father caving in to that thought, so he said, "And what if Phoebe recognizes Bobby and herself in him?"

"She believes she gave birth to a daughter, who died. Why would she think the boy was her child?"

"Because she is uncannily perceptive."

"Mr. Wyndham, I make no excuses for my son. He was brash and thoughtless and behaved unchivalrously towards your sister..."

"Is that what you call seducing an innocent girl?" Edgar snorted.

Josiah waved his hand dismissively. "Call it what you will. He made a mistake. But he hasn't been given the chance to mature and to redeem himself." He paused to let the weight of the words settle on them. "I ask only that you give me the name of the family who adopted the boy. We can, of course, do nothing if they don't agree to give him up."

"You'll buy him," Edgar accused.

"Did you not sell him?"

Edgar couldn't deny it. He had offered the doctor and midwife a ransom to find a decent family to care for the child, and to hold their tongues. The family had also been well recompensed.

"Of course, I can try and find him myself, but you may not wish your name to come up in my enquiries."

Albert stated, "Mr. Miller, you will allow us to ponder this before we give you our decision. Perhaps you would be good enough to return tomorrow." He rang for the butler.

"I will indeed, Mr. Wyndham. Thank you."

"Pringle will show you out," Albert said. "Good day."

When Josiah had gone, Edgar exploded. "You can't mean to let them raise the boy, Papa! Think how dangerous that could be!"

"He's right, Edgar. Phoebe thinks she lost a girl. And I *do* want to see my grandson and ensure that he is raised properly."

"Do you think they'll do a better job with him than they did with Bobby?" Edgar asked snidely.

"Actually, I do. I expect they have learned from their mistakes. Edgar, I've tried to forget about the boy, as if by not acknowledging him, I can pretend that he doesn't exist. But we have to face the fact that he *is* a Wyndham - your nephew, my grandson. And suddenly I feel heartbroken that we've abandoned him."

"It was *your* idea, Papa! I never wanted to do that to Phoebe!"

Albert shook his bent head in regret. "I know, I know. I, too, made a mistake. But I can still atone for it."

"Would we tell Phoebe?" Edgar asked with faint hope, but knew the answer.

"It might push her over the edge. She must never know."

Chapter 3

July 1st was another sizzling, sunny day, and spirits were high.

The Stepping Stone Marathon would begin from the Seafords' Pineridge Inn. Not only was there a flotilla of yachts, skiffs, launches, and canoes rocking on the waves, but also a host of hotel guests watching the antics from the veranda and lawn. Others at the neighbouring Country Club paused their tennis and golf games to watch the races begin.

"I didn't think it would be so... popular," Alice confided to her friends. She felt embarrassingly underdressed in her swimsuit. The new styles were much sleeker and more revealing than the old-fashioned woolen ones.

"I told you this was serious business," Esme said with a smirk.

"It's a bit rough out there today, ladies, so be careful," Stephen Seaford told them. "I'll be in one of the rescue boats with Major Thornton, if you need help."

"Are your sisters participating?" Esme asked him.

He didn't quite manage to hide his surprise as he replied, "They're busy with other things." It was the summer people who partied and played, while the locals catered to their needs.

"Yes, of course," Esme said awkwardly, feeling foolish. She knew that Nancy Seaford had her market garden to tend, as well as helping with the cooking. Nancy rowed over to Wyndwood and other islands most mornings with fresh milk, eggs, and produce.

The girls were delighted when Arthur Spencer joined them. He had recently returned from his tour of duty. Having arrived in England just before the Armistice, he had then been part of the Allied troops that marched into Germany. He and Alice became acquainted during his stay at Chas and Ria's English home, Priory Manor, and had been corresponding regularly since then.

Like his brother, Freddie, Arthur was tall and lean and easygoing, yet focused on forging a career in journalism. But Alice realized it wasn't only that shared interest that sustained their friendship. Even in England she had sensed a mutual attraction. So she was thrilled that he would be spending the summer here as well, and then would be sure to see him at the university the rest of the year.

"It's been a while since any Spencers won the cup, so I feel it's my duty to restore the family honour," Arthur jested.

"Well I won't let Maud or Hazel win," Esme declared, referring to his younger sisters.

"Those Roland fellows might be a challenge," Arthur said, eyeing Troy's younger brothers, Stuart and Eugene.

"Don't discount Derek either," Esme warned. "The Carlyles are no slackers."

"Hmm. Then there are the unknowns - all the newcomers on the lake."

"Well, you're taller than any of them, so that should give you an advantage."

He chuckled. "Esme, I have every faith in your Wyndham spunk, but I fear that the Thornton doggedness may win out."

"I expect to be standing on the podium with you this evening, Arthur. So good luck!"

The men's race was called, and he went to the shoreline. The women's race would begin five minutes later.

Alice was delighted to see Arthur taking a bit of a lead and excited to be a part of the event. But she was nervous when she lined up on the beach beside the other contestants. The starter's pistol gave her a jolt, as did the initial plunge into the cool water.

Being in the lee of the wind, the first couple of islands were easy enough, and Alice made up time on land with Ria's strategy. But the rough water between Driftwood and Red Rock made swimming difficult, and Alice struggled to keep up with Esme and the rest. A wave crested in her face, causing her to choke. Startled, she sank for a moment. Seeing the many boats hovering about as she surfaced, she was suddenly back in the Irish Sea, gasping for breath, surrounded by lifeboats that made little effort to scoop out the screaming, bleeding, dying people. She was momentarily paralyzed with fear. Hearing Ria shout her name as she began sinking again, she managed to thrash her way back to the surface. But she seemed to have forgotten how to swim.

Esme heard Ria's cry of desperation, and looked back. Seeing Alice flailing about, she turned around immediately. Chas and Stephen were already on their way to Alice's side. Stephen kicked off his shoes and dove in just as Esme reached Alice and tried to keep her afloat.

"I've got her," he said to Esme. "You keep on."

"There's no point," she replied.

Stephen drew a spluttering Alice to the side of the runabout, and Chas hauled her in. Then Stephen helped Esme over the gunwale and clambered in after her.

Despite the heat, Alice was shivering. Chas wrapped her in a large towel and rubbed her arms.

"I'm so sorry," she said between coughs, fighting back tears. "It was... I was..."

"The *Lusitania*," Chas guessed.

She nodded as tears streamed down her face. "I'm sorry, Esme. I've spoiled your race."

"Tosh! It's just for fun and Fliss is bound to win anyway. Alice, *I'm* sorry that this reminded you of that terrible ordeal."

Ria pulled alongside in *Dragonfly*. She had the children and Johanna with her, as well as Olivia and Richard. "Alice, thank God you're alright!"

"She had a flashback," Chas said, glancing meaningfully at Ria.

"Oh, Alice!"

They looked at one another with a wealth of shared heartbreak. "I'm alright now, Ria," Alice assured her. But once they were back at Wyndwood, and Ria had taken Alice into her arms, she wept again.

"I'm afraid I'm such a rabbit."

"Nonsense! Those memories ambush all of us sometimes," Ria confessed. "And hopefully that will occur less often. But now you need to rest, and then allow yourself to enjoy the evening."

Resting up for the ball that usually lasted until daybreak was also a tradition. Once Ria had the others settled, she joined Chas in their bedroom.

"I've never felt so anti-social, and I really wish we didn't have this event to face tonight," he confessed.

"I'm not in the mood for it either. But I know that if we don't make an effort, then we will become ever more isolated. Controlled by the past. We have to move on, no matter how hard that might be."

"I know you're right, my darling. And I also know that you have worked miracles as usual." As she joined him in bed, naked in the heat of the day, he added, "So let's take advantage of our time alone."

They fell into an easy sleep after their lovemaking.

The children, however, were too excited to rest for long because they were allowed to dress up and participate until they dropped from exhaustion. Otherwise, it would be almost impossible for them to sleep with the music playing until dawn.

They had a light supper, since another would be served about midnight, and then eagerly climbed into their costumes.

"Oh, Mummy Ria!" Sophie exclaimed when she saw her.

Designed by Jack's mother, Ria's costume was a turquoise tiered satin dress that mimicked the segmented body of a dragonfly, each tier fringed with black beads. A sequined net cape cascaded to her waist at the back, and its ends were attached to spangled cuffs at the wrists, so that when she spread her arms, glittering wings took flight. The outfit was completed by a silver and azure headpiece that looked like wings embracing her forehead.

"I agree! You look stunning, Ria," Jack said.

"I love this so much, I think I shall wear it every year. I will become the legendary dragonfly lady," she quipped.

"You already are that, my darling," Chas affirmed. "I said on our wedding day that I was marrying a fairy princess, since a couple of your attendants were dragonflies."

She smiled in fond remembrance. "Jack, I think your mother should become a couturier. She is so talented."

"She has her hands full just catering to family and friends," Jack replied with a chuckle. Never one to be idle, his mother, Marie, had decided to use her love of design to make couture-inspired clothes for her daughters. When Ria had seen those, she had commissioned costumes for the ball.

Sophie had chosen to be a flower, so she was encased in a swirl of pink petals, while "pilot" Charlie had an aviator's helmet and goggles along with a credible suit and silk scarf. Alice felt resplendent in her medieval gown, and Johanna was excited that she had been allowed to choose something from the costume trunk.

Jack was wearing a short-sleeved striped jersey he'd picked up in France, with a handkerchief around his neck, and a beret worn at a rakish angle. Now that he was a gentleman, he could dress as a Bohemian.

Chas had selected an old pirate costume from the Thornton cache, saying it seemed only natural with his scarred face and "peg leg".

With the fairyland decorations, lights draped through branches and along the eaves, and a scattering of gigantic blue potted hydrangeas sent up from the Wyndholme greenhouses, the cottage and pavilion had been transformed.

"I think a stiff drink before the hordes arrive is called for, don't you, Jack?" Chas asked.

"Definitely!"

Prohibition didn't prevent them from serving liquor, since this was a private party, and they had great stores of it put down. Ria opted for a cool glass of champagne rather than the cognac that Chas poured for himself and Jack.

"And we should be celebrating something else today," Chas said. "The official end to the war." Although the fighting had stopped with the armistice last November, the treaty signed on June 28th at the Paris Peace Conference formally ended the hostilities between Germany and the Allied Powers.

They raised their glasses solemnly. Now that the numbers were tallied, they were staggering, unfathomable - 13 million dead, 68,000 of them Canadians, and another 20 million wounded.

"Although I'm not convinced that the Versailles Treaty won't set the stage for future conflict," Chas conjectured.

"Surely not!" Ria cried, horrified.

"The terms are harsh. Germany will be bled dry by the reparation payments. If you keep kicking a dog when he's down, he'll eventually bite back."

Ria couldn't imagine going through another cataclysmic war, this time with their children or grandchildren risking their lives. "Wasn't the League of Nations created to prevent more conflicts?"

"Quite so, my darling. And I expect it should be run by women."

"Absolutely!"

They were joined by the crowd from Silver Bay, except for Zoë. Richard and Max accepted drinks as Olivia explained, "Zoë sends her regrets, but is staying home with the baby."

"I can imagine how hard it must be for her," Ria sympathized, "but I had hoped that she would come. As a first step."

"I worry about her," Olivia admitted, taking Ria aside. "She seems so remote, as if she's living only in the moment with the baby and otherwise, in her memory. And she hardly lets him out of her sight, as if she fears that he'll disappear from her life as well. She refuses to have a nursery maid, other than one to do the laundry, and never leaves Ethan to sleep alone. He's either in his crib beside her bed or in the cradle next to wherever she is. It's as much as I can do to persuade her to go for swim or a paddle in the canoe. And that's practically the only time I have alone with my grandson."

"You know it's her nature to be completely engaged, mind and soul, with whatever she undertakes, Aunt Olivia. Her love for Blake was all-consuming, as I expect her love for the baby is now."

"I do know, and I realize how unhealthy that can become when there is no other passion in her life. If only she would finish her degree that she had once been so adamant about pursuing, or volunteer at the orthopedic hospital, where they could surely use her massage skills."

"I expect that will come in time, Aunt Olivia. It's only been a year. Zoë is not one to be idle for long."

"You're quite right, Ria. I should trust my daughter more. But God forbid if anything should happen to that child!"

Ria had been disconcerted to see how much Olivia had aged during the four years Ria had been away. Zoë's grief, Max's shell-shock, and Richard's ongoing melancholia had etched her face and streaked her hair grey, though she was only forty-seven. Olivia was like a mother to her, and Ria felt her burdens deeply.

"I will try to spend more time with Zoë, Aunt Olivia. Engage her in our old pursuits."

"Thank you, my dear. I know how close you two and Max have always been."

The orchestra was tuning up, but they could hear boats approaching as the sun set fire to the horizon.

As expected, Fliss had won the ladies' race, and despite a noble effort, Arthur had lost - narrowly - to Stuart Roland.

"Once again, well done, muggins!" Chas said as he kissed her cheek. "I knew you wouldn't let the side down. You look radiant, by the way."

"I feel it in this exquisite costume! Jack's mother is so clever, isn't she?" As "starlight", she had a scintillating gown and headdress that seemed to spark light from the beaded metallic fabric.

"I always knew that I would have to keep love-struck men at bay when you grew up."

She giggled.

But she *was* popular, and Stuart Roland was immediately at her side when he spotted her, saying, "Well, you're certainly the star tonight, Felicity. We champions should lead off the dancing, don't you think?"

"Of course!"

She had no lack of partners, and Jack noticed that Fliss had a natural grace and charm that not only put people at ease, but also drew them to her. Stuart Roland seemed particularly enchanted, and Jack realized that Stuart, like the other rich young men, saw Fliss for more than her wealth. Perhaps it was time to escalate his own efforts.

When the orchestra began "Under the Moon" - the signature tune from his brother-in-law's Broadway musical - Jack swept in to claim the dance. The music was slow and sensual, telling of a young man's moment of falling in love under a summer moon.

See the moonlight shimm'ring on the tranquil bay,
Silvering the trees along the shore.
See her silhouetted as she comes my way.
See it kiss the girl that I adore.

"You look beautiful, Fliss," Jack said as he drew her close.

"Thanks to your mother."

"Oh, no, it's much more than that," he said softly.

She blushed. The implication of this simple statement accompanied by an admiring and probing look was more powerful than the idle flattery of the younger men.

He held her tenderly, his almost imperceptible caresses so sensual that she had no wish to talk, just to be held in his arms.

Aroused and hopeful, Fliss felt that he was surely in love with her as well.

"There is something magical about Muskoka nights, even when there isn't much of a moon," he murmured while the last few lines played:

Summer is fleeting and in our brief meeting
Our hearts are beating so true,
Under the moon, I'm over the moon
For you

They parted reluctantly when the song ended. "May I claim another?" he asked as the band struck up the livelier For Me and My Gal.

"As many as you like!"

"As many as your other admirers will allow," he replied with a smile. Tantalize her, but don't lay it on too thick, he told himself. So he said breezily, "Being reminded of my brother-in-law, I've been charged with finding an island for Hugo and Emily, preferably with a cottage that they can use this August. Hugo was very specific about what he wanted, most importantly a music room with fabulous views. But I haven't had any luck. Do you have suggestions?"

With sudden inspiration, she exclaimed, "I know the perfect spot! Moonglow Island!"

"Moonglow?"

"You know the three islands that we own to the west of Thorncliff? And that Rafe and Sid are taking the largest one, Sunset, and Chas and Ria will have Sunrise, the smallest one, because they already have this place? Well the other island is Moonglow. And it's mine as well, so I'd be happy to give it to them."

"Didn't your father buy them to preserve the privacy of Thorncliff?"

"Yes, from strangers. But I would adore having Emily and Hugo as neighbours!"

"That would be splendid!" Especially since Jack intended to own Thorncliff. "But you mustn't give it to them, Fliss. They have plenty of money," he said with a grin.

"I just had another thought! Until their cottage is built they could use Chas and Ria's Inn at Spirit Bay."

"Perfect!"

"Oh, do let's go and talk to Chas about it!"

They found him in the sitting room, conversing with some elderly guests. "I do beg your pardon, but I really must have a word with my brother. I promise I shan't keep him long," Fliss said graciously.

They went into the library, which was being kept aside tonight for family who wanted a few minutes of privacy from the activities. Usually it served as a smoking room for the men, but since young women were now smoking quite openly, there was no need for the men to sequester themselves, except to talk business.

"What's so important that it couldn't wait until I heard more about Mrs. Buxton's grandson's 'infernal new motorboat'?" Chas asked as he poured himself a cognac and offered one to Jack.

When Fliss had excitedly explained, Chas said, "Ah, yes, Moonglow, so named during your poetic adolescent phase." While she blushed, he said to Jack, "It's officially Island 49 or some such thing."

"Oh, *do* say that you think it's a brilliant idea!" Fliss urged.

"It's a brilliant idea, muggins."

She threw her arms around him.

"You see why women are no good at business, Jack? They become so emotional," he teased.

"And you can see that Chas is back to his old self when he makes silly remarks," Fliss countered affectionately. They had always loved sparring.

"So now you can use your Thornton business acumen and come up with a fair price," Chas said. "Jack's right that you can't just give it away. And you can't ask him, since he has a vested interest." Chas suppressed a grin.

"I shall ask Stephen," she announced. "He knows everything about the lakes."

Chas laughed. "Clever girl!"

"So what will you charge them for renting Spirit Bay for a month?" she challenged.

Chas pondered for a moment as he lit a cigarette. "They'll owe us a concert."

"You see why Daddy said that Chas was hopeless at business?" she asked Jack.

"Looks like you've inherited all the brains, Fliss," Chas acknowledged. "You may have to look after me in my dotage."

"You mean once you've frittered way all your money on fast boats."

"Precisely."

"Well, I think that Moonglow is a perfect name for Hugo and Emily's island," Jack said. "I'll go and have a closer look at it before sending them a telegram."

"May I show you?" Fliss asked.

"You and who else?" Chas asked, arching an eyebrow at her.

"Oh, Chas, do I really need a chaperone? That's so tediously old-fashioned!"

Jack intervened. "I'm certain that Lizzie and Claire would like to see it as well."

"Of course," Fliss said, slightly deflated.

"Now, what say we hit the dance floor again?" Jack suggested.

"Go via the veranda, and try not to let Mrs. Buxton see you," Chas implored. "I need a few minutes to myself."

Fliss went to him with sudden concern and touched his arm. "Are you in pain?"

"Just a bit weary. I haven't had this much excitement since my last air battle."

"Oh, *do* be serious!"

"I am!" But he grinned at her and said, "Don't worry about me. Just go and enjoy yourself." He kissed her lightly on the forehead.

When the French door had closed behind them, Chas gratefully slouched down in the overstuffed leather armchair.

On the veranda, Jack and Fliss turned right so that they could go to the pavilion through the breezeway between the house and the kitchen wing, avoiding the other guests. No one was on the west veranda, and only the box room and lavatory windows overlooked it at this point. So Jack stopped Fliss and drew her into his arms. He kissed her softly and chastely and lingeringly. When he released her he whispered, "I've been longing to do that."

She looked at him breathlessly. "Oh, Jack!"

He took her hand and said, "We'd better go before Chas comes out or someone else takes advantage of this quiet spot."

Fliss gripped his hand tightly and beamed at him. She was ecstatic, for his kiss had been everything that she had always imagined, and surely meant that he loved her. Jack was not a callow youth just trying to steal a kiss, she was certain.

Jack was sure that the attentions of other suitors would now be wasted on Fliss. She was reluctant to relinquish him to other partners, but they both knew their duty.

"Showing off those lovely muscles, I see," Sid said as she danced with him. "Very sexy. Reminds me of old times."

Jack was careful not to encourage Sid's flirtation. The last thing he needed was Rafe's jealousy. "You're certainly getting your share of attention."

Glamorous and arresting, Sid's harem costume was more suited to the vaudeville stage than a ball. It revealed a hint of bare midriff below the tasseled bodice. Only the longest points of the elaborately beaded, jagged overskirt reached her knees, and the diaphanous chiffon pantaloons beneath did little to hide her shapely legs.

"How divine! One likes to make an impression."

"Sid, you would do that even if you weren't half naked. I'm surprised that Rafe didn't object."

"Ah, but you see, a harem costume is most fitting. I am but a kept woman."

"Ha! It would be more appropriate to say that you obviously wear the trousers."

She laughed delightedly. "I *have* missed you, Jack."

Back among his guests after his brief respite, Chas was receiving his own stares from people who hadn't yet seen him. But he knew he had to harden himself. He had thought of wearing a full-face mask, but decided he should just get the worst over with.

As they danced, Sid said to him, "The piratical look suits you. Your burns aren't even that shocking anymore."

"That's because you're used to me."

"I have to admit I'm terribly jealous of Ria." She paused significantly before adding, "She's managed to steal the show after all."

"I had no doubt of it. But you win for most outrageous costume."

Sid laughed. "Do I detect a note of censure?"

"I expect some elderly gentlemen may need their heart medicine."

"While their wives are furiously fanning themselves to keep from fainting at the audacity of exposed knees. Just as they would have at a naked ankle before the war."

"True enough. But I really can't envision women walking around quite that undressed in another few years."

"I'll wager that you're wrong! You'll have noticed that swimsuits keep shrinking."

"Well, I don't expect you'll hear too many men protesting."

She laughed. "By the way, you're dancing quite well."

"For a cripple, you mean."

"Better than two left feet," she jested.

But Chas was finding it difficult, and tiring for his good leg, which was compensating so much for the other, and where an old bullet wound still made itself felt at times.

Ria sensed that when she finally had a chance to dance with him. "You should rest more, Chas."

"What, and pass up an opportunity to hold my delectable wife in my arms instead of listening to the matrons despairing about the frightful behaviour of modern young people?"

"Are they?"

"Not their own offspring, of course."

Ria laughed. "Of course not! So has anything really changed?"

"Only the music. Jazz instead of ragtime."

•   •   •

Lizzie had dreaded this moment, although she had envisioned it countless times. She would be aloof, disdainful, polite, of course, as befitted a lady. But her heart was thumping and she felt an angry blush creep into her cheeks. He was more handsome than ever, and his betrayal stabbed her anew. She had tried to avoid Rafe, but he finally waylaid her attempt to escape him. They stood in the shadows behind the marquee that extended the dance floor tonight.

Rafe was surprised at his own reaction, the intense desire that suddenly flooded through him. "Lizzie Wyndham. Beautiful as always, I see. Would you care to dance?"

"I think not," she said, turning away.

He grabbed her arm, and she drew away as if she'd been burned. "Don't touch me!"

He chuckled. "Come, Lizzie. Have you forgotten how much fun we had in New York?" For two tantalizing evenings.

"Obviously you have. I waited for you, Rafe," she said bitterly, annoyed with herself for admitting it, for letting him see the depth of her disappointment.

He was pleased, if a bit surprised. "Still the virtuous virgin then?"

Maliciously, she said, "Unlike your wife, whose charms have been much appreciated by others." She had almost said "Jack", but realized that she could be jeopardizing his relationship with the Thorntons.

He snorted. "You think I don't know that your brother fucked her? But he wasn't good enough for her. She chose me."

"In that case, I don't think we have anything more to say to one another."

"You still don't know the ways of society, do you, Lizzie? The guttersnipe hasn't been eradicated yet."

It took all her self-control not to punch him in the face, thereby confirming his statement. Her eyes blazing, she said icily, "I don't play games, if that's what you mean."

"Then you'd better learn, if you want to belong. It takes more than fancy clothes to make a lady. Knowing how to flirt, to flatter, be witty and gay - that's what confers class."

"Bugger off."

Rafe laughed wickedly. "Still the Lizzie I know and love." And damn it, he did! He remembered the moment he fell in love with her. It was at Delmonico's that November night in '16, when he had given her the gold locket from Tiffany's. The genuine joy on her face had momentarily revealed the soft core beneath the armour forged by a difficult and impoverished childhood. He had wanted to look after her then, be the magnanimous lover who would delight in laying the world at her feet. But she had wanted marriage, not a fling. During his years in the German prisoner of war camps, he had looked forward to her chatty yet intimate letters, and had almost convinced himself that he would ask her to marry him when he returned. If Sid hadn't taken him up on his long-forgotten offer of marriage, he might well have.

Of course, Lady Sidonie was a feather in his cap. He was tremendously proud of her beauty, her careless charm and noble lineage, and enjoyed the envy of other men. He tried not to worry that Sid might still be in love with Chas, with whom she'd had an intense affair before the war, when Chas had been at Oxford with her brother. Like Rafe's prize horses, Sid was his to flaunt. Sex was good and they had ample means to enjoy life extravagantly. Lizzie hadn't approved of his gambling, and so would have been a poor companion after all. But he still desired her.

•   •   •

"I'm sorry about what happened to you today, Alice," Arthur Spencer said as they danced.

He felt her sag a little in his arms as she replied, "It's too embarrassing."

"Not at all! God knows, the *Lusitania* sinking was a horrific experience. Have you given any more thought to writing about it?" He'd suggested that to her in England last year.

"I have, but can't face it." And she feared that if she told her story, people might recognize her as the unnamed girl in Theadora Prescott's gripping account of the disaster - the girl who had saved the life of her friend, a heavily pregnant young woman who then lost her baby. She couldn't risk exposing Ria's secret.

"Think of it as an important historical document. Not just a catharsis for yourself."

"That's even more intimidating."

"Just write from the heart. Don't worry about how it reads. Your editor will do that." He smiled. "I'll volunteer."

"Would you?"

"Of course! And I'm planning to interview all our friends about their war experiences."

"I think people are trying very hard to forget, and don't want to talk about that."

"I know Freddie doesn't," he said of his brother. "But their stories shouldn't be ignored, or, God forbid, completely lost. The time will come when they need to be heard." He led her to the veranda when the song ended. "I think we have a unique opportunity to capture the essence of our times. Not in any sentimental or exploitative way. More of a moral obligation to record these monumental events for future generations."

"I do see your point." She smiled at him. "I will try."

Because she suddenly seemed young and fragile, he assured her earnestly, "I will help, Alice. Anytime it seems overwhelming, you must let me know."

His warm eyes held hers with a deeper promise.

The heart-thumping moment was interrupted when Esme joined them saying, "You two look as if you're plotting something."

"A book," Arthur answered. "At least Alice is."

"So you're not going to bother with university after all?" Esme asked.

"Oh, but I am!" Alice affirmed.

Esme harrumphed and said to Arthur, "I don't know why Alice feels she needs a career when she has a small legacy from her father, and Chas and Ria to look after her."

"I realized that I needed to fend for myself when my father sent me to boarding school in England because his new wife didn't want me around. I decided then that I wanted more than anything to be a writer. Beside, Chas and Ria are only my guardians, so I don't expect them to support me once I turn twenty-one."

"Tosh! They're devoted to you," Esme said.

"Still..."

"I think you'll be a successful author," Arthur declared with admiration.

Esme felt a pang of jealousy. Her lifelong friend seemed quite smitten by Alice and her literary ambitions.

Arthur had completed a year at the University of Toronto before signing up. Because Alice would be starting in the same program – English and History - she eagerly questioned him about the courses.

Feeling superfluous, Esme took a proffered glass of champagne from one of the maids and drank it down in annoyance as she walked away. Why should she be upset that two of her best friends were so attuned to one another? It wasn't as if she had any romantic interest in Arthur anyway. But it really was too bad when friends started pairing up and ignoring others! And making her feel keenly the lack of a similar relationship. And of the disconcertingly blank future awaiting her.

Relieved to finally be finished with school, Esme had no ambition for higher education, nor was that even admired in her circle. Grandmother had always pooh-poohed the idea, and maintained that too much education would ruin a girl's marriage prospects. Despite that opposition, her sister, Zoë, had fought hard to convince their parents to allow her to attend university, which she had for two years, but what good had it done her in the end? Zoë was, after all, content to be a mother.

Esme knew that her goal was to find a suitable husband so that she could settle into a life of happy domesticity and charitable works, but had to admit that it seemed a rather anemic ambition, and not nearly as exciting as writing a book or driving ambulances or doing something else important and noteworthy.

Wanting to be alone, Esme marched down to the dock, aware that spooning couples sneaking away from the cottage would claim the lakeside paths.

"You look as though you could use a smoke."

Startled out of her disgruntled ponderings by the disembodied voice, she sought to locate the speaker. Although lights glowed on the dock, the boats were moored three and four deep, so there was a flotilla of ever-darker shapes swaying gently before her. She finally noticed the glow of a cigarette and discerned Stephen Seaford sitting in one of the shadowed boats. He was in charge of them for the evening.

Stephen knew he should have stayed silent, and not address her so casually, but he wanted her to know that she wasn't alone. People thinking themselves unobserved often did or said things not intended for an audience, like cursing or picking their noses.

"I could indeed!" she replied. "And that looks like the perfect place to have one. May I join you?" Instantly she regretted her words. It didn't do to put him on the spot that way. As hired help, how could he refuse a guest's request? Having made a breech of etiquette, she felt awkward now.

But he didn't hesitate as he replied, "Sure thing!"

There was a faint hiss as he threw his cigarette into the lake, and then he clambered over the other boats to her side. He had a firm grip on her hand as they stepped from one launch to the next, setting each bobbing, and trying to keep their balance. She fell against him once, but he steadied her, and she laughed with slight embarrassment, surprised at his strength and her own reaction to him. For this moment in the dark, it was easy to forget that he was staff, and she longed to be held in his arms.

They sat side by side on the plush leather bench of a mahogany launch, and she knew that it was highly inappropriate for her to be alone with him like this. But she felt rebellious.

After he lit their cigarettes, Stephen said, "We could see the stars better if we took the boat out farther into the darkness, but I don't think your Uncle James would approve of our borrowing it."

"Goodness, no! He's always rather frightens me."

"Why's that?"

"He's so... proper and judgmental. And he's never been very nice to Ria. How can you tell all these boats apart, especially in the dark?"

"Each one has a personality. And not always that of the owner, although you can infer a lot about a person by his boat."

"So what does this one say?"

"Judging by the scratches, your Uncle James isn't a good driver and has no interest in boats aside from their utility and comfort. But he does like to have the best, and cost is no consideration."

"You're right," Esme replied. "I prefer driving our Dippy, so what does that say about me?"

"That you take time to enjoy your surroundings."

"Spot on! And actually I like canoeing best of all. It makes me feel as though I'm part of the lake. What about you?"

He shrugged. "I love these mahogany launches, of course. I've worked with Ditchburn and Minett in the winters, so I know how painstakingly they are built. And I'm thrilled to be working with Major Thornton on his speedboat. But I also enjoy a good row in my skiff, which I built before the war."

"So you want to work with your brother?"

"Sure thing! And be on the forefront of boat design. The Major's giving us that opportunity. He's actually bought into the business, so we have no lack of resources. It's tremendously exciting."

"You're lucky that you have a passion for something."

"Don't you?"

"Gosh, I don't mean to sound pitiful. I really wanted to do something useful in the war, like Zoë and Ria. It seems that all of you who were there... belong to a different club or... secret society. That the rest of us are excluded, can't know, wouldn't understand, won't be told. That whatever we do is much less important. Gosh, I'm talking rot. I think I must have had too much champagne."

He laughed, but not mockingly. "I admire your honesty, Miss Wyndham. We don't talk about the war because we want to forget, and we sure as hell don't want our friends and families to ever see the things that we did. So yes, there is a gulf of sorts. But not something that you need feel guilty about. I expect you did your bit for the war effort with fund-raising and Red Cross work and the rest, just like my mother and sisters."

"I know that it's absurd to feel that I've missed out on something monumental. I wouldn't have wanted to experience what Ria and Alice and little Sophie did. But it's hard not to feel guilty when so many are forever gone from our lives, and even those who came back are damaged. My brother Max... worries me at times."

"The anguish of loss ties us all together, whether or not you were there." Stephen's brother Roy had been killed at Passchendaele.

"I expect you're right."

"By the way, that was very good of you today to give up the race to help your friend."

"Oh, but I couldn't have done anything else!"

"We were nearby."

"But I was closer. It's no matter anyway. There's always next year."

The lively sound of *Jazz Baby* drifted down to them, and Stephen said, "Won't you be missed?"

"I doubt it. Gosh! But I mustn't keep you!" She jumped up, once again feeling silly.

"I have nothing to do at the moment anyway, so don't leave on my account."

"No, no! You're quite right. I'm being a poor guest. I really must allow some eager partner to tread on my toes."

He laughed fulsomely. "As bad as that, is it?"

"At times," she replied with a grin, glad at his amusement.

When he had her safely on the dock, they stared at one another for a poignant moment under the lights, and then Esme lowered her gaze as she said, "Thank you, Stephen. That was a welcome break."

"My pleasure, Miss Wyndham."

"Would you call me Esme?" she dared to ask, staring at him again, knowing that she was going beyond the bounds of propriety. And was excited.

He grinned. "When it's appropriate, I'd be pleased to!"

She didn't know exactly what had just happened to her, but Esme practically bounced back up to the pavilion, her heart bursting with elation, cheerfully singing along with the song flowing across the rocks and into the night.

'Cause I'm a Jazz Baby.

I wanna be jazzin' all the time.
There's something in the tone of a saxophone
That makes me do a little wiggle all my own.
'Cause I'm a Jazz Baby...
She wondered when she could see Stephen again. And imagined dancing with him.

•   •   •

At Silver Bay, her sister, Zoë, could hear the lively music that the darkness carried far out onto the lake, but she felt no pang of regret that she wasn't at the Ball. These days she dreaded the thought of socializing, of struggling to find clever things to say, or even of appearing interested in what others had to relate. She was content to be here alone with Ethan.

She had just finished breast-feeding him and now patted his back gently as she stared at Ouhu, where a single light at the end of the dock quivered across the water towards her. As if it were reaching out to her. *Oh-you-who* it called to her, the playful island name so typical of the Carlyles' sense of humour.

For blissful, brief moments she could almost imagine that Blake was still there, that he would suddenly appear in his canoe. And each time, the profound sadness of his loss would wash over her in a choking wave of misery.

She ignored the promise that he had exacted from her - to get on with her life should something happen to him. In any case, baby Ethan *was* her life now. What else was there for her?

On the lakeside path leading to the cottage, Freddie Spencer cursed his treacherous heart when he spied Zoë in the dim light that spilled from the sitting room onto the screened veranda. She had the baby pressed to her shoulder, and swayed gently with him as she gazed out at the lake. Her long dark hair was tied loosely at the nape of her neck, and cascaded girlishly to her waist.

He'd hoped that the months he and his wife, Martha, had spent alone together in Europe would have strengthened their relationship, but he realized that he was still in love with Zoë. And wished, guiltily, that he were free to show her how deeply.

Having not seen her since those gentle spring days at Priory Manor over two years ago, Freddie was now apprehensive. Her grief was sure to envelope him. He was actually glad that Martha and his sister Emma were with him, since they would help to diffuse the tension.

Zoë was startled out of her reverie when she heard footsteps ascending the veranda stairs, but was pleased to see them.

Martha, who had nursed with her in England, had been her Maid of Honour, while Freddie and Emma had, of course, been lifelong friends.

As they joined her on the screened porch, Martha said effusively, "We couldn't wait any longer to see you and the baby, Zoë! Oh, isn't he precious! Do let me take him for a moment."

Her arms suddenly free, Zoë felt it only natural to hug Freddie. Of course he had written to express his condolences last year, but as she hadn't seen him since Blake's death, their embrace was more than a homecoming welcome. It was fraught with their mutual grief, his unexpressed love, and her need of comfort.

Martha seemed slightly surprised at the obviously intense emotions and said, "Goodness, we didn't mean to make you weep!"

Emma, who had lost her fiancé as well as her eldest brother, had been a stalwart friend since Zoë's return from England. She said, "Grief catches you anew the first time you do anything - see old friends, observe traditions, that sort of thing. Surely you must feel that as well." One of Martha's three brothers had been killed in '17.

"Yes, of course," Martha agreed, and tried not to feel jealous that her husband was so ardently consoling another woman. Zoë was, after all, her friend, and had introduced her to Freddie.

And because Martha was there, Zoë felt safe in Freddie's arms, and grateful for his support. Blake had been a close friend of his.

Freddie thought his heart would break to see her so wounded and alone. Holding her in his arms just stoked the fire of his passion, which he knew he must hide from everyone. How hard it was to resist stroking her hair, her cheek.

"I didn't feel inclined to go to the ball tonight either," Emma admitted. "And now I'm glad of a respite. If we're not intruding, Zoë."

Freddie released her reluctantly, and she hastily brushed away tears. "Not at all. I know that I shouldn't brood, but making the effort to go to a party is beyond me. Do sit down and I'll fetch a bottle of wine." The servants were all working at the ball.

"Let me help," Freddie offered.

She asked him to choose something from the butler's pantry. While he was opening a bottle of champagne, he said, "Let us know if there is anything we can do to help, Zoë." Figuring that if it didn't sound too personal, she might well take him up on the offer.

"Thank you, Freddie. I just feel numb at the moment. Content to be with my family, with no aspirations other than to be a good mother. When I think of how I criticized Mama for choosing a domestic life instead of pursuing a career in music, I feel so ashamed. She knew what was important. At least to her and to us." In a moment of unexpected candour, she added ruefully, "Of course, it's not what I had envisioned for myself."

"You're not planning to return to the university then?"

"Heavens no! I would be lost among the eager young women who intend to change the world."

She had once been such a crusader, keen to tackle inequities. "What about your massage therapy?" he asked as they loaded glasses onto a tray.

"I treat Ellie regularly, and Ria and Chas for their injuries. And other friends. How is your leg wound?"

"Sometimes painful and hard to ignore, but the leg is still mine, and with so many worse off, I shan't complain."

"Massage does help the healing process. You must come to me for treatments as well, Freddie."

The thought of her touching and massaging his thigh was almost unbearable, but how could he reject her offer? "Thank you, Zoë. Will you make a career of it?" He recalled discussing that at their last meeting.

"I shouldn't think so." With a self-deprecating chuckle she said, "I seem to have disappointed other people, and surprised myself."

"You mustn't ever think that, Zoë. Each of has to find our path, which isn't always as we had hoped or intended. Life sometimes sidetracks us, but we eventually find our way." As they returned to the veranda, he said, "Martha will tell you all about what she discovered on our European jaunt."

"It was a revelation!" Martha enthused as she handed the baby back to Zoë and accepted a glass of champagne.

"Welcome home!" Zoë said to them as she raised her glass in a toast. "So do tell, Martha."

"You know how I was forever drawing buildings when I had a moment, to try to educate myself about architecture? Since the university wouldn't admit me into the program because I'm a woman," she added snidely.

"How could I forget the times I had to amuse myself while you did a 'quick sketch' on our walks?" Zoë reminded her with a chuckle. To the others she added, "It wasn't so bad on our outings around Cliveden, but in London there were just too many 'interesting' buildings."

"Yes, well, you should have seen the ones in Italy!" Martha reported with glee. "Fortunately, Freddie has the same habit, so it was enormous fun, even if we were trying to outdo one another."

She threw him a loving glance, which made him feel like a cad. They *had* enjoyed their travels, and he did care for her.

"If you compare the drawings, you'll see that Martha's are much more artistic than mine," Freddie demurred.

"But his are so obviously the precise work of an architect," Martha admitted. "So he's convinced me to study art and learn more about architectural history. And instead of designing buildings, I'll be showcasing them!"

"What a splendid idea!" Zoë said.

"Quite honestly, once Freddie showed me the tedious details that are involved in architectural drafting, I realized that I wouldn't have been keen on that part anyway. That's not to say that I won't offer ideas on the overall design."

"And Martha can do an artist's rendering of my projects, which will surely be more attractive than the geometric drawings."

"That sounds like an ideal partnership," Zoë said. "Will you return to Ottawa?" Martha had grown up there, and the Spencers had lived there since their father had become a Senator.

"No, I'll be starting a practice in Toronto," Freddie said. "I had thought to take the summer off, but Chas already has a commission for me, as do Justin and Troy."

"You could become the cottage and boathouse designer of Muskoka," Zoë suggested. "Then you could easily spend all summer here."

"That's actually a good idea," Freddie admitted. "I noticed that Max's cottage is almost completed." He had designed that as well.

"He and Lydia should be able to move in a couple of weeks," Zoë said. "I think it will be good for them to be on their own. The boys don't understand about Max's shell-shock, and can be a handful at times," she added, referring to her younger brothers, Rupert and Miles.

"He doesn't look well," Freddie said. "So drawn, and not at all like his jovial old self." He and Max had gone overseas together and had thus forged an even closer bond during their wartime service.

"I worry about him, but fortunately, Lydia is a pillar of strength."

The baby had fallen asleep, so Zoë put him into the bassinet beside her chair.

"I'm still sweltering and would dearly love to shed this costume. How be we girls have a skinny dip and leave Freddie to watch the baby?" Emma suggested.

"We couldn't!" Zoë replied.

"Why not? Freddie doesn't mind, do you? And he promises not to look."

"Happy to oblige," Freddie agreed.

"Come along, Zoë," Emma urged. "It's not like you to be reticent. And Martha has to experience the lake properly. She's already enamoured with it, so now she needs to feel its silken caress."

"Emma! That sounds almost indecent," Martha protested, and then giggled.

Freddie was grateful to his sister for invoking such a light-hearted mood. "I promise to alert you the moment the baby stirs," Freddie assured Zoë.

She went off to fetch towels, and the three girls chatted gaily on their walk down to the change rooms in the boathouse. Zoë had turned off most of the lights in the house, so that little spilled into the dark night. A spider web of clouds drifted across the sliver of moon.

Freddie poured himself another glass of champagne. He felt at home here, and knew every inch of the cottage intimately, since he had essentially built it for Zoë. Although she and Max had commissioned the design for their parents, he'd imagined himself sharing it with her when he created it. And because it had been his first commission, it held a special place in his heart.

But now he would have to design a summer home for Martha and himself on his parents' island, Driftwood. He should feel more enthusiasm, but had to admit that he was more excited by Chas's enormous boathouse, and his other commissions. His own place would have to wait.

The girls were enjoying their refreshing swim. "This is heavenly," Martha said. "Even if a bit frightening. I swear if something touches me, I'll scream."

"The fish won't bother you, but there might be the odd bit of seaweed churned up from the depths of the lake," Emma said. "But no monsters."

"I'd forgotten how delicious this is," Zoë admitted. "Especially on dark nights when you feel like you're floating amongst the stars."

"Much preferable to dancing with sweaty partners," Emma said.

Zoë laughed. "You do cut to the heart of things, Emma."

"That's just my legal training. Besides, there aren't any interesting new men at the party."

In the ensuing silence, Zoë could almost feel Emma's sorrow as she was reminded of her fiancé. Cliff Sinclair had been the son of her father's law partner, who, together with Emma's eldest brother, Archie, had planned to take over the firm. Now both lay in foreign graves. Emma and Cliff's sister were planning to step into the breech when they had finished their law studies.

A sudden explosion of fireworks from nearby Oaktree Island startled the swimmers. It looked like a shower of shooting stars - beautiful, if only the noise weren't so disturbing, Zoë thought, since it boomed and echoed alarmingly across the nighttime water. She thought instantly, protectively, of Max.

•   •   •

Back at the Old Cottage, Ria was comforting the children and cursing Helena under her breath. Max came into the sitting room as well, where the sound was at least somewhat muffled. He looked deathly pale.

"Come and sit with us, Max," Ellie said, indicating a chair beside her. "Troy was determined that I should practice my dancing, so I'm completely done in." She had only swayed to a couple of slow tunes with him, but felt frustratingly exhausted. Otherwise they had just been talking to old friends and Troy's brothers. His parents hadn't come, which was just as well, Ellie thought, since she was not strong enough to deal with their hostility.

Lydia rushed in, her look of concern abating somewhat when she saw Max. Snuggling up against him, she took his hand reassuringly. "I thought you said there wouldn't be any fireworks, Ria."

"I expect that Helena arranged those," Ria replied angrily. The Oakleys of Oaktree Island were particular friends of Helena's, and indeed, it was through them that she had met the Wyndhams five years ago. "Troy, would you kindly find her and tell her I'd like a word?"

"Oh dear, I sense a battle brewing," Ellie said with mischievous pleasure.

"She should realize the consequences of her thoughtlessness."

"What is this command performance all about?" Helena demanded a few minutes later.

"I wanted you to see what effect your precious fireworks have on the children." Sophie and Charlie were both clinging to her, and cringing whenever there was another blast.

"It's almost midnight. Children should be in bed," Helena retorted.

"Sleeping through what sounds like an air raid?"

"Don't be absurd! They're being fired from Oaktree, which is at least half a mile away. And how do you expect the children to develop backbone if you mollycoddle them?"

Chas and Jack joined them and, forestalling a scathing response from Ria, Chas said, "The fireworks have unsettled a number of guests, Helena, not just the children. Surely you can't accuse us of being spineless?"

Confronted by war heroes, she was momentarily speechless.

As if on cue, several other veterans came into the sitting room, Lyle Delacourt saying, "I had my fill of pyrotechnics in France, but I suppose there are some who are still amused by them. Surely not you, Ria?" he added.

"My fault, I'm afraid," Helena admitted. "Just trying to keep up traditions."

"Some aren't worth it," Stanford Vandemeer, another wealthy American, drawled.

"This calls for something a bit stronger than wine, don't you think, Chas?" Marshal Fremont added, "Medicinal, don't you agree, Ellie?"

"Absolutely!" Ellie affirmed.

"Do excuse me," Helena said, flushed with embarrassment. She swept out of the room.

After a moment, Lyle Delacourt said, "Did we pass muster, Chas?"

"With glowing colours," Chas replied as he handed out snifters of cognac.

"You arranged that little charade!" Ria accused with a grin.

"I knew that you were planning to lambaste Helena when I saw Troy fetch her," Chas explained. "I thought the point would best be made by others. The Doughboys were happy to oblige."

"It's not as if we're lying, anyway," Lyle Delacourt said. "I don't need any reminders of my time in hell." He sported an eye patch not only because he was dressed as a pirate, but also because he had lost an eye in France. The shrapnel that removed it had left a scar across his cheek.

"You're all priceless!" Ria said. They had been welcome visitors at her English home, Priory Manor, so another bond had formed between her and these once less-intimate summer friends. She had grown particularly close to Troy, who had been stationed at one of the hospitals near the WATS. He had saved her life when she'd been wounded, not only through his transfusion research, but also by donating his own blood to her. She now affectionately called him "big brother".

"Anything for you, my friend," Lyle said, raising his glass to her.

The drinks helped to relax people, but there was a noticeable sense of relief when the blasts, booms, and whistles finally stopped. The band struck up again, and people drifted back outside. The children were exhausted, so Johanna took them up to bed, with Ria promising to tuck them in shortly.

"I'm ready for my bed as well," Max said.

"I'm sorry, Max," Ria commiserated. He had always enjoyed staying up to watch the sunrise after the ball.

"No need. We all have to adjust, don't we?"

As they left, Lydia held onto Max as if she were trying to keep him from breaking apart. He seemed so frail that Lyle said, "Poor chap."

"It might help if you veterans got together for a chat occasionally," Ellie said to the others. "Make it a golf outing, and then spend some time just talking through your war experiences. I think that helps."

"That's a swell idea, Ellie!" Lyle said. "Since most of us won't talk to anyone else about that. Of course we'll have to include Ria. She even has a couple of medals." He grinned at her.

"Oh no! I'd be happy to leave you men to it. How be I provide dinner afterwards?"

"This sounds better all the time! I haven't forgotten what you managed to whip up at Priory Manor, despite wartime shortages."

"I'll volunteer to organize it," Troy offered.

"That's jake!" Lyle said. "And right now I fancy a dance with the wondrous Lizzie."

She had just come in for a break, and did indeed look stunning, Jack thought proudly. Her Spanish costume was shimmering gold, fringed with black, the bodice fitted to the hips, from which multiple layers of skirt cascaded. She smiled at Lyle and took his arm, saying, "I daren't refuse a dashing pirate."

Lyle was an accomplished dancer and they did an energetic Foxtrot to a lively rendition of *Blues My Naughty Sweetie Gave to Me*. Lizzie's mother had cut the layers of her skirt on the bias, saying, "That way it will flow beautifully when you sway." So Lizzie knew that they made an impressive couple.

And looked more carefully at Lyle. Tall and athletic, he was good looking enough, despite his scar. With the backing of supreme wealth, he was self-assured and suave - which also meant that he could have any woman he chose. So, how to play her cards?

"You must have learned from the Castles," she quipped, referring to the famous ballroom dancers, Vernon and Irene.

"Clever girl! I did actually. Mother paid $1000 an hour for us to have private lessons."

Lizzie tried not to let her jaw drop. As a servant, in those lean years before the affluent Wyndhams had acknowledged them, she had earned $150 a year.

"Outrageous, isn't it?" he said with amusement. "I think Vernon hadn't wanted to come to Pittsburgh, so he quoted a ridiculous sum, but Mother called his bluff. The Castles spent nearly a week with us. Mother arranged for the Fremonts and Vandemeers to join us as well, so Vernon got more than he had bargained for. The Castles did oblige by demonstrating the Foxtrot for a soiree Mother arranged. Vernon, poor chap, was killed in an aeroplane crash in Texas last year when he was training pilots. I wonder if Jack or Chas ever ran into him when he was in the RFC."

"They've never mentioned it."

The next tune was the melodic waltz, *If You Were the Only Girl in the World*, so they kept dancing. She allowed him to pull her closer than was considered proper, and, having had her own dance training when she was in New York, was able to follow his lead effortlessly as he whirled her about, her billowing skirt sometimes wrapping sensually around his legs. Some of the other dancers stopped to watch and allow them more room.

There was applause when they finished.

"You've been practicing," Stuart Roland accused.

"Not at all. We're just naturally good together," Lyle said, with a meaningful smile at Lizzie.

She felt the thrill of conquest.

"Shall we?" he asked when the orchestra struck up *For Me and My Gal*.

"Oh, yes."

They danced another before Lyle suggested, "Let's cool down with a glass of champagne."

They chose a quiet spot on the west veranda, where smudge pots smoked to deter mosquitoes. Lyle pulled off his eye patch, saying, "With this thing on, I almost believe I can see again when I take it off. What do you think?"

She was surprised at how much his glass eye resembled his real one. "It's a work of art."

"So it is! Most people can't tell it's fake. At least not until they realize it doesn't move much. I have eyes for different occasions. This is my evening wear."

"But it doesn't glitter," she jested.

He laughed. "The pupil is larger because the light is lower, so they tell me."

"It's amazing." She touched his scar gently and said, "You must let me photograph you. You have such a strong and expressive face."

He grabbed her hand and seductively kissed her wrist. "Definitely. I've heard you're quite accomplished. An artist, in fact."

"It runs in the family." Lizzie owned a studio in Toronto, where she took acclaimed portraits of society people, earning herself not only accolades, but also a great deal of money.

They were staring at each other, and Lizzie did find it disconcerting to realize that his one eye was expressionless. She concentrated on the other.

"There you are, Lyle!" Adele Fremont said. "Do come and dance. You're the only one who really can."

"I'll look forward to another whirl, Miss Wyndham," he said as he got up to take Adele's outstretched hand. She shot Lizzie a haughty glare before going off with Lyle.

There was her competition, Lizzie realized. And because the Fremonts and Delacourts had been friends for decades, the families would be expecting Lyle and Adele to marry. She would have to play her cards carefully indeed.

In the sitting room, Ria had just returned from bidding goodnight to the children when Grayson, looking pale, said to Ellie, "Would you accompany me please, Dr. Carlyle?"

"Yes, of course, Grayson."

She leaned on Troy as they followed him into the kitchen, where a blast of heat greeted them. Ria was right behind them, surprised that there was no bustle or clatter of dishes, only someone sobbing.

The servants were standing around in shock, watching Branwyn Grayson as she knelt on the floor beside Mrs. Hadley. She shook her head and moved aside to let Ellie take her place. The young scullery maid, Jane, sat in a chair wailing and rocking back and forth. Mrs. Grayson put an arm about her and said softly, "Hush, child."

"What happened?" Ria asked with dread. Chas, who had also followed them in, put his arm about her shoulder.

"She let out a sharp gasp and collapsed," Grayson said.

A broken platter and scattered shrimp vol-au-vents lay in front of her.

"Ellie?" Ria asked.

"I'm afraid there's nothing I can do for her, Ria. She must have had a massive heart attack."

"Dear God!" Ria sank down on her knees, and took the dead woman's hand in hers. "Oh, Mrs. Hadley." She bit back tears, knowing she should be strong in front of the servants.

Chas pulled her up. "Come, my darling."

"We have to stop the Ball," she said.

"If I may suggest, we should carry on," Grayson said. "It would be better for us all. Mrs. Hadley would not have wanted it otherwise. She always took great pride in her work and in the family."

"But it seems so heartless and disrespectful," Ria said.

"There's nothing more we can do for Mrs. Hadley tonight."

"I agree with Mr. Grayson, M'am," Olivia's cook, Mrs. O'Rourke, said. "I've known Mrs. Hadley nigh on thirty years. Started as her kitchen maid, and we've been best of friends ever since. I'll do her right proud tonight, if I may," she said with determination. "We'll have plenty of time to grieve."

"We'll take her up to her room, where Mrs. Grayson will lay her out. She has experience with such things," Grayson said. "And I will see to arrangements in the morning."

"I ain't sleeping upstairs with no body!" young Jane said. "I just wanna go home!" She began howling again.

"You can sleep in our cottage, Jane," Grayson assured her. "Perhaps a drink is called for to steady everyone's nerves."

"By all means. Thank you, Grayson," Chas said. "I know we can rely on you."

He led Ria out of the kitchen, saying quietly, "Why don't you take a few moments in the library to steady your own nerves, my darling? And I can make your excuses if you want to retire."

He looked at Ellie, who nodded. She and Troy followed Ria. "It doesn't seem right," Ria said as Troy handed her a cognac and a handkerchief.

"That's the way it is," Ellie stated, although what she really wanted to say was, *It isn't right that a dozen people are sweltering in a hellishly hot kitchen with the wood stove burning when its 90 degrees outside, and working slavishly long hours for a pittance so that the rest of us can eat and drink and be merry.* "Might I suggest you do something about the ventilation in the kitchen? I don't know how anyone can work in that heat."

"I've already been talking to Freddie about redesigning the kitchen. Do you think that contributed to her death?" Ria asked in consternation.

"Not directly, although I'm surprised that no one has fainted in there. From her swollen legs and ankles, and the fact that she was overweight, I suspect Mrs. Hadley had a heart condition, so the extra stress of the heat would not have helped."

"I asked her if she wanted to retire when we closed the hospital," Ria said, referring to her city estate, Wyndholme, which had been used for convalescent soldiers during the war. Mrs. Hadley had remained in charge of the kitchen. "But she said she wouldn't know what to do with herself. That we were all the family she had, and could she stay on. Of course I was delighted, much as I knew she was getting on in years. She said that one of the things she always looked forward to was her early morning dip in the lake, before anyone else was up." It had made Ria realize that she knew virtually nothing about the people who worked for her and lived in her home, other than those moments when their lives intersected. It was only Grayson she had come to know better.

Richard and Olivia came into the library saying, "Chas told us what happened."

"Grayson and Mrs. O'Rourke insist we keep the ball going. Are they right?" Ria asked.

"They've chosen that way to honour their friend," Olivia said. "Mrs. Hadley would have been terribly embarrassed to think that guests were being sent home because of her."

"It's going to be a long night," Ria sighed.

"You go up to bed, and Richard and I will carry on. It is, after all, a Wyndham ball, not just your responsibility."

But Richard looked as if he wished he were quietly at home. Everyone had to carry on, despite pain or grief or fear. That, too, was the way it was. "If the servants can manage, so can I," Ria assured them.

Olivia smiled at her.

But it was more difficult and exhausting to be cheerful and witty than Ria thought.

She was fetching a cup of tea from the dining room for her mother-in-law when she found Phoebe looking puzzled. "Is there a problem, Phoebe?"

"I just caught a glimpse of Mrs. Hadley in the mirror, but when I turned around, she wasn't there. She doesn't usually come out of the kitchen.... Ria, why are you staring at me like that? Stop it! STOP IT!" Phoebe clawed at her own face as if she could erase the expression of horror on Ria's.

"What's going on?" Edgar asked with concern as he rushed into the room. He took hold of his sister's hands and managed to pull them away from her face before she hurt herself. "Phoebe, stop!" He looked questioningly at Ria.

She grabbed the back of a chair to stop herself from shaking. "Phoebe just saw Mrs. Hadley… who died more than an hour ago."

"Oh, Phoebe!" Edgar said compassionately, taking his sister into his arms. "Let's go home. It's late and everyone's tired."

"I did see her," Phoebe whimpered. "I did."

"I know, sweetheart."

"How could she have?" Ria asked Ellie and Troy when she rejoined them in the sitting room.

"I don't know, Ria, but the same thing happened when Toby died." Ellie said. "Daphne was there." Toby had been the Wyndwood caretaker. "Phoebe must have some heightened perception. Something the rest of us haven't experienced. If you believe in an afterlife, then is it difficult to believe in ghosts?"

"Is that what makes her crazy?"

"What does that mean? That someone perceives and thinks differently? I don't know anymore, Ria. I once thought I did, but… sometimes I question my own sanity."

"We're all overtired," Troy said. "It's been an eventful evening, and we should get home. But do let us know if there is anything we can do, Ria."

"I shall. And thank you."

What had once been an exciting night had become an ordeal. Ria could hardly wait for it to end.

•   •   •

Mrs. Hadley was laid to rest in the Port Darling cemetery as per the instructions she had long ago left with Grayson. He explained to Ria, "She spent so many summers here that she felt this was her home more than the city. "I won't get lost here," she told me. And she loved the lake, since she grew up by the sea."

Ria was quiet when they returned from the simple ceremony. "You seem to be pondering something profound," Chas said to her.

"I was thinking how right Mrs. Hadley had been to choose to be interred up here rather than in some massive cemetery in the city. Do you think we could be buried on the island?"

"That wouldn't be allowed, Ria."

"Well, I don't want to go into the family vault. So you can sprinkle my ashes here."

"That's still a long way away, my darling. And I daresay you will outlive me."

"We'll mingle our ashes and scatter them to the wind. Then we'll be forever together and a part of Muskoka."

Chas held her while she mourned the loss of another happy fragment of her past.

Chapter 4

Fliss hadn't expected to lead an expedition when she'd offered to show Jack Moonglow Island, but she was happy just to be in his company. And, of course, she loved spending time with her friends. So she and Jack were in the lead canoe, followed by Lizzie and Claire, and then Esme and Alice. They had surprised her with a picnic basket that Olivia's cook had put together for them.

Moonglow lay less than a quarter of a mile to the west of Thorncliff. It was rugged and rocky and peppered with second-growth pines and hardwoods. Among the granite slopes and cliffs were a couple of sandy coves where they could beach the canoes.

"This would be a perfect spot to build a cottage," Fliss said when they had clambered up the bluff from the beach. "From this point you have views of the lake to the east, west, and south, and a sheltered spot for the boathouse and dock."

"It's glorious!" Claire agreed. "I can already imagine it."

"I'll take pictures of it, so that we can send them to Emily and Hugo," Lizzie said.

"You can photograph the entire island," Jack suggested.

"I'll just sit here and sketch," Claire said. Jack had been teaching her to draw and paint since she was old enough to hold a pencil, so like him, she always carried her small sketchbook. "I'm a bit tired."

Jack squatted down beside her as the others set out. "Are you alright, sweetheart?" She looked flushed and her breathing seemed a bit ragged.

"Oh, sure. I'm still not over that wretched flu." She coughed.

Jack looked at her with concern. Always slender, she seemed to have grown thinner lately. "You should let Ellie examine you."

"I'm fine, Jack, and happy just to sit here and be inspired."

"You're getting really good."

She grinned. "My goal is to be at least as famous an artist as you."

He went off, chuckling.

Claire whispered into the wind, "Please God, don't let it be that!" She tried to still the manic thumping of her heart, which seemed to reverberate through her.

She thought it was just as well that Jack had talked her out of becoming a teacher, which had been her long-time dream, because she didn't have the energy to even contemplate attending the Normal School for training. He'd reminded her that she would lose her career when she married anyway, as women teachers were expected to be single. And now that she didn't need to earn money, it really wasn't fair to take jobs from people who did.

After her initial disappointment, she realized with mounting excitement that she now had the leisure and means to pursue her art, which she loved. Esme had suggested that she should see paintings by the Old Masters in person, so wouldn't a European jaunt be an educational adventure! It was what Ria and Zoë were to have done under the guidance of Cousin Bea five years ago, but the war had intervened. So Esme and Claire had already begun planning their Grand Tour for this year or next, with the expectation that Cousin Bea would oblige as chaperone, and failing that, perhaps Esme's mother, Olivia, would step in.

It took the others a while to explore the seven-acre island, and Claire was already feeling better - and thus happier - by the time they returned.

"You should see all the blueberry bushes in the middle of the island," Alice told her.

"We have an annual blueberry-picking party here," Fliss said.

"I think it's perfectly enchanting and romantic," Alice declared. "Imagine having an entire island to yourself! I don't mean like Wyndwood or Thorncliff, which are most impressive, of course. But something smaller and more intimate, like this."

"You should have Sunrise Island, Alice," Fliss said offhandedly. "Chas and Ria don't need it."

Alice blushed. "Oh, I didn't mean..."

"Of course not. It's my idea," Fliss assured her. "I'll suggest that it be your wedding present."

Alice blushed hotter, but allowed herself to consider the delightful possibility. "Golly!"

"What if she never marries?" Claire asked devilishly.

"That's not likely to happen," Esme said. "I do think she has at least one ardent admirer, who shall remain nameless, but is someone dear to all our hearts." And she earnestly hoped that Alice and Arthur would eventually marry, since they seemed eminently suited.

"Do stop!" Alice pleaded.

The girls giggled.

Lizzie snapped more photos of them.

They spread the picnic on a cloth and helped themselves to tiny sandwiches of cucumber and egg and ham, moist fairy cakes with fresh strawberries, and cool lemonade from thermoses.

Lizzie said, "I think Hugo and Emily will be delighted with this."

"Stephen told me that the going rate for vacant land is about $100 an acre. So I expect I should ask $700 for the island," Fliss speculated.

"That hardly seems enough," Jack replied.

"Jack! You're supposed to be bargaining *for* Hugo, not *against* his interests!" Lizzie scolded.

"But if something seems too cheap, it won't be valued as highly," he countered. "There should be a bonus on islands, since they'll have this all to themselves, as Alice pointed out. Believe me, Hugo will think he's getting a bargain if you asked $2000 for it."

"But since Emily is a friend, I wouldn't expect her to pay more," Fliss said. "No, I've quite made up my mind."

It was what Jack had once earned in a year. He needed to keep his perspective, even though he was now worth almost a quarter of a million. He could see how easy it was to slide into the excesses of affluence, to pay a workingman's weekly wage for a bottle of champagne, as Chas did. And yet, wouldn't that be expected of him, once he and Fliss were married? Wouldn't they need a showpiece of a home in which to throw lavish parties? The Thorncliff cottage was one of the largest on the lake, so at least he would be set with that. He was now eager to move his future forward.

When they dropped Fliss off at Thorncliff, Jack said, "Shall we play tennis tomorrow?"

"Oh, yes, do come over!" Fliss entreated. She felt bereft that they were all going back to Wyndwood, leaving her with only her mother for company, unless Rafe and Sid were back from their activities. Fliss often canoed to Silver Bay, or to visit Chas and Ria, but Thorncliff itself wasn't as much fun now that Chas was no longer there.

So Fliss was happy when the Wyndwood friends, along with Lydia, Max, Chas, Ria, the children, and Johanna arrived for tennis the following day. Claire had been persuaded to come along, although she claimed she was too tired to participate. Zoë had chosen to stay at home.

They changed partners regularly, and Johanna was thrilled to be invited to play a set.

While they were watching from the pavilion veranda, Lizzie said to Chas, "I wonder if I might ask a great favour?"

"Certainly."

"I thought it would be a good idea for me to have a darkroom up here to process my photos."

"And you want to use some space at the Inn?" he said astutely.

"Yes! If that wouldn't inconvenience anyone. I'm sure that Emily and Hugo won't mind, once they move in."

"By all means, Lizzie. I'll give you a key. Get Jack to show you how to drive the Dippy and then you can use that to get back and forth."

"Thank you, Chas! How generous!" Now she could do a portrait of Lyle Delacourt, as she had promised him.

As if she had conjured him up, he suddenly strolled onto the pavilion. "Glad to find you all here," he said, although it was Lizzie he focussed on for a meaningful moment. "I've been given the task of inviting all the islanders to attend a Full Moon Sing-Song followed by a dance. It's Belinda's idea," he acknowledged, referring to his youngest sister. He handed out the invitations. "Everyone is to come in a canoe or rowboat, or a motorboat if you can't manage otherwise. We're going to raft all the vessels together out on the lake and sing. Belinda thinks it will be impressive if we can assemble lots of people."

"That sounds smashing," Ria said.

"It's still a couple of weeks away, but Belle wanted to be sure that everyone had plenty of notice," Lyle said.

Chas offered him a drink, which he gratefully accepted.

"Did I hear talk of a party?" Sid inquired as she swept onto the veranda.

Lyle explained and she replied, "How divine! You people certainly have the most clever ways of amusing yourselves. I've just met the very charming Eatons, who've invited us all to a soiree next week at which some famous tenor will be singing. Apparently he's been quite the rage in Europe, and will be performing with the Chicago Opera this season. So he's going to be resting and rehearsing at Kawandag for a month." Which was Sir John and Lady Flora Eaton's stately summer mansion at the north end of the lake.

How tedious, Lizzie thought. She loved musicals, but she found the operas that Hugo had taken her and Emily to in New York melodramatic and antiquated. But if she wanted to fit into the upper class, she needed to be informed and enthusiastic about all the arts. So she was amused to hear Lyle say, "I have the greatest respect for people whose voices are finely tuned instruments, but I'm afraid that opera assaults my poor brain and has me running for the exit."

"So you have a tin ear as well as a glass eye," Lizzie quipped.

Jack shot her a "watch yourself" look, but was relieved when Lyle laughed appreciatively.

"Ah, Lizzie, you do have the measure of me!"

"And now I should like to capture you as well. On film. I'm going to set up a summer studio in the Spirit Bay Inn, but I think perhaps an outdoor portrait would suit you better."

"Anytime, Lizzie."

"I have my cameras here, so why not tomorrow? I can fetch my processing equipment from the city later."

Rafe was annoyed to see Lizzie flirting with Lyle. He would just have to warn his friend about the cunning vamp.

"Did you bring your tennis racquet?" Ria asked Lyle.

"I'm afraid that my attempts at one-eyed tennis have been abysmal," he admitted.

"You and I could have a fair match then," Chas jested.

"Do put on some music," Sid said to Rafe. "I feel like dancing."

"That's more my style!" Lyle pronounced. "Shall we, Milady?" he asked Sid.

"Oh yes, let's!"

They twirled about the large empty pavilion, Sid's laughter punctuating the music.

"We can't let them have the dance floor all to themselves," Rafe declared. "Come and shake a leg, Lizzie."

He had put her on the spot, and seemed to gloat. But she wouldn't give him the satisfaction of besting her. "Yes, of course," she said graciously, assuring herself that she cared nothing for Rafe now. It was Lyle she wanted, and she would focus on that thought while Rafe held her, too tightly and suggestively. And for Jack's sake, she needed to stop alienating Rafe.

"A studio, eh? Perhaps I should have my portrait done," Rafe said.

"As you like. I expect that you've changed since the last one I took." She tried to be noncommittal, to keep the sarcasm out of her voice, but Rafe chuckled.

"Scheming to ensnare Lyle now, are you?" he whispered to her.

It took all her willpower not to tense. Calmly she replied, "I don't know what you mean. I've obviously never *ensnared* anyone."

"Not for want of trying."

"We had fun once, Rafe. But don't blame me for the choices *you* have made," she said in exasperation. "My loyalty to you apparently meant nothing. I understand better now the man that you are, and am actually very happy to move on with my life." She said it with such dignity and lack of contempt that Rafe was momentarily speechless.

Lizzie was relieved that the dance was over and Lyle came to claim the next one.

Sid coaxed Chas onto the dance floor and seemed to be enjoying herself rather too much. Annoyed by the unruly women in his life, Rafe grabbed Ria for a dance, but was so distracted and moody that she said, "Oh dear, I feel rather like I might as well be a broom that you're dancing with."

"I realize I prefer horses to women. They're much less complicated and demanding."

Ria couldn't help laughing, although she realized that he was serious. "We're not so complicated, Rafe. We need only to be revered and romanced, cherished and celebrated. In song or poetry."

"Don't mock me, Ria!"

"Then stop thinking that women are here only for your pleasure and convenience! We don't take kindly to the bit between our teeth these days."

He grumbled as he walked off to fetch himself another drink.

While the others danced, Jack and Fliss trounced Esme and Alice on the court.

"Come for a stroll with me," Jack said to Fliss after they had cooled off with a frosty glass of lemonade.

"We're a great team, aren't we?" Fliss said eagerly as they walked along the shore path to the east.

"Unbeatable, I'd say," Jack replied with a grin.

"So will you be my partner for the tournament?"

"Well of course I would, but isn't there a rule that you can't play with the same person you did in the previous one?"

"*Last year* to be precise, and since we haven't had the tournament since 1914, I don't think that rule applies, do you?"

"Since it's a Thorncliff tournament, I think you can make whatever rules you like. So, yes, let's take on all comers."

She was surprised when he took her hand, and squeezed his joyfully.

When they were out of sight of the house and tennis pavilion, Jack stopped and turned to her, looking deep into her eyes as he said, "Fliss, Chas is my greatest friend, as you know, and through all your wonderful letters during the war, I'd come to think of you as an equally dear friend. But since I've been back and had the opportunity to know the enchanting and accomplished young woman that you've become, that has grown into something deeper."

Wide-eyed, breathless, Fliss felt herself melt as he kissed her tenderly.

"You're still young, but very mature for nineteen, and I don't want to wait any longer to marry. Would you consider becoming my wife?"

"Oh, Jack! Do you really mean that?"

She quivered when he stroked her cheek. "Oh yes. I can't imagine anyone I'd rather spend my life with," he said, not untruthfully. Among the heiresses, there was no one as amenable and likeable as Fliss. And Ellie was no longer his for the taking.

He kissed her more passionately, and when he released her, he was momentarily concerned to see tears streaming down her face. "Fliss?"

She wiped them away hastily as she said, "I'm deliriously happy! I've been in love with you for years! This is all I've ever wanted!"

She laid her head against his shoulder as he embraced her - and his future. "You don't know how happy you've made me," he said. "As long as I have your family's blessing, I shall be *over the moon!*" He pulled a small silver box from his trouser pocket and handed it to her. "I was hoping you'd say 'yes'."

Inside was a deep blue oval sapphire surrounded by a starburst of sizable diamonds. Although he had bargained, he had still spent a small fortune on it, but knew it was important to appear affluent and generous to his bride. And what difference would a few thousand dollars make once he had Fliss's millions?

"Oh, Jack! It's exquisite!"

"I thought it was the colour of the lake on a sunny day, so it would always remind you."

She kissed him, and he enveloped her in another joyful hug. Surely no man could be happier than he. Lizzie was right to say that although Fliss didn't have the natural beauty of her brothers, she had the elements that allowed artifice to make her more alluring - fine bone structure, flawless complexion, a tall and lithe body, which was becoming fashionable. Her newly short, marcelled hair complimented her narrow face and emphasized her best features. A few more lessons from Lizzie on the subtle use of make-up to enhance her pale eyes and narrow lips and other men would surely admire his classy wife.

"Now I should talk to Chas," Jack said. "And you'd better hide that ring for the moment. The women are sure to notice."

She beamed broadly as she took his outstretched hand. "I'll wait up at the cottage. I'm sure Chas will be happy for me."

Back at the pavilion, Lyle said, "Alas, I must be on my way. I have more invitations to deliver. Thank you for this delightful interlude. Lizzie, shall I come by tomorrow afternoon?"

"Perfect!"

"Tie and tails?" he jested.

"If that's how you clamber over rocks."

He laughed.

"Think about what you'd like as a backdrop," Lizzie said as she walked down to the wharf with him.

"You're the artist, what do you recommend? Rocks by the sounds of it."

"I see you sitting on a granite outcropping staring pensively into the distance. And standing, leaning against a pine with the lake in the background."

"And gazing at the photographer?"

"Perhaps. We'll have to try different poses." She actually hadn't meant to make it sound risqué, and hid her amusement.

He didn't, however, and said, "I shall look forward to it!"

As she watched him pull away from the dock, Lizzie thought that she could even fall in love with Lyle. Unlike Rafe, Lyle had a basically cheerful temperament.

While Fliss ran up to the house, Jack approached Chas and asked to have a private word. Ria was playing tennis with the children, and the others were still dancing. Claire was reading a novel on the pavilion veranda.

So Jack and Chas strolled toward the house.

"Chas, I've just taken the liberty of proposing to Fliss. I expect I should have asked you first, but I wanted to be sure she was willing."

Chas wasn't all that surprised. He suspected that Fliss had a crush on Jack, and had noticed how well they'd been getting along these past months. But more like best friends, he thought. "Are you in love with her?"

Jack knew he had to be careful. There was little to indicate that he was completely smitten. "She's lovely, utterly charming, great fun to be with. I care deeply for her and want to make her happy. So, yes, I certainly do love her. Perhaps not with the searing passion that you and Ria share. What you have is rare. This is something quieter, but no less real. And I'm absolutely thrilled that she wants to share her life with me. I've never felt anything so exciting or heady!" Which was indeed true, and must have shown. "You're the best friend I've ever had, Chas. You know I'll look after Fliss. Cherish her."

"And you know I'll hold you to that." He looked sharply at Jack, and then held out his hand. "Welcome to the family, brother-in-law."

Jack could hardly contain his joy.

"You should know that half of Fliss's inheritance is in a trust fund for her children."

"Our children, you mean. Good!"

"Find Fliss and we'll go and tell Mumsy."

Marjorie Thornton gave her blessing and suppressed tears at the thought of her baby leaving her. She admired the engagement ring and said to Fliss, "We'll plan a wedding for next summer."

"Mummy, I can't wait until then!"

"We'll leave you to talk about it," Chas said. "Then you can come to the pavilion and we'll announce this to the others with champagne."

When the men had gone, Jack departing with a wink, Fliss said, "I've waited the whole war for Jack to return! Haven't we learned that every moment is precious, that we don't know what might happen tomorrow? I don't need a fancy wedding, just something elegant and intimate, like Emily had. Perhaps I should ask Jack's mother to make my gown. Emily's was so modern and chic, wasn't it? Quite deevie! We'll have the wedding here on the Labour Day weekend, so we'll have the whole summer to plan, Mummy. Oh, isn't this just too thrilling!"

"Will you be happy, my angel?"

"Oh yes! How could I not be, with Jack?"

"We'll have to talk about wifely obligations. Or perhaps I will ask Ria to talk to you. Perhaps that would be best."

"Let's go and tell the others!" Fliss took her mother's arm, and they strolled down the path.

Chas had meanwhile taken Rafe aside, anticipating that he might spoil Fliss's joyful moment with a sour reaction. Chas knew that Rafe had never liked Jack.

"I won't allow my sister to marry that scheming upstart!" Rafe hissed. They were standing on the croquet lawn.

"Don't be absurd," Chas retorted. "Jack's a Wyndham. His grandfather was already a millionaire when our father was still a telegraph clerk. I would - and did - trust Jack with my life, and I will with my sister."

"He's using her and us. He doesn't love her."

"He loves her well enough. More than you love Sid, I'd wager."

"He was fucking Sid, you know. In London."

"As were you, before you had any intention of marrying her."

"You're a fool, Chas, to be so completely taken in by Jack. You'll regret it."

"I doubt it. Jack will make Fliss happy. And he'll prevent us from losing everything that Pater built up. You'll be grateful to him one day."

Rafe practically spat as he marched away.

So Fliss was a bit disappointed when he didn't appear at the pavilion for the engagement announcement. But the others were happy for them, the girls eager to admire the ring. Fliss immediately decided that Esme, Claire, Alice, and Sophie should be bridesmaids, and Lizzie, the photographer. She wanted Ria to be Matron of Honour, and Jack had obviously chosen Chas to be Best Man. Max, Edgar, Rupert, and Miles would be groomsmen.

"Let's carry on the festivities at the beach," Ria said. "We need to get back soon, as Father has summoned us all to a family dinner."

"I think it's about something momentous," Max said.

"Like what? Is Helena expecting again?" Ria asked sarcastically.

"Your father and Uncle Albert have been closeted with Papa on several occasions, but they've all been tight-lipped."

"We'll find out soon enough," Ria said. "Now let's swim!"

Esme had deliberately left her bathing suit in the boat so that she had an excuse to return to the dock in the hope of seeing Stephen. But she was surprised to discover him shirtless, his trousers rolled up, and standing in the shallows splashing his head and chest. Men's swimsuits always covered their torsos, so he was rather indecently exposed.

"I do beg your pardon, Miss," he said, quickly picking up his shirt, which lay discarded on the dock, and putting it on. But because he was still wet, it clung to him, emphasizing his strong muscles.

"Not at all," Esme said, hoping her blush seemed like just a bit of sun on her face. "What better to do than cool off in the lake in this heat?" she said inanely. "I just came for my bag."

"I'll fetch it if you like," he said, hoisting himself effortlessly out of the water onto the wharf. He moved with the ease and grace of a cat, she thought.

"It's the only one left in the boat," she said as he clambered into Chas's launch.

She thanked him when he handed it to her, but made no move to leave as she watched water dripping off his ruffled hair, disconcerted and embarrassed at the strong desire to run her fingers through it. "And it's Esme," she said with a smile as she finally collected herself and realized that she must seem foolish, staring at him like an eager puppy.

"Yes, of course." His smile was so sincere and friendly that she had to fight the impulse to stay.

The others were already in their suits when Esme arrived at the east change house, and on their way to the diving rock and beach further along.

Sid caught Jack alone for a moment and said with a smirk, "Well done, *brother-in-law*. You've certainly landed on your feet. And isn't it convenient that we'll be so close. When we get bored with the Thornton siblings, we can resume our *friendship*."

"You're outrageous, Sid!"

"Just realistic, darling. That sweet little thing isn't enough of a woman for you. But I do feel sorry for her. She's so utterly besotted that she doesn't yet realize she's just another one of your stepping stones."

Jack was no longer amused. "She is all I could ever hope for in a wife, and I expect that she'll be loyal and faithful," he retorted looking pointedly at Sid.

She snorted at the dig. "Ah, but will you be?"

•   •   •

Ria had to admit that her father's cottage, Westwynd, which had been built during her absence, was impressive. Of course, it was Helena who had pressed for a place that would rival the Thorntons' and Oakleys' for opulence, and make Ria's Old Cottage seem pedestrian in comparison. It had always irked Helena that Ria had inherited the cottage and the palatial Toronto estate, Wyndholme, from Augusta rather than James, the eldest son. The recent addition of a conservatory that could double as a ballroom now ensured that Westwynd was the grandest of the Wyndwood cottages.

It was in the new wing that the Wyndhams, dressed in their finery, gathered for pre-dinner drinks. With its many arched windows overlooking the lake, the room had absorbed the heat of the day, but breezes wafted in through the open French doors, and people wandered out onto the balustraded flagstone terrace. This was Ria's favourite part of Westwynd, since it reached almost to the water's edge.

Zoë had once again declined to attend, and Ria had known that Sophie and Charlie were not invited, so nineteen of them sat down at the long oak table in the dining room under the glittering crystal chandelier. Liveried staff served the tantalizing dishes prepared by the French chef.

It was over the Muskoka lamb that Jack said, "I have an announcement to make. Felicity Thornton has agreed to be my wife."

"Oh, how wonderful!" Olivia cried. "Congratulations indeed."

"Another bond between our families, eh, Chas?" Richard said with a smile. "Well done, Jack!"

"You must let us know what we can do to help with the preparations," Irene volunteered, which annoyed Helena, who had been about to make the offer. She had not taken to Irene, Albert's second wife, a widowed nurse and not "quality" as far as Helena was concerned. She conveniently ignored the fact that Lady Flora Eaton had been a trainee nurse before her marriage into that mercantile empire.

"There must be an engagement party at least," Helena said.

"I've already begun organizing it," Ria assured her. "But I'd be grateful if your staff could help out again." Although Helena didn't have thirty servants like the Oakleys, the staff wing of Westwynd could house at least twenty, with accommodations for the personal maids and valets brought by visitors.

"Of course."

"Now let me tell you some other news," James said. "We have found buyers for our mills."

There were gasps of amazement.

"This area is almost lumbered out. Albert and I wish to retire rather than expand further north and west, which we would need to do, and Richard has been plagued with ill health. Edgar and Max have no interest in lumbering, and Henry's staying in England. We felt this was a good time to sell, while the mills are still profitable. Albert, Richard, and I will divide the assets of these and our other Wyndham enterprises, and each shall provide his children with an equitable share. None of you will be poor, to say the least."

"What about Jack's family?" Ria asked.

"I shall see that they are provided for," Richard said immediately.

Ria wasn't surprised that her father and Uncle Albert didn't make similar offers. Albert had disliked and distrusted Jack from the start, and was still only coldly civil to him. "Uncle Richard, you have enough dependents to look after. I'd be happy to share my portion with Jack and the girls," she said before Jack could respond. She challenged her father, not really expecting anything from him, nor did she need his money when Chas had more than the entire Wyndham fortune. But she was hurt at his dismissive answer nonetheless.

"You did well out of your grandmother, and have an assured financial future with Chas."

"Thank you, Ria and Uncle Richard, for your generous offers. But I've done very well in my own ventures, thanks to my small inheritance from Grandmother," Jack assured them proudly. That $25,000 *was* a pittance compared to the worth of the family, if not to the general public. "I don't expect anything more, and will happily provide for my sisters." Of course it was easy for him to say that with Fliss's fortune soon to back him. But it still rankled that his family hadn't been included even in some small measure. James and Albert might yet regret their cavalier treatment.

Back at the Old Cottage later, Ria said, "I'm sorry that the family has treated you so shoddily, Jack! In fact, it makes me fume!"

"Thank you, Ria, but I can truly say that I prefer not to be beholden to my uncles for my success. Uncle Richard, of course, has been most generous in buying us a house, and I shall never forget that. But it's exhilarating to think that my own investments have paid back ten-fold."

"And already made us richer as well, Ria," Chas said. "Jack has the touch of Midas."

Jack laughed. But he felt rather like he did.

•   •   •

"Mama, does Max *have* to play such angry music?" Miles whined to Olivia.

Max was doing a ferocious rendition of Rachmaninoff's Prelude in C# Minor. He was hunched over the grand piano, pounding out the haunting chords as if that could excise the demons from his mind.

"It's not how *you* play it," Miles added, when Olivia looked worriedly at Max.

Max had heard and suddenly looked up with a grin - like the cheeky boy he used to be, Olivia thought, with hope - and said, "Is this better?" He launched into the exuberant *Russian Rag*, which was based on the Rachmaninoff piece.

Miles smiled and said, "That's crackerjack!"

When he'd finished, Max got up from the piano, and went to give his mother a quick embrace. It took all his willpower to not let her see how fiercely he held himself in check. "Don't worry about me. Not having to go into the family business has freed me. I've decided I'm going to study music at the Conservatory."

Olivia was thrilled, not only at this seeming transformation in character, but also at his choice. "That's wonderful! You do have talent, Max."

"I realize that I love music more than anything. And it's helping me to heal." He tousled his youngest brother's hair, and said, "And I'll be out of *your* hair soon anyway, as our cottage is almost ready."

"I don't *want* you to leave," Miles said seriously.

Max laughed. "I'll be within spitting distance. And you can visit whenever you want. And not have to listen to me playing when you don't care to."

"Will you write your own music?" Miles asked.

"Oh, yes. I've been toying with ideas." He returned to the piano and played a few compelling phrases. "Just wait."

"I think your brother will do great things," Olivia said cheerfully to Miles.

Max noticed how much younger she suddenly looked, and felt guilty for having added to her burdens. It really was time for him and Lydia to move into their own cottage. Pretending took too much energy.

Chapter 5

In winter, Esme found it hard to drag herself out of bed in the mornings, but summer dawns beckoned her. Especially when she had friends or, in this case, cousins staying with her, she relished the time to herself while the others still slept soundly. Throwing on a simple dress, she crept from the girls' dorm. After a quick wash, and leaving her long blonde hair loose, she tiptoed downstairs, and into the misty morning. It seemed as if the wispy clouds had come down to rest overnight upon the calm water and were just beginning to rouse themselves, blushing to be caught by the rising sun.

Esme paddled north, past Westwynd, and then closer to the shoreline of Thorncliff than usual. She was disappointed that the boathouse doors were still firmly closed, and Stephen Seaford wasn't doing something on the docks. She knew that he and some of the other male staff slept above the boathouse, but could see nothing from her vantage point.

It was just as well, she thought, for what would she say to him? What would he think if she seemed to be seeking him out? And for what purpose? Despite her parents' liberal views, she knew that any kind of relationship with Stephen would be inappropriate. The fact that she was smitten by his healthy good looks and vitality was something that she would have to hug to herself.

She continued paddling around Thorncliff, lost now in the magic of the dawn.

She was startled when a familiar voice said, "You're out early."

She turned to see Stephen fishing from his skiff between Sunrise and Sunset Islands. And felt a thrill of pleasure. "I love the early morning before others are about. It makes me feel as if the lake belongs to me," she said.

"Yes. It's like that all day once the tourists and cottagers leave," he said with a smirk.

Esme giggled. "We do rather infest the lakes, don't we?"

"We don't mind sharing, especially when it provides us with the funds to live in paradise year round."

"You mean you put up with us," she quipped.

"It's more of a *symbiotic relationship*, as my school teacher used to say," he explained with a grin. "We need one another. For instance, the Thorntons can't manage all their watercraft without help, and require a chauffeur for the yacht. The cottagers appreciate the fresh produce from our farm. The tourists need the rooms in our inn and the boats that Mac rents. We need the money."

"Is that why you work for the Thorntons in the summer, instead of building boats with Mac?"

"Major Thornton in particular knows how difficult it is to find men experienced and knowledgeable about motorboats, and ensures I'm paid handsomely. We have all winter to build boats."

"I'd love to see the lake in winter, when it's frozen solid and blanketed in snow," Esme said wistfully.

"It's bleak, but beautiful, especially when snowstorms whip across the vast whiteness and even the islands seem to disappear. But it can be dangerous too, when you're out on the lake and a sudden squall blows up. Toby had to stay over with us a few times when he couldn't make it back to Wyndwood." Toby had been the Wyndhams' steamboat pilot and caretaker who had lived on the island year round. He had died in 1917. "But some find the winters long and dreary."

"That's when you hunker down by the fire with a good book."

"Sure thing!" There was a noticeable tug on his line, and Stephen reeled in a good-sized trout. He snapped its head against the gunwale to kill it and tossed it into his bucket of water. "That's enough for breakfast at the inn. The Indians always have some for us as well." He put away his fishing rod and said, "I have a thermos of hot coffee, if you'd care to join me. Only one cup, though."

"I don't mind," she said, paddling up to him.

He handed her the steaming cup first. The coffee was strong and sweet. "Cigarette?" he asked.

"Yes, please." She took one from him, but threatened to tip the canoe as she leaned towards him to have it lit.

"I can light it, if you like," he offered.

"Thank you." She felt her cheeks flush as she watched him place her cigarette between his lips. She was thrilled when she then put it between her own lips, because it was almost like a kiss. When she handed him the cup, he made no effort to avoid the spot where her lips had left a moist impression.

A loon suddenly surfaced just a few feet away from them. Esme had always been fascinated by these black-and-white striped and speckled diving birds with their red eyes and intriguing calls. It sat still, turning its head this way and that as if it hadn't taken notice of them, and gave a throaty, lunatic trill.

"It's laughing at us," Esme whispered.

"More likely warning us off. There's a nest close by."

"Or it doesn't like sharing the fish with you."

"That too."

The loon reared up, flapped its wings, and then settled down again. It glided effortlessly through the water, still cackling. Esme noticed another loon rounding the end of Sunset Island. Two tiny brown chicks were nestled on her back.

"Oh, look!" she exclaimed. She had never seen the babies so close.

The mother loon's wail was answered by the male, who paddled quickly to her side, and seemed to usher her away from the boats. Then he dove, coming up moments later ahead of her with a small pickerel clamped in his sharp black beak. He spent several comical minutes manipulating the flapping fish until it was oriented head first in his beak, and then proceeded to swallow it whole.

"And here I thought he was bringing her breakfast!" Esme said.

"She can fend for herself, although he might bring some minnows for the chicks."

"You know their habits?"

"This pair's been nesting around here for years, and there's another couple near our inn."

"Gosh! The same ones? Do they... stay together for life then?" She had been about to say "mate" but it suddenly seemed too suggestive a word.

"Looks like it."

The male disappeared again while the female sailed along unperturbed towards the lee of Sunrise Island.

"Zoë wrote a pantomime once about the loon being the 'Spirit of the Lake.'" Esme told him about the short, allegorical play. Poignantly, she recalled the amusing rehearsals, that summer of 1914 when Blake had still been with them, but not yet married to Zoë. Esme herself had had an adolescent crush on the handsome and brilliant Dr. Carlyle.

"Your sister is very clever. I think of loons as the voices of the lake."

"But competing now with motorboats," Esme said with a smirk.

He chuckled. "But theirs is the haunting sound that stays with you."

"And soothes you. Did you know that Ellie - Dr. Carlyle - does a wicked loon call? Apparently she's had more than one loon completely perplexed."

Esme thought Stephen's laugh engaging and charming. "Do you fish here every morning?" she asked.

"Most days, if I haven't been chauffeuring until the wee hours. It saves my family money and the guests rave about the fresh fish. So I really should go and deliver my catch."

"Perhaps I'll see you some other morning."

He smiled. "Sure thing."

•   •   •

The lake was serene. The few clouds perfectly reflected in the water were dissolved by Chas's paddle. The pain that screamed in his leg seemed like an affront to the tranquility of the morning. He cursed the fact that he'd have to undergo yet another surgery - the tenth in the past year - which might relieve the torment this time. Or not. Sometimes he wondered if it was worth it. Wouldn't Ria be better off not being tied to a disfigured cripple?

Rounding the south end of Ouhu, he was puzzled by something splashing in the water between it and Picnic Island. Then stunned when he realized it was Ellie, feebly struggling to stay afloat. And losing the battle.

Chas paddled madly over to her, praying that she would resurface. But there were only bubbles.

For a split second, he wondered if he was fit enough to dive in after her, but knew he had no choice. In the still, clear water, her red hair fanned out before him like siren seaweed. He grabbed one of her flailing arms and kicked hard to pull her up. But his damaged leg was weak, and he could get little force behind its fluttering, agonizing attempts. The healing wounds in his arm and shoulder protested the strain and he felt that he might lose his grip on her. As he fought, he realized how much he wanted to live.

His lungs were bursting when he finally broke the surface. Grabbing onto his canoe, he drew Ellie against it, and was relieved when she began coughing and gasping.

He held her in the circle of his arms, as she seemed too weak to support herself, and could feel her trembling.

"Dear God, Ellie! What are you doing swimming out here alone?" he demanded, angry as a scared parent is towards a foolish child who has endangered her life.

"Exercising," she croaked. But she was dismayed by the pounding of her heart and weakness that made it seem like too much effort even to breathe. An effort that she sometimes wondered was worth making. "We swim every morning, and I was half-way back from Picnic Island."

"So where is Troy?"

"In the city, on some mysterious wedding business."

"Eleanor Carlyle, you are the most stubborn girl I know."

"Even more than Ria?"

"Well..."

"I need to regain my strength! Otherwise, what kind of wife will I be?"

"Troy loves you, Ellie."

"He fell in love with the old me. Not this pathetic creature I've become."

Her despair cut him to the quick. "Nonsense! You may not realize it, but you *are* making progress. You just have to be more patient, and kind to yourself."

"Giving the doctor advice now, are you?"

"The same sage advice that you gave me. I do understand, Ellie. You don't know how many times I've told myself that Ria would be better off without me. But deep down inside I don't really believe that. The old me is still there somewhere, and still as much in love with Ria and life as before. You and I have difficult and lonely battles to fight, so let's help each other. Keep each other strong in spirit while our bodies heal."

She put her head on his shoulder and sobbed.

"Pact?" he asked when she had regained her composure.

"Pact."

"And now I think it would be a good idea if we got out of the water before we succumb to hypothermia."

Chas pulled down the gunwale, swamping the canoe a little as he helped Ellie flop in, and then clambered in without tipping them both back into the water.

"So why are *you* out by yourself this morning?" she asked.

"Sometimes I just need space for self-pity," he replied wryly.

She grinned at him. "The old you is definitely making a comeback."

"I'm not sure that's a compliment, considering how you've always disapproved of me," he jested.

"Only your hedonistic lifestyle. There are things about you I would never change."

"Glad to hear it."

"Chas... don't tell Troy. I don't want him fussing or worrying, or feeling that he has to nurse me like a child."

"It'll be our secret, as long as you promise not to do it again. At least not until you're well enough to swim in the Stepping Stone Marathon."

"I'll make it my goal for next year."

His warm and encouraging smile made her realize how lucky she was to have friends like him, and just how damned lucky she had been that he'd appeared when he did. It suddenly terrified her that she hadn't had the strength to save herself. Or, for a moment, even the inclination.

●   ●   ●

When Lyle arrived at Silver Bay in his gleaming mahogany Minett runabout that afternoon, Lizzie felt a thrill of pleasure. In his casual beige duck trousers and white shirt, his sleeves rolled up to reveal tanned arms, he looked deliciously tempting.

"Do you want colour photographs as well?" she asked him. "Not hand-painted ones. Autochromes. They're gorgeous but expensive. And one of a kind."

Lyle grinned. "Shoot away, Lizzie. I'm intrigued."

"Let's start with you in the boat. The colour plates take longer to expose, so you have to hold absolutely still for at least a second. And hopefully there won't be any waves."

Lizzie set up her tripod on the dock and put a yellow-orange filter on the lens to subdue the blues. She had him turn partway towards the camera, drape one hand carelessly over the steering wheel, and smile invitingly. She also shot several black-and-white plates with her "view" camera, and then some snapshots with her rollfilm Kodak.

"Where to next?" Lyle asked.

"Spirit Bay sounds like it might be ideal, and I want to see where my studio will be."

Olivia had suggested that Lizzie take someone along for propriety, which Lizzie thought ridiculous, since she had looked after herself as well as her sister Emily in New York, and had often been alone with her boss, the famous society photographer, Anders Vandeburgh. But such were the outdated conventions of the upper classes, which were important for preserving one's reputation. So Esme, Alice, and Claire were happy to tag along.

"It's delightfully atmospheric," Alice said when they had docked. The large, sheltered bay was detached from the activities on the lake, the drone of distant motorboats no more than the buzzing of a mosquito. "I can see how this could be haunted."

"I sense a story brewing," Esme said.

"Oh, yes!"

"Lizzie might even capture the ghost on her camera," Claire speculated.

"You certainly could with your paints," Esme said.

"Yes, I could! May we have the key to the inn, Lizzie?" Claire asked her sister.

The girls wandered up to the house.

Lizzie said to Lyle, "That rocky point is perfect for what I have in mind."

"I'm game. For whatever you have in mind."

She smiled coyly.

As they walked along the ridge, Lyle said, "You need a packhorse to carry all this equipment."

"Oh no, you'll do splendidly!"

He chortled. "So I have a job?"

"It's yours for the taking."

"And here I was, wondering how I was going to entertain myself this summer."

The rocky background and dappled light on the treed slope of the point were perfect for the photos Lizzie had envisioned: the pensive wounded veteran, the Ivy League athlete, the seductive lover.

Lyle said, "Do you realize how flattering and tantalizing it is to have a beautiful woman staring at you so intently?"

Now it was she who became flustered by his probing, one-eyed gaze as she took a few more photos.

On the crest of the point, she had him lean against the decaying gazebo, one ankle crossed over the other, and gaze out at the lake, his family's island visible in the distance.

"This one will be a statement of the times - a victim of the old order turning his back on the crumbling past and looking toward the future."

"So you're a philosopher as well," Lyle said, impressed.

"I think that artistic photographs have something to say about the world. They're not just a flattering likeness, although I can do those as well."

Back at the inn, they hauled a wicker chair onto the veranda, and Lyle was instructed to lounge there, with his feet up on the railing and a cigarette casually held in one hand.

"So have you now captured the essence of me, lovely Lizzie?" he asked.

"And stolen your soul," she teased. "It's what some cultures believe - some of the native American tribes for instance. Crazy Horse never allowed his photo to be taken." So Anders had told her.

"Oh, I do believe that," Lyle replied.

The girls joined them, Claire saying, a bit breathlessly, "You should see the waterfall, Lizzie! I'm going to paint it some time."

"And the inn is deevie," Esme enthused.

"We'll have to explore it," Lyle said. "Come along, Lizzie."

Claire stayed on the veranda to rest while Alice and Esme headed out to the point.

As he and Lizzie looked around inside, Lyle said, "Why should I be surprised that Chas bought an entire inn just so that he could have a mainland property for his boats? What will he do with this building, aside from allowing you to set up a studio?"

Lizzie explained about Emily and Hugo staying there in August, and exclaimed, "This rotunda room will be perfect for Hugo! It needs only a grand piano."

She felt rather awkward as they wandered among the bedrooms, but Lyle didn't try to take advantage of the situation, leaving Lizzie to wonder whether that showed his respect for her or meant that he wasn't all that interested in her.

Needing a water supply, she chose one of the bathrooms as her workspace. "I've decided I'm going to do outdoor portraits for anyone who is interested. They're so much more immediate and relevant than formal studio ones."

"So you'll become the roving Muskoka photographer?"

"Why not? I expect that people may even want photos of their cottages and dogs."

"Say, that's a thought! I'm sure my parents would, as well as having a family portrait. How about it?"

"Sure!"

"I think it's very adventuresome of you to have a career."

"I consider photography an art form more than a job."

"True enough. But you have to be a businesswoman as well. I can't imagine either of my sisters doing it."

"You may be surprised what we modern women can accomplish when given the opportunity."

He chuckled. "You're quite right, of course. I should know better, having seen what girls like Ria did during the war. And I don't think I'd ever underestimate you, Lizzie."

When they stood on the upper balcony of the thrusting bay, Lyle gazed out at the lake as he said, "My father is buying a factory in Toronto. It makes precision stainless steel surgical and other instruments, like our company. He wants me to manage it, since my brother is mostly responsible for our Pittsburgh operation."

"So you'll be moving to Toronto?" she asked in surprise.

"That's the idea. I hadn't been that keen on it at first." He turned to look at her. "But living in Toronto is becoming more appealing all the time."

"At least you'll have lots of friends around."

"Precisely." He stroked her cheek with the back of his index finger as he said, "I hope you'll have time for me in your busy schedule."

"Oh, I think I can squeeze you in," she jested, delighted with how things were working to her advantage.

He laughed. "I shall look forward to that!"

•   •   •

For a moment Chas wondered if he had passed into the next world, or was having an intensely realistic dream. Except when he was heavily medicated, he hadn't been free of pain since he'd been shot down over a year ago. But he opened his eyes to find Ria lying next to him, sleep still soft upon her face in the glow of dawn.

He moved his crippled leg, and despite some soreness of the muscles from the unaccustomed strain he had put on them yesterday when saving Ellie, there was no deep nerve pain. He could hardly believe it! He almost wept as he gave a silent prayer of thanks.

He gathered Ria exuberantly in his arms.

"Mmm. Is it morning already?" she murmured sleepily.

"A glorious, magical morning! The dawn of the rest of our lives!"

She chuckled as she opened her eyes. "What's precipitated such jubilance?"

"There's no pain, Ria! It's vanished. Like someone finally withdrew a knife."

"Oh, Chas!" She hugged him fiercely. "Oh, thank God!"

He kissed away her joyful tears, thankful that he had never succumbed to the black urges of despair. Somehow he had rejoined the world of the living.

When he told Ellie later that morning, she said, "I expect that the peroneal nerve had been compressed, perhaps even by scar tissue from your numerous operations. You did something that released the pressure on the nerve, which is what another surgery could have done. You'll be fine now, Chas," she affirmed with a big grin, wishing her nerve problems could be as easily resolved.

"I had a rather vigorous swim yesterday," Chas said, catching Ellie's eye. "Could that be responsible?"

"I daresay it could. Strange how things sometimes work out, isn't it?" she replied. "I've always said you have good Karma."

Chapter 6

"Mummy Ria, look how pretty it is!" Sophie exclaimed. She was examining a soft, deerskin bag with colourful beading.

The Indian girl selling her crafts smiled broadly but said nothing. She was dressed in a fringed buckskin dress, also decoratively beaded, as was the band across her tawny forehead. Her long black braids were intertwined with bright red ribbons. Other natives from the encampment in Port Darling were selling sweet-grass baskets and porcupine-quill boxes.

Ria knew that the Ojibwa had been here long before the settlers, but had been moved by the government to an Indian Reserve on an island in Georgian Bay. But many came back every summer to the "Indian Village" along the river.

"Would you like to have it, ma petite?" Ria asked.

"Oh, yes, please!"

"And what about moccasins? Grandmother would never allow me to have any, but I think we could all enjoy a pair. You can wear them without stockings."

They took time selecting their treasures, as Chas was at the Seaford Boatworks.

Ria, Alice, Esme, Claire, Johanna, and the children had come along to drop Lizzie off, so that she could catch the next southbound steamer to Gravenhurst. She was going to the city to collect her photographic equipment. Ria suggested that she bring her mother back as well, since Marie had agreed to create a wedding gown for Fliss. When Ria offered the Spirit Bay Inn for her accommodation, Jack admitted that his mother would be happier there, rather than staying with family.

Port Darling was a bustling, lively place, especially on a sunny day. The swing bridge was open as the majestic *Sagamo,* the largest of the steamship fleet, was locking through to the upper lake. Many of the hundreds of passengers had disembarked to spend the half hour stop wandering about the wharves licking ice cream cones and buying handicrafts from authentic Indians. Cottagers tied up their runabouts and went to shop at Carver's General Store or enjoy a dockside refreshment at Mercer's Drugstore and Ice Cream Parlour. Guests of hotels in the village paddled or swam nearby.

The Seaford Boatworks and Livery was north of the locks, past the drugstore and the Dockside Tea Room and Dancehall. It overlooked Chippewa Bay, which narrowed once more before opening into the lake.

The Boatworks was a large, barn-like building that was dim inside despite tall windows. The stench of varnish overwhelmed the fragrances of the various types of wood used in boat construction - oak and cedar for the frame, and the expensive mahogany imported from the Philippines and Honduras for the decking. There was a cacophony of saws, hammers, drill presses and the like as each employee went about his own specialized job. Chas was delighted to see the skeleton of his new racer taking shape.

Because the beauty of a boat lay not only in the lines, but also in the finishing, Chas appreciated that Mac was a stickler for time-consuming perfection, which included at least eight coats of varnish, sanding yet again between each coat. He even made his own butter-coloured putty that filled in between the narrow strips of dark mahogany, giving the decking an elegant pinstriped look.

Extending in front of the workshop was the livery, with half a dozen wet slips for the skiffs and canoes that the Seafords rented to vacationers. It was here that Chas found Mac, among a haphazard clutter of papers and drawings in his office.

"I don't know how you find anything on that messy desk of yours," Chas said in greeting.

"I sure as hell won't if anyone touches anything," Mac replied with a grin.

He and Chas were the same age, and Mac had been working for the Thorntons since he was twelve. With their mutual love of boats, they'd long had a friendly relationship beyond that of master and servant. Now, of course, they were partners.

Chas sat down in a battered old chair as he announced, "Well, I've bought the neighbouring property, so you can think about expanding. But I suggest that we build in brick. It'll be warmer than this draughty old place, and safer in case of fire."

"Terrific! We'll be able to bring the upholstering on site as well. I've already managed to hire some more men for the winter."

"Stealing them from Ditchburn's, are we?" Chas asked with a chuckle.

"You pay too generously, Chas. But some of the chaps are happy to come home to Port to work, rather than living elsewhere. And thanks to you, I can actually afford to get married now," Mac confessed.

"You mean Audrey Carver hasn't given up on you yet?" Chas knew that Mac and Audrey, whose father owned the General Store at the end of the wharf, had been courting since before the war.

"Yeah, well, I wasn't sure I was coming back, so I didn't propose before I left for France. But she didn't give up on me."

"Lucky for her."

Suddenly rummaging among his papers, Mac found and then handed Chas a letter, accompanied by a sly grin. "I was asked to give you this."

It was addressed to Major Chaz Thornton.

Dear good and kind Sir,

You will need a good caretaker for your inn. My husband is a hard worker. He can chop firewood and cut grass and fix anything. I can clean and grow a garden. Please will you give us a chance?

Your humble servant,

Mrs. Roderick Mayhew

Chas looked at Mac. "You obviously know what's in this."

"She came to me for advice, once she heard that you'd bought the inn."

"It's probably a good idea to have a caretaker."

"It would help to keep people like Mayhew from moving in uninvited," Mac said.

Chas snorted.

"Don't get me wrong. He's a decent chap, but a bit desperate at times. He and Sky and their two-year-old son have been squatting in an abandoned shack on the edge of the village for the past two years. You can see daylight through the boards, so you can imagine how cold it must be in winter. I feel for them, her and the kid especially."

"So if I gave them the position, they'd have a decent place to live, but wouldn't be there illegally. *Is* he a good worker?"

"Yes, when he has a job. He was gassed at Ypres, so his lungs aren't strong. He gets a bit of a veteran's pension but it doesn't go far. He's tried working in the boatworks and mills and such, but can't take the sawdust and fumes. So he does odd jobs for people. That's fine in the summer, when there's lots to do, but the winters are hard. He loves to fish and read, but otherwise, is the most unambitious and contented chap I know, even if he's a bit too fond of the drink at times."

Chas could sympathize. "Can he afford illegal booze?"

"Makes it himself."

"Enterprising of him."

"As far as I know, he's not selling any. Yet."

"What about the wife? Sky, did you call her? That's an unusual name."

"She's Ojibwa, and because she married a white man, they're not allowed to live with her people. And she doesn't have it easy living in the village, I can tell you! But she's the strength of that family, and keeps Mayhew in line. She's been helping out at our inn. Walks the two miles each way every day. Her sister looks after the boy at the Indian camp, but I think Sky's with child again, so it's going to become more difficult for her. You'll need someone at Spirit Bay or the local hooligans could become a problem, Chas, and I'd vouch for Roderick and Sky."

"Where do I find him? I'll stop and see her at Pineridge on my way back."

"He's doing yard work for most of the local hotels. Today, I think he might be at the Northern Lights, just below the locks."

Chas found the others sitting on a bench on the wharf eating ice cream cones. Charlie flourished his toy tomahawk. "Look!"

"Quite the little Indian!' Chas said, for the boy sported a feather headdress and moccasins.

"We couldn't wait any longer for our ice cream," Ria said in mild rebuke.

"I will forego mine. Hmm, I see you've all gone native."

Laughing, they held their feet up in unison for him to see their new footwear. "These are the most comfortable things I have ever worn," Alice declared.

Chas told Ria about the Mayhews, and she agreed that it would be good to have resident caretakers, who might also be able to keep an eye on Wyndwood during the winter. "Do you want to come along while I talk to Mayhew?" he asked.

"Of course!" To the others she said, "You can wander about, and we'll meet at the boat in about half an hour."

The river and locks bisected the village, which rose steeply on either side. South of the bridge they passed another boatworks, the library attached to the Community Centre, and the white-framed Anglican church where Ria and Chas had spent most summer Sunday mornings of their childhoods. Beyond the Orange Lodge and two-room schoolhouse was the Northern Lights Hotel, whose deep property ran down to the river. A tanned fellow with scrunched-up sleeves and a well-worn cap was trimming a cedar hedge.

"I'm looking for Roderick Mayhew," Chas said.

"Then you are in luck, my good Sir, since you have found him in tolerable health and vigour," Mayhew said with a British accent somewhat flattened by years away from the Mother country. He smiled disarmingly, wiped his hand on his trousers, and held it out to Chas to shake. He had a firm grip.

Chas introduced himself and Ria, who received a decidedly cheeky grin.

"VC, DSO and bar, MC, Légion d'honneur," Mayhew rhymed off. "I've followed your exploits Major Thornton, and I must say that we in Port Darling are proud to claim you as our own. You've been summering here since you were a little shaver, so I've heard." A violent cough wracked him. "Beg pardon. Came up to Muskoka to breathe again and found my destiny. Well, well, to what do I owe this esteemed pleasure?"

Ria and Chas realized that his flamboyant speech was part of his nature and charm. He had already won them over.

When Chas had explained that they needed a caretaker for the Spirit Bay property, and that Mac Seaford had recommended him, he said, "Stout fellow, Mac. Now would I be wrong in thinking that my dear wife instigated this confluence of serendipity?"

Chas grinned and said, "She did write to me, as she seems to have anticipated our needs. Very astute of her."

"Indeed. Indeed. A treasure above all earthly riches, my Sky. Well, Major Thornton, Mrs. Thornton, I can't tell you how chuffed

I am to be offered this sinecure! You have your man, if you'll take me as you find me."

"It's hardly a sinecure, as there will be considerable repair and maintenance work involved," Chas pointed out.

"I do beg your pardon! To me it will seem as though I am just pampering my beloved home. You need have no fears, Major Thornton. Spirit Bay shall be a showpiece."

"That's reassuring, Mr. Mayhew, but you haven't even asked the terms."

"If my family can live within the precincts of that glorious abode in a little corner of paradise, then I will be happy with enough to put food upon the table, Major Thornton. And perhaps have the use of a skiff?"

Chas laughed. "Yes, indeed. And I think you'll find the terms generous, Mr. Mayhew."

"Then you gild the lily, Major Thornton. Now there was a chap here recently who claimed he flew with you."

"Yes, Captain Cracknell."

Chas hadn't realized that his manner conveyed wariness until Mayhew said, "Bit of a bad apple, is he?"

"Just trying to readjust, I think."

"Indeed. Indeed. But if he becomes a problem, you'll let me know?"

As they returned to the wharf, Ria laughed and said, "It appears that you have a new champion. And if Crackers gets out of hand, Mr. Mayhew will take him to task."

"By overwhelming him with rhetoric, no doubt!"

While Ria and Chas had been on their mission, the girls and Charlie had wandered about the island that lay between the lock and the dam. There were several boat liveries along the shore, and the new cinema on the hillside, with a pool hall on the lower floor. On the curve of river across from the island was the Indian camp - a collection of wooden huts and tents and smouldering campfires beneath tall pines. Older women and young children were weaving baskets and beading; men were carving wood and cleaning fish that they had caught that morning. Their movements seemed relaxed and instinctive. To Alice it appeared a gentle tableau of some earlier time when the natives had lived in harmony with their surroundings.

A young man in a birch-bark canoe set out with a bucketful of fish probably destined for one of the inns on the lake. Charlie waved his tomahawk in greeting when the Indian passed close to the shoreline where he and the girls stood. The man looked over and nodded his head in acknowledgement.

A young man came up behind them and yelled, "Hey, ya dirty Injun. Stop gawkin' at the white girls like that!"

"There's no need for that kind of language!" Esme objected indignantly.

The Indian raised his fist. It was not a violent gesture, but it was powerful.

"Don't you threaten me, ya lazy, good-for-nothin' Redskin!" To Esme the guy said, "Ya see? Gotta keep 'em in their place! The government threw 'em out years ago, but they don't know when they're not welcome."

"They seem to fit in quite naturally here," Alice countered. "And obviously the tourists like them."

"Yah so ya buy their trinkets, but ya don't have to live with 'em. Thieves and drunks, the lot of 'em! So... you girls going to the moving pictures?" he said suggestively.

"No, we are not," Esme stated coldly, and ushered the others away.

"Hey, just trying ta be friendly!" The lout shouted after them.

"How dare he!" Esme hissed. She looked at Sophie and Charlie as she said, "That was very disrespectful of that fellow to insult the Indian. It's because of attitudes like that that we still have wars."

Although the others were thoughtful, little Charlie said, "I like to be an Indian."

"As well as a pilot?" Alice asked him with grin. "You think those feathers will help you fly?"

"Mais oui!" He spread out his arms like an aeroplane and zoomed around in front of them.

When Alice mentioned the incident to Ria and Chas in the boat, she and the others were told about the new caretakers of Spirit Bay. They met Sky at the Pineridge Inn.

Like Spirit Bay and so many other hostelries on the lakes, it had evolved from the original farmhouse, having sprouted wings on either side, anchored by square towers. Red-roofed in contrast to the crisp white of the walls, it beckoned a welcome from far out in the lake.

Sky was pinning bed sheets onto the laundry line in the yard behind the inn. While Roderick was in his early thirties, Sky seemed a slip of a girl barely out of her teens. Her long hair snaked down her back in a thick plaited rope. Although she was petite, she exuded vitality, and her demeanor was that of someone much older and wiser. Esme thought that Sky had probably had to grow a tough shell to live among the rednecks of Port Darling.

Her eyes sparkling with delight, Sky said seriously and simply, "Thank you, Major and Mrs. Thornton. We will make you proud."

Later than evening, Ria said to Chas, "You seem to be lost in thought."

"I've decided to reinvent myself and change my name."

"Chas!"

"I mean the spelling. Sky spelt it 'Chaz'. See how much stronger that looks? 'Chas' is somehow soft and mellow and not the stuff of a competitive racer. 'Chaz' is sharp; has more presence. More in tune with the jazz age."

"Then you should spell it 'Chazz'.

"Very droll!"

She kissed him provocatively, and whispered, "I like the soft and mellow you."

Chapter 7

Ria heard a strange droning noise, coming ever closer. Doubting her senses, she rushed outside. Surely it was the exhilarating hum of an aeroplane! The sound flooded her with memories of England, of watching Chas flying, of herself soaring above the cloud-shadowed meadows and huddled villages.

Suddenly it appeared - a giant silver bird both magnificent and ungainly looking, its belly hanging beneath an immense span of wings. It sank down like a gliding gull to skim across the water, and headed for the large front dock.

Ria ran down the path as it nosed up to the wharf. She recognized the pilots, who waved to her - Billy Bishop and William Barker, or the two Billies, as Chas called them.

"Is Chas here?" Bishop called to her.

"He's in Port Darling, but will be back shortly."

"We just dropped Margaret and a friend at Kawandag," he said of his wife. Kawandag was the summer mansion of her uncle, Sir John Eaton. "So we wanted to show Chas our latest purchase. What do you think?"

The Curtiss HS-2L did indeed look like a flying boat, its nose curving up and two triangular water wings sloping down on either side of the front fuselage. The wings were an enormous 74 feet long, studded with eight sets of struts, and crazily crisscrossed with wires. Small floats on the lower wingtips kept them nicely balanced on the water.

"It's magnificent!"

"It is indeed," Jack said, joining her.

The children raced excitedly down the rocky slope. "Is it Papa?" Charlie shrieked. "Is it Papa?"

"No, mon petit poussin," Ria said, grabbing him before he could run too close to the plane. She was unsettled by the fact that he still expected his pilot father to come for him. "These are friends of Daddy Chas." She could feel him deflate as if he had been puffed up with air.

"Care for a flip?" Bishop asked Ria with a grin. "While we wait for Chas?"

Remembering Chas's fear of her flying, she hesitated only a moment before replying, "Super!"

"What about you, Jack?" Bishop asked.

"Sure! I was thinking of buying one of these."

"Can't fly it yourself. You need a co-pilot at the very least. Some have a crew of three."

"May I co-pilot?" Ria asked hopefully.

Bishop laughed. "I have every faith in your abilities, Ria, but this damn thing is the devil to fly. The controls are so heavy that Will needs help during takeoff, because of his arm." Barker's left elbow had been shot away in the air skirmish that had won him the Victoria Cross. "Besides, you don't have a licence, and we have enough problems with the Air Board as it is."

But Ria wasn't too disappointed as she put on the helmet and goggles he passed her. Tilda, the maid, ran up to the cottage to fetch her a jacket, for most of the staff had now come down to behold the wondrous sight.

"We have room for one more," Bishop said.

"Oh, may I?" Alice asked immediately.

"Of course!" Ria said. "I'd always promised you a flight."

They put Jack in the forward-most single cockpit, and Ria and Alice into the side-by-side ones right behind him. "You almost need a shoehorn to get in," Ria joked.

The two pilots sat behind them, with the engine and pusher prop to the rear of them, beneath the top wing.

Ria laughed to see the astounded expressions on the faces of her cousins as they skimmed past Silver Bay, Miles jumping up and down on the beach and Rupert waving wildly. She was thrilled as they lifted up into the wind. Alice, beaming but nervous, clutched Ria's hand.

For twenty minutes they soared and circled above the deep blue lakes and dense forests, the whole landscape like a map come alive. On the return leg, they flew low over Port Darling to the thrill of the holiday-makers below.

Having heard the roar of the plane, Chas was already outside the Seaford Boatworks. He knew he shouldn't be surprised to see Ria in the cockpit, but had to suppress his sudden anger. Damn her for taking such a risk, and involving Alice! And yet he knew he was being irrational. "Bishop-Barker" was emblazoned on the sides of the fuselage, and Barker especially was an excellent pilot. Ria could hardly be in better hands, as long as the men were sober - a reputation that, unfortunately, they didn't always have. But then Chas knew all too well that alcohol helped to blur haunting memories and to blunt the lingering pain of wounds.

He scrambled into his boat and sped for home. The Curtiss was already tied up at the front dock when he arrived, and drinks were being served on the veranda.

"Gin Rickey," Bishop said, holding his glass of that cocktail up to Chas in welcome. "That's what we're calling the new bus. What do you think?"

"You certainly made an impression in Port Darling. How is it to fly?"

"A pain, quite literally. You have to keep constant pressure on the rudder bar, so if you're up for any length of time, you can hardly walk when you get back," Bishop said. "I prefer flying a scout, but they don't take passengers."

"We're going to offer air service between Toronto harbour and Muskoka, for all you businessmen who need to get back and forth in a hurry," Barker chimed in enthusiastically. "And give sightseeing flights to tourists up here."

"That's sure to be a success. It was super!" Alice exclaimed.

Ria was amused to see Alice eyeing twenty-four-year-old Will Barker with interest. Tall, handsome, personable, he radiated the energy of a man determined to accomplish great things. The fact that he was a wounded war hero added to his appeal.

"We'll be flying from the Grand Muskoka Hotel to start with," Bishop said.

"And then we'll try our luck with it this winter in Palm Beach," Barker added. "Apparently it's become a fashionable place for the rich."

"Now Chas, you can't believe how absurd the Air Board is being," Bishop declared. "They require us to take flying tests before issuing us pilot's licences!"

"And the most insulting thing is that we can fly circles around the inspectors because some of them never saw more action than training novices in Toronto!" Barker added with disgust.

Chas could sympathize. Barker was Canada's most decorated war veteran and Bishop was second, and both had been Lt.-

Colonels in the RAF. With seventy-two victories, Bishop was Britain's top Ace. An insult indeed.

"That confirms my decision not to fly anymore," Chas admitted.

"Ria says you're going to get your thrill from boat racing." Bishop said. "At least you don't need a licence for that!"

"I noticed that the Curtiss has a Liberty engine. I'm going to modify some that I bought, and try them in my race boat."

"We don't get much more than 65 miles an hour out of our 360 horse power," Bishop admitted. "But it gets us to the city in a couple of hours."

"Instead of seven or more by train and boat," Ria said, throwing Chas a meaningful glance. "That's exciting."

"Book me in for a honeymoon flight to Toronto with my new bride, if she's willing," Jack said with sudden inspiration. What could be a more dramatic leave-taking than that? And wouldn't that give him some added prestige?

Chas bit his tongue. He didn't want Fliss flying either, but knew he would sound ridiculous if he protested. Barker, too, had been badly wounded, and had almost died in a crash, but he had obviously recovered his nerve, and had even taken the Prince of Wales for a flight while still on his crutches and with his useless left arm in a sling.

"Done!" Bishop said to Jack, and held out his glass to Ria for a refill. "So what do you think of the British airship that just crossed the Atlantic with the first passengers?"

"I expect that most people wouldn't care to spend - what was it, four and half days? - cocooned in a dirigible," Ria said. "I'd rather enjoy that time dining and dancing aboard an ocean greyhound."

"But just think of the possibilities when we have heavier-than-air craft whisking people across the Atlantic in a day or less!" Barker said. "That's the sort of future I plan to invest in."

Later that evening when Chas was already lying in bed while Ria slipped into her nightgown, she said, "You were angry, weren't you? About my flying today."

"Was I?"

"I know you too well. You didn't want me flying and I chose to disregard that." She would never say "disobey" because she felt no one had a right to expect any sort of archaic "obedience" from her.

"Should that surprise me?"

"You're evading the question."

He lay staring at the raftered ceiling for a long time before replying, "You might understand how I feel if you'd crashed your plane and felt fire licking at you."

"Oh, Chas, I do understand!" She went to sit beside him. "I was terrified on the ship for most of our journey back from England. I know it was irrational to think that we would sink, but I couldn't escape the fear." Nor could Alice, which was why they had only been apart at night, in their respective, but adjoining bedrooms. "But I don't expect other people to stop travelling on ships or flying in aeroplanes just because of our experiences."

"You're right, of course," Chas admitted.

She ran her fingers across his scarred cheek. "But I know you were motivated by love, so I will forgive you," she said with a grin.

He grabbed her hand and pulled her on top of him. "Forgive me? I don't recall asking."

•   •   •

Ria felt a little thrill whenever she saw the words "Priory Manor" in the return address. Not because it meant that Lance Chadwick had written to her, although she was always glad to hear from him, but because she was instantly transported to the delightful English country estate that had been her home for almost two years. How glad she had been that Lance had managed to buy it from the aged widow, because it wasn't completely lost to her now.

Priory Manor, Hampshire
Dear Ria,

Addressing this to your lakeside summer home, I can imagine how happy you are to be back, since you always spoke with such longing about it. I had hoped that my sons and I could visit your magical Muskoka, but the boys have other plans for our summer together, while their mother is visiting friends in Deauville. I felt I owed them this time, since I missed so much of their childhood during the war. In any case, I have a promising colt competing in some minor races, and my youngest, Philip, is particularly keen on horses. I expect he will want to take over the stables one day, while Christopher is mad about aeroplanes and can hardly wait to be old enough to join the RAF.

But I blame you as well for my latest endeavour, which is learning to fly. When you took me up for that daring escapade in France, I understood completely your enchantment with soaring high above the clouds and the earthbound mortals who exist in their passing shadows. A magnificent realm where few people have ever ventured, it appeals to me to transcend the ordinary, to feel so completely unfettered.

It's odd how numb I'd felt since the war ended, almost as if I were only truly alive while being under fire or waiting on the sidelines to be called back to duty at any moment. I thought at first it was the head injury, which still gives me crushing pain at times. I'd even thought of buying back my commission, but am truly fed up with the military and all the bungling that resulted in so many pointless deaths. But the exhilaration of flying has finally restored my senses, my life.

So I've bought a surplus Avro 504K, and prepared a strip of the meadow as a runway. Of course you must fly the plane whenever you're back in England! I've named it 'Dragonfly' in your honour, since I recall what an affinity you have with those insects. And wasn't that what you called the Rolls you loaned to the WATS?

I must say that I'm surprised Major Thornton has no intention of buying an aeroplane, or indeed, allowing you to fly. Perhaps he will change his mind in time. I know many men who are still profoundly shell-shocked, some unable to settle back into civilian or even family life. Even sadder to see those who are maimed or unemployed begging on street corners. How quickly a grateful nation and its people forget. These vagrant veterans are no longer heroes, just nuisances that people attempt to avoid.

But enough about the misery! Of the good things to come out of the war are the strong friendships established with colleagues, since what we all shared can never be truly understood by those who weren't there. Don't you find that? You must be especially pleased that Lady Antonia is now nearby. Yes, I can see her readily embracing your adventuresome colonial life. You must let me know how she makes out at the Regatta.

So I look forward to visiting you another summer, or welcoming you to your erstwhile home. In the meantime, I shall delight in reports of your exploits. Do give my regards to Major Thornton.

Sincerely, Lance

"Don't scowl, Chas," Ria said when she finished reading the letter aloud, as she wanted no misunderstandings about her relationship with Lance. "He's as much a friend as Toni and the others." Lance had been a career officer in the cavalry, and stationed near her WATS camp in France. Their lives had often intersected, and she had enjoyed his attentions when she had been emotionally adrift from Chas. But she had never succumbed to his advances.

Chas harrumphed. Surely Ria must realize that the chap was still smitten with her. Even if nothing had happened between them, as Ria claimed, Chadwick had obviously not given up trying. Did he buy an aeroplane mainly to impress her, or lure her back to England? And how dare he imply that Chas was shell-shocked, and infer that may be affecting their marriage.

"Why did you tell him I didn't allow you to fly?" he demanded in annoyance.

"I didn't say it like that, Chas!" Ria retorted. "I just mentioned that I longed to fly and you didn't."

"What business it is of his anyway?"

"I told Sybil and Carly the same thing," she explained, referring to other WATS friends. "What else does one write about in letters?"

"Less personal things." If Chas didn't feel so wretched and ugly, he wouldn't feel so threatened by another man.

Ria sensed his mood, and was touched by his new vulnerability. She put her hand on his, saying gently, "You needn't be jealous, my love. I know that Lance isn't above a bit of one-upmanship," she added shrewdly. "Wait until I tell him that we're going to be racing boats!"

He chuckled and drew her hand to his lips. "*We* are, are we?"

"You bet! Try to keep me out of it!"

"I'd rather not," he said, gazing at her lovingly. "So how many more people did you enchant with tales of Muskoka, and who plan to descend upon us?"

"Everyone I met, of course!" she replied wickedly.

Chapter 8

"I think this engagement picnic is a charming idea," Marjorie Thornton said. She was sitting with the older Wyndham women on the wide veranda of the Spirit Bay Inn.

It had been only a week since the Mayhews had moved in, but already the place looked less shabby and neglected. The rotten boards on the dock had been replaced, the lawns had been mowed, the tennis court rolled, and Mayhew had supervised the painting crew that had been hired. Sky had given the interior a thorough scrub-down, and glued up the wallpaper in the reception rooms as a temporary measure. The tables in the dining room were covered in fine linen cloths, and sprouted slender vases of bright daisies from the garden.

Staff from the various Wyndwood cottages, under the supervision of Grayson, were in the kitchen preparing the food, or circulating among the guests offering glasses of champagne and lemonade.

"I only wish that Joseph could be here with us," Marjorie lamented, the loss of her husband keener in such situations. "I've never seen Felicity so happy."

"They do make a handsome couple," Olivia said.

Fliss and Jack stood arm-in-arm at the wharf, along with Ria and Chas, greeting the guests, who were fast arriving. Animated and smiling, the betrothed couple seemed joyfully in love.

"Felicity has certainly blossomed," Helena observed.

"It's not easy to see your baby so grown up and going off to start a family of her own," Marjorie bemoaned.

"Ah, but just think of the fun you'll have when you can spoil your grandchildren," Olivia pointed out.

"Yes, of course! And how lovely for them to have all these little ones to grow up with."

The youngest children, supervised by their nannies, were already splashing about in the shallow water at the beach.

"You should have brought the children, Helena. They would have enjoyed playing with their cousins," Olivia said.

"Jimmy's too young and there's no one who's Cecilia's age except Charlie, and he plays too roughly."

"Surely not," Olivia argued, since she knew well enough that Cecilia was the bully. "In any case, a little boisterousness among children isn't harmful. And the twins seem to be enjoying themselves, so I'm sure Jimmy would have as well."

He was actually a couple of months older than Edgar and Daphne's twin boys, but wasn't developing as he should. Because he was passive, almost vacant, and didn't prattle and explore like most one-and-a-half-year-olds, Helena was mortified that others might notice. The doctor said he could just be developmentally delayed, and there wasn't any cause for concern as yet.

She was grateful for the distraction of Jack's mother, Marie, joining them, although Helena didn't relish the obligation to welcome a former actress into the family circle. She did not, however, disdain Jack's sister Emily, since she was a Broadway star and had married into a wealthy old New England family.

"This must be a very proud day for you," Olivia said to Marie.

"It is indeed," Marie replied. Despite her brave words to Lizzie about knowing the ways of society, she was anxious, and planned to become a wallflower among all these intimidatingly affluent and powerful people. She was also wary, for she knew all too well their fickle ways, and how tenuous was her family's foothold among the elite. Being French-Canadian only made her feel more an outsider, although Lizzie maintained that Marie's residual French accent gave her a somewhat exotic cachet. Jack's marriage would cement their acceptance, but Marie counted on nothing until it was a *fait accompli.*

Few could fail to notice how elegant she was in her fashionable dress. Now that the stress of poverty and overwork had been lifted from her, she looked younger than her forty-six years, and was still beautiful. Thirty-four-year-old Helena was not pleased to see her husband, James, admiring his sister-in-law.

"I feel truly blessed with my children, and delighted to welcome Felicity into our family. She's such a sweet girl," Marie said warmly, feeling that something else was required of her.

Down at the dock, Jack felt his heart lurch when Ellie and Troy arrived. Of course he had seen her at the ball and on a few other occasions since he had returned from England, but each encounter stoked his lingering desire for her.

Ellie embraced Fliss and then Jack, saying sincerely, but with her own doubts, "I wish you every happiness."

He held her perhaps a bit too long. She could sense his regret that their intensely passionate affair would remain something bittersweet in their past. She had been afraid to see him again, that first time they met after five years. Afraid that seeing, touching, being with him would re-ignite the flame, that her love for Troy might not be strong enough. But she was relieved to discover that Jack was well and truly in her past, much as she would always feel close to him.

"I think it's so exciting that you're going to be married here soon," Fliss said.

"Yes, in three weeks," Ellie replied, hugging Troy's arm. "And the place already looks so lovely!"

"It's amazing what a bit of paint and grass trimming can do," Chas said.

"Go and have a tour," Ria suggested, "and we'll join you shortly. You can stay in the royal suite for your honeymoon."

"Royal?"

"It's in the tower and has its own bathroom," Ria explained.

"And Ria plans to let the Prince sleep there if he comes to visit," Chas added with a smirk.

"Then I can hardly wait!" Ellie declared.

When the Fremonts and Delacourts arrived, Adele Fremont said to Ria, "What a deevie idea to own a hotel! And what clever invitations." Ria had sent them out on the picture postcards of the inn.

"Do enjoy yourselves. There's plenty to do, and you can use the bedrooms to change into your swimsuits," Ria said.

It didn't take long for the guests to challenge each other to games of tennis, Ping-Pong, billiards, and croquet.

Alice, her skirt hiked up, was wading in the cascading stream, talking to Arthur Spencer, who was sitting on a rock. Claire was perched nearby doing a watercolour painting. Wanting to be close to Stephen, who was managing the boats, Esme was at the beach with Johanna and the children, and throwing him surreptitious glances.

In the shade nearby, Zoë and her sister-in-law Daphne were sitting on blankets with their babies. Ethan was crawling about, but Sally was only three months old and perched in her mother's lap.

"What an idyllic scene," Lizzie said, snapping a photo of them. She was determined to create an album of memories for Jack and Fliss, so everyone would be in her lens today.

Lyle, already in his swimsuit, said, "Do join us for a dip, Lizzie."

Adele Fremont came running up to him, giggling. "We'll race you over to the point," she said, grabbing his arm as his sisters, Belinda and Blanche, joined them. "Do take a picture of us first, Lizzie."

Lyle smirked as Adele twined herself around him. Lizzie took the photo with her Graflex camera and then said, "The rock is a perfect spot for a group picture. Round up some others and I'll meet you there."

More than a dozen joined in the free-for-all swim, including Sid and Rafe, Max and Lydia, and Blanche Delacourt's fiancé, Frank Sheridan. It had already struck Lizzie that Blanche was blasé about her engagement. Indeed, she was sometimes quite cruel to Frank, who seemed an amiable fellow. Yet another family alliance that didn't take into account the desires of the betrothed. Hopefully Lyle could break away from that antiquated tradition.

Lizzie hurried to the point with her two hand-held cameras and scrambled down the rocky headland, arriving before they did. The first photo showed the laughing group swimming toward the Graflex; in the next, they were clambering out. Lizzie took several shots of them stretched out on the granite slope, some still partly submerged. Removing her "barefoot sandals", she hitched up her skirt, securing it under her belt, and waded in with the smaller Kodak camera to shoot them from the vantage point of the lake.

The algae made the rock slippery, so Lizzie stepped carefully. She bent over to get one shot at almost water level, and when she straightened up, she slid backwards and off a drop in the granite shelf. As she fell, she raised the camera protectively above her head. She sat breast-deep in the water, laughing along with the others to hide her embarrassment.

"Splendid save!" Lyle said as he slid down the rock to help her up. She realized that her cream lawn dress clung to her more revealingly than did a swimsuit.

Rafe was scowling at her as she held onto Lyle's arm. When he had her safely on the sun-warmed rock, Lyle said, "Now we need a picture of the dedicated and drenched photographer. May I?"

She handed him the Kodak, showed him what to do, and then sat down on the granite, drawing up and hugging her knees so that her nipples weren't too evident through the thin material.

"I noticed that there's a gramophone in the lounge," Adele said. "Who wants to go back and dance?"

"I'm you're man!" Stanford Vandemeer said, splashing enthusiastically into the water beside her.

Most of the group joined them, including Lyle's sisters. Adele kept glancing back and seemed peeved that he was staying.

In her stylishly skimpy swimsuit, Sidonie stretched out seductively on the rock. When Max and Lydia went to explore the point, Lyle sat down next to Lizzie, who said to him, "Your photos are ready. I can show them to you when we get back."

"Splendid! Perhaps I can help you develop today's. I'd be interested to see the process."

"Certainly," Lizzie replied. "I'll be doing them tomorrow, if you want to come by. I'm actually staying here to keep my mother company."

Rafe snorted and swam off.

"Do bring me a glass of champagne, darling," Sid shouted after him, but he ignored her. "I expect I shall have to fetch it myself," she complained to no one in particular as she waded into the water.

"You didn't hurt yourself, did you?" Lyle asked Lizzie when they were alone.

"Just my pride," she said with a smile.

"I was hoping you'd be at the Country Club dance on Wednesday."

"I didn't have an escort."

"You can always join our party. We usually go unless something else comes up."

"May I? That would be delightful!"

"Just send word, and your chariot will arrive."

"To go next door?" she asked with a laugh, since it was only a few minutes to the Clubhouse.

"Ah, but you don't want to be walking that stretch alone at night."

"You're so right! Wait until you see what I have to show you!"

"I hardly can!" he replied with a salacious grin.

"In one of the photographs," she explained. Slipping on her shoes and grabbing her cameras, she said in a hushed voice, "It's the ghost!"

•   •   •

Neither Lizzie nor her mother had chosen the "Royal Suite", as Ria called it, since it would undoubtedly be Emily and Hugo's room when they arrived. But she had selected a lovely corner one with windows overlooking the ridge as well as the bay. She was thrilled that her mother had agreed to stay here for most of the summer, which allowed Lizzie to as well. Marie had admitted that the city house felt too big and empty without her children and the boarders she had become used to catering to these past five years. It would also give her a chance to spend time with Emily, whom she rarely saw. In the meantime, she would craft Fliss's wedding gown and the bridesmaids' dresses.

Claire had chosen to stay with Esme, and Jack preferred his boathouse accommodations. Chas had given Lizzie the use of the Dippy, so she was back and forth to Wyndwood, sometimes dining at Silver Bay or The Point, and often trolling about the lake looking for interesting landscapes to photograph. She was amused to think how comfortable she had become with summer life on the lake now that she was no longer here as a servant. How she had hated that summer of 1914! And she was proud of not only having learned to drive the boat, but feeling at ease with it, even though it only went nine miles per hour.

She changed into a sleeveless white, V-neck frock with large black polka dots and black sash at the dropped waist. It was simple but stunning, perfect for dancing, and made her feel every inch one of the smart set. *Adele Fremont, eat your heart out*, she thought as she examined herself in the mirror and tilted her chin in the air.

Laughing gaily, she grabbed Lyle's photos and rejoined the party. The dancers had pushed the furniture aside and taken over the lounge. As she watched Lyle fox-trotting with Adele, she thought again how smoothly and masterfully he moved, as if he embodied the rhythm of the music. He was astonishingly sexy.

As soon as the tune ended, he was at her side. "Shall we go into the rotunda lounge?" she suggested.

No one else was there, although people were sitting on the veranda outside.

"You did say ghost?" Lyle asked.

"I can't believe it myself. I'm sure it's some sort of flaw in the plate, or a processing mistake, or a trick of the light." She had been shocked and mystified when she had seen the picture. It was the one of Lyle leaning against the gazebo on the ridge. Behind the structure hovered a faint smudge that eerily resembled a human shape.

"Good God!" Lyle said. "This isn't some sort of camera trick, is it?"

"No, it's not!" she said indignantly.

"Sorry! I didn't mean to suggest you were trying to put one over on me, Lizzie. It's just that... it seems... unbelievable!"

"I know! I've been over this with a magnifying glass, trying to determine what caused it. But I can't find anything." It wasn't even as if it were a double exposure of Lyle, since the pose was quite different.

"You know what this means? That you were wrong. We can't leave the past behind. It's always with us."

"Very clever! Is that how I should present this?"

"Why not?"

"Why not indeed. Have you heard about the Cottingly Fairies that two children photographed in England? The photos have been checked by experts and are not considered fakes. Arthur Conan Doyle - you know, the Sherlock Holmes author - is a spiritualist and has stated that he believes those pictures are proof not only of fairies, but of an afterlife."

"Hell!"

"Hopefully Heaven," Lizzie riposted with a chuckle. "I expect that consoles a lot of people."

"I'm sure you're right."

"Anyway, I may just keep this aside for an exhibition some time. If I have permission from my subject?"

"Of course! As long as I'm invited."

"Naturally! Now have a look at the other photos."

Lyle examined them carefully and then sat back. "I feel as if you did capture my soul, Lizzie. They're... outstanding!"

"Thank you."

She couldn't miss the new admiration in his eye, and felt triumphant. He was particularly impressed with the colour Autochromes, which were displayed in a diorama, since the glass plates needed to be lit from behind.

"These are astonishing! The colours are so rich. And true. You are indeed an artist. Whatever you normally charge, I'll double. And consider I'm getting a bargain."

"Ah, but I'm not cheap," she said.

"No, I'm sure you're not." He paused and then asked, "What did you do to put Rafe's back up?"

So that bastard was trying to ruin her chances with Lyle! "I defended my virtue. What has he been saying?"

Lyle looked at her carefully. "That you're a social climber and can't be trusted."

She guffawed. "That's rich! He seems to have forgotten that I have aristocratic relatives in England. Rafe thinks that because my father was estranged from his family for marrying the woman he loved, rather than one chosen for him, I'm somehow less a Wyndham than my cousins. Rather absurd, don't you think? I won't deny that things were sometimes difficult in my childhood, but Jack has invested my inheritance from my Wyndham grandmother brilliantly, and I make a very comfortable living myself, so I actually need to be wary of fortune hunters," she added flippantly.

He laughed.

"In any case, Rafe should look to his own marriage before casting aspersions."

"Ah, yes, the delectable and carefree Lady Sidonie."

"Who exacted a very lucrative pre-nuptial contract before agreeing to marry Rafe."

"You're bitter about him," Lyle said astutely.

Lizzie thought it prudent that she come clean. "We were practically betrothed when he went off to war. His letters were filled with love and longing." How glad she was now that she had kept them, since they proved that she and Rafe had never actually been lovers, at least in the physical sense. "He had a picture of me, taken by Anders Vandeburg, and told all his comrades that I was his girl. So you can imagine how surprised and hurt I was when he arrived home with Sid." She smiled up at Lyle. "But I've come to realize that it was only an infatuation, and that we really aren't compatible. I'm not fond of horses and gambling, which appear to be his main pursuits. And there are more intriguing men around."

They gazed at each other for an intense moment. Lizzie was sure that if there hadn't been people outside the windows, he would have kissed her. Instead he held out his hand and said, "Shall we go and dance?"

"Oh, yes."

• • •

Phoebe plunked herself down on the blanket between Zoë and Daphne and said, "Oh do let me hold my teensy-weensy niece!"

Daphne handed the baby over reluctantly.

"She's such a doll," Phoebe enthused. "Dear little Sarah. You're auntie is so happy that you have her name."

Daphne looked at Zoë with alarm. Zoë was used to Phoebe's claim that she communicated with her long-dead sister, but Daphne had only come to know Phoebe well since her marriage to Edgar three years ago.

"We're calling her Sally, remember?" Daphne asked Phoebe, who ignored the question.

"Your Auntie Sarah has promised to be your guardian angel. Isn't that swell?" Phoebe asked as she bounced the baby on her knees.

"It certainly is," Zoë said. "And she would now be telling you that babies mustn't be jostled so vigorously. You'll make her ill."

"The twins like going for horsy rides," Phoebe said dismissively, referring to Daphne's older boys.

"Sally is still too little and has to be handled more gently," Zoë cautioned.

"Oh, all right then!" Phoebe snapped, handing the baby back.

Daphne took Sally with obvious relief, and excused herself just as Ria joined them.

"Does Ethan want a horsy ride?" Phoebe asked.

"He's happily engaged with his toys. Best not to agitate children when they're quiet," Zoë advised.

"You're being a boringly typical mother, and not allowing children to have any fun!" Phoebe muttered in disgruntlement. But suddenly realizing that she was alone with Ria and Zoë, she became excited as she said conspiratorially, "My friend, Silas, might be coming today!"

"Your friend, Silas?" Ria asked, incredulous. "How did you meet him?"

"Oh, he was paddling by one day and we talked," Phoebe prevaricated. She didn't want anyone to know where they regularly met in case someone stopped her. As her family undoubtedly would.

"What do you know about him?" Zoë asked.

"He's a poet and he's shell-shocked. He sees dead people too!" She threw Ria a defiant look.

Ria and Zoë exchanged glances. They were accustomed to Phoebe's fantasy world and her twisted grasp of reality, but had never been comfortable with it.

"Where does he live?" Zoë asked.

"Toronto. But he's staying up here with friends. I think you'll like him. But don't say anything to the others yet!" She drifted off humming *Pretty Baby*.

"Phoebe never ceases to surprise me," Ria admitted. "Although I should know better by now."

And Ria didn't even know about Phoebe's baby, Zoë thought. Phoebe had written to Zoë about it in England, asking her to find out from Blake why her baby had died. Zoë heard the true story from Ellie once she was back home.

"Do you think that there is a Silas?" Zoë asked.

"God knows! Maybe she saw a chap in a canoe and has made up the rest. She still talks to that freaky Maryanne, although Edgar won't let her take the doll out of the house anymore." Phoebe's two-faced doll had always given Ria a chill, especially when Phoebe made it talk with a creepy and accusing voice. "She really is too much alone, you know."

"She doesn't fit in with Esme's crowd, partly because they're younger." Phoebe was twenty-one, the same age as Daphne. "And Daphne's actually a bit frightened of Phoebe. She's seen her when she has her *turns*, and sometimes hurts herself. Daphne is scared that Phoebe might eventually lash out at someone else, like the children." Neither of them knew that Phoebe had done precisely that, and inadvertently killed her mother.

Zoë took Ethan into her arms and hugged him protectively. "I can't blame Daphne." Much as she knew that Blake had felt Phoebe needed compassion as well as counselling. Would he be disappointed in her attitude, and that of his sister Daphne? So many of Zoë's thoughts went through the filter of *his* mind.

They were joined by friends - some claiming chairs nearby, others lounging on blankets spread on the sun-dappled lawn next to Zoë and Ria. Staff came by with more refreshments.

Ellie said, "This is a fabulous place, but what will you do with it?"

"Have lots of parties, I suppose," Ria said.

"And accommodate all the people that Ria keeps inviting to Muskoka," Chas added.

"How lovely for them," Ellie said.

"What Ellie really means is that it's an extravagance and should be put to better use," Emma Spencer said astutely.

Ellie laughed. Before she could respond, Emma's brother Freddie said, "Let me guess what Ellie would do with it. Turn it into an orphanage."

"Or a hospital," Justin Carrington suggested.

"A convalescent retreat for maimed soldiers," Emma conjectured.

"Or a home for unwed mothers," Jack said. He remembered all too well his conversation with Ellie the first time they had been invited to the Thorntons' opulent Toronto mansion, Thornridge, which she had considered indecently large for one family.

"You all know me too well," Ellie conceded.

"Only the original farmhouse part of the inn is insulated, so the rest can't be used in winter," Chas said. "Thank God, or I'm sure Ellie would try to make me feel guilty about keeping it all to myself." He grinned at her.

"Well, at least one poor family will benefit from it," she replied.

"Benefit? The Mayhews think they're in paradise," Ria said.

"Precisely," Ellie remarked. "Doesn't that make you feel good?"

Emma chimed in. "Isn't it wonderful to have the power to so effortlessly change people's lives? Practically on a whim?"

"I have a feeling you haven't heard the last of this, Chas," Troy cautioned.

"Don't I know it!" Chas replied.

Zoë excused herself from the good-natured banter, saying the baby needed changing, and took him up to the inn.

Freddie watched her sadly, and caught his wife looking at him suspiciously. He smiled reassuringly. "Who's up for a game of croquet?"

Ethan's nappy was dry, but Zoë sometimes found it too painful to be around happy couples. They could move on with their lives, but her war would never be over.

She took the baby up to the tower lookout and was relieved that no one was there. All the windows were open, so lovely breezes infused the vaulted room, carrying the sounds of laughter, the thunk of tennis balls, the splashing of swimmers. Ethan was restless, so she let him crawl about the floor while she chose one of the wicker chairs close to a window. In the far distance, a white steamship sliced through the deep blue of the water. A seaplane suddenly swooped across the sky above it, reminding Zoë how much had changed.

She cursed under her breath when she heard footsteps ascending the stairs.

"Oh, hi, Sis," Max said. "I didn't think anyone was up here."

"So both Wyndham twins are wet blankets," she said with a smile, happy to see him.

"Lydia and Toni just started a game of Ping-Pong against Emma and Maud, so I thought I'd slink away for a bit."

"You can join me if you like." They had always been close, and Zoë was daily thankful that he had survived.

"Sure thing!"

"I just saw Bishop and Barker fly by, and thought how strange it is to hear aeroplanes overhead."

"With them and ever more motorboats, our lake will never again be silent."

"Do planes bother you?" she asked.

"Not as such, although when they're close, the noise suddenly thrusts me back into the trenches. Not fearfully, like thunder. It's just a sudden memory, like when I bite into a Cadbury bar and am momentarily a kid again, buying chocolate from the supply boats."

"I know exactly what you mean." Whenever she heard *You Made Me Love You*, she found herself blissfully in her husband's arms again, he, pondering her quizzically as if surprised to find himself falling in love with her.

Ethan was tugging on Max's trouser leg, trying to pull himself up, and babbling away happily.

"Hey little man, want to visit with Uncle Max?" Once he was on Max's lap, Ethan patted his face and chortled. "You want Mr. Trout, do you?" Max puffed out his cheeks and flapped his lips like a fish, sending the baby into hysterics.

Zoë watched them with delight. Ethan brought such light and laughter into their lives, and she was hopeful that when Max and Lydia had children, Max would regain some of his youthful exuberance. Pray God she was right.

Chapter 9

Ellie was cautiously optimistic as the cool water soothed her feet. She was convinced that she was making progress. There was definitely less pain, and she walked more confidently, not relying so much on her cane. Even yesterday's party at Spirit Bay hadn't completely exhausted her.

She and Troy had already had their early morning swim, and were sitting side-by-side on the dock, fluffy towels wrapped around them and steaming cups of coffee cradled in their hands.

Summer mornings would always be like this, she thought joyfully. It would be their special time, even once they had children.

"Troy, I should tell you before we're married so that there are no surprises. I want us to have a few years together before we start a family. We both need to establish our careers. Don't you agree?"

"Absolutely!" After a moment's hesitation, he looked carefully at her as he asked, "You *do* want children, don't you?"

For a moment she considered seizing the opportunity to back out of the marriage. She kept waffling in her conviction that it was the right thing to do, and had once again suggested that they wait until her health improved, but Troy had prevailed.

"I'm not one to coo over babies. But I do want *your* children." She returned his assessing gaze. "Very much. And I know that we women can be good mothers as well as professionals. One of my heroes is Dr. Emily Stowe. She was Canada's first licenced female physician, although she had to go to New York to get her medical training. My grandfather was a doctor, and supported her efforts to establish a medical college for women in Toronto. Her daughter was the first graduate. I would have gone there, too, if U of T hadn't finally relented and allowed women into medicine. It was because Dr. Stowe and her family had a cottage on Lake Joe that my grandfather first came to Muskoka, and ended up buying Ouhu. So I'm grateful to her for that as well."

"What happened to the women's college?"

"It closed, except for the dispensary, where women continued to seek the advice of women doctors. That grew into the Women's College Hospital. Olivia Wyndham's just been asked to sit on the Board of Directors, and agrees with Lorna that I should see about getting a job there, even if I can only manage part-time." Lorna was Ellie's friend as well as her doctor. Lorna's mother, Irene, had married Albert Wyndham, so Lorna was Phoebe and Edgar's stepsister.

"Does that appeal to you?"

Ellie was thoughtful for a moment. "Yes, it does. Being in a caring environment where women can honestly and openly deal with issues related to them is really important. And it wouldn't hurt for them to know how to prevent pregnancy."

"Isn't it illegal for you to talk about birth control?"

"Stupidly, yes! Because men make the laws. If women had any say in the matter, most wouldn't want a dozen children to care for, nor the risk of frequent pregnancies."

"I sense a crusade. A dangerous one," Troy said with concern.

"Aren't all crusades fraught with danger? And don't you possess illegal condoms?"

"Well... yes."

"Because you're educated about conception and how to prevent it, even if that came from your peers. Shouldn't the poor and working classes also have access to protection? I've seen women who didn't realize that sexual intercourse caused their pregnancies. One thought it happened through kissing. Another thought that once she was married, God automatically gave her a yearly child."

"I do see your point, Ellie."

"Don't worry, Troy. I do know how to be discreet. A little private education on matters relating to a woman's health is surely not going to ruffle any legal feathers."

"What about religious ones?"

"Ah, well, that could be a problem if an outraged patriarch accuses his wife of going against the will of God by trying *not* to have more children. But I'm sure I can deal with men like that."

Troy laughed. "I'm certain you can!"

"As for our family planning, I managed to get a Dutch cap - the Europeans are much more realistic and forward thinking about contraception. Apparently, we won't even know it's there."

He grinned. "I can hardy wait to try it out."

She ran her fingers along his thigh playfully and then said soberly, "I'm afraid that my not getting pregnant for some years will just confirm your mother's opinion about my unsuitability as a wife."

"I'm sure she'll appreciate her grandchildren all the more once she does have them."

Ellie was quiet as she pondered her children visiting a home where she was not welcome. Troy seemed to sense her thoughts, because he squeezed her hand and said, "I expect she'll come around, given time. Let's not allow my mother to spoil anything, including this blissful morning."

But Ellie wasn't as sanguine that Troy's mother would ever accept her. She just hoped that it would never jeopardize their future.

•   •   •

"You have one less visitor to worry about this summer," Chas said to Ria as he handed her a letter. "David says that much as he'd delight in seeing Muskoka, his schedule has been fixed and doesn't allow him the time."

"David?" She looked at the letter. "Oh! The Prince! A pity he doesn't get to try out the Royal Suite."

"I'm relieved he's not coming, because I had promised him a flight."

"Barker could take him up again."

"True. And could actually fly him up from the city, but I think that Barker will be doing that air race to New York during David's few days in Toronto. In any case, we're invited to a reception for His Royal Highness at the Yacht Club." The Thorntons and Wyndhams had for decades been members of the Royal Canadian Yacht Club, situated on the Toronto Islands. Bracketing their Muskoka summers were many pleasant days of boating on Lake Ontario. "Apparently he wants to dine with Canadian officers whom he met in France. Wives and girlfriends are invited to join us afterwards for an informal dance."

"What fun!"

Ria was happy to discover that Jack and Justin had also been invited. Rafe grumbled at not being included, but Chas pointed out that he and Sid would be at the horse races in Saratoga anyway.

"That's not the point," Rafe said. "It just confirms that those of us who were prisoners of war are not given much consideration or respect from anyone. Other chaps think that we were lucky bastards who got to sit out the war, especially if you didn't make at least half a dozen attempts to escape. Some think that we were fools to get captured, or cowards who took the *easy* way out. They have no idea what hell it was, nor do they wish to know. We're just an embarrassment," he added bitterly.

"Surely it's not as bad as that," Chas said.

"Easy for you to say, great Canadian hero," Rafe scoffed.

"In any case, this dinner is for officers whom the Prince actually met, so you're not the only veteran excluded," Chas pointed out.

But Rafe was not mollified. He had fought and suffered for fucking King and Country.

•   •   •

Phoebe had almost given up hope that Silas would appear, so she was thrilled when she noticed the canoe approaching. But she was still upset, so she greeted him with, "Why didn't you come to the picnic yesterday? I was looking forward to seeing you there!"

"I'm sorry that I disappointed you, Phoebe," he apologized, sitting down beside her. "But I did say that I'm not ready to meet your family and friends yet."

"*You* didn't disappoint me. Just the fact that you weren't there."

"Ah, a fine distinction, that."

She smiled and put her arm through his. "At least you're here now," she said, leaning against him.

"You keep me grounded."

•   •   •

Lizzie was surprised to see Lyle arrive at Spirit Bay with his sister Belinda, who said, "I hope you don't mind my tagging along, Lizzie. But I was so impressed with your pictures of Lyle that I thought I might try my hand at photography. Just for amusement, you know. I'm really keen to see the process."

Lizzie's initial annoyance disappeared instantly when she realized that befriending Belinda might help her win Lyle. Nineteen-year-old Belinda was cheerful and friendly, unlike her older sister, Blanche. "You're most welcome, of course!"

Lizzie ushered them into the converted bathroom, where heavy black curtains blocked out the light from the window and could be drawn across the closed door. She had set up tables next to the sink, and put a plank across most of the bathtub, leaving the water accessible. All the chemicals and trays were neatly arranged and labeled, and the rest of the equipment was readily to hand.

"Quite a laboratory you have here," Lyle proclaimed.

She grinned, glad to have impressed him. "I've already finished some preliminary steps, which have to be done in complete darkness. So I have the negatives of one of the films I shot yesterday, and we're now going to develop photos of the best ones."

She showed them the contact sheet, and explained some of the process she had gone through to produce the negatives. She talked about the importance of knowing your paper, correct temperatures for the chemicals, experimenting with exposure timing, and some of the science of optics as she set up the enlarger. She turned off the main lights and turned on the safe ruby light, explaining that the unexposed paper wasn't sensitive to that wavelength. After the positive had been exposed through the negative, she immersed it in the developing bath. They were amazed to see an image appear.

"It's like magic!" Belinda said. "Look, it's us lounging on the rock!"

"The shot that dunked the photographer," Lyle added with a chuckle. "Will you have such dedication to your art?" he asked his sister.

"I will go to heroic lengths for perfection," she retorted with a grin.

"Now we have to stop the developing process," Lizzie said. "This is the 'stop bath'." When she had finished the fixing and washing, she said, "Now we can hang this up to dry."

"And work on the next one," Lyle said. "I didn't realize how labour intensive it was."

"And timing in the various stages is critical to the picture quality," Lizzie explained. "There are also certain darkroom techniques, like dodging and burning, that you can use to achieve the perfect exposure."

"I'd be most grateful if you'd teach me how to do all this," Belinda said. "It would be the cat's meow to take good photos, even if I'm never as accomplished as you, Lizzie. Lyle says you have to have an eye for setting up the shots as well, which I realize I may not have."

Lyle said, "Do you think it's fair to expect Lizzie to spend time teaching you?"

"I'd be happy to," Lizzie decided. "Anders Vandeburgh was gracious enough to teach me, so I'm willing to pass along what I know. Besides, it will be fun to have company."

The name of the famous American society photographer was not lost on Belinda and Lyle. "So I'd be like a pupil of his by proxy!" Belinda said. "How keen!"

She beamed at Lyle, who chuckled and said, "Are you willing to spend all the time and effort it takes to succeed at this? Give up much of your leisure activities?"

"You mean being tolerated by Blanche and Adele and their friends, who try to find ways *not* to include me?" she asked snidely.

"Now, Belle," he warned.

"Well, I'm willing to try. Surely I can decide to stop anytime if I change my mind?"

"Of course you can," Lizzie reassured her. "Since you're not planning to make a career of it, you should just enjoy it."

"Can we start right away?" Belinda asked eagerly. "I'll have to get my own camera, of course. But in the meantime, could you show me how to take a proper picture? We'll make Lyle stand by the gazebo."

He and Lizzie looked at each other, recalling the ghostly picture, which no one else had yet seen.

"Sure thing," Lizzie said. "But let's start at the waterfall."

The clear stream burbled over the rocks in its haste to dive into the lake. It was a picturesque spot and bound to provide a successful photo for a beginner. Lizzie positioned Lyle on one of the granite boulders, elbow atop one raised knee, and his chin resting in his palm. She showed Belinda how to set up the shot and then let her take it. After a few more with different poses, Belle said, "You join him, Lizzie, and let me do it all myself this time. Now sit back-to-back, leaning against each other."

She asked them to wade in the trickling water, so Lyle obediently took off his shoes and socks and rolled up his trousers, while Lizzie kicked off her barefoot sandals. Belle instructed them to hold hands as if they were picking their way across the brook. She captured them laughing when Lyle slipped and Lizzie prevented him from falling.

"I must get a photo of you two dancing. You do it so well."

"Stop-action shots are harder to take," Lizzie explained. "You'll need more practice."

"Then just pretend that you're dancing."

Lyle held out his arms to Lizzie with a barely-suppressed grin, and Lizzie went into his embrace, wondering what Belinda was up to. Was she possibly *trying* to get them together? Belle obviously didn't like Adele much.

When she had finished the roll of film, Belinda was too excited to wait to see the results, so they had to process it immediately. A few turned out a bit blurry or overexposed or crooked, but she had managed some very fine pictures. Lizzie was flattered by the ones of her and Lyle. They did look good together, and she was already imagining their wedding photos. "Elizabeth Delacourt" had a very fine ring to it.

Chapter 10

For those who didn't know the lake intimately, unexpected shoals and getting lost amid the many islands made nighttime boating dangerous. So Stephen Seaford chauffeured most of the Thorntons and their friends to the Delacourts' Full Moon Sing-Song, while Chas and Ria took Ellie, Troy, Justin, Toni, Freddie, and Martha in *Windrunner*, all having agreed that they had no intention of dancing until dawn like their younger siblings.

Despite entreaties to join them, Zoë stayed home with her parents and younger brothers.

The sun-breathed wind had dropped, so the lake was calm and reflected the violet afterglow of sunset, oddly brighter than the darkening sky, as if it clung jealously to the light. It had been an almost perfect summer day, not overly hot or moistly oppressive, so the moon shone crisply as it rose in the cloudless twilight.

The Delacourts' Thunderbird Island was among a small archipelago near the south end of the lake, mostly owned by a group of American friends, including the Fremonts, Vandemeers, Sheridans, and Rolands. All the shoreline lights of Thunderbird had been turned off, and only a few soft glimmers from the uphill cottage filtered through the trees. There was already an impressive armada of boats bobbing gently together when Chas and the others arrived. They tied up next to Edgar and his group, and were handed bottles of champagne and crystal goblets that were flowing from the dock, passed jovially from one boat to the next.

There were shrieks of merriment at the frothy popping of corks, some of the young men shaking the bottles to see whose cork flew highest.

Spotlighted by the moon on the dock, Belinda Delacourt strummed a few chords on her ukulele, making the crowd fall silent. "Welcome everyone! Thank you for making this evening even more magical. You're required to sing a few songs before we allow you ashore to carouse."

People chuckled. Stuart Roland yelled, "Send more champagne to wet the whistle!"

"We have rivers of it. We're going to sing moon and summer songs. So I'll start you off with *Under the Moon*."

She was enthusiastically competent on the ukulele, and the crowd joined her singing with equal exuberance. They warbled *By the Light of the Silvery Moon, Moonlight Bay, Shine on Harvest Moon, By the Beautiful Sea, In the Good Old Summertime*, their mingled voices drifting heavenward and spreading out like ripples across the echoing nighttime water.

When Belinda asked if anyone wanted to lead any other songs, Marshal Fremont piped up, "I know the perfect one. It's new, so you may not know the lyrics yet, but you will, believe me! You can always hum along." He had a strong and confidently melodic voice.

I've got the blues, I've got the blues,
I've got the Alcoholic Blues.
No more beer my heart to cheer,

Good-bye whiskey, you used to make me frisky,
So long highball, so long gin,
Oh, tell me when you comin' back again?
Blues - I've got the blues
Since they amputated my booze.
Lordy, lordy, war is well, you know,
I don't have to tell.
Oh, I've got the alcoholic blues,
Some blues.
Prohibition, that's the name,
Prohibition drives me insane.
I'm so thirsty soon I'll die,
I'm simply goin' to 'vaporate, I'm just that dry.
I wouldn't mind to live forever in a trench,
Just if my daily thirst they only let me quench.
And not the Bevo or Ginger Ale,
I want the real stuff by the pail.
I've got the blues, I've got the blues,
I've got the Alcoholic Blues....

He barely managed to finish amid the chuckles and cheers. The Americans were beginning Prohibition in six months, and people, including the songwriters, were already anticipating the inconvenience.

"Down with the 18th Amendment!" Marshal concluded, to supportive whoops and whistles.

"Have you heard this one?" Rafe yelled.

Four and twenty Yankees, feeling very dry,
Went across the border to get a drink of rye.
When the rye was opened, the Yanks began to sing,
"God bless America, but God save the King!"

There were appreciative hoots.

"I don't understand," Ria said. "We have Prohibition as well."

"Ah yes, but we can still manufacture booze and sell it to the Yanks and the Quebecers, since they just repealed their wartime temperance," Chas explained. "It's not illegal for us to *have* alcohol, just to buy it in Ontario. We can actually import our own cellar stock from Montreal."

"Which, of course, makes perfect sense," Ria said sarcastically.

"Basically, our provincial government doesn't care if our distilleries sell outside the province. They just don't want us selling it to each other."

There was a splash and a roar of laughter. Troy groaned when he heard his youngest brother, Eugene, say, "Stuart's so dry he's swimming to shore!"

Troy knew that once easy-going Stuart was traumatized by his war experiences, and was overindulging in alcohol to forget them. "I hope Mum isn't outside hearing all this, or the boys will be in for it when they get home." The Rolands' island, Ravenshill, was close by.

"Everyone come and party!" Belinda declared.

The canoes and skiffs drew up on the beach, allowing the motorboats to pull up to the extensive docks, where lights had suddenly glowed to life.

They were ushered up the flight of stairs outside the sixty-foot long boathouse to the party room above. With a gleaming hardwood floor, warm basswood-stripped walls and ceiling, and the French windows open to the night and extending the space onto a long balcony, the room was cheerful and inviting. A bar was set up along one end, next to tables of food. Maids and footmen offered refreshments, although people could also help themselves. A Negro band at the other end surprised most of the guests.

When they launched into a lively rendition of *Blues My Naughty Sweetie Gave to Me*, Ria whispered to Chas with glee, "Grandmother would have been scandalized! Shall we?"

Now that his leg was no longer painful, he was building up strength in his weakened muscles, and was able to dance remarkably well.

Esme snuck away as soon as she could. She was pleased to find Stephen in the Thornton yacht. The sixty-foot day cruiser had a luxurious glassed-in cabin with an arched ceiling and elaborate woodwork crafted from gleaming mahogany. There was also a galley and a head. The open area in the stern offered a plush leather bench and more wicker chairs for passengers out on picnic or sightseeing tours of the lakes.

"What? Bored already?" Stephen asked with a grin, putting down the book he had been reading by the dim light of a lantern.

"Gosh yes! You don't mind if I camp out here for a while?" She was glad that they were in the cabin, and thus not visible from the boathouse balcony.

"Not at all."

"What are you reading?"

"*The Doomed* by Montgomery Seaton."

Esme was impressed. "What do you think of it?"

"It's powerful."

"Did you know that Ria and Chas met the author in Antibes when he was writing the novel, and that he pretty well put them into it?"

"That explains why I felt I already knew those characters! And makes it even more interesting."

"It was before Ria became an ambulance driver, so she began to feel jinxed after she read the book. I won't spoil the plot, but you'll see what I mean. And Ria said that the boozy flapper is very much based on Seaton's wife, who was trying hard to seduce Chas and every other handsome officer around."

"Then I feel sorry for Seaton."

"Yes, but wasn't it cheeky of him to use Ria and Chas?"

"I'm sure authors are always drawing from bits of their own and other people's lives."

"Do you read a lot?"

"Whenever I have time. It's a way of experiencing the world and being challenged by new ideas. Fortunately, we have a good library in Port Darling, thanks in large part to the generosity of the summer people, especially the Thorntons."

"So what's your favourite book?"

"Anything by Thomas Hardy, but particularly *Far From the Madding Crowd*."

"I love his books, too! But Mama thinks they're too dark and rather scandalous. I read them anyway," she said with a mischievous grin. "I just put covers from 'acceptable' books over them."

Stephen's laugh was rewarding.

Esme was tempted by a jazzy version of *That's-A-Plenty*, the music emanating through the open windows probably audible as far as Wyndwood.

"Would you care to dance?" she asked tentatively. "Here?"

"You know that it's not appropriate for us to mingle like this," he said, his eyes betraying his desire.

"Tosh! Things have changed." She held out her arms.

He extinguished the lantern, and Esme could hardly contain her joy as she sank into his embrace.

"I'm not much of a dancer," he admitted, so they swayed slowly, despite the buoyant music.

He drew her ever closer through *The Vamp* and the *Midnight Trot*, drinking in her fresh scent as he nuzzled her hair, knowing how dangerous this was. Not only because he was falling for her, and encouraging her obvious infatuation, but also because he could jeopardize his job and his reputation. He released her reluctantly. "You really should get back or we could both be in serious trouble."

She was about to protest, but realized that he had more to lose than she, if they were discovered like this. A twenty-two-year-old servant seemingly seducing a naïve eighteen-year-old girl would not sit well with Chas or her family. Who would believe that she had instigated it?

"Of course. But it's been fun!" she said, as he helped her out of the yacht. "We'll have to do it again." She threw him a promising look as she sauntered away, swinging her hips to the music and occasionally turning back to glance his way.

What the hell am I getting into? Stephen wondered. But damn it, he wasn't about to relinquish her. She was right that things had changed. But so much that a servant could marry into virtual aristocracy?

•   •   •

"Come for a walk," Lyle said to Lizzie as they finished a dance. "I want to show you our other islands, Peek-a-Boo and Wistful."

"How can I resist places with names like that?" she asked.

The shore path was illuminated as far as a point, where a humpback bridge crossed the ten feet of water to a small, rocky island boasting a gazebo.

"This is Peek-a-Boo," Lyle said.

"I can see why," Lizzie replied. Another bridge led to a larger island, so that sandwiched Peek-a-Boo was only visible to passersby on the lake at certain angles.

"This is where we come for private swims. The girls like to skinny dip here."

"It's definitely inviting. And so that must be Wistful Island. Why 'Wistful'?

"Because it seems to be yearning for something. To be bigger or more isolated so that it has its own presence and isn't just an adjunct to Thunderbird."

"That's delightfully imaginative."

"Thank you."

"You named it?" she asked, impressed.

"I did, but my siblings may recall our long-ago discussion differently," he said wryly. "Anyway, there's a guesthouse there, which we kids used when no one was staying. Our clubhouse. We still retreat there when we want some time to ourselves."

The bridges were lined with fairy lights, but beyond that lay only the undisturbed night.

"Mind your step," Lyle said, taking her hand. "The rocks and roots can easily trip you up."

The island was bathed in moonlight, the granite gleaming, the trees casting strong shadows. The windows of the sizable guesthouse reflected the indigo lake.

"I feel it!" Lizzie said in surprise. "The wistfulness."

He laughed. "Well I thought you might want to take some photos here. My parents were so impressed with the ones you took of me that they want a family portrait and pictures of the cottage."

"I'd be happy to oblige. And I have some ideas already."

"I thought you might."

He stared at her in the moonlight and then took her into his arms. She allowed the kiss and responded to him, but drew away when he became more ardent. "I... think we should get back before we're missed," she said with reluctance and yet a hint of longing for more. A good girl, tempted. As indeed she was.

"We'll continue this later then," he promised. "We're about to be invaded anyway."

They could hear the clatter of many footsteps on the bridges and some lively chatter. One girl, flourishing a bottle of champagne in one hand and a brimming glass in the other, said, "Oh, we can dance on the bridge!" which she proceeded to do. She giggled when she spilled the wine and then drained the rest of her glass in one go. A couple of young men cheered her on.

"Here's to Prohibition!" she toasted, refilling her glass.

•   •   •

There was barely time to catch a breath between parties and events during the hot July days. Whenever there was an opening on the cottagers' social calendars, Lyle took Lizzie and Belinda on photography outings around the lakes, often with others - like Blanche and Adele, Frank Sheridan and Stanford Vandemeer - tagging along as well. They clambered about waterfalls, climbed to cliff tops, and canoed up the tranquil Shadow River where the majestic wilds seemed at once to rise from the water and sink below it, in perfect reflection, tempting and taunting the photographer's lens. While Lizzie taught Belle the secrets of the darkroom, Lyle would take in a game of golf next door at the Country Club. They would meet him there for ice cream sundaes or cool drinks afterwards, Belle invariably enthusing about the photos they had just developed. She was an apt and dedicated student, pleasantly surprising Lizzie, who had assumed her to be just a bored rich kid looking for diversion.

So Lizzie was puzzled not to see Belinda when Lyle appeared one afternoon in late July. "Mother insisted that Belle accompany her to tea at the Sheridans'. Apparently they have visitors with an eligible son. Belle will hate that, of course," he added with a grin. "She doesn't want any interference on the husband-hunting front, and has actually been lobbying to attend Bryn Mawr College. Anyway, I'm still game for an outing if you are. I've brought a picnic lunch."

Much as she liked Belle, Lizzie was excited to be going out alone with Lyle. Her mother had no objections, and as it was a blistering, steamy day, being on a breezy boat would be heavenly.

"We'll go up the Joe River, which is navigable now that John Eaton had it dredged. He figured it was faster getting to the Lake Joe train station that way than down through Port Sandfield."

With unexpected nooks and rocky narrows, it was strikingly picturesque. They explored Little Lake Joe, a lobe of the larger lake, which was still relatively uninhabited. It was when they were at the top of the lake and furthest from home that the wind suddenly picked up and black clouds ominously billowed in. With the rumble of thunder at their back, they sped down the lake.

"Is it dangerous to be on the water in a storm?" Lizzie yelled into the wind.

"Yes. Did you notice any likely cottages where we can seek shelter? People on the lakes are good about accommodating boaters during storms."

"No, I haven't." But she searched frantically as the storm exploded violently above them, the clouds opening with a torrent of rain. Lightning knifed around them. The white-capped, wind-whipped waves slammed against the boat throwing more water over them and threatening to flip the boat.

"There!" Lizzie shouted above the roar of the motor and the heavenly cacophony.

Lyle zoomed up to the dock and jumped out to tie up. The boat rocked violently. He helped Lizzie out and grabbed their bags.

No one answered their knock at the little cottage.

"Damn!" Lyle swore. But when he tried the door, it opened. "Some people don't bother locking."

With little about but shabby furniture, there was nothing much to steal, Lizzie thought.

"Hello? Anyone home?" Lyle called out, and did a quick recce when there was no answer.

"I feel guilty dripping all over the floor," Lizzie said. She was soaked through.

Lyle returned a few minutes later with several soft towels. "Don't worry," he said when she took them reluctantly. "I'll leave the owners enough money to buy new ones."

The storm raged outside, thunder applauding the blinding lightning. Lizzie wasn't often afraid of storms, but the wind howled and ripped at the cabin as if it would tear off the roof. It had also sucked away the heat of the day, leaving her shivering in her sodden clothes.

Lyle rubbed her arms with a towel and said, "There's plenty of kindling here. Why don't you take off your wet clothes? They should dry in no time once I've got a fire blazing."

When she hesitated he said, "I brought large towels, and I won't look."

She went into one of the tiny bedrooms and gratefully peeled off her clinging garments. She wrapped one towel tightly around herself and draped the other over her shoulders, but still felt awkward returning to the sitting room, to the welcoming warmth of the fire. She hung her clothes on a ladder-back chair that Lyle had thoughtfully set before the fire.

She thought how sexy he looked in his waterlogged clothes, but said, "You should dry off, too."

He returned from the bedroom a few minutes later with a towel wrapped around his waist. "Well, Miss Wyndham, shall we partake of our picnic en déshabillé?"

She laughed. "It would be worthy of a photograph, if I weren't concerned about the potential for scandal."

They sat close by the fire as they ate cold chicken, lobster, and strawberries, and drank champagne. When they had finished, Lyle threw a cushion onto the floor and stretched himself out on the hooked rug, his hands behind his head. Lizzie was disconcerted by the way he was eyeing her. As though he were mentally divesting her of even the towels.

"Why not join me?" he suggested.

"I think that would be too dangerous."

"I didn't think you'd shy away from danger."

"Lyle, I've never... I'm saving myself for marriage."

"Naturally! But that doesn't mean you can't have a bit of fun beforehand. I promise I won't take your virginity."

"I thought that women weren't supposed to enjoy sex," she said coyly.

"Ha! I was quickly disabused of that Victorian notion at college. Let me show you, luscious Lizzie." He held out a hand to her.

A dozen thoughts whirled through her head. Jack had always warned her of men's attitudes - *Why buy the horse when you get free rides?* But would allowing Lyle to take some liberties tantalize him and strengthen her hold on him? And damn it, she was tired of being virtuous, and desperate for some intimacy. Let him seduce her.

"What if someone returns?" she asked.

"No one will be travelling in this storm."

She went into his arms, surrendering herself to his passionate kisses. He unhooked her towel and trailed his fingers lightly down the length of her, saying, "You're just as beautiful as I had imagined."

She moaned when his lips teased her breasts, and was moistly eager for his probing fingers. He took her hand and showed her how to caress his rigid manhood. She cried out and gripped him tighter when he brought her to a shuddering climax.

He kissed her tenderly and said, "You're marvellous."

"Am I a fallen woman now?"

"No, just a delicious vamp."

"What else did you learn at college?"

He laughed. "I did actually study metallurgy, since that's relevant to the family business. The other lessons were a bonus."

She cuddled up against him, throwing one leg over his and laying her head on his chest, giving him a playful nibble. "And you're a quick study," he said with amusement as he stroked her back.

The storm stopped as abruptly as it had started, although distant rumblings meant it was still heading down the lakes. As the sun reappeared, Lyle said, "We should probably take our leave, much as I hate to cut short this delectable picnic."

Lizzie climbed back into her still-damp clothes, not bothering to dress in the privacy of the bedroom. She didn't realize that Lyle was observing her until he said, "It's as sexy watching you dress as seeing you naked. Come here, my siren." He pulled her tight and kissed her deeply.

Lizzie wondered how he could possibly *not* fall in love with her now. Or she with him.

Chapter 11

"Aunt Olivia, I'm not feeling well, so I think I should go and stay with Maman," Claire said.

Olivia put her hand on Claire's brow. "You're feverish. Of course we'll take you to be with your mother, if that's what you wish."

"I don't want to infect anyone here. I'm afraid I might have influenza again."

Olivia saw the fear in Claire's blue eyes, and realized how thin she had become. "You have had a bad go of it, haven't you? I noticed that you've been coughing more lately. We'll ask Eleanor to have a look at you. You know that Richard is still debilitated from his bout."

Claire nodded, grasping at hope from those words.

Esme offered to pack, insisting that Claire lie in bed and supervise. "I've been pushing you too hard, haven't I? I should have realized you weren't completely recovered," Esme said.

"Tosh! I don't want to just sit around and miss all the fun," Claire assured her. "I thought I was getting better."

"Well, you must come back to us as soon as you can! And I'll visit you every day."

"And tell me about all the outings I'm missing?"

"Of course!" Esme flashed her a mischievous grin. "And all the fascinating new young men who would be eager to dance with you."

Claire giggled. "Are there any? Fascinating new young men?"

"Oh, there are bound to be. All of our friends are expecting visitors some time this summer. Anyway, you'll be back on your feet in no time, and then you can dazzle them."

"I hope so."

Miles had been dispatched to fetch Jack from The Point, who arrived looking concerned. "How are you, sweetheart?" The flush of fever couldn't hide her underlying pallor.

"Frustrated! I don't want to waste any more of the summer being ill."

"Well, there's no better place to recuperate than in a chaise lounge on the veranda overlooking the lake, and with Maman fussing over you," he replied.

Esme offered to drive them to Spirit Bay, but they stopped at Ouhu to see Ellie first. She confirmed that Claire had a temperature of 101, and then listened carefully to her chest.

"Take a normal breath. Now exhale completely, give me a quick cough, and then inhale deeply." She moved the stethoscope. "And again. Again."

Claire had a coughing fit. Ellie rubbed her back soothingly until she stopped. "OK, just a few more."

Ellie's face gave nothing away. "Have you had night sweats?" she asked.

"Yes."

"And chills?"

"Sometimes"

"Have you been eating well?"

"I haven't had much of an appetite. It's too hot."

"And I know that you've been very tired. Your pulse is a bit fast. Does your heart feel like it's pounding at times?"

"Yes."

"Have you noticed any blood when you cough?"

Claire looked at her with horror. "NO! I would have come to you right away if I had! Oh, please don't tell me…"

"I can't be sure of anything until we run some tests. But better to be safe," Ellie said with a reassuring smile. "Come along. Let's get you tucked up in bed for now."

But Claire couldn't suppress tears. Jack took her into his arms, and looked questioningly at Ellie. She couldn't meet his gaze as she said, "I have to run some tests to rule out tuberculosis."

Jack was stunned. He hugged Claire to him as she cried even harder.

"How can that be?" Esme asked, thunderstruck.

"Claire's father died of it, so she could have been infected by the bacillus at a young age. Apparently many of us are, but it doesn't often develop into disease. We've been finding that some of those who had the Spanish Influenza last winter are now exhibiting symptoms of TB, the flu having weakened the body, thus allowing the bacillus to flourish. If this is the case, then the good thing is that we'll have caught it early, and there will be every chance of recovery. And I could still be wrong."

But Jack doubted it. If he hadn't been so caught up in his own affairs, he would have realized how emaciated and listless his once bright and bouncy youngest sister had become these past months. She felt almost skeletal in his embrace. Cursing the gods, he squeezed back his own tears as he said to Claire, "You will have the best care that money can buy. It won't be like Papa, I promise you." He kissed the top of her head, and then picked her up in his arms and carried her back to the boat.

"I'm going to make arrangements and then meet you at Spirit Bay," Ellie said to him. "Get Claire settled into a sunny room with good air circulation, close to the lavatory and a veranda, if possible."

Esme tried to be strong, to show Claire that she had every faith that she would be well again. But they all knew how deadly consumption was, even if it took years to kill the patient. So she drove through her tears.

"This is damnable!" Ellie said to Troy as he took her to The Grand.

"You're convinced that she has TB?"

"I heard the distinctive râles."

"Poor kid!"

"It's bloody unfair!" Ellie knew how hard this would be on Jack's family, since he had already lost three siblings. But she was hopeful that Claire could be cured.

Although there were two large sanatoria in Gravenhurst, Ellie wasn't surprised to find that they were full beyond capacity, some patients already housed in tents. The Lakeview Sanatorium, the newest and most modern, was private, and beyond the reach of most people, so their waiting list was considerably shorter. But the expansion, which would soon be completed, was to house war veterans, under an arrangement with the government.

"I've compromised my principles," Ellie complained to Troy after she had finished her telephone calls. "I've always felt that people were equal, and the privileged shouldn't be able to pull rank on others when it came to medical or other aid. But I found I had to play the name game to expedite matters. I assured them that yes, Claire was one of THE Wyndhams."

"Ah, but all you're doing is going to bat for your privileged person," Troy said. "No downtrodden or salt-of-the-earth can afford those exorbitant rates."

She laughed. "You're quite right! You're obviously determined to keep my conscience in check."

•   •   •

Lizzie, meanwhile, was unaccountably nervous as she and Lyle pulled up to the dock on Thunderbird Island. She had never really spoken with his parents, and had sensed hostility from Blanche, who was obviously bosom buddies with Adele Fremont.

"Mr. and Mrs. Delacourt, I can't tell you how pleased I am to be here to create a memory album for you," Lizzie exclaimed.

"Lyle speaks very highly of your artistry, Miss Wyndham," Mrs. Delacourt said graciously. "Indeed, we were most impressed by your portraits of him."

"Thank you. I hope to do equal justice to the rest of the family. If I may suggest that we begin on the veranda?" Which was wide and substantial, as if it were just another airy room of the spacious cottage.

Once she was in her element, it was easy to command them to do her bidding. She had them seated in casual poses as if they were about to partake of afternoon tea. "If it's your habit to smoke a pipe or cigarette, gentlemen, then please do so. Mrs. Delacourt, could you perhaps have that book in your lap? Belinda, do you ever sit on the floor and lean against the wicker settee?"

Belinda laughed and said, "How did you guess?" From her spot beside Lyle she sank down onto the rug and propped her head on her elbow, which rested on the seat next to his knee.

"Blanche, perhaps you could relax into your chair a little?" She was sitting perfectly upright on the edge of the seat as if she were about to rise majestically. Lizzie felt her gazing disdainfully down her nose at the lowly photographer.

"I think not," Blanche replied.

Lyle shot her an annoyed look, but Lizzie just said, "As you wish. It's how posterity will see you."

"Which means you'll forever look like your corset's too tight," Belinda said with glee.

"Don't be foolish!" Blanche snapped.

"What a lovely family group!" Adele Fremont said as she arrived on the veranda. "You don't mind if I watch?"

"I certainly don't," Lizzie said. She didn't at all mind the opportunity to outshine her competition, considering Adele vapidly pretty, and no match for Lyle. Or her. She did wonder if Lyle had ever seduced Adele as he had her.

After she had taken several shots, Lizzie had them move to the balcony of the boathouse ballroom, and photographed them from the dock. On Peek-a-Boo Island, the family took various positions in the gazebo, and on Wistful, Lizzie had them lean against or perch on rocky outcroppings at the edge of the water.

"If I could use a canoe, I'd like to have you standing on one of the bridges," she said.

"By all means," Lyle replied.

"I think that we will leave the rest to you young people," Mrs. Delacourt said. "There are quite enough photographs of us already."

Lyle helped Lizzie into a canoe. She paddled over to the bridges and suggested the siblings have fun with poses. Lyle sat on the railing as if he were about to launch himself into the lake. Belinda laughingly pretended to push him, and gave Blanche, who never changed her regal stance, bunny ears. Cigarette in hand, Gregory looked relaxed but less playful, as befitted the responsible older brother with his pregnant wife at his side.

"Do come and join us, Adele," Blanche implored. "After all, you're practically family."

Blanche linked arms warmly with Adele and gave Lizzie a challenging smirk.

In response, Belinda hooked her arm through Lyle's and leaned against him like an adoring younger sister. Lizzie was amused to see that possessiveness as a declaration against Adele's encroaching on the family.

Blanche pronounced that she had had enough. "Come along, Adele, I fancy a swim."

"Well, if we're finished then I shall go for my sail," Gregory announced.

"Splendid!" Lizzie said. "Could you come past the rocks on Wistful so that I can capture you against that backdrop of distant islands?"

"Sure thing!"

"Do you want some more photography lessons while I take some shots of the cottage and islands, Belle?" Lizzie asked.

"You bet! I'll go and fetch my new camera. I bought what you said I should, Lizzie. A Graflex like yours. It finally arrived yesterday." Belle had been using Lizzie's Kodak in the meantime.

Belinda scampered away, leaving Lyle and Lizzie alone. They strolled over to Wistful Island. "It won't take long for Greg to come around the point," Lyle said. "But enough time for this." He took her in his arms and kissed her passionately. She was glad that the guest cottage shielded them from the main island as he pressed her hard against him. When he released her, both of them breathless with desire, he said, "We'll have to find more opportunities for picnics *en déshabillé*."

Lizzie managed to grab her camera and take a succession of shots as Greg sailed past. When Belle rejoined them, Lizzie said, "You see that the Graflex is the best camera for action shots? Now let's look at how we can portray and convey a mood. Wistful Island might best be photographed on an overcast day or when just a ribbon of sunlight breaks through a bank of clouds, sparking diamonds off the water. So keep taking pictures under different light conditions. And think about what angles are best. Try to find a unique vantage point or highlight some feature. Like that wild daisy that's found a precarious foothold in the rocks. If I get down to its level, it becomes the focus in a landscape of rock and water."

"And becomes a philosophical statement," Lyle added with a grin, which Lizzie returned.

"How clever!" Belinda enthused. "I do see what you mean."

"As Jack, in his artistic guise, always tells me, you need to look at the world differently, with new eyes, without preconceptions," Lizzie explained. "A boat is not just a vessel, but lines, and curves, and textures, and surfaces that reflect light - a thing of esthetic as well as functional beauty. Let's capture some waves washing up on the rocks. Get so close that you can see the lichen and the crystals of quartz."

They spent over an hour traversing the three islands for interesting shots, Lizzie occasionally asking one or both of them to figure in a picture. She captured some wonderful snapshots of brother and sister that revealed their deep affection for one another. Both sitting on a sloping rock, Belle resting her cheek on her drawn-up knees and grinning mischievously at Lyle, who had his ankles crossed and his head thrown back in a hearty laugh. Lyle reclined with his hands cupped behind his head while Belinda was about to tickle him with a downy tuft of grass. The aftermath, with Lyle chasing a giggling Belle. Catching her and drawing her, protesting, toward the lake as if intent on throwing her in. Lizzie felt privileged and happy to be a part of this carefree intimacy.

"Do stay for luncheon, Lizzie," Belle invited when they returned to the cottage. "I'm sure it will be fine with Mother."

"Well, if I'm not intruding..."

"Adele stays whenever she wants to. There's always plenty of food."

But Lizzie felt intimidated now that she was once again a guest. And Adele, of course, did join them. But actress Lizzie was soon on top form.

The large formal dining room with a table long enough to seat twenty was rather sombre, but the family apparently ate most of their meals in the bright, relaxed morning room beyond, with its massive plate glass windows overlooking the lake, and an inviting sitting area that opened onto the veranda at one side. Lizzie preferred that to the all-encompassing veranda of Ria's cottage, which dimmed the interior rooms, even if it did keep them cooler. Yes, she could enjoy staying here.

"What prompted you to take up photography, Miss Wyndham?" Mrs. Delacourt asked.

"I'm not as skilled with the paintbrush as Jack and Claire, but had been told that I have an eye for composition. When I had the opportunity to study under Anders Vandeburgh, I became enthralled with this newer art form."

"That's all very well, but why on earth turn it into a career?" Blanche asked.

"I like the independence and the challenge."

"I suppose for people who don't consider marriage and family to be the focus of their lives, it is essential to have a career," Adele said dismissively. "Otherwise I don't see the point of one."

"It's not only entertaining, but also rewarding in other ways," Lizzie said. "Men seem to be able to manage both. Why shouldn't women?"

Lyle suppressed a grin, but Belle didn't bother.

"Do you mean that we should compete with men?" Adele asked, aghast.

"Not at all. But making use of one's God-given talents is surely a good thing. So being compensated for one's work shouldn't demean it."

"Quite right!" Belinda declared. "Haven't we been proving that we can do all kinds of things that people had once thought women couldn't or shouldn't? Look at Ria. She can fly airplanes and drive ambulances and win medals for bravery."

"And she runs a fine household and kitchen," Lyle said. "If she weren't married to Chas I could be quite smitten with her."

"Don't talk rot, Lyle," Blanche admonished.

"Haven't you heard of the *New Woman?*" Belle countered.

"Only the ones with too much makeup and too few morals," Mrs. Delacourt said. "Now, Miss Wyndham, is it true that your mother is designing Felicity Thornton's wedding gown?"

"Yes, and the bridesmaids'. My mother's artistry lies with fabrics and design. She's hired some women to do the actual needlework, of course." Only because there wasn't time for her to do them all herself, but they didn't need to know that. Marie was still sewing the wedding gown.

"How... interesting. And *modern.*"

"She's designed all your clothes, hasn't she?" Belinda asked. "I think they rival Paris fashions, and I'm so envious!"

They were adapted copies of Paris fashions, but Lizzie wouldn't tell them that. "Yes, I am lucky. My mother is actually French."

"Quite an artistic family, what with your sister being a *showgirl,*" Blanche drawled.

"She and Hugo will be here for August, and I'm sure they will give a concert to our friends, based upon their latest Broadway success."

"How exciting!" Belle exclaimed.

"Lady Sidonie couldn't say enough about how wonderful the musical was when she and Rafe saw it in New York recently. Hugo and Emily are buying an island and plan to become regular summer residents. Hugo finds himself inspired by Muskoka, so I expect that his next masterpiece will be conceived here."

"Will your sister give up the stage when she has a child?" Adele asked.

Lyle snorted a laugh, nearly choking on his wine. "I think Lizzie was referring to a musical conception, not a Biblical one."

"I know that!" Adele shot back. "I was just wondering whether Emily will retire to nurture her children."

"That's what nannies are for," Belle said. "Don't tell me that your mother spent all day every day *nurturing* you."

"Belinda," her mother cautioned.

"Of course not!" Adele retorted indignantly, the implication being that only the lower classes looked after their children. "But I wouldn't have wanted my mother to be on stage! How... grotesque!"

"I'm sure that none of us would have wanted your mother to be on stage either," Belle said flippantly as she buttered her bread.

Lyle chuckled and Lizzie hid her grin with her napkin.

"That's quite enough, Belinda," her mother admonished.

"You seem to have had a rather... Bohemian life, Lizzie," Blanche said. "What with your father being... estranged from his family. Wasn't he an artist of sorts?"

"Yes. He studied in Paris and London. An unconventional childhood does set one apart from others. Which is not always to one's detriment. It provides a broader perspective on life." Lizzie challenged Blanche with her direct gaze, confident in her own beauty and aplomb. *Take that and shove it up your arrogant, upper-class ass!*

•   •   •

Ellie steeled herself as she and Troy arrived at Spirit Bay. She had found that a cheerful and matter-of-fact demeanor helped to put patients and their families at ease.

Lyle, Belinda, and Lizzie, who had arrived only a few minutes earlier, greeted them grimly on the veranda.

"We should be leaving," Lyle said. "I'm terribly sorry, Lizzie. Do give Claire our best regards."

He seemed anxious to get away, probably worried about those kisses, about whether she'd poisoned him, Lizzie thought. "Have we become lepers?" she asked Ellie snidely as the Delacourts left.

"Unfortunately there's a lot of fear and misinformation about TB. You might as well harden yourself to it now. And you'll have to be tested as well," Ellie replied.

Jack and his mother had settled Claire into the Royal Suite with its screened windows in the four sides allowing for excellent ventilation, and a private bathroom. It was to have been their honeymoon suite, Ellie thought with but a moment of regret, realizing that their wedding needed to be moved elsewhere now, although it was only a week away. Guests would not feel comfortable here, even if Claire were already at the sanatorium by then.

"What a delightful spot for you, Claire!" Ellie said brightly. "OK, so I've arranged for you to go to the Lakeview Sanatorium tomorrow to have an x-ray and sputum culture done. That will give us a definitive answer. If they turn out to be positive, then the Lakeview will put you on their waiting list." She didn't add, "near the top".

"In the meantime, we will do what we can for you here. So this is the regimen. Complete bed rest. No getting up for anything except to use the toilet and wash. Lying flat or propped up with some pillows, but no sitting in a chair. Never get chilled and try not to cough. No writing at the moment, very little reading, talking only when necessary, lots of sleep, plenty of nutritious food, and most of every day spent on the veranda in the fresh air. Jack, if you can manage to fit wheels onto this bed, then she can easily be moved back and forth. The idea is to rest your lungs as completely as possible. So no crying either, OK?" she added, as she stroked the girl's head. "You can get better, Claire, but it will take a lot of work from you. Lying about doing nothing is damned hard, as I know."

"Do you really mean that, Ellie?" Claire asked.

"Absolutely! And when you start to improve, you can do more and more things. Get back to your painting, write letters, take gentle walks, swim. And eventually you'll be able to resume a normal life. But it will take time, perhaps even a few years, and you have to follow the doctor's orders religiously."

"Yes, Doctor!" Claire said, hope glistening in her eyes.

"Remember *that* when you get bored and feel like rebelling," Ellie said with a grin. "And I hate to disappoint you, but friends must curtail their visits, at least until the fevers have subsided. You can't have any kind of stimulation, and even though laughter is good for the soul, it isn't for your lungs at the moment."

Esme and Claire both looked crushed.

Ellie said, "Let me explain just a little about what goes on when the tubercle bacilli infect your lungs. Your body's immune system, which protects you from disease, sends out an army to kill the invaders. This army starts by building a wall around the germs, to contain them so that they can't infect other parts of the lungs. Most of your lungs are still perfectly healthy, so stopping the invaders as soon as possible is crucial. This wall, however, is very delicate at first, and takes time to harden into a scar. During that time, any sort of strain on the lungs can cause the wall to rupture, which allows the germs to spread. Then your body has to start again, and work even harder to contain the larger numbers. So you see how important rest and quiet are?"

They nodded.

"So, short visits a few times a week, and Esme does all the talking. Your big challenge, Claire, is to cultivate equanimity. You must be calm in spirit as well as body, and keep a positive outlook. That will most definitely put you on the road to recovery.

"The other vital thing you need to do is to contain your germs so that you don't infect others. That involves always covering your mouth with tissue paper or a handkerchief when you cough or sneeze, and then burning that. I'm going to go to the pharmacy in Port and get you a sputum cup. I'll explain how to use that later, but you mustn't swallow anything that you cough up." Turning to Marie, Ellie said, "Mrs. Wyndham, I'd like you to take Claire's temperature at regular times daily. I'll draw up a chart where you can record the numbers, and give you a recommended diet sheet. And please ensure that Mr. Mayhew doesn't go near Claire, since his lungs are already weak."

"Oh God, what about everyone at Silver Bay?" Claire asked in a panic.

"You mustn't distress yourself, remember? Ellie chided gently. "I will let them know how to cleanse the cottage. Sunshine and fresh air kill the germs quite promptly, and the cottage has excellent cross-breezes, so I don't think many will still be lingering there."

"The baby?" Claire looked stricken.

"Is strong and healthy. Now stop worrying."

But Zoë was not as sanguine as her sister-in-law. She grabbed the child in a fiercely protective hug and said, "Oh my dear God!"

"TB isn't as contagious as people think, not like influenza," Ellie reassured her. "Claire would have had to cough on Ethan or share his cup or spit on the floor, none of which she would likely have done, so don't worry, Zoë."

"How can I not? How could a baby survive consumption?"

Ellie didn't tell her that most under a year old didn't. "My nephew has a healthy immune system. Make sure he keeps getting plenty of fresh air and sunshine. Why don't you move in with Ria for a few days while the cottage is scrubbed to make sure that every possible germ is eradicated?"

Zoë and Ethan did, while Esme and the boys stayed with Max and Lydia. Olivia supervised the cleaning, which involved wet dusting all the surfaces, and putting the upholstered furniture, rugs, and the mattresses in the girls' dorm out into the sunshine for a day.

"Zoë's even afraid to be near *me*," Esme complained to Ellie the following day. "I told her she should perhaps spare a thought for poor Claire, but she just got annoyed with me."

"Are you worried at all? About yourself?" Ellie asked.

"Not really. Claire and I have been sharing a room for the past month, but we've always had the windows open, and the sun shines in late in the day."

"If you had been sharing a closed-up room all winter I would be concerned, but I expect you're probably quite fine. Doctors and nurses who work with tubercular patients actually seem to contract it less than the general population. I'll arrange for you to have a tuberculin test. If it's negative, then you'll have nothing to worry about. If it's positive, it will mean only that you've been exposed to the bacillus, not necessarily that you have an active case, and we'll do further tests."

They and Troy were in the Thorntons' yacht, offered by Fliss and driven by Stephen, and heading to Spirit Bay to pick up Claire and Jack. A comfy chaise lounge was set up for Claire in the glassed-in cabin, out of the wind but with the open doors inviting gentle breezes through. Ellie had agreed to allow Esme to accompany them, Esme maintaining that Claire would be upset anyway, and that she might be able to keep her cousin calm.

"Isn't it a beautiful day for a boat ride?" Ellie chirped as Jack tucked a blanket around his sister, for she was chilled despite the heat.

Claire gave a wan smile. She was pleasantly surprised to see Esme, who explained, "Ellie said I could come as long as I'm not a chatterbox." She had also warned Esme that she mustn't cry despite whatever transpired today.

Jack had convinced his mother that she shouldn't come along in case she became too emotional and upset Claire. Marie should have a good supper ready for the patient's return. Lizzie should get on with her work. It didn't help for people to drop everything and hover over the patient, Jack had said, paraphrasing Ellie. Claire needed neither additional guilt nor activity surrounding her.

It was a pleasant two hour drive, the yacht slicing sedately through the gentle swells. Esme pointed out a few interesting sights to Claire, but otherwise was happy to sit quietly beside her beloved cousin. And she was able to observe Stephen at the helm in his captain's uniform, feeling strangely proud of him.

Fliss had sent along a picnic lunch, which they ate en route, Esme having to coax Claire to eat more. "Ellie says you have to eat whether you feel like it or not. That's your job right now."

An impressive rocky bluff bulged into the lake with Gravenhurst in view beyond it, at the end of the bay. Stephen pulled the yacht up to a long wharf in a cove alongside the cliff and next to a sandy beach.

The grey sanatorium topped with a pink roof, was set against a lush backdrop of trees, high above the water.

Esme said she would stay in the boat, and watched the others traipse up to the imposing building with trepidation. Ellie struggled with her cane in one hand, and with obvious support from Troy. Jack carried Claire as easily as if she were down-filled.

Esme allowed herself a few brief tears. A hand squeezed her shoulder and she went gratefully into Stephen's arms.

He stroked her hair as he said, "I'm terribly sorry about your cousin."

"She's my very best friend! I couldn't bear it if anything happened to her!"

"They do good work here, Esme. People do leave again."

Esme was comforted by his words as well as by his reassuring touch. This was not a seduction, but a companionable intimacy, which felt so right, as if they had been friends forever.

And as if to prove Stephen right, a group of patients - for they were wearing dressing gowns over pajamas - shuffled with measured steps to the gazebo on the rocky headland. A few sporting bathing suits under their robes picked their way down to the beach.

Esme poured two glasses of wine from the open bottle, and said, "You didn't have much to eat. There's still plenty of food here."

He took a small cheese and cucumber sandwich, but said, "I shouldn't drink. I'm on duty."

"They'll be ages, I expect. Just a glass." She touched hers to his, their eyes locked as they sipped.

"I wish I had known Claire all my life, as I have my other cousins, especially since she's the only one who's my age. But she grew up poor in the city. Did you know that?"

"We heard rumours about Mr. Alex being disowned by the family. Toby had been very fond of him."

"It was disgraceful! My grandparents were tyrannical, and I shan't forgive them for that. But finally Claire and the others have a chance at a decent life, and now..." She didn't want to cry again.

"The best thing you can do for your cousin is to continue to be cheerful and encouraging. I'm impressed with your strength and compassion, Esme."

She gazed at him in happy surprise, wanting to throw herself into his arms and kiss him. Instead, she nibbled on a sandwich.

Troy came down to the boat and said to Esme, "The doctor wants to give you a tuberculin test."

Between the rocky cliffs lay a grassy ravine sprinkled with wildflowers, the path following it up to the extensive lawn. Patients sitting on benches amid colourful flower gardens greeted them cheerily. The long, three-storey building with its jutting bays curved towards the sun. Scaffolding caged a large new wing, from which the cacophony of saws and hammers disturbed the tranquility of the setting. As they stepped onto the entrance porch, Esme realized that the many bays contained private screened balconies for the patients.

Only a few years old, the facility didn't resemble a hospital so much as a comfortable hotel. She caught a glimpse of a sitting room with a fireplace, lined with bookshelves, and an inviting dining room overlooking the lake.

Troy ushered her into the medical director's office. His face bristling with formidable whiskers, Dr. Mainwaring rose to greet her. "Well, Miss Wyndham, we shall hopefully soon put your mind at ease. We're just going to give you a little injection under the skin, and Dr. Carlyle can read the results in a couple of days."

"What should I expect?" Esme asked.

"If you've been infected, a raised red lump will appear within forty-eight hours. That won't mean that you have an active case, but it will mean further investigation is warranted," Dr. Mainwaring said.

"That didn't hurt at all," Esme said when he had withdrawn the needle.

"Well, young lady, you are done. Your cousin is being X-rayed and should be finished shortly. But I will have a diagnosis for her before she leaves. I've ordered tea to be served in the lounge if you wish to partake."

"Thank you, but I think I shall return to the beach."

"Quite so! It's where I would spend more time if I could." He had a kind smile.

When Esme arrived back at the boat, she poured herself another glass of wine.

"Are you scared at all?" Stephen asked, sitting down beside her.

"Not for myself. Oh! I just remembered that you and I have shared a coffee mug! That's as dangerous as a kiss!"

"Oh, I wouldn't say that." His eyes held hers.

"I think it would be terribly sad to have to come here and never have been kissed," she said, looking at his lips, longing for them to touch hers. But she knew she might be putting him at risk. In more ways than one. They could too easily be seen here. So she turned away and took a sip of wine.

"But the patients can kiss each other," Stephen pointed out. "I have a friend who works here, and she says that there are always romances blooming, once the patients are no longer confined to bed."

"That makes sense. What does your friend do here?"

Stephen was amused that she seemed jealous. "Anne works in the kitchen. She's a terrific cook and great fun." He took pity on her and added. "She's married to one of my best friends. We were all kids together. He works at the Ditchburn factory."

"I see." She flashed him a smile.

"Have you heard that Major Thornton has hired me to work for him at Wyndwood?"

"No, I hadn't."

"He called it a secondment, but Miss Felicity accused him of stealing me. The Major had already warned me to prepare my assistant to step in at Thorncliff. But I'll still be asked to drive this yacht, since he's not that comfortable with it."

"Where will you live on Wyndwood?" Esme asked, thinking how close he would be to Silver Bay.

"I'll be working there, for sure, but also at the Boatworks experimenting with the engine for the racer. So I'll be living at home. The Major's giving me a runabout to use."

"Will you still go out fishing in the mornings?" They had met a couple of times now.

"Sure thing. There's good fishing behind what you call the Stepping Stone islands, but we don't usually let our guests know," he added with a grin.

Esme could tell by the others' faces as they returned to the boat that the news wasn't good. Claire was weeping.

Ellie said briskly, "Claire has a small lesion in her left lung." Her illness was a bit more advanced than Ellie had hoped. "But still caught in good time. Claire might be able to move in within a few weeks."

"May I visit her here?" Esme asked, swallowing hard to keep her own tears at bay.

"Eventually."

Esme took Claire's hand and squeezed it reassuringly. "I'll write every day that I can't see you," she promised.

•   •   •

Lizzie kept breaking down as she was processing the photographs from Thunderbird Island. She wept for Claire, but also for herself. Why was life so cruel? Why keep tantalizing her with visions of what might be, only to snatch away her dreams and crush them to dust?

The other Wyndhams would weather this, but she and Claire and Jack were the newcomers to this society, the ones who had been poor, the *Bohemians*. So surely it was through some fault of their own that they carried pestilence.

She hadn't been surprised that Belinda hadn't shown up today to help with the processing. Lizzie was bitter when she'd finished. Although the pictures were bloody damned good! She poured herself a strong gin and tonic and sat on the veranda eviscerating a cigarette. Still fuming and raging at the gods, she didn't notice the canoe at first. But as it came closer she saw that it was Belinda, who waved at her.

Lizzie ambled down to the dock. Belle didn't approach very close, saying, "I'm not allowed to come ashore. In fact, I'm not even supposed to be here, but I wanted to apologize for not showing up earlier to help."

"It doesn't matter."

"It does to me!" Belinda said vehemently. "I *wanted* to come, but Mother says that it's not safe. I'm terribly sorry about Claire."

"She'll be going into a sanatorium soon to get well."

"I'm so glad! Perhaps I'll be allowed to come back then."

"You know you're welcome any time."

"Thanks, Lizzie. Have you processed yesterday's photos?"

"Yes, and I think you'll like them. Especially the ones of you and Lyle."

Belinda looked down in embarrassment.

Shit! Do they think the fucking photos are contaminated?

"Mother will pay for them of course, but wondered if you might hold onto them for the time being."

"If you like." And she would obviously have no more commissions from anyone in their social circle.

"I don't! Oh, this is all so awkward!"

"Isn't it just? Look, it was kind of you to come, Belle, but don't get into trouble on my account."

Belinda drew herself up. "Well, I'm determined to continue my lessons! So I will see you when I can. Wish Claire the best of luck for me."

"I will. Thank you."

"Lyle... isn't... allowed to see you."

"Ah, yes, he's a dutiful son."

"It's not as simple as that, Lizzie."

"He wasn't inclined to linger yesterday."

"It was just the shock of the moment. He does care about you, Lizzie. A lot. I wish with all my heart that things could be different."

"So do I, believe me."

Belle looked at her tearfully. "Lyle and Adele have been expected to marry since they were practically children. They had an understanding of sorts before he went off to war. We heard that your father died of consumption. Mother says that it runs in families.... Father told Lyle that he needs a supportive wife to help him succeed in his new life in Toronto, so it was time to stop mucking about. If things had happened differently, he might have escaped. I really wanted you to be my sister-in-law."

Meaning that that obviously wasn't going to happen. *You bloody, cowardly bastard, Lyle!*

"Me too."

"I hope you'll be OK."

"I'm a survivor... Don't change, Belle. Don't let yourself be worn down by convention and expectations and rumours and ignorance and narrow-mindedness."

"I won't! Can we always be friends?"

"Of course. I shall count on that."

"Promise!"

"Yes. And you follow your dreams and your heart. Go to college if you want. Be a rebel."

"I will! But don't make it sound as though I won't see you again this summer!"

Lizzie shrugged. "I'll keep in touch anyway."

Belinda paddled away sadly.

Lizzie raged inwardly. But could she really blame Lyle or his family? The spot where Ellie had injected the tuberculin in Lizzie's arm yesterday was beginning to swell and redden. *Fucking hell and damnation!*

•   •   •

Jack had immediately moved into the Spirit Bay Inn to keep a safe distance from all the children on Wyndwood and to help Claire. Ria, Chas, and Alice arrived later that afternoon to visit.

"Johanna says to tell you that she's praying for you," Alice said to Claire, sitting next to her bed on the second floor balcony. Alice had already spent her tears and was determined to be chipper.

"You shouldn't have come. The children..."

"Ellie said we'll be just fine, especially if we're outside or in a well-ventilated room, and if we wash our hands well. But she did say we mustn't tire you. Now do look what we've brought you! First of all, Sophie made you this." As usual, Sophie had used some of her supply of dried wildflowers to create a delightfully artistic card. The elegant handwriting inside read, "We love you lots and lots, Claire. Get well soon!"

"She's making you a book. And Charlie drew this. I think it's supposed to be a portrait of Ace."

Claire grinned at the comical dog.

"Rupert and Miles wanted you to have these until they can buy you new ones." Alice handed her a pair of binoculars. Claire glowed with delight. "This is how you adjust them," Alice explained.

Claire did and then looked through them. "I can see forever!"

"And I've brought you some books from Ria's library."

Sipping cocktails on the veranda downstairs, Jack said to Ria and Chas. "The doctor said that the cure could easily take two or three or more years."

"Dear God! Poor Claire! We shall have to keep her spirits up," Ria declared.

"I'm going to rent a house in Gravenhurst for Maman so that she can be near Claire," Jack said. How thankful he was that he had the means to do that, as well as to pay for Claire's expensive stay at the private sanatorium.

"Just let us know if there is any way we can help," Chas said.

Jack was grateful, but more terrified about his future than he had ever been during the war. Despite his obvious support, would Chas allow his sister to marry a man infected with tuberculosis? Wouldn't Chas be concerned that it might flare up - as it had with Claire - and thus endanger Fliss as well as any children they might have? And what if he was already ill? Apparently people in the early stages weren't even aware that they had TB. How would he get on with his life's work if he had to spend years in a sanatorium?

Compulsively Jack rubbed the spot on his forearm where the doctor had injected the tuberculin yesterday. No lump. Yet.

•   •   •

Jack wished that Troy wasn't always with Ellie. Like a watchdog. She had been his confidante during the war, and he had opened his soul to her as he never had to anyone except Lizzie. Even with Chas he was mindful of his words.

Now all he wanted was to speak to Ellie again with that easy understanding they had shared. Alone.

But that obviously wasn't to be.

He was optimistic when he presented his forearm to Ellie to examine. She ran her fingers down it, carefully feeling for any swelling, even though there was no redness. Her touch was naturally sensual, reminding him of their lovemaking. Sex with other women had never been as all-consuming as with her.

She smiled at him. "No reaction."

"Thank God, since I have to look after my family!" He was delirious with joy. He still had a viable future.

But Lizzie was not so fortunate. The inside of her elbow was red and hot and swollen. "More tests for you, I'm afraid," Ellie said. "Although it's probably latent - as it is in most people - meaning that you're not ill. So take comfort in that for the moment at least. I'll arrange for you to have x-rays at the Lakeside San as soon as possible."

"But will people think differently even if I'm not ill? Won't they always wonder? And avoid me? Is it hereditary, as some people think?"

"No. It only seems to run in families because they live in such close proximity. If they don't exercise good hygiene to counteract the disease, then others can certainly fall ill. That's why it thrives in overcrowded areas and is considered mostly a disease of poverty, although the wealthy are no more resistant to it in the right circumstances."

"Tell that to the Delacourts! They won't even come near us. And I no longer have a job up here, thanks to this! Damn them all to hell!" she said as she stormed off.

"I'm sorry, Jack," Ellie said. "I do know how hard this is for you all. Bad enough worrying about Claire's recovery, but dealing with fear and prejudice isn't easy."

"I know that Lizzie's a bit rough when she gets emotional, but she really is devastated."

"I'll do what I can to educate people and change attitudes. Let's hope that you won't have to admit both of them to the sanatorium."

"God forbid!"

•   •   •

Lizzie's X-rays and sputum analysis showed no incipient disease. The relief to her family, if not so much to herself, prompted a celebration. Finishing a bottle of champagne, Lizzie went to bed, wondering if she had any future in Muskoka.

Chapter 12

"Mama, could I ask Stephen Seaford to the Regatta Ball?" Esme inquired.

Olivia was taken aback. Carefully she said, "I don't think it would be fair to him, my chick. He's not used to the ways of society, and would probably feel awkward, especially since he works for the Thorntons."

"But, Mama, you've always said that we should respect all people, no matter their status in society."

"Of course, but that doesn't mean that we subject them to uncomfortable situations."

"That sounds hypocritical. You mean that he's not good enough to socialize with us!" she accused.

"I mean that crossing barriers of class in either direction isn't easy for anyone. What's behind this?"

"I like Stephen. He's helping Chas build boats and I thought that he shouldn't be treated as just a servant." She tried not to sound scathing, but it irked her to think that her mother's professed liberalism was a tender thing that wilted when put to the test. "Grandfather Wyndham was a poor immigrant, but because he, unlike the Seafords, was ruthless, he amassed a lot of money and that, ironically, made him better than his neighbours."

"Esme! How can you say such things?"

"Because they're true! Since we don't have to work all hours of the day to make a living, we can read books, and play music, and visit museums and galleries and concerts. Which supposedly makes us cultured. Which makes us superior. Which is how the moneyed distance themselves from the rest of humanity. It's utter rot! I can't believe that you, of all people, Mama, are such a snob!"

Olivia was shocked by this tirade. "Esme, what on earth has gotten into you?"

"A sense of justice!" she spat before running from the room. She was still seething when she finally stopped at the top of the Dragon's Back to catch her breath. It was one thing for her family to do good works among the poor, but quite another to befriend a "servant". She wished she could just run away. Preferably with Stephen.

From this highest point on the island, Esme had a commanding view over Ria's point and the vast lake beyond. Scoured and scarred, the rock was mostly bare of vegetation, which gave her the sense that she sat on the top of the world as she plunked herself down on a giant boulder. From here she could easily see the SRA Country Club, and the attractive Pineridge Inn next to it. She allowed herself to daydream about living there with Stephen. No other visions of her possible future excited her as much. She didn't even care that she and Claire could no longer go to Europe. That was too far away from Stephen.

It was Zoë who confronted her when she returned. "Do you want to talk?"

"Mama put you up to this."

"She said you were upset. Do you have a crush on Stephen?"

Esme tried not to glare at Zoë, since she knew how shattered her sister was over the death of her husband. But she couldn't resist saying, "Blake wasn't wealthy either. Why is Stephen not as acceptable?"

"It doesn't come down to money, Esme. It's a matter of intellectual compatibility."

"So now you're saying he's not smart enough to be my friend!"

"Not at all. He's very accomplished in his field. But what do the two of you have in common? There's no high school in Port Darling, so he won't have more than a grade eight education."

Esme was momentarily speechless.

"Do you remember how Blake and I wrote to each other constantly? How we discussed all kinds of things that we both felt passionate about?" Because Esme looked deflated, Zoë said, "I don't know anything about Stephen, so I can't have an opinion about him, one way or the other. If you like him, you need to explore what the attraction is, beyond the physical. Of course he's a handsome man. But what would sustain your relationship?"

"This family always analyzes everything to death!" Esme retorted in frustration.

•　　　　　•　　　　　•

Ria reluctantly handed Ethan back to Zoë, her arms aching to cuddle a child of her own. "Let's enter the canoe race at the Regatta. I know we haven't practiced together at all since '14, but surely it will come naturally to us." As she had promised Olivia, Ria was trying to engage Zoë in some activities. They were sitting on the veranda of the Old Cottage.

"No thanks, Ria. Ethan and I are content to watch, aren't we, pumpkin?" She smiled lovingly at the baby as he chortled over the rattle that he flailed about.

Ria felt that she was somewhat superfluous, the mother-child circle being exclusive.

"Zoë... you need to do things for yourself, have some fun. Ethan couldn't be in better hands than your mother's, and I know that Johanna would look after him splendidly, and I daresay your nursery maid would as well."

"I have no need of anyone's help. I'm perfectly happy to spend my time with Ethan."

"Motherhood shouldn't consume you."

Zoë frowned. "It's what I want."

Ria put her hand on Zoë's arm. "You're a wonderful mother. But you also need to move on with your own life. I can imagine how hard it must be for you..."

"Can you?" Zoë demanded, her eyes blazing. "You still have Chas. You were on the brink of despair when he was hovering between life and death. But you have no idea what it's like to plunge over that precipice. The only thing that gives me any joy or sense of purpose or future is my child. Why should I indulge in silly games and frivolous parties? Do you think I should be looking for another man?"

"Well... no, but..."

"Then why shouldn't I do exactly as I please? Why are you all trying to make me forget Blake and 'move on', as though there is anything to move towards? Why can't I just be left alone?"

Ria had never seen Zoë so livid. "Of course. I'm sorry, Zoë. We're all just trying to be helpful."

"Then don't presume to know how I feel or what's good for me!" Zoë got up and marched off, furious with herself as much as Ria and everyone else. How dare they make her feel guilty for how she chose to live her life! But why was she so sensitive to their intervention? Was it because she sensed some truth in their words? She was even angry with Blake for trying to exact that promise from her, to "move on" if anything happened to him. Surely he hadn't thought her love so shallow that she could easily do that.

She was in such a state as she hurried along the west veranda that she collided with someone as she rounded the north corner. A strong arm steadied her and Freddie said, "I do beg your pardon, Zoë."

"It was my fault, not watching where I was going."

"No harm done, eh chum?" Freddie asked Ethan. The child chuckled and waved his rattle excitedly.

"He's showing it off," Zoë said. "Auntie Ria just gave it to him."

"And a very fine one it is!" Freddie said, grinning broadly at Ethan. To Zoë he said, "I've just come to show Chas the drawings for the boathouse."

"I hope you're managing a holiday as well, not just working all summer for your friends. That seems quite unfair."

"Not at all. You know how much I love to design buildings."

"Yes, but you should have a chance to relax and heal."

"I do, but I also don't like being aimlessly idle." He smiled tenderly, grateful for her concern. "There's only so much sailing and swimming I can do. Martha has been assiduous in the massage you taught her, so I am definitely on the mend. And I like the idea of putting my own stamp on Muskoka through my designs. So what could I do for *you*, Zoë?"

Her ire having melted away, she replied, "Actually, I *have* been thinking that I'd like a place of my own. Something small, just for the two of us, and living atop a boathouse really appeals to me." The idea had been nagging her that she needed some independence, and not just live like a guest in her parents' homes, being forever a child herself. She had her $25,000 inheritance from Grandmother, and her father had given each of his children a sizable fortune on the dissolution of the Wyndham enterprises. She needed to consider a city residence for herself as well. "Maybe not the fanciful playhouse you designed for Rupert," she added with a grin, reminding him of that summer of 1916 before they had both gone overseas.

"OK, then I won't make it ship shaped," he said with a chuckle. "Look, I'll deliver these to Chas and meet you at Silver Bay. Then you can show me where you want to put the boathouse, and we'll discuss the layout." He was excited not only to be doing something for Zoë, but also to have an excuse to spend some time alone with her.

With the baby squirming in her arms, Zoë wandered along the path towards her parents' cottage, trying to envision where she wanted her place. It definitely had to have an unobstructed view of Ouhu, so that she would feel as though Blake were still nearby. There had to be a sandy beach, but also sufficient depth for a boathouse, and sheltered enough to be protected from winter ice, she knew. So she was seated on a granite outcropping about halfway between Max's cottage and her parents' when Freddie found her.

"What do you think?" she asked him.

He examined the site quickly but expertly. "Just about perfect, I'd say. I'll anchor the building to this rock, which can be the foundation for the kitchen at least. We don't want any open flames right above the boats because of the danger of gasoline fumes igniting."

He sat down beside her. "Let me take the baby while you tell me what you want in the cottage."

Her arms tired, Zoë was grateful to hand him the restless child. Ethan seemed content with his new perch. Zoë had noticed that he was intrigued by the deeper tones of men's voices, and appeared to pay attention to them as if he were already preparing himself for his manly role. It suddenly struck her how much he needed a father. But his uncles and her male friends would have to suffice, since she had absolutely no interest in marrying again. Even considering it felt like a betrayal of her vows and her love for Blake.

That it was comforting to have Freddie around wasn't at all the same thing.

They discussed the layout, Freddie insisting that she plan room for at least one servant.

"As a VAD, I learned how to boil eggs and make tea and toast," she informed him with a grin. "Matrons usually considered that our most valuable contribution."

"Martha said that was only because the trained nurses were jealous of you do-gooders."

She laughed, for the volunteers had been mostly middle and upper-class girls eager to do their bit for the war effort, and undaunted by the sometimes horrendous tasks that confronted them when the regular nurses were overwhelmed by the ceaseless flow of patients. Zoë had a scar on her wrist from an operation for dangerous sepsis, picked up from handling a patient's suppurating wound. It ached arthritically at times.

"But I concede that help with the household and in the kitchen is probably essential," Zoë admitted. "I just don't want to be surrounded by servants. I like my privacy."

"But you'll still want a space big enough for friends to gather."

"Of course! Not a ballroom though," she jested.

"Noted! I think I can design something quite special for you, Zoë." The sort of place he would like for himself, if he could share it with her. An intimate love nest.

•   •   •

Ellie and Troy's wedding was held at The Point on Wyndwood, last minute notices going to all the guests regarding the change of venue. They would also spend part of their honeymoon in the boathouse, since Jack was no longer there.

Ellie had flattered and coerced Lizzie into still being the official photographer.

"Shall I wear a mask?" Lizzie asked sarcastically. "Or a sign around my neck saying 'officially not poisonous'?"

"My sanctioning your presence should count for something, Lizzie."

She snorted. "Sure! The Delacourts didn't even want to touch my photographs!"

"If you run away, they'll think they were justified."

Lizzie glowered at her, but realized the truth of her words. *Fuck them all!* She would be there, and they could just go jump in the lake if they didn't like it!

Her indignation made her belligerent and touchy, which Jack noticed, so before they left Spirit Bay, he implored, "Be nice. They will come round and realize that we're not a danger to anyone. Just don't make it more difficult for yourself or burn any bridges."

"It wasn't me who burned bridges! Belinda as good as told me that Lyle and Adele are engaged!"

"There are other men."

"Are there? You say that so blithely. Show me another guy who's interested in me. Preferably someone I could like for more than his money."

"So you actually fell for Lyle?"

She hesitated to admit it even to herself. "I could have."

"Then he's a fool. Look, sweetheart, rise above it all. Just be a confident aristocrat. Disdainful if necessary, but charming and all that rot. You know how to play the game."

"Yes, we always have to play games, don't we? Do you know, I almost wish that I were infected, and had given it to Lyle. Then Adele wouldn't want him, and we could still be together."

"Like vampires."

"Why not?"

Lizzie took along the Delacourts' photos, not wanting to be reminded of what could have been.

The bride and groom had invited just their closest summer friends, so all the young American cottagers near the Rolands were in attendance. Troy's brothers had managed to come as well, Felix being Best Man. Ellie's sister, Daphne, was Matron of Honour. Practical as always, Ellie had bought a chic evening gown of ecru satin overlaid with a black Chantilly lace tunic, which she substituted today with Ria's knee-length ivory lace wedding jacket.

Having worn that jacket at her own wedding in England, it was hard for Zoë not to weep as she watched Blake's sister walk slowly up to the minister - one with Theosophical leanings - who conducted a simple celebration of marriage on the rocky point of Wyndwood.

Jack concentrated on his own upcoming nuptials, knowing that he needed to push his feelings for Ellie firmly into the past.

Lizzie took no notice of the other guests as she shot the wedding photos. In addition to the stiff formality of the usual pictures, she also liked to use unconventional locations and poses. She captured the newlyweds cuddling in Troy's boat, Troy pushing Ellie on the tree swing that Gareth had rigged up for the children, and sitting thoughtfully, Ellie's head on Troy's shoulder, on the boathouse veranda overlooking the lake towards Ouhu.

Daphne had organized the luncheon, with the staff from Tumbling Rocks and Silver Bay helping out in the kitchen at the Old Cottage. Tables were set up in the pavilion and an adjacent marquee.

Lizzie was sitting with the Wyndhams, her work finished, having adamantly refused to take photos of all the guests. She deflected glances from Lyle, as if he were a stranger.

After the meal, Lizzie went up to the table where Lyle sat with his siblings, the Sheridans, and the Fremonts. She forced a smile as she said, "I haven't had a chance to deliver the photos, so here they are."

She plunked the package onto the table in front of him, and challenged him with her gaze.

Belinda picked them up immediately, not giving Lizzie a chance to see if Lyle would have. "Do let's look!" After perusing a few she exclaimed, "Oh, they're fabulous!"

"And quite safe," Lizzie assured them sardonically.

Adele said, "Perhaps we should hire Lizzie to take our wedding pictures, Lyle."

Lizzie knew that Adele had no such intention, but threw that out just to make sure that Lizzie was aware of the betrothal.

"Next April, if you're free," Adele added smugly to Lizzie.

Lyle looked away.

"How kind of you to think of me, but I shall be in Europe. I'm going to visit my cousin, Lady Beatrice, and we plan to spend the winter at her villa in Cap d'Antibes. Do excuse me."

She had cabled Cousin Bea, asking if she could visit. Beatrice had been delighted, and Lizzie was looking forward to discovering the Riviera, about which Jack had been most effusive. Why the hell not take advantage of family connections? She would undoubtedly meet some intriguing and wealthy, even titled men. A bigger world beckoned, and Lizzie was itching to move on. It was actually cathartic to feel sorry for Lyle, who would be forever stuck with prissy Adele.

Lyle looked at her in astonishment, which changed into profound regret. Had he thought that he could wile away long winter nights in Toronto making love to her, Lizzie wondered angrily.

She smiled saucily at him. *Fuck you, Lyle Delacourt.*

•   •   •

The guests departed in the languid heat of the afternoon, some to sleep off the champagne, others to practice for the SRA Regatta the following day.

Ellie and Troy had a refreshing swim and then retired to their boathouse suite. It had been almost two years since they had made love. As Ellie lay in Troy's arms afterwards, gazing out at the lake through the French doors, she said contentedly, "What bliss!"

"We should have a room like this above our boathouse," Troy said. "With a view of Picnic Island."

"That would be glorious!"

"I have a small wedding present for you." Troy took a paper from the bedside table and handed it to her.

Ellie was stunned when she opened it. "It's a deed! To Island 37. Is that Picnic Island? You *bought* it?"

"It's what you've always wanted, isn't it?"

"Yes, but... Troy! Can we afford this sort of extravagance?" She was momentarily concerned that his lifelong familiarity with wealth might be a difficult habit to break.

He chuckled. "Oh, it was very extravagant. Cost me all of $10."

"What?!"

"And that was mostly an administration fee. It's not big enough to build on, so it has no real value."

"How marvellous!" Ellie tried not to cry. She knew it had not been a noble ambition to covet that picturesque spot, but for her it had always seemed a treasure. Now it was hers. With sudden realization, she asked, "Was this your mysterious wedding business in Toronto a few weeks ago?"

"It was, actually."

How ironic that he had gone to the city to purchase this for her, while she had almost drowned swimming back from the island in his absence. "I thought I couldn't be happier, but this is... so thoughtful and... overwhelming."

He kissed her and said, "You're so easy to please."

Pulling herself together, she retorted, "I beg to differ! It took someone special to convince me that I truly wanted to be a wife." She grinned and said, "And I'm afraid that's the only present I have for you."

He gazed at her tenderly. "I want nothing more. Except for you to be well again. And I'm sure that will happen." As he stroked her cheek, he added, "In the meantime, you'll be able to enjoy setting up a home, with an office, of course, so that patients can come to you." They were planning to spend a few days in the city, searching for a house.

"An adventure!"

"Not a European honeymoon, I'm afraid."

"We'll do Paris some day. This is really so much more fun right now."

"I know that you mean that. I can't tell you how much I love you, Eleanor Roland."

"Just tell me often."

"Or show you," he said, nuzzling her neck.

"Even better."

•   •   •

Silas took Phoebe into his arms and swung her about exuberantly. Feeling his excitement, she laughed delightedly. When he set her down again he exclaimed, "I've written a poem! A beautiful one. Not a tormented thought or gruesome word. And it's all because of you, Phoebe. You've brought me back from the brink."

She responded eagerly to his kiss. There lovemaking was a celebration of his joy and hope.

When he collapsed on top of her, spent, he said in anguish, "Oh, God, Phoebe, I've never made love to a girl before. You should have stopped me."

"Didn't you like it?"

He saw the wounded look in her eyes. "Of course I did! But I've taken advantage of you. Compromised you."

"Poppycock! I wanted to make love to you. Does that make me wicked?"

He kissed her gently. "No, only honest."

"Does that mean we can get married?" she asked hopefully.

"I expect we should. You are my muse, Phoebe."

Her laugh rang out through the woods, mingling with the trilling of the birds. "Can we go and tell Papa right now?" she asked eagerly.

"Yes. Well. I suppose we should," he said tentatively, overwhelmed with events. He hadn't considered marriage and settling into a responsible routine, finding it difficult just to take care of himself. So a moment of careless abandon had just launched him into a life-altering future.

Even being in the canoe with Silas was an unaccustomed thrill for Phoebe. She was suddenly his and a part of him. They would always do things together, like Ria and Chas or Edgar and Daphne. She would never again be alone, or feel left out at parties, where others seemed to speak a different language that she couldn't comprehend.

Silas was sweating by the time they reached Tumbling Rocks. What the hell was he doing? Yes, he loved Phoebe in certain ways, and she did inspire him. But could he truly share his life with her?

He had no more time to think. When they had docked, Phoebe gleefully pulled him up to the cottage.

Finding her father and step-mother, Irene, in the sitting room, Phoebe blurted out, "Oh, Papa, Silas wants to marry me! Isn't that splendiferous? He's such a clever poet, and his mother has a bookshop in the city, so we'll always be surrounded by books. He was a lieutenant in the war, don't you know."

The enormous summer home was intimidating enough, but meeting Phoebe's rather formidable father, Albert, made Silas's throat dry and palms wet. Under the searing scrutiny of Phoebe's father, he shriveled.

"Come into my office, young man," Albert ordered.

Silas gave Phoebe a half-hearted smile and followed her father with trepidation.

When they had settled into the leathery office, Albert demanded, "What are your intentions?"

"As Phoebe said, Sir, I would like to marry her," was all he could manage.

"Phoebe is... rather special."

"Indeed she is, Sir. She sees the world differently from most people I've met. She's so insightful, refreshing, honest. You know exactly where you stand with her." As Albert scrutinized him, Silas added, "Although I expect you were referring to her hearing voices, talking with God, seeing dead people."

Albert's eyebrows shot up in undisguised surprise. "That doesn't concern you?"

"I understand completely. She has helped me to regain my equilibrium, Mr. Wyndham. Rescued me from the hell of the trenches. I want to share my new life with her and make her happy." He tried to say it with total conviction.

"That's all very well, but I know nothing about you, young man, or your people."

"You might have known my father, Samuel, many years ago. He worked for J.D. Thornton before he died of pneumonia." It had never seemed important to tell Phoebe about his link with her world, which is another reason he felt so comfortable with her. She wouldn't care.

"Good God! Sam Robbins! Of course I remember him. J.D. had great expectations for him." And had bought his widow a bookstore so that she had some means to support herself and her son – this young man standing before him. Albert wasn't the only one who wondered if J.D. had another reason for being so generous to the lovely widow. "Well, I'll be damned!"

After a thoughtful moment, he said, "This is unexpected and quite wonderful!" He pumped Silas's hand vigorously. "Phoebe may seem strong and confident at times, but she is fragile, easily hurt. She doesn't understand artifice and pretence. And her candour can present difficulties socially."

"I promise I will look after her, Mr. Wyndham."

Edgar was not as convinced as his father that Phoebe's marriage was a good idea, since he knew how difficult her world sometimes became. It would take a strong and compassionate man to deal with that. He doubted Silas had ever seen her in the throes of a fit. He seemed a gentle but weak man, possibly not up to the challenge.

But how could Edgar dampen Phoebe's ecstasy and future happiness? He was not about to interfere yet again in his sister's life, still burdened with guilt over the affair with her baby. A boy who was now no longer far away from his unsuspecting mother.

Chapter 13

Now that Silas Robbins was to become part of the Wyndham clan, Phoebe insisted that he join them in their activities. She had already delighted in taking him around Wyndwood and introducing him to all her relatives, leaving Ria, in particular, flabbergasted. Silas was real after all, and an amazingly decent chap at that. "Will wonders never cease?" Ria said to Zoë.

So on Regatta day, Silas found himself thrust into the life of the privileged at the SRA Country Club. He hadn't initially considered that he was marrying into such a supremely wealthy family, so the realization that he need never concern himself with making a living, but could just indulge in his poetry, was extremely heady. Doubts about marrying Phoebe vanished. He could be a gentleman poet, and even travel to intriguing places to feed his imagination. So it was with growing confidence that he mingled with the many Wyndham friends at the Club.

Phoebe was proudly showing him off to everyone, and bubbling about their September nuptials. "We're going to have our honeymoon in the Rocky Mountains," she told Lizzie. "At the Banff Springs Hotel. I just loved it when I was there with Papa and Irene, and I'm sure that Silas will be inspired! We're going to stay until it closes for the winter."

"Even crazy Phoebe has managed to snag a husband," Lizzie whined to Jack when she caught him alone for a moment.

"A fortune hunter, I expect," Jack said dismissively.

There had been no Regatta for the last two years of the war, so people were eager now to resume that annual tradition. As usual, hundreds of vessels were moored or bobbing at anchor, and the neighbouring uninhabited "Silly Isles" were invaded by people lounging on blankets with brimming picnic baskets to hand. So popular were the events that spectators made the long journey from Toronto, returning home on special overnight trains. Thousands flocked in from the cottages and resorts on the three big interconnected lakes. Hotel launches sported colourful bunting, and trailed canoes and skiffs for their guests who were entering the races.

Esme and Alice battled hard to win the women's canoe race, Jack and Fliss triumphed in the mixed, with Justin and Toni coming in a respectable third, and Arthur won the sailing cup. Max and Freddie gave two of the Roland brothers a crowd-pleasing dunking in their final canoe tilting competition - a modern-day jousting event - to win that event. Zoë had agreed to come and watch for a while, baby in tow, of course, and was grateful to Freddie for having coerced Max into participating. Laughing and dishevelled, he was once again her lighthearted and fun-loving brother.

The races that generated the most buzz, however, were the motorboats.

The Seafords had installed a new Packard Liberty V-12, 360 horse power engine in Chas's pre-war thirty-two foot *Windrunner*. Stephen rode as his mechanic, and would be monitoring the competition, the course, and the engine, making any necessary adjustments and suggestions during the race.

As Chas pulled alongside Edgar, he shouted over, "You haven't a hope, Wyndham!" And gave him a big grin.

But he wasn't so sanguine when he saw that Stanford Vandemeer and Frank Sheridan both had newer runabouts. *Windrunner* had been designed to be a fast boat, but one that could carry almost a dozen passengers. The sportier boats with long decking, fewer seats, and powerful engines had the advantage.

Claire, looking out at the lake from her veranda bed, could hear the throaty roar of the boats long before they streaked past the opening to the bay. Aside from the delightful wind-dances of the many sailboats earlier, these were the only other events she could see. Esme and Alice had promised to come over later to tell her all about the day.

The race covered several circuits of an oval course, marked out by buoys, its turns tight and challenging. Those at the Club could see only one end, and Ria watched breathlessly as Chas pushed relentlessly around the curve, seeming about to tip the launch, spray shooting high above it. Edgar took them more sedately, especially after Stanford skidded and spun out on one of his, nearly colliding with another boat. The engine of one of the other contenders began spewing flames, which were quickly doused by the mechanic. All this excitement elicited gasps from the enthralled audience.

Chas won, just beating out Frank Sheridan, and Edgar, well behind, came in third, while several other boats had engine problems and didn't finish the race. There were huge cheers and the blaring of boat horns for the victors as they returned.

Frank congratulated Chas, "Well done! But I'll best you at the Port Sandfield Regatta next week!"

"Want to bet?" Chas replied.

"Damn right!" Frank asserted with a laugh.

Ria popped the champagne and handed Chas and Stephen each a glass when they had docked at the Country Club. "To your - our - first victory!" she said as they clinked glasses.

"That looked thrilling," Esme said as she joined them.

Not feeling it was his place to respond, Stephen just grinned. Chas said, "Yes, but we can go faster. And we will. I'm happy with the engine, but we can only push this hull design so far. Don't you agree, Stephen?"

"I do, Major. The more streamlined cedar hull of the new boat will make it lighter, but you can still have the mahogany decking."

"Good point. We want it to look majestic as it trounces the competition. But for now, you can tinker with the engine to see how much more horsepower you can coax from it for next week's race."

Esme was delighted that Chas was treating Stephen as a knowledgeable equal.

"So when Chas gets his new gentleman's racer, I'll take over this one and give him some competition," Ria announced.

"We'll see about that!" Chas retorted.

With the races over, the crowds departed. Members of the Summer Residents' Association would return later for the Regatta Ball.

Lizzie wasn't inclined to go, not wishing to see Lyle and Adele and the others, although this was one of the premier events of the summer. When her mother urged her, Lizzie told her what had happened with Lyle.

"I made a mistake when I married your father. Oh yes, I loved him, but part of that grew from how well he treated me. From his wealth. When that was no more, I had only the man, and he was weak, unable to care for his family. Love can't flourish on an empty stomach. Make sure your heart is tempered by good business sense. Jack has it right. The money will make him happier than any woman alone could. Lyle would be no good for you if his family disapproved of your union."

Lizzie knew she was right. Having experienced poverty and witnessed how it had eroded her parents' marriage, she had no wish to be tied to any man who wasn't substantially well off.

"So rise above them. Show them that you have class. Make him regret that he lost you. Meet someone new. But don't hide here," Marie advised.

"Yes, Maman."

"Wear your shimmering blue silk. I'll make you something special for Jack's wedding."

Lizzie grinned. "I will!" It was one of her favourites, and she had been saving it. Sleeveless and sinuous, the gown was a frostwork of crystal and onyx beaded embroidery. The stunning teardrop aquamarine and diamond earrings that Jack had given her for her birthday completed the outfit.

Marie was overwhelmed with pride for her children. Jack looked dapper and every inch a successful gentleman in his tailored formal black suit, while Lizzie was breathtakingly lovely. How could she truly regret having married Alex when she so admired and loved the children they had created?

Jack and Lizzie strolled over to the clubhouse in the gathering twilight. He was meeting Fliss there, the new Thorncliff boatman bringing Rafe and Sidonie as well.

Launches were pulling up to the docks where lanterns glowed invitingly. Music was already emanating from the long ballroom wing of the U-shaped building, and people wandered in and out of the French doors onto the flagstone patio. The two shorter wings housed billiard and Ping-Pong tables, and a bar lounge with cozy leather chairs where older gentlemen had already gathered to smoke cigars and talk business. Jack knew that deals were made as readily at these events as in offices.

The women were arrayed in their finest gowns, diamonds sparkling on nearly every bosom. But it was Sidonie who attracted the most attention when she swished into the room. Her seductive, midnight-blue gown, shot with silver and trimmed with jet sequins, was the perfect canvas for an exquisite peacock brooch studded with sapphires, emeralds. black opals, and diamonds set in yellow and white gold. Those who hadn't yet met her were eager for an introduction, so she was quickly surrounded by admirers.

Jack took Fliss's arm proudly, impressed that she managed to look confidently regal while being completely outshone by Sidonie. "You look absolutely lovely, Fliss," he said sincerely.

She beamed at him. "Thank you. I do think it must sometimes be a burden to be as beautiful as Sid," Fliss opined without rancour or envy.

Jack laughed, but thought her very astute. "You're probably right. But I expect Rafe may feel that even more keenly when he has trouble getting a dance with his wife. That's quite a work of art that Sid is sporting."

"Isn't it just! Rafe had the brooch made for her at Tiffany's when they were in New York. Sid wanted something more spectacular than Ria's dragonfly." Which Chas had commissioned from Tiffany's in 1914, and Ria was wearing tonight, as she usually did. Jack had the impression that it was her talisman.

"So what would you fancy?" he asked.

"I already have the best thing of all," she replied, displaying her ring finger. "But perhaps a matching necklace?"

"We'll drop in at Tiffany's in London, and you can tell them what you want. Earrings as well, don't you think?" He marvelled at his ability to offer this extravagance.

She hugged his arm. "I'm so excited I can hardly wait for our honeymoon!" They would be spending some time in London, where Jack had business to conduct with Lord Beaverbrook. Then they would head off to Lady Beatrice's villa in Cap d'Antibes, with a stopover in Paris.

"It can't come soon enough for me," Jack said truthfully, anxious to seal the deal.

She blushed. At Marjorie's request, Ria had recently explained marital intimacy to her, which had embarrassed them both and left Fliss apprehensive.

Lizzie, meanwhile, was trying hard to be graciously sociable. The Delacourt crowd seemed to be avoiding her, aside from Frank Sheridan, Blanche's fiancé, who said as they danced, "Bad luck about your sister. Hope she'll be OK, poor kid."

"Thank you. Why aren't *you* afraid to dance with me?" she challenged.

"One of my good friends went into the Saranac Sanatorium in New York two years ago, so I do know about the illness and understand what you're going through. I pray that she'll survive."

His look conveyed much more. That he was in love with this unfortunate girl, but knew he had no future with her. He'd been forced to give her up, and would now be shackled to bitchy Blanche, poor bugger.

Despite everything, Lizzie didn't lack for partners, although there was no one who interested her.

Lyle eventually cornered her, saying, "Will you dance with me?"

"Are you allowed?" she taunted.

"Lizzie, we need to talk."

"I don't think there is anything left to say."

"Please." He stared at her intently.

"Our song, isn't it?" she asked as he took her into his arms to *If You Were the Only Girl in the World*.

He winced. "I didn't want it to be this way, Lizzie. But I'm honour bound to marry Adele."

"That's not the impression I had when we had our special picnic," she sneered. "It was ungentlemanly and insulting of you to take advantage of me like that!" She tried to pull away, but he held her tightly and whirled her around so that she couldn't possibly escape from him.

"No, Lizzie. It was because I was falling for you," he murmured. "Hoping to get out of my commitment to Adele."

"But obviously you didn't."

"It goes beyond my desires and needs. I should have known that. Which is why I want to apologize. I never meant to hurt or mislead you."

Her eyes shining with unshed tears, she retorted, "I can't forgive you that easily! We *were* good together, Lyle. I thought we had something exceptional. Now please let me go." The plea was as much an appeal to stop tormenting her as to physically release her.

He did so reluctantly.

She rushed out into the night air, suppressing tears of anger and bitter disappointment. Realizing that she was in love with him.

•   •   •

Esme was getting used to sneaking away from dances in search of Stephen, but was still incensed that it was necessary. Since he wasn't on duty tonight, he would be home, so she made her way to Pineridge, and was surprised to discover a newly constructed wooden platform at the edge of the Seafords' property. Guests were using it as a dance floor, since music from the clubhouse infused the night.

Stephen had hoped, and indeed, expected, that Esme would wander over, so he had been lounging about the waterfront. He went up to her, saying, "Instead of having guests complain that the music was keeping them awake, we decided that they should join in the fun. Dad intends to build a roof, but that may not happen this summer."

"How clever!" Esme said with delight, sensing there was a bit of nose-thumbing at the exclusive Club as well. "You'll have to learn how to dance now, won't you?"

"I will if you care to teach me."

"Oh, yes," she replied, staring at him in the light of the half-moon.

"Somewhere more private," he suggested.

As they walked over to a stand of pines beside the lake, Esme said, "Don't you think that the war changed a lot of things? Like making us less class conscious?"

"Somewhat. But not to the point where I could feel comfortable dancing at the Regatta Ball," he said, as if reading her thoughts.

"Well, that's just wrong! You're as much a champion as Chas for winning the race today. It was your ingenuity that made the boat go faster, and Chas obviously relies on you."

"Perhaps, but only gentlemen can belong to the Club."

"Tosh! What does being a gentleman entail? Look at my cousin Jack. He was a waiter at The Grand, then he went off to become an Ace and a buddy of Lord Beaverbrook, and now he's about to marry Felicity Thornton."

"He's worked hard, for sure. But he's also a Wyndham."

"My Wyndham grandfather was just a poor immigrant whose family homesteaded in the backwoods. Like yours," she countered.

Stephen chuckled and said, "I won't win this argument, will I?"

"Absolutely not!"

"Then I really must learn to dance properly. In case I'm ever invited," he added with a smirk.

When he took her into his arms she melted against him. It felt so natural. Her attempt to teach him to waltz became less a lesson than an excuse to hold one another. She shivered with desire when he ran his fingers down her bare arm. When they were interrupted, they were barely moving.

"I was wondering what was shimmering down here. Thought it might have been the ghost from Spirit Bay, but I see you have a real visitor," Stephen's sister Jean declared with a hint of censure.

They sprang apart, and Stephen said, "Esme... Miss Wyndham was teaching me to dance."

"Oh yes," Jean drawled skeptically. "Well, perhaps *Miss* Wyndham would care to come in for a cup of tea, if she's not expected at the ball."

Esme realized that she would look ridiculous going into the inn in her bejewelled evening gown when everyone else was in work-a-day or leisure clothes. It was obviously her dress glittering in the moonlight that had given them away. "Thank you for the kind offer, Jean, but you're quite right that I must return to the ball. Do excuse me."

Under his older sister's scathing scrutiny, Stephen didn't offer to walk Esme the short distance back to the Club.

"What the hell are you doing, Steve?" Jean asked. "*Esme*? Have you lost your mind?"

"I like her."

"Don't be stupid! She's a nice enough rich kid, but not for the likes of you."

"Who's to say?" he retorted.

"Getting above yourself now that the Major has involved you in his racing, are you?"

"Stop being so negative, Jean. *Esme* is right that things have changed, that lines are blurred. You'll never accomplish anything different if you don't have some vision and ambition."

"Ambition to marry a Wyndham?" she asked, incredulous. "You might as well hope to fly to the moon."

"Why not?"

She snorted. "Just don't lose your job over this foolishness, or the partnership with the Major, or Mac will have your hide."

Stephen tried to refute her logic when she left him alone, but knew that she was right. His growing affection for Esme was a dangerous and probably unrealistic indulgence. He had no place in her world, and how could he expect her to fit into his?

Chapter 14

Ellie was delighted with the house she and Troy had found in the Annex neighbourhood, not far from her family home in Toronto. She had always loved that area of the city, just north of the university, with its dignified Victorian and Edwardian homes - some mansions, to be sure - sitting comfortably and solidly on quiet, tree-lined streets. Having belonged to a doctor, the house had a side entrance to a small waiting room with lavatory, and a sizable office, keeping the rest of the substantial residence private. With nine additional rooms and two bathrooms, it was larger than Ellie felt they needed, but Troy had impressed upon her that it was a good buy for $8000. If they had to convert any other dwelling to provide office space, it would be more costly.

They would take possession in mid-September, and Ellie was excited at the idea of furnishing and decorating their home. But for now, she was also happy to be back at the lake. And that she was on hand when Claire was informed that her room at the sanatorium was ready.

She and Troy were at Spirit Bay, along with Ria, Chas, Alice, Fliss, and Esme to bid farewell to Claire. Stephen was once again chauffeuring the Thornton yacht, but Ellie suggested that only Claire's immediate family accompany her this time.

Although sad to see her cousin leave, Esme was also disconcerted that Stephen avoided making eye contact with her. And feared there was a problem. She hadn't met him out fishing in the early morning since the ball nearly a week ago. Because Jean had seen them together, Esme speculated that his family was against their friendship as well. That was so unfair!

As they stood on the dock, waving goodbye to Claire, Ellie said, "How lucky it was that you had this place to offer her while she awaited admittance to the San. It's actually quite amenable to hosting invalids or convalescents. Even if only in the summer."

She looked pointedly at Chas, who guffawed and said, "What are you suggesting?"

"The Thornton Children's Retreat, where disadvantaged kids recovering from rheumatic fever or broken bones or pneumonia or whatever can spend a week or a month or the summer enjoying some fresh air and sunshine. Zoë could be involved with any physiotherapy required. She needs something like this to bring her back to life. Ria can organize the place like she did the soldiers' club in England, I'll be the doctor, Mum can be in charge of the medications, and we could even have a small lab to test samples, which Troy could look after." She had been giving this a lot of thought since the conversation about the inn at the engagement picnic.

They were all speechless for a moment. "What, no job for me?" Chas ribbed.

"You can take the patients on scenic boat tours in your new yacht. And help us raise funds. We won't charge them, of course, so we'll need lots of donations to run it."

"Doesn't the Hospital for Sick Children have a summer facility on Toronto Island?" Chas asked. "I'm sure we've donated money to that."

"Yes, the Lakeside Home for Little Children," Ellie said. "But they deal with more serious and infectious cases, like TB. I was thinking about the children convalescing at home in the smoky summer heat of the inner city, living in overcrowded and unsanitary conditions."

"But I bought this place for my boats. I don't want to have kids swarming all over them or falling off the cliff," Chas protested half-heartedly.

"You have a mile of shoreline."

"Only half a mile," Chas corrected.

"Section off the point and boathouse and put in a new dock for the retreat. Besides, we'll have succeeded if the children are well enough to get up to mischief. Just imagine how many lives you can touch and enrich."

Ria and Chas exchanged glances. She said, "I think it's a super idea!"

Remembering their pact when he had saved Ellie from drowning, Chas realized that this would help her to heal as much as the children. He grinned. "As long as Ria doesn't want to adopt them all. But 'The Spirit Bay Retreat' has a better ring to it. And you're going to need an endowment fund, so I'll start it off with $25,000."

"Oh!... Good Lord!... Thank you!" Ellie exclaimed in astonishment, throwing her arms around him and then Ria.

"I have only one stipulation," Chas said. "That you have the title of Executive Director and draw a decent salary, as determined by your Board, which will include Ria, Troy, Jack, Fliss, Justin, and me."

"I can agree to that," Ellie said happily.

"We'll have our work cut out for us, deciding what needs to be done to prepare for next summer," Ria said. "This is exciting!"

"It feels good to take the initiative for positive change, after the long war years of just reacting to situations," Troy mused, smiling lovingly at Ellie.

"You're right," Chas agreed. "And your wife is a very clever psychologist."

"You weren't hard to convince, " Ellie replied with amusement.

"How could I resist your and Ria's appeals?" he teased.

"Chas is too modest to admit that he likes helping people," Alice alleged.

He laughed.

"There's plenty of room to add at least a couple of beds to the Royal Suite, so we could have over sixty children at a time," Ria speculated.

"And if each one stayed an average of three weeks, and we had this place operating from mid-June until mid-September, we could help about two hundred and fifty children in one summer," Ellie declared.

"I'll organize concerts and other fund-raising events when we're back in the city," Fliss offered, having done plenty of that during the war.

"I can help with those," Alice volunteered.

"Me too," Esme said, glad to have something useful to do this winter. "And may I help you as well?" she asked Ria. "I want to learn from your experience in England."

"Of course you may! There are all kinds of less pleasant tasks, like bookkeeping, which I'm happy to share," Ria added with a laugh.

When Jack heard about the scheme, he remembered what Ellie had said to him the first time they had visited the Thornton mansion in Toronto. "I always knew you'd get Chas to ante up for a children's home, Ellie! You can count on our patronage as well." How important he felt saying that! "And I'd be happy to manage the investments."

"Which I know you'll do brilliantly. Thanks, Jack."

He was inordinately happy to be able to help out.

Zoë was more reticent. "I do think it's a wonderful idea, Ellie, but I'm not sure how much I can contribute."

"Ethan really doesn't need you all the time, and you must find something else that gives you a sense of purpose and fulfillment. I know that you would be perfect to oversee the children's rehabilitation. So please consider it. And Ethan can come with you, as there won't be any contagious children there. It's not as if you'd be spending all that much time at the Retreat. I expect my brother would have been completely supportive." It didn't hurt to use Blake as in incentive to motivate Zoë.

She winced. "I daresay you're right. And I will think about it." But at the moment, her heart wasn't in it.

Ellie knew not to push the point, expecting that Zoë would eventually embrace the idea. She had all year to think about it.

•   •   •

"A noble venture, indeed!" Roderick Mayhew said when Chas explained the plans for the Inn. "I trust that my services will still be required?"

"Rest assured that they will," Chas said. "In fact, I've been discussing some alterations to the layout with my architect friend, Frederick Spencer. We thought it best to expand the staff quarters by putting the nurses, cooks, and so forth into the back wing that your family now occupies. And to build a separate house for you. Perhaps set up near the road to act as a gate house, since we will be erecting a fence."

Mayhew looked astonished and was momentarily speechless.

"So I thought that you and I could wander around and decide where best to place it."

"Indeed! Indeed! Our own dwelling, you say? My word!"

He glowed even more when Chas suggested a spot on higher land, which had an extensive vista of lake.

"I've asked Mr. Spencer to design a three bedroom house with the sitting and dining rooms overlooking the lake. And a big veranda, of course."

"You're too generous, Major!"

"Not at all! You will have your work cut out for you, keeping everything well maintained now that the place will be used for more than the occasional guest or party, even if it does sit empty for almost nine months of the year." Chas turned to look at Mayhew. "And you're to inform me if there is any work for which you require help. I'm well aware that your lungs are damaged, and don't expect you to jeopardize your health."

"Most considerate and magnanimous. Thank you, Sir."

Suddenly pensive, Chas said, "Mr. Spencer's brother was gassed at Ypres. He didn't survive."

Solemnly, Mayhew said, "I'm thankful every day that I did."

Chas nodded. "As am I. Now." Their shared remembrance momentarily dissolved the difference in class. Chas was sure that Mayhew also heard the terrifying echo of the guns in his dreams.

"One more thing. Can you handle a carthorse?" Chas asked.

"Indeed, I can."

"Good, then I will arrange for you to have one. I noticed that there was a wagon and an old sleigh in the barn. That way you can easily fetch supplies from Port Darling."

"Will these riches never cease?"

"They have for the moment!" Chas said with a laugh. "Now let's mark out where to put the fence. It's going to be wrought iron, and you need only supervise the installation."

Work had already begun on the stables and paddock.

"Capital idea to have a fence about the property," Mayhew stated. "We had a bear sniffing a mite too close for comfort the other day, but Manitou scared him off." He patted the large puppy's head proudly, chuffed that he now had the means to keep a dog, especially one as beautiful as this blue-eyed Siberian husky.

"We certainly don't want any wildlife getting close to the children or the horses," Chas agreed. "So did you name him Manitou because he lives in Spirit Bay?" It was the Ojibwa word for "spirit".

"Indeed, I did. What could be more appropriate?"

"Well, Manitou will have the run of the place and probably steal the children's hearts," Chas said, scratching the dog's ears.

"He's good with Thomas," Mayhew said, referring to his two-year-old.

"You'll have to get him a sleigh so that Manitou can pull him about in the snow," Chas suggested with a grin. "That'll make them both happy."

Roderick Mayhew was dumbfounded a few days later when a parcel arrived from Eaton's. It was a child's sled, and the accompanying note read, "Save it for Christmas. From Santa Claus."

•   •   •

"I haven't seen you out fishing." Esme startled Stephen, who was in Chas's boathouse tinkering with *Windrunner's* engine.

"I've been busy," he replied, tensing at her presence; not looking up from his work.

"Preparing for the next race, I suppose."

"That's right."

Undeterred, but concerned by his curtness, she climbed into the boat and sat down. "If I teach you to dance, will you teach me something about engines?"

He looked at her in surprise, and showed her his grimy hands before wiping them on a cloth. "You don't really want to cover yourself in grease, do you?"

"Ria did when she was fixing her ambulance."

"For King and Empire, but she doesn't anymore," he pointed out.

"Well, I'll do it if that means we can still be friends." She stared hopefully, longingly at him.

Her vulnerability melted his resolve to avoid her. "We can still be friends without your sacrificing your hands."

She returned his smile, and was once again reminded of how well spoken he was. If he'd had no formal education beyond elementary school, that didn't affect his grammar, and probably wouldn't have helped his mechanical skills. Dress him in a tailored suit and he could easily pass as a gentleman - one who would set many hearts a-flutter. She admired Jack for being a self-made man, and respected Stephen in the same way. They hadn't had everything handed to them on a silver platter from birth. She'd be sure to mention that to Zoë.

"That's a relief!" she said joyfully. "But will you tell me a bit about what you're doing?"

When he had explained how he was tuning the exhaust to increase the effective horsepower, she admitted, "That's too clever for me. I will happily stick with my new job."

At his inquisitive look, she said, "You've heard about the Children's Retreat at Spirit Bay, haven't you?"

"Yes, and we're all impressed with the Major and Mrs. Thornton's generosity in converting the old inn into a convalescent home. And I can't tell you how thrilled the Mayhews are that the Major is building them a house."

"Well, Ria said that I could help her organize and run it."

"An interesting challenge."

"I'm excited do be doing something so useful and important. But it's unfortunate that the place can't be used in the winter as well."

"It would be impossible, even if the building were insulated. Once the ice starts to form and the boats can't bring passengers to Port Darling, there's no easy way to get here. Or back to the city again." He might as well spell out the realities of living here. If that didn't discourage her, then perhaps they did have a future together.

"Are you all stranded here in the winter then?"

"It's not as isolated as it used to be, now that there's a train station only twelve miles away in Bala. So we do get mail fairly regularly, and other supplies brought in by sleigh. Many of the innkeepers and even some of the shopkeepers, like the druggist, close up and live elsewhere in the winter, and don't return again until the steamers are back on the lakes in the spring. Since old Doc Rumbold died last year, we don't even have a doctor in the village. Any kid wanting to attend high school has to board with a family in Bracebridge, but not many parents can afford to send them. It's deceptive, because in summer, Port is bustling with activity, as you know, but the rest of the year it's a bit like a ghost town."

"Gosh! It sounds like a pioneer adventure."

"I suppose it still is. And not a life that many choose."

"But you like it?"

"I was born here. I love the lake in all its moods. I like the winter silence and tranquility. The only time I ever went to Toronto was when I enlisted, and I knew right away that I could never survive there." He watched her reaction carefully.

She seemed thoughtful and then said, "But there must be lots of winter activities. There's a community centre and a library at least."

"We curl and skate in the bay. There's a Christmas carnival. Occasional square dances that I never attend. Sure there are things to do, but no real cultural events once we can't make it to the Opera House in Gravenhurst. No glittering balls or fancy parties."

"You mean the ones I usually run away from?" She shot him a sly look, realizing he was trying to discourage her by painting such a bleak picture of life in Port Darling.

He chuckled. "Maybe. But I expect you'd miss them."

"You shouldn't make such assumptions," she countered.

They stared at one another, but the pregnant moment was interrupted by the coughing roar of an aeroplane as it descended nearby. They went out onto the dock and watched Bishop and Barker land the behemoth flying boat, which was obviously heading for the wharf at the point. They hurried along the shoreline path to greet the pilots. Not far behind them, Rupert and Miles came running from Silver Bay, shouting gleefully. By the time the two Billies had nosed up to the large dock, most of those from the Old Cottage were there.

"Ria said to drop in anytime," Bishop said to Chas. "Nearly lunch time, isn't it?" he added with a cheeky grin.

"Of course!" Chas said.

When the two pilots were on the dock, Bishop said, "Actually, you mentioned that you had an ace mechanic, Chas. The engine's running a bit rough, so we didn't want to head back to the city with it misfiring."

"You're in luck, because Stephen's right here," Chas said, introducing him to the pilots. "He's been fine-tuning the Liberty V-12 that he recently installed in my launch."

"Isn't that dandy!" Barker said cheerfully, since it was the same engine that powered their plane. "You won't mind having at look at ours then, Stephen?"

"My pleasure, Colonel. May I say how much I admire you both for your wartime exploits and also for your visionary enterprise."

"By all means," Bishop quipped.

"While Stephen investigates, we can offer you lunch," Ria said.

"And I wouldn't say 'no' to one of those doozy gin rickeys you concoct."

"Could we have a flight later?" Rupert asked. Miles was bobbing with excitement beside him.

Bishop laughed. "Sure, if your parents approve."

"Crackerjack!" Miles yelled as they went charging off home.

"Will you stay to lunch as well, Esme?" Alice asked.

"I expect I could. The boys can tell Mama where I am," Esme replied. She would have preferred to watch Stephen work, but at least she could see him again later.

They had drinks on the front veranda while the staff was alerted to provide additional fare for the visitors. Lunch was always a cold collation of various meats and cheeses, fresh bread, pickles and relishes, seasonal salads and fruits, tarts, squares, and cookies, all laid out on the dining room buffet where people helped themselves. They took their plates out to the long refectory table on the screened east veranda.

"So I see that Bert Cracknell wrangled some money out of you for a Curtiss Canuck," Bishop said to Chas.

He replied casually, "Oh, it's just a loan to an old comrade. I hope he makes a success of his venture."

"Had us scrambling to find a new pilot," Barker said. "But there are lots of good men out there."

"Competition for us if we don't hire them," Bishop said with a chuckle. "Mind you, Will's put together a crack team to do some stunt formation flying. We're all involved in the CNE this year." The Canadian National Exhibition was held annually at the Toronto waterfront at the end of August.

"What sort of stunts?" Alice asked.

"Flying in the squadron V-formation, peeling off at each side and plunging earthward, pulling up smartly back into formation. Pairs flying towards each other and one diving under the other at the last second. That sort of thing," Will explained.

"Golly!" Alice exclaimed, looking at him with alarm and admiration.

"That's sure to thrill the crowds," Ria said.

Grayson waited until they had finished eating before coming out to announce, "Stephen informed me that the aeroplane is repaired, gentlemen."

"Capital!" Bishop said. "Let's go see what the problem was."

Esme was eager to tag along.

Stephen was sitting on one of the dock benches smoking a cigarette. "A couple of the ignition wires were damaged, so they'd short out whenever they touched the metal," he explained. "Luckily, we have spare wires, so I've replaced them."

"Good chap! I don't suppose you'd consider coming to work for us? Lots of excitement in the city, " Bishop said.

"Not a chance!" Chas interjected. "Stephen's my right-hand man. Besides, he has boats in his blood, not aeroplanes."

"Like you, it seems," Bishop replied.

"That's right. I say, why don't we race you to the north end of the lake? I'll take as many passengers as you, just to make it fair," Chas said with a grin.

"Want to put money on it?" Bishop retorted.

Chas laughed. "Hardly, since I know you'll win. But it would be rather fun to see how well we can keep up. You owe me, Bish!"

"I never back away from a challenge!"

"May I come on the boat?" Esme asked immediately.

"And me?" Alice asked. Strangely, she had no fear of being on a boat, particularly since she could now drive one. It was only ocean voyages that she dreaded.

"Sure," Chas replied.

"You're not leaving me behind," Ria informed him.

"So you'll have the two boys..." Chas began to say to the Billies.

"And me, if I may," Olivia said she and her youngest sons approached them.

"Mama!" Esme said in surprise.

"Flora Eaton told me what a thrilling flight she had to the city," Olivia said.

"And did she tell you what her husband thought of that?" Bishop asked with a smirk.

Olivia laughed. "Indeed she did." To those who hadn't heard, she explained, "John met her at the Toronto harbour and was livid. Asked her how she, a mother of five, could risk her life like that. Then he drove so erratically up Yonge Street that she finally told him that the perils of flying were nothing compared to the danger of being in the car with him in his present state. He laughed, and harmony was restored."

"But when we took Sir John up later, he complained that the sense of danger was sadly lacking," Bishop said.

"I'm sure it will be exciting enough for me," Olivia confessed.

"Stephen will come with us, so we'll each have five," Chas said.

"You're on!" Bishop agreed.

"Starting now," Chas said with a grin.

"Oh, unfair advantage!" Barker protested. "We have to suit up our passengers."

"This cripple has to limp to the boathouse," Chas replied, moving swiftly now that he was becoming accustomed to his stiff leg.

The others laughed as they rushed along the path. They heard Bishop shout, "Fraud!"

There was a lighthearted but urgent mood as they piled into the launch. It felt a bit like a cat and mouse chase, Esme thought. As if it really mattered that they outrun the plane.

Chas pushed the *Windrunner* to her limit. Esme found it exhilarating to slice through the water at such a speed, the wind snatching her breath and sculpting her hair. The familiar landscape of the lake zipped past so that it flowed into a new panorama.

They were more than halfway up the lake when the plane caught up to them. It hovered overhead for a while, mocking and teasing, and then moved on, zigzagging around to give the passengers more of a view, but never straying too far from the boat.

When they reached the small lighthouse island not far from the Eatons' summer home, Kawandag, Chas waved his arm in defeat. The plane waggled its wings and then headed southwest to give the passengers a bird's-eye view of a smattering of the other sixteen hundred Muskoka lakes.

"Whatever you've done to the engine, she's definitely faster," Chas said to Stephen when they returned to the boathouse. "We should leave Frank Sheridan and the others bouncing in our wake in tomorrow's race."

In fact, *Windrunner* won all the local races that Chas entered. At the Bala Regatta, he took along three extra passengers to prove that his boat was more than a racer. Ria, Alice, and Esme were on board. With the other boats in close pursuit, Esme found it even more thrilling than racing against the aeroplane. When they all toasted their victory afterwards, she was delighted to be able to clink her glass to Stephen's. Surely he was one of them.

Chapter 15

Sidonie sat at her dressing table in her silk negligee, applying a light dusting of powder to her face and cleavage. Fliss and Jack were hosting a soiree at Thorncliff that evening with his sister, Emily, and her husband, Hugo Garrick, performing from his new Broadway hit. The Garricks had settled into the Spirit Bay Inn the previous week, after the place had been sterilized of any lingering TB bacteria.

Sid was looking forward to the evening, but also took a quiet moment to enjoy the view of the lake from her window. She felt surprisingly content. There was always plenty to do, interesting people to converse and flirt with, and moments of healing solitude. Here she could forget about all that she had lost, at least for a time.

Rafe came out of their bathroom scowling. "What's this?" he demanded, holding out her diaphragm.

"A Dutch cap."

"I know that! But why do you have it?"

"It's obvious, isn't it? So that I don't get pregnant."

"In case it's not mine?"

"Don't be so insulting, darling. I just don't wish to have a baby." She would never tell him that she didn't want a child because she had lost everyone and everything she had ever loved, and was afraid to have her heart broken again.

"But I do. Don't I have a say in this?"

"Not if you aren't going to carry it inside you for nine horrid months."

"So when will you be ready to have children?"

She should have noticed his increasing anger. "God knows. Perhaps never. I have no intention to feel ugly and cumbersome," she replied dismissively.

"We'll see about that!" he said, grabbing her wrist and pulling her up roughly.

"You're hurting me!"

He ripped off her wrap.

"Rafe, stop this instant! What are you doing?" she asked as he pushed her onto the bed.

"Exercising my rights," he snarled.

"I'm not in the mood."

"But I am!"

Scared now, she squirmed and punched, but he grabbed her wrists and lay heavily on top of her.

"Please don't do this, Rafe."

Not bothering with any foreplay, he tore into her. She stifled her cries, not wanting the rest of the household to know of her humiliation.

When he rolled off her she accused, "You bastard!"

"Your husband. Remember that," he threatened.

"Go to hell!"

"Not without you, Milady."

When he had stormed from the room, Sid rolled over and wept more abandonedly than she had ever allowed herself to after the deaths of her husband and brothers and other friends. For the first time in her life she felt truly alone.

She declined to come down to dinner, pleading a headache, and lay in bed with a cool cloth over her reddened eyes. And she ordered one of the maids to move all her belongings into a guest bedroom.

●   ●   ●

Fliss had decorated the white and gold ballroom with black netting sprinkled with scintillating silver beads and sequins to simulate a starry night sky. A glittering golden ball dangled from the central chandelier in imitation of a full moon. The grand piano had been wheeled in from the music room, which wasn't large enough to hold tonight's many guests.

Emily and Hugo began their performance with *Under the Moon* and then another tune from that show, before dazzling the appreciative audience with selections from the new musical.

While people helped themselves to refreshments in the dining room afterwards, the servants prepared the ballroom for dancing.

Sidonie downed several glasses of champagne before she had a chance to waltz with Chas. "Your brother is a brute," she told him.

He noticed how tense she was and frowned. "What's he done?"

She almost told him, but said only, "Profoundly disappointed me. I wish now that I hadn't married him."

"Surely it isn't as bad as that."

"At the moment."

"Is there anything I can do?"

"If only you could, my dearest friend." She stroked his cheek lightly, the intimate gesture inviting an embrace. The longing in her eyes spoke volumes more. "If only you could."

Ensnared by her need, Chas drew her close. "Did he hurt you?"

"Yes. In too many ways. I'm not sure if I can forgive him."

Recalling the effervescent, free-spirited girl he had once made love to, Chas said, "Sid..."

"No! Don't sympathize or I will lose what little control I have left. I'm sorry now that I even mentioned it."

He looked at her in confusion.

"I just wanted to know that someone still cared. Excuse me."

But he didn't let her go. "Sid, You know that I do."

"Yes. But never enough!"

Her anguish was so raw that he couldn't respond. A moment later, the veil had once more descended and she said, "I have no one to blame but myself. I'll just have to live with Rafe. Or not," she added flippantly as she sashayed away.

Ria had noticed the exchange and approached Chas with some trepidation. "What was that all about?"

"Sid is having second thoughts about marrying Rafe."

"That's hardly surprising. But surely none of our concern."

"Except that we should support our friends when they're in need."

"Of course. But you can't give Sid what she needs without breaking your own vows," she said snidely.

"Ria!"

"It's obvious she's still in love with you, Chas."

"I haven't encouraged her."

"I should hope not! But she's realized that Rafe isn't you after all."

"It's more than that. Rafe has done something, but she wouldn't tell me what."

"And if you confront him with vague suspicions, he will realize that his wife has gone whining to his brother, and that will cause even more discord between them. If Rafe's being cruel to her, Sid won't stand for it anyway. You have to stop trying to be the chivalrous hero, Chas."

Her sharp gaze challenged him. "You're right, of course," he admitted, somewhat reluctantly. "They have to work out their differences themselves."

Damn Sidonie for making Chas feel responsible for her, Ria fumed.

•   •   •

"I'm not coming to Saratoga Springs with you."

"But Sid, North Star is running in the premiere race, the Travers Stakes. It's a big society event. Just your cup of tea," Rafe said.

He had found her drinking alone on the pavilion veranda. She was still cold towards him, and he realized how seriously he had jeopardized their relationship when he had discovered that she had moved out of their room and locked her door against him.

"Look, Sid, I'm sorry about what happened yesterday. I lost my head."

"You raped me!"

"That's rather harsh."

"It's the truth! The archaic law might not consider it that, but if you had any sense of decency and affection you would respect the fact that my body is *not* your property, to be used as and when you wish."

He looked contrite. "I do love you, Sid. What can I do to make amends?"

"I've been giving that a great deal of thought. First of all, we will continue to have separate bedrooms. That is how it's done in polite society in any case. Percy never questioned it," she said, referring to her first husband. "I value my privacy. So be sure that you tell Freddie to design two master suites in our cottage. Secondly, you can double my allowance." He had already given her half a million dollars, which had been part of their prenuptial agreement. She was also entitled to a quarter of his net worth should they divorce for any reason except marital infidelity on her part. Rafe had added the stipulation that they be married at least five years before that condition was valid, so she knew that she couldn't leave him. Yet.

"You want $25,000 a year?" he snorted.

"If you can easily risk $50,000 on one horse race, then surely you can afford half of that to ensure your wife's happiness."

"Is that it, or am I to be further punished?" He was leaning against the railing, staring down at her.

"I shall be going to London for the autumn and will spend the winter on the Riviera. You may do as you wish." Thankfully, she still had her substantial Grosvenor Square townhouse in London from her first marriage.

He was damned if he was going to let her run away from him. "Sounds like fun. I'm game."

"And one more thing. I want to rename our island Blackthorn." The name of her ancestral Elizabethan estate, which she had so loved.

"Done! All of it." He sat down beside her and coaxed her hand into his. He raised it to his lips and kissed each finger sensually. "Do I have to woo you every time I want to make love to you?"

"Yes. And you had better do it well," she added with a smirk.

"Sounds exciting!" He took a blue Tiffany box from his pocket and said, "Let's start with this." It was to have been for her upcoming birthday, but this was more important.

"You can't buy my forgiveness, you know," she said, reluctant to open the box, knowing that she would need to be grateful to him. It felt too soon after yesterday's outrage, after being convinced that she hated him.

"I know that."

"I'm not ready for intimacy. You really hurt me."

He was taken aback by her uncharacteristic vulnerability. "Look, Sid, this is an apology, not a barter for sex. Let's say it's the beginning of my wooing. I'll play by your rules."

The earrings were exquisite teardrop sapphires dangling from a string of perfectly matched diamonds that looped around the sapphires and from which larger diamonds formed petals at the bottom.

"They're beautiful. Thank you, Rafe," she said simply.

He stroked her cheek. "Say you'll come to Saratoga with me."

She saw the tenderness in his eyes, so reminiscent of Chas. Perhaps there was hope for them after all. "Alright."

Chapter 16

"But, Mama, Ria said that Alice may go, and she's letting us use her launch," Esme entreated.

"I don't think it's wise for two young girls to drive that distance alone," Olivia replied.

Esme and Alice were planning to visit Claire at the sanatorium. Now that her fevers had stopped, Claire was allowed to receive visitors.

"Honestly, Mama! We're not *that* young! Chas gave us navigation charts of the lakes, so we know the route exactly." Flippantly she added, "I promise we won't pick up any men."

"Esme!"

"Well, what are you worried about, Mama? That we'll be abducted by white slavers? We can outrun them in *Dragonfly*."

"Don't be sassy! There are all kinds of difficulties that you could encounter. It's at least twenty-five miles, and you have to lock through at Port Darling."

"I've helped do that a dozen times, so I do know how. Couldn't you please trust me, Mama?" Esme pleaded.

"I'd be happier if you went on one of the steamers," Olivia confessed.

"They take ages, since they have so many stops to make." Esme tried to suppress her mounting frustration.

"Perhaps if you took the boys along..."

"That's too many people to visit Claire at one time, and the boys would just get bored if they have to wait around. I don't want to have to look after them," she added pointedly. It was insulting to think that thirteen and fifteen year old boys should somehow be *her* guardian when she had always been required to be theirs.

"Zoë wasn't much older when she went off to war. How can this little jaunt cause you any concern at all?" Esme challenged.

Olivia couldn't stare down her headstrong daughter, so she conceded, "Well... alright."

"Smashing! I'll ask Mrs. O'Rourke to prepare a picnic lunch for us."

Esme hadn't told her mother that Chas had suggested she stop in at the Seaford Boatworks and ask Stephen, who was working there today, to point out some of the danger spots. With fluctuations in the water level, especially after a hot and dry summer, hidden shoals could suddenly become a hazard.

They arrived in Port Darling as boats, including one of the steamers, were filing in to lock upstream, giving the girls plenty of time to talk to Stephen. Esme felt excited and nervous as she went into the Boatworks. Stephen's face lit with happy surprise, and she smiled broadly at him.

When she told him what they were up to, he said, "That's adventuresome of you."

"Do you think so? Mama wasn't pleased, but finally relented when I pointed out that at least I wasn't going off to war, like Zoë did."

He chuckled. "It's always good to keep things in perspective."

He showed them the same route that Chas had pointed out, and said, "Be careful not to wander out of the channel in this area, since there are some underwater rocks that aren't deep enough in August. And anytime you spot seagulls that look like they're standing instead of swimming, steer well clear!"

They laughed.

"Do you need help locking through?" he asked.

"Thanks, but I think that Alice and I can... *should* manage, just to prove ourselves capable."

"Enjoy your trip, and please do give my regards to Miss Claire."

"We will. Thank you, Stephen."

Their eyes locked for a meaningful moment, which wasn't lost on observant Alice. On the way back to the boat, she accused, "Esme Wyndham, you didn't tell me that you had a romance brewing with Stephen!"

Esme was shocked.

"Don't deny it! You both look love-struck! Oh, do tell!"

"Did you truly think that he is as well?"

"Absolutely!"

Esme said elatedly, "I think I *am* in love, Alice! But you mustn't tell anyone! Promise?"

"Of course, but why not?"

"He's not from the right social strata, according to Mama," Esme said.

"Oh, dear. That could make things tricky for you," Alice sympathized. Then she grinned and said, "But I can't see that stopping you."

Esme giggled. "You already know me too well."

"I think you are more Ria's sister than Zoë's at times." With her blonde hair, Esme even looked a bit like Ria.

"Zoë can be quite stubborn when she needs to be."

"True enough. Anyway, you have to tell me how all this came about."

Esme was eager to talk.

"So you'd be happy to marry him and settle down in Port Darling?" Alice asked.

"I think so. Of course, Mama will insist on a long engagement. Zoë was twenty, but Mama probably wouldn't have approved of the quick wedding if Zoë hadn't been working in England in wartime. Gosh, wasn't it fortunate that she and Blake didn't wait? At least they had a little time together, and a sweet baby."

"Stephen's a bit older, so he may not want to wait much longer."

"Perhaps we'll elope!" Esme said with a smirk.

"You wouldn't!... Would you?"

"Only if it were really necessary," Esme assured her. "But I suppose I shall have to wait until I'm twenty-one before I could even do that, since I can't marry until then without my parents' permission. Unless we just lived in sin."

"Esme!" Alice admonished, and then giggled.

But Esme wasn't at all certain that Stephen would risk everything to be with her. Hadn't he made it plain that he intended to stay in Muskoka? If he really loved her, he would surely wait for her to come of age.

Having pretty well memorized the chart of Lake Muskoka, which she didn't know as well as her own lake, Esme drove confidently and quickly. She was pleased to see familiar landmarks, like the stately Beaumaris Hotel. Since it was about halfway, they stopped there, letting the boat drift offshore while they ate sandwiches and drank lemonade, and envisioned their futures.

It was sobering then to enter the sanatorium, where people's lives had been put on hold, if they survived at all.

Claire's room, on the second floor, was bright and cheery with a tall window and French double doors that opened onto her private, sunny veranda. The screened windows on two sides overlooked the rugged granite bluff and sparkling water. She was reclining on a chaise lounge fitted with a mattress.

"Oh, how wonderful that you could come!" she greeted them.

"This is delightful" Alice proclaimed, as she and Esme drew up chairs.

"It is. I love looking at the rock and watching the passing boats on the ever-changing lake, and wish I could paint them. I'm not allowed up yet, but at least I'm not flat on my back all day anymore."

"Do you sleep out here then?" Esme asked, for the wheeled bed stood waiting.

"Oh yes. We're only allowed to sleep in our rooms in winter, so for now that's where we wash and dress. Mary says we have to spend our days out here no matter the weather. Mary has the room next door, and we usually leave the partition open between our balconies, but the nurses close it when we're supposed to be resting or they think we're talking too much." Claire grinned. "Mary says that it sometimes snows in."

"Gosh!" Esme exclaimed.

"I'm not looking forward to that! Mary says the nurses cocoon us in a dozen blankets, and then wheel us out here for a good part of the day. The windows are only closed if there's a blizzard."

"So that they don't have to shovel you out," Esme said with a grin.

"You do look better," Alice observed, for Claire was no longer so hollow-cheeked and wan.

"I *feel* better! All we do is eat six times a day and rest, and I can barely do either anymore." She never thought that she would complain about having too much nourishing food to eat when there had often been too little in her childhood. "I haven't even been allowed to read anything but letters, so thank you both for my daily mail! It's keeping me from complete despair. But I'm itching to get up and do something. If my fever doesn't return, I'll be able to take my meals downstairs in the dining room next week. But I still won't be getting properly dressed, even though there are men around," she giggled.

"We heard that, so we've brought you something pretty," Esme said, handing Claire a parcel. "In case there's a special fellow you want to impress."

"Oh, they're divine!" Claire said of the sky blue silk pajamas and Oriental-style satin dressing gown embroidered with exotic and colourful flowers.

"Next time we'll have to bring you a fur set," Alice quipped.

"Jack is getting me a fur coat and hat and mitts and all that. Mary even has a fur blanket."

"How long has Mary been here?" Esme asked.

"Since the place opened three years ago. She's having weekly pneumothorax treatments now, which she says aren't quite as bad as they sound. They inject air into your chest to collapse your lung so it can heal."

"Good Lord!" Alice exclaimed. "Do you have to have that done as well?"

"Only if I don't make good progress, the doctor said." Claire was crestfallen as she confessed, "I can't imagine being here for years. Even the people who are healing and are allowed out for exercise have to have two-hour rests mornings and afternoons, and be in bed by nine."

Being deprived of mental and physical stimulation, Claire had been making up stories to entertain herself. First they were about being cured, so she envisioned herself swimming and painting and dancing with a handsome young man who would be her future husband. But once those had become stale, she conjured up elaborate spirit worlds and fairylands, and imagined how they would look when she was finally able to paint them.

"Ellie did say that it would be a challenge to be idle and resting," Esme reminded her. "Now we mustn't ask you any more questions. Matron was adamant that we do most of the talking. If you end up worse after our visit, she won't let us come back."

So they caught her up with the latest news until a nurse came in with a glass of milk and raw egg, and declared that it was quiet time. Esme and Alice promised they would visit as often as possible, but of course, that would become difficult once they returned to the city in a few weeks.

It was late afternoon when they headed back north. Alice drove the first leg of the journey, with Esme navigating them through the narrows and islands. As they were nearing Beaumaris, they detected a change in the throaty roar of the engine. Esme noticed black smoke coming from the exhaust and told Alice to stop the boat.

"Oh dear, the temperature gauge is reading too high," Esme said. "When Edgar taught me how to drive, he said it shouldn't go above 170."

"I knew I was too inexperienced to take the helm," Alice lamented.

"Tosh! You didn't do anything wrong. We'll let the engine cool down for a few minutes."

But when Esme tried to restart it, she had no luck. "I hate to admit it, but we need help." She tooted the horn in an approximation of the SOS distress signal. "I'm sure someone will come to our aid."

After a few minutes, Alice said, "Oh, look! There's a boat heading out from that island."

They waved their arms wildly.

"Rather handsome fellows coming to rescue us," Alice noted as the runabout closed in.

"It seems that we're picking up men after all," Esme said. They giggled.

"Will your Mama be scandalized?"

"Unfortunately not. I recognize the driver. Martin Daventry. From the publishing house, you know?"

"Golly!"

"The cottagers around here belong to the Beaumaris Yacht Club and have their own golf course and tennis courts, so we don't often see them at the Country Club, although most do belong to the SRA. I danced with Martin at the Regatta Ball. But I don't believe I've met his passenger." The Beaumaris crowd rarely came to SRA dances, because it was a long way to go and more difficult at night to navigate the river that connected the two lakes.

As the men pulled alongside, Martin said, "Miss Wyndham. A pleasure to see you on our lake. Allow me to introduce Ted Lorimer. I'm attempting to convince him that his family needs a cottage in Muskoka."

"Surely no persuasion is required now that he's seen it for himself," Esme said.

"Spot on, Miss Wyndham," Ted Lorimer replied. "And the more I see of what other beauties abound here, the more inclined I am to become a member of this illustrious summer community," he added with a grin.

Esme was used to the flirtatious remarks of confident young men, but Alice blushed.

"Gentlemen, this is my very dear friend, Alice Lambton. She's a ward of Ria and Chas Thornton."

"A pleasure, Miss Lambton," Martin Daventry said. "Ted and I were inspired by Major Thornton's exploits, and met while we were both training to be RFC pilots at the School of Aeronautics at U of T. But the war ended before we could be deployed."

"How fortunate for you," Esme said, knowing that his only brother had been killed at Passchendaele.

"On the contrary. We're dashed fine pilots, but had no chance to cover ourselves in glory. Now, ladies, how may we render assistance?"

"The engine won't start because I think it overheated," Esme explained.

"We'll tow you over to our island. Then we'll take you home and you can send your mechanic along to fetch the launch," Martin suggested.

The men coupled the boats together by securing ropes around the cleats. Then they slowly made their way to a small, verdant island.

"Welcome to Neverland," Martin Daventry said when they had docked.

"How charming!" Alice exclaimed.

"How could we not give it a literary name, being in the book industry? Treasure Island was out, Crusoe is that island over there in the distance, and Tempest wasn't whimsical enough," Martin said. "May I offer you some refreshments before we head out?"

"Thank you, but we're expected home, and mustn't be late," Esme said. "Perhaps another time?"

"Absolutely!"

Martin drove at a leisurely pace to allow for conversation, so Esme said, "Mr. Daventry, you may be interested to know that Miss Lambton has published articles in *Home Fires*, and is writing a book."

"Esme!" Alice protested.

"Indeed? What's the subject?" Martin asked, almost warily.

"Friends have been trying to persuade me to write my account of the *Lusitania* sinking," Alice admitted reluctantly.

"Good Lord!" Ted Lorimer exclaimed. "You were on the *Lusitania*?"

"It's where I met Ria Thornton. We sort of saved each other."

"Now *that* I am interested in," Martin said. "People claim to be saturated by anything to do with the war, but in a few years, memoirs and thinly disguised fiction will become the rage," Martin predicted. "And I intend to be ahead of the game. You'll give me first option on it, won't you, Miss Lambton?"

"Of course, Mr. Daventry!" Alice could barely hide her excitement.

"Tell me more about your work. But first, shall we drop the formalities and call each other by our Christian names?"

After they had locked through in Port Darling, they tied up along the wharf outside the Seaford Boatworks. Esme had intended to go in by herself to speak with Stephen, but the others accompanied her. And she noticed that he was not as pleasantly surprised by her visit this time.

"Have you had a problem, Miss Wyndham?" he asked with concern as he came to her side.

She explained what had happened.

"You did the right thing to shut off the engine, or it might have caught fire. I'll see to it tomorrow. Can I give you a lift home?"

"That won't be necessary, my good man," Martin Daventry said dismissively. "We shall accompany the ladies."

Esme hid her irritation at his condescending manner as she said, "Did you know, Martin, that Chas is in partnership with the Seaford brothers? They're building him a gentleman's racer, as well as other boats. You might have seen Chas and Stephen win a few races this summer, including the one at Beaumaris."

"Yes, of course. But I didn't realize that Chas had gone from banking to boat building. Well, shall we be on our way, Esme?"

Esme threw Stephen a surreptitious and sympathetic glance.

He grimaced. Chas had never patronized him, but others of the upper class had, so that wasn't what bothered him. It was seeing Esme the object of admiration from the kind of men that her family wanted her to marry. How could he possibly compete?

•   •   •

"Mama practically said 'I told you so'. Papa pointed out that Alice and I had responded to the situation appropriately, and no harm was done. And Chas told them that no one was to blame, since you discovered that seaweed had clogged the impeller and prevented the engine from being properly cooled," Esme said to Stephen. "I got Chas to explain that to me so that I can speak of it with some authority," she added with a laugh.

She was sitting in Ria's boat at The Point while he was making further repairs to the engine. It had been almost a week since they'd had a chance to talk in private.

"I'm sure you impressed those young men," Stephen said.

"Put them in their place, you mean."

"They're here every day, so I doubt that's the case."

Was he jealous, Esme wondered. Surely that meant that he truly cared for her.

"Martin is trying to encourage Alice to get to work on her book, and to persuade Chas and Ria to write their own memoirs of their wartime experiences."

And Ted Lorimer was targeting Esme, Stephen thought. He managed to be on hand occasionally to tie up Daventry's Ditchburn, and had noticed Lorimer's interest in her.

"I suspect that Arthur Spencer's a bit put out by Martin's zeal, because he thinks that Martin has designs on Alice. So he has valiantly become her protector." And therefore visited daily as well.

But, of course, Stephen couldn't engage in any territorial claims over Esme. He cursed inwardly when he heard what was surely Daventry's launch. "Your company's arriving, I think. Is it tennis at the Country Club today?" He tried to keep his tone light, and not allow any bitterness to creep in, but Esme sensed it.

"An outing, with some other friends coming along. Ria invited the Beaumaris crowd to stay here so they can attend the dance at the Country Club tonight. I'll try to sneak away, if you want another lesson." She looked at him hopefully.

He grinned and said, "I think I do need more practice."

She smiled happily.

He walked down to the dock with her, arriving at the same time as Alice and Arthur, just as the launch pulled in. Stephen tied it up and then accepted the overnight bags that were handed to him.

The two elegant young women with chic hats were introduced as Martin's older sister, Esther, and younger, Lucy.

As they chatted on the dock, Ted suddenly ran his forefinger provocatively along Esme's cheek, startling her.

"I do beg your pardon," he said. "But I had this sudden inspiration for a slogan for soap - one of my father's new accounts." His father had an advertising agency. "*For skin that he will love to caress.*"

"Isn't that a bit risqué?" Martin Daventry asked.

"Not at all. Sexual innuendo is being used in all kinds of ads these days. And Esme could be the face of Snow Pure Soap. What do you think?" he asked her. "You could be the model for our artist."

Stephen tried not to clench his fists.

"Gosh, I'm flattered, but no. Mama would never allow it either." For once she was glad to be able to use that as an excuse.

"A pity," Ted Lorimer said. "But I still like the line, which you inspired, Esme."

"You'll have to pay her royalties then," Arthur Spencer said.

"In some form or other," Ted acknowledged, giving Esme a wink.

"I'll show you to your rooms," Alice offered, "and then we can head out on our picnic."

Esme was staying at the Old Cottage for a few days, kipping in with Alice and Sophie. She preferred being there, not only because she was closer to Stephen, who was usually working in the boathouse, but also because she chafed under her mother's rules and expectations. Besides, now that Claire was gone and Zoë had her own room, she had no one sharing hers, so it was more fun to be here.

After their outing, the friends had a pre-dinner swim in the west bay near the boathouse. Esme could sense Stephen watching them, and tried not to respond more than civility dictated to Ted's flirtations.

Stephen had to admit to himself that he was damned jealous. In her sleek, modern swimsuit that was more revealing than concealing, Esme was incredibly sexy, and undoubtedly aroused the other men as well as him. He would have enjoyed indulging in the carefree playfulness of these privileged young people. But he had to stop imagining taking her into his arms with only the scantiness of their wet bathing suits between them. And he had to stop fuming that Ted attempted to do just that with Esme. Like an eel, she kept eluding his grasp, but Stephen wondered how long it would be before Ted won.

He didn't actually believe that she would be able to sneak away to meet him outside the Country Club that evening, but stood in the shadows of a copse of trees at the boundary of the property, waiting. Since it was Wednesday night, the dance didn't have to end at midnight as it did when Saturday gave way to the Sabbath. But he'd wait until he saw the Wyndwood crowd leave, even if he had to stay up half the night. Part of him knew that it was stupid to be enthralled with someone so far above him. So unattainable.

It was close to midnight when she appeared, like a wraith, hurrying toward him as if by instinct. When he took her into his arms, their kiss seemed so natural. He pressed her to him as though they could meld their souls.

Breathlessly, she said, "Oh, how I wish I could stay! But they'll miss me. Stephen…"

He stopped her with another searing kiss. "Don't say anything, Esme. Just go."

But as she turned reluctantly to leave, Stephen became aware of three unusual things: the increasingly strong smell of smoke, more pungent than the local fireplaces and campfires; a red glow above the treetops; and the faint but frantic chiming of church bells.

"There's a fire in Port Darling!" he cried.

As he ran off to the Inn to get help, Esme rushed back to the Clubhouse. She told Chas and Ria, who were ostensibly acting as chaperones for her friends.

Suppressing his fear of fire, Chas said, "I'd better go and help. I hope it's not the Boatworks. Ria, why don't you take the girls home in *Windrunner*, and I'll round up some chaps to come with me."

"We can all help with the bucket brigade," Esme stated, remembering how the others had fought the fire at Wyndwood in '14, while she had been tasked with looking after her younger brothers and Grandmother.

"She's right," Ria said. "And I'm not letting you go alone," she added firmly to Chas, fearing that he might have a paralyzing attack of nerves when confronted by flames.

The Wyndwood crowd headed out, while Fliss and Jack offered to fetch Ellie in case her medical help was required. The word spread, and others, like Lyle and his party, also hopped into their boats.

When Chas entered the narrows where the lake flowed into the curving river, they could see flames shooting high above the trees, the brightness lighting their way. The ominous crackling and snapping was terrifying. But they were still awed by the conflagration that was reflected in the still water of Chippewa Bay. It appeared that hell had opened before them, Esme thinking - foolishly, she knew - that they might be sucked down into it.

Up on the hill to the north of the lock, the Crowhurst Hotel was ablaze and the Methodist church beside it was already alight. Then a house on the other side of the hotel caught fire. They threatened the wharf-side shops below them, including the Seaford Boatworks. Villagers, some still in their night attire, had formed bucket brigades, while volunteer firefighters had only one hose, which made little impact on the inferno.

"Dear God!" Ria exclaimed. "The entire north end of the village could burn down."

"There's so much inflammable stuff in the Boatworks," Chas said gravely, thinking of the gasoline and varnish and volatile solvents inside.

They also knew that if the fire spread into the woods that hugged Port Darling, everything from here to the Spirit Bay Inn and beyond could go up in smoke. Forest fires often burned for weeks, incinerating thousands of acres. The flames might even race along the wooden bridge and consume the rest of the village to the south of the river, and head towards Beaumaris.

Chas parked the launch at one of the docks on the far side of the island, near the dam, and they scrambled out. "You ladies stay here," he said. "It's too dangerous to get close to the Boatworks."

"That's an order," Martin said sternly to his sisters.

"Absolutely!" Ria said, looking sharply at Alice and Esme before she followed Chas.

"Ria, go back!" he urged.

"Not without you!"

"There's no time to argue."

"Then let's go."

He shook his head as they hurried off, accompanied by Arthur, Martin, and Ted. Esme was pleased to see that their new friends were eager to help, since they had doffed their dinner jackets and rolled up their sleeves.

Esme said to Alice, "You should stay here, but I'm not their ward, so I don't have to obey."

"Piffle!" Alice retorted. "Anyway, I will heed the spirit of the command, if not the letter. I'm sure that there are things we can do to help without getting too close to the Boatworks or the fire."

"I'm game!" Lucy declared.

"You could organize a spot for Ellie to set up a clinic," Esme suggested. "See if the community centre can be used as a shelter for all those who will be without beds tonight. Perhaps borrow blankets and pillows from inns south of the lock."

Esme ran along the shoreline of the island, up the slope to the swing bridge, and down the other side to the wharf. Strong men dipped buckets into the water and then passed them along a line of willing hands to finally be poured onto the flames or the buildings that were in imminent danger. The employees of Carver's General Store were hastily piling merchandise onto their supply boat - a large steamer that made twice-weekly deliveries to cottagers. The druggist next door was likewise moving out boxes of supplies from his shop onto a wagon, fearing the worst.

At the Boatworks, Stephen and Mac were dragging out tins and barrels and passing them to Chas and the others, who put them into the skiffs that the Seafords rented by day, as well as the seaworthy boats that had already been moved out from their slips in the workshop. Arthur wet tarps and threw them over each load. Young men were asked to take the boats far out into the bay, away from the dangerous heat and sparks.

An explosion caused Esme to duck and cringe. Another building on the hill had ignited, raining ashes on them. There were more explosions, and Esme saw a flaming can shoot up, followed by a barrel, which sprayed its blazing contents over a wide arc that nearly reached them.

"Christ that's McFarland's Carpentry Shop!" Mac shouted. "It's filled with paints and solvents." And it was directly above them.

Esme was scared, not so much for herself as for Stephen, who had climbed onto the roof, which he was soaking with water from the buckets that were being passed along and up a ladder to him. She could feel the heat of the inferno that was creeping ever closer, see the still-hot sparks that sizzled out as they hit the wet roof. Stephen had wisely poured water over himself, but looked vulnerable amid the fiery shower. No one spotted her as she joined the short bucket line, relieving one of the teenagers who'd offered to row a skiff to safety.

The thick black smoke had become nauseating, laced now with toxic fumes from burning paints and turpentine.

Jack, Troy, Freddie, and Justin arrived with several pumps that they had wisely picked up from friends as well as from Wyndwood, Jack having alerted all their neighbours. They spread out along the wharf to spray the buildings that were in the greatest danger and within reach of the relatively short hoses. Stephen was able to come down from the roof, and the bucket brigade took a break.

It seemed that nothing could save the buildings up on the hill. Everyone had to draw back from the continuous explosions. The people who lived in the vicinity were rescuing as many of their precious belongings as they could, aided by fellow citizens and guests from nearby hotels. Everyone was out helping, and wary, wondering when they should start looking to save their own homes and businesses.

Alice had arranged for Ellie to use the community centre, south of the lock, where weary people were coming to be refreshed by tea and sandwiches provided by ladies from the Women's Institute. Alice, Esther, and Lucy were charged with informing the populace, but didn't go beyond the bridge, to which people were retreating in any case. Some arrived with horse-drawn wagons piled high with random furnishings and even cages of squawking chickens and the family cow plodding along behind.

Ellie was treating minor burns and abrasions, a wrenched wrist and sprained ankle, and people overcome by smoke. Mr. Crowhurst, whose popular hotel was now in ruins, was among them. He had valiantly helped his guests to safety, but tears streaked his smoke-blackened face as he said, "We'd got them all out. All of them, even though we barely managed to reach the staff sleeping in the attic. But there was a young war widow who realized with great anguish that she had failed to take the string of pearls her husband had bought her for their wedding. I tried to stop her from going back inside." He lowered his head and shook it. "No one saw her come out."

"How tragic!" Ellie commiserated. "But you did what you could and saved many lives, Mr. Crowhurst. You mustn't blame yourself. You're a hero, you know."

His shoulders shook. She patted him on the back and handed him a double shot of brandy in a teacup. "Doctor's orders," she said. She had brought a supply of booze to help calm nerves, possibly the most useful aid she could give tonight, she though wryly.

Back at the wharf, more powerful pumps had arrived from some of the lake resorts, and managed to spray the shops and homes bracketing the blaze. Thankfully, it was still a calm night, and the fire finally lost its rage.

Stephen, Chas, and the others began to relax.

"Well done, chaps!" Chas said. "And ladies."

"Esme, your mother would rake me over the coals if she could see you now," Ria chided her cousin.

"Do I look as much like a chimney sweep as you do?" Esme asked with a chuckle.

"Most definitely!"

"That was plucky of you to join us," Ted said in admiration. They all had smudged faces and sooty clothes.

"I hate being left out," she quipped.

Stephen went around shaking everyone's hand in gratitude. To Esme he said, "I'm afraid you've spoiled your lovely gown, Miss Wyndham." He subtly stroked the palm of her hand as he held it momentarily, giving her delicious shivers.

"It's of no consequence," she replied. "I'm glad I could help."

Troy said, "Ellie brought a supply of fortifying spirits, so we should go and find her."

Mac stayed behind to make sure all was well, although he and his staff would wait for a while before unloading the boats, which were now tied up along the wharf. So Stephen joined the group of friends who made their way up to the bridge.

They were nearing the pharmacy, where Mr. Mercer was already confidently restocking his store, when Stephen noticed a quick sleight of hand by a couple of locals. Trick Butcher, who was helping to move things back inside, grabbed a bottle of "medicinal" scotch from a crate and passed it to his brother who tucked it under his jacket and dashed away. When Mr. Mercer realized a bottle was missing, he said, "Hey, who's been pilfering my goods? You up to no good again, Trick Butcher?" His real name was Patrick, but he hated being named after an Irish saint, so he'd shortened it to something that had punch.

"Weren't me, Sir. It was that Injun there. Saw him pass it to a friend."

"Liar. You took it," the young Indian accused.

"Who you callin' a liar, you dirty Injun!" Trick Butcher said. He was a beefy, pugnacious bugger, whom Stephen knew all too well. He stood belligerently in front of the Indian, and put up his fists, ready to fight, as always.

Esme realized that she had encountered Trick Butcher earlier in the summer, when he had once before insulted an Indian, and made a pass at her and Alice. She had already considered him a scoundrel then.

Stephen said, "Back off, Butcher. I saw you steal the bottle and pass it to your brother."

"Fuck you, Seaford! It was him took it! Better watch your place don't burn down next time the Redskins set fire to the village."

The Indian suddenly grabbed Butcher by the front of his shirt. "Don't spread lies like that, you no-good white trash. My people don't set fires. Or steal."

Butcher threw the first punch, and the two began brawling. Esme recoiled at the violence, and was fearful for Stephen when he went to intervene. The druggist snatched the case of liquor and scuttled inside.

"Enough, or we'll fetch the constable!" Stephen said as he attempted to pull Butcher off. But the brute turned on him and tried to plow him in the face. Stephen ducked quickly enough that he didn't get the full force of the blow, but it still grazed his chin.

Esme cried out.

"Let's get the ladies away from here," Chas said, putting his arm protectively around Ria.

Ted did likewise with Esme.

Jack, who had grown up scrapping in the slums of Toronto, helped Stephen immobilize Butcher in an arm lock, while Troy calmed down the Indian and urged him to walk away.

Esme turned around to see Butcher struggling against Stephen and Jack, shouting, "Fuck off, you fuckin' Injun-lovin' toffs!"

"Sorry you had to witness such deplorable behaviour," Ted said to Esme. "It's a rather stark reminder of how primitive these backwoods villages still are."

"I'm sure there are plenty of places in Toronto where people brawl in the streets," she retorted, stung by his criticism as if it were already her community.

"Ah yes, but not areas that *we* frequent."

It was true, of course, even if it smacked of arrogance. "I'm fine now, thank you," Esme said, as she disengaged herself from Ted's embrace.

They met Alice and the Daventry girls at the bridge.

"I don't know about this younger generation. They just can't take orders," Chas jested.

"Not when there's work to be done," Alice replied with a grin. "But I assure you that we were never in any danger."

Martin seemed about to say something when his sister Esther warned, "Remember that I'm older than you."

They all laughed, and then joined the others streaming into the Community Centre.

There were a lot of shaken people inside. Some of the Crowhurst Hotel guests and staff, who had lost everything except the nightclothes in which they stood, looked dazed. Others had already settled down to sleep in the dim reaches of the room. The elderly and mothers with young children had been invited into the homes of generous citizens a safe distance from the fire. A few locals who had lost their homes wept softly.

Esme was glad to see Stephen come in with Jack and Troy, the bully Butcher obviously having been dealt with.

"I'm almost out of 'medicine'," Ellie informed them. Still frail, she looked exhausted. "So I'm writing prescriptions that I'm sure Mr. Mercer won't mind filling tonight."

Esme said, "Stephen will need some to deaden the pain in his jaw."

"How did you manage that?" Ellie asked as she noticed the swelling.

He told her while she examined him. "As if things weren't bad enough tonight! Nothing broken and no loose teeth. But ice and a stiff drink are called for. The ice being for your chin, not for the drink," she added with a grin.

"Is there any indication of what caused the fire?" Chas asked her.

"Mr. Crowhurst says it started in the hotel kitchen, but he doesn't know how. Thank God he's so vigilant about doing a walk about the hotel before he retires, or there could have been a much bigger tragedy. These old wooden buildings are like kindling, especially after the hot, dry summer we've had."

"The fire might not have gotten out of control if the village had a proper fire engine, and not just a supply of buckets and a hose," Chas said. "I'm going to buy them one."

"That's a super idea!" Ria said.

"And essential when we have the Spirit Bay Retreat going," Chas pointed out.

"Quite true," Ellie agreed. "We'll have to make sure we have a good fire prevention and escape plan there."

Troy put his arm about her and she leaned her head wearily on his shoulder. "Time for bed," he announced.

Esme had no opportunity to talk to Stephen that night. Chas declared that there was nothing more to be done, and took his group back to Wyndwood. They had a cleansing swim and then fell into bed just as dawn was breaking.

While the others were soon fast asleep, Esme finally had the luxury to relive those passionate kisses, joy bubbling inside her. Surely Stephen was as much in love as she.

•   •   •

"This is damned awkward," Chas said to Stephen a few days later. "Richard Wyndham asked me to talk to you. He's concerned that Esme's become a little too fond of your company. What's that about?"

"We're just friends," Stephen said warily, not looking at Chas.

"I have no problem with that. But she's still quite young. Girls that age love to flirt, and constantly have a crush on some chap or other. Perhaps you shouldn't encourage her friendship at the moment. Give her a chance to grow up." Having seduced Ria when she was Esme's age, Chas felt like a hypocrite. But he realized it wasn't so much Esme's age as the difference in their status that concerned Richard and Olivia about a blossoming relationship.

"Yes, Major."

Because he liked and respected Stephen, Chas advised, "Give yourself a chance to get established with the business. Then you'll be on a more equal footing."

But Stephen couldn't imagine that he would ever achieve the kind of success that had catapulted Jack Wyndham into the illustrious society to which he belonged in any case, just because he *was* a Wyndham.

Almost as if he had read Stephen's thoughts, Chas said, "When we start winning important international races, people will take notice of Seaford Boatworks. Just wait and see! Now, let's talk about the trial runs we're going to do in October."

The new displacement-hull racer, *Windrunner II*, was almost finished. All the resorts, except a few that catered to hunters, closed down by the end of September. So once the summer traffic was no longer an impediment to speeding on the lake, Chas and Stephen would put the boat through its paces. Before the lakes iced up, they would transport it to Toronto, and then to Florida for regattas in Palm Beach and Miami.

"I saw Greening's *Rainbow* at Ditchburn's the other day," Chas said. "She's a beauty. But so is ours. I'll expect you in Toronto in February."

Stephen hadn't given much thought to the fact that he was going to be travelling with Chas and *Windrunner II* to whatever races Chas decided upon, whether in North America or Europe.

Stephen was suddenly excited. Surely his mingling with this elite crowd would raise him a notch or two in the Wyndhams' estimation of his suitability.

He could be patient. Would Esme be, or would suave Ted Lorimer wear down her resistance?

Chapter 17

"It's a veritable castle!" Antonia exclaimed when she first saw Wyndholme. The city home that Ria had inherited from her grandmother was a rambling Gothic confection of towers and turrets, elegant bays and oriole windows, balustrated porches and terraces, all crowned by elaborate tracery and whimsical gingerbread.

When Ria's grandfather had built it for his aristocratic bride in 1863, there had been only four houses in this rolling woodland outside the city. Now known as Rosedale, it had become one of the most fashionable enclaves of Toronto's wealthy, whose mansions were crowding up against the sprawling grounds of Wyndholme.

"The tower rooms were my domain, where I was a princess," Ria said. "I'm sure the children will love playing there as much as my cousins and I did. Of course, they haven't seen inside yet, because the renovations have only just been completed." When she had gone to England in 1915, Ria had turned Wyndholme into a convalescent hospital for soldiers, which Aunt Olivia had capably administered until the government had taken it over. It had required some months after the Armistice for the patients to be discharged or relocated. So upon their return from Britain, Ria, Chas, and the children had stayed at Thornridge until they had been able to open their Muskoka cottage for the summer season.

Now Ria, Chas, Jack, Fliss, Justin, and Toni had come to the city for a couple of days to attend the reception with the Prince of Wales, and would be staying at Wyndholme.

"I don't think that much of the décor or furnishings had changed since the place was built, so I've had a lark redecorating everything," Ria explained.

"Nary a sombre Victorian drapery nor shred of flowered wallpaper has escaped her ruthless onslaught," Chas teased.

"For which you will be eternally grateful," she shot back.

Marble imported from Italy as well as the finest mahoganies and oaks had been used in the construction, and these could shine now that they no longer competed with busy walls and the clutter of heavy furnishings and elaborate bric-a-brac. So even Chas was struck by how bright and modern and welcoming the house was. "Hmm. Ruthless is good," he conceded.

She laughed.

"You *have* done wonders, Ria," Justin said. "Made the place your own."

"And a showcase for the art that Chas has been collecting since he went to Oxford," she said of the Renoirs, Monets, Van Goghs, Cezannes, Picassos, and others that she planned to hang throughout the reception rooms. "Including some of Jack's and mine," she added with a grin. "Wait until you see the indoor pool I've had built."

It extended beyond the conservatory that housed exotic flowering plants and massive palms.

"Oh, it's fabulous!" Fliss declared when she saw it.

The glass walls echoed the pointed arched windows in the other rooms and overlooked the terrace and rose gardens on one side, the orchard on another, and seemed to drop off into the wooded ravine at the end. Like the conservatory, the high ceiling had a stained glass dome that showered down rich colours. The pool was a mosaic of tiles depicting a rocky island with a Jack pine sculpted by the wind, which, along with the sparkling pink and grey granite flagstones, instantly conjured up a sense of Muskoka.

"I think we will visit often," Antonia quipped.

"I do hope so!" Ria said. "Part of the fun of having all this is sharing it with friends."

"We'll have to start a new trend," Chas suggested. "Pool parties."

"Super idea!" Ria agreed. "In fact, I asked Cartwright to ensure that the pool was ready so that we could inaugurate it today." Cartwright, the head gardener, had been supervising the workmen, although Grayson had been in the city a few times during the summer to check on things and hire extra staff to prepare the house for the family.

After the long train journey, they enjoyed their swim even more. They would dine at the King Edward Hotel this evening, since the reception with the Prince at the Yacht Club on the Toronto Islands was tomorrow.

"We will fall back on our skills as WATS and make our own beds and breakfast," Ria said as they sipped their pre-prandial drinks on the terrace. Beyond the sweetly scented rose garden before them lay themed formal gardens, some sunken, one secret, all punctuated with sculptures and water features, like fountains and reflecting pools. The tennis court beyond was well hidden. "I told Grayson not to bother about us, as we're only here for two nights, and Mrs. Cartwright could provide us with the essentials."

"That's a cakewalk after what we endured in France," Toni replied.

"Precisely what I said to Grayson when he balked. Fortunately, he's never too scandalized by my behaviour."

"You'll have to show me what to do," Fliss said. "I expect it must give one quite a sense of accomplishment to be able to provide an edible meal."

Chas chortled. "Ay, there's the rub. Will your boiled eggs be a perfect melding of a golden, creamy centre embraced by a firm yet tender white globe, or will you be able to bounce them like rubber balls?"

"You can test them for us," Fliss joshed.

"Grayson told me that young people no longer want to go into service," Ria said. "During the war, they discovered that working in a factory or shop gives them more money and freedom. So we may yet have to fend for ourselves."

"Gosh! I shouldn't like that at all," Fliss said. "There are so many more interesting things to do than cleaning one's house."

Chas laughed. "I think that we will be able to entice people to work for us by paying them more than they could earn in a noisy, smelly factory. Who wouldn't rather serve cocktails here, among the roses?"

"I'm grateful that I don't have to deal with our various mills and factories," Justin admitted, referring to his family's enterprises. "Happy to leave them in Simon's hands, and have a nice, bright, quiet office in my Grandfather Keir's building overlooking Main Street."

"Sounds much too quaint," Ria jested.

"Since I'm only going to be sitting on a few boards and racing boats, I've been wondering what else I should do. Ever since Andrew Carnegie died a couple of weeks ago, I've been thinking that the world needs a new philanthropist," Chas announced. "Did you know that he gave away over $350 million?"

"I don't think we have that much spare change," Ria joked.

"*The Star* reported that he built eight of Toronto's libraries, over 100 others in Canada, and more than 2000 in the rest of the world," Chas continued.

"The Guelph and Launston Mills libraries are both Carnegies," Justin said.

"What a legacy to leave, don't you think?" Chas asked. "Just think of all those millions of people who now have free access to books, to knowledge, in a large part, thanks to his generosity. And libraries are only some of the many institutions and initiatives that he funded."

Jack silently agreed, since he had been one of those who would otherwise not have had access to books, which he had gobbled up in his effort to educate and improve himself, having had to drop out of school at fourteen when his father died.

"Your family has donated to all kinds of good causes," Ria said. "More than we Wyndhams ever have. Grandmother was rather tight with her money, perhaps because she had grown up as a somewhat impoverished aristocrat."

"Impoverished because they insist on maintaining crumbling castles that their noble heritage burdened them with," Antonia said tartly. "My family would be much happier - and warmer - in a modern place like this!"

They laughed.

"If you're serious about following Carnegie's example, then I suggest you set up a charitable trust fund," Justin said.

"I'll start it with $2 million capital," Chas decided. "And ask you and Jack to help administer it, Justin. You ladies can be trustees, and we'll invite some of our other friends to sit on the board that determines how to allocate the funds."

"Do we really have that much to give away?" Ria asked in awe.

"We won't starve," Chas replied. "Especially with Jack multiplying our money daily." He opened another bottle of champagne and they toasted the new Thornton Foundation.

"Perhaps you'll even earn a knighthood," Ria speculated. "Then I would be Lady Ria."

They laughed.

"Sorry to disappoint you, my darling, but the government is going to ban honours and titles for Canadians," Chas said. "The knighthoods granted to those who some think were war profiteers have apparently left a sour taste with many Canadians. Politicians are alleging that the practice is undemocratic."

"Just my luck to miss out!"

"Ah, but there shall be a *Lady Ria*," Chas declared with a grin. "I'll name our new day cruiser that."

"I've told Justin's family that I prefer not to be introduced as Lady Antonia. It seems somehow pretentious here," Toni said.

"And many years from now, people will have forgotten that you actually have a title, and will think you just a batty old dear if you ever use it," Ria teased.

"Especially in Launston Mills," Justin added with a chuckle.

"The honours that you earned yourself are just as likely to impress, my darling," Chas pointed out to Ria, referring to the Military Medal she had received from the King, and the Croix de Guerre and Silver Star from the French. The Prince of Wales had been at her hospital bedside when she had been awarded the latter. "You'll have to wear them tomorrow. We men are expected in full kit."

"I refuse to wear my khaki!"

"Then pin them to your gown. That's sure to make an impression."

Chas was absolutely right. Men were admiring: women, astonished. The medals looked particularly striking against her glittering teal and black gown.

The Prince said to her, "Mrs. Thornton, how delightful to see you looking so much better than when we last met in France. And how clever of you to wear your medals. It makes us realize that it was not only men who confronted danger with great courage on the front lines. We should have included you in our banquet."

"How kind, Sir, but I do believe that when we are not wearing khaki, we might be accused of diverting attention from the topic at hand."

He laughed delightedly. "Quite so! Quite so! Well, Lady Antonia, I had heard that you'd married one of our valiant Colonials."

"Indeed, Your Royal Highness?"

"The King took me to task for not moving smartly enough to secure your hand," he said with a twinkle in his eyes.

"I'm honoured that His Majesty thinks so highly of me, Sir."

"We all do, Lady Antonia. Britain's loss is Canada's gain."

"You're too kind, Sir."

"Not at all," he replied, gazing at her in admiration. To Fliss he said, "Miss Thornton, I understand that you are betrothed to another of our heroes."

"Indeed, Your Royal Highness. The wedding is in a matter of days. And I'm so looking forward to my first trip to Britain."

"A pity I shan't be there to play host. It appears that it will take me three months to traverse this delightful country."

"I am sorry that you couldn't find the time to visit us in Muskoka, Sir," Ria said when she danced with the Prince.

"I expect I shall be back, so I will certainly keep that in mind for the next time, Mrs. Thornton. I must confess that I would have enjoyed spending an idle day or two with an old friend. And Chas did go on about the beauties of his summer home when we were at Oxford, so I'm determined to see it for myself."

"Being on an island allows for plenty of privacy, Sir."

"Even this island reception is more relaxing, and what a splendid view of the city across the bay!" The Royal Canadian Yacht Club was on Toronto Island, but the clubhouse itself had burned down last year. So the Prince had just laid the cornerstone for the new building, and marquees served to shelter the guests from the brisk winds and prying eyes.

"There do seem to be a number of boats hovering offshore, waiting to catch a glimpse of you and the activities," she pointed out.

"One does enjoy the enthusiasm of the people, but it can be wearing and even dangerous. Especially when we have incidents like today at the Exhibition, where I was giving a speech to some 27,000 veterans. I had not been in favour of going into the crowd mounted, in case they surged towards me, which they did. It was fortunate no one was hurt."

"Including yourself, Sir," Ria said astutely.

He smiled. "Indeed! I felt more threatened than I had in the trenches."

Chas later amused the others with an account of what had actually happened to the Prince. The friends were having a nightcap among the tropical foliage of the conservatory, the French windows open to the warm night air.

"The veterans began cheering and yelling when they saw him, and broke through the security barriers like a tide, which hemmed David and his horse in so tightly that the animal couldn't even rear up. Then he was plucked off his nervous steed and passed over the heads of the veterans - like a football, was how he put it. Dishevelled and shaken, he finally ended up on the platform, clutching his crumpled notes, and managed to deliver his speech. I give him a lot of credit for that, since it must have been very unsettling, and could have been a disaster," Chas said.

"Imagine if the Prince had been crushed by his admirers!" Fliss said.

"Wouldn't that have given Canada a black eye," Toni added.

"And the world would have lost a nifty dancer," Fliss declared.

Despite the gravity of the situation, they couldn't help laughing.

"To say nothing of losing our future King," Chas reminded her. "Who, by the way, seemed quite taken with you, Fliss. How many dances did you have?"

"Three."

"You'd better watch out, Jack," Toni said. "The little man has his eye on Fliss."

"Is that any way to talk about our future King?" Ria teased.

"He's terribly charming, of course, but strikes me as a boy in men's clothing. Or in this case, uniform," Toni riposted.

"He spent most of the time talking about Chas and Jack," Fliss said. "He claims that they are shining examples of the best that the Empire has to offer the world. I said that I thought the Empire *was* the world, which made him laugh and rather preen."

"So that's why he told me that you were a breath of fresh air," Chas said.

"He told *me* that he rather envied my escaping into a new life in the Colonies," Toni said. "Away from all the stuffiness of tradition and hidebound thought. I had the distinct impression that he would prefer *not* to be King."

"I expect that he may modernize the monarchy, which wouldn't be a bad thing," Chas said. "Make royalty more accessible to the people, and aware of how their subjects actually live. The fact that he was at Oxford and then in France with us gives him a better sense of his own generation. But he'll have resistance from the old. The King raked him over the coals when he found out that David had gone up for that flight with Barker in the spring. David desperately wants to learn how to fly, but the King forbids it. Too dangerous for the heir."

"So instead, the King sends him into the wilds of Canada to be trampled by adoring mobs," Justin said.

"Quite so!"

"Don't you just love irony?" Toni said.

•   •   •

"Freddie showed me the drawings for my cottage. It's going to be perfect," Zoë told his sister Emma. They sat on the granite outcropping that would support the kitchen and spacious living room with fireplace. The dining room, bedrooms, bathroom, and large screened veranda - a sitting room for fine days - would stretch out over the actual boathouse. Off the master bedroom would be a private sleeping porch, while an open veranda would run along the west side, overlooking the sandy beach and sunsets. "I'm going to call it Wyndhaven."

"I was impressed by the design, and wish I had something like it for myself," Emma admitted.

"Couldn't you?"

"One day, I expect, My salary won't stretch that far, so I'll have to earn enough first," Emma said with a grin. Although her father had a partnership in a successful law firm and was a Senator, the Spencers didn't have the immensely deep pockets of many of their summer friends. Emma would begin working for the firm in

September, and would become a junior partner once she proved herself.

"I feel quite a dud at times, doing nothing but spending time with Ethan, being financially complaisant, contributing nothing to society. But somehow I can't muster the energy or enthusiasm. I don't even like to admit it to myself." And got annoyed whenever anyone else hinted at that.

"I still find myself adrift at times, wondering where my life is going, whether I really want to devote myself to law. Trying damned hard to forget about the future that Cliff and I had envisioned for ourselves. Seeing only a long, lonely stretch of years looming ahead."

"Oh, Emma!"

"But then I just take one day at a time. Try to find something that brings me some contentment. Being with family and friends helps. You're lucky that you have the baby," Emma said as she ruffled his strawberry curls. "He's starting to resemble Blake more all the time."

"Yes, he is." Zoë hugged him close, but Ethan wasn't having any of it. He squirmed and fussed, struggling to get off Zoë's lap.

"Looks like he wants to explore."

"All the time! He can crawl really quickly, so I almost dread the time he starts walking and then running."

"You should rethink having a nanny for him, before he wears you out."

Zoë hesitated. "I know it's stupid, but I'm terrified whenever he's out of my sight. It's like leaving his father all over again, thinking that he's only a few miles down the French coast from me and that we would meet again in a matter of weeks. And then he just disappeared from my life. Because I wasn't there to watch over him. Illogical, I know, because I couldn't have done anything to stop the air raid, and most of the patients and the nurse in his ward survived. So Blake would take me to task for thinking that way. Tell me to get my head examined," she said with a sad smile. "But I can't help how I feel."

"I do understand, Zoë. But Ethan also needs the freedom to just be a kid. I suppose it's a good thing that so many of our friends are about to have babies. They'll become companions for him. His circle of friends, like we have."

"Lydia and Max are thrilled that she's with child. I haven't seen Max so happy in a long time."

"We're all still raw from the war, but we'll heal. Being different from who we were isn't necessarily bad."

"You're so right. Max has immersed himself in his music and is composing some chillingly haunting tunes."

"Why don't we drop in on him and Lydia? I think I hear laughter emanating from their cottage."

It was only a couple of minutes walk along the shore. On the veranda they found Esme and Alice poised over a Ouija board, while Lydia sat beside them and Emma's bother Arthur perched on the railing. Max was playing *Ragtime Nightingale* on the piano inside.

"The Ouija can't make up its mind if Lydia is going to have a boy or girl, so we think she'll have both," Esme told the newcomers.

"Possibly not at the same time, though," Lydia said.

"It affirmed that Alice is going to write a bestselling book..."

"... and that Esme will marry the man of her dreams, although it took its time deciding that," Alice finished Esme's sentence.

"Who is the intended?" Zoë wanted to know.

Her sister smirked. "My secret."

"Arthur, it's your turn to ask something," Alice said.

"I want to know if Emma's going to be Prime Minister."

They laughed.

"A question about yourself," Alice said to Arthur.

"Ask if *he's* going to be Prime Minister," his sister teased.

"Never!" Arthur retorted. "OK, ask if Ontario's going to repeal the Temperance Act in the October referendum. Then I can scoop the story."

"Art, you're hopeless!" Emma lamented with a chuckle.

"Do you have any messages for anyone here?" Esme asked the board.

The planchette moved hesitantly at first, and then sped down to the letter "Z". "For Zoë?"

YES, it acknowledged. Then it started to spell. MOVE ON.

"NO!" Zoë cried. "How dare you, Esme! You did that deliberately! How could you?" She was practically hysterical.

Esme and the others looked at her in astonishment. "What are you talking about, Zoë? What does it mean?"

"You know that's what Blake told me! To move on if anything happened to him."

"I didn't! Honestly, Zoë!"

Zoë was thunderstruck. "Oh my God! Blake? Are you here with us?" Tears were streaming down her face. "Oh, Blake!"

Lydia took the baby while Zoë crumpled onto a chair and buried her face in her hands. Max, having finished playing, heard the cries and hurried out to the veranda. He took his twin into his arms as she wept.

Esme and Alice were afraid to touch the planchette.

•   •   •

Soft, shifting clouds often slumbered on the still lake in late summer until the sun struggled to rise, later every day. Zoë loved to watch the undulating mists that allowed momentary glimpses of islands, like the Carlyle's Ouhu, and then shrouded everything until the sun chased away the last frolicking strands.

She was wading on the beach, the water warm in the cool dawn, and looked up to see Blake coming out of the fog towards her.

She couldn't believe he was actually there, smiling as he moved ever closer. With an ecstatic cry, she ran heedlessly into the water and threw herself into his arms. They embraced fiercely and kissed passionately. He loosened her pinned-up hair, and ran his fingers though it.

"I knew you'd come back!" she said breathlessly, sobbing with joy. "Why have you been gone so long? I've been dead without you."

"I can't stay, my love," he said, tenderly brushing away her tears.

"But why?" she asked in a panic. "You can't leave me again, Blake! I'll go with you!"

"No, Zoë. You have to look after our baby. Remember I told you that you have to move on."

"NO! Not without you!"

"You promised me."

"I didn't! I can't! I need you, Blake."

She kissed him again as if she were sharing her life force with him.

"It's time to go, Blake," Vivian Carrington said as she materialized out of the haze. She was floating on her back with her long raven hair spread around her like an aura.

Blake looked at Zoë sadly. "I have to leave, my love. But you know I'm always with you."

Zoë tried to hold onto him, but he slipped out of her grasp and floated ever deeper into the lake towards Vivian. Zoë tried to follow him, but her feet sank into soft, sucking sand. "Blake!" she screamed and heard only the raucous shriek of a seagull in reply. She flailed at the enveloping mist as if she could grab Blake from it, but he was gone and there was nothing to disturb the calm lake.

The dream had been so intensely real that Zoë was surprised to find herself in bed, her pillow damp with tears.

•   •   •

"Lyle's disappointed that you're never at the Country Club dances anymore," Belinda said to Lizzie. They were sipping lemonade on the veranda of the Spirit Bay Inn. Belinda canoed over to visit occasionally, secretly. They didn't process any films, since that would have given the game away, but Belle enjoyed talking to Lizzie. "You two danced together so beautifully."

Lizzie felt there was nothing to say.

"Adele's now trying to convince Father that she and Lyle really don't need to live in Toronto. He could just go and check up on things at the factory once in a while. She doesn't want to be too far from Blanche. I think *they* should get married!" Belinda said in disgust.

Lizzie laughed.

"I mean it! Neither one of them cares all that deeply for her fiancé. They're getting married because they need rich, amenable husbands to look after them. So they're all going to be miserable and pretend that they have ideal marriages, while they take lovers."

"That's very cynical. And sad." But Lizzie agreed with her. "Don't any of them have the guts to get off that merry-go-round before it's too late?"

Belle was stung at the implied criticism of her brother. "Lyle tried, Lizzie! If... well, I'm sorry to have to say this, but if you weren't carrying TB, which could flare up like Claire's and become a danger to your family, he might still have been able to persuade our parents to accept you as his wife."

"How did you know that?" Lizzie asked, outraged that Ellie must have told people.

"Blanche was determined to find out, so she asked Olivia Wyndham if you were as contagious as Claire, and she replied that you only had a latent case, which posed no threat to anyone at the moment."

Blanche was a clever bitch, Lizzie thought.

"Ellie said that a lot of people have been infected by TB and don't know it, or ever will because they don't get sick," Lizzie said.

"I know it's unfair, and I think Lyle would have taken the risk. But..."

"Your parents don't think that I'm good breeding stock."

"Lizzie!"

"Isn't that what it amounts to?"

"I suppose so."

They silently pondered how different things might have been.

"And what about you, Belle? Are you going to college?"

She snorted. "Mother says that college girls have a reputation for being uninhibited and either too brainy to land a husband or not the kind of women who even want one. I think she means lesbians."

Lizzie laughed. "Oh, dear!"

"Father won't pay for me to go to college, so there you have it!"

"What will you do then?"

"Escape from Pittsburgh as quickly as I can," Belinda announced. "So I'm going to find myself a husband from Boston or Toronto or even Europe."

"Presumably someone you can love."

"Of course. Maybe I'll be one of those glamorous American heiresses whose daddies buy them titled, if impoverished, husbands. Then I can lord it over Blanche and Adele. *The Duchess of Cheeses is not receiving visitors today because she's dining with the Queen.*" She giggled.

"I *am* going to miss you, Belle," Lizzie said with amusement.

"I'll miss you terribly, Lizzie! If you see any likely fellows for me, do steer them in my direction. Then I can come to Europe, too." She grinned. "Now I'd better go, since Esme and Alice are expecting me. A group of us are going to have a picnic on something called the Huckleberry Rock near Beaumaris. Their new friend, Martin Daventry, says there isn't a finer lookout in all of Muskoka."

Which she had to agree was the case. Starting out in a leafy woodland, they were unprepared for the rising stone that soon dominated. It wasn't just the sweeping, eagle-eyed views of the lake and forests beyond, but also the rock itself that was stunning. They were used to the granite outcroppings that defined Muskoka, but this one was so extensively bare and powerful that it seemed like the very sinews of the earth. Grasses, junipers, and white pines struggled to survive in small pockets of soil, but these were mere scabs on the vast, muscular pink granite.

"Gosh! Why have we never been here before?" Esme asked no one in particular.

The young Spencer sisters, Maud and Hazel, shook their heads, while their brother Arthur said, "Someone's been keeping this jewel a secret."

"My family knows the owners," Martin Daventry said. "They allow the neighbours here to use it."

"Just not the rest of us," Arthur said. "So I can't even write about this hidden treasure."

"Sorry, old chap," Martin said.

"But I can capture it on my camera," Belinda declared. She thought that she might just want to capture yummy Martin Daventry as well.

Chapter 18

Ellie and Troy were reading their mail on the veranda at Ouhu. The distant sounds of hammering were satisfying, since it meant that their new cottage was daily growing.

"My cousin Rainer has sent us his very best wishes on our nuptials, and has invited us to visit him some time," Troy said.

"Is he the heir to the crumbling ancestral castle in Bavaria?"

"Yes," he said, reminded afresh that his gentle and favourite cousin Ernst, the heir apparent, hadn't survived the war.

Troy's German mother had met her American husband in Baden Baden when both had taken the waters there for their health. Although Troy dismissed his noble lineage as insignificant, his uncle was Baron Aldrich von Ravensberg. Troy's family had spent many holidays amid the Alpine mountains and meadows, so being at war with Germany had been difficult. It was why Troy had chosen to work with the Harvard Medical Unit on the French coast, where he wouldn't be required to kill.

"Rainer is back at his job with the German Consulate in London, but he says that we must come for some mountain air at Ravensberg, and he plans to visit Muskoka one day."

"I do hope so! And I would love to see the spooky medieval castle where you spent so many summers. But I don't know how we would manage a European vacation with the Children's Retreat and your studies taking up all our time."

"True enough. Perhaps after I finish my degree we can take a month off in the spring."

Troy realized that his brother Felix was at the helm of the runabout that was racing towards the dock. He went down to greet him.

"Can you and Ellie come quickly?" Felix asked. "Mom's fallen and hurt herself badly."

Troy rushed back up to the cottage to tell Ellie.

"Of course we must go! But will she accept help from me?"

"She has no choice."

"Dr. Albright has a cottage over near Port Sandfield..." Ellie began.

"He's out on a golf course somewhere, Felix said. And it's urgent."

Ellie was nervous as she and Troy sped over to Ravenshill. With good reason, for as soon as Erika Roland saw Ellie she turned away and said haughtily to her sons, "Diese Frau soll mich nicht anfassen!" *That woman is not allowed to touch me!*

Troy must have failed to tell his mother that Ellie knew German. He looked embarrassed and angry, but Ellie said, "Sie müssen sich keine Sorgen machen." *You mustn't distress yourself.*

Erika was startled.

"You're obviously in a great deal of pain, Mrs. Roland. Do allow me to help you. I believe I already see the problem, and any delays in treatment could cause permanent damage."

"Very well."

"You've dislocated your shoulder," Ellie said, examining her more closely. "I can give you something to take the edge off the pain before I begin the procedure to fix it."

"Just get on with it, please."

Ellie took Erika's affected arm and positioned it at her side, elbow bent. Ellie's manipulations were slow and gentle. She rotated the arm outward, stopping whenever the muscles tensed or spasmed. And suddenly the shoulder popped back in.

"Oh!" The severe pain was instantly relieved. "Gott sei Dank! How... miraculous. Thank you, Dr. Carlyle."

"It's Roland," Ellie reminded her mother-in-law. "There's going to be some discomfort, so I will leave you with medication. And you'll have to wear a sling while the muscles and tendons heal. You can see your own doctor when you return home."

Troy gave Ellie a grateful smile, and then asked, "How did this happen, Mom?"

"I was coming down the stairs and felt a bit light-headed, so I grabbed onto the railing, but fell anyway. That was how I wrenched my shoulder."

Ellie had trussed her up in a sling, but was concerned by Erika's shallow breathing, as well as the dizzy spell. "I just want to listen to your chest."

She wasn't happy with her examination. "Mrs. Roland, I believe you may have a heart condition."

"My heart is broken, Dr. Carlyle. That is no surprise to me." She looked accusingly at Ellie, implying that she was partly responsible. "Thank you for your help, but I don't need anything more from you," she stated dismissively. "You may present your bill to my husband."

"Mom!"

"Your mother has had a shock and needs to rest. I'll wait in the boat," Ellie said, touching Troy's arm in a gesture that requested he be gentle with Erika. "Payment is not necessary, Mrs. Roland. We are family after all."

"Since you did not have a proper Christian wedding, you are not married in the eyes of God. Or in mine."

"Mom, that's enough!"

Ellie just walked away, trying not to feel wounded by those scathing words.

Troy wasn't long in following her. "Damn Mother for her intransigence and rudeness!" he swore as he started the engine.

"I didn't expect her to change her attitude towards me just because I helped her, especially since she didn't want me here in the first place. Don't be angry, Troy. I'm afraid that she may have congestive heart failure."

"Good God!"

"It's not necessarily imminently fatal if she gets help. Make sure that she does. And spend some time with her so that you won't regret it when it's too late." He had been to see his family only twice this summer. "I don't ever want you to stay away because of me."

"You're too nice, Ellie."

"Ha! No one has ever accused me of that before!"

When a cheque for $10 arrived from the Rolands two days later, Ellie cursed her mother-in-law silently and burst into tears.

Troy soothed her, but she complained, "I'm sorry, I'm not usually so sensitive." It was the damned flu that had left her emotionally volatile.

"This is unforgivable! I'm sure Dad wouldn't have done this without Mom's insistence. I'm sorry, sweetheart."

"At least he got my name right - Dr. Roland," Ellie said between sobs. "You can thank them for that when you give the cheque back."

"You can be sure that I will!"

Shortly thereafter, Erika Roland took to her bed, and wielded her considerable power from the sick room.

•   •   •

Claire seemed so dejected that Jack's excitement about his wedding in two days was dampened. He and Lizzie had come to say goodbye, since they would be leaving for England in a few days, Lizzie travelling with the newlyweds as far as London. Then she would stay with Cousin Beatrice.

Claire had been delighted to be up and sketching, and have her meals in the convivial dining room, but her fever had returned and she had started coughing up blood, so she was now on strict bed rest. "For three months!" she wailed. "It'll be almost Christmas before I'm allowed up again, except for baths."

"Your lesion needs more time to heal, so that when you are able to be up, you won't relapse," Jack assured her. Dr. Mainwaring had informed him that if this forced bed rest didn't produce any improvement, then he would put Claire on pneumothorax treatments to completely rest the infected lung.

"I'll have forgotten how to walk by then. What's the point anyway? I'm not likely to get out of here. Except by the back door, as they say here." She meant in a coffin.

"You mustn't think like that," Jack soothed her.

"My friend Mary, next door, died last week. She'd been here for three years. It didn't do her any good."

"I'm sorry, Claire. But look at all the people who *are* cured. Ellie said that you would find this challenging and tedious, but you *can* get well. You have to believe that and keep your spirits up."

But Claire just turned her head away as tears trickled down her cheeks.

"Jack's rented a lovely house for Maman, just a short walk from here," Lizzie said brightly. "Esme's already asked if she could come and stay there sometimes so that she can visit you."

"You're both going away," Claire said forlornly.

"Fliss and I will be back in a couple of months, sweetheart."

Lizzie felt guilty that she was deserting her sister. It could just as easily be her lying there, confined more than any criminal, railing against the gods. "I'll write you chatty letters regularly, so it will seem as if I'm here with you."

"Telling me all about the things that Esme and I would have seen on our Grand Tour," Claire lamented.

"You'll get there one day," Lizzie assured her. "Keep that goal in mind. If anyone can beat this, Claire, you can. You have heaps of the Wyndham determination and persistence."

"Known as stubbornness," Jack teased gently. "Which is a good thing, by the way."

"Doctor Mainwaring said that you may do some light reading - magazines and cheerful books with not too much intellectual stimulation or excitement. Or romance," Lizzie said with a grin. "Apparently you're not to be emotionally aroused."

Claire managed a giggle. "There's a chap I sort-of met in the dining room. He's one of the new officers who've moved in. Our eyes kept meeting, so I think he rather fancies me. Now I won't even see him again for ages. Not that they let us mingle with the men anyway. But Mary said that you can still find ways to meet secretly." She was saddened anew at the thought of her dead friend.

"How's your new porch mate?" Lizzie asked.

"She's fourteen, and cries a lot."

"She's probably scared and homesick."

"Maybe you can help her be strong as well," Jack suggested.

"They call being here 'chasing the cure'," Claire mused. "Which makes you think that the cure is elusive, hard to grab and hold onto."

"Especially for those who give up," Jack said pointedly. "But I have every faith in you and this place, sweetheart." Dr. Mainwaring had assured him that about two-thirds of the patients were cured. Which still meant that a third died, but he wouldn't dwell on that. "Now tell me what else you need for the time being." He had brought her luxurious, warm furs to keep her well bundled, and Lizzie had brought a bright lipstick, a sassy hair band, and an elegant bed jacket that their mother had made.

"I want to see lots of pictures of your wedding. Oh, how I wish I could be there! Esme said that the bridesmaids' gowns are divine."

"I'm going to develop the photos before I pack up all my equipment," Lizzie said. "And I will definitely make copies for you."

"Now I want something from you, Claire," Jack said. "You're fighting a war. To win it, you need to be a stalwart and obedient soldier. Think of Mainwaring as the General and Matron as the Colonel. Promise me that you will do all you can to obey, with cheerfulness and hope."

"Didn't you say that the Generals made a hash of things in the war?"

"Not all of them. Certainly not the Canadians," he said with a grin. "Come along - a solemn promise, followed by one of your radiant smiles."

"Alright."

He hugged her tenderly, and prayed to a God that he no longer believed in that she would survive.

•   •   •

Esme was frustrated. She hadn't been alone with Stephen since the night they kissed. She didn't find him out fishing in the early morning, and the few times he had been in Ria's boathouse, Chas had also been there. She could hardly call on him at Pineridge or at the Boatworks, but why didn't he make an effort to be available somewhere? It was almost as though he were avoiding her again.

Her family would soon close the cottage and return to Toronto, so she wouldn't see him until next June. How could she bear that? She was planning to stay with Aunt Marie in Gravenhurst occasionally so that she could visit Claire, and realized that she might be able to meet Stephen as well somehow. At least until the ice froze Port Darling into winter isolation. Surely he could visit his old school chums, Anne, who worked at the San, and her husband, since they lived in Gravenhurst.

It was the Labour Day long weekend, and this evening was the Summer's End Ball at the Country Club. Esme was determined to see Stephen tonight, even though Ted Lorimer would surely monopolize her again. A large crowd was coming over from Beaumaris in chauffeured yachts, so none of them would be staying at Wyndwood this time.

But now she was in Port Darling for the Regatta. Because Chas was racing again, she hoped to talk to Stephen.

The faint stench of charred wood still lingered, although the devastation was not that obvious from the wharf, where Mercer's Drugstore and Ice Cream Parlour was doing brisk business, as was the Dockside Tea Room next door. Citizens and visitors alike were enjoying the last pleasant days of the dying summer.

Chas and Stephen barely beat Frank Sheridan this time. "I'll best you next summer, Thornton!" Frank warned.

"Wait until you see what the new racer can do before you lay any money on that," Chas replied.

"I'm going to have to bet on you from now on, not Rafe's horses," Ria said ruefully to Chas. They'd heard that North Star had come in second - a respectable showing for the colt in the prestigious Saratoga Springs race, had family money not been riding on him. Ria had lost only $500, and wondered how Rafe must be feeling, having lost $50,000. He and Sid were expected back today, in time for Fliss and Jack's wedding on Monday, and he would probably be in a foul temper. Ria actually felt sorry for Sid.

Esme managed to bump into Stephen and pass him a note. "SRA tonight," was all it said, but he knew what she meant.

He deliberated on whether he should meet her. What was the point? Perhaps it was better to let her think he didn't care enough. But he couldn't resist seeing her again, perhaps for the last time this year.

So he had been waiting for over an hour when she finally joined him in the copse. He hadn't intended to kiss her, but she had turned her face expectantly to his. It was so sweet and full of promise, how could he let her go?

"I don't want to go back to the city. I wish I could stay here with you," she pleaded.

"That isn't possible, Esme."

"Why not? I... I love you, Stephen. We could get married."

He was at once exultant and worried, since Chas's advice was difficult to ignore. "Oh, Esme. It's not that simple. I wish things could be different, but what future do we have? Your family would never approve."

"I don't care! I'll challenge them!"

"You're still so young," he said, brushing errant strands from her flushed face. "Give yourself time to experience the world. To be sure."

"I am!" Why was he being so resistant? Why didn't he admit that he loved her?

"You're idealistic. You don't realize what you'd be sacrificing."

"Oh, I do. But you obviously don't want me! How could I have been so wrong about you?" she asked with an anguished cry.

It took all his willpower not to follow her when she ran off. Surely it was better that way.

Part 2: 1922

Chapter 19

Claire was glad that she had worn her fur coat, for there was still a breath of winter in the spring air. She realized that she was unconsciously doing the "TB tread" - the measured, plodding pace that had been instilled in her once she had been "put on exercise". *Never get tired out, never get out of breath, never run.* Good Lord, as if she'd dare take that risk!

She had obeyed Jack's edicts, and followed the sanatorium rules to the letter. Well, mostly, she thought with a giggle. And if she didn't relapse, she might be able to go home before the end of summer. She was to start swimming and do some light paddling, more walking, easy games like croquet and golf putting.

She shuffled to her favourite spot on the very edge of the granite bluff. The lake side of a rocky hump was hollowed out, with a tucked-in ledge that made a perfect and secret place to sit, as if it had been deliberately carved. Cupping the sun, it was sheltered from winds, and completely private from all angles but the lake. Perched thirty or more feet above the water, it overlooked a small cove and even higher bluff to one side. Claire often sat here to sketch or just watch the boats pass by. And to meet Colin.

The past long and difficult three years had tested her, sometimes beyond endurance. She made friends, only to forever lose them. Been terrified when she'd coughed up blood, fearing that she would drown in it, as some did. She had endured a year of weekly pneumothorax injections to collapse her diseased lung. Spent a lifetime resting in bed or on her "cure chair", breathing icy air. Perhaps hardest was the mind-numbing boredom of doing nothing. So she took solace in noting the minutiae of life from her balcony - the shapes and textures of the clouds, the sounds of the rain and the wind, the kaleidoscope colours of sunset and sometimes the dancing northern lights, the winter blizzards that powdered everything with sparkling snow, the winking stars that spoke to her of greater realms before lulling her to sleep. They had given her a new appreciation of life and the wonderful complexity and sheer beauty of the universe. Her paintings had become more powerful, Jack told her.

Gradually she'd been allowed up, sometimes to relapse, but then longer stretches when she was able to mingle with other patients, attend the weekly moving pictures shown in the sitting room, learn to play bridge. Linger with Colin in the library or by the letterbox until one of the staff chivvied them to be on their separate ways. Romances were discouraged, even thwarted.

The very fine town band sometimes came to entertain them, and carolers added to the festive Christmas celebrations. Emily and Hugo gave concerts in the summer, much to the delight of the staff and patients. Sometimes a travelling troupe of actors would stage a performance on the lawn. There were sleigh rides in the winter, and boat trips in the summer.

Lately she had been giving watercolour-painting lessons to interested up-patients, which she enjoyed enormously. That was the untapped teacher in her, she thought with a chuckle, recalling her erstwhile ambition. Colin had no talent, but he attended the classes just to be near her.

Claire sat down on the sun-warmed rock, happy to see one of the majestic white steamships sailing out of Gravenhurst Bay. That meant that the summer people would be arriving soon - her family and friends. Although Esme, Jack, and Fliss did visit every couple of months, and Maman came by every other day, summers allowed others to drop in.

But she was a bit surprised to realize that her very closest friends were now here, at the San, among the people who shared the same hopes and fears, pains and struggles, joys and sorrows. No one from outside could understand what it was like here, with death hovering around them, their lives paused, their goals redefined. Colin said it was like the bonds forged among comrades in the trenches.

Colin Sutcliffe was the young officer whose eyes had captured hers on her first day in the dining room, almost three years ago. He'd been a Lieutenant in the Princess Patricia Light Infantry, and had escaped being wounded on several battlefields. Leaving the trenches because of tuberculosis wasn't a noble way to end your war, he had told her wryly. Transferred here from a military TB hospital, he had been "chasing the cure" for four years. And finally seemed to be winning.

The soft scuffle of shoes on the rock alerted her that he was coming. He would stand for a moment near the edge and make sure no one was nearby, his bird-watching binoculars put to good use. Then he would slink around the boulder to join her.

She smiled happily and went into his arms.

"Miss Wyndham, you're looking flushed," he said, mocking Matron, between kisses. "Are you taking too much exercise?"

"I've hardly moved at all," she replied with a giggle.

"But your heart is racing," he said after another kiss. "You must be thinking impure thoughts."

Claire stifled a laugh. "The General and the Colonel would have us on the carpet if they ever caught us like this," she said, referring to Dr. Mainwaring and Matron. Colin had liked Jack's analogy.

"Perhaps they'll discharge us."

"If only! More likely they'll lock us up at opposite ends of the building."

"Quite frankly, I prefer this kind of exercise over any other. So now that we've run a marathon, let's rest."

The rock seat was just wide enough for two. Colin took her hand with a contented sigh. His TB scar still shrinking, he was easily short of breath, whereas she had nearly full expansion of her damaged lung again.

Colin was tall and lanky with dazzling blue eyes and straight sandy hair that he was forever brushing off his forehead.

"I've had this wonderful view of the rocks and lake for so long that I'll actually be sad to leave, in some ways," he confessed.

"I feel that too!"

"Obvious to anyone who has seen your portfolio of paintings, my love. So I was wondering how you'd feel about staying up here. Living in Gravenhurst, I mean. Once we're married."

They'd been secretly engaged since Claire's twenty-first birthday a month ago, and intended to tell their families as soon as they were released from the San. They didn't want to jinx their plans. Maman was very fond of Colin and his widowed mother.

Loving to cook and entertain, Marie had begun taking in visiting relatives of other patients - just Claire's friends at first - but her place had become so popular that she had a steady stream of guests. She didn't charge them because Jack said she was now beyond needing the money, and running a boarding house would demean their status. But grateful visitors brought hampers of food and delicacies, and Marie had made a new circle of friends, many with the wealth and stature of the Wyndhams. Colin's mother, Julia, had neither, but she was one of Marie's favourite guests. Comfortably middle-class, her husband had been a small-town lawyer.

"I would adore living here if we could have a house overlooking the lake!" Claire assured him.

"Mum said that your mother's place is delightful."

Jack had bought Marie a house when a suitable one had become available. He considered renting a waste of money. In fact, he was constantly buying and selling properties these days, Claire realized.

"Except in early spring, when the bay is infested with logs. You could walk across it then. I'm always amazed that the steamers get through." The house was next to the San grounds.

"Yes, well you can blame those Wyndham mills for that eyesore," he teased. Although the family no longer owned them, the Wyndham name was still faintly visible on the buildings.

"I expect that Maman will want to move back to the city once I'm released. Or even get married, since Dr. Chamberlain is rather keen on her." Gordon Chamberlain was the widowed father of Claire's porch-mate, Ruth, and frequent guest of Marie's. Claire was thrilled for her mother, and even Jack approved of the courtship. "Perhaps Jack would give us this house as a wedding present."

"That's extravagant!"

"Not for him," she said with a grin. "And I've come into my inheritance from my Wyndham grandmother." It was only $1000 a year for 10 years, but still a sizable amount to most people. "And Jack's been giving me a very generous allowance, which he's invested for me." She could hardly believe that he could afford to give her, Lizzie, and their mother each $500 a month. $500 would once have been enough to sustain their entire family for a year.

"So I'm marrying an heiress," he quipped.

"Only a very minor one. Do you truly want to live here?" she asked with mounting excitement as she began to envision their life together.

"Yes. I expect I can start a viable law practice, or buy into one." He had completed his law degree just before going off to war. "You can teach art and sell paintings to the well-heeled summer people."

Claire rested her head on his shoulder. "At times like this, I'm so glad I came to the San."

•   •   •

Lyle Delacourt was lingering on the corner opposite Lizzie's Paris studio, trying to decide if he should go in, when she stepped out. His heart cartwheeled when he realized that she was more beautiful and sophisticated than when he had last seen her three years ago. She could be a *Vogue* fashion plate for Chanel, which she was undoubtedly wearing. Ending just below the knees, her sleek dress scandalously exposed her shapely legs, American fashions not having caught up with Paris ones yet.

He withdrew into a doorway as he watched her stride confidently down the street. He should just walk away, but her allure was too strong. So he followed her.

It was a warm May day, fragrant with flowers that spilled colourfully from window boxes. When she arrived at Les Deux Magot café, the maître d' immediately escorted her to an outdoor table that seemed to be awaiting her. A moment later a bottle of white wine and two glasses were placed before her.

Still he hesitated. She was obviously expecting someone. She took a cigarette from her stylish handbag and placed it into a long holder.

He approached and offered her a light, saying, "May I sit down?"

"Lyle!" She gazed at him in astonishment. "Yes... of course. What on earth are you doing here? Belle never told me you were coming to Paris." Her heart pounding, she offered him some wine, which he gratefully accepted.

"I had business in London. Adele and Blanche insisted on coming along to do some shopping in Paris, but I didn't know how much time I'd have here. They're at Molyneux's right now, having their final fittings, so we're leaving in a couple of days." He had sworn Belle to secrecy, not knowing if he dared to see Lizzie, and yet not wanting her to think that he didn't care at all.

"Too bad that Belle didn't come along."

"I tried to persuade her, but she said that much as she'd love to see you, she wouldn't survive two weeks alone in Adele and Blanche's company without losing her mind or contemplating violence."

Lizzie laughed. "Yes, I can imagine her saying that."

He stared at her with such longing that she felt herself soften. She had sworn that she would never allow any man to ever have emotional control of her again. Love made you lose power, over yourself as well as your relationship.

"You look wonderful," he said with admiration. "Belle told me that you've already made quite a name for yourself here."

"I adore Paris! It's so vibrant and filled with interesting, artistic people, including plenty of ex-pats." It was also incredibly cheap to live here, for the franc had been greatly devalued by the war, worth only about four American cents now. "Of course, it's not so pleasant in the winter, which is why I spend some of that at my cousin's villa in Antibes." Where she occasionally met Rafe and Sidonie, who wintered in nearby Cannes.

A handsome, broad-shouldered young fellow came up to them, saying, "Elizabeth, tell me you're not really going back to boring,

Prohibitionist Toronto for the summer." He plunked himself down on one of the other chairs at her table.

She chuckled. "Not Toronto, Hem. Muskoka."

"Ah, then you're forgiven. I've seen the photos, but whether I believe your claim that it's superior to our lake in Michigan, remains to be seen."

"You can ask one of my Muskoka friends. This is Lyle Delacourt, whose family travels all the way from Pittsburgh to summer on our lake. Lyle, this is Ernest Hemingway, who is a foreign correspondent for the *Toronto Star.*"

"And budding author, don't forget," Hemingway said as the men shook hands. "Be assured that Elizabeth will one day scintillate on the pages of my novel."

She laughed. "Will you join us for a drink?" She motioned to the waiter.

"A scotch, if you're paying," he replied cheekily. "So, is your poet cousin-in-law still here?"

"He sailed yesterday. He didn't think he should leave Phoebe and the baby alone for more than a month." Lizzie had been surprised when Phoebe and Silas spent three months in Europe last year – Phoebe accompanied by a lady's maid who was a trained nurse, in case she had one of her "turns". Silas had been anxious to return to Paris, but Phoebe, enthralled with her new baby, hadn't wanted to travel, and agreed that he should go alone. "Although he feels that Paris is the place for him to perfect his craft."

"He's damn right there. Ezra calls America 'a half-savage country'," Hemingway said of his friend Pound. "I don't suppose Canada's all that different, in the cultural sense."

"We're young, just finding our vision and voice," Lizzie countered.

"Which is why you're in Paris," Hemingway snorted.

"Ah yes, but I bring a different perspective, a 'freshness', as I believe you once called it," she said.

He chuckled.

"Daventry House recently published a slim volume of Silas's poetry," Lyle informed them. "I hear it's being well received."

"Good for him!" Lizzie said. "Anyway, I can't tell you how thrilled Silas was that you introduced him to Joyce and Pound, Hem," she added. Irish author, James Joyce, also lived in Montparnasse, as this Left Bank district was known.

"Ezra says he's got talent, but has to allow himself to draw on those darker thoughts that come from his wartime experiences. Poetry doesn't have to be pretty. But it needs to be truthful,"

Hemingway stated. "Ezra let him read Tom Eliot's latest poem, 'The Waste Land', which he just finished editing, and says it seems to have had a profound effect on Robbins."

"I think he'd love to move here and become a disciple of famous ex-pat authors, but knows that would never work for Phoebe and her family, so he's planning to spend at least every spring in Paris." He didn't stay with her, of course, and had initially taken a room at the Ritz, but had then found himself a small flat not far from her own.

"I daresay that'll suit him in other ways as well. I hear he frequents some of the... *less salubrious* nightclubs in Montmartre," Hemingway confided, giving Lizzie a meaningful glance.

It took her a moment to catch his drift. "Oh! You mean...? Good God! I wonder if Phoebe knows."

"I don't suppose the spouse usually does, unless it's flagrant, like with Cole. But Linda knew what she was getting when she married him."

Linda and Cole Porter lived in a mansion a short walk from here, and entertained extravagantly. Lizzie had been invited to a party where the entire Ballets Russes had been hired to entertain. Cole, having written a few hit tunes, admired Lizzie's brother-in-law, Hugo Garrick, and his successful Broadway musicals.

The homosexual, bisexual, cross-dressing, and playful sensuality so readily accepted in Paris no longer shocked her. Hemingway's friend and mentor, Gertrude Stein, lived openly with her lover, Alice Toklas, and Lizzie sometimes attended their stimulating Saturday evening salons where she met artists, writers, and intellectuals.

But, Christ! What would happen to Phoebe if she ever found out that Silas preferred men?

Lyle raised a knowing eyebrow, not all that surprised at the implication. He found Silas a decent enough chap, if somewhat fey, lost in his own meandering thoughts and surprised to be asked his opinion about anything but books and poetry. Lyle wondered if Silas and Hemingway had even gotten along, the latter exuding an almost overpowering maleness.

"I've butted in long enough, and will leave you to reminisce," Hemingway said. "I'm meeting Ezra anyway. Thanks for the drink, Elizabeth."

"You and Hadley will have to come to dinner before I head off for Canada."

"Sure thing!"

When he left, Lizzie said, "Hem and Hadley are a dear couple. You'd never know that he's often broke, and always grateful for a free drink or meal."

"Do you go by 'Elizabeth' now?"

"Yes. Lizzie Wyndham was a waif who couldn't shake off her past."

They gazed at each other regretfully. Although they hadn't consummated their relationship, she thought of him as her first lover.

"So you're coming to Muskoka for the summer?"

"I'm looking forward to seeing my family. And... I'm getting married in October, so my fiancé and his sister will join me there for the last few weeks of August."

Lyle's heart sank, although he knew he had no future with Lizzie. Now that he had a daughter, there was no question of divorcing Adele.

Living with her had been worse than he'd imagined. Because she seemed more like a sister than a wife, he needed a few stiff drinks before he could even feel aroused by her. Not that she cared much for sex. He was surprised that they had actually managed to produce a child. Lyle was relieved when Adele frequently went home to Sewickley, the community outside Pittsburgh where their families lived, leaving him happily alone in Toronto for months at a time. But he would put his foot down if Adele tried to take Caroline with her. The baby was only six months old, and was with her grandparents at the moment, but she was the only thing that made his marriage tolerable. Adele had declared that she would eventually give him another child, hopefully a boy, but if not, he would have to make do. He had found a young widow in Toronto who was amenable to his attentions and needs, without demanding all his free time.

"Belle didn't tell me." But how could he have missed that dazzling diamond ring on Lizzie's finger?

"I haven't told her yet." She didn't know why she'd hesitated, since Belle had become a confidante of sorts.

"I suppose it's that Count fellow that Belle mentioned."

"Comte Étienne de Sauveterre. We met in Antibes the first winter I was there with Cousin Beatrice." They had eventually become lovers, Lizzie finally seduced by his considerable charm and the expensive "baubles" that he bestowed on her. She had also succumbed to the less inhibited French attitude to sex, premarital or otherwise. Étienne had been surprised to discover that she was still a virgin.

"He makes wine somewhere in the south of France?" Lyle asked.

She turned the bottle around so that he could see the label, Château Sauveterre. "His family has owned this for generations." "This" being the impressive château pictured against a backdrop of hills. "The vineyards and estate are near Avignon."

"So you'll give up your studio?"

"Jack bought it for me, and the flat above it, where I live, so I will keep them, even though I won't be working as a portrait photographer after our wedding. Étienne says that I should treat my photography as art. Have exhibitions."

She loved her flat and studio in the Latin Quarter, above the vanilla and chocolate-scented patisserie on the ground floor, and overlooking the Seine, with a glimpse of Notre Dame Cathedral from her balcony. With the franc still losing value, it wasn't a good time to sell anyway. Besides, it was important for her to retain some independence. Étienne was not likely to be faithful, so having a pied-à-terre in Paris suited her well.

Cousin Bea had warned her early on that Étienne had a reputation as a playboy, and both of them had been surprised when he proposed to her in Antibes in February. The fact that Lizzie was related to the Marquess of Abbotsford and the Earl of Leamington through her Wyndham grandmother surely conferred some nobility to her, but Étienne seemed most impressed with Jack, whom he considered an astute businessman. Jack had flown over from London last fall when he'd been there on a business trip, and the two men had gotten along well. Jack certainly approved of Étienne and his management of the profitable winery, and was absolutely delighted with the engagement. Jack had agreed to bestow a yearly income of $20,000 on Lizzie, with $5000 of that going into a trust fund for her children, which he and she would administer. That made her wealthy in her own right.

"Ah, here he is."

The Comte kissed her warmly and lingeringly on the lips, which made Lyle squirm. He wasn't used to such public shows of affection, especially when he longed to do the same.

When she introduced them, Étienne said, "Ah yes, you and your sister are in the photo hanging in Elizabeth's studio. A masterpiece."

Lizzie blushed slightly, hoping that Lyle wouldn't think it was there to remind her of him. She was fond of it because it had been such a carefree moment on Thunderbird Island, which now seemed poignant, like a rose crushed between the pages of a well-loved book.

The waiter had brought another glass and bottle. Lyle drank deeply while he assessed de Sauveterre. He hadn't expected him to be so young, no more than thirty, and already in possession of a title. He had that sleek, casual, continental look and manner that seemed at once rakish and effete. His dark hair, unrestrained by Brilliantine or pomade, curled softly to his open-necked collar, where he sported a silk cravat. It would surprise Lyle if de Sauveterre didn't have a string of women in thrall, which also angered him on Lizzie's behalf. He didn't feel like a hypocrite, since he wouldn't have needed a mistress if he'd married her.

"Your wine is very fine, Monsieur," Lyle said in French.

De Sauveterre's eyebrows shot up. "Your French is commendable, Monsieur. For an American."

"My mother believes that a cultured person should speak French, although we don't have much use for it in Pittsburgh."

"Indeed. But of course, you must have French ancestors. Delacourt."

"Generations ago. They were Huguenots." Protestants who had fled France because of religious persecution by the Catholic state and church.

"Ah yes."

De Sauvettere was Catholic. Because of her mother's beliefs, Lizzie had been raised Catholic, although her father had been Anglican. Like Jack, she had never been faithful to either religion, being more of an atheist. But there had been a time when she, a hungry eleven-year-old, had seriously considered becoming a nun. The appeal of a clean, ordered life with a full belly and no earthly concerns had been powerful, if short-lived.

Although she didn't attend mass, she loved to wander through the myriad beautiful old churches and cathedrals tucked into alcoves and side streets throughout the city. One of her favourites was right across from the café - l'Église Saint-Germain-des-Prés, reputedly the oldest in Paris. And she often listened to the choir practicing at Notre Dame, their voices rising hauntingly into the arched rafters and stirring her soul.

"I must say I was amused by Elizabeth's Canadien accent. But I do believe it is influenced more by Paris now than Montreal." He picked up her hand kissed it.

Étienne had teased her about it at first, calling her a delightful peasant, so she had worked hard to drop her archaic Québécois idioms and slang, and cultivate an upper crust Parisian accent.

Étienne poured them each another glass of wine, saying, "Have you Americans not yet tired of Prohibition? You will forgive my saying that no civilized society deprives its people of the joys of the grape or the freedom to choose wine over water." He smirked. "But then of course, I am biased."

"Indeed. We manage to stock our cellars despite restrictions. In fact, I've heard that the White House also has a good supply of illicit booze."

De Sauveterre laughed. "Ah, you Americans make criminals of good citizens and help to make the true criminals rich. I do not blame so many for coming to live in France."

"The fact that the dollar is so strong against the franc is a great incentive." Lyle couldn't resist making the dig.

"Perhaps, but that also allows Paris to become the breeding ground for a new intellectualism, as well as avant-garde artistic movements. It is the artists and thinkers who often cannot afford to live in polite society otherwise, especially without the muse they find in the bottle," he added with a disarming grin.

"Chas has been collecting work by some of the artists I've met at Gertrude Stein's salons," Lizzie said. "Like Matisse and Picasso. He's asked me to keep a look out for new talent." Étienne had only accompanied her to the salon once, declaring afterwards that he could do without the company of brash, opinionated American women who looked and behaved like men.

"You must buy some for your own pleasure as well, mon amour," Étienne suggested. "Before all our best art goes to America."

"I have the sketch that Picasso did of me," she reminded him.

"Ah yes. He loves beautiful women. Too well. I shall have to keep my eye on him," he said as he gazed warmly at Lizzie.

"Paris is certainly looking better than when I was here last," Lyle stated.

"Ah, you were a Doughboy."

"Arriving in time to stop the Germans from overrunning France in the Spring Offensive. I was wounded at the Marne. And you, Monsieur?"

De Sauveterre shrugged in that nonchalant Gallic manner. "I was with Intelligence."

Lizzie thought she had better intervene in this one-upmanship. "I'm glad the city wasn't heavily damaged by the war. The architecture is so opulent and beautiful. I'm afraid you will find Toronto very drab and ordinary, mon cher," she said to Étienne.

"I've become rather fond of it," Lyle said.

"Belle told me that you have a lovely house on Davenport Hill overlooking the city, close to Casa Loma."

"Dwarfed by Sir Henry's baronial castle, but much cozier," Lyle said with a smile. "He told me he needs another million to finish it, but I've heard he's actually in financial straits, and may have to sell."

"Good Lord! I don't think anyone but the Thorntons or Eatons could afford to buy it!"

"The Eatons' Ardwold is almost next door, and more to my taste. I expect you heard that Sir John died of pneumonia few months ago."

"Yes, I had." To Étienne she said, "Forgive us for chatting about people you don't know. But the Eatons have a cottage on our lake as well, so you may meet Lady Flora this summer."

"And is Jack's wife not a Thornton?" he asked.

"Yes."

"Then they are not strangers. I am interested in knowing about your friends." He leaned over and kissed her, saying, "Something came up and, regretfully, I must attend a business lunch. I'm sorry I cannot stay, mon amour. But I am looking forward to a quiet evening at home," he added, running his finger suggestively along her cheek and neck, leaving Lyle in no doubt that they were already lovers. "Monsieur, I'm delighted to have met the man in the photo, and will look forward to seeing you again this summer."

"My pleasure," Lyle responded politely, if untruthfully, as the men once again shook hands. He wondered if the Comte was going off to meet a mistress.

As, indeed, was Lizzie. Having hardened herself, she tried not to let it bother her. She would be Étienne's wife, the Comtesse, the mother of his children, who would be the heirs to his fabulous estate. Not that the title had any real significance since the French Revolution abolished nobility. But it still impressed, and was even beyond the dreams of little Lizzie Wyndham. So emotion shouldn't come into the arrangement, as long as he was kind and affectionate. *Let your head rule your heart*, her mother had cautioned before Lizzie left Canada.

De Sauveterre greeted friends at other tables with the double cheek kiss and then swanned off.

"Are you happy, Lizzie?" Lyle asked.

"Very. Are you?" she shot back.

He winced. "I have a beautiful daughter."

"So I heard. Congratulations. Belle says she has yet another excuse for spending time with you in Toronto. Would you like to join me for lunch?"

"Very much."

"So is Belle truly in love with Martin Daventry?" Lizzie asked after the waiter had taken their orders.

"Madly, I'd say. She was beside herself when she heard that he'd been seriously injured in that plane crash last fall. She's spent most of the time since then in Toronto to be near him, staying with Esme."

"She says he'll be out of his back brace soon."

Billy Bishop had been flying Martin back to Toronto from a business meeting when he crashed the Sopwith Dove on landing. Bishop suffered head injuries and a smashed nose, but Martin, sitting in the front cockpit, had broken his back. At first they had feared that he might be paralyzed, but thankfully, the injury had not been that severe.

"Bishop's not flying anymore, because he's had vision problems since the crash, and just moved to England. And Barker's finding there's not enough business to keep the company going, so he's joining the new Canadian Air Force. It's too bad they couldn't make a go of it. I'm impressed with the daily air service between London and Paris."

"I use it whenever I want to go to England," Lizzie said.

"In any case, I'm expecting an engagement announcement soon. Belle's already making publishing suggestions to Martin," he added with a grin.

"That doesn't surprise me!"

"You probably heard that Daventry published Alice Lambton's memoir about her *Lusitania* ordeal, and it's been a great success."

"Yes. Ria sent me a copy."

"Belle said that you photographed the battlefields and cemeteries when you first came over, and thinks that those pictures could be turned into a book."

"There are illustrated Michelin Guides out to the battlefields, so perhaps not."

"It seems rather macabre and dangerous to make them tourist attractions. There must be tons of unexploded shells lying about. Why did you want to go there?"

"To better understand what you men went through. To see and record how the war ravaged the countryside. To pay homage, I guess." And she was always on the lookout for an opportunity to get a good shot, and to make a name for herself.

But she had been astonished at the scale of the devastation. Entire villages annihilated; historic cathedrals and medieval towns reduced to piles of rubble. The countryside desolate - scarred and pock-marked by water-filled craters, crumbling trenches, rusting barbed wire, smashed planks, torn up railways, broken trucks, impassable roads. The only trees left standing were amputated black stumps poised eerily against the apocalyptic backdrop, which her camera had so starkly captured. And everywhere there had been graves, sometimes single wooden crosses leaning forlornly, but too often, an entire crop of them.

She was horrified by the bodies – or bits of them - being recovered from the mud, and sometimes frightened by the mad or desperate men who were salvaging whatever useful objects they could scrounge from the debris. She had been moved by grieving widows and mothers who made long journeys to locate the graves of their men. And she was still haunted by the shell that had exploded deafeningly close, vapourizing the farmer who was trying to reclaim his land. She'd captured him on film only moments before, as he stood, a lone, bent figure against the horizon, perplexed by his brutalized domain.

Perhaps now that the lacerated landscape had begun to heal, it was time to exhibit the photographs, which were damned good.

"You should know that Étienne's only brother, the heir, was killed in the First Battle of the Marne, so there was no question of Étienne being allowed near the front lines after that," she told Lyle.

"Did I seem disdainful?" he asked with a contrite smile.

"A bit. But perhaps no more than Étienne is of Americans," she said shrewdly.

"Touché." He laughed. "May I see your photos? After lunch?"

She hesitated. "If you like."

Lizzie thought it odd to be walking so companionably back to her studio with Lyle. She had been unsettled at the prospect of seeing him this summer, so this unexpected meeting eased her concerns. She realized that she didn't truly hate him, that her dampened love could still flare into a consuming flame if she allowed it to, which she wouldn't now that she had Étienne, and that she really did like him. Perhaps they *could* be just friends.

•   •   •

Ellie stood at her brother's graveside with tears streaming unchecked down her face. It wasn't only for him that she wept. It was for the thousands of other young men and a few women who were his eternal companions in this field of death. Nearly 11,000 of them, one of the cemetery workers had told her. It was unfathomable, and yet she knew that there were hundreds if not thousands of other military cemeteries scattered about France and Belgium. Archie Spencer lay in one near Ypres.

A brisk breeze blew off the Channel – it was always windy along this coast, Troy said – but Blake's grave, at the bottom of the long slope, was sheltered somewhat by the shifting dunes behind. Yet Ellie shivered under the glaring sun, and Troy hugged her close.

He recalled only too vividly that heart-wrenching day when he had been here with Zoë, at Blake's funeral. Then, the earth had been raw and churned up with the many burials. Now, the gentle green swards of grass between each row conferred serenity. The wooden crosses had been replaced by simple white headstones, all identical save for the names, ranks, and regimental insignia carved into each. Families could provide a small motto at the bottom. Blake's read, "Beloved son, brother, husband, father: forever cherished and remembered".

Workers were interring remains brought from smaller graveyards; others were planting or tending the flowers in the endlessly long lines of narrow gardens that strung the headstones together.

The Boulogne-to-Paris train, which ran between the cemetery and the sea, slowed and lingered for a moment, allowing passengers a glimpse of the battalions of graves marching up to the impressive monument on the hilltop, punctuated by the Cross of Sacrifice – a sword imbedded in a tall stone cross – which made this shrine even more poignant. The inscription on the massive Stone of Remembrance dominating the broad terraces read "Their name liveth for evermore".

But it shouldn't be this way. They should have had a chance at life.

As the train moved on, Ellie placed her bouquet of roses on Blake's grave and stroked the stone as if comforting him. "I'll see you at the lake," she murmured.

Troy suppressed his own tears.

He had finished his doctoral degree the previous month, so they had finally embarked on their delayed honeymoon. They'd spent a week in England, staying with Ria's cousin, Lady Beatrice Kirkland, at her London townhouse as well as her Thames-side estate. Troy had been to both during the war. They spent ten memorable days in Bavaria at Troy's cousin's ancient castle, and a luxurious week in Paris. Now they had come to the French coast so that Troy could show Ellie where he and Blake had worked. Not that there was any evidence of the seaside hospitals, although here, at Étaples, there had once been seventeen of them with 22,000 beds. Ellie couldn't fathom that either. Where Troy had been stationed, at the Harvard Unit further up the coast, there were once again just colourful farmers' fields undulating to the edges of cliffs.

Ellie turned away from the grave and took a deep breath of sea air before saying, "I'm ready to go home."

•   •   •

As soon as he had rung the doorbell, Freddie Spencer realized what day it was. Blake had been killed in the air raid four years ago. It was too late to leave, but Zoë smiled as she opened the door.

"You've just missed Max," she said as she ushered him in.

Three-and-a-half-year-old Ethan came running up to Freddie gleefully saying, "Look what Uncle Max made!" It was a paper airplane, which Ethan tried to launch, but drove it into the floor. He shrieked in frustration. Freddie squatted down, put the plane in Ethan's hand and then guided the throw towards the ceiling. The plane swooped through the wide entrance hall and curved into the sitting room as if in invitation for all to follow. Ethan giggled and ran after it, as did the silver tabby, Pearl. There were squeals of delight as the cat leapt for the plane.

"Planning to be a pilot, is he?" Freddie asked with a grin.

"Today. Or whenever Miles talks about how he's going to fly. But when Rupert gets him interested in his crystal radio set, he wants to be an engineer like his other uncle." Rupert would be starting his engineering studies at the university this fall. "Would you like a cup of tea, or a drink?"

"Is Emma home yet?" His sister rented the upper floor of Zoë's Annex house. "She asked me to come by and hang a picture for her."

"Not yet. She's been working late these days."

"Then I'd love a drink."

Knowing what he liked, Zoë poured him a scotch and added a splash of seltzer water. She took a sherry for herself as she joined him in the sitting room.

Freddie relaxed as he sank into the sofa. He liked this house, which he had advised her on when she was buying. It was typical of Annex houses, blending Romanesque arches and decorative brickwork with fanciful Queen Anne turrets and nook-like porches. His place, only a few blocks away, was similar, with more elaborate terra cotta trim, but one day he would design his own house.

He always felt comfortable here, unlike home these days, where tension seemed to be a third member of his household.

"Something smells delicious. Not vegetarian, I'd wager," he added with a grin.

Zoë laughed. "I will treat you to a vegetarian meal some time and you'll be amazed. Today it's just a simple beef stew." Although Zoë preferred being a vegetarian, Ellie insisted that her nephew not be deprived of meat. Zoë now knew how tricky it was to get all the essential nutrients, so she was trying to discover and devise new recipes that provided healthful meals without meat. But she did serve chicken and fish, and either beef or pork once a week.

"I'm impressed that you're such a talented cook. Emma raves about the meals." Zoë had learned to cook from her sister-in-law, Daphne.

Although a small kitchen had been built in the apartment upstairs, Emma usually ate with Zoë, which both they and Ethan enjoyed. Zoë had decided that she wanted no live-in staff, so a cleaning lady came twice a week, and Zoë did all the cooking and washing-up herself. She took pride in her abilities, and was pleased that she had so much control of her life, even if she was surprised at her new-found domesticity. She was even teaching Esme to cook.

"Will you stay for dinner, Uncle Freddie?" Ethan asked as he went over and leaned against Freddie's knees.

"I'd like nothing better, chum, but Aunt Martha's expecting me home soon." Ethan looked dejected, so Freddie said, "But how be you and I build something with your Meccano set on Saturday?"

"Could we, Mummy?" Ethan asked excitedly. He was still too young to build anything on his own, but his various "uncles" were always happy to oblige. Except Max, who claimed he had no mechanical ability, and so he was teaching Ethan to play piano.

"Of course." To Freddie she said, "How *is* Martha? She hasn't been over to visit in ages. Always working or with other commitments." Zoë had begun to feel snubbed, but she knew that Martha was having a hard time since her second miscarriage a few months ago. It was as if she didn't want to be around children just now.

Freddie didn't have that much artistic work for Martha that she couldn't come to tea occasionally, so he also wondered why she seemed to be avoiding Zoë. "Still grieving, but immersing herself in activities to keep busy. How are *you* doing?" Freddie asked.

She saw the compassion in his eyes and knew what he meant. "It's hard to believe it's been four years - except when I look at our son. Sometimes I still can't accept that Blake's really gone." Especially after that recurring dream where she runs to him in the water, but he abandons her yet again. "Mostly I just get on with each day. Try not to think too much about the past." Or the future. She smiled sadly. "It helps to have friends who knew him and understand."

Freddie often dropped in, even without Martha, partly because his sister lived upstairs, but also because he wanted to support Zoë. And, of course, to see her.

Zoë didn't want to admit to herself how comforting and reassuring it was to have him relaxing in her parlour. A tiny, niggling thought, which she refused to acknowledge, regretted that he wasn't free. After all, she had no intention of marrying again.

"I have to admit that I'm a bit upset at what Max just told me," Zoë confessed. "Now that he's finished his studies at the Conservatory, he and Lydia are moving to Guelph! They've found a delightful property not far from her family's estate. He says that the peace of the countryside will inspire his music, and Lydia wants the children to grow up with horses and the freedom of the outdoors." They had a two-year-old boy and a three-month-old girl. "I know it's not that far, but I'll miss him popping in every few days." Which he had easily done, since the Conservatory of Music was only a few blocks away.

"That really is too bad. But I expect you'll be visiting back and forth, and at least you'll be close in the summers."

"Thankfully! Actually, I can hardly wait to get up to Muskoka. You know how I adore the cottage."

Freddie smiled gratefully, and had to admit that he liked it better than his own, which he'd finally built.

"Mama and Lydia have both offered to lend me their maids for a few hours each week, And Ria said I can send the laundry to The Point, so I won't even need to find anyone to help me out."

"Sound ideal."

"Will you be up much this summer?"

"Now that I have an office in my cottage, I do plan to be there a good deal. Besides, I have a few more commissions there."

"That's wonderful!"

They heard the front door open and Emma called out, "Smells scrumptious!" as she came into the room.

Ethan was zooming his airplane and launched it as he said, "Look, Aunt Emma!"

She ducked as it hurtled toward her, which sent the child into gales of laughter.

"Good grief, we have planes flying about the house now!" Emma exclaimed. To the adults she added, "I could murder one of those," referring to their drinks. Zoë fetched her a scotch and refilled Freddie's glass.

"Rough day, Sis?" Freddie asked, as she slumped onto the sofa.

"Brutal! Remind me why I was crazy enough to go into law. I still have hours of work tonight. I don't know what I'd do if I didn't have Zoë looking after me so well," she said as she gratefully took the drink. "I just had another woman come to inquire about divorce - a war bride. Apparently hubby didn't turn out to be at all what she'd expected. He'd bragged about his job at a factory, making her believe that he was at least the foreman, if not quite the owner, and was appalled to find herself living in a shabby flat and struggling to make ends meet."

"Some of our boys did swagger around a bit over there, especially since they were better paid than the British soldiers. But how can she afford a divorce?" Freddie asked.

"A small legacy from an aunt in Britain, which she's not telling hubby about. But her real problem is that he's perfectly content, so he won't divorce her or give her any grounds to divorce him. I think she's just going to leave him and return to England. There were too many quick marriages during the war that weren't well founded, so the divorce rate has really spiked. I think that people should live together for a few years before they commit to marriage."

"That may seem practical, but I doubt that society would ever condone that," Freddie opined. "But I do think that divorces should be easier to obtain. If people really love each other, they don't need the law to force them to stay together. If not, then they should have a chance to rectify their mistake."

"Well, I am scaling back so that I can take a month at the cottage this summer," Emma said. "I'm *so* looking forward to it! I never realized how lucky I was to spend three months there, in the old days. In the meantime, I indulged myself and bought a painting that reminds me of Muskoka and your paintings from Edelina, and the ones that Ria and Chas have from her friend, Tom Thomson."

"I see what you mean," Freddie said when they had gone up to her apartment and examined the canvas. "A.Y. Jackson. Isn't he one of that group? What do they call themselves?"

"Group of Seven. Yes. He was also a war artist, like Jack."

"It's very evocative," Zoë said. An autumnal red maple was poised on the edge of a cascading stream.

Freddie was reluctant to leave after hanging the picture, and felt his heart sink as he walked into his own home just a few blocks away. The house itself was beautiful, but the atmosphere was chilly and unwelcoming these days.

"You've been drinking," Martha accused when Freddie gave her a peck on the cheek. Although not quite a teetotaler, since she enjoyed the occasional glass of wine, Martha did not approve of Freddie's habit of savouring a relaxing pre-dinner whiskey.

"I had a drink with Emma and Zoë. Who, by the way, sends her love and wonders when you can come to tea."

"Does she? So what were you doing there *this* time?"

"Hanging a painting for Emma," he explained, annoyed and disturbed at her bitter tone. "What's wrong, Martha? You seem upset."

"Why should anything be wrong, other than the fact that I'm still in mourning and no one else seems to care. Including you." She looked at him tearfully.

He sank down beside her and put his arm about her. "Oh, darling, how can you say that? I know it's harder for you, since you were carrying the baby, but he was mine as well." Although Freddie had to admit that at barely four months, the child had not seemed all that real to him yet. After the shock and sorrow of her first miscarriage, he hadn't allowed himself to invest emotionally in this pregnancy yet. "Ellie said..."

"I *know* what Ellie said! Next time could be just fine, but hold off trying for a while." She wrung her hands, and looked at him with sudden fierceness. "Let's go away, Freddie. To Europe. Let's wander around France and Italy like we did on our honeymoon. Let's move to London. I love London." Her youngest brother was living there, managing one of the family companies, and wrote enticing letters about his life, which she read with increasing envy.

"I wish I could take the time for a holiday, but you know I'm busy with important projects. I can't possibly spend a month or two in Europe just now." He ignored the irrational plea to move.

"I'd rather be there than at the cottage."

"But I'll be working in Muskoka."

"I was serious about moving to London."

"Martha, I've established a career here. I can't just drop everything and start again."

"Why not? We're still young. Life feels so sterile here. I hate it! I want to be surrounded by beautiful old buildings and fabulous cathedrals."

Freddie hung his head to hide his frustration. "Look, I'll try to scale down my work, hire another assistant, and perhaps we can take a few months off in the fall."

"You just don't want to move away from Zoë."

The words rang out like a death knell.

"What do you mean by that?"

"That you summer people are an incestuous little group that doesn't readily welcome outsiders! That you're more in love with her than me!" she screamed.

"Martha, for God's sake, calm down and listen to yourself. That's just nonsense!"

"Is it? Is it, indeed? I've seen the way you look at her. How you dote on her son. How you're always finding excuses to visit her."

"She's a dear friend and has been for as long as I can remember. And so was Blake."

"Ah yes, and I was just a convenient consolation prize when you knew that you had lost her to him."

She was right, of course, but he had committed himself to his marriage, and had tried hard to make it work. For a moment he considered that this might be the opportunity to get out, but divorce was still scandalous and left women, in particular, with a tainted reputation. He couldn't do that to Martha. "Am I such a bad husband?"

She was speechless for a moment. "No, but... I don't feel that you're completely here with me."

"We've had a rough time lately, darling, especially you. Why don't you go home to Ottawa for a few weeks? Allow your mother to pamper you and just rest. Then when we're at the cottage, we *will* have more time together."

"Yes, perhaps I should. I do need a change."

So did Freddie.

•   •   •

Felicity Wyndham was happy with her new home in many ways. As large as thirty-five-room Thornridge, but more elaborate, it announced to the world that Jack Wyndham was a highly successful man with good taste. Freddie Spencer had designed a grand, somewhat Gothic, English country manor house in warm stone, with gables and thrusting chimneys. Tall, leaded casement windows in bays invited plenty of light into elegant, high-ceilinged rooms. But there was nothing medieval in the modern interior that had flourishes of Art Deco. Balustrated flagstone terraces perched over a wooded valley and stream, and led to formal gardens. It was certainly a showpiece.

But situated north of the city amid rolling farmland on the edge of the ravine that connected with Thornridge, it was far from the intimate and friendly community where she and Jack had spent the first two years of their marriage. Because Jack's mother pretty well lived in Gravenhurst, he and Fliss had had his Annex home to themselves, while he and Freddie made plans for the new estate. Zoë, Emma, and Ellie lived only a few blocks away, Alice and Arthur were nearby at the university, Esme often stayed with Zoë, so friends had been close by, and Fliss relished the informal gatherings resulting from an evening stroll or telephone call to drop in. Now she felt isolated.

Of course, she was closer to Ria and Chas here, and especially to her mother, who too often had Thornridge to herself and was lonely when Rafe and Sid spent most of the winter on the Riviera and elsewhere for race meets and jaunts. So whenever Jack was away on business trips, Fliss went to stay with her mother.

And Jack had assured her that they would have neighbours within a few years, since he planned to develop the area with estate homes, as the city was continually creeping northward. Of the five hundred acres that he now owned, they would keep only thirty for themselves. And with restrictions on minimum lot sizes of five acres, they would be assured of only the very best of neighbours.

There was a knock at the connecting door, and Jack walked into her bedroom. "Good morning, sweetheart. How are you feeling today?" he asked as he sat on the edge of her bed, kissed her cheek, and put an arm around her. She pushed the breakfast tray away and snuggled contentedly up to him. Now that she was pregnant again, she relished these intimate moments when he came to her room and held her in his arms, making no other demands.

Which, of course, he knew all too well.

"Perfectly fine. I think that Baby has made his peace with me."

"A boy, is it?"

"Must be, having given me so much trouble," she replied with a grin.

"I'll wager it's a girl. Much more likely to distress her mother, especially these modern fillies."

She laughed. "Then her father will have to keep a tight rein on her."

Jack had been exultant when Alexander John Wyndham had been born, just thirteen months after their wedding. That pregnancy and delivery had been relatively easy.

But Fliss wasn't looking forward to it all again so soon, especially since this one had caused a great deal of morning sickness for the first three months. She'd had only one summer between pregnancies. But Jack was delighted, and lavished tender care and thoughtful gifts on her once again. And now that she was feeling better, she was excited to be moving to the cottage soon – her favourite place, and where Mummy would constantly be with them.

"Are you off downtown now?" she asked.

"Yes, I am." He sometimes worked from his home office, but felt it was important to get out of the house. So he had an office in a building he owned on Bay Street, in the heart of the city. It was run by an extremely competent secretary, hired for her formidable skills and definitely not for her looks or sex appeal. Jack wanted no distractions or temptations.

His sex life with Fliss was adequate, if not exciting, and he spent his energies on his work, thus avoiding the need to look elsewhere. The last thing he wanted was any hint of scandal that would hurt Fliss or alienate Chas. He had more than he had ever dreamt of achieving, so why risk it all for a woman? In fact, there wasn't a single one who even tempted him, Ellie no longer being available and Sidonie, far too dangerous.

He took much more pleasure from a good business deal than from a roll in the hay. Oh yes, life was good.

"I've just sold Uncle James one of the properties in Palm Beach," he said, trying not to sound smug. He had demanded top dollar for the land - ten times what he had paid – thereby having the added satisfaction of getting a bit of his own back on his cold uncle. Helena had been agitating for a winter place ever since the Oakley's had invited them to their palatial dwelling fronting Lake Worth.

Jack had been alerted to the business possibilities in Florida when Bishop and Barker had mentioned their own plans to head south. Unfortunately, they hadn't done well against the stiff competition in airline service around Florida, Cuba, and other islands. But Jack and Fliss had also gone to Palm Beach that first winter, and Jack had realized that the super-wealthy Americans were starting to congregate and build lavish mansions there.

So Jack and Fliss went to Palm Beach every winter, staying for a month or six weeks at the posh Breakers Hotel, while he continued to make investments and business connections. Now they were going to build their own ocean-side villa. Jack sometimes had to pinch himself to realize that he was not only hobnobbing with America's great movers and shakers, but that he was actually one of them.

The Palm Beach season was only January to early May, but it was *the* place to be and be seen. Chas and Ria were there when

Chas was racing. Fliss had to admit that she loved the climate, the exotic flowers and stately palm trees. Jack had suggested, even on their first trip, that they invite Marjorie to come along, which she gladly did, and Fliss had noticed that the warmth and sea air were good for her mother. She was grateful to Jack for his kindness and thoughtfulness, and having a winter place that suited Mummy was an added bonus. Jack had said that there was no reason why Fliss, Marjorie, and the children couldn't spend entire winters there, even if he had to be in Toronto or off in Europe, where business also beckoned. "You'll be as grand a society hostess there as here, sweetheart," he'd said, obviously proud of her. And Fliss loved to entertain.

In fact, she was in the midst of planning yet another dinner and soiree - the last before heading north to Muskoka.

Jack got off the bed and looked puzzled for a moment as he reached into his pocket. "Look what I've found," he said handing her a small packet.

She opened it gleefully. "It's a key!" She looked at him quizzically.

"To your new Nash Roadster. I thought you wouldn't always want to drive the Cadillac..."

"Oh, Jack! A little sports car! How wonderful!"

It always pleased him to make her happy. It seemed so little in return for her inheritance, which had given him such power.

•   •   •

"For God's sake, Ria, did you have to encourage him to come?" Chas snapped.

"I didn't!" she retorted. "You heard what Lance said last year."

Chas hadn't been happy about visiting Priory Manor when they had been in England the previous spring for one of his races, but Ria had been determined to see their erstwhile home. So he had agreed to take her to tea with Major Chadwick, but had warned her that he would draw the line at letting Lance take her up for a flight in his private aeroplane. Chas had felt like an outsider as Ria and Chadwick had chatted happily of shared experiences in France, of which he had not been a part.

"You urged him to come over," Chas accused.

"I did nothing of the sort! He's been eager to come ever since I first talked about Muskoka. Just like Sybil and Carly," she added pointedly, referring to her British WATS friends, who, along with their husbands, had visited two summers ago.

"Then you should have discouraged him," he grumbled.

Chas was in one of his moods again, which Ria usually managed to ignore if she couldn't coax him out of it. She had hoped that once the severe pain was gone, he would become his old, easygoing self again, but he still suffered from bouts of anger, or restlessness, or depression, as well as arthritic aches. Of course she tried to be supportive, but sometimes she lost her patience.

"He's bringing his sons to explore Canada, and visiting stables here and in the States to purchase horses. Including Rafe's," since North Star had won some major races after all. "So don't make this into something it is not. They'll only be in Muskoka for two weeks, and they're staying at The Grand. I didn't even offer them the boathouse."

He glared at her, and she stared defiantly back.

"Mummy, Daddy! I got a letter from Philip saying he's coming to visit! Isn't that keen?" Sophie asked, as she waltzed into the room.

Chas frowned, but Ria said, "It certainly is, ma petite." Sophie had met Lance's youngest son, who was only two years older than she, during their visit to Priory Manor. Having become an extremely proficient rider under Uncle Rafe's tutelage, Sophie was eager to see the horses and Clive, the stable boy, who had been her friend. So Philip had accompanied her to the stables, and then invited her for a ride through the countryside. He thought it wizard that Priory Manor had once been her home and that she now lived in enormous and wild Canada, where she knew real Indians. They became fast friends that afternoon, and corresponded regularly.

Ria noticed that Sophie, now twelve, was transforming from a pretty child into a beautiful young woman. Ria felt ancient, realizing she would soon have to deal with her daughter's amorous suitors.

"Will I be able to take Philip riding?" Sophie asked.

"Of course," Ria said, before Chas could veto the idea. "And canoeing. Major Chadwick said the boys are eager to participate in the Regatta."

"Oh, yes! We'll do the mixed doubles race. Philip's been practicing his rowing at school, and plans to enter the single skulls. He said that they're staying at The Grand, but why can't they use the boathouse, like our other visitors do?"

Ria looked at Chas. He never denied Sophie anything that was reasonable, but from the outset, he hadn't liked her friendship with Philip. The last thing he wanted was continued contact with the Chadwicks. Even more than Ria, he realized that Sophie would be a knockout, and worried that she, so trusting and loving, would be hurt by predatory men. As his daughter, she was also very rich.

Because Sophie's mother, being estranged, had never told her daughter that her grandmother was the famous French actress, Dominique Rousseau, Ria and Chas hadn't revealed that either, especially since Dominique wanted nothing to do with her granddaughter. But Chas could see that Sophie had inherited some of her grandmother's sensual magnetism. Only in her early fifties, Dominique was still a renowned beauty, and always the mistress of a powerful or titled man.

Noticing Ria's glance, Sophie appealed to Chas. "Please, Daddy, could they stay here? Then it would be easier for me to make sure Philip really does know how to canoe." She looked at him eagerly. "Won't he be surprised when I take him in the boat to play tennis at Thorncliff or the Club?" She took great pride in being able to drive the runabout by herself, even though she did it under the supervision of Stephen or someone else.

Chas couldn't resist her appealing grin. He smiled half-heartedly as he said, "As long as you show him that you are your own woman, poppet."

She giggled at being called a woman.

"Oh, I shan't let him tell me that I can't do something just because I'm a girl," she reassured him.

Or course that wasn't what he meant, but he figured she and Philip were both too young to cause concerns on the sexual front. In a couple of years, it would be a different story.

"Yes, alright," Chas agreed. "You can write and tell him."

"May I send a telegram?"

"OK. But we won't press the point if they don't accept," he added, hoping that Chadwick would decline.

But the response came quickly, accepting the "delightful and kind offer".

Chas dreaded the visit.

Chapter 20

Esme looked back with amusement at Charlie as he exclaimed that Mercers made the best ice cream on earth, so she was startled when she collided with someone coming into the drugstore.

Strong hands steadied her. "I do beg your pardon, Es... Miss Wyndham," Stephen Seaford said.

Esme felt a visceral shock at his touch.

For the past two summers she had avoided and ignored him as best she could, treating him as merely Chas's business partner. If she had been dismissive, she had never been condescending, although she had at times been tempted to consider him just a servant. It would have been a way of retaliating for the anguish of his rejection.

She had cried herself to sleep for weeks at the end of that summer of '19. Then she had become angry. Who the hell did he think he was that he could spurn her like that? Oh God, she had made such a fool of herself! What had she seen in him anyway? Maybe she had fallen for him precisely because their relationship was inappropriate – a way of rebelling against her mother and those old-fashioned expectations and restrictions. Or perhaps it had been simply a fleeting summer romance under the moon.

But when the rage and embarrassment had evaporated, she was still left with an aching void, the yearning to be held in his arms, just to be with him.

Ted Lorimer had become an ardent suitor that winter, and she enjoyed his company. He persuaded his family to buy a cottage, so he now spent summers on Mystic Island near the SRA Golf and Country Club. "Father thinks it's an excellent opportunity to do business from here," Ted confided to her. "And so he rewarded me with a junior partnership in the company. Of course, I'm expected to make good deals on the golf course," he'd added with a self-deprecating smile.

Everyone, including Esme, was expecting that Ted would soon propose to her.

She had avoided meeting Stephen's eyes, afraid of what she might or might not find there. But now they stared intently at one another. Was it regret and longing she saw in his?

"Stephen's wearing your ice cream," six-year-old Charlie said with childish glee.

"Oh, I am sorry," Esme said, flustered, as she backed away from Stephen.

"It's no matter," he replied, pulling out a handkerchief and cleaning his shirt. "I'm afraid your ice cream might be spoiled. Perhaps I could buy you another?"

"Thank you, but that's not necessary."

"It's dripping all over the place," Charlie pointed out between licks of his own double-scoop cone.

"That won't matter outside," Esme retorted, feeling foolish now.

"I'll let you get on your way then," Stephen said, moving aside to allow them to pass. Alice, Sophie, and Johanna were also with her.

Out on the wharf, Esme took a few half-hearted licks from her cone, but with her stomach in a knot, she had no appetite for it. She tossed it into a garbage can and then knelt on the edge of the dock to rinse her sticky hand in the water.

"That was a waste! I could have eaten it," Charlie exclaimed, gobbling up his own at his usual furious pace.

"And give yourself a stomach ache again?" Johanna countered.

"Baloney!"

"Charlie!" Johanna chided, but they all laughed.

When they walked over to the boat, Alice said quietly to Esme, "You're still in love with Stephen."

"Would it make a difference if I were?"

"He hasn't married yet, as far as I've heard."

"I can't open up that wound. Be prepared to be hurt all over again."

"So you'll settle for Ted, who's rich and charming and popular."

"Don't reduce it to that, Alice! I *do* like Ted."

"So do I. So do a lot of girls, in fact. But do you love him? Trust him?"

"I can't talk about this right now," Esme said as they reached the runabout.

Coming out of Mercer's Drugstore, Stephen watched them climb into the boat, resisting the urge to go and help. With her blonde hair cropped stylishly short, Esme had matured from the schoolgirl of three summers ago into a sophisticated young woman. Even more out of his reach.

As if she could feel his gaze, she looked up at him – sad and confused - and then turned away.

He had allowed himself the faint hope that she might still love him, despite the fact that they had barely talked these past two summers. Touching her again, breathing her scent, had re-inflamed his banked desire. But he wasn't sure that her feelings had survived the charismatic onslaught of Ted Lorimer or the Wyndhams' intention to separate them and undermine their relationship.

That Esme was afraid of being rejected by him again didn't even occur to Stephen.

•   •   •

Stephen realized that his life had, in some ways, been on hold these past three years. The dedication to boats and racing had helped him to suppress his longing for Esme. No other woman had captured his interest, although some had tried. As he returned to the Boatworks, he wondered if and how he could possibly re-establish a connection with her.

Chas had arrived to examine *Windrunner III*, which was now ready to be tested.

Windrunner II had won races in Palm Beach, the Thousand Islands, Buffalo, Toronto, and at all the local regattas. But the team was particularly proud of their Fisher Trophy win in Miami in 1921, especially since they beat Harry Greening and his Ditchburn-built *Rainbow I*, which had snapped up that prize in the Detroit leg of the Fisher Trophy the previous September. It was a prestigious race that tested the endurance and reliability of boats as much as their speed. It was held over three days with 50-mile heats around a tricky two-mile oval course. Between heats, the contenders' engine hatches were locked down and no work could be done until the race began again the following day. It meant that Stephen had to make any adjustments in the few minutes before the race, or during it. So it was a great testament to the Seafords that *Windrunner II* had required nothing more than a quick spark plug change.

The Fisher rules restricted boats to marine engines, but Chas also wanted a boat powered by what he considered a superior Liberty aircraft engine, for other races. So the Seafords had built the smaller *Windrunner III*.

"She's beautiful," Chas said. The 26-foot runabout was sleek, with a pointed stern. Her black hull made an attractive contrast to the auburn gleam of the highly varnished mahogany decking. The leather upholstery in the two cockpits – the one for passengers being forward of the engine compartment – was a rich forest green.

"She should average around forty miles per hour in a race and can be pushed to fifty or so," Stephen said.

"Good, because we're going to race her in the APBA Gold Cup in September," Chas told Stephen and Mac, who were impressed and excited. "We'll get a jump on Harry, who's decided to go for the Gold Cup as well, but his *Rainbow III* won't be ready for this year's race. And he's undoubtedly going to have some edgy innovations, like he had with his other boats, and which we haven't even considered."

"So you feel more confident racing against Gar Wood?" Mac asked with an incredulous chuckle. "Didn't he post an average of 70 miles per hour last year?"

"In a hydroplane with two 500 horsepower Liberties." Gar Wood had won the coveted British Harmsworth Trophy with *Miss America*. But the American Power Boat Association had recently changed their rules to allow only displacement, not stepped hulls, and a maximum 625 cubic inch engine. With his deep pockets, Gar Wood had also been dominating the Gold Cup Race against ever fewer challengers. "I heard that Wood paid $250,000 to win the Harmsworth."

"God Almighty!" Mac exclaimed.

"But *Miss America* doesn't qualify for the Gold Cup this year, so we'll see what Wood can do with a true gentleman's runabout." Which was required to be able to seat at least four people, although only the pilot and mechanic needed to race. "Let's take *Windrunner III* out for a trial run, Stephen."

"Not until we've christened her, Commodore," Mac said, fetching a bottle of champagne from the icebox.

"Oh, Lord, you're not going to start calling me that!" Chas protested.

"Why not? It's a great honour that the SRA has put you in charge of the fleet, so to speak."

"Indeed, but that's probably to stop me from entering at least one of the local races," Chas said with a laugh.

"You're a great ambassador and terrific role model for boating, Chas," Mac said. "So, here's to you, Commodore, and to *Windrunner III*. May you conquer all!" He poured a bit of the champagne across the bow and they clinked glasses.

•   •   •

With all the wrinkles ironed out over the past two summers, the Spirit Bay Children's Retreat now ran smoothly and efficiently. Esme spent a great deal of time in the spring interviewing and hiring university students to cook, clean, and look after the children and their activities. Some of them were themselves from impoverished families, and attending university on scholarships funded by the Thornton Foundation.

Maud Spencer, who was studying Household Science, recommended fellow students for the kitchen staff, and planned the menus, based on scientific principles of good nutrition and the awareness that poor children weren't used to fancy dishes. Fresh eggs and milk from the Seaford farm, and daily servings of meat or fish were like ambrosia to them.

Matron was not only in charge of her nurses, but also of the general running of the place, with Sky Mayhew supervising the cleaning and laundry staff. Students helped Ria and Esme manage the accounts, the ordering of supplies, and the transportation of the patients, including accompanying them to and from the city.

As the children regained their strength, they were encouraged to do outdoor activities, learning, when necessary, to swim, fish, canoe, play croquet and tennis, and ride ponies. Evenings, there was always a bonfire at the beach in good weather, with a singsong, and some stargazing when Ellie's brother, Derek, or their professor father came by. Once a week, the children were taken on an afternoon cruise in Chas's forty-five-foot yacht, *Lady Ria*, piloted by Stephen.

Every day after lunch were the reading circles, held indoors or out, and often run by Esme, Alice, and Arthur. Esme was amusing the youngest with Beatrix Potter's *Peter Rabbit* and other tales, Alice was reading *The Wind in the Willows* to an older group, and Arthur was regaling the eldest with the spunky *Anne of Green Gables*.

Although never deprived of books, five-year-old Thomas Mayhew always sat in on story time. He had the run of the place, and enjoyed playing with the other children, who didn't know enough to make racial slurs by calling him a half-breed like the locals did. Indeed, some were from immigrant families who were themselves struggling against prejudice and suspicion.

Sophie took her responsibilities as assistant tennis instructor very seriously, and Charlie enjoyed playing with Thomas, under the watchful eye of Johanna, while Ria spent time mothering the ones who were homesick or still bedridden.

"Ria finally has her houseful of children," Ellie quipped to Chas.

"But thankfully they all have homes to go back to," he replied.

Ellie checked on the convalescents daily, thrilled herself with how well the Retreat was working out. In the winters, she did some work at Women's College Hospital, so children of patients there were referred, while the bulk came from the Hospital for Sick Children. But more doctors were hearing about the Retreat and referring patients.

Ellie herself was stronger now, able to walk without a cane, although she sometimes had residual pain, especially when she was tired or had been on her feet all day. It had been challenging to adjust to her limitations, but the Retreat gave her a great sense of purpose and accomplishment. Her small private practice had become little more than writing prescriptions for booze that people couldn't get any other way.

She was delighted and relieved that Troy had been accepted as an assistant professor of biochemistry at the University of Toronto, so there was no longer any worry that they would have to move away.

The only blemish in their lives was that Erika Roland still refused to acknowledge Ellie as Troy's wife. He was required to visit - even spending some of the Christmas holidays in Pittsburgh - but he couldn't take Ellie along. She tried not to let him feel guilty about leaving her behind, but it stung.

Now that Troy had a job, and because she was twenty-eight, Ellie thought it was time for them to start a family. Not that it would make any difference to her mother-in-law. Felix had married and already produced the first grandchild, which had been another black mark against Ellie.

With so many family and friends having babies these past few years – her younger sister, Daphne, already had four - Ellie was actually excited at the prospect of having her own. As was Troy, she knew, though he never pressed her. He was a popular uncle, and so good with Ethan that Zoë even trusted him to look after the boy when she helped out at the Retreat.

Ellie was pleased that Zoë had eventually agreed to provide massage and physiotherapy for the recuperating children. But she still seemed to live too much in her own closed little world. Any attempts to entice her to social events aside from family dinners failed miserably.

It was nearing the end of June, and the children were already noticeably healthier and happier after two weeks of increasingly warm and dry days spent outdoors. Some were lamenting that they had only a week left in this paradise. Sicker children were grateful that they would be staying longer.

Troy and Ethan were watching a tennis game while Zoë was attending to a young girl who was recovering from multiple injuries after having been hit by an automobile.

"May I play?" Ethan asked Troy.

"Perhaps not today, since the older children are having their turn," Troy explained. Sophie had begun to teach Ethan, who was enthralled by the game.

"I'm going to be a champion, like Sophie." She had won the Junior Cup at the Thornton Tournament for the past two years.

"I expect you will, buddy."

Ethan jumped up and tried to run for a stray ball, but moved awkwardly. When he returned, he was panting, and leaned heavily against Troy, saying, "I don't feel good, Uncle Troy."

Noticing his flushed face, Troy touched Ethan's forehead and said, "You're a bit too warm. Let's find Aunt Ellie."

Troy heaved him onto his shoulders, which the child loved, and they went up to the veranda. In case Ethan had something infectious, Troy didn't take him inside, but asked one of the staff to summon Ellie.

Ethan was sitting listlessly on Troy's lap when she joined them.

"He has a fever," Troy explained.

"He does indeed," she said with concern. She felt his pulse, which was much too fast.

"My knee hurts," Ethan told her.

She looked at it, and frowned. It was slightly swollen and red. He cried out when she touched it gently. "Let's get him home so I can examine him properly."

The fear in her eyes when she looked at Troy floored him.

"I'll fetch Zoë while you carry Ethan down to the boat," she said.

Zoë came running, with Ellie following as quickly as she could. "What's the matter, pumpkin?" Zoë asked as she took the child from Troy.

"Mummy, I hurt," Ethan began crying.

Zoë looked at Ellie, who said, "He has an inflamed knee."

"Meaning?"

"I can't be sure yet." But her worst fear was confirmed when she examined him.

She gave him a strong dose of Aspirin and tucked him into bed. "I know you're going to be a very brave boy, chum. But you must tell Mummy when things hurt. And you have to stay in bed. No getting up and running about, even if you're feeling better. OK?"

"I can't play tennis?"

"Not for a while." She almost choked on a sob.

The cat jumped up on Ethan's bed and lay down beside him, staring intently at him.

"Looks like Pearl's going to look after you," Ellie said brightly, before Zoë could shoo the cat away.

Pearl gently put a paw on Ethan's chest, as if to confirm Ellie's words.

"We'll leave her to look after you for a few minutes while I talk to your Mummy."

In the dining-sitting room across the hall from the child's bedroom, Ellie tried not to reveal her own anxiety as she told Zoë and Troy, "It's rheumatic fever."

"Oh dear God!" Zoë cried. "Are you sure?"

"I wish I were wrong. We'll see how the arthritis behaves. You can expect it to travel between joints every few hours or days. The Aspirin should help relieve the pain and swelling. But I also heard a slight heart murmur," she confessed, meaning that he had some carditis – inflammation of the heart.

Zoë covered her mouth as if she were trying to hold herself together. They all knew that rheumatic fever could be fatal if the heart was compromised. It was one of the leading causes of death in young people. At best, he would probably still be left with some heart damage.

"I knew I shouldn't have taken him to the Retreat!" Zoë snapped.

"He didn't catch it there," Ellie reassured her. "It's most likely a result of that sore throat he had a month ago, remember? The one he probably got from Rupert. It must have been a strep infection. That's what appears to trigger rheumatic fever in some people."

"Will Rupert get it, too?"

"Possibly not, since it's much less common over the age of sixteen."

"Is there nothing you can do?" Zoë looked pleadingly at Ellie.

"I'm afraid not. Strict bed rest for probably two or three months. Aspirins. And prayers, I guess." This, from an atheist who was going to be sending her own prayers, at least to Blake, who she felt sure was here with them. "I can arrange for a nurse...."

"No. I'll manage. I'm sure Mama will help."

"We all will, Zoë," Troy assured her.

"Perhaps you could move one of the cots on my sleeping porch into his room, so I can stay with him at night," Zoë suggested. He often came and slept with her when he was ill or frightened, but would need to be undisturbed in his own bed.

By the end of the day, Ellie had informed the family and closest friends, and had set up a roster of volunteers so that Zoë wasn't overwhelmed with well-meaning visitors.

Mrs. O'Rourke sent over meals from the Silver Bay kitchen, and one of the maids came by to do the cleaning and washing up, leaving Zoë free to tend to Ethan.

When they were having dinner at their own cottage that evening, Troy asked Ellie, "So what *is* the etiology of rheumatic fever?"

"That's still a mystery. There seems to be a genetic component that makes some people more susceptible after strep infections. My mother's sister died of it when she was fifteen. And we don't know what causes the heart damage. That doesn't appear to be the strep bacillus itself. I haven't dared to tell Zoë that although I'm confident Ethan will recover, he will be prone to future attacks. And each one causes more damage. Sometimes children don't survive even the second one."

"Dear God!"

"I'll have to warn her eventually, but she'll want to wrap Ethan in a cocoon and keep him away from the world even more than she already does. After about age sixteen, it appears that children become less likely to have recurrences."

"That's a long way away for the poor kid," Troy said soberly, since Ethan was not yet four.

Ellie couldn't suppress her tears.

Ethan's arthritis migrated between his knees, ankles, elbows, and wrists as if it were a demon scurrying about to find a way out. He cried when the pain flared and even the touch of a blanket was excruciating, but Aspirins helped. As did the nettle and ginger tea that Mrs. Grayson, with her knowledge of herbs, prepared, and which Ellie said was safe for Ethan to drink.

Although Zoë was reluctant to leave his side, Ellie insisted that she take time to rest and to go for a swim or a paddle, saying, "You'll be no good to him if you get sick as well."

Esme, Olivia, Ria, and Ellie helped to nurse him through the terrifying first days. Busy with her own four children, Ellie's sister, Daphne, baked Ethan's favourite cookies and other treats, while his other aunts and uncles came by to entertain him, giving Zoë a few hours to herself every day. She didn't go farther than her beach until after his acute fevers had passed, and was grateful for the break and company once Ethan was feeling well enough to get restless.

Freddie was a frequent visitor, bringing a handsome teddy bear with him one day. "I found this fellow wandering about Port Darling looking for a home. Do you have room for him?" he asked Ethan.

"Oh yes!"

"He says his name is…" Freddie put his ear up to the bear. "Honeysuckle? No. Oh I do beg your pardon, Mr. Bear. Of course, honeysuckle is a flower."

Ethan giggled.

"Ah yes, your name is Huckle-*bear*-y."

Ethan took him eagerly.

"Hazel says Hucklebeary needs some clothes, and will make them for him," Freddie said of his youngest sister. "So you can tell her what Hucklebeary should wear, when she comes to visit."

Zoë and Freddie moved out to the party-sized screened veranda once Ethan had fallen asleep. She was grateful that this wasn't one of those blistering summers when it was impossible to cool off, even at night. She had a private, airy sleeping porch off her bedroom, but hadn't needed it so far this year.

Freddie fetched a bottle of wine and poured them each a glass.

"That was so kind of you, Freddie. I expect that Hucklebeary will be his favourite new companion, next to Pearl. Who has turned out to be a devoted nurse. It was quite uncanny - as if the cat knew that he was deathly ill, and wouldn't leave his side until he started to rally. Now she still sleeps with him, but does go off to roam about outside."

"That's a good sign that Pearl believes he's on the mend."

She smiled. "You're right, of course. And I finally feel as though I can relax a little," she confided. "I was so afraid..." She couldn't finish the thought. In the depths of the night, when Ethan had cried out in pain, she had begged Blake for help, saying, "I need him more than you do, my love." And young Ethan had been spared, but whether he could resume a normal life remained to be seen.

Fighting the urge to take Zoë into a comforting embrace, Freddie said, "He's got his parents' spunk and determination. I expect he will heal."

"Is Martha not back yet?" she asked.

"She's at her family's summer house on the Ottawa River with friends. She says that it's been too long since she spent any time there." She had been away for two months now, and Freddie was actually relieved that she wasn't here at the moment, as she would surely find fault with his regular visits to Zoë's Wyndhaven.

But he was surprised that she seemed in no hurry to come back. *I've realized how important old friendships are,* she recently wrote. *I can understand now why your circle of friends is so close, and regret that mine has been allowed to languish since the start of the war. So I'm planning to stay a few more weeks at least. Perhaps for the rest of the summer, since I don't expect that any of you will miss me terribly in Muskoka. Of course I am distressed to hear about Ethan, and will send a note to cheer him. I imagine that you are lending him and Zoë your unfailing support.*

He could almost hear the sarcasm in her voice.

•   •   •

"Arthur and I slaved over this," Alice quipped to the group of friends as she handed out the pages of clues. "So we want to see some interesting results. There'll be a prize for the first team to bring back all the treasures, but the grand prize goes to those who find the most imaginative or amusing things."

"Gentlemen – and ladies – start your engines!" Arthur said.

They were going out, mostly in couples, for a treasure hunt. Esme and Ted were together, but since she was the more experienced driver and knew the hazards of the lake better, she was driving his new Seaford launch. Belinda was with Martin Daventry, Maud and Hazel Spencer took Derek Carlyle, whose family still had nothing faster than a Dippy, while Rupert and Miles Wyndham took Sophie, Charlie, and Johanna in their runabout. There were several other groups, so a dozen boats zoomed off when Arthur shouted, "Go!"

Ted read the list to Esme, and they discussed ideas. "Some strategy is called for," he said. "We should be able to combine some of these in one location. *Something old. Something white. Something heavy. Something light.* OK so old rock, white flower, heavy rock, light flower."

"Hardly creative," Esme said with a chuckle. "But I do know where we can find some fossils, and you can't get much older than that."

"*A brochure from a resort hotel that charges $2.50 per day.* The Grand will be more expensive. The Pineridge Inn might fit that. It's the closest and they probably also have newspapers for *The latest news headlines from Toronto.* Trust Arthur to want that!"

"Not the Pineridge," Esme said quickly. She didn't want to request a brochure for a game that Stephen's family would consider a trivial waste of time. "One of the hotels in Port will probably do, and we can buy a newspaper at the general store and pick up some popcorn for *Something light.* Then we can go to the Indian village for *Something that was one thing but is now another.* How about a deerskin bag for that?" She was already heading towards Port Darling.

"Well done! Next: *A sign of the times.*"

"I have a cloche hat in my bag. You can't really wear one without short hair, so that is doubly significant."

"Perfect, I'd say. *Something celebrated in song.* That's a bit tougher. We can't exactly haul down the moon. I'll just present you! *A Pretty Girl is Like a Melody*, as Irving Berlin said."

Esme laughed. "*The Maple Leaf Rag* would be easy."

"Not as much fun, but it works. *Something sparkly.*"

"Sand from Silver Bay," Esme said instantly. "It has flecks of gold and sparkles beautifully in the sun."

They arrived at Port Darling, tied up the boat, and went for their items. "What about *A geometric shape that delights more when full than empty?*" Esme asked. "We should be able to find that here. How about an ice cream cone?"

"Too messy."

"Just the cone."

"Pick one up if you like, but I have a better idea. I'll show you later."

After they had accumulated their finds and were on their way back to Wyndwood, Ted said, "Just stop in the lee of that island, would you?"

She did, puzzled. Ted pulled a square box out of a compartment in the boat and said, "How's this for *A geometric shape that delights more when full than empty?*"

She took it reluctantly, anticipating what it held. Trying to formulate an acceptable answer.

It was an astonishingly beautiful diamond caressed by brilliant smaller ones.

Before she could respond, he said, "I was hoping you'd agree to marry me. I haven't talked to your father, because I wanted to know how you felt."

"This is magnificent, Ted. I'm truly honoured." She looked away, suppressing tears. She hated to disappoint him, but suddenly realized that she couldn't commit to marrying him. Not when she still loved Stephen, and wondered if she had any future with him.

"But?"

"I... need time to think. I'm sorry."

He relaxed. "Of course! You know that I'm crazy about you, Esme." He kissed her seductively. "Perhaps you can give me an answer by the end of the summer?"

"Most assuredly." He hadn't spoken of love.

The scavengers straggled in, with Derek and the Spencer girls arriving first. The treasures collected occasioned plenty of merriment.

"A chicken?" Alice asked Derek, for *Something that was one thing but is now another.*

"It was an egg, and actually we took it a step further, since it will also be tonight's dinner – so, past, present, and future."

"Trust the biologist to come up with that!" Eugene Roland teased.

The songs brought the most variety – honey, roses, baseballs, teddy bears, dolls, and several American flags.

But the one that unsettled people was the actual sign that someone had borrowed from a shopkeeper in Port Darling, for *A sign of the times* - "Gentiles only".

"What does that mean?" Sophie asked.

"That Jewish people aren't welcome," Arthur said.

"What are juice people?" Charlie wanted to know.

"Jewish. It's a religion. Like we're Anglican, and other people are Catholic, or Presbyterian, or Methodist," Alice explained.

"It's all rather silly and unkind," Esme said to placate the children. "Now let's see if Alice and Arthur can actually declare a grand prize winner." She didn't want to win because it would somehow bond her more closely with Ted. So she was immensely relieved that Belinda and Martin did.

•   •   •

During the past two summers, Bishop and Barker had often dropped in at The Point, but no one had expected to hear an aeroplane over the lake since they had ceased operations. So there was excitement and curiosity when a floatplane pulled up to the dock.

Grayson was the first to greet the guest, who chuckled to be met by the butler. "Captain Bertram Cracknell to see Major Thornton."

Chas was already coming down the path, putting on his welcoming host persona despite his apprehension. "Crackers! Good to see you, old chap. Where did you fly in from?"

"North Bay. What do you think about my modified Jenny?" Two long and narrow pontoons had replaced the wheels of the Curtiss Canuck.

"It has little boats on!" Charlie exclaimed as he raced along the dock.

"Sure does," Bert said with a laugh.

"Works well, does it?" Chas asked.

"As long as the water is relatively calm. Wouldn't take her on the ocean, but great for bush flying. Lots of lakes to land on."

"So you're flying up north, are you?"

"Yup. Taking supplies and mail to remote mining camps and such. Flew a chap out who needed medical attention."

"What happened to barnstorming?" Chas asked as he ushered Bert up to the house.

"People are getting jaded by it. Couldn't compete with the wing walkers in any case. Decided to try my luck in a new frontier."

"Can I pour you something?" Chas offered when they had settled into the library.

"Sure can. Whatever you're having. So, you still have a supply of booze."

"Grayson, with great foresight, put plenty of it down when the war started. We were augmenting the supply by ordering from Montreal until the government shut down private importing last year, so we're relying wholly on our cellar now."

"Most people aren't so lucky. There's some mighty poisonous moonshine about. Fine scotch, this," Bert said. "It's criminal to keep it from a man."

"Yes, well, hopefully when we get rid of the present Ontario government next year, the new one will see sense."

"They say that Quebec managed to repeal prohibition in '19 because women didn't have the vote there."

Chas laughed. "Quite possibly. Although there are enough self-righteous men around who think they have an obligation and right to dictate their idea of morality to the rest of us – and too many of them are in government. I have yet to figure out why it's illegal to buy ice cream on a Sunday."

Bert chortled. "Too sinfully good, I'd say. Mustn't be allowed to enjoy ourselves on the Sabbath."

"Quite so!"

"You're Charlie's a handsome little chap. Looks more and more like you."

Chas ignored the comment, but wondered what was coming. "So, things have been going well for you?"

"Winters can be slow, although I have skis to replace the pontoons. Just getting some lucrative contracts going, but thought I should invest in another surplus Jenny and keep her on wheels. Can get one for less than $1500 now. Course I know I owe you, and could pay some back, but thought you might like to invest in a partnership, now that Bishop-Barker's been dissolved. Thornton-Cracknell Air Service. What do you say?"

Chas kept his anger in check. Bert wanted to capitalize on his fame, but he wouldn't put his name to an enterprise that was bound to fail. He knew that the two Billies had worked damned hard to make their company successful, even if they had pulled some silly stunts, like terrifying crowds at the CNE by flying dangerously low over the grandstand. So if they couldn't make a go of it, Bert probably wouldn't either.

"I'm not interested in a partnership, thanks all the same." Chas stared hard at him to show that he wasn't prepared to be blackmailed to that extent. Let the bastard try, if he dare. Justin Carrington hadn't been able to find any real dirt on Bert, although there was a girl in Peterborough whom he might have gotten pregnant. But she married someone else, and there was no scandal. "But I'll give you an interest-free extension on the loan for another... let's make it five years, if that helps." Chas didn't want him coming back too often.

"Sure would. Appreciate that, of course. And if you could spot me another $1500, I'll be well set up for my new enterprise. Bound to make money, this one."

"What is it?"

"Ferrying supplies." Bert gave him an enigmatic grin. "Hard to come by in some of these places, so they pay well. Damn well."

Chas wondered what exactly he was implying, but didn't want to hear any details. "Because we *are* old chums, I'll give you a cheque and you can sign me a promissory note." If another fifteen hundred would get Bert out of his hair for a few more years, and give him the chance to make a successful business, then so be it. In fact, Chas didn't care if Bert ever paid him back, but it would do no good to let him know that, or he'd be calling regularly to see how much more he could weasel out.

"Much obliged. If I could have a wee drop more of these fine spirits, I'll be on my way."

•   •   •

"But why do you have to stay there?" Phoebe whined. "It's only a fifteen-minute boat ride from here."

Feeling guilty for wanting to escape, Silas said placatingly, "This is a tremendous honour, Phoebe, and an opportunity to mingle with fellow poets and authors. The legendary Charles G. D. Roberts and Bliss Carman, the unofficial poet laureate, will be there! I want to spend as much time as I can in their company, learn from them, and be accepted into that literary circle. There are lectures and activities from morning until night, so it doesn't make sense for me to go back and forth." Through the efforts of his publisher, Martin Daventry, he had been invited to read his poetry at the Muskoka Assembly of the Chautauqua on nearby Tobin Island. His recompense was an all-expenses-paid week at the Epworth Inn, owned by the Assembly. He was up especially early this morning since he could hardly wait to go there. "This is so important for me, birdie."

She liked that pet name since she *was* a bird is so many ways. "The birds were gossiping. They said you were going away because you don't love me anymore."

She looked at him with such enormous, hurt eyes, that he sank down onto the bed beside her and took her hand. He was afraid she would have one of her "turns" – as everyone so euphemistically called her psychotic episodes - which seemed to come on when she was upset or frustrated or frightened. "Then the birds were wrong, and naughty to spread lies."

"But you haven't made love to me in a long time. Not since you went off to Paris." She ran her other hand suggestively down his chest and hips, and along his thigh. From the outset, he had been surprised that she was always looking for an opportunity to seduce him.

He tried not to show his discomfort because Phoebe picked up on things so uncannily, as if she could read minds. In fact, he tried to discipline his thoughts so that nothing inappropriate went through them at all when he was with her.

He was grateful that they had separate bedrooms here at the cottage as well as in his father-in-law's Rosedale mansion. Albert had insisted that the city house was too large for just himself and Irene, and it would be less disturbing for Phoebe to live in familiar surroundings. At Tumbling Rocks, Albert and Irene had just moved into a small new cottage next door, leaving the large one to Phoebe and Edgar, whose expanding family needed room to spread out. Edgar, of course, had his own house in the city. So Silas felt that he was always just a guest in someone else's home.

"A fellow isn't always in the mood, birdie," he replied to Phoebe's accusation as he took her straying hand firmly in his and kissed it. "I've been distracted, filled with exciting ideas, working long hours, as you know." Which was another convenient excuse he would push out of harm's way. "But that doesn't mean that I don't love you," he said, and he did, but not with a passionate lover's heart. In that way, he was living a lie. "Perhaps we can have a romantic dinner – just the two of us – when I get back. In the meantime, be happy for me, birdie. This is so good for my career."

"Of course I am, Silas. But why can't I come along then?"

"The invitation is only for me, and you couldn't bring the baby in any case."

Mention of their daughter, Sylvia, instantly brightened her. Phoebe spent lots of time with her, but always under the watchful eye of the baby's nurse. Phoebe had her own nurse, Brenda, in the guise of her companion/lady's maid. Edgar had wanted to ensure that Phoebe didn't inadvertently harm herself or her child, since he had dealt too often with her more violent outbursts, one of which had resulted in their mother's death.

•   •   •

"I hadn't realized this was so popular!" Alice said to her friends. She was researching to write an article about the Muskoka Assembly of the Chautauqua for *Our Times*, formerly called *Home Fires*, the British magazine published by her *Lusitania* friends Lady Meredith Powell and Theadora Prescott. Arthur would be writing one for *Maclean's* magazine, so they were accompanied by his sisters, Maud and Hazel, as well as Esme, Ted Lorimer, Derek Carlyle, Belinda Delacourt, and Martin Daventry.

They were at the Epworth Inn on Tobin Island, where every chair on the spacious veranda was occupied, and people perched on the railings and lined the walls to listen to the morning lecture, presented today by renowned poet Wilson MacDonald.

Alice had spoken to him briefly and wondered how this slight stick of a man with his retiring, if self-assured manner could keep all these people interested. But as soon as he began speaking, he was transformed. He gave an entertaining and thought-provoking lecture on "The Development of Canadian Poetry", and followed it with selections from his own works. His passion resonated through his thin frame; his shyness dissolved in the cadence of his words. With the skill of a consummate actor, he became a conduit that brought his poetry to vibrating life.

The audience was mesmerized.

"This is my latest work, which, I'm sure you'll agree, is in tune with the ideologies of the Muskoka Assembly. It's entitled *Out of the Wilderness.*"

I, a vagabond, gypsy, lover of freedom,
Come to you who are arrogant, proud, and fevered with civilization -
Come with a tonic of sunlight, bottled in wild, careless acres,
To cure you with secrets as old as the breathing of men;
Come with the clean north wind in my nostrils,
To blow out the dust and the smoke of your lives in a great blast of beauty;
Come with a chaos of wildflowers, grouped in a lovely disorder,

To shame all your gardens of maddening, cloying perfection.
I have in my veins all the sweet unrest of the wild places....
After the applause had died down, MacDonald said, "Now I have the pleasure of introducing to you one of our up-and-coming Canadian poets, Silas Robbins. Mr. Robbins will be reciting more poetry this afternoon at 4:00 o'clock at the Poet's Tree, which you will find on your map of the island."

Alice felt nervous for Silas, having to follow such a theatrical performance. But Silas, too, had a more forceful on-stage personality, as if his written words were the inner man relieved of the burdens of civilization – that need to have an acceptable social persona. His poetry was not so much of the old Romantic tradition, like MacDonald's, but influenced by the philosophy that Phoebe had inspired, and sharpened by his suppressed war experiences. Which gave him a unique voice, she thought, feeling proud of him.

"Oh, well done!" Martin said, when Silas had finished. "Well done, indeed!"

Silas was rather overwhelmed by the wholehearted praise from his friends as well as others in the audience.

A couple about his age came up to him, the young woman beaming as she handed him her copy of his poetry book, saying, "Mr. Robbins, it was thrilling to hear you read the words that have so impressed us. Do let me introduce myself. Mildred Kirkbride, and this is my brother, William. Willie and Millie, people like to tease," she added with a chuckle. "Would you sign your book for us? William aspires to be a poet. Perhaps we'll have a chance to talk sometime? We're here for a month."

"How delightful. Yes, of course! We could take a stroll in the woods after lunch," Silas suggested.

"Splendid!"

"Miss Kirkbride, would you be willing to be interviewed about your experiences and impressions of the Assembly for magazine articles?" Alice asked, having taken an instant liking to the confident and friendly young woman. She and Arthur had already interviewed the Reverend Charles S. Applegath, who had founded the Muskoka Assembly, based on the principles of the American Chautauqua movement.

"By all means!"

They strolled down to a rocky outcropping near the water while the others said they would explore some of the woodland paths with enticing names like "Ghost Trail", which led to the "Bay of the Singing Sand". The Assembly owned over two hundred acres and two miles of the island's shoreline.

"So what enticed you to come here for a month?" Alice began.

"I'm a high school English teacher, you see, and I'd heard that not only were there illustrious authors and academics giving lectures here, but also that a Reading Circle and Poetry Prize were to be inaugurated this summer. Emphasizing Canadian literature, I must add, which is woefully lacking in our schools as well as in our national conscience. I've been delighted with the intellectually stimulating presentations."

"The Reverend Applegath told me that the foundations of the Chautauqua movement are to provide nourishment for the body, mind, and soul."

"All admirably enhanced by this magnificent setting! We spend our afternoons swimming, canoeing, playing tennis, and so forth. In the evenings we have musical concerts, plays, moonlight cruises, masquerades. I can't tell you how beneficial this has already been for William." He had wandered off with Silas, so she confided, "Our father is a Presbyterian minister, as was his father. The expectation was that William would follow the tradition, but he doesn't believe in the church dogma and rituals, so the more liberal views espoused here are opening his mind to new possibilities. Particularly since there are so many clergymen here."

Several had bought lots and built cottages on the property, Alice had learned.

"That gives him permission to dissent from the philosophy of his upbringing."

"It's seems rather Theosophical, the culture here," Alice stated.

"Oh, very much so. Find God in Nature. Who can argue with that?" Mildred said brightly. "I lost my fiancé in the war, and find the platitudes of the church woefully lacking."

"Oh, I am sorry," Alice said.

"One must forge ahead. I am grateful, though, that William's health kept him out of the war. He had rheumatic fever as a child, so his heart is damaged."

Alice wondered if Zoë would ever be grateful for that with Ethan. And hoped that would never be necessary.

Meanwhile, Silas had persuaded William to quote a passage from one of his own poems. They stood on a bluff that overlooked a beach where children were building sandcastles and adults were bobbing in the gentle swells created by a passing motorboat.

"That's very powerful. And dark," Silas commented. William's words conjured madness.

"You'll wonder what inspired it, no doubt. My father's religious melancholia. He suffers bouts of such extreme fear that he cannot function for days on end."

"Fear of anything in particular?" Silas was thinking about Phoebe, and the terrors that sometimes paralyzed her.

"Dying, and burning in hell. He believes he is unworthy of God's love and forgiveness, although I have no idea what sins he feels he committed. Other than being too morally upright and perhaps unforgiving and judgmental. It is I who will burn in hell, not he."

William's look sent a naked shiver of excitement through Silas.

Chapter 21

Bloody veins of sunset coursed through the cobweb clouds that everyone hoped would stay tethered to the western horizon. The island friends were heading over to the Chautauqua Assembly on Tobin Island for a lecture about the stars by Professor Carlyle, which would begin as soon as night enveloped them

Stephen Seaford was driving them in *Lady Ria*, which had a head and galley in the glassed-in cabin, and provided plenty of seating there and on the open deck in the stern for the thirty-odd people aboard.

"It's never the same twice on the lake, is it?" Ted observed. "I don't really notice the sunset in the city, but here it's always an event."

Esme was struck by the implication of those words, because he was right. In the city you might glimpse a rosy sky above the rooftops, but you never saw the sun actually setting. How wonderful it must be to live on the lake year-round and witness that glorious sight every fine day, even throughout the long winters when darkness descended early. Stephen knew, and she suddenly envied him that.

"You can tell that Ted's a newcomer to summers on the lake," Derek Carlyle said with a chuckle. "He's still in awe."

"Don't tell me you're jaded," Maud Spencer teased. She and Derek had been seeing a lot of each other in the last couple of years, and were pretty well going steady.

"Never!"

"It occurs to me that Ted hasn't had the chance to look through Dad's telescope yet," Ellie said.

"An oversight on my part," the Professor confessed. "You can't escape that obligation, Ted."

The others laughed, since they loved going to Ouhu to explore the heavens.

That was something else they couldn't readily do in the city, which was encased in a perpetual aura of light, Esme thought. There were many millions more stars twinkling brightly in the Muskoka firmament.

When they had docked at the Assembly and each paid their twenty-five cents to attend, they mingled with the Epworth Inn's guests, who were now so numerous that many slept in tents.

It wasn't long before they met up with Mildred and William Kirkbride, and further introductions were made. Phoebe felt William staring at her, but he looked away as soon as she turned her probing gaze on him.

She liked Mildred, who exuded a cheerful buttery aura, but William was enshrouded by his own gray shadow. He seemed haunted, like Silas when she'd first met him. Perhaps it was little wonder that the men had become such good friends.

Silas had mentioned that it would be fun to take his fellow poet along on their annual autumn trip to Banff, pointing out that she would be preoccupied with the baby a lot of the time anyway, and William would appreciate the inspiration of the mountain scenery. "It would be like having a brother along," he'd told Phoebe.

She felt sorry for Silas, being an only child, since she'd always had Edgar to look after her. Henry, too, when he'd been here, but he was content to live in England now. And Silas had seemed so much happier lately, having taken William under his wing. So she couldn't think of any reason to object, as long as they didn't ignore her, as men were wont to do when together.

"Delighted to meet you, Professor," Mildred said. "We're so looking forward to your talk. I feel privileged having met so many esteemed speakers here that I've already booked us in to stay next summer!"

"How kind, Miss Kirkbride. I hope that my little talk will not disappoint."

Standing on a rise, Esme noticed Stephen paying his attendance fee, and remembered how interested and knowledgeable he was about the stars.

Their eyes met across a sea of people, who seemed momentarily to fade into the background.

Ted took her arm, saying, "Let's find a seat."

Chairs had been set out on the lawn away from trees that would obstruct the view. As it began to grow dark, the professor gave an entertaining lecture about man's long association with the visible universe, and then all the lights in the inn and grounds were extinguished so that the audience seemed to be drawn into the night sky.

Ted sought and captured Esme's hand, stroking her palm seductively with his thumb. Was she foolish to even think about Stephen when Ted was such a determined suitor?

The professor pointed out various constellations and explained the Perseids meteor shower, which would be active from now until almost Labour Day, with the most shooting stars – sometimes over a hundred an hour – visible in mid-August.

He concluded by advising, "The best way to see the meteor shower is to haul a blanket outside and lie down. It's always more fun with friends and even better with your sweetheart - as long as you're married, of course." The audience laughed and clapped in appreciation.

"We'll have to try that," Ted whispered to Esme.

But she was picturing herself lying next to Stephen.

•   •   •

Lizzie was surprised that she had missed the lakes. Having only come here for the first time eight years ago – initially as a servant – she realized that she had become rather enchanted by Muskoka.

She had just spent two weeks with her mother in Gravenhurst, visiting Claire at the Sanatorium every day. They had gone for walks in the extensive grounds, and Claire had managed to introduce her to Colin. It was obvious that they were in love, but Claire was not forthcoming when pressed for details. Marie, meanwhile, had started to create Lizzie's magnificent wedding gown.

Now Lizzie was savouring a pre-dinner cocktail on the veranda at Thorncliff, where she would be staying for the rest of the summer. Claire should be released from the San in a few weeks and would join them here, while their mother would return to the city to prepare for her own wedding to Gordon Chamberlain. Lizzie was excited that the newlyweds would then travel to France for their honeymoon, timed to attend her October wedding. Jack would be there, of course, but Felicity would be too late in her pregnancy to travel. She hoped that Claire would feel able to come, but Emily and Hugo would be back on Broadway, and she doubted that any of her other Wyndham relatives would make the journey. Which, strangely, saddened her for a moment. As did the thought that she'd be living so far away from here, even though she loved France. Well, she would just have to visit occasionally, especially when she had children, who should know their Canadian cousins.

"I told you we'd be early," Sidonie chided Rafe as she breezed onto the veranda. "Hello, Lizzie."

Fliss had arranged a family dinner party to welcome Lizzie.

"I'll have a very large one please, Jack," Sid said with the hint of a mischievous grin at the *double entendre* before she indicated the cocktail.

Rafe gave Lizzie more than a familial peck on the cheek, as he said, "Welcome back, lovely Lizzie. Paris obviously suits you."

It was somehow different when she ran into him and Sid on the Riviera, as if they were on equal terms. Here, Rafe could always make her feel like a scheming upstart. "It's Elizabeth, remember?"

He chortled. "Perhaps to your continental friends." He scooped up some caviar offered by one of the maids before asking, "So when is the Comte expected to grace us with his illustrious presence?"

"Don't be an ass, Rafe," Sid admonished. "You sound as if you're a jealous pleb about to guillotine the aristocracy."

He hooted. "I suppose you're looking forward to consorting with peers, Milady."

"Indeed, I am."

"Étienne will arrive in a couple of weeks," Lizzie said to interrupt the bickering.

"Then I shan't be going to Saratoga this year," Sidonie announced. "It's become such a bore, in any case."

Lizzie and Jack exchanged meaningful looks. They needed to deflect the obvious rancour between these two.

"I understand that Major Chadwick is interested in your stables, Rafe," Jack said. "Isn't he arriving this week?"

"Yes, he is," Sid chimed in. "Another peer for me to consort with." She smirked.

Jack suspected that she was already high on cocaine. She had been using it in England during the war, and he knew she hadn't dropped the habit because she occasionally offered him some, saying it was easier to obtain than booze.

He could understand her sorrow at losing the most important men in her life, and ending up with Rafe. But what he couldn't fathom was her complete indifference to her two-year-old daughter, Elyse. She was a delightful and beautiful child who was too much neglected, left behind with her grandmother and her nanny for weeks on end while her parents went to horse races and jaunts to New York and Atlantic City. Although Rafe was obviously delighted with his daughter, he was often too busy with his horses when he *was* home, and probably wouldn't be all that attentive until Elyse could ride. So Jack and Fliss spent more time with her than her parents, and Ria and Chas, especially, had taken her into their warm embrace.

Zoë didn't attend the dinner, of course, although Ethan was recovering well. She was reading him a bedtime story when she heard a boat approaching. Her spirits lifted, since it sounded like Freddie's runabout. He'd been down in the city for a week, and she'd missed his almost daily visits.

"Hey, chum, you're looking better," Freddie said to Ethan. "Looks like Hucklebeary and Pearl have been good nurses."

Zoë thought that Freddie seemed strained while he entertained Ethan. So when she had tucked the child in and she and Freddie went out to the screened veranda, she said, "You look as though you could use a drink."

"Several, in fact."

When Zoë had fetched a scotch for him and a glass of wine for herself, he said, "Martha's leaving me."

"What? Oh, Freddie! Why?"

He shook his head and looked at her in bewilderment. "She met up with an old beau in Ottawa, and said she realized that we got married too quickly. That we weren't really in love, but just caught up in the wartime frenzy to live fully."

Zoë put a sympathetic hand on his arm.

"And I think she's right. We had a lot of fun together, at first, but we don't have much in common other than our love of architecture. That's sometimes enough to keep people together, but she wants something different from life than I do. She wants to live in Britain, and it just so happens that her old flame has landed an important job there. So she's going over. Not with him, initially, but staying with her brother, who lives in London. Martha said that in a couple of years we can apply for a divorce."

"I'm so sorry, Freddie. I'd really hoped that you two would be happy."

He shrugged. "We tried. I suppose I'll have to give her grounds. Adultery and desertion are the best options, Emma said." Since he would never drag a respectable woman into the courts, he would have to find a whore who would claim she had been with him. It was all rather sordid.

And in the meantime, he had neither a wife nor the chance to woo Zoë, for fear of involving her in this. "I'm sorry, Zoë, I shouldn't burden you with this distasteful business."

"Oh, but you mustn't hesitate to tell me things, Freddie. We're friends, after all."

"Which I greatly appreciate," he said brightly, making sure that he kept their relationship easygoing. "So if I could trouble you for another drink, I'll tell you about my latest project."

•   •   •

"This is wizard!" Philip Chadwick exclaimed as they picked their way down the rock next to the cascading Bala Falls. "There are actually people *swimming* here."

"It seems tame enough," his older brother, Christopher, said somewhat disdainfully. "Not exactly Niagara Falls."

"But delightfully picturesque," Lance Chadwick said to soften his son's sarcasm.

Chas was beginning to find Christopher's schoolboy arrogance trying. Probably the only thing that kept the teen from lording it over "the Colonials" was his respect for Chas, the Ace pilot hero, whom he planned to emulate when he joined the RAF. He became an eager kid when he urged Chas to recount his aerial adventures. But it bothered Chas that the boy seemed to have taken against Ria, as if he realized and resented that his father was in love with her.

"Swimming here isn't the safest thing to do," Ria cautioned. "There isn't a lot of water coming down the north falls at the moment because it's been a relatively dry summer, but it can certainly become dangerous when there is. And you have to be careful not to get caught in the current, especially from the south branch." Which plunged steeply and dramatically, the turbulent water thrashing its way into the Musquosh River. "Someone drowned last year."

"Don't tell me that you haven't swum here," Lance said to Ria, since he knew all too well how daring she was.

She laughed. "Who can resist flirting with fast water?"

"May we dip our toes in?" Sophie asked.

"If you sit on the edge of those rocks near the bottom you may," Ria said. "Toes only!"

Delighted, Sophie and Philip went off to do just that. Both had on their moccasins over bare feet, Philip, chuffed to have such exotic footwear.

"Me too!" Charlie said, trying to squirm out of Ria's firm grasp.

"Not without someone holding onto you," she said.

Chas couldn't easily sit down on the rock with his stiff leg, so Justin Carrington volunteered.

They were a large group who had come on this outing to show the Chadwicks around the lakes. Chas was grateful that there were so many friends to help entertain their guests, not leaving the onus on him and especially Ria. Antonia, of course, also knew Lance, who had been a frequent visitor at the WATS camp outside Calais.

But Chas had an idea that would not only get the Chadwicks out of his hair for a few days, but also give them a real taste of backwoods Canada. "There's a sort of rite-of-passage that a lot of us chaps did when we were about your age, Christopher. It's a canoe trip starting from here and then branching off down the Moon River to Georgian Bay, and back via various lakes – over seventy miles."

"I could do that."

"There are challenging rapids, and twenty-some portages – that's where you have to carry your canoe to avoid waterfalls or to reach the next lake. Sometimes those can be a mile long. You have to take your tent and all your supplies as well. Not something for the faint-hearted."

"There's nothing like it. I felt like a man when I returned," Rafe declared. "And I was only fourteen at the time."

Chas was secretly amused at this wholehearted support from his brother, and knew it was because Sid had been flirting quite outrageously with Lance.

"Father, that sounds like capital fun! Could we?" Christopher asked.

Philip had heard and chimed in, "I bet the Prince of Wales would have had a go if he'd known about it." He had been impressed that Prince Edward had been so enamoured of Canada that he'd bought a ranch in Alberta. So Philip had convinced his father that they should go out west. They would take the train out to the Rockies from here, and stay at the Banff Springs Hotel, at Ria's recommendation. She had heard enough about it from Phoebe and Silas.

Lance looked askance at Chas. "How would we find our way on this trek?" he asked.

"I'll hire an Indian guide for you. Mrs. Mayhew has relatives who I'm sure would be happy to oblige. You couldn't be in better hands."

Philip hooted with glee.

Some of the young people, having been at the falls often enough, had stayed at the ice cream parlour by the harbour.

Esme was thoroughly frustrated. She had been contriving to "accidentally" meet Stephen, not seeking him out as she had that summer of '19. But she hadn't encountered him on her early morning canoe forays to their former haunts, and he was never outside alone when she went by the new boathouse at The Point. And now here he was in charge of the *Lady Ria*, sitting onboard reading a book, while Ted was lavishing such flattering attention on her that she should just give in. But she couldn't. Damn Stephen!

She didn't notice his surreptitious glances at her.

Alice and Arthur Spencer, meanwhile, had decided to explore, taking the narrow dirt lane alongside the small hydroelectric plant and old millstream that rushed into the river.

Daringly they held hands, and Arthur said, "Alice, we're kindred spirits, don't you think?"

"Most definitely!"

"I can't imagine not spending my life with you. I'm not in a position to marry yet; I have to get settled in my job and make some money. But will you wait for me? I love you, Alice, and would be the happiest man alive if you'd agree to become betrothed to me."

She stopped and looked at him in astonishment. Then she threw her arms around him. "Oh, Arthur! Of course I will!"

He looked around quickly, and, not noticing anyone, kissed her passionately.

But he had missed seeing a woman seated on the veranda of the Roselawn Lodge, who had watched the encounter with bittersweet interest.

"I have my inheritance from Father," Alice said. "It's enough to give us a start, and we wouldn't have to wait to get married. I'll be desolate if you're in Launston Mills and I'm in Toronto." They had seen each other almost daily at the university these past three years.

"Let's discuss it over a cup of tea. Perhaps this inn serves some."

Beaming with joy, they gripped hands and walked up to the ornate veranda of the gabled main house. Dotted with pockets of silver birches, pines, and outcroppings of rock, the lawn stretched invitingly down to a small, riverside beach.

"Excuse me, Madam," Arthur said to the lady relaxing on the veranda. "Does the inn have a tea room?"

"I'm afraid the restaurant is closed this summer. We take our meals at the tourist home across the road. So I'd suggest someplace in the village itself. One of the ice cream parlours perhaps."

"It just seems so pleasant here," Arthur said, "with a view of the falls upstream, but without the crowds."

"It's a fairyland," the lady stated with a wistful smile.

During this conversation, Alice had the growing conviction that she had seen the lady before. Then it struck her. Surely it was Lucy Maud Montgomery, the beloved author of *Anne of Green Gables* and so many other delightful stories! But would word not have spread that a famous author was staying in Bala?

"Thank you, Ma'am," Arthur said, but Alice hesitated to leave. She just had to know.

"Excuse me, Madam, but am I mistaken in thinking that you're L.M. Montgomery?"

Arthur looked shocked.

The lady suppressed a grin. "I'm Mrs. Macdonald."

"Oh, I do beg your pardon!" Alice blushed in confusion.

"And that is only who I plan to be on this holiday. It makes my husband happy. But, if you'll keep it a secret, I will confess that you *are* right, young lady." Their expressions caused her to chuckle.

"This is a great honour, indeed!" Arthur said. "I've been reading your *Anne* to the older children at the Spirit Bay Retreat. That's a convalescent hospital for disadvantaged children on Lake Rossseau. Many have never read a book, and they adore her."

"I'd like to hear more, if you have a few minutes to join me."

After they had explained about the Retreat, Arthur said, "Alice is an orphan, and a ward of the Thorntons. She's the Canadian correspondent for *Our Times*, and has published a book."

"Arthur!" Alice protested. Embarrassed, she explained to L.M.'s quizzical look, "It's just an account of my experiences on the *Lusitania*."

"Oh, how tragic for you, my dear. Is that how you were orphaned?"

"No, my mother drowned when the *Empress of Ireland* sank, and my father succumbed to the Spanish Influenza."

"As did so many," L.M. said sadly, having lost her beloved cousin in the 1918 flu pandemic. "Will you keep writing?"

"I expect I shall, as I really don't know how to do anything else," Alice admitted. "Or wish to."

L.M. laughed. "That's certainly a good reason. Are you also a writer, Mr. Spencer?"

"A mere hack, I'm afraid. I'm going to be a reporter for the *Launston Mills Observer*." Justin Carrington, who helped to manage his grandfather's paper, had given him the job. Arthur hoped to become an editor for a big-city newspaper or a magazine like Maclean's one day, but this was a solid start.

"Launston Mills is not far from where I live, and the largest town around. I will look forward to reading your articles, Mr. Spencer. Now do tell me about your summers on the lake. It seems like such an enchanted life."

They talked about their islands and the summer friends that Arthur, in particular, had grown up with. They mentioned the balls and theatricals, regattas and moonlight cruises, bonfires and singsongs, picnics and excursions, like the one that had brought them to Bala today.

"I expect you realize how very fortunate you are," L.M. said.

"We certainly do," Alice replied. "I, more than anyone, perhaps, since I'm still a relative newcomer to this world."

"Will you be writing a story set in Muskoka?" Arthur asked L.M.

"I've been sitting here absorbing the breathtaking beauty around me. Daydreaming. So perhaps I will, one day." She gazed out at the river.

"Well, we mustn't interfere with the creative process any longer," Arthur announced. "It's been a tremendous pleasure to meet you, Mrs. Macdonald."

"Yes, indeed!" Alice chirped.

"Will you keep me informed about your literary career, Miss Lambton?" L.M. asked. "You can write to me at the manse in Leaskdale."

"Oh, may I? How wonderful!"

"And I'd enjoy a visit, if you end up in Launston Mills as well." She looked at them shrewdly.

"Actually, we just became engaged," Arthur confided proudly.

"Ah, I thought so! Well, it's a delightfully romantic place to do that."

"I'll never forget this day," Alice proclaimed.

"Nor shall I," the author admitted. "Now remember that you haven't seen me."

•   •   •

"This is a truly magical place, Ria," Lance said when she joined him on the open second-floor deck of the large boathouse where he and his sons were staying. Chas would come down shortly, so this was the first time during the visit that they were alone together. "And the accommodation is first class. It's tremendously soothing to listen to the water lapping gently below you, and the haunting calls of the loons echoing across the lake."

"It is delightful, isn't it? Chas and I sometimes sleep here."

The children were messing about in the bay below, Miles and Rupert Wyndham showing the Chadwick boys the tricks to canoe jousting for the SRA Regatta tomorrow. There was plenty of laughter from the participants and spectators whenever one of the boats got dunked.

"It's been tremendous for the boys. I can't tell you how splendid that trip down the Moon River was." Which surprised him, since he had thought it was just a way for Chas to get rid of them for four days. "The scenery was astonishing and the camping really gave us a chance to connect with nature and each other."

"I noticed that the boys enjoy the Indian names your guide, Ben, gave them," Ria said with a chuckle, since they hadn't stopped calling each other "Amik", the beaver, for Philip, and "Makwa", the bear, for Christopher.

"And appropriate they are, too! Clever of the chap to have pegged them so quickly. Philip feels he's part Indian now, and is a confirmed outdoorsman with an addiction to Muskoka blueberries. He already wants to come back next year. And Chris did some growing up."

Lance had confronted Christopher about his surly behaviour towards Ria, and the boy had responded, "Mother didn't come on this trip because she said she had no desire to associate with Mrs. Thornton. If she was your mistress during the war, then she doesn't deserve my respect."

Lance had almost smacked him, but had kept his temper, his reasonable tone more forceful than anger when he'd retorted, "That's very presumptuous and insulting of you to malign Mrs. Thornton like that. She and Lady Antonia have never been more than courageous friends with whom I shared some wartime experiences. I trust you will be man enough to admit that you have been mistaken, and will become civil to our hosts." Of course he would never tell Christopher that his mother had a string of lovers, and that their marriage had never been more than a convenient business arrangement.

Chris had stomped off into the woods, and had returned, stony-faced, only when the delicious aroma of freshly caught fish roasting over the fire had enticed him back. "Makwa" indeed! But as they had sat around the fire under an incomparable, starry sky, listening to Ben's native tales, Chris had mellowed.

Watching the activity in the bay, Lance said, "Sophie's a lovely girl. Just delightful, which of course we knew when we first met her." Sophie had assumed that they were married when he and Ria had walked into her mother's flower shop in Calais six years ago. That was about the time he had begun to fall in love with Ria.

She caught an unguarded look of desire and longing in his eyes, quickly shuttered, but it unsettled her. How she wished she could just have an uncomplicated friendship with him like she had with Justin, who had also been in love with her once. She was relieved to hear Chas's distinctive tread on the bridge that led from the hillside stairs to this second storey deck.

"I'll fetch drinks," she said, going into the sitting room where a bar was set up.

"I can't tell you how grateful I am for your suggestion to do the Moon River jaunt, Chas," Lance said.

"We did it a few times, and never told our parents about Rafe nearly drowning when we capsized in some rapids, or they might not have let us go again."

Hearing the exchange, Ria was relieved that they were finally on a first-name basis. She had cringed every time they had addressed each other with stiff formality as "Major".

"We girls were always rather put-out that the boys wouldn't let us go along," she said as she handed them cocktails.

"It was your parents who wouldn't let you go, not us," Chas corrected.

"Applesauce! We would have had a chaperone, but you said it was far too dangerous for girls. Then I discovered that entire families, including infants, do that circuit."

Chas chuckled. "But I'll wager that the women and children don't carry the canoes. Sometimes chaps just want to be left to their own devices, and not have to be chivalrous or worry about stripping off for a swim."

She smirked.

"Will you be racing your new boat at the Regatta tomorrow?" Lance asked. Chas had taken him and the boys on an exhilarating ride up to the head of the lake in *Windrunner III*.

"As SRA Commodore, Chas is now in charge of the sailboat and motorboat events," Ria explained. "So I'm racing instead."

Lance gawked at her and then burst into laughter. "I shouldn't be surprised, but is that really any safer than flying?"

"Chas thinks so."

"It's not my idea, Lance, believe me," Chas said.

"He won't let me use the newest boat, so I'm driving *Windrunner II*."

"Which can be pushed to 40 miles per hour," Chas pointed out.

"Good Lord!" Lance exclaimed.

Despite Ria's fearless confidence, Lance was nervous when he watched her race the following day.

There was a brisk wind, and the lake was rougher than usual. Frank Sheridan, in his new gentleman's racer, took the lead by seconds at the starter's signal, so *Windrunner II* bounced in his wake as Ria tried to pass. Her stern started to drift in the turn, threatening to spin out, but she corrected quickly and pushed harder to make up time. Stanford Vandemeer's boat right behind her was not so fortunate, as it caught a rogue wave and flipped over, amid shrieks from the spectators. Stanford and his mechanic surfaced and signaled that they were alright, and a rescue boat went over to help. The mechanic, it turned out, had a broken collarbone.

It was an exciting, tight race, but Chas had trained Ria well, and Stephen, who rode as her mechanic, offered sage advice, so she beat Frank by half a length, much to his dismay.

"This year I thought for sure I'd win!" he said to her. "So much for my male arrogance. Well driven, Ria."

She flashed him one of her enchanting smiles. He wasn't the only one to think what a damn fine woman she was.

•   •   •

Phoebe had her arm wrapped firmly around Silas's, happy that he was spending the entire day with her at the Regatta, and not going off to the Chautauqua Assembly as he did most days, at least for the morning lecture. He had taken her along once, but she had found the talk "Canada's Evolving Identity on the International Stage" boring, although Silas and the Kirkbrides hadn't.

She and Silas had come today with Edgar and Daphne, who were just watching the events and no longer participating. Daphne had declared that boat racing was too dangerous for a father of four, so Edgar had given it up. It was too difficult to compete against Chas's boats, anyway, even if Ria was driving them now. But damn it, he'd enjoyed the thrill of racing!

How did women manage to be so sweet and accommodating when you first married them, and then slowly gain the upper hand in such a deceptively nice way that you couldn't possibly disappoint them by going against their wishes? Ah well, he still enjoyed speeding about in his boat even if there was no potential glory in it.

So Edgar clapped enthusiastically for his cousin, proud of Ria for beating the men.

The docks were milling with spectators and participants preparing for their own events, while others spread out on the terraces and lawns. A child darted out from a sea of legs and collided with Edgar. "Steady on, lad," he said as he grabbed the tyke. And suddenly had a chill of dread, for he recognized the boy. It was his own nephew, Phoebe's illegitimate child. Edgar and his father had been keeping a discreet eye on him over the past three years.

"Sorry!" the boy said.

Phoebe looked at him curiously. "Do I know you?" she asked, certain that she had seen him before.

The five-year-old shrugged. But, of course, Edgar could see the resemblance to his father, Bobbie Miller, as well as to Phoebe – her mouth and eyes in particular. Edgar was unnerved, so afraid that she would somehow recognize herself in the boy.

Phoebe squatted down and stared at him as she said, "I seem to have a spare lollipop. Cherry, my favourite. Would you like it?"

The child nodded and took it.

Just then, Rosie Miller, his aunt, came looking for him. "There you are, brat!"

He squealed and started to run off, but she grabbed him, and he giggled as he tried to squirm out of her grasp. "Behave yourself, Luke, or you won't come along next time!" she warned as she smacked him.

Phoebe gasped and Edgar, barely controlling his anger, said, "There's no need to slap the child."

"He's a little devil, Mr. Wyndham, and doesn't listen."

"I expect he's just high-spirited. Boys that age are."

"Is he your brother?" Phoebe asked, realizing what seemed familiar to her. He had Bobbie's broad forehead and dark hair with the distinctive curl over the widow's peak.

"Good grief, no. He's the son of some distant cousin who died, so my parents adopted him. Although God knows what possessed them at their age! And now *I* have to mind him!"

"Oww, stop pinching!" Luke wailed at Rosie, who had a firm hold of him with both hands.

"I'm *not*, brat! You're such a little liar! So you'd better watch out or I *will*!"

As Rosie hauled him off none too gently, he looked back with a mischievous grin, waving his lolly.

How he resembled Phoebe at that moment! Dear God, what had they done, allowing the boy to live near her?

•   •   •

Stephen stood among the trees on the edge of the Pineridge Inn property, watching the activity that spilled from the SRA Country Club into the cool August evening. Charcoal ribbons of clouds, backlit by a nearly full moon, were congregating overhead, as a sharp breeze chopped up the lake.

Ria had invited him to attend the Regatta Ball this evening, maintaining that today's victory was his as much as hers, thanks to his critical advice. He had waffled and finally dressed in the requisite black tie that Chas had bought him for post-race events, and then realized that he would feel completely out of place, even if Ria and Chas included him in their party. It was one thing to dine with them when they were in Palm Beach. But for him to suddenly join people who had always known him only as a chauffeur and mechanic would undoubtedly prove awkward for them and uncomfortable for him.

So he waited here in case Esme came to seek him out. He wasn't hopeful, but how else might he see her alone, unless she initiated the contact? He could hardly go calling on her, cap in hand.

His heart leapt when he spotted her walking towards him.

Esme had schemed to sneak away, but was constantly waylaid by someone. Finally Ted was dancing with Belle and in animated conversation, so he didn't see her leave. But when she stepped out onto the terrace, she hesitated.

But damn it, if she didn't talk to Stephen, how would she ever know if he still cared? She began to walk along the brightly lit dock. If he wasn't waiting for her, then that would be the end of it.

But what would she say to him that she hadn't before? She stopped and began to head back.

Stephen stepped out from the shadows and started to go after her, but Ted, coming in search of her, was closer.

Esme looked back towards Pineridge and caught a movement at the edge of the aura of light that spilled from the Inn's roofed dance pavilion. The figure seemed to be looking towards her, and then turned and walked away. She knew it was Stephen. Had he been waiting for her after all? She fought the urge to run after him.

"If you came out for a breath of air, you probably got more than you bargained for," Ted said.

In her thin, sleeveless gown, she did feel chilled. Ted removed his dinner jacket and draped it about her shoulders.

"Thank you."

"I don't suppose you have an answer for me yet," he asked.

"I'm afraid I haven't."

"Perhaps you need some convincing," he said, drawing her into his arms and kissing her.

She pulled away, saying, "We'll be seen!"

"Does that matter so much these days? We're practically engaged. What's wrong, Esme? You seem distracted."

"I'm sorry. I'm just tired, Ted. It's been a long day." And she realized that Stephen was still watching.

•   •   •

"She's terribly beautiful," Fliss said to Jack. "It *is* hard to take your eyes off her."

Jack realized, somewhat guiltily, that he had been staring at Véronique de Sauveterre. "And she knows it, too," he said. With her hypnotic, ice-blue eyes, helmet of shingled black hair contrasted by a spangled headband that dripped crystal beads down to one shoulder, and the dramatic Vionnet gown that bared her flawless, tanned back and emphasized her alluring curves, Étienne's twenty-three-year-old sister was definitely the star of the evening.

Because none of Lizzie's friends and few family could attend her wedding, Fliss had planned this as an engagement party.

As Lizzie had expected, Étienne deemed Toronto ugly and uninteresting, its best feature – the lake – mostly spoiled by factories, railroads, and warehouses. Although he did acknowledge that Jack's estate north of the city was delightful. She had gone down to meet him and Véronique, and they'd spent only two days there.

But he and his sister were suitably impressed with the luxuries afforded by Thorncliff in such a majestic and wild setting. They'd just had a superb dinner of freshly caught lake trout, renowned Muskoka lamb with all the trimmings, and blueberry pie. Étienne had been rather surprised when guests had arrived for the soiree arrayed in dazzling gowns and diamonds, although Lizzie had primed him about all the financial titans and captains of industry he would be meeting tonight.

Étienne oozed charm naturally and was an instant hit, especially with the women. Lizzie was so proud of him, and gloried in her role as the future Comtesse. The Delacourts and others could no longer look down their long noses at her. How satisfying it was to see the envious glances that Blanche, now married to pleasant but unexciting Frank Sheridan, and Lyle's wife, Adele, gave them.

She didn't even mind that her future sister-in-law had stolen the limelight. Being a French film star, Véronique was used to the attention, although not many outside of France knew about her.

"How did you get into film?" Belinda Delacourt asked her. "Were you on the stage?"

"Oh no, I was never an actress. But when I was in Cannes with Étienne three years ago, Alphonse Dupont, the director, saw me on the beach and told me that I was the face of his new heroine. When I protested that I had no training, he replied that I needed only to keep the camera as enchanted as he was." She had a tinkling laugh. "Fortunately, I have found that quite easy."

"I'm not surprised," Martin Daventry said appreciatively, earning a sidelong glance from Belinda.

"How exciting!" Alice said. "Would you allow me to write an article about you for *Our Times*?"

"But of course!"

"I'm surprised that Hollywood hasn't come calling," Ted mused.

"I had an offer from Cecil DeMille to do a movie with him, but I have no desire to leave France."

"That's a pity, since we don't get to see French films. You have no wish to become another Gloria Swanson?"

Véronique smiled graciously. "But in France I *am* as famous as she."

Ted chortled. "I do beg your pardon!" When he asked, "Have you done any postcards or magazine pin-ups?" the other men knew he was referring to nude photos, which Hollywood stars were starting to do, but for which the French were already famous. Naturally, the girls didn't know that.

She smiled. "It is all part of the publicity. Very artistic, of course."

"You must send us some," Esme said innocently.

"They are for the studio, not for me," Véronique replied.

"I see. Is it fashionable to be suntanned in France? My mother is always telling me to cover up, which is difficult if you want to have any fun outdoors," Esme said.

"Quite the latest fashion, thanks to Coco. Chanel, that is. She is one of my great friends. She says that pale people look like they are dying of – how do you say? – consumption? And that being bronzed by the sun gives health and vigour. It is the mark of a modern woman not confined to boudoirs or sitting idly in the shade."

Esme wasn't the only one wondering how naked Véronique had to be outdoors to develop such an even tan on her back. Her sleek burgundy gown draped scandalously low to her waist, where two thin, bejeweled shoulder straps met, forming a flattering and eye-catching V across her back.

Glasses of champagne were handed around by the staff, and Jack called for everyone's attention. "Ladies and gentlemen, thank you for coming this evening to help us celebrate the upcoming nuptials of my sister Elizabeth and Comte Étienne de Sauveterre. I wish them every happiness - which shouldn't' be too difficult in beautiful Provence in a château filled with exquisite wines."

"You can expect plenty of visitors," Stuart Roland chimed in amid the laughter.

"And I must say that we would be savouring the Comte's wines this evening if he'd been allowed to bring some with him," Jack said. "In any case, I ask you to raise your glasses in a toast to Elizabeth and Étienne."

"To the Comte and Comtesse!" people said.

"And now Emily and Hugo will entertain us with some of their Broadway hits, and then they'll be allowed to enjoy the rest of their holiday," Jack said, grinning at his sister.

Emily and Hugo loved their Moonglow Island cottage, and had been relaxing there for a couple of weeks, and looking forward to another month of quiet, creative activity. Their summer friends were always eager to know what next Broadway success would originate from their Muskoka getaway.

Emily said, "Hugo wrote this song for me, but it touches every lover's heart. And tonight I'm dedicating it to my beloved sister and her fiancé."

She launched into *Under the Moon*. As usual, the audience was mesmerized.

An orchestra took over after the short concert, with Lizzie and Étienne leading the dancing. When Jack danced with Véronique, he was somewhat disconcerted and tempted by the sensual feel of her naked back. It would be so easy to slip a hand under the flimsy silk and slide it around to her obviously bare breasts. It had been a long time since he had felt the thrill of the chase.

"Your sister Emily has an astonishing voice," she said to him.

"Yes, even I'm impressed. She's become much more accomplished than when she sang around the house as a kid."

"That is a great love her husband has, to write such beautiful music for her."

"They seem happy and well matched. What about you? Is there no great love in your life?"

"There have been some, but why should I tie myself to one man when so many are appealing?" She looked him boldly in the eye.

Jack felt his blood stirred.

Lizzie was torn about dancing with Lyle, especially to *If You Were the Only Girl in the World*, but she could hardly refuse him a dance.

"Is the Comte enjoying himself?" Lyle asked her.

"I think he's suitably amazed by Muskoka, especially that people own entire islands."

"Rather than immense châteaux?"

She smiled. "Well, having an island is somewhat exotic, I suppose. There's really nothing to compare in Europe, is there?"

"Will you miss it, Lizzie?"

"Sometimes, I expect. But I'll be back."

"I do hope so."

Étienne, waltzing with Sidonie, said of Lizzie and Lyle, "They dance remarkably well together."

"Like a professional team, I'd say. The rest of us usually stop to watch."

"It is my luck that Monsieur Delacourt did not dance Elizabeth to the altar then."

Sid laughed.

"Jack tells me that you spend winters in Cannes, Lady Sidonie."

"We do. My parents have a villa there, so Rafe and I rent something nearby for a few months. I can't abide the bitter winters here, nor in London, I have to admit." She still had her Grosvenor Square townhouse, so she spent part of the autumn there before meeting Rafe in the south of France in December. He was preoccupied with his horses, and complained that she never wanted to stay in Toronto.

"I expect that Elizabeth will wish to spend some time with Lady Beatrice at Cap d'Antibes, so we must get together."

"That would be delightful," Sid said, wondering if he had left that statement deliberately vague and open to interpretation.

He smiled down at her.

She chuckled to herself. So the Comte had a roving eye. How delightful!

•   •   •

"Are you coming down to the beach, sweetheart?" Jack asked Fliss. He and twenty-two-month-old Alexander – Sandy for short - were both in their swimsuits.

Fliss was reclined on a chaise lounge on the veranda, feeling drained after yesterday's party, and the baby was very active today. She felt too large to even consider getting into a bathing suit. "I couldn't, Jack. Do keep a close eye on Sandy. You know how fearless he is of the water."

"Of course. Don't worry, and get some rest. That was a marvellous party yesterday. You always outdo yourself, sweetheart."

She smiled wanly. "Well, I'm afraid you'll have to look after our guests today."

He and Véronique had already beaten Lizzie and Étienne at tennis earlier this afternoon, and the engaged couple had just gone canoeing. Jack had seen Véronique head out in her swimwear earlier.

There were several small sandy beaches interrupting the rocky shoreline of the island, but the largest was at the "diving cove". Here a cliff reared up at the end of the bay and formed a perfect diving platform. Being a third of the way around the twenty-acre island from the house, it was also quite private.

Jack was not surprised to find Véronique lying face down on a towel, her bathing suit pulled down to her buttocks. Her avant-garde beach pajamas – sexy, flowing, diaphanous trousers and long jacket – lay discarded in the sand.

"I beg your pardon," Jack said. "We didn't mean to disturb you."

As she sat up, she held onto the front of her skimpy sleeveless crimson maillot – more daring than anything Jack had yet seen on a beach. The skin-tight pantaloons only reached to mid-thigh and weren't covered by the usual short skirt, which would have afforded some modesty. She had also dispensed with the requisite stockings and slippers, so she was mostly, and enticingly, naked, the thin, wet jersey not leaving much to the imagination.

"Not at all. Perhaps you could help me?" she asked as she fumbled to find the back of the straps, which buttoned at the shoulders.

Jack managed to help her without touching her too much, knowing this would be a disastrous time to allow any sort of intimacy to occur. He was glad to slide into the cool and sobering water with Sandy, who hadn't bothered to wait for him.

Véronique sat on the beach, one bent knee splayed on the sand and the other tented up. Jack couldn't help thinking it an invitation. He sat in the shallows while Sandy splashed about.

"You have a wonderful kingdom here," she said as she lit a cigarette.

Jack laughed. "Hardly that!"

"Are you not the ruler of all you behold?"

"Mostly, I suppose."

"To have a private beach like this... it is a privilege."

"We do rather take this for granted. There is still so much unspoiled and uninhabited land, even on these lakes."

"The water is so soft, and I like that I don't have to wash the salt off after a swim."

Jack knew that he was suffering from not having had sex in over four months when the arousing image of licking the salt off her popped into his mind. He was relieved when she butted out her half-smoked cigarette in the sand and pulled on her sheer jacket. She put her large-brimmed hat on, and drew the towel up over her bent knees.

"Do you know what is bad about having nothing but beauty to define you?" she asked, but didn't wait for an answer. "You have an obligation to look after that beauty, knowing well that it is a losing battle. I have what? - perhaps another ten or fifteen years before I am considered too old and will be replaced by some young ingénue? And in the meantime, I must ensure that I don't get sunburnt or have strange tan lines or eat tasty pastries or smoke too many cigarettes, because they might give me wrinkles, make me fat, destroy my complexion." She seemed inordinately sad.

"Then you mustn't think that all you have is your beauty," Jack suggested.

"Ah, but what else have I? Not talent. I'm no Dominique Rousseau." Jack knew that that famous stage actress was Sophie's grandmother.

"Everyone has some sort of talent. You're just not aware of yours yet."

"Oh, but I am. I give pleasure." She smiled seductively at him. "What can women do but be wives and mothers. Lovers."

"Artists, writers, doctors, lawyers..."

"Not for me! When you have a daughter, will you want her to have such a man's profession?"

"I expect my daughter will become a shrewd businesswoman."

Jack had a sudden shock of intense fear when he realized that he hadn't been watching Sandy. He didn't hear any splashing and looked around in a panic to see, with immense relief, the toddler standing waist-deep, peering into the water. "Peepee all gone, Daddy."

Véronique burst into a trilling laugh. Jack thought her utterly bewitching.

He couldn't imagine that he would rue the day when the de Sauveterre siblings had come into their lives.

•   •   •

Sophie was tearful on the day that the Chadwicks were scheduled to leave, and the boys, stoical. They were up early for one last canoe jaunt around the island and morning swim. It was just before lunch, when their bags were loaded into *Windrunner*, ready for Chas and Sophie to drive them over to the train station on Lake Joe, that they were startled by an unusual sound.

"That's an aeroplane!" Christopher shouted.

"It's Barker!" Miles said, recognizing the giant seaplane.

"We arranged a surprise for you and the boys," Ria explained to Lance. "Will's going to give you a tour of Muskoka by air and then fly you down to the harbour in Toronto. Stephen's heading out now and will see that your luggage gets aboard the train, so you need only pick it up at Union Station."

"But this is marvellous!" Lance said. "What a tremendous treat!"

"Especially since you'll be piloted by the Empire's most decorated war hero, who has twice flown the Prince of Wales," Chas added. "Barker and his co-pilot will join us for lunch, as there's no great hurry now. I'm sure the boys will be thrilled. We've invited Miles and Rupert to dine as well."

"That's most thoughtful," Lance said sincerely.

"This is probably Barker's last flight in the Curtiss HS-2L. He's been selling off the company's planes, since he's now a Wing Commander in the CAF, and Bishop's already in England," Chas said.

It was a lively lunch and a terrific send-off for their guests. When Ria and Chas had a quiet moment to themselves afterwards, she said, "That was the cat's whiskers! Thank you, Chas, for being so kind to our guests."

"The flight was your idea, if I recall."

"But you persuaded Barker. Probably with a nice big cheque, but still."

He laughed.

"No, truly, Chas. I know how much you disliked their coming, but you helped to make their trip memorable. And I hope you don't resent Lance quite so much anymore."

"I couldn't possibly resent every man who's in love with you, my darling, or there'd be hardly anyone to talk to," he teased as he kissed her hand.

"Applesauce!"

He crooned to her:

Whispering while you cuddle near me
Whispering so no one can hear me

Each little whisper seems to cheer me
I know it's true, there's no one dear, but you,
You're whispering why you'll never leave me
Whispering why you'll never grieve me
Whisper and say that you believe me
Whispering that I love you.

She gazed at him tenderly, realizing that he still wasn't the self-confident pre-war Chas who'd had the world at his feet. She saw past his scars, but he didn't. "You should never doubt it," she assured him. "I have to admit that I'm glad our visitors have left. I feel surprisingly wrung out in this heat, and just want to be lazy."

Chas hoped that it would be a long time, if ever, before he needed to concern himself with the Chadwicks again.

He hadn't counted on Sophie and Philip.

Chapter 22

"Be a good chap and bring the gramophone for us," Ted said to Stephen. The men in the party were already carrying the baskets of food, picnic rugs, and buckets for berrying.

"That's hardly Stephen's job," Esme said, trying to keep her tone light, but annoyed that Ted was treating Stephen as a servant.

"That's alright, Miss Wyndham. I don't mind," Stephen said. In fact, he was glad that he could accompany them on the hike up the Huckleberry Rock rather than waiting in the boat or hanging about the Wild Cedar Lodge where they had docked.

Chas had offered the use of *Lady Ria* to Alice and her friends for an outing. They were starting out with a picnic lunch at the lookout, some of the group never having been there, including half a dozen city friends of the Daventrys and Lorimers, as well as Lizzie, Étienne, and Véronique.

It was an easy but long climb through the pine-needled woods and up the rock. Dottie Bellinger, the sister of Ted's friend, Harry, had worn her fashionable high-heeled pumps despite being warned, and kept grabbing Ted for support when she tripped or slipped.

"You are an ass, Dottie," her brother scoffed.

"One must keep up appearances, as Mother always says," she retorted. From a wealthy mercantile family, twenty-two-year-old Dottie was stylish, and carried herself with supreme confidence. Esme had met her several times, but had never warmed to her. Especially since she was always angling for Ted's attention.

Today, she was obviously intent upon impressing the Comte. Her scarlet lipstick and kohl-vamped eyes hardly seemed suitable for a picnic. "Besides, they're so much sexier than flat shoes."

She was right of course, Esme thought. The heels somehow made women's newly exposed calves seem more alluring.

"Sexier indeed," Ted agreed. "But so impractical. The things you women do to yourselves!"

"Only to attract you men, of course," Dottie shot back. "Don't you think I'd rather be barefoot? Actually, that's a good idea!"

She took off her shoes and, urging the others to go ahead, slipped off her silk stockings. She ran to catch up with them. "Ouch, the rock is as hot as sin!" she protested.

"May I offer a piggyback ride?" Ted asked, passing his bag of gramophone recordings to Harry.

"Oh, how gallant!" She put her shoes back on and jumped onto his back, not at all bothered that her skirt rode up when Ted wrapped his arms around her knees. He was obviously struggling with the extra weight, and had to put her down several times to rest. Harry took over for a while, but brother and sister bickered so much that Ted resumed the task. He almost dropped her once when his foot caught in a crevasse and unbalanced him.

With Stephen lagging respectfully behind the crowd, Esme hated this expedition.

When they arrived at the lookout, Harry exclaimed, "What a view!"

"You can see Port Darling, where you locked through, in that direction," Martin Daventry explained, pointing north. "And Bala, way over there. That's where we're going later to see the falls."

"It must be spectacular here at sunset," Alice mused.

"And an amazing place to lie down and watch the Perseids meteor shower, which will be at its peak soon," Derek Carlyle observed.

"I wouldn't relish trying to find my way back down in the dark, though," Maud Spencer admitted.

"But we wouldn't, because the most activity occurs just before dawn."

"What kind of *activity* are we actually talking about?" Dottie jested. "Sounds delightfully risqué to me."

Martin said, "Well, I feel chuffed just having managed this climb in the daytime." Belinda Delacourt, who had held his arm the entire way, grinned happily at him. They were engaged to be married next summer.

"Then let's celebrate!" Ted said, opening the hamper that contained several bottles of champagne on ice. Corks popped, flying over the cliff, and the wine was poured into waiting glasses.

"Congratulations to Martin for his complete recovery from the plane crash, and also for successfully coercing the lovely Belinda to marry him!" Ted looked hard at Esme, who squirmed. "And, of course, to our special guest and his soon-to-be-bride," he added, lifting his glass to Étienne and Lizzie.

Stephen set up the gramophone while the others ate sandwiches and cookies. Then he sat on a boulder some distance from the party, having a smoke.

Esme went over and offered him some food and a glass of wine, saying "You shouldn't have been asked to do this."

"I'd rather be here," he said, engaging her eyes.

They stared at one another searchingly, but were interrupted when Ted said, "How thoughtful you are, Esme. Of course Stephen must be fed. Now let's dance."

Toot, toot, Tootsie, Goo'-Bye! Toot, toot, Tootsie, don't cry, rang out incongruously across the ancient rock and dispersed over the cascading treetops to the lake.

It was during the lilting slow tunes that Esme felt awkward dancing with Ted under Stephen's gaze, realizing that she wished she could be in Stephen's arms instead. Recalling, with sudden poignancy, swaying with him under the moon.

Stephen felt just as miserable watching. After that fiasco during the Regatta Ball, he had begun to think he had lost her. But there was a spark of hope in the way she had looked at him just now. How right the song was that was playing.

A pretty girl is like a melody
That haunts you night and day
Just like the strain of a haunting refrain,
She'll start upon a marathon
And run around your brain.

When the group headed off to pick blueberries and huckleberries, Derek cautioned, "Watch out for bears. They're very fond of the berries as well."

"Bears!" Dottie bleated. "No one warned me that this would be dangerous!"

"Just continue to make lots of noise, which will alert them that you're coming, but back off if you actually see one," Derek advised. "They need the berries more than we do," he added with a grin.

"Dottie doesn't have any difficulty making noise," Harry ribbed.

"I think I'll stay here with the gramophone," she declared.

As the others headed off, Dottie realized that she would be all by herself, with only Stephen for protection, so she stumbled after them. They didn't have far to go to find heavily laden bushes. Eating while they were picking, they soon had purple fingers and tongues, which occasioned plenty of amusement.

Lizzie snapped some photos of the group, and then she and Étienne went off to explore other views.

Dottie surprised Ted by smudging a particularly large and juicy blueberry on his cheek, leaving a lavender mark there. She squealed with delight and ran off – not moving far or fast in her heels – in obvious invitation for him to follow and retaliate with some playful tussling.

But Ted just hurled a fistful of berries at her. "Vixen!"

She laughed delightedly, and threw some back at him.

"You'll never get the blueberry stains out of your clothes," Maud informed them.

Harry suddenly stared at his sister with a look of terror on his face. "Behind you!" he yelled.

She screeched and dashed back to the group, where Harry had a handful of berries ready, which he crushed onto the sleeve of her white blouse when she ran into his protective embrace.

"Oh, you beast!" she accused as she punched him on the shoulder.

"It seems to me that you started it by assaulting our host."

"It was just a bit of fun."

"Precisely. We're enjoying it immensely," Harry assured her.

"You scared me to death! I thought there was a bear. I need more wine! Anyone else coming?"

"I will," Esme said, glad of an excuse to get back to Stephen, even though she wouldn't have a chance to talk to him alone.

The others declared that their buckets were full enough and followed.

While they were savouring another glass of champagne before heading back down the hill, Eugene Roland asked Ted about his new job with the family firm.

"It's a fun challenge convincing people that they need something that they don't, or didn't realize they did, and then persuading them to buy it," he replied.

"Horsefeathers! You can't do that!" one of the girls said.

"If the newspaper ads tell you that you'll have wrinkles by the time you're thirty if you doesn't use Pond's Cold Cream, then you're likely to buy it, aren't you? Or if Dottie sees sad-looking Suzy who can't get a date because she has – horrors! – halitosis, then Dottie will buy Listerine as well, just to be on the safe side."

"It's easy to prey on women's insecurities," Harry said. "That's hardly a challenge."

"If I drape a sexy flapper with a come-hither gaze across the hood of a Cadillac, I expect that you will consider a Cadillac before a Chevrolet when you buy a car," Ted assured him.

"You're going to use your psychology training to manipulate people?" Esme asked.

"They're eager to know how to improve themselves. I'd go so far as to say that the vast majority like being told what to do and how to think."

"You mean the great unwashed," Harry chimed in.

"They have more money than ever before, but little experience with how to spend it. We're doing them a favour," Ted stated.

"That is so condescending and arrogant!" Esme fumed.

"Don't be so yawn-making, Esme," Dottie chided languidly. "Is there any more giggle-water?" she added, holding out her glass for a refill of wine.

"Think of it this way, Esme," Ted said. "The Seafords make dandy boats, but who aside from us knows that? So we create an ad that shows a beautiful, sleek launch carrying happy, good-looking young people, and mention that Seaford Boats win international races, and, presto! any number of guys are now tempted to buy a launch and will consider a Seaford if they do. Everyone wins." He grinned. "And Chas has hired me to do just that."

Of course that made perfect sense, and Esme felt a bit foolish for reacting so angrily. She caught Stephen's wry look.

Harry tried to pour himself another glass of wine, but the last of the bottles was empty. "Dottie, you little piggy, you finished the champers!"

One of his friends said, "Not to worry. I have some ganja." He pulled out his silver case and gave Harry a marijuana cigarette, and offered some to the others. "There's enough to share."

Most of them declined, agreeing with Esme when she said, "I've had plenty of champagne, and this isn't the best place to get hopped-up. Somebody might prance off a cliff." Not that she and most of the others hadn't tried marijuana at some time, but she much preferred the familiar buzz from wine and cocktails. Yet cannabis was easier to obtain than bootleg liquor.

"I'm surprised it isn't illegal yet," Stuart Roland said as he took a deep drag and then passed his cigarette to Véronique. He was obviously pleased that she was staying close to him on this outing, her arm often entwined with his.

"At the same time as outlawing booze?" Harry groused.

"It'll come," Derek predicted. "Haven't you been reading the rubbish that Emily Murphy wrote in *Maclean's* about the 'drug menace'? No scientific facts to substantiate her outrageous statements, but the articles have been scaring people who don't know any better. Mum says that doctors used to prescribe cannabis for all kinds of ailments, including migraines." His mother was a pharmacist, and her father had been a doctor. "But now you're going to become savage, immoral, raving lunatics," he warned the smokers with a grin.

"Mama was quite distraught when she read Emily Murphy's dire warnings," Esme confessed. "And, of course, made me swear I would never touch the stuff."

"And being the obedient daughter that you are, you never have," Alice teased, for they had giggled together over a smoke last winter.

"I find Murphy's journalism extremely racist," Arthur said. "She blames 'aliens of colour' for peddling poisonous drugs to bring about the degradation of the white race. It's propaganda designed to lobby for tighter immigration laws."

"That's what happens when you give women a voice and power," Ted quipped. "Isn't Murphy a judge?'

"First female police magistrate in the British Empire," Maud clarified.

"Then I hope she's more familiar with law than she is with science," Derek said.

"She's obviously adept at marketing her cause," Ted rejoined. "When has government - or industry - ever allowed truth to stand in the way of *progress* or profits?"

"You'll go far with that attitude, old fruit," Harry ragged.

"Ted for President!" Stuart Roland declared.

"Prime Minister, you ignorant Yank!" Harry corrected, and they burst into riotous laughter.

Esme's eyes met Stephen's and she suddenly felt ashamed. Ted and some of the others might be amused by glib repartee, but they were so caught up in their own pleasures and sense of entitlement that everything else was trivialized.

"Cripes! I just realized that there's no loo here," Dottie looked so stricken that the others couldn't help chuckling. "What's a girl to do?"

"Not drink so much champagne, for a start," Lucy Daventry said snidely.

"You can head back to the boat or the Lodge, or make use of that stand of trees down there," Ted suggested.

"And risk encountering a bear?" Dottie demanded. "No thank you, I will make a run for the Lodge."

"Not in those shoes," her brother snorted.

"You can wear mine," Esme offered. "I'm used to going about barefoot in the summer. And I think that Ted's back can't offer any more rides." She had noticed that he'd moved stiffly when they'd danced, although he hadn't complained.

"I think I wrenched it a bit when my foot slipped," he admitted.

Eager to relieve herself, Dottie accepted Esme's offer, the rubber-soled canvas espadrilles being an almost perfect fit. "But I'm not going alone! Anyway, I'm sure I'd never find the way."

It was rather confusing, as there was no real path until you reached the woods, so Ted said, "I'll show you, and the rest of you can follow more leisurely with Martin."

Dottie moved remarkably quickly, probably in desperation to get to the toilet. They were out of sight before the others had gathered the things and set out.

"Are you sure you're alright, Esme?" Martin asked as she picked her way across the rock, occasionally cooling her feet on the clumps of grass. "Perhaps you should wait here until someone can bring your shoes back."

"That would take much too long," she protested. "I'm fine."

Stephen was annoyed by the situation, but could hardly offer to carry her.

They were getting close to where the woods thickened, about three-quarters of the way down, when Esme stepped on the edge of a tussock and felt a needle-sharp pain in her ankle. She cried out and then screamed when she saw the mottled snake rattle its tail and slither across the rock into a clump of junipers.

"Jesus Christ!" Stephen swore, dropping the gramophone and rushing to Esme's side. He had recognized the venomous Massasauga rattlesnake.

Esme was hysterical. He gripped her firmly by the arms and said, "Calm down, Esme, or you'll just make it worse. Will you trust me?" He stared hard at her, willing her to relax so that the poison wouldn't rush through her veins.

Wide-eyed with terror, she nodded. He picked her up and sat her on a nearby boulder, shouting to the stunned group, "Does anyone have something stronger than wine?"

Étienne handed him a hip flask, saying, "My best cognac."

Derek had meanwhile borrowed Alice's sash and went to help. "Have you done this before?" he asked as he tied a loose tourniquet above the bite.

"I've seen it done," Stephen replied.

Stephen pulled out his pocketknife and sterilized it in the flame of the match Derek lit. Then he knelt down, doused the bite with the alcohol, and quickly made an incision across the two fang marks.

Esme tried not to cry out, but couldn't stop her tears. Arthur had a supportive arm about her in case she fainted, while Alice gripped her hand for moral support.

"What the hell?" Martin exclaimed amid the gasps of the others.

"He's trying to evacuate the venom," Derek, the biologist, explained.

After swilling some brandy, Stephen sucked at the incision, spitting out the blood and venom, over and over again.

"Christ, won't he get poisoned?" Martin asked as the group watched, dumbfounded.

"Probably not. As long as he doesn't have any sores in his mouth," Derek replied, and then asked Esme, "Did you step on the rattler or just startle it?"

"I don't think I stepped on it."

"Snakes control how much venom they use, so you may not have gotten a big dose if it was just warning you," Derek tried to reassure her.

Stephen finished by rinsing the wound and his mouth with the remainder of the cognac, and said, "Try to relax, Esme." He picked her up and carried her as quickly as he dared over the rough terrain. "How bad is it?"

"Hurts like the devil."

"You're very brave," he murmured to her.

She had her arms around his neck, and would have been thrilled to be held like this in different circumstances. "I'm so scared," she confessed.

So was he, though he wouldn't let her see that. He knew a kid, years ago, who had died from a rattlesnake bite, but no one had known what to do then, and the person who had survived the procedure he had just performed had still became dangerously ill. Hopefully Derek was right, and the snake hadn't injected much poison. And hopefully he hadn't made a mess of things with his incision.

Ted was thunderstruck when he saw Stephen carrying a bleeding Esme along the dock to the boat. "What happened?"

"She surprised a venomous rattlesnake, which bit her," Stephen replied, furious that that stupid bitch with her fancy shoes had caused this.

Dottie shrieked. "There are poisonous snakes here? With those and bears, you still suggested I go into the woods?" she accused Ted.

"This isn't about you, Dottie," Lucy growled.

"Perhaps you could make some room, Miss Bellinger," Stephen said brusquely as he pushed past Dottie. He took Esme into the cabin and settled her, with a cushion, in a reclined position on one of the leather benches.

While he fetched the first-aid box, Ted sat down beside Esme. He took her hand and said, "Tell me what happened, sweetheart."

"I'm feeling really sick." The pain was excruciating; she had gone deathly pale, and was faint and nauseated.

"Of course you are! My poor darling."

Stephen bit his tongue as he offered her some Aspirin, the only thing he had. He wasn't happy that the wound was starting to swell, the poison having taken hold despite his efforts. She was obviously in shock, so he covered her with a blanket and advised, "Stay as still and calm as you can, Miss Wyndham. Mr. Lorimer, she shouldn't talk or be disturbed in any way. I suggest that everyone except Miss Lambton and Mr. Carlyle stay here so that I can get her to the doctor more quickly."

"He's right," Derek said, taking Ted aside. "It's important that the toxins don't travel too rapidly to her heart."

Ted was shocked by the implication. "Alright, but I'm coming along."

"I'll bandage the wound," Derek offered. "So you can get going, Stephen. Best take her to Ellie, since she has a lab at the Retreat, and is likely there."

Watching the boat pull away, Dottie said, "Well, we seem to be stranded."

"Thanks to you and those ridiculous shoes," her brother accused. "I'm leaving you home next time."

"Don't be beastly! I hadn't intended this to happen!"

"We have the Lodge at our disposal, so we should make the best of it," Belle suggested, barely controlling her temper. "Anyone who wants to go home can catch the next steamer that comes by."

Wishing he had one of the fast launches, Stephen was still grateful for the 250 horse power engine, and pushed *Lady Ria* to her limit. Fortunately, they were able to get to the upper lake quickly by using the new small-boat lock beside the dam, the *Lady Ria* only just fitting into it.

It was helpful to have Derek monitoring Esme, checking that the tourniquet wasn't too tight to cut off circulation, and moving it higher as necessary to stem the toxic spread.

Another blessing was that Troy's boat was docked at Spirit Bay. Stephen bolted up to the Retreat. "I'll arrange for a bed," Ellie said when he had explained the situation. To Troy she added, "It's a hemotoxin, so there could be internal bleeding. I'll need a blood count right away and we'll have to be prepared to do a transfusion."

Esme was in obvious agony when Stephen scooped her into his arms and carried her into the Retreat. What luck and irony that Ted had injured his back.

"Take her into the sunroom," Ellie instructed. There were daybeds set up in the hexagonal ground-floor room, but none of the children required them at the moment. One of the staff that Esme had hired was quickly arranging some bedding, while another – a medical student – was asked to fetch various items from Ellie's dispensary.

Derek told his sister about Stephen's first-aid while she replaced Alice's sash with a rubber band. The swelling was creeping up Esme's calf.

"Well done, Stephen!" Ellie said as she examined Esme, listening to her heart, checking her pulse, which was too fast. "Now we need to do a bit more of the same. But first I'm going to give you some morphine for the pain and to relax you, Esme, so try not to worry. We'll fix you up. And what about you, Stephen? Do you have any tingling or numbness in your mouth? A metallic taste?"

"No."

"Nausea, headache, blurred vision?"

"No."

She checked his pulse. "Excellent!"

When the student returned with suction bulbs, antiseptic, and a scalpel, Ellie said, "I'm going to have to ask the rest of you to step outside while we get to work."

One of the nurses came in carrying basins and saline solution, and Troy took a blood sample off for analysis and typing.

Stephen was loath to leave Esme, but knew he had no place by her side now. With a reassuring smile, he squeezed her hand and said, "Stay strong, Esme. You'll be fine." He had deliberately not called her 'Miss Wyndham' because he wanted her to know that he still cared for her. When she had recovered, he would tell her how much.

Grateful tears quivered on her lashes. "I haven't thanked you." She clung to him for a moment, and he reluctantly disengaged himself.

"There's no need," he said gently. "Just get well." He had to restrain himself from caressing her cheek, kissing her lips. But she saw the tenderness in his eyes.

While Ellie was pleasantly surprised, Ted was taken aback by Stephen's familiarity, but then reasoned that he and Esme had known each other for years, and perhaps were on less formal terms when alone. There surely couldn't be anything else going on.

"You can go and fetch the others now," Ted said to Stephen.

"Yes, Sir."

"Before you leave, Stephen, will you give Troy a blood sample? I want to ensure you haven't been adversely affected by your courageous action, and we may need you as a blood donor, if you're willing."

"Of course!" he said. He knew that Troy had saved Ria's life in France by donating his blood when she'd been wounded, which was why she called him "big brother".

When Stephen returned several hours later, Ellie declared Esme out of immediate danger, but he didn't have a chance to see her because she was still undergoing treatment.

"Your blood work was normal, but I want to take another sample just to be sure there haven't been any delayed effects. Are you still feeling alright?" Ellie asked him.

"Just fine. Will you need me for a transfusion?"

"No. Esme has Ria's more rare blood type "B", so we'll use Troy if necessary. Anyway, Esme's holding her own and may not need any blood, despite what we've been sucking out of her." Ellie smiled warmly at him. "You've done your good deed for today."

Stephen was working in the small office at the back of the new boathouse at The Point the following afternoon when Richard Wyndham found him. "My family and I wish to thank you for your quick-thinking heroics yesterday, Stephen. Dr. Roland said Esme was lucky that you managed to eliminate some of the poison so quickly and slow down the rate of its spread." He paused and added, "That was very noble of you to endanger your own life."

Stephen got up from his chair and faced Richard squarely. *Damn the torpedoes*, he thought. "There's no need for thanks, Mr. Wyndham. I love Esme and would give my life for hers if necessary."

Richard was completely taken aback – by the sentiment, the honesty, the courage in expressing those feelings. "I... see," he stammered.

Stephen could have taken it a step further, accusing Richard of not thinking him good enough for his daughter, but he figured it was more effective to leave it simply at that. "Please give her my sincerest wishes for a speedy recovery."

He was right. Richard was impressed with his quiet dignity. And seemed conflicted as he said absently, "Indeed I will. Thank you."

Before he left the boathouse, Richard looked back at Stephen as if examining him with new eyes.

•   •   •

Four days later Esme was reclining on a chaise lounge on the veranda at Silver Bay, resting her bandaged leg and sipping beef tea to build up her blood. Ellie had made a ring of cruciform incisions around the bite as well as at the upper edge of the swelling on her calf, and mechanical suction had been applied on and off for several hours. "You're going to look like you've been cross-stitched for a sampler," Ellie had jested. Troy had done blood and urine tests every two hours that first day, but luckily she hadn't needed a transfusion. A nurse had sat up with her all night, while Ellie and Troy had camped out in the lounge in case Esme took a turn for the worse. Now she had only Aspirin to take the edge off the ache from the incisions, the intense pain from the venom thankfully having disappeared. Ellie assured her that there had been no permanent damage, although the bite itself might take a while to heal.

Ted had visited her every day, bringing a dozen red roses and other treats. Esme had been disappointed that Stephen hadn't come. But on the second day one of the attendants brought her a bud vase embracing a single perfect daisy, telling her, "The gentleman said that he's delighted to hear you're doing so well, Miss, and to pass along his best wishes." She knew it was from him, and expected that he had carefully selected the daisy from the colourful gardens at Pineridge.

Alice joined her on the veranda saying, "How wonderful to have you home again! Stephen asked me to give you this."

Esme took the note with hope and apprehension.

When can we talk? it read.

"Is he in the boathouse now?" Esme asked Alice.

"Yes, but you can't walk that far yet."

"I don't intend to. I'll take a canoe," she said with a grin.

"Nothing can stand in the way of true love," Alice teased.

"Is it, do you think?" Esme asked earnestly.

"If you mean do I believe Stephen's hopelessly smitten by you, and would battle bears and rattlesnakes – and fathers - for his lady-love, then yes. And I already know how you feel."

She was to stay off her foot, so Esme used her crutches to make her way down to the dock. "Sorry to cut your visit short, Alice. I'll see you later."

"I'm counting on being the first to hear the news."

Esme felt elated as she paddled the short distance to The Point, but nervous when she reached the boathouse. She pulled into one of the empty slips. Stephen was just putting the engine hatch of *Windrunner III* back into place.

"Is this a good time?" she asked, her heart pounding.

He hadn't expected her so soon, but he might as well get it over with. "Sure thing."

He helped her manoeuver onto the edge of the dock, and then pulled her up and handed her the crutches.

"I'm happy to see you looking so well," he said.

"Thanks to you."

They stared at each other searchingly, expectantly.

"Esme, I…. When you opened your heart to me three years ago, I wasn't truthful."

She was breathlessly hopeful.

"I should have told you how much I loved you. I shouldn't have let anything stand in the way of that. Not your parents' disapproval or your age or the difference in our social status. I know that Ted Lorimer is keen on you. In fact, I've heard that he intends to marry you."

Esme tried to interrupt, but Stephen wanted to say his piece. "I couldn't let that happen without telling you. In case you still…"

She dropped her crutches and went into his arms. Their embrace held all the thwarted passion of the past three years. "Why have you waited so long?" she asked after their searing kiss.

He could hardly blame her father, so he said, "I wasn't sure I could make you happy. We have such different lives, and I can't be anywhere but here, even for you. This is my life - the lake, the boats, the inn. Could you make it yours?"

"Oh yes! I love it here, too."

He chuckled. "You may not say that in the depths of winter."

"We'll keep each other warm."

"Indeed we will." He kissed her deeply, joyfully. "But what will your parents say?"

"They'll point out all the potential problems and then give us their blessing. Ultimately, they want me to be happy. Papa recently remarked that you were a 'decent chap', as if he had some new insight. In any case, I'm twenty-one and have my own money, so I can do as I please. Gosh, you don't mind that I have money, do you?"

He laughed heartily. "Not at all. But I'm not marrying you because of it either." He pulled something from his pocket. "Will you accept this as a place-holder for a real engagement ring?" It was a blue plastic gem set in a copper band. "It's a Cracker Jack prize."

Esme burst into laughter. "I adore it! You mustn't go to any great expense to buy me a ring."

"It won't be showy like Belinda's or Lizzie's, or anyone else's that you know, come to that."

"Oh! But what about *your* family? Will they accept me, or think me a snob?"

"If you don't expect to be waited on hand and foot, they'll adore you. As I do."

"Let's not wait any longer! Let's elope!"

"We'll do this properly, Esme Wyndham," he said stroking her cheek. "No one will be able to say that we went against our families' wishes."

"Then let's go and tell them now."

Esme had been right. Her mother said to her, "What about Ted?"

"He's been great fun to be with, but I don't love him, Mama. I was in love with Stephen before I even met Ted. He has his pick of girls, anyway."

"But Esme, my chick, can you really live in such a small village, where people are often parochial and narrow-minded?"

"Stephen certainly isn't like that. He's well read and thoughtful and fair and kind. You can't accuse The Reverend Buckminster and his wife of that either," she said, referring to the pastor of the Anglican church they attended in Port Darling. "Or Mr. and Mrs. Mayhew."

"Won't you miss what the city can offer? The concerts and plays and such?"

"There are other entertainments here. Perhaps *I* will give concerts at the community hall," she added with a grin. She didn't play piano as well as her mother, of course, or Max, but she was talented.

Olivia laughed. "Perhaps you will! If you're certain that you'll be happy, my chick..."

"Oh, Mama, I'm deliriously happy!"

Richard meanwhile was talking to Stephen in his office. He had only needed to remind himself of what had happened to his younger brother, Alex, who had married despite his parents' objections, and the ensuing tragedy of his life, to realize that it would be a mistake to disapprove of the match. Esme was bound to have her way, and Stephen was an honourable, hard-working chap.

He said, "Esme has come into her inheritance from her grandmother, and has a generous income from her trust fund..."

"Which will remain her money. I have no need of it. I *can* provide for her, Sir. Not as lavish a lifestyle, of course, but our Boatworks is doing well. We have more work than we can handle, so we're hiring again."

Richard nodded. "Your handiwork is gaining recognition, rivaling Ditchburn, I hear."

"Major Thornton's success on the racing circuit has certainly helped."

Richard shook his hand. "I will entrust you with my daughter's happiness, Stephen. And if ever there is anything we can do to help out, you mustn't be too proud to ask."

"Thank you, Sir!" Stephen could hardly believe his luck.

"I've promised my children each a house as a wedding gift, so you must find or build something suitable. And don't stint on it. Esme is used to certain luxuries," he added with a smile.

"That's most generous, Sir!"

Richard and Olivia exchanged approving glances as they all met in the sitting room. "This calls for a bottle of champagne!" he said.

•   •   •

"I can't believe I've been thrown over for a servant!" Ted ranted. "Is this a cruel joke, Esme?" He had come to visit her that afternoon, and she had broken the news to him as graciously as she could.

"Stephen's not a servant. He's Chas's business partner."

And Ted had to work with the Seafords on their advertising campaign. "So if you were already in love with him, why did you lead me on?"

"I'm truly sorry, Ted. Stephen and I had a misunderstanding, and I guess I was lonely, so I relied too much on your company. I thought that my heart was free to love again, but it wasn't. You have so many women friends, like Dottie, that I didn't expect you'd actually fall in love with me."

He harrumphed.

"Lucy is crazy about you. She'd be much better for you than Dottie," Esme said with a grin.

Ted laughed despite himself. "You're really special, Esme. I wish..."

"If you can forgive me, perhaps we could still be friends?"

She looked at him so guilelessly and hopefully that he couldn't resist her plea. "Of course we can," he agreed, but she could see that he was deeply hurt. "Just don't invite me to the wedding." He kissed her hand and guffawed. "A Cracker Jack ring! I've been doing things all wrong!"

But Stephen presented her with a real ring the following week. He had ordered it from the Eaton's Catalogue, and Esme knew that Lady Flora Eaton had some magnificent pieces, including a diamond tiara, created by the in-house Eaton jewellers. It was modest but beautiful – a sapphire flanked by diamond chips, set in white gold.

"It's perfect!" she enthused, certain that it suited her much better than the ostentatious diamonds that Ted had offered her.

She had never imagined that she could be so ecstatic. But how fleeting such euphoria usually was.

•   •   •

Esme hadn't seen Claire since before her encounter with the snake, but she had written to tell her about the engagement. So she was excited to be going to the Lakeside Sanatorium on the day Claire was to be released. Family and friends were also along to take Claire on a celebration picnic en route to Thorncliff, where she would stay for the rest of the summer.

It should have been a gloriously happy day, but Esme could tell immediately that something was wrong. Claire looked pale and haunted.

"I can't come to Thorncliff," she told them, her eyes brimming. "Colin's had a relapse." It took all her willpower not to break into heart-rending sobs. The doctor hadn't even allowed her to see him.

Jack took her into his arms. "But you can't do anything to help him, sweetheart."

"I can visit him every day, once his fever comes down. I'll stay at Maman's house, if you'll let me." Her mother had already returned to the city to prepare for her wedding to Gordon Chamberlain.

"By yourself?" Jack asked with a frown. "That probably wouldn't be a good idea."

"I'll stay for a while," Esme offered. Things were falling into place for her September wedding, and she wanted to spend time with Claire before preparations became too hectic.

"I will, too," Alice said. "Then it will be like old times."

"Of course you can use the house," Jack said. "I wasn't planning to put it up for sale." He was thinking of giving it to his mother as a wedding gift, so that she and Gordon could use it as a cottage. Nor would he sell the city house once Marie no longer needed it, since she would be living in Cobourg. It was his first property, generously given to him by Uncle Richard, so it had nostalgic as well as real value. Jack liked the security of owning real property, not just stocks that fluctuated seemingly on a whim, and needed to be constantly monitored.

"The picnic is a lovely idea, but perhaps we could just have it at the house, which I'm eager to see," Claire suggested.

The rambling beige bungalow was tucked into the trees, with its back turned to the rocky bluff that formed part of the Sanatorium grounds. It had its own tiny bay, and views up the lake as well as down to the busy harbour, where the afternoon train was being met by a fleet of steamers and sleek motor launches. The house seemed to have grown over the years, with bays and wings tacked on, including a small sunroom giving onto a spacious veranda.

Claire loved it instantly. And had an inspiration.

When they had toasted her return to health with champagne, she said, "Colin and I have been engaged since my birthday."

There was a stunned silence for a moment, everyone thinking how much more tragic that he was so ill, but Claire went on before anyone could speak. "So I think that we should get married as soon as possible, and I will bring him here and nurse him myself."

"But, Claire..." Jack started to protest.

"I know better than anyone what to do! And even if... he doesn't recover, it will give us some time together." She seemed desperate to seize a chance at happiness.

"If you can manage and it won't compromise your own health, then I think it's a splendid idea," Esme said, feeling terribly sad for her cousin. Her own joy seemed rude in the face of this tragedy.

"I don't care about myself, except if I couldn't look after him properly," Claire confessed.

Jack wasn't happy about any of this. Couldn't Claire be re-infected, especially if they were living as husband and wife? But he couldn't extinguish that spark of hope that reignited her old radiance.

"There's much to discuss with various people before you could do that," he said. "Including Colin and his mother."

"But tell me if we may use this house," Claire urged.

"You may have it if you wish," Jack offered. He would have bought her one in any case, and would find something else for his mother if she wanted to have a summer place in Muskoka. And that joyful smile on his little sister's face was worth more than anything.

When he managed to speak to her alone later, he said, "Colin seems a decent fellow, Claire, but perhaps you shouldn't set your sights on a future with him. He may never be able to support you. Now that you can rejoin society, I expect you'll meet plenty of other chaps."

"You mean rich ones?" she shot back. "I don't aspire to being wealthy like you and Lizzie. I wouldn't even feel comfortable living in a mansion or château. I'm perfectly content if I have enough food to eat and a fabulous home like this to call my own and to share with Colin. I love him from the depths of my soul. I can't see a future for myself without him, Jack."

For a moment, he envied her that contentment that made such modest demands of life. Who was he to deny her that? He chucked her under the chin and said, "Let me know how I can help. I'm giving Lizzie $20,000 a year, so you shall have the same."

"That's much too much, Jack! My present allowance is more than adequate."

"To ensure that you're well set, let's make it at least $10,000, and I will set up a trust fund for your children, as I have for Lizzie's. If you ever need more, you must let me know."

"Oh, thank you," she said, hugging him excitedly.

"But you must promise me one thing," he said, eyeing her sternly. "You must look after yourself as well."

"I will. Cross my heart!"

It was an anxious week before Claire was allowed to visit Colin. She had been grateful to Esme and Alice for staying with her and sharing her new freedoms, since it took time to adjust to not having a strict routine. They tried to distract her with easy outings and activities.

One day, they took the 100 Mile Cruise on the majestic *Sagamo*, which started with breakfast aboard as they steamed up the lake towards Beaumaris. Because the ship also carried mail, freight, and passengers bound for hotels, it not only stopped at major resorts, but also made mid-lake transfers with several of the smaller steamers of the fleet, which serviced other parts of the lakes. It was a dramatic moment when the *Segwun* nudged up against the mighty *Sagamo* on one side and the *Cherokee* on the other, with the even smaller *Ahmic* beside her. Gangways secured, passengers and baggage moved from one ship to another, depending upon their destinations. It was an impressive manoeuver.

After they locked through at Port Darling, the orchestra that had just come aboard began playing popular tunes on the aft deck. They had another relaxing meal while they passed their own familiar part of the lake, glimpsing Wyndwood and Thorncliff in the distance. At the head of Little Lake Joe, the ship stopped for an hour so that passengers could enjoy Natural Park, and the magnificent view of Mirror Lake from the rocky summit. Claire wasn't up to the steep climb, so the girls sat in the shade along the shore and chatted about their upcoming weddings.

"Emily said I may wear her wedding gown," Claire informed them. "She's sent to New York for it."

"That's an exquisite dress!" Esme enthused. "So chic. I'm going to be rather Victorian in my mother's gown, although we're altering it so that the sleeves are less puffy and I don't need a corset. No bustle, thank God! It's quite beautiful, and I know that Mama was disappointed that Zoë couldn't wear it."

"You should see the one Maman's creating for Lizzie. It's modern and dramatic and has an enormous lace train."

"As befits a princess?" Alice asked, posing a wild daisy in her hair as if it were a crown.

"Or at least a Comtesse," Claire replied. "She even gets to wear a diamond tiara that's been in the family for generations."

"Wouldn't it be keen to go to the wedding?" Alice mused. "The ceremony in a cathedral and the reception at a château!"

"It would be," Esme agreed. "But, honestly, I'm looking forward to our simple ceremony in the little white church in Port Darling, followed by a party at The Point." Although only family and very close friends were invited, Silver Bay wasn't large enough, so Ria had offered her place.

"I wish I didn't have to wait until *next* summer to get married," Alice said so dolefully that the others laughed. Ria And Chas had pointed out that Cousin Beatrice would want to attend the nuptials. And besides, Ria wanted her to come along to Antibes this winter, because Chas was planning to race on the Riviera, and they could shop in Paris for the wedding gown and trousseau. Arthur had agreed that it would give him time to get settled into Launston Mills.

"But you're still so young, Alice," Esme teased. She was only a year older.

Alice threw the daisy at her.

"Anyway, I do think it's strange that Stephen and I will be coming to Antibes with you," Esme said to Alice. "At least for a few weeks. Chas has a race in Italy as well. In the meantime, I'm going to buy a motorcar, and then I can drive down to Gravenhurst to visit you until the snows come," Esme said to Claire. "Stephen says that the lakes can be treacherous for boating in the autumn, even before they begin to freeze."

Claire began to fret about being so far away from Colin, so she was happy to re-board the steamer and head south once more. They had another delicious meal in the elegant dining room just before docking at Gravenhurst in the early evening. Despite not doing much, Claire had found it a long and tiring day. She realized that she needed to build up her strength and stamina to be able to look after Colin properly. But she also knew that she needed to do that gradually, much as she wished to accelerate her fitness regimen.

She was nervous when, a few days later, she finally stepped onto Colin's porch, where he was reclined on his cure chair.

He looked at her sadly, and turned his face away when she tried to kiss his lips. "You shouldn't do that."

"I don't care!"

"But I do. Don't feel bound to me, Claire. It wasn't an official engagement."

"It is now that I've announced it to my friends and family, so you can't back out," she quipped.

"It's not fair to you, my love. I may never leave here, except by the back door."

"Don't even think that!" she chastised him. "You know that you have to stay positive and focused on regaining your health. Anyway, I plan to whisk you away from here as soon as you're allowed out of bed." She grinned at him and told him her plan.

"You'll be putting yourself at risk," he protested.

"No more than the doctors and nurses who work here."

"I don't deserve you."

"Tosh! Anyway, you're stuck with me." She took his hand in hers. "I love you so much that I don't want to live without you." She kissed him tenderly on the forehead.

"Trying to lay responsibility on me, are you?"

"No pressure. Only incentive," she replied with a warm smile.

The nurse bustled in and said, "Enough of that now. He needs to rest, as you know very well, Miss Wyndham."

"Indeed, but I also know that patients benefit from having something to look forward to."

The nurse smirked.

Of course Dr. Mainwaring had objections, including the fact that Colin couldn't be readmitted if necessary on the government's tab. Claire assured him that she would cover the costs if it came to that, and promised to bring him in for regular check-ups. Since the pneumothorax injections hadn't helped Colin, there was nothing that the Sanatorium could do for him now that Claire, with her first-hand experience, couldn't at home.

"Be vigilant about your own health," Dr. Mainwaring advised.

"I've been well-trained," she assured him. "And I will have daily help from the village so that I don't waste my energy on housekeeping."

"Keep in mind that sexual excitement will be detrimental to Mr. Sutcliffe."

"Yes, doctor, but I'm sure that support from a devoted spouse won't be."

"I daresay you're right, Miss Wyndham. I wish the pair of you the very best of luck," he said sincerely.

As the summer waned, Claire and Colin were married in a small and quiet ceremony on the veranda of their new home, which they christened "Hope Cottage".

•   •   •

Esme had never before missed the Labour Day weekend and Summer's End Ball at the lake, but she had insisted on going to watch Chas and Stephen race for the APBA Gold Cup in Detroit. Alice had come along to write an article for *Our Times*. Ria refused to be left behind, although she still wasn't feeling well. A touch of flu, she thought, as she was unusually tired and often had no appetite, but Chas was concerned that she hadn't been herself for weeks. She promised him that she would consult Ellie as soon as they returned.

Stephen and Mac had arrived a few days earlier with *Windrunner III*, and had put her through her paces to make sure that she had survived the train trip without harm.

With their wedding only two weeks away, Esme was thrilled to be at Stephen's side for this important event.

But she was astonished at the popularity of the various races. A flood of spectators lined the river – half a million of them. With the roar of the engines and the chattering of the crowd, Esme was suddenly bursting with an overwhelming desire that Chas and Stephen win this prestigious trophy.

Windrunner III had a dozen competitors, one of them Commodore Gar Wood. With a few more Commodores around, Chas was now glad that he, too, could claim that title.

He got off to a terrific start and, although challenged, was never overtaken on the first 30-mile heat. His best lap was an impressive 42 miles per hour. Three boats dropped out with engine and other problems, including Edsel Ford, son of Henry and now president of the Ford Motor Company.

Gar Wood led on the second day, but *Windrunner III* passed him within four laps and once again finished victorious.

Esme, Alice, and Ria could hardly contain their excitement on the last day of the race. *Windrunner III* was leading again and seemed to have the event tied up when, with just five miles to go, she suddenly slowed down. Her propeller had struck some floating debris, which had bent the blade. Without causing serious damage, Chas couldn't push the runabout, and limped in, finishing last in the heat.

Although *Windrunner III* was greeted with tremendous cheers, she didn't have enough points over the three-day event to win.

"I'm not sure I'm cut out for this world of racing," Esme admitted glumly at dinner that evening. "I was so sure we'd win!"

Chas chuckled. "You'll get used to it, Esme. That's part of the fun, not being guaranteed a victory until that trophy's in your hand."

"But it's so unfair that you lost because there was something floating in the river, not because the boat wasn't fast enough!" Esme said indignantly. "She was the best!"

"We can consider ourselves lucky that we didn't have more damage. When Harry Greening was racing *Rainbow II* in Buffalo, a wave punched a twelve-foot long hole in the underside and the boat sank," Stephen said.

"And ironically, *Rainbow I* won the race, but Harry no longer owned her. He'd sold her to a chap in Buffalo," Chas said.

"Which is another reason why you won't sell any of your boats, and we need more boathouses," Ria teased.

"So what do you chaps think about building me a stepped-hull runabout?" Chas asked Mac and Stephen.

"Chas!" Ria protested.

"Not an out-and-out racer, like the Harmsworth boats, but a practical launch that's faster than we can manage with a displacement hull. There are plenty of races around where we can test her. And it'll appeal to the chaps on the lakes who want a bit more speed. Good for business."

"Sure thing, Chas," Mac said with a grin. "*Windrunner IV.*"

•   •   •

Ria joined Chas on the veranda, having just returned from Spirit Bay.

He didn't look up from his newspaper as he said, "Listen to this. The Toronto police shot and killed a rum-runner, and four cops now face charges. Seems that it's not a federal crime to bootleg, so they had no right to fire at the fleeing boat. You'd think that incidents like this would make the provincial government repeal the Temperance Act. Otherwise, we'll start getting the kind of violence that we keep reading about in the States."

When she didn't reply, he glanced up, surprised to see her looking as if she were in shock. "Ria? You saw Ellie, didn't you? What did she say?" he asked with growing concern.

She sank into the chair next to him. "I can't believe it. Not after all this time." She gazed at him with tears rolling down her cheeks.

"Ria! Tell me!"

"Ellie says I'm pregnant!"

After a stunned moment Chas took her joyfully into his arms. "Good God! How wonderful! Miraculous!"

"I'm afraid to believe it," she said amid the laughter and tears.

"Is Ellie certain?"

"She says I'm three months gone. I've been so busy I hadn't noticed that I'd missed my periods. But that explains my fatigue and occasional nausea."

"But how?"

"Ellie said that there could have been a blockage or scarring caused by the infection, which has disappeared or at least diminished over time. She said that many doctors, especially old country ones, are not well versed in women's ailments. She wants me to be followed by a specialist at Women's College Hospital, in case there are any complications."

Everyone was excited for them, including the staff. This time Grayson allowed himself the privilege of giving her a quick hug. He knew how she had mourned the loss of her child, how delighted she was with her adopted family, and how generously she had taken his own two-year-old son, Alastair, into her maternal heart. He couldn't have been happier for her.

"I'll be a big sister again!" Sophie declared with glee.

Alice observed, "So if the baby's due in mid-March, it means that we won't be going to Europe."

"I'm afraid not. Sorry, Alice," Ria said.

"I'm not! Surely I should get married before the baby's born because otherwise all the preparations and such will be too much for you. How about December?" she asked with a big grin.

Ria laughed. "You never wanted to go abroad, did you?"

"I'm still not comfortable with oceans. And I don't need a Parisian trousseau. It wouldn't be all that useful in Launston Mills."

Chas chuckled. "You're wedding should be exactly what you want it to be, Alice."

"Wyndholme is like a castle, especially at Christmas."

"Then so be it!"

Only Charlie was not thrilled with the news. He cuddled up to Ria and said, "Will I still be your petit poussin?"

"Always and forever," Ria assured him as she ruffled his hair. But having seen the fuss that was made over other people's babies, he had already decided that he *really* wasn't going to like this one.

Part 3: 1926

Chapter 23

Jack awoke to feel her trailing kisses down his belly. He groaned as she aroused him and then lowered herself onto him. Her languid, teasing movements were driving him mad. She giggled when he flipped her onto her back and plunged into her, feeling her convulse before his own release.

"You're a witch," he accused as he nibbled her ear. "How will I be able to leave knowing that it will be months before I see you again?"

She stretched contentedly. "Don't wait so long."

"It's hard enough for me to come here twice a year as it is. And next time I promised to bring Fliss, so this will be impossible, except for a few snatched moments."

Véronique pouted.

He loved Fliss more than he ever could Véronique, although with that protective, contented affection of old friends. But he was physically obsessed by his sister-in-law. She was a delicious - and expensive - toy.

Jack had tried to resist Véronique, but they had been inadvertently thrown together by Lizzie and Étienne in Paris, at the Château, and even in Antibes.

With the franc still dropping and now worth only thirty to a dollar, Jack continued to buy real estate in Paris, and had a competent manager who looked after his properties. Lizzie had alerted him to the fact that a few wealthy Americans had started going to the Riviera in summer. Her friends, Sara and Gerald Murphy, had convinced the posh Hotel du Cap to remain open for them, and had enjoyed their first summer so much that they had built their own villa. Since their friends were joining them there, Lizzie was convinced that it was the beginning of a new trend. So Jack was buying property along the Côte d'Azur, and even a few small hotels, which were among the first to stay open year-round.

Cousin Beatrice let him use her villa whenever he was in Antibes, and it was in its secluded cove where he had finally surrendered to Véronique's persistent advances. It had been magnificent, if laced with guilt, but he reasoned that Fliss couldn't be hurt by the affair if she didn't know about it.

So they were discreet. Of course it was only natural that he would treat his sister-in-law to dinner or attend the premier of her latest movie. Even Fliss loved to hear about that. But Jack never lingered all night at Véronique's Paris flat, which overlooked the Luxembourg Gardens, not far from Lizzie's usually vacant apartment where he stayed.

"Oh, Jacque! I forgot to use the Dutch cap."

"Christ, Véronique! I can't have any bastards, understand?" He glared at her. She had sworn at the outset that she would never make any demands on him or try to undermine his marriage. He owned the building in which she lived, but, privately, he gave the rent money back to her. Everything needed to appear above-board.

"And my career would be ruined," she said archly. "So don't concern yourself. I know how to get rid of it."

"I thought your government made abortion illegal." Even contraception, now that the French were anxious to rebuild their decimated population.

"I know where to get one. It wouldn't be the first time."

If he was a bit shocked, he wasn't really surprised. Of course he knew that she had other lovers when he wasn't here. In the war he had seen the importance of protecting against venereal disease, which is why he usually used a condom as well, although she insisted that she was clean and that it was more fun without one. Every so often – like just now when he had drifted off and she had taken him unawares - she managed to get her way.

"Must you go, mon amour?" she asked, trying to pull him back into her rumpled bed. She was insatiable.

"It's already after midnight and I have an early start." He was sailing to New York, where he would take the train down to Palm Beach in time to help Fliss close up their ocean-side mansion for the season. He was already looking forward to seeing the children.

Three-and-a-half-year-old Kate was such a delight and Sandy, who would soon be six, always missed him terribly. Fliss was seven months pregnant, so this sexual interlude in Paris had been most welcome.

He also had some business to conclude in Florida. Last year he had already seen the warning signs of the Florida real estate boom becoming untenable, so he had dumped all his speculative holdings, some of his colleagues telling him that he was crazy to sell when prices were shooting up even before the properties had changed hands. But Jack realized that the buying frenzy had artificially elevated the prices that soon no one would be willing or able to pay. He had a knack for getting out of investments before they cooled or collapsed. Once again he had been right.

"Did you bring me something to remember you by?" Véronique asked, lying down in a provocative posture of surrender.

"Don't I always? Cover yourself up, you temptress."

She grinned at him as she threw the corner of the sheet carelessly across her abdomen, not hiding much.

He handed her a rope of perfectly matched pearls with an exquisite diamond cluster fastening. He was taking a double strand home for Fliss.

"Oooh-là-là! They will be perfect with my little black Chanel dress."

"Don't entice too many men with them."

"There is no one like you, Jacque," she said as she draped them across her firm breasts. The artist in him wanted to sketch this siren wearing nothing but pearls. The man longed to rejoin her in bed.

The wise man wouldn't return.

•   •   •

In another part of Montparnasse, Silas Robbins and William Kirkbride sat in a café sipping illegal absinthe.

"Why can't we stay?" William asked as he signaled to the waiter for more drinks. They were due to leave tomorrow.

"You know very well that it was difficult enough to get Phoebe to agree to my going away for a month without her," Silas replied.

"I mean not go back at all. We have no life there, just clandestine meetings snatched from a mediocre existence. Don't you feel liberated here? Free to be your *true* self?"

Of course he did. As Silas looked around at the stylish crowd seated at the outdoor tables on this balmy night, he wished just as fervently that he could stay in Paris, rub shoulders with famous as well as struggling writers and artists, and not feel a crawling guilt whenever he and William were together. And here they weren't considered criminals.

"I can't leave Phoebe. I promised her family I would look after her."

"Such an honourable man," William scoffed. "If you ignore the fact that you have a lover. I doubt that would go over well."

"Are you threatening to tell her?" Silas demanded, fear and anger jostling with a sense of relief. He hated the lies and subterfuge.

"Why not, if it revolts her enough to throw you out." The waiter brought the vilified green liquor and a jug of ice water. He perched silver slotted spoons over the glasses and added a sugar cube atop each. The men then drizzled the water over the cubes until the drinks transformed into fragrant, opalescent elixir.

"And what would we live on? I have little money of my own, and have been supporting you with Phoebe's."

"We make enough from our poetry to live a Bohemian life here."

"In an unheated garret without plumbing? No thanks."

"You wouldn't mind if you really loved me."

"Don't play that pathetic card with me. I've risked everything for you!"

"I just can't stand the thought of you going back into her bed. Still loving her."

"It's a different kind of love; I've told you that. She's a dear pal, and the mother of my child."

"She's sucking the life out of you."

"She *gave* me my life back, and now she needs me. And so does Sylvia."

"Phoebe should be in a fucking lunatic asylum."

"Shut up, Will, or this will be the end of our friendship!"

William snorted. "*Friendship*. Is that all this is?"

"Christ, you're a bastard!" Silas threw down some money and got up to leave.

"I'm sorry, Si. Let's not ruin our last glorious night here. Forgive me."

He looked so pathetic that Silas conceded, "Only if you're willing to accept the status quo."

William stared hard at him, and then promised, "For now."

•   •   •

From the time she was very little, Drusilla knew that she could fly. In her dreams she soared above the lake, darting and hovering, swooping and gliding. But it wasn't until she met the fairy who lived in a wondrous and magical land behind the waterfall that she took wing.

Thus began the children's book that was already being hailed as a classic. It was Claire's fanciful paintings of fairylands, which she had created at the Sanatorium to offset her boredom, and Esme's reports about Spirit Bay that had inspired Colin to write the story, initially for the invalids there.

In the book, a group of children convalescing at a summer retreat become friends. When they meet Faith, the fairy behind the waterfall, they are given the power to transform themselves into their animal soul mates at will. Drusilla, crippled by polio, can become an iridescent, flitting dragonfly, light as thistledown. Lewis's heart has been weakened by rheumatic fever, but his loon persona swims great lengths underwater and soars masterfully over the lake. Oliver, whose eyesight is dim even through thick spectacles, becomes an observant and keen-eyed owl. Catriona, recovering from TB, scrambles up trees and pads stealthily through the woods in the guise of a cat. Using their newfound powers and aided by Faith and her fairyland friends, the kids solve the mystery of Spirit Bay.

With Claire's richly imaginative and colourful illustrations, the book was also a work of art. Daventry House had commissioned an entire series of these heartwarming adventures, which had the added benefit of giving sick children hope. Although he hadn't yet met Ethan, Colin had been thinking about him when he created Lewis, the loon, and Ethan loved the book. That they could actually make a living through their fun, creative endeavours was a thrilling bonus.

For Colin, this new career as a writer suited him better than the stresses of running a law practice. He was finally free of lesions and shadows on his lungs, but as Dr. Mainwaring had cautioned him and Claire, they still needed to be careful and always vigilant about any signs of recurrence. A sedate life would be beneficial. There was no room for complacency.

Claire woke every morning giving thanks that Colin had survived when too many of their San friends hadn't, taking nothing for granted, feeling blessed that their precious and beautiful year-old daughter, Merilee, was healthy.

At first, Claire had been afraid to be so blissfully happy, in case that was snatched from her by some vindictive fate. But that fear of potential future sorrow would have robbed her of so much joy, so she lived one day at a time, and filled each with love and delight. Colin had flourished under her nurturing care and buoyant spirits.

They reveled in the splendour of their surroundings, which Claire continued to paint, selling the pictures for significant sums to well-heeled cottagers and tourists.

Although they were a contented little family, friends and relatives enriched their lives. She wanted nothing more than for this gift of glorious days to continue.

•   •   •

"Wake up, sunshine," Stephen said as he ran a finger down Esme's arm. "Time for our morning dip."

"Noooo," she protested, pulling the quilts over her head. "Too cold."

"Softie," he teased, drawing the blankets back down. He kissed her bare shoulder sensually.

"Mmm," she mumbled, still heavy with sleep as she turned towards him.

"Since it *is* a bit early..." Stephen began.

When they lay replete in each other's arms after their lovemaking, Stephen said, "Now we really do have to get up."

"You can swim. I'm going to have a nice, long, hot shower-bath."

"Softie."

"It's only May! I never swim this early. Between the ice floes," she added with a grin.

"That's because you're a city girl."

"Not any more. Just sensible."

"I'll let you off because the baby might not like it," he said as he kissed the soft mound of her belly. She was four months pregnant.

Stephen was red-skinned and shivering when he joined her in the shower after his quick plunge.

"Admit it was cold," she said.

"Bloody freezing."

"Softie."

She squealed when he tickled her.

Esme loved the roomy five-bedroom house that Freddie had designed for them, and which they called "Seawynd", a combination of their names and homage to the Seawind line of boats the Seafords were now building, based on their success with the *Windrunners*. Because it perched on the rocky shore of Chippewa Bay, she had wanted something like a year-round cottage, with airy rooms that flowed into one another, well-lit with large picture windows and lots of French doors that gave onto verandas, open and screened, as well as a sleeping porch off the master bedroom. She had agreed with Freddie that it should be built of wood and stone to fit naturally into the landscape, rather than brick, which sat more comfortably on formal streets. So it looked as if it had been carved out of the granite, pine-bearded hillside.

It was thoroughly modern, with private bathrooms for the master and guest suites, central heating with cozy radiators in each room, as well as a couple of fireplaces, and a "servantless kitchen".

Because the village had reliable hydroelectricity brought in from Bala, she was able to have a Frigidaire refrigerator, dispensing with the icebox, and a Westinghouse electric range, which meant no hauling of dirty coal or wood or ashes, and odourless heat at the flick of a switch. There was no need to have a stove blazing throughout the summer so that water could be boiled or food prepared. The new stainless steel cutlery didn't require polishing, like silver. And because Esme had learned how to cook simple meals from Zoë and Stephen's sister, Nancy, and Stephen helped with the washing up, they had no servants, only Widow Harrison coming in twice a week to do the cleaning and laundry, and sometimes to help with a dinner party.

The villagers had taken to Esme quite readily once they'd realized she wasn't a spoiled heiress above fending for herself. She had quickly become aware of the resentment by some of the locals of the "summer people", much as they relied on these seasonal residents for their livelihood. But she had become an active member of the Women's Institute, had raised significant funds through her rich friends for a library expansion, helped to organize and direct the village children in theatricals, and gave the occasional piano recital on long winter nights.

It had also been at her instigation that the WI approached the local council and suggested the community actively seek a resident doctor. They agreed that the village would pay $450 a year for a Medical Officer of Health, who would also run a private practice. Their advertisement in the Toronto newspapers, compellingly written by Esme with input from Alice and Arthur, had enticed Dr. Douglas McIvor, a dynamic and dedicated young man who loved the outdoors, and couldn't believe his luck in securing such a fine community. The residents warmed to him immediately, especially the young women. But it was Nancy Seaford who won his heart, and they were getting married in the autumn.

Esme and Stephen had their meals at the informal dining table in their sunroom overlooking a stunning vista of the bay, the village, and the narrows that led to the lake. She loved the changing panorama – the windswept winter isolation punctuated by torch-lit skating parties, the summer steamships carrying merry holidaymakers who waved gleefully in passing, the fires of the Indian Camp shimmering alongside the moon across the dark water. Sometimes she was overwhelmed by the sheer beauty of sunsets or undulating northern lights or the prefect reflections of autumn colours materializing out of the morning mist. Her heart sang with joy.

"The Indians are back," Esme pointed out, noticing more tents at the camp scattered among the tall pines and maples. They returned to their reserves for their winter.

"Then we know that the tourists aren't far behind."

"It seems like we've been preparing for them for months," she said wryly.

Stephen chuckled. "You thought that we locals just twiddled our thumbs all winter when we weren't building boats."

"Well..."

"Admit it!"

"Of course I realized that someone was constructing cottages and docks and such."

"And repairing buildings, and hiring staff for the inn, and chopping wood for summer fires, and cutting ice."

Since the cottagers had first come to the Stepping Stones area of the lake, Stephen's family had been cutting wood and ice for them in winter. So when the harvest began, he took her to watch the team of a dozen men supervised by his father as they sawed heavy blocks of ice out of the lake, which were then hauled by horse-drawn sleds to the ice houses, including Wyndwood's, and packed in straw and sawdust, ready to last through the hottest summer.

"Gosh, that looks dangerous!" Esme had exclaimed. Stephen had already warned her to stay off ice until he checked it first, saying that it could be deceptively thin in places, especially on the river. But these men were balancing on the edge of open, frigid water as they manoeuvered the massive chunks.

"We've never lost anyone, or any horses, but some of the other ice harvesters have," Stephen had explained. It was big business on the lakes, some of them even supplying the railway companies.

Much to his relief, Esme actually enjoyed the winters, even if they did feel too long when they dragged into April. But how beautiful the landscape after a howling, blinding blizzard or a soft cascade of fluffy flakes that congregated inches thick on every twig and bough. Once the ice was solid enough, they occasionally took their horse-drawn cutter across the lake from Pineridge to Wyndwood to check on the shuttered cottages, ensuring that no vandalism or storm damage had been done. Esme had been awed by the utter, uncanny silence on still days, and the somewhat forbidding solitude of being the only people on the vast lake. She could understand why Stephen would feel such a visceral connection to this place.

Their jaunts to racing venues with Chas and Ria – like March in Palm Beach – and Christmas with Esme's family in Toronto were interludes that provided a stimulating contrast in their lives, but she was always, and surprisingly, happy to be home again.

For the past few weeks, Stephen had been busy preparing the boats for the cottagers. She had watched him putting her family's boats in at Silver Bay. Hauled up on slings into the boathouse rafters for the winter, the launches dried out and the seams opened up. First he lowered them, still cradled, so that the wood would swell in the water to prevent leaking, which took days. Once they were seaworthy, he serviced and tested the engines.

"Today I'm at Thorncliff, so don't expect me for lunch," Stephen said. Esme helped out at Pineridge, so during the summers they took most of their meals there. "Mrs. Smedley likes to spoil me." The Smedleys were long-time caretakers of Thorncliff, living in their cabin year-round. Esme and Stephen visited them several times each winter. The old dears were getting on, plagued with rheumatism, and probably wouldn't manage another winter there. Fewer cottagers had year-round staff now, especially on islands.

"She's dotes on you like a proud grandmother."

"And thinks I'm jolly lucky to have won a lady like you," he said with a grin.

"It seems to me that *I* did the pursuing."

"If that got out it would ruin my reputation."

Esme laughed, and Stephen was overwhelmed with love for her. "I'm glad that you'll be home well before dark. I'm not happy that you have to drive past the Butchers' place," he said with concern.

More and more cottagers were motoring up in the summer, many of them leaving their automobiles at the SRA Golf and Country Club. But until they arrived, the rough, two-mile-long road to the Club and Pineridge was quiet and deserted past the few houses and the Butchers' shack on the fringe of the village. Esme had learned how to change a tire, but any other problems with the car might necessitate walking back to town.

She'd already had unpleasant encounters with Trick Butcher. Whenever he saw her drive past, he would mockingly tip his cap to her in such a way that he was also giving her the finger. She hadn't even known what that meant until Stephen had explained the obscene gesture. He had fumed.

"Trick's been making trouble ever since we fired his brother," Stephen said. Jake Butcher had been pilfering expensive mahogany from the workshop. Stephen and Mac hadn't thought him as rotten as Trick, which was why they had given him a chance – he was a good mechanic. But he had probably been goaded into stealing from them.

Someone had broken into the Boatworks a few days ago, but only the petty cash and some tools appeared to be missing. Stephen suspected that Trick was behind it, and not bored teenagers making mischief, which is what the local constable thought. "Trick would have taken more valuable stuff," the cop had pointed out.

"Trick seems to have it in for you for some reason," Esme worried.

Butcher never passed up an opportunity to mock Stephen, saying things like "Boots gettin' a bit tight, are they, Seaford?" or "Sure that hat still fits?" Because Stephen had married "above his station" and went to glamorous races and places with Chas, a few of the redneck villagers were jealously nasty.

"We used to have schoolyard tussles, so nothing's really changed there."

"Brawls, you mean," Esme corrected, knowing Stephen was downplaying Trick's viciousness. "Well, don't worry about me. Rufus will look after me," Esme said. Hearing his name, the black and white Siberian husky jumped up and came to her side, and she rubbed his head affectionately. She did feel a great deal safer with him around, and not just from jerks like Trick Butcher. She had encountered a bear on the Pineridge road one day when she'd been mired in a muddy rut, and Rufus's aggressive howls had scared him off. She had been closer to the inn than the village, but the walk through the rustling forest to get help had been nerve-wracking, and she had been grateful for her devoted companion.

"At least I have the motor again." Not that there was much protection in a touring car that had only a ragtop and open sides, but it went faster than the sleigh. She had learned the hard way that it didn't take much to get stuck on the hills in Port after even a bit of a snowfall, having to be towed home by a team of horses to the amusement of the locals, especially the Butchers. So the handsome McLaughlin-Buick had to be put away in November, and it was usually mid-April before it came out of hibernation.

"Well, be careful. Love you, sunshine," he added, giving her a kiss. "When I've finished at Thorncliff, I'm going to take *Windrunner V* out for a test run, so I'll stop by the Inn. Now I've got to go."

She took her coffee out onto the veranda as she watched him scamper down the hillside to the boathouse. They had no beach, although the water was shallow along the shore, with a hard sandy bottom interspersed with the shelving granite. The house faced south, and in the shelter of the bay it basked in the sun, making it feel much warmer outside than it actually was. She would take a few more minutes to enjoy the view and breathe the fresh morning air before heading out herself.

Esme glowed with love as she waved to Stephen before he sped off towards the narrows. Could anyone be happier and more contented than she?

Seawynd was the last house along this sparsely populated shore, with cottages much further along where the river opened into the lake. But Mac and his wife, Audrey, lived next door, and were just leaving - three-year-old Grant perched on his father's shoulders - as she and Rufus drove past.

Audrey's family was one of the oldest in Port Darling; with their general store and supply boats that delivered groceries and sundries to cottagers twice weekly, the Carvers were also the most wealthy and prominent citizens – who, along with Douglas McIvor, owned the only other automobiles in the community. Audrey had attended high school in Bracebridge, one of the few in the village who had, and was particularly grateful to have Esme as a friend with whom she could discuss books as easily as business. She spent a few hours at the Seaford Boatworks every day looking after the accounts while Grant visited his grandmother.

"Do you want a lift?" Esme asked.

"No, thanks. It's a beautiful morning for a walk," Audrey replied.

"I'll pick you up at 7:30 then," Esme said, referring to the Women's Institute meeting that evening. The community-minded new mayor of Bracebridge, newspaper publisher George Boyer, was determined that the town should have a hospital, and Esme was in charge of the WI drive to help raise funds for it. She was convinced that the summer residents would be as eager to have one in the area as the locals. What would have happened to her if Ellie hadn't been able to treat her at Spirit Bay for the snakebite?

Esme felt a frisson of discomfort when she approached the Butchers' tumbledown house, because Trick was in the front yard chopping wood. He stopped, did his usual rude cap salute, and then smashed his axe down onto the block while staring belligerently at her. It was a violent gesture that implied a threat.

She shivered as if she could almost feel the bite of the axe, but then chided herself for letting her imagination run wild. He wouldn't dare harm her or Stephen! As if sensing her panic, Rufus whined, and she felt a new fear - for him. She wouldn't put it past Trick to hurt her dog.

Fortunately, the road repair crew had already dealt with the winter damage, filling the potholes with gravel, so she was able to move at a fair clip, but she was glad when the lake finally came into view. There were a few cottages along this stretch of the road, but they were still closed up.

Her summers were busy at the Retreat as well as at Pineridge, and she was excited by the coming season, since she was about to see how well several of her initiatives worked.

The Seafords had needed to expand the inn, and she had suggested that it made more sense to construct a separate building, in case of fire. So a brand-new, two-storey annex flanked the main lodge to the north. It had a small lounge and games area, and each room had a private bath. Stephen's older sister, Jean, had thought those an extravagance, and a waste of space and money, but Esme had pointed out that this would put Pineridge a notch above most of the other resorts on the lake, and attract a new, moneyed clientele. The annex rooms commanded a higher price - and were already fully booked for the summer.

Last year, at her suggestion, they had expanded and enclosed the dance pavilion, adding a stage and a bar area that sold ice cream and beverages – non-alcoholic, of course. They'd hired a band and invited cottagers and tourists from other resorts to attend the thrice-weekly dances, for a 10-cent charge. It had been a tremendous success, with people sometimes lining up to get in, and as many as a thousand coming in an evening. Other days, the building was used for theatricals performed by travelling troupes, and a weekly costume party and private dance for the guests, which Esme organized. During the day, it was a place for the young people to hang out and dance to a gramophone or stage their own plays. The ice cream bar drew people from around the area who didn't want to go as far as Port Darling or who just craved a refreshment when out boating, since the bar at the Country Club next door was only open to SRA members.

Esme was drawing on her own experiences of summer life to give guests a taste of the same. They were a hit, and so was she.

Her in-laws had quickly discovered that her natural charm and easy social graces were admired and appreciated by the guests. After their initial reticence with her – she was a Wyndham, after all - Stephen's parents had quickly succumbed to her warmth and eagerness to fit in and be useful. His younger sister Nancy, who was only two years older than Esme, had taken to her immediately. Only Jean was resistant to Esme's friendship and ideas.

"She has no husband or life of her own, aside from the Inn," Stephen had explained when Esme had been upset by Jean's hostility. "She plans to take over from Mum and Dad when they're ready to slow down, and I expect that she sees you as a threat. Your ideas have already transformed the place."

"Shouldn't I help out then?" Esme had asked, disappointed.

"You should just keep doing what you have been, and don't be afraid to make suggestions. Jean is the one who will have to adjust, and she should be jolly grateful to have your help!"

Stephen was immensely proud of her, and delighted with how readily and wholeheartedly she had embraced his life and his family.

She stopped at Spirit Bay to see how the preparations were coming, as the first group of children would be arriving in three weeks. Winter took its toll on unheated buildings – doors warped, windows stuck, the plumbing usually leaked somewhere, and paint flaked. But the Mayhews were excellent caretakers.

Rufus would stay until Esme was ready to go home, because he loved to romp with the Mayhew's husky, Manitou, and they had thirty fenced acres to call their own. It was where Rufus boarded whenever she and Stephen were away.

Things were more hectic at Pineridge, since it was opening in a week. With her years of experience hiring university students for the Retreat, Esme had taken on that responsibility for the Inn these past two summers, since they could no longer manage with just locals. Separate accommodations had been built behind the inn for the students.

"Hello, dear," her mother-in-law, Edith, greeted her. "I like what I've seen of your staff so far."

Esme was amused that they had become "her" staff.

"I'm so glad, Mum!"

"You wouldn't believe how many inquiries we've had since we announced that we have a children's program and dining room. We're still turning people away. What a grand suggestion that was!"

Esme's other innovations for this year were to have day-long programs run by qualified students to engage the children in activities, both indoors and out, leaving their parents free to relax or head out on their own adventures. There was now also a separate, supervised dining area for the kids, allowing the adults the luxury of quiet, civilized meals.

"You'll just have to expand again next year," Esme said with a grin.

"Don't think that Dad isn't considering it!" Edith said. "A south annex, so we'll look balanced, is how he put it."

Esme supervised the students' training, and gave them a talk before their afternoon break. She emphasized that courtesy, helpfulness, and genuine cheerfulness were essential. "Think of them as guests in your own home. We all need to make them feel comfortable and appreciated. No matter how arrogant, whiney, or downright ornery they are, you will resist the urge to push them into the lake."

They laughed.

"So make every effort —within reason – to ensure that their stay is pleasant and memorable. That doesn't include allowing anyone to take liberties. If that occurs, you will report it immediately."

A girl raised her hand and asked, "Has that happened?"

"We had a fellow last year who was a bit too fond of patting the waitress's backside. So we had one of the chaps wait at his table instead. We think he got the message."

They seemed to appreciate the support. "Just remember that if you do your job properly, we're on your side. Never hesitate to ask for advice or report a concern. And try to enjoy yourselves as well. You are allowed to use the beach in your free time, as long as you don't interfere with the guests."

"You're good at the big-sister act," Jean said when the students had gone off duty.

Esme wondered why Jean always made interactions with her sound so negative, but said congenially, "I've had practice with two younger brothers."

"I'm sure you'll have the staff well trained before July."

Esme was puzzled. "July?"

"You don't intend to keep working when you start to show, do you? It's not seemly for an obviously pregnant employee to be greeting the guests."

Esme was stung. "I hadn't realized I was actually an employee, since I don't get paid."

Jean waved her hand dismissively. "You know what I meant. It's how guests see you. But don't worry, dear, we'll manage just fine without you."

Esme didn't fail to catch the sarcasm in her voice.

But she put it out of her mind when she heard the throaty roar of *Windrunner V* as it approached. She hastened down to the dock to meet Stephen, impressed by the rooster-tail spray shooting up behind the elegant racer. She heard the engine backfire as he throttled down. Suddenly there was a tremendous explosion, fragments of the boat hurtling into the air as flames engulfed it. Esme screamed.

Jerry and Mike, two of the students in charge of the Inn's watercraft for the summer, had also been watching the racer approach. "Christ Almighty!" Jerry shouted as they ran towards a runabout. Esme was already in the boat.

"You should stay here, Mrs. Seaford," he advised.

"That's my husband!" Esme cried.

They zoomed towards the burning launch, although it was now an inferno. Stephen must have jumped off, Esme kept telling herself. If he could.

But the deep lake was still cold enough to paralyze limbs, endangering even the strongest swimmers. Surely he had worn his racing life vest.

By the time they were close to *Windrunner V*, there was no possibility of saving anyone on board. Trying to control her panic, Esme looked frantically about water. And then she spotted him. He was drifting, motionless, held up by his lifejacket. "There!" she yelled, desperately afraid, praying to God that Stephen was alright. Promising anything to make that so.

The first close look terrified her. He had a bloody gash across his forehead, his hair, eyebrows, even eyelashes were singed, and his face looked sunburnt. Mike eased the boat up beside Stephen, and Esme took over the controls so that both young men could haul him in.

She wrapped herself around his cold body, there being nothing aboard to warm him. "Stephen! Wake up! Please be alright!"

She was sure he was breathing, but it seemed a lifetime before he stirred. "Esme?"

"Oh, thank God!" she wept.

•   •   •

"I'm convinced the boat was sabotaged," Stephen said to Mac when he was comfortably ensconced in his sitting room. He'd been blown out of *Windrunner V*, but, miraculously, hadn't been seriously hurt – a mild concussion, some superficial burns, and a wrenched shoulder. Douglas McIvor had stitched up his head and ordered a few days rest.

Esme cuddled beside Stephen, clutching his hand. She realized that if the explosion had happened elsewhere on the lake, where no one would have seen it, he would probably have died of hypothermia before he was found.

"I did notice a smell of gas before the explosion," Stephen said.

"So if someone had tampered with the fuel lines or fittings and the engine timing, it was a recipe for disaster." Mac began.

"Exactly!"

"But who would want to kill you?" Esme asked, astonished and alarmed.

"I doubt if it was done to kill anyone. Rather to destroy the expensive racer and undermine our reputation," Mac said.

"Jake Butcher, you think?" Stephen asked.

"I can't imagine any of our employees doing it. I expect that Trick would have talked him into it. But how and when? You would have noticed something amiss if he'd done it before he was fired, and he hasn't been in the shop since."

"The break-in!" Esme suggested. "Perhaps it wasn't to steal anything, but to damage the racer. They took things to make it just look like theft."

"Christ, you're probably right, Esme!" Mac conceded.

"But we could never prove anything," Stephen said. "Even if the boat hadn't sunk. Who's to say it wasn't my mistake?"

"We know better, but how do we convince everyone else that our boats are safe and reliable?"

But Esme was more concerned with the Butchers' malevolence. It terrified her that Stephen was the target of Trick's spitefulness. Ironically, partly because of her.

Chapter 24

"This is delicious, as usual," Freddie said. He dined several times a week with Zoë and Emma now that he was on his own.

"Mummy's vegetables are getting better," Ethan opined. He had eaten earlier and was playing with his train set in the living room adjacent.

They laughed. Having grown up with multi-course dinners that always included a variety of meats, Zoë liked to keep meals simple. Today it was plenty of tender vegetables baked beneath a cheesy mashed-potato topping, and apple crumble with ice cream for dessert. Ethan loved to help Zoë crank the ice cream churn.

"I had another potential client come in today who was surprised that Spencer and Sinclair are both women," Emma said as she helped herself to more. "He blathered and blustered a bit, and was ready to walk out when I suggested that he might be more comfortable talking to one of junior *male* partners. You should have seen the relief on his face."

"But how unfair!" Zoë exclaimed. "I'm sure you'd handle his case brilliantly, whatever it is."

"One of the junior partners is always coming to me for ideas and arguments in his cases," Emma conceded with a chuckle.

"He's just flirting with the boss's daughter," Freddie teased. Their Senator father was still nominal head of the firm.

"He is rather cute, but, alas, married." Emma sighed.

"May I work for you, Aunt Emma?" Ethan asked. "Mummy says I shouldn't argue, but I'd like a job where I *could!*"

They laughed heartily. "I would be delighted to have you work for me, chum. But you'll have to study hard so that you can make *good* arguments."

"May I, Mummy?"

"I don't see why not," Zoë replied, although she wondered if his heart would stand up to the rigours of a high-powered, demanding career. So far, they had been lucky that he hadn't had a relapse of rheumatic fever. "But for now, you need to get into your pajamas."

"But it's not even dark yet!"

"It will be soon, and I expect that Uncle Freddie will read to you before bed."

"Maybe he'd rather read to me on the front porch, since it's so warm, and I shouldn't like the neighbours to see me in pajamas."

The adults suppressed grins.

"No arguments," Zoë stated.

"Yes, Mummy." To Emma, the seven-year-old said seriously, "I *do* need to learn how to win my case."

That had them in stitches again. He grinned happily.

"Well, I promised Laura that I'd go to the pictures with her this evening," Emma said. Laura Sinclair was the daughter of the other senior partner in the law firm, and would have been Emma's sister-in-law if her brother, Cliff, had survived the war. Emma had persuaded Laura to study law as well, so that they could eventually take over from their fathers. "Yummy Douglas Fairbanks in *The Thief of Bagdad*. It's supposedly swashbuckling fun. Do you want to come along, Zoë? I'm sure Freddie wouldn't mind looking after Ethan."

"That's perfectly fine with me," Freddie agreed.

"Thanks, Emma, but I'm looking forward to the concert from Pittsburgh on the radio tonight." She enjoyed this new invention that brought the world into her sitting room.

While Zoë did the washing-up, Ethan sat on the sofa beside Freddie, with Hucklebeary on his lap and Pearl curled up beside him. They were reading Rudyard Kipling's *The Jungle Book*. Ethan had been excited to learn that Aunt Ria had worked with the author, and Mummy had met him when they were in England. Tonight they read *Rikki-Tikki-Tavi*, about a brave mongoose.

"Could I have a mongoose?" Ethan asked when they had finished. "I shouldn't like to get bitten by a bad snake like Aunt Esme did!" He was awed by her scars.

"We don't have mongooses in Canada. Or is it mongeese, I wonder?"

Ethan giggled.

"But there aren't any bad snakes on the islands, and certainly none here in the city, so you don't have to worry," Freddie assured him. The story *was* quite scary. "Anyway, I don't think that Pearl would be fond of sharing the house with a mongoose."

"Alright, young man. Time for bed," Zoë said as she joined them.

He knew better than to protest. She and Freddie tucked him in.

"We'll continue with the stories in a few days, chum," Freddie said.

"Why can't you stay here, Uncle Freddie? Aunt Martha's not waiting for you anymore."

"Somebody has to live in my house. It would be very lonely and sad otherwise."

"You wouldn't need a house if you were my Daddy. You could live here."

Zoë was embarrassed. "Go to sleep now, pumpkin."

Back in the living room, she said, "I'm sorry, Freddie."

"Don't be. He's right, Zoë."

She looked at him, speechless.

"I've been meaning to broach the subject with you, now that my divorce has been granted."

"Freddie..."

"Hear me out, Zoë. I know that you had something special with Blake and that I could never replace him in your heart. You think that you'd be betraying his memory by marrying again, but you know that he'd want you and Ethan to be happy. I love you, and have for a very long time, as you probably realize. Being with you so much these past few years, I already feel like we *are* a family. Let me love you, look after you. We could have a wonderful life together, the three of us."

He was right that she enjoyed his company and relied more and more on him. "Freddie, I love you as a dear and cherished friend. But I'm not sure that I can ever feel more than that. It wouldn't be fair to you."

"That's enough for me and for a good marriage, Zoë. You might even grow to care more, if you gave us a chance."

He took her into his arms and kissed her tenderly. She moaned at the sweetness of it, of being caressed, of being the desire of a man's passions after all these years. But then she was suddenly struck with guilt. There were tears in her eyes when she drew away.

"I... can't. I'm sorry, Freddie."

He looked at her ruefully and stroked her cheek. "I'm here whenever you need me."

Zoë wept when she sat at her dressing table brushing her long hair. Freddie's kiss had rekindled a long-dead spark. Suddenly she ached for intimacy, for the comfort of someone lying next to her or being cradled in his arms. It was eight years since Blake had died.

She was haunted by the tune, *I'll See You in My Dreams*:

Tho' the days are long, twilight sings a song,
Of the happiness that used to be,
Soon my eyes will close, soon I'll find repose,
And in dreams you're always near to me.
I'll see you in my dreams, hold you in my dreams,
Someone took you out of my arms, still I feel the thrill of your charms;
Lips that once were mine, tender eyes that shine,
They will light my way tonight, I'll see you in my dreams.

She ached for the dream where Blake embraced her poignantly on the beach, but it rarely came now, and she felt as if he had truly abandoned her.

She had promised him not to cut her hair, but it suddenly felt heavy and oppressive. She longed to chop it off and rejoin a world that had moved on so energetically without her.

•   •   •

"The fire of 1862 was a sight to behold, flames leaping from one building to the next. We all tried to help, of course, but buckets of water did no good, and we were driven back by the intense heat and roiling smoke. Ma and I stood right here with the other townspeople, watching what seemed to be rivers of fire flowing towards us, " Keir Shaughnessy said to Alice. "But thankfully, the wind changed."

They were sitting in her motorcar in downtown Launston Mills, and she was gathering information for the weekly feature she wrote for his newspaper – "A Look Back". That had been her idea after hearing a few fascinating tales from him about the town's history, and he had approved wholeheartedly. They would eventually put the collection together as a book, which the Shaughnessy Book Bindery would print.

Justin Carrington had told her that his grandfather seemed rejuvenated by her interest and the positive response that her articles had generated. He was the kind of grandfather she would love to have had, and enjoyed her time with him. They had another bond, for she had been a friend of his granddaughter, Justin's sister Vivian, who had held her hand as they had gone into the Irish Sea with the doomed *Lusitania*. She had been touched to see that the poem she had written in memory of Vivian had been framed and hung on his parlour wall.

"So everything east from here, right down to the river, was destroyed – the entire original settlement. But people eventually thought that a blessing in disguise, because you can see the handsome brick buildings that replaced the old wooden ones."

She agreed that the wide Main Street had a pleasantly harmonious collection of three-storey commercial blocks, each proudly flaunting individually with decorative trim. The Shaughnessy Block, which he had built, was one of the finest, and housed the newspaper office where Arthur worked.

"Some people even thought that the fire didn't go far enough up the street," Keir chuckled. "But the rickety shops to the west were soon torn down and replaced."

"How did the fire start?"

"Well, Ma had thought it was the vigilantes she had encountered earlier that evening, who had threatened to burn down a brothel."

"Golly!"

He laughed. "It was wild here in those days, especially when the lumbermen came into town in spring after being in the bush all winter without booze or women."

"That sounds like a story in itself," Alice said with relish.

"Indeed! Especially since the Chief Constable was one of the patrons of the establishment. Anyway, it seems as if the fire was started in the slum known as Shantytown by my own ne'er-do-well cousin. Whether deliberately because he was quarrelling with the landlord, or accidently, was never established."

"Your stories sound like the makings of a novel," Alice mused. His mother had arrived here when the tiny community of a few log cabins by the river and mill had been newly carved out of the wilderness, so the evolution of the town over the past ninety-odd years intrigued Alice.

"I hope I'm still around when you write it," the eighty-eight-year-old said shrewdly.

She looked at him in surprise. She had written very little fiction, but had had a couple of short stories published this past year in the American fashion magazine *The Delineator*, which went to well over a million homes. She had been excited to earn $300 for each of those.

"You'd be just the girl to do it. That was a great accomplishment to be published by *The Delineator*. It puts you in the company of Rudyard Kipling, L.M. Montgomery, and a host of other famous authors," he said with a twinkle in his eyes. "Megan's been reading the magazine for decades, and was impressed by your stories and so proud of you," he said of his wife.

"Golly!"

"Anyway, I have a hundred more tales for you. And a few secrets," he confided with a grin. "But for now, I believe Megan's expecting us back for tea."

Alice enjoyed life in Launston Mills. Ria and Chas had not only given her and Arthur Sunrise Island, complete with a Freddie Spencer-designed cottage, but also a beautiful Queen Anne style house, which was just around the corner from Grandfather Keir, as she had come to think of him. And she was glad that she had friends here like Justin and Antonia, as well as the Shaughnessy clan she had come to know.

Grandfather Keir had been so impressed with Arthur's journalism that he had promoted him to editor last fall, which was a huge honour for someone so young.

"He's afraid Arthur will be snatched up by a big-city paper," Justin had explained. "And the two of you have injected such energy and sophistication, significantly raising the circulation of the newspaper. Our competition is hurting," he'd said of the other newspaper in town. "I think Grandfather's afraid that even Lord Beaverbrook might entice Arthur away, after that complimentary letter he sent."

That had been to congratulate Arthur on his book – *The Heroes Among Us: Tales from the Great War* - which Daventry House had published. It was a collection of his interviews with war veterans, including his brother, Freddie, Chas, Rafe, Justin, Jack, Troy, Lyle, Stephen and Mac Seaford, Roderick Mayhew, a reluctant Max Wyndham, Silas Robbins, Colin Sutcliffe, and with the added focus on women's important contributions - Zoë's VAD nursing, and Ria and Antonia's ambulance-driving in France. He felt that women's often-dangerous jobs were being ignored or forgotten, and had deliberately not added "heroines" in the title. As far as he was concerned, gender shouldn't be emphasized by such pejorative words. His research that fleshed out all their stories detailed a cross-section of events and experiences, and was already being lauded as an important piece of Canadian history. Alice was so proud of him, and thrilled to have had some editorial input.

Jack, who kept up his social and business connection with Max Beaverbrook, had sent the powerful press baron a copy of the book. A glowing review in Beaverbrook's hugely successful London paper, the *Daily Express,* had resulted in a contract for British publication of *The Heroes Among Us,* and a very happy Martin Daventry.

The book had precipitated another bonus – an invitation to tea with L.M. Montgomery at the Leaskdale manse last autumn. It had been a glorious thirty-mile drive through the glowing and burnished countryside to the little village that had been the author's home for fourteen years, and where she'd written most of her novels.

"Oh dear, I can see why LM sets all her stories in PEI," Alice had said as they arrived. The village was little more than crossroads nestled amidst vast farmland, having none of the charm of Prince Edward Island, and only the trickle of a creek nearby. "I think I, too, would want to escape into my imagination if I lived here."

Arthur had laughed. "Well, I can understand why she enjoyed Muskoka so much."

"I would shrivel up if I couldn't go there every summer," Alice had confessed.

The Macdonalds had since moved to Norval in the Halton Hills west of Toronto, and Alice hoped that its riverside setting provided more sustenance for LM's soul.

"It was refreshing to read – and be reminded about – our valiant veterans, Arthur," the famous author had said as they nibbled freshly baked cakes in her parlour. "Sometimes I think we dwell too much on the dead, but the survivors also made tremendous sacrifices - still coping with injuries and haunted by memories - as you so poignantly pointed out. Do you know, a reader took me to task for 'glorifying war' in *Rilla of Ingleside.* Some people just don't understand, do they? We *need* to remember and honour those who gave so much."

Alice had been thrilled and overwhelmed by LM's praise of her articles and short stories. Alice and Arthur had gone to Prince Edward Island for a delayed honeymoon, and sought out the enchanting places mentioned in LM's novels, so a lively discussion of PEI had ensued. It had been a magical afternoon.

Alice had been particularly captivated by a small bronze statue in the parlour, which LM explained was called the Good Fairy.

Gazing heavenward, her arms exuberantly outstretched, she radiated such joy that Alice decided that she would like to have a Good Fairy, and that she must buy one for Claire and Colin as well. She might well be the fairy who lived behind the waterfall.

Before they left, LM had confided with a grin, "I am writing a book set in Muskoka – an adult novel I'm calling *The Blue Castle*. But that's still a secret."

•   •   •

"Please, Daddy, may Philip come to visit for a month?" Sophie pleaded. Mummy had already agreed but she knew that Daddy needed to as well. She had found him reading the newspaper in the morning room at Wyndholme.

Chas was taken aback. "A month?"

"Or six weeks. It's a long way to travel, so he wants to make it worthwhile. He loved his last visit. Christopher can't come because he's in the RAF. Philip is going to start his veterinary studies in London this fall." He had decided that he wanted to know everything he could about horses, which was a large part of veterinary education.

"So he's coming on his own?"

"Yes. It means that you and Mummy don't have to entertain Major Chadwick," she added astutely.

As Chas pondered his reply, Grayson came into the room. "Excuse me, Sir, but there's an officer from the Provincial Police who would like to speak with you."

"Oh! Well, best *not* show him into my study, since we don't need to draw attention to the alcohol," Chas said, as there was a drinks trolley set up there. Although it wasn't illegal to drink in one's own home, the cop might wonder where his supply came from after all this time. Policing the illegal liquor trade was one of the OPP's main jobs these days. "I'll see him in the conservatory."

"Very good, Sir."

"Daddy, what about Philip?"

"Yes, alright, darling."

She gave him a quick, joyful hug.

Chas wondered what the OPP could possibly want from him.

"Inspector Emery from the Criminal Investigations Branch," the fellow said, greeting Chas with a firm handshake as he entered the conservatory. "Good of you to see me, Major Thornton."

"Not at all. How can I help you, Inspector?"

"I understand you know a Bertram Cracknell."

"Indeed I do. We flew together in the war."

Emery nodded. "I followed your exploits. Well done, if I may say so, Sir. And since then, have you had any contact with Cracknell?"

"I loaned him some money to buy aeroplanes."

"On what terms?"

Chas was puzzled. What had Crackers done? "Is that relevant?"

"Were you in partnership with Mr. Cracknell, Sir?"

"No. I had no expectations except that he might one day pay back the loan."

"So you don't know what work he was engaged in?'

Chas noted the use of the past tense in the last two questions. What the hell did that mean? "He said he was flying supplies into remote northern communities."

"Did he tell you what kinds of supplies?"

"He did not and I didn't ask. Can you tell me what's going on?" Chas demanded.

"Mr. Cracknell was ferrying illegal alcohol into those mining camps."

"I see." The Ontario Temperance Act was becoming increasingly unpopular, so many ordinarily law-abiding citizens were buying and selling illicit booze, and authorities often looked the other way, or were themselves involved. After all, it wasn't a criminal offence. The papers were filled these days with stories of bribery, corruption, and the huge profits made by the liquor industry.

"But he was also flying it into the United States," the Inspector said.

"Which doesn't seem to worry our government much," Chas pointed out. The distilleries were allowed to export their goods, and if some of it found its way into the States, it really wasn't Canada's problem. Maclean's Magazine recently estimated that 100,000 North Americans were involved in smuggling booze into the U.S.

"It does concern a certain criminal element, however, who don't take kindly to rivals. Have you heard of Al Capone, Major?"

"He's an American gangster, I believe."

"He is indeed. A bootleg king you might say, in charge of a large network of criminals, including the Purple Gang in Detroit. A violent bunch. We're investigating the shooting death of Mr. Cracknell."

"Good God!"

"We found his promissory note to you in his belongings. Do you have any idea about his business contacts, legal or otherwise, Major?"

"None at all. I haven't even heard from him since I gave him the money four years ago. Where did this happen?"

"Windsor, which is a hotbed of rum-running. There's also the possibility that it was a botched hijacking of the booze. Any information that you might have could be helpful."

"I'm afraid that I can't help you, Inspector. Damn shame about old Bert."

"By the way, Mr. Cracknell seems to have done quite well for himself. He's got a fancy place in Hamilton. Not on this scale, of course," the Inspector said, glancing about the enormous glass-walled and domed room filled with potted palms and exotic flowering plants – just one of Wyndholme's many opulent rooms. "He's left his pretty widow quite well off. I wonder why he never paid back the money you loaned him." He looked suspiciously at Chas.

"As you can see, I don't need the money, Inspector," Chas said casually. "Bert, being a sharp businessman, would wait until it was due next year, because it would generate plenty of income for him in the meantime. Amazing what you can make on the stock market these days."

Fortunes, the Inspector had heard, if you had at least some money to invest. He was satisfied with the explanation.

Poor bloody bastard, Chas thought when the cop had gone. Had the flying business been so bad that Crackers had to resort to smuggling, or were the enormous and quick profits just too tempting?

Of course he was sorry that his erstwhile friend had died so brutally and needlessly, but he couldn't help feeling a small measure of relief that his own secret was once again safe.

But Chas hadn't yet realized that more dangerous than Bert's knowledge of Charlie's parentage was Charlie's resemblance to his three-year-old half-brother, Drew, as well as to Chas himself.

Chapter 25

"Why hasn't Uncle Freddie come to see us?" Ethan asked disconsolately.

They had been at the cottage for several weeks, but Freddie had visited only briefly before they left Toronto.

"He's working," Zoë explained, but knew it wasn't just that. Her rejection had wounded him.

Although Ethan was constantly distracted by visits from his many aunts, uncles, and cousins, he obviously missed Freddie. He replayed the song, *My Buddy*, on the gramophone.

Nights are long since you went away,
I think about you all thru the day,
My Buddy, my Buddy, No Buddy quite so true.
Miss your voice, the touch of your hand,
Just long to know that you understand,
My Buddy, my Buddy, Your Buddy misses you.

Zoë tried to ignore her own surprising loneliness in Freddie's absence. Traitorously, longingly, she recalled his soft kiss full of rapturous promise. Could she possibly open her heart to him? Begin another phase of her life? She remembered how she had once accused Blake of not letting go of the past – his infatuation for Vivian Carrington. Hadn't he realized the futility of that, and then fallen deeply in love with her? Wasn't she just as guilty now of resisting a new love?

She had finally bobbed her hair and felt a tremendous freedom. Perhaps it was time to move on.

Zoë was suddenly frantic as she pulled out a sheet of paper and began writing:

Dearest Freddie,

Ethan and I miss you terribly. I have come to realize that you are such an important part of our lives that we are diminished by your absence. Is that love? Would that be enough to sustain us? I know only that I – we - long for you to be here with us.

I confess that I'm apprehensive, yet excited. May we take things slowly? Can you be patient with me?

With deepest affection – dare I say, love – Zoë.

Freddie arrived three days later. He gathered Zoë into his arms. "I will do anything to make you as happy as you have just made me," he promised.

As it turned out, they didn't take things slowly. They were hungry for each other and made love that night on the sleeping porch, serenaded by the gentle lapping of the waves and the distant call of loons.

They were married quietly in the Port Darling church three weeks later.

•   •   •

"You can't manage the girls and drive the boat on your own, so I'll come along. And stay down at the dock," Ellie said to Troy. He was going to introduce two-month-old Jacqueline to his parents.

Troy hated that he couldn't bring Ellie in the first place, but to have her waiting by the boat like a servant made it all worse. Yet he could understand her concern that he'd have an inquisitive three-year-old aboard who rarely sat still, even if the baby would be fine in her bassinet.

Troy still spent a few days with his family in Pittsburgh right after Christmas, but Ellie had put her foot down at his taking Ginnie along. If the grandparents wanted to see her, they could include Ellie or wait until summers at the cottage. Troy had agreed with her, but his mother had been incensed.

Ellie knew how difficult all this was for Troy, but when it impinged on their family life – and in this case, the safety of the children - she was adamant.

She had brought her fishing rod and flies that her father had tied – it was one of his hobbies - and set about angling from the dock. "Might as well catch our supper," she said with a grin.

Troy had to chuckle at her aplomb. But his good humour was quickly tested.

"So, you finally have time for your mother," Erika snarled. She was ensconced on a chaise lounge in the sitting room. Rarely leaving her sickbed, she had grown bloated and querulous.

Stuart had warned Troy that she was becoming impossible. She constantly berated him about his drinking, so he had married quickly – if not wisely – just so that he could escape.

"Good to see you, Troy," his father, Howard, said with a warm smile. "And Ginnie!" He opened his arms and the child went over for a big hug.

"Come here, Virginia, and give your grandmamma a kiss," Erika ordered.

The child went reluctantly, knowing Mummy wasn't allowed to visit, and Grandmamma was scary, like a witch. She wasn't at all like Granny, who was cuddly and funny.

"You're a pretty little thing, I'll give you that," Erika said. To Troy she added, "So, you have another daughter."

"This is Jacqueline," he said, showing the baby cradled in his arms, but didn't hand her over to his mother.

"What a precious little doll!" Howard exclaimed.

"Very sweet," Erika said, almost dismissively. "But is she going to give you an heir?"

"We cherish our girls, Mom," Troy said firmly, suppressing his anger.

"Of course, but every man wants a son. I gave your father five strong boys, and Felix has two already. It's a wife's duty, but I suppose that's too much to expect of yours."

"It's wonderful to have some girls in the family now," Howard interceded quickly.

But Troy fumed. "Mom, I have been patient with you, and Ellie's been a saint. But I'm not going to tolerate your disparaging my wife, especially in front of our children," Troy declared in German, not wanting Ginnie to understand what was happening. "If your granddaughters are not as important as the grandsons, then there is no reason for us to visit."

"No, Troy, don't leave like this!" Howard implored.

"I'm sorry, Dad. You're welcome at our house any time, but until my entire family is truly welcome here, I won't be back," Troy declared as he took Ginnie by the hand.

"That scheming hussy has turned you against me!" Erika cried. "I knew she would destroy all the goodness and nobility in you."

"On the contrary! She's saved me from your tyranny. You did this to yourself, Mom, and you have to live with that."

Although he knew he was right, Troy would regret that he had parted so bitterly from his mother this last time that he saw her alive.

•   •   •

"So the Prince actually slept here, in the boathouse," Philip said as he and Sophie stood on the upper deck. Patrick and Gareth were hauling his luggage into one of the bedrooms.

"Just one night, but he thought it was the cat's whiskers." Sophie had already written to Philip about the Prince of Wales's stopover in 1923 en route to his ranch in Alberta. "Daddy took him for a breeze around the lake in *Windrunner IV* after they went canoeing, and he said he'd thoroughly relished both modes of transportation, but that zooming across the lake at sixty miles-per-hour was somewhat more thrilling. We invited a few of our closest friends to join us for dinner before attending the big ball at Thorncliff. I was allowed to go, and the Prince very graciously danced the Foxtrot with me."

Sophie had been absolutely thrilled. She would never forget that magical September night when the Thorncliff ballroom had scintillated with extravagant gowns and glittering jewels. The jazz band had been superb, and the party had lasted until the wee hours, when the Prince had finally decided it was time to retire.

"Because it wasn't an official visit, he travelled as Lord Renfrew, and the newspapers didn't report his trip. But Daddy had alerted the guests about whom they would be meeting, and some of the ladies were in such a tizzy! I think they practiced their curtsies for weeks."

"So at the end of this visit, I expect I'll be able to tell my friends that I danced with a girl who danced with the Prince of Wales," Philip said.

Sophie laughed delightedly. "And you can tell them that you slept in the same bed as he did."

She didn't understand the implications of that, but Philip burst into laughter. "I feel privileged! I say, but it's good to see you again, Sophie!" He looked at her with admiration, for she was a beauty.

He was eighteen and very handsome, she thought, feeling a flutter of excitement. Their correspondence had made them good friends, but she was already in danger of developing a crush on him.

"I'm so glad you can stay for a month! You should see what Daddy's bought. You'll love waterskiing. Daddy saw it demonstrated at a boat event in Palm Beach, and I'm sure we're the first on the lake to have Awka-Skees. They're faster and more fun than the aquaplane," she said, referring to the curved board that you stood on and which was towed behind a boat. Philip and Christopher had thought that a great lark last time. "But what do you want to do first?"

"Canoe around the island and then have a swim, if you're game."

"And how!"

"I'm determined that you and I will win the mixed canoe doubles at the Regatta. You don't know how chuffed Chris and I are about the trophy we won for jousting last time."

A three-year-old boy came charging down the hillside stairs and across the bridge to the deck. Ten-year-old Charlie followed more sedately.

"First you have to meet my little brother, Drew," Sophie said.

"A great pleasure to make your acquaintance, Drew. You sister speaks very highly of you in her letters." Drew shook Philip's outstretched hand with a giggle at the formality. "You take after your big brother. Hi, Charlie. I was just saying how I'm looking forward to the Regatta. How be you and I enter the men's canoe doubles?"

Charlie was surprised that an eighteen-year-old would be interested in doing anything with him. "That would be wicked!"

Philip quickly became a part of the family, the boys enjoying his visit almost as much as Sophie. He gladly helped out at Spirit Bay while she taught tennis, and being an expert equestrian, he gave Drew riding lessons. He played golf with Charlie and sometimes went fishing with him in the early mornings.

Philip mastered the skill of waterskiing and couldn't get enough of it. Each of the eight-foot-long boards was attached to the boat towrope, and the skier used hand ropes that were anchored to the curved tips, in order to steer. After a few failed attempts, Philip was able to start from the water rather than dive into it, and kept signaling to Chas to speed up. He got up to thirty miles an hour, and was able to carve some sharp curves.

Philip was impressed that Chas had been one of the team of drivers who'd helped Harry Greening and his *Rainbow IV* establish a new world record last autumn on this lake. It had been a 24-hour endurance test, run over two 12-hour days. *Rainbow IV* had covered more than 1200 miles at an average speed of 50 miles an hour. Philip asked Chas if he would take him around the 19-mile course and teach him how to drive a boat.

Chas did, and after a few lessons in *Dragonfly*, let Sophie take over as instructor.

He wasn't happy with this visit when he noticed how well Philip and Sophie got along. She was more energetic and effervescent than usual. They had riotous fun dancing the Charleston on the boathouse deck, both the wildly exuberant solo version, which Charlie and Drew did with them, and the partner version, which took some practice to co-ordinate.

Ria loved hearing all the laughter that counterpointed the jazzy music drifting up from the lakeside.

One evening, as Sophie and Philip prepared to go to a dance at the Country Club with Alice and Arthur, Sophie wanted to show Chas and Ria how well they had mastered the dance. "This is the perfect dress for the Charleston. Just watch."

She looked stunning in a sky-blue, beaded and fringed frock with splashes of pink sequins over an indigo silk underskirt that reached just below her knees. She had a matching headband, and blue suede T-strap high heels. The requisite long strands of beads were actually real pearls that she had received for her birthday. She needed no kohl or mascara to accent her large eyes, but she was wearing some lipstick, and looked decidedly older than sixteen.

When she and Philip danced, first singly and then together, the long strips of her overskirt twirled and shimmered.

"You've become very accomplished," Ria said, clapping. At thirty, she wasn't beyond doing the Charleston, of course, but hadn't mastered it like they had. They'd even added a few of their own touches – a flirty backward look and kick when they were sideways at arm's length. It all looked so delightful.

When they had gone, Ria said, "You shouldn't scowl so much, Chas. It ruins your good looks."

"Ha!"

"Can you really find any fault with Philip?" she asked astutely.

"No," he admitted reluctantly. "But Sophie's too young to start falling in love."

"Applesauce! This is exactly the age when girls have pashes. I've talked to her about sex, and what sort of behaviour is acceptable."

"And what would that be?"

"A bit of kissing and cuddling, if it felt right."

"Which can be highly dangerous, as we very well know."

"It was different then. You were going off to war, and I didn't know if you'd be coming back to me."

Chas harrumphed. How could a virile young man not be inflamed by his sexy daughter?

"It's a glorious time to be young and carefree," Ria said. "So much of our youth was stolen by the war, so don't begrudge them this."

"Of course I don't. I just don't want her marrying him and going off to live in England," he jested.

Ria laughed, but she knew that what he really didn't want was Lance being related to them. But how ironic if Sophie became mistress of Priory Manor! "If there's a romance blooming, it will likely just be the first of several for both of them. Remember how infatuated I was with Justin at that age?"

"Yes, but he didn't reciprocate."

"Not until later, when I was already in love with you."

"That was my luck then," Chas said with a smile.

•   •   •

Sidonie thought that she would probably miss this view of the lake from her beautiful island cottage. Sometimes. But she doubted that she would ever come back.

She had just gained possession of a villa on the Riviera, bought from Jack, sight unseen. He knew what she wanted and assured her that this property with a private beach at Juan-les-Pins would be ideal. He had rented it last year to F. Scott Fitzgerald - author of *The Great Gatsby,* among other novels - and his wife, Zelda.

Rafe was at the races, and Sid had just delivered Elyse into her Grandmother and Aunt Felicity's care. So she began her letter.

Dear Rafe,

I realize more than ever that we were never meant to be together. You want more children, as you keep reminding me; I don't. I despise "Toronto the Good", and find that even Muskoka has become a bore. I need to live among people who know how to enjoy life fully and are not afraid to revel in pleasure.

So I'm leaving. I won't hold you to our pre-nuptial agreement if you're willing to give me two million. Once that's in my account, I will provide you with a reason for divorce. That way, your reputation will be intact and Elyse need not be ashamed of both her parents, or blame your philandering for my departure.

She should stay with you, since you she is the product of your desires, and I have nothing to offer her. She reminds me of two painful events – her conception and her birth. Be good to her, as she deserves at least one loving parent. And when you remarry, don't ignore her in favour of your new children, or let your wife treat her badly.

It hadn't been hard to dismiss Elyse when she was a squalling infant, but now that she was becoming a charming little girl, Sid was in danger of falling in love with her. But she didn't ever want her heart engaged and disturbed again.

I'll be living at Juan-les-Pins, and you may bring her for a visit if you wish.

She stroked that out and wrote instead:

It's probably best if I stay out of her life altogether. It will be easier for her to despise me instead of longing to be with me.

We did have some fun times, didn't we? I wish you and Elyse only the best.

Affectionately, Sid

Dearest Chas,

Don't think badly of me for leaving. It's better for everyone this way.

Perhaps I dwell too much in the past - all those wonderful times we had when we were young and carefree at Blackthorn. It was surely another world, wasn't it?

I trust that you and Ria will help to look after Elyse, especially if Rafe isn't an ideal father. She's fortunate to have so many loving relatives around.

Do come to visit me if you're ever in Antibes.

Love always, Sid

•   •   •

The "Cousins Party" had been instigated when Sophie mentioned to Ria that she and her brothers had over a dozen cousins on Wyndwood and neighbouring islands. Now that Drew was old enough to enjoy playing with the others, Ria thought it would be fun for all the children to get together. She rarely saw her half-sister and brother, Cecilia and Jimmy, so this would be a good excuse to have them over to mingle with their relatives.

When they also included Ellie and Troy's two girls, who were cousins of Edgar and Daphne's five kids and Zoë's Ethan, and Justin and Toni's three, who were cousins of Max and Lydia's three, they had nearly two dozen children. And because he was almost like a member of the family, Ria invited Grayson's six-year-old son, Alastair.

They held it a week after the Regatta, at which Sophie and Philip did win the mixed doubles canoe race, while he and Charlie achieved a hard-won third in the men's.

Alice helped organize it, as she had been staying at The Point this past week, since Arthur had to go back to work. He was lucky to get all of July off, but worked very long days in August while others had their vacations, so he had insisted that Alice stay in Muskoka and enjoy the fine weather. Much as she loved her cottage, she didn't relish being there alone, so Claire, Colin, and baby Merilee were going to stay with her next week. It would be a nice change of scene for them, and they could also spend time with Jack and his family. After that, Alice was planning to visit with Esme. Arthur would be back for an extra long Labour Day weekend, when they would close their cottage.

Tables were set out on the open-sided pavilion east of the Old Cottage, spread with paper, pencils, boxes of Crayola crayons, paint brushes, and watercolour sets. "Draw or paint whatever you like," Ria told the children as they arrived.

"Are there prizes?" ten-year-old Cecilia wanted to know.

"No, this is just for fun. But we're going to have a treasure hunt later."

"Oh," Cecilia drawled as if that were a great bore.

Her brother, Jimmy, had developed slowly, and although he could now read a little, he wasn't a typical eight-year-old. He gravitated toward the younger kids – the half dozen between ages five and seven - and giggled with them as they drew comical pictures.

Their parents overlooked the activity from the east veranda, while Alice, Sophie, and Philip supervised the kids. Ria's father, James, hadn't come, probably feeling out of place, being a generation older than the other parents. Jack had brought Elyse, who was still with them. Fliss had stayed home with three-week-old Joseph.

"He's quite a handsome fellow, that young Chadwick. Has his father's looks and charm," Helena said to Ria. "Do you think it's wise to allow Sophie to spend so much time alone with him?"

Ria always bristled when Helena criticized her. "Do you mean going out canoeing or horseback riding together? Sophie knows how to conduct herself, and Philip is certainly a gentleman. I think all that chaperones accomplished was to make young people find ways to be sneaky and meet secretly."

"Eluding them was half the fun, wasn't it?" Ellie said cheekily.

Jack had a sudden stab of longing as he was reminded of their passionate trysts.

"Oh, yes!" Phoebe said, thinking about her own affair with Bobby Miller.

"This flapper notion that anything goes will backfire, you mark my words," Helena said. "In the end, reputation is everything, and a girl can lose hers much too quickly and easily these days."

"People thought us very brazen when we drove men about in France, especially since not all of them were wounded," Antonia said, for they had chauffeured the brass as well on occasion. "But we were only *fast* when driving," she quipped. "Freedom and responsibility don't make us forget the values that were instilled in us as children. At some point, parents have to trust that they did a good job, and not rely on constant supervision to ensure that their offspring have a moral and social conscience."

"Unfortunately, that doesn't work for everyone, as we know," Helena said pointedly, looking at her stepdaughter.

She was referring to Ria getting pregnant before Chas went off to war. Chas could sense Ria beginning to fume.

But it was Phoebe who inadvertently diffused the situation. "Grandmother is glaring at you, Helena," she declared. "Isn't it interesting that she always comes when you're here? You must have done something to upset her."

Helena looked startled and then angry. "Do stop your nonsense, Phoebe!"

"Didn't Hamlet say about his father's ghost, *There are more things in heaven and earth, Horatio, than are dreamt of in your philosophy?*" Max said.

"Yes, indeed," Silas agreed. "We don't all see the world the same way. Which we can probably tell by looking at the children's artwork."

And which some of the adults proceeded to do, offering encouraging comments. But Ria and Jack were surprised by Jimmy's drawing of Elyse. It was an amazing likeness that also captured her exuberance.

"This is wonderful!" Ria enthused.

Jimmy beamed. "I draw what I see."

"Then you have a very fine eye, young man," Jack said.

"Would you like me to give you some lessons in watercolours?" Ria asked her brother.

"Hot dog! Could I?"

"You'll have to ask your parents, but I'd be happy to teach you."

Jimmy ran over to his mother, his gait still awkward as if he didn't have complete control of his limbs. He was bouncing up and down when he talked to Helena. She frowned and he looked crestfallen, so Jack went over and said, "Your son has a remarkable talent, Helena. Ria and I will be happy to help him nurture that."

She could hardly refuse without seeming churlish and unfair. So when she agreed reluctantly, Jimmy shouted, "Hooray! Hooray! Hooray!"

"Do calm down, Jimmy," Helen ordered. "It's not seemly to be so loud."

"It's nice to see such enthusiasm," Chas said, taking Jimmy by the arm. "So let's go play baseball."

"Me too?"

"Of course."

"Girls don't play baseball," Cecilia scoffed.

"Yes we do," Sophie said. "At least here at The Point."

"But it might ruin my dress!"

"You can just watch if you like," Ria told her annoying little sister.

"May I play as well, Mummy?" Ethan asked.

"He's getting good at batting," Freddie told Zoë.

Ellie said, "You know to stop before you get too tired."

"Of course, Aunt Ellie."

She and Ria were so glad to see that Zoë was allowing Ethan to play with the other children. Surely that was Freddie's influence. Ellie had assured them that exercise was good for Ethan, so Freddie had been teaching him tennis and canoeing as well. Ellie was convinced that the more normal a life Ethan led, the stronger he would be and, thus, perhaps less susceptible to a relapse. And she didn't want him thinking of himself as an invalid. His heart murmur was not that severe.

Ethan was so proud to have a father of his own, and Ellie was delighted that Zoë had finally given in to Freddie. "Come on, Daddy," Ethan said, taking Freddie's hand. "Let's play ball!"

In the valley behind the house, a makeshift baseball diamond had been laid out. The fathers helped the littlest ones with batting and there were plenty of outfielders to run for balls, so there was squealing and laughter among the kids and the adults, especially when Alastair Grayson hit a home run, the ball bouncing past all the little hands right into the Back Bay.

The women watched from the fringes, and Helena said to Ria, "You're giving that boy ideas above his station, as I've mentioned before."

"The world is changing, Helena. Thank God!" Ellie intervened. She knew only too well the antipathy between Ria and her stepmother, and how little criticism it took from Helena or James to upset her friend. "With hard work and determination, Alastair could become Prime Minister."

"Eleanor, you have the most *lively* imagination," Helena retorted.

Ellie grinned at Ria.

When the rousing game was over, the children went into the cottage where lemonade, desserts, and ice cream were laid out on the long dining table. When Drew darted in front of Cecilia to snatch a chocolate cookie, she snapped at him, "Andrew! You should wait until your guests have selected theirs!"

Although Charlie was always telling his little brother what to do, he didn't tolerate others doing it, especially Cecilia, whom he had never liked. He said, "Don't be so bossy, Cecilia."

"Andrew has to do what I say because I'm his aunt," she stated.

Charlie was two weeks older than Cecilia, so he grinned and said, "Yes, Auntie."

"I'm not *your* aunt!" she said indignantly. "You're just a poor orphan that Victoria adopted."

The words hit him like a physical blow. "You're just stupid!"

"I am *not*! You're a liar and have no manners!" She flounced off.

Sophie had heard and went over to put her arm around Charlie's shoulder. Because they were both orphans, she had always been protective of him. In French she said, "Don't let that brat upset you. Mummy and Daddy chose us. Her parents had to take what they got."

That made him laugh, although Cecilia's words had wounded him. So he was distracted and moody when they started playing wildfire tag.

Older kids were teamed up with the younger ones, and all were reminded that the lake and boathouses were off limits, but they could run and hide anywhere else on the five acre Point. Sophie and Philip were "it" or "the fire". When they found and touched someone in a team, the tagged kids joined the fire and helped to locate the next group. The last ones tagged were the winners. Everyone could evade the fire, but that became more difficult and thrilling as the fire grew.

Charlie grudgingly took charge of Drew and led him down to a rocky nook on the slope near the steamer dock. When they sat down, they were also screened by ferns and blueberry shrubs, and when the fire approached, they could dash along the shoreline path in either direction. It would be easier to escape when the pursuers were funneled down the narrow path.

"We'll run around to the billiard room when they come, either through the back of the house or the front," Charlie said.

"I know a good place to hide," Drew said.

"No you don't. You're just a baby."

"Am not!"

"Shut up or they'll hear us!" Charlie snapped.

Drew sulked.

They heard plenty of squealing as the fire grew, and the quiet moments between captures became increasingly suspenseful.

"Get ready to run," Charlie warned as he listened for the rustling of underbrush or the muffled tread of footsteps. With so many players, it was hard to keep the little ones from giggling, so that and the consequent shushing alerted them to the wildfire flowing down the granite slope from the house.

"The back way!" Charlie said, grabbing Drew's hand. They raced along the tanbark path past the new boathouse, but had been spotted, so the others were in hot pursuit. Philip was particularly fast and managed to touch Drew just before he and Charlie reached the house. The others lagged behind.

Panting, Philip said, "Good strategy, Charlie. But I won sprinting races at school. So come and join the fire."

The pursuers gathered; Sophie counted heads and declared that they had only two groups left to find, so they set out stealthily again. Charlie's heart wasn't in the game, so he told Drew to stay with the others because he had to go pee. Instead, he went into the library, stole a couple of cigarettes from the humidor, and then slunk back to his erstwhile hideout.

He'd taken the odd cigarette before, although they were out of bounds. But he was almost eleven, so he should be able to smoke if he wanted to. He didn't suck too deeply on the cigarette at first, because it usually made him cough, but then he felt quite grown up as he let the smoke linger in his mouth and swirl about his head as he puffed it out. Soon he felt a pleasant buzz in his head, and the far-off revelry of the others didn't impinge on him. He could just sit quietly and think about his real parents.

He'd been almost three when his mother had died of the influenza. He could still remember her softness and the lilt of her voice, but he had to study the one small photograph he had of her to remind himself what she actually looked like. She would be forever young and beautiful. Whenever he smelled lily-of-the-valley, he thought instantly of her with a crushing longing.

He had never seen his father, and knew only that he had been a great British pilot hero, handsome and noble, and that he had loved Charlie dearly. So he must have died, but Maman never knew how or when. But what if he had survived the war and come looking for them, only to find them gone? One day he would go to England and France and discover more about him.

It wasn't that he didn't love Mummy Ria and Daddy Chas. After Sophie had told him about her bleak months in a French orphanage with the nuns, he realized how lucky he had been that they had taken him into their hearts and home. But if his father was still alive, he wanted to know him, to belong to him as well.

It wasn't until after his second smoke that he became aware of a different sound. The others were shouting for him and Drew. He suddenly grew cold with fear. Why were they seeking Drew?

He ran over to the valley behind the house.

"Where's Drew?" Ria asked when she saw him. "Charlie!"

"I left him with the others. I... I had to use the bathroom. I told him to stay with them."

"He was *your* responsibility!" Chas scolded. "You should at least have told Sophie so she could keep an eye on him!"

Charlie trembled at the cold anger that emanated from Daddy Chas. He was rarely furious, so each time it felt momentous.

"Where do you think he might have gone?" Jack asked.

"I don't know! He said he knew a good place to hide, so maybe he thought he could keep playing."

"Where?" Chas barked.

"I don't *know!*"

"Is there any place that's special to him?" Troy asked gently, realizing the boy was almost in tears.

"He likes the boats. We sometimes watch Stephen." Who wasn't here today.

"We've already checked the boathouses," Chas said, but he could see the horror on Ria's face as she considered another possibility. "No, Ria!" he shouted as she raced towards the new boathouse. He tried to run after her, but couldn't move as quickly. Jack realized what was happening, and managed to intercept her before she could go inside.

"Let me go, Jack!" she demanded as she struggled in his grasp.

"No, Ria! Let me have a look."

"And me," Troy said.

Chas took Ria from Jack. "Don't panic, my darling," he said as he held her close. "He's probably hiding out somewhere and thinks it's a great lark that no one's been able to find him."

Ellie had joined them and said, "I'm sure Chas is right, Ria. You can't expect Drew to be any less adventuresome than you," she teased.

The others were walking the paths and shouting, "Come out, Drew. The game's over!"

Jack and Troy checked the clear water around the boats and under the docks, and were vastly relieved to find nothing. Just as they rejoined the others, there was a happy shout from Max, saying, "We've found him!"

Ria almost collapsed with relief in Chas's arms as they all made their way over to the base of the "Dragon's Back" cliff behind the Graysons' cottage. Drew was perched about a quarter of the way up the steep, shaggy slope, and shouted, "Mummy, Daddy, I can't get down! I'm scared!"

Philip was already scrambling up to rescue him.

"Alastair remembered telling Drew about the little cave in the cliff," Max explained. "And it's a lot easier to climb up than down, as I know only too well." He'd been stuck there once as a youngster.

The crisis wasn't over, since it was a hazardous descent, which they did backwards, their faces pressed to the rock. There were gasps when Drew slipped, but Philip was protectively below and caught him easily. He guided Drew slowly and safely down and into his anxious mother's arms. "You shouldn't have gone off alone like that, Snuggles!" Ria chided as she squeezed him tightly.

"But Mummy, I had the bestest hiding place. The fire didn't find me."

Sophie said, "But you have to play by the rules. You mustn't scare us like that again, OK?" She ruffled his hair.

"OK."

"Thank you, Philip," Chas said. "You obviously knew what you were doing."

"Father takes us climbing in the Lake District sometimes."

Sophie beamed at him. Then she said, "It's time for the corn roast, everyone!" So they headed down to the fire pit, where the servants were already preparing the treat.

"And high time for some drinks," Chas said, as the adults settled into chairs on the broad steamer dock nearby. Grayson handed around welcome glasses of wine, but Helena decided there had been quite enough excitement for one day, and dragged an unhappy Jimmy away, Cecilia being anxious to leave. Corn on the cob was much too messy to eat.

"I feel very sorry for my little brother," Ria said.

"I think it's a great idea of yours to tutor him in art," Ellie said. "It would be good for Jimmy to spend time in an environment where he's appreciated. I expect he'll blossom."

"I keep forgetting that he actually *is* my brother, since we rarely see him, but I plan to be a better big sister, even if I have to wrestle Helena to steal him away for a while."

The others laughed at the image that conjured.

The rest of the party unfolded as planned, and everyone had such fun that Ria promised they would do it again next year, which was how it became an annual tradition, with activities changing as the cousins aged.

Johanna was back from her half-day off, which she and Gareth, Grayson's stepson, had spent in Port Darling. They were engaged to be married in the fall. Once Johanna had prepared Drew for bed, Ria went to tuck the boys in.

When she kissed Charlie, he said, "I'm sorry about today, Mummy. I didn't think anything bad would happen to Drew."

"And thankfully nothing did," she reassured him, realizing he was feeling guilty and unhappy. "But you see how important a big brother's job is."

"Daddy's still mad at me."

Chas always said goodnight to the children downstairs, and Ria hadn't detected any censure in his interaction with Charlie.

"No, he's not, mon petit poussin. He was scared earlier, like I was, but that's all behind us. Now go to sleep, the pair of you. It's been a busy day."

But Charlie wasn't convinced. Daddy was disappointed in him at the very least. After all, Drew was *his* son, not an adopted orphan. At this moment he wished that Drew would fly to Oz with Dorothy or fall down a rabbit hole into Wonderland, and just disappear from their lives, so things could be as they'd been before he was born.

But maybe *he* should be the one to leave. Maybe it was time to search for his real father.

Charlie didn't sleep much as he pondered his plans. So he rose well before dawn, packed a bag while Drew slept angelically, snuck into the kitchen where he took a large hunk of cheese, ham, a loaf of bread, and cookies from the pantry, and a thermos of lemonade, grabbed some cigarettes and matches, and then set out in the Dippy, which was really his boat now that Sophie was driving *Dragonfly*.

The Disappearing Propeller Boat was a skiff that had a motor located in the centre, and a propeller that could be raised into a housing, and would do so automatically if it struck something or was beached. That meant that it could go anywhere a canoe could. But he'd have to paddle it for a while, since the distinctive put-put of the engine might awaken his parents. He was never up this early.

He knew more or less how to get to the Lake Joe train station. He had his ice cream money and had borrowed Drew's, which he hoped was enough to buy him a ticket to Montreal, and then he would have to find some way to get onto an England-bound ship.

He had only a moment's regret as he paddled away. Sophie would miss him, of course, but she had Philip now. Mummy would cry, but Drew would soon cheer her up. Daddy had his own son – the golden boy, blonde and beautiful, like his parents.

Charlie didn't realize how much he looked like the pre-war Chas – or Drew - even though his hair had grown darker over the years.

When he actually left Wyndwood behind, he suddenly felt afraid. But excited as well. He was Huckleberry Finn, ready for any adventure.

The lake seemed to be exhaling smoke, which sometimes thinned to reveal the darker shapes of islands. He knew this area well enough that he wasn't concerned about paddling into the enveloping mist.

No one was unduly worried when Charlie didn't show up for breakfast, as he sometimes went fishing in the morning. But when he didn't appear by mid-morning, Ria and Chas became concerned. When they realized that he had taken his and Drew's allowance, clothes, and food from the kitchen, they were deeply worried.

"Perhaps he thought I was too harsh with him yesterday," Chas confessed. "But he needs to face up to the consequences of his actions. How immature and foolish to run away!"

"I know how that feels," Ria reminded him.

Chas, of course, remembered what had instigated her running away in '14. "Surely I'm not as bad a father as yours!"

"Of course not! But you know that Charlie has been insecure ever since Drew was born. Sophie overheard Cecilia spiting him for being an orphan. Surely that hurts."

"I found this note under his pillow," Johanna said excitedly as she handed it over.

I'll write when I get there. Don't worry. Love, Charlie

"Get where?" Ria pondered. "Sophie, has he ever mentioned someplace he wants to go?"

She shook her head.

"What about when he grows up?" Chas added astutely.

Sophie thought for a moment. "He *has* said that one day he'll go to England to find his father."

Ria and Chas were staggered.

"He must be heading for the train station," Chas said. "Stephen can go down to Bala and Gravenhurst, in case he took that route, although that's not likely because he'd have to lock through. And someone should go to the Lake Joe station via Port Sandfield. I'll go up the river, since that's the way he knows."

"Philip and I will go via Port Sandfield," Sophie said. It was a longer, but less complicated route.

"Capital!" Chas said. "We'll meet up at the station."

"But Chas, how will Charlie find his way among all those islands beyond the river?" Ria asked.

"If he gets lost, my darling, we *will* eventually find him," Chas reassured her. "That might be easier than if he actually gets onto a train."

"Then you take the main channel and I'll skirt to the south," Ria said. "I'll ask Max to come along as an extra pair of eyes."

"Good idea."

"May I go with you, Mummy?" Drew asked. "I want Charlie to come home!"

"You wait here with Johanna, in case he comes back on his own," Ria replied, giving him a big hug and a kiss.

Drew was how Ria had pictured Reggie. But if she favoured him because he was uniquely hers, she also loved her adopted children. Somehow she would have to make sure that Charlie knew that.

Chas set out in *Windrunner IV*. The hydroplane had won numerous races and could do over 60 miles per hour. He realized that Charlie could have arrived at the station by now, the Dippy's maximum speed being nine miles an hour, and the distance, about twelve miles. But Chas couldn't go much faster along the winding, often shallow river with narrow rock cuts. Then he had to weave his way among some islands, but once he was in the large open stretch of Lake Joe, he was able run at full speed again. The next train for Toronto didn't leave until 1:20, so he had plenty of time, whether to catch Charlie before he left, or to follow him to the city.

But Charlie and the Dippy weren't there, the stationmaster had not seen a boy travelling alone, and no tickets had been sold to a lad for the morning train. It was a relief of sorts. Likely the cantankerous Dippy had had engine problems, which was not unusual. Stephen had taught Charlie how to deal with some of the issues, but if something else had gone wrong, it would take the boy a long time to row the skiff. And since Chas hadn't spotted him along the main channel, he must indeed be lost.

He was impatient to begin looking, but had to wait for the others to arrive. None of them had found Charlie. They left instructions for the stationmaster to call through to the Pineridge Inn if Charlie showed up – and to keep him here. Chas got out his chart and said, "We need to do an organized search. Sophie, you head south along the west shore, and go into all the bays and around islands. Ria, you do the same going north, and I'll circumnavigate all the islands west of the river. Let's meet back here in two hours."

Lake Joseph was long, sometimes very wide, and riddled with coves and bays, and had a fair share of the 400 islands that dotted the three big lakes.

They had no luck, and Charlie hadn't arrived at the station. Chas telephoned over to the Seaford Boatworks to see if Stephen had found him, but that also proved to be negative. He asked Stephen to round up some help – Jack, Justin, Troy, Freddie, Edgar - and suggested areas that they might search. Whoever found him should phone through to Pineridge and Chas would keep checking back. Otherwise, they should all meet at the train station at 6:00 PM.

Ria was becoming frantic when they still hadn't located Charlie by then. She could barely eat the sandwiches that Stephen's mother had sent along, but Chas told her that she needed to keep up her strength. "Something must have happened to him," she said disconsolately. "Even if he were rowing he would have been here by now."

"That's a long way for a lad his age to row," Justin said. "I expect he's made plenty of stops."

"But someone should have spotted him by now!"

"Perhaps he headed back and is now safely at home," Troy suggested.

"Sophie, why don't you take Mummy back via the river, checking any little inlets on the way," Chas suggested. "And Max can take over *Windrunner III.*"

"No, Chas! I have to help. It'll be dark soon," Ria protested.

"You and Sophie are tired, Ria, and I expect that Drew will be anxious about all of us. The poor kid doesn't know what's happening."

It had been the right card to play.

Philip said that he'd keep searching with Max.

A tearful Drew threw himself into Ria's embrace when she arrived home, and although she was distraught that Charlie hadn't come back, she had to keep up appearances for Drew. So she managed to eat a little dinner and read him a bedtime story. But he was too worried and afraid to sleep alone, so Ria cuddled up with him in her bed. Exhausted, she fell into a restless sleep.

Chas didn't want to disturb her when he returned, the men having had to give up the search as darkness descended. With plenty of shallows and shoals outside the main channels, it would be treacherous on the lake in the dark, and they were likely to get lost as well.

Chas refused to think that anything truly bad had happened to Charlie. Perhaps he hadn't even planned to catch a train, but had just wanted to get away by himself, and was camping somewhere. Perhaps a night under the stars would bring him rushing back home tomorrow. But if he had boat problems, he could be stranded somewhere, so they would resume the search at dawn. At least it was a relatively mild night with no storms threatening.

Chas sipped a large cognac as he poured over his nautical chart yet again. Charlie knew that he would need to travel slightly northwest at the mouth of the river to thread his way through the islands and get across the lake to the train station, but they had searched that area twice.

But what if Charlie had miscalculated? What if he had gone too far north and ended up in Little Lake Joe, a long branch off the main lake? The morning had been cloudy, and he might not have known where west was amid the confusion of all the islands. They hadn't explored far into Little Lake Joe, and there was a large bay partway up.

Ria woke at midnight, frantic as she realized that Charlie must still be missing. She found Chas in the library. He calmed her when he explained his thoughts, telling her he would set out as soon as it was light enough.

"A night in the open won't harm him," he said. "It's just like camping."

"But what if he's hurt? What if he broke a leg or an arm? You know how temperamental that engine is. I can't bear the thought that he's in pain and alone." Or the unthinkable – that he'd fallen out of the boat or had capsized and drowned. "Oh God, Chas, I can't bear to think about it."

He held her and rubbed her back. "It's too easy to imagine the worst. He's a sensible, capable boy. Stay positive, my darling."

"This might be the perfect time to tell him that you're his father. He's obviously not going to let go of the fantasy that he'll find you one day."

"And if he knew, what would he have said yesterday to Cecilia's nasty taunt? Wouldn't he have been tempted to tell her the truth? And how would that serve him if people knew he was my bastard? We can't risk his future, Ria. Right now he is my legitimate, adopted son."

"But, Chas, he's dreaming and longing for something he already has. Isn't it cruel to keep the truth from him?"

"When he's older and mature enough, we will tell him."

Chas couldn't imagine how wrong that decision would prove to be.

•   •   •

Charlie dipped his aching, swollen wrist into the cool water. He didn't think it was broken, because he could wiggle his fingers. But he couldn't paddle. That damned engine had played him a nasty trick when he'd tried to restart it.

He knew he had been hopelessly lost when the stupid thing conked out. But then the sun had come out and he had paddled west before his wrist had begun to ache too much. But it was only a large bay, and there were no cottages around to ask for help. He had pulled up to a sandy shore and here he sat.

He still had food, and had replenished his thermos with lake water. A couple of cigarettes had helped to calm his panic. All day he looked for passing boats to hail, but none came down this deserted inlet. He had seen the *Sagamo* in the distance as it made its way up to Natural Park on its 100 Mile Cruise. But no one could see him. He was little more than a faraway speck.

He had hoped that Mummy and Daddy would find him, but he had told them not to worry. So what was he to do now? Nobody would be looking for him. He had refused to cry so far, but there was hardly any light left in the sky now. He crawled into his boat and put a warm sweater on. He didn't like being completely alone in the dark.

He lit another cigarette, which helped to keep the mosquitoes away. Something – a bat likely – swooped and darted above him. Daddy said that they ate mosquitoes, which was good, but Charlie had also heard that they could get tangled in your hair, and some were vampires. He took a shirt out of his bag and tied it over his head so that it also draped around his shoulders. Then he sank down into the bottom of the boat to make himself smaller.

He hoped that there weren't any dock spiders around. Daddy said they were actually "fishing spiders", since they caught and ate minnows as well as insects. On the docks at home, they scarpered away like lightning when they heard your tread, but he had seen some clinging to rock faces, and they terrified him. As large as his hand, they would suddenly raise themselves up in a menacing stance. They could run on the water and dive down into it. And they were poisonous.

At dusk he had been awed to see a moose come down to the lake for a drink. He prayed to God there weren't any bears.

The haunting cry of a loon nearby was strangely reassuring. He wasn't completely alone.

But still he couldn't stop the tears. After a good sob, he decided that he needed to have a plan. So tomorrow he would ignore the pain and try to paddle out of this forgotten bay.

As he lay back in the Dippy, he became aware of the many layers of darkness. There was no moon, but the lake glowed eerily with the reflections of the vast multitude of stars, some of them dropping out of the sky or shooting across in a fiery arc. The Milky Way was an endless, bright cloud, which seemed to billow out of the black treetops, and was oddly comforting.

Maman was up there somewhere, wasn't she? And looking out for him? Sophie had told him that their mothers were their guardian angels, and would never let anything bad happen to them.

Whip-poor-wills trilled; crickets chirped; a bullfrog bellowed. His fears eased and he fell into a deep sleep.

•   •   •

Chas had urged Ria to go back to bed with Drew while he kipped in one of the guest rooms. He didn't sleep much, and was already underway before sunrise. Grayson supplied him with thermoses of hot tea and cold lemonade, sandwiches, and Charlie's favourite cakes.

Chas had left instructions for the others to await a message at Pineridge before setting out. Somehow he was convinced that he would find Charlie in that bay.

The mist was still rising when he did. He took his son into a fierce embrace.

"Daddy! I was so scared. I didn't think you'd come!"

Chas told him how they had all searched for him.

"I'm so sorry I ran away."

"Charlie, you are as much my son as Drew. Always remember that. Mummy and I love you dearly. Please don't ever do this to us again."

Charlie wept on Chas's shoulder.

•   •   •

Esme was so happy to have Alice staying over, especially since she had been ordered to rest and do absolutely no work, which made the days long and tedious without at least some distraction. Douglas McIvor had determined that she was carrying twins, and was concerned about her blood pressure, which was too high. Not surprising since Trick Butcher's continued antics disturbed her.

One day last month she'd been talking to Sky Mayhew on the wharf outside Mercer's Drugstore. Although there was plenty of space to walk around them, Trick had barged between them, pushing them apart roughly, as he sneered, "Don't block the way, ya dirty squaw."

Rufus had sensed Trick's hostility and jumped on him, growling.

"Get this fuckin' dog off me or I'll kill it!"

Esme had taken Rufus by the collar and calmed him, but the dog was wary and upset.

Trick's contemptuous leer raised her own hackles. "Don't be so rude!" she'd countered.

"Ya don't own this village, Injun-lover," he'd snorted.

Another time she had arrived home to find a dead skunk festering on the doorstep. It had obviously been shot. Last Sunday, they had come out of church to discover two of their car tires slashed.

When Rufus barked in the night, Esme would tense and listen for sounds of an intruder, although Stephen reassured her that it was probably only a nosy raccoon that the dog was warning.

"It's disturbing how one's paradise can so easily be violated," Esme admitted to Alice as they sat on the veranda. "I love it here, of course, but now I feel unsettled at times. Even scared."

"I can imagine!" Alice had been horrified at Stephen's close escape in the explosion. "Hopefully this Butcher creep will get tired of harassing you."

"I rather doubt that, since he never lets up on his hatred of the Indians, so Sky told me. We can only hope that he moves away, like his brother Jake did when he found a job in Orillia."

Stephen arrived home bearing baskets of food, still warm, from the Inn. They dined on the open deck, the mosquitoes hardly bothersome at this time of year. Jazzy music from the dance hall above the Dockside Tearoom flowed across the bay.

Constable Bob Bayley arrived as they were finishing dessert. He had a badge, but no uniform. Not that it mattered, since everyone knew that he was the law in Port Darling, and incorruptible.

"You heard that Old Zeke died last week?" Bayley asked, referring to the village drunk.

"One too many?" Stephen volunteered, wondering where this was leading.

"A bit too much poison. Turns out that he bought his tainted supply of moonshine from Trick. A couple of others in the area are sick and Trick himself was deathly ill. The OPP from Bala have been on the case, and Trick's been charged with manslaughter. Thought that might give you some peace of mind." He had been sympathetic to their troubles, but couldn't find any witnesses or evidence to indict Trick.

"Much appreciated, Bob," Stephen said, delighted to see Esme visibly relax.

"You take good care of yourselves now," Bob Bayley said with a warm smile.

•   •   •

"The birds are upset," Phoebe said, wringing her hands in agitation. "There's going to be an angry storm."

And Phoebe always became distraught during storms, so Silas waffled. He should stay here this afternoon to look after her.

"Please don't go, Silas."

"But William is reading his poetry at the Assembly and I promised to be there."

"William!" she scoffed. "It's always William, William, William! Don't look at me like that!"

"Like what?"

"With those dead eyes. Oh God, he's stolen your soul!"

"Who has?"

"William! Silas, stop looking like that!" There were only deep, dark holes where his eyes should have been. She dug her fingers into her cheekbones as if she were about to pull off her face.

Silas grabbed her hands, but she shook him off violently. "Don't touch me!"

Having heard Phoebe's scream, the nurse, Brenda, bustled into the sitting room. She took Phoebe into a motherly embrace. "There now, dearie, things will be just fine. The weather is unsettling today, isn't it? Smothering. Do we sense a storm coming? Perhaps a bit of medicine would help, and then you'll have a lovely little lie-down. What do you say, dearie?" She motioned for Silas to leave, which he did with guilty relief.

Phoebe nodded. The veronal always made her drift into a pleasant world where nothing hurt or frightened or threatened her.

Silas found four-year-old Sylvia playing with Edgar's youngest children. She was such a quiet and serious little child, and he desperately hoped that she wouldn't become like her mother. Or him, for that matter. Too much imagination, too sensitive, too guilt-ridden. So he was glad that she had the constant company of her boisterous cousins.

"Mummy's having a rest, and Daddy's going off to do some work, so I'll see you later, munchkin."

She threw her arms around him fiercely, and didn't want to let go. No doubt she had heard Phoebe shrieking, and was scared. Her own nurse was unobtrusively nearby. He disengaged himself gently. "Daddy mustn't be late."

She nodded sadly.

As Silas set out in the canoe, he had a moment's regret. If he were a responsible father, he should be taking Sylvia out for a walk or a trip to the ice cream parlour – anything to get her away from the atmosphere of Tumbling Rocks for a while. But she did have her cousins, and he didn't really know how to deal with children, other than reading to them. Sylvia loved cuddling up to him as they shared their favourite stories.

But the rhythm of the paddling soothed him. It was why he always chose to canoe the two miles over to Tobin Island. He relished these tranquil moments when he was alone, skimming through the water like the loons that sometimes popped up beside him.

He noticed the colossal thunderheads in the west, but thought the foaming, sun-kissed mountains merely beautiful and awesome.

•   •   •

"Philip and I are going canoeing," Sophie told Ria.

"Keep an eye on the weather," Ria advised. "I think this heat is going to break, so we could be in for a nasty storm." They had been sweltering these past few days, and a cleansing rain would be welcome.

"We'll just paddle around the island," Sophie assured her.

Because Philip was leaving tomorrow, they wanted to get a few more of his favourite activities in, and it was too hot to play tennis or ride. Chas had promised to take them water skiing later.

As they headed up the west side of the island, they realized that there was indeed a storm brewing, but they weren't prepared for how quickly it swooped down on them. They had just reached the end of the north shore when the light wind suddenly burst into a gale, and black clouds gobbled up the sun as they rumbled and tumbled overhead.

Sophie thought about heading across to Thorncliff, which was the nearest cottage, but they couldn't fight against the wind and waves that now threatened to swamp them. So they stayed close to shore, Philip shouting to her, "Let's aim for the beach around the point."

She nodded and paddled faster as lightning forked around them, unleashing a deluge of stinging rain. Thunder ruptured the air and rattled their bones. She was truly scared. But fortunately, they were now on the leeward side of the island, and the Shimmering Sands was only a few more strokes away.

Painful, pea-sided hail pelted them by the time they beached the canoe. Philip flipped it over and leaned it against the granite outcropping. "Get underneath," he said.

She pressed against the rock, and he sat down beside her. Hail pounded on their cedar-strip roof as the wind roared like a wildfire through the trees. They heard the snapping of branches; something large hit and bounced off their shelter. Sophie shrieked, and Philip put his arm comfortingly around her shoulders.

"Bloody hell, but you have extremes of weather here," he said. "Hot enough to melt candles one minute, and then raining ice pellets and..." As if to finish his sentence, the wind snatched the canoe and hurled it into the trees at the other end of the cove. Philip instinctively pushed her down onto her side and wrapped himself around her to shield her. They faced the immutable rock, grateful for its solid presence and the bit of protection it afforded as branches flew past overhead. Fortunately, the precipitation had become liquid again.

Like a rampaging beast, the storm screamed down the lake, leaving a traumatized silence in its wake.

Sophie rolled over to face Philip, excited by the closeness of his strong body, grateful for his chivalrous protection. "Thank you for looking after me."

"My pleasure."

They looked at each other searchingly, having fought the suppressed desire that had been building these past weeks. He kissed her chastely.

She had never been kissed before and was surprised and thrilled at how pleasant it was to feel his soft lips on hers.

"So that you don't forget me," he said with a grin as he helped her to her feet.

"I could never do that!" she assured him, and then boldly kissed him back.

He laughed as he drew her into a hug. This time the kiss was more passionate, but she responded as his tongue sought hers.

"Oh, hell, I'm going to miss you, Sophie!" he said when he finally released her. He had promised his father to comport himself as a gentleman, which meant absolutely no seducing Sophie.

"Can't you come back next summer?"

"I don't know. I'll certainly try. In the meantime, may I tell everyone that I have a Canadian girlfriend?"

"Gee! Of course!" She glowed with pride and happiness.

He took her hand as they assessed the damage. "Hell, that would have hurt," Philip said as he picked up a golf-ball-sized chunk of hail.

The canoe was smashed, so they began walking along the path to the point. Trees and branches were down all along the route, and they had to clamber over or under them, in the case of those that had been plucked right out by their massive roots. In the dripping, calm, sunny aftermath, it seemed incredible that the wind had had such power.

Ria and Chas had seen few storms that violent, so they were deeply worried about Sophie and Philip. Chas reassured Ria that they were sensible kids, and bound to have found some shelter, perhaps at Westwynd or Thorncliff. So they were vastly relieved when the two walked in, soaked and bedraggled, but unharmed.

Silas wasn't so lucky.

He was out in the open water at least a mile from any shore. The storm bore down on him like an avenging Valkyrie. The lake itself turned black and sinister, the waves licking at his canoe like ravenous flames.

When it flipped him over, he struggled to hang onto the overturned canoe, as the rough water washed over him. But suddenly he saw old comrades beckoning, and knew that this was right. He should have died with them long ago. And torn between Phoebe and William, he would finally be free of *that* anguish and guilt as well. It was sweet little Sylvia whom he regretted leaving as the hail bombarded him.

•   •   •

"He was already dead. Inside," Phoebe muttered when Edgar had broken the news to her. There had been no way to soften the final blow. She looked at her brother with tormented eyes. "*Was* he real, Edgar?" She had begun to doubt her own reality, which had always seemed so different from others'. But if he had been imaginary, couldn't she force him to still be here? And why would her body ache so much for his gentle touch?

"He certainly was, and he loved you and Sylvia, Phoebe." Or at least he had seemed to at the outset, but Edgar had begun to worry that Silas was drawing away from her.

"Then why hasn't he come to me? I can't see him, Edgar! Make him come back! SILAS!"

Edgar tried to take her into his arms but she went rigid as she screamed. Brenda hurried in, armed with a hypodermic needle. "Now, dearie, settle down and let Brenda give you something to help the hurt."

But Phoebe could hear only the howling in her mind, like a giant wounded animal begging for relief. She held her head and shook it, but still it wailed. She began pounding her temples with her fists, trying to make it stop. She didn't know it was the echo of her own relentless screams.

Edgar fought hard to subdue her, for she had uncanny strength. Albert and Irene helped him, so they were at least able to prevent Phoebe from injuring herself.

Daphne had sent the children next door to the grandparents' cottage with their nannies. Although she felt desperately sorry for Phoebe, the unearthly shrieks unnerved her, and she stayed in the kitchen, brewing strong tea.

The cottage next door wasn't far enough away to stop the tortured sounds of unbridled grief. Sylvia knew that something bad was happening to her mother. Large tears rolled down her cheeks.

She would never forget that day of the evil storm when Daddy never came home and Mummy went away for a long, long time. Somehow she had known it would happen.

Chapter 26

"This place is perfect, just as you said, Jack. Oh, I know it's too big for one person, but it announces that I am a woman not to be trifled with. Except in an amorous manner," Sidonie added with a grin

Jack laughed. They were having cocktails on the stone terrace of the Villa Blackthorn, as Sid had renamed it. It was a three-storey, champagne-coloured mansion perched above a private sandy beach and surrounded by gardens lush with exotic flowers, riotous roses, fragrant eucalyptus, majestic palms, and umbrella-like stone pines, which still grew in thick groves in the area. With a staff of twelve, including three gardeners, a chauffeur, and a boatman, Sid was hardly alone in the house.

Jack, Lizzie, and her two boys – along with their nanny - were overnighting so that the adults could party at the chic, new, Art Deco Hotel Provençal, virtually next door. Lizzie was living at Cousin Bea's villa a few miles away, near the tip of Cap d'Antibes, and Jack had joined her there for a couple of weeks while he conducted business. His room here at Blackthorn – one of a dozen elegant guest suites - had tall French windows that opened onto a small balcony overlooking the sea.

"Not for a me a modest abode that shrinks into an anonymous crag or hides behind walls, but a place that commands attention and elicits envious admiration."

"Just like you, Sid," he teased.

"Precisely." Her smile suddenly faded as she admitted, "My soul feels at peace here as it hasn't anywhere else since the war. Strange, isn't it? I don't even have much desire to spend time in

London, although I'm keeping my townhouse for now. I expect I'll want to escape from here occasionally."

"Don't you feel lonely?" he asked, although he knew that her parents lived in nearby Cannes, which was what had brought her to the Riviera initially.

"Hardly, darling! I already have old friends from London who've booked themselves in for most of the winter, and plenty of new friends, some of whom you'll meet this evening."

He was excited, since they were dining with Sid's neighbours, the American millionaire, Frank Jay Gould of railroad fortune, and his third wife, Florence. Frank had also invested heavily in the Riviera, and had built Le Provençal, with its casino, where Jack planned to indulge a little to establish his credentials, but not lose too much. He had worked too damned hard to toss his money away on the turn of a card. But he hoped to make a new business connection.

"I took your advice and invested in French government bonds," Sidonie informed him. Rafe had balked at giving her $2 million, so she had settled for $1.5. Because Jack had been managing Chas's investments, he had more than quadruple what Rafe had left of his inheritance. So Rafe was bitter about sharing any of it with a wife who had socially embarrassed him by running away. But he did want his freedom now.

"Frank said that was very astute, since he's done the same. And Florence is a woman after my own heart. We can party until dawn and then still play tennis and swim before noon. She's so impressed that I can drive my launch, and take her aquaplaning. Seems I learned something useful in Canada after all," she chuckled.

Jack had to admit that this lifestyle suited her. She looked relaxed in her slinky beach pajamas, which she had thrown over her skimpy swimsuit.

Earlier today she had taken him for lunch up to Eze, a precipitous village carved out of a cliff-side. She had driven her luxurious and ridiculously expensive Isotta-Fraschini wildly, but confidently, along the hairpin curves. Jack had just held his breath. But he had to admit that she seemed in control of the car and of her life.

He enjoyed sitting here companionably in the late afternoon sunshine gazing out over the turquoise shallows and blueberry depths of the sea toward the distant, smoky hills, breathing in the fragrances of sweet heliotrope and spicy lavender that splashed their envied purples along the terrace gardens. People were bronzing themselves on the beaches that curved away toward Cannes, and speeding off in motorboats from Le Provençal's jetty.

The devastating hurricane, which a few weeks ago had razed a large section of eastern Florida killing hundreds and leaving over 40,000 homeless, had been like a death knell to the Florida real estate boom. Thank God he had gotten out last year, for land was now selling at one-hundredth of its previous, overinflated value, bankrupting plenty of speculators.

He had heard from his caretaker that his own property in Palm Beach had sustained only minor damage, the brunt of the storm demolishing Miami. But it had made him realize that many would seek somewhere else to spend their winters and their dollars. There had long been an aristocratic presence on the Riviera, which was now augmented by affluent Americans, so others would soon follow suit. For the past few years, the Cunard line had been offering direct sailings from New York to Marseille.

So Jack had decided that he would invest in more property here. And since Juan-les-Pins was relatively undeveloped, despite having the finest beaches on the Côte d'Azur, he was convinced it would eventually thrive, particularly with the opulent Hotel Provençal and its classy casino now drawing the younger moneyed set.

Jack watched Lizzie, who was still down at the private beach playing with her sons under a large umbrella, and said, "I expect that Elyse would flourish here."

"No, Jack. Don't start on that again. I'm no good for her. We'd just end up breaking each other's hearts. I need my freedom."

Yesterday evening, the three of them had dined with Lizzie's friends, Sara and Gerald Murphy, at their Villa America partway down the Cap. It had been obvious that they were absolutely devoted to their three children, so when Sara discovered that Sidonie had a daughter living with her father in far-off Canada, she had remarked with surprise and sadness, "How can you bear it?"

Sid had been stung, although she knew damn well that she was a failure as a mother.

"Excuse me, my Lady," the English butler said as he came out to the terrace. "There's a telephone call for you."

When Sid returned, she smirked as she said, "Oh, I do love a little intrigue!"

"What's happening?"

"We have an extra guest joining us for dinner at the hotel. You'll see. But now I'm off for a long soak in the tub. Help yourself to cocktails or whatever."

But Jack wanted a clear head for tonight, so he went for a brisk swim and then took three-year-old Alain for a paddle in the warm shallows. He was glad he had some time to spend with Lizzie and his young nephews. Because Cousin Bea wasn't arriving here until next month, Jack would visit her at Bovington Abbey after his business in London and before heading back to Canada. And, of course, he was going to spend a few days in Paris en route.

Jack was rather concerned about Lizzie. When he had asked her whether she was happy, she had replied cautiously, "I adore spending time with my boys. I hadn't really expected, but had hoped that Étienne would be as lovingly attentive after our marriage as before, but he has his various pursuits, and doesn't usually invite me to come along to his races and such." Étienne was even more involved in car racing, and liked to gamble on the horses, which he knew she disapproved of. "He says he values my role as wife and mother, but..." she trailed off. "I don't have any friends at Sauveterre, and I feel as if the staff barely tolerate me – a foreigner, even if I do speak the language – but when Étienne is not around, some of them become rather surly."

Despite her polished act, Lizzie didn't have the inborn sense of entitlement or air of superiority that it took to effortlessly lord it over the servants, and they recognized that as a failing in her. The only ones she trusted were the British nanny she had hired and her own lady's maid.

To her surprise, Lizzie disliked the Château itself, which was lofty and chilly and in the middle of nowhere. Étienne hadn't wanted her to waste money redecorating to provide at least some modern and welcoming rooms, so none of it felt like hers, and all of it was a dreary mausoleum. The neighbours were mostly peasants, and the owners of other large estate wineries in the area were of an older generation, with no one Lizzie could really relate to. Avignon was a beautiful, medieval city, but it was ten axle-breaking miles away, and she didn't know anyone there either.

"So I'm always happier here or in Paris, where I have friends like the Murphys," she had told Jack.

She met Sara and Gerald when they first arrived in Paris five years ago, and soon became part of their inner circle. Gerald, who had taken up painting, especially appreciated Lizzie's artistic photographs, and had helped to arrange a successful exhibition for her in Paris after her marriage.

Étienne also wasn't interested in spending any more time at Sauveterre than necessary to make sure the winery was working well, but they often went in different directions. In winter, he liked to ski in Switzerland, but never invited her along. Although she didn't know how to ski, she was willing to learn, but he said it wasn't practical with the children.

He preferred summers in fashionable, high-society Deauville, but Lizzie found the English Channel uncomfortably cold, and that north coast, unpleasantly windy. When the Murphys had persuaded the Hotel du Cap to stay open for them in the summer of '23, they had invited her and Étienne to join them. Since Cousin Bea's villa was very close by, she and Étienne had gone there, and partied with the Murphys at the Hotel and on the deserted beach at La Garoupe, which Gerald discovered and recovered from beneath tons of seaweed. Pablo Picasso and his family had stayed at the Hotel as well, so they were a small and merry group. But Étienne had soon declared it too hot and socially dead – the casinos in the area also closed for the season - and returned to Deauville, where, Lizzie suspected, he kept a mistress. Why else would he have encouraged her – six months pregnant at the time - to stay on with her American friends? His desertion had been sharply painful, but now she was used to it.

The times they actually spent together, Étienne was the perfect husband and father, proud of his beautiful family, but mostly Lizzie found herself alone with the children. Now that the Murphys had their own villa nearby and a Paris apartment only blocks from hers, she spent plenty of time with them, and was grateful for their unstinting friendship.

Jack said, "I like your friends. They're lively and amusing, and the Murphys seem to have made an art of entertaining."

"They do have a knack for living well, and inspiring others. Hem was reluctant to meet them because he doesn't trust really rich people, but now he's one of their pets," Lizzie said of Ernest Hemingway, whom Jack had also met last night. Hemingway had just published his wildly successful first novel, *The Sun Also Rises*. Lizzie was saddened to discover that Hem and Hadley had separated. Only last year, they and their young son visited her at the Château for a few days on their way to Antibes.

"Well, I feel better about your being so far away when I know that you have friends like that. Perhaps you should think about buying your own villa here."

"I have considered it, but Cousin Bea says she enjoys our company and doesn't know how much longer she'll want to travel down here. She's in her late 70s, isn't she? Anyway, she said that it's good to have someone using the place so much. It feels like a second home to me."

"Maybe she plans to leave it to you."

"That had occurred to me, too. I'd adore that!"

"Will you come to visit us next summer?"

Although she hadn't known Sidonie long or well, having her here gave Lizzie a link with home, which she appreciated. Sid was, after all, Jack's sister-in-law. And she certainly didn't hate her anymore for stealing Rafe.

Lizzie tried to ignore her longing for Toronto and Muskoka, and particularly for Lyle. She knew from Belinda that he and Adele were practically separated, she spending most of her time in Sewickley, their daughter shared between them. "Yes, I think I will come home. Julien will be two and more able to travel. It's time the boys met their cousins."

"See if you can persuade Sid to come along. I really hope that she doesn't completely abandon Elyse."

"I will certainly try," Lizzie promised. "Now I had better bathe, and dress for dinner."

Jack did as well, and awaited the ladies on the terrace. He was always impressed with how flawlessly beautiful Sidonie was, her aristocratic upbringing adding an alluring sang-froid. Tonight she shimmered in silver-swirled black, the jewels of her fabulous peacock broach providing the only – but eye-catching - colour.

"What a privilege to escort two such ravishing women," Jack said, for Lizzie looked exquisite in a black-spangled jade chiffon frock with a dramatic, layered handkerchief hemline that zigzagged from knee to calf. "Shall we?" he asked, offering each an arm.

"Henri will drive us," Sid declared.

"But the hotel is only a stone's throw from here," Jack protested.

"It's all very well to stroll over during the day, but in the evenings one needs to make an entrance. Besides, I mostly drive myself around during the day, so what would Henri do if I didn't make him work at night? In any case, he has made me his responsibility, and wouldn't hear of my walking home in the dark, even with you, Jack."

The chauffeur had, in fact, once astutely told her that the war had broken him as well, but that she had given him a new purpose in life. So he had become her champion, and ensured that she reached her bed safely, especially when Sid had overindulged, and he and her maid practically had to carry her to her room.

Florence Gould was about Sid's age and, thus, a couple of decades younger than her dapper husband. A soft, blonde beauty glowing in a white frock, she was a dramatic counterpoint to Sid, with her severe raven shingle and dark dress; together they made an exponential impact. Lizzie, with her rich auburn hair and green gown, provided the colour in this triumvirate of glamour.

They had just ordered cocktails when a waiter escorted a gentleman to their table. Lizzie was stunned to see Lyle, her heart softening when she noticed the premature grey in his hair and his drawn look that accentuated the scar across his cheek and eye. She wanted to run her fingers along it to erase the strain.

After introductions had been made, he said to Lizzie, "I'd heard from Belle how much you enjoy the Riviera, and since I was in Europe on business, I thought I'd stop in for a visit. The staff at your cousin's villa informed me that you were staying with Lady Sidonie tonight. I hope you don't mind my intrusion."

"Not at all. I'm delighted that you came." They looked at each other longingly, each recognizing the loneliness in the other, and recalling their passion of seven years ago.

"I'm staying at the Hotel du Cap," Lyle said, "But all of this is wonderful. Rivals our Muskoka a bit, doesn't it?"

"Just a little, I think," Jack agreed with a chuckle.

The superb dinner was accompanied by bottles of Château de Sauveterre vintages, which Frank Gould had thoughtfully ordered. Étienne had ensured that all the finest hotels on the Riviera offered his wines.

In order not to bore the women, the men spoke only casually about business, but at one point Florence said, "It never ceases to amaze or delight me that Frank has such rare clairvoyance in matters of business."

"Isn't she a peach?" Gould asked the men proudly. "I proposed to her the moment I first met her." He beamed at his wife.

"Oh dear. The Fitzgeralds are back," Florence said, having spied Scott and Zelda breeze in. To her guests she explained, "Of course we got to know them last year when they rented your place, Sidonie. They can be very amusing until they get zozzled, and then they become impossible."

"I agree!" Lizzie said. "They're friends of the Murphys, so I've seen them quite often. At a dinner party at Villa America this summer they indulged in too many of Gerald's potent cocktails, so we didn't know what had happened to them when the rest of us sat down to dine in the garden. We soon discovered that they were crawling about among the vegetables when they started hurling ripe tomatoes at us. One hit me and slid down the back of my gown. The Murphys were terribly embarrassed and incensed, and the Fitzgeralds haven't been invited back since. I think they're quite mad, especially Zelda."

"It's one thing to be outrageous, and quite another to be immature and rude," Sid opined.

Jack grinned at her, since she relished being slightly outrageous.

"Frank forbids me to have anything more to do with them," Florence said, smiling at her husband affectionately. "He had them evicted last time for dancing on the tables."

"Damn nuisance, they are," Frank grumbled.

After dinner, the group moved out to the terrace to dance under the moon, the night still resplendent with the warmth of the day and grasping at memories of summer.

"May I entice you onto the dance floor, Comtesse?" Frank invited Lizzie.

"Do be careful, Elizabeth," Florence cautioned. "He's an insatiable, demon dancer." To Jack she added, "Shall we?"

Jack managed the Charleston, and when they swayed to Irving Berlin's romantic *Blue Skies*, Florence said, "Any chance that we can meet? We have a villa in Cannes as well, which we only use for entertaining."

Jack wasn't unduly shocked, but had to think quickly to not alienate her or her husband. "How wonderfully tempting. But you should know that I am happily married, and not seeking any dalliances."

"What a pity," she said, stroking the nape of his neck sensually. "Frank and I are happy, too, but everyone sleeps with everyone here. It's so amusing, and what else is there to do?" It almost seemed like an existential question. "Do let me know if you change your mind."

When Lizzie and Lyle finally danced, it was to resume that fluid union that had always made them seem as one when they moved. And it felt delicious to be held so firmly and yet tenderly in his arms, Lizzie thought.

"God, I've missed you, Lizzie. If I could turn back time, I would do things differently. Is it too late for us?"

Her look practically invited a kiss, which excited him. "I don't know, Lyle. We have our families now. It's not easy to change things."

"Would you, if you could?" he challenged her.

She hesitated, but realized it was time to stop the games and pretense. She no longer considered being a Comtesse as a symbol of success. What did a worthless title matter when she was unhappy in her marriage? "Oh, yes."

"Then couldn't we try? Couldn't we start by pleasing ourselves just a little? Spend some time together? I can stay for a week."

"I'd like that."

Joyfully, he drew her closer. "I love you, Lizzie. No matter where we end up, I want you to know that."

She laid her head gratefully on his shoulder. "No man has ever said that to me and actually meant it."

"Then you've known the wrong men. Can I take you and your sons on a picnic tomorrow?"

"Yes, how delightful!"

The Fitzgeralds were hard to ignore, especially since they were now drunk. Sidonie overheard Scott pester two young Frenchmen, asking if they were "fairies", while Zelda stepped onto the dance floor and gyrated to some music in her own head, rather than the jazzy rendition of *If You Knew Susie* that the band was playing. She seemed completely oblivious to everyone else as she lifted her skirt above her waist and began some sinuous movements.

"Christ almighty!" Frank swore, gesturing to a couple of men, discreetly clad as guests, who went over to Zelda and escorted her out. Scott followed, protesting and threatening the beefy bouncers.

The other guests had stopped and watched in fascination and amusement, and now there was a buzz of chatter.

"You see, she always manages to get attention, even if it's the wrong kind," Florence said to the others. "It's as if she can't stand to be ignored."

"Which must be difficult for her when her husband is the celebrity," Sid remarked. "I enjoyed his *Gatsby* novel."

"Did you? I must read it," Florence said. "I have to admit that I worry whether Frank and I will somehow appear in whatever story he was working on last year. He was constantly asking probing, personal questions, like how ruthless had Frank's father been to amass his millions, and had we slept together before we were married. Of course we tried to laugh it off, but he was like an annoying mosquito, always seeking blood."

Lizzie and Lyle didn't join the others when Florence suggested they do a spot of gambling in the casino. Dancing gave them an excuse to hold each other. While others drifted back into the ballroom away from the creeping chill of the night, they cuddled closer as they swayed under the moon.

Jack wanted a relatively early night, so Lizzie and Lyle parted reluctantly at 2:00 AM.

Jack had just settled into his comfortable bed, curtains open and windows cracked to permit the night air to slink in, when Sidonie crept into his room.

"Sid," he protested when she slid into bed with him.

"It's like old times, isn't it? Remember how much fun we had in London?"

"Yes, but things have changed. You're my sister-in-law now."

"You can't convince me that Fliss satisfies your needs. Or that you don't still want me."

He realized that she was more intoxicated than she seemed. "You are an utterly desirable and irresistible woman, but I do love Fliss, and am not willing to risk hurting her."

She pouted for a moment, and then asked, "You do still love me, don't you, Jack?"

Sensing her desperation, he replied, "Of course I do, Sid. You're a dear friend, and what we had will always be a treasured memory."

She settled into the crook of his arm. "May I stay here for a while?"

He snuggled his head against hers in confirmation as he said, "Sure."

"I thought of reverting to my maiden name, but decided I wanted to remain a Thornton. That way I can always imagine myself to be Chas's wife. Damn! I must be spifflicated because I've never admitted how much I love him. Promise me that you won't betray my secret!"

He was disconcerted by the intensity of her emotion. "Yes, of course I promise. But you have to try to leave the past behind, Sid."

"I *am* trying. There's too much sorrow there."

•   •   •

Lizzie was inordinately excited and could hardly wait for Lyle to arrive the following morning. Jack had taken the car that she kept down here to go about his business, but said he'd be back by dinner.

It was gloriously warm, and since she didn't want to go too far with the baby, she suggested that they just head down to La Garoupe beach. Bea's villa was perched atop a steep cliff, with steps carved out of the limestone, leading down to a secluded cove with a concrete pier and a sliver of sand, which wasn't ideal for small children.

So they went the short distance in Lyle's rented car, laden with beach umbrellas and blankets, and a hamper of food prepared by the chefs at the Hotel du Cap. The Murphys would normally have been here on a day like this, but they were going back to the States for a few months, and Lizzie was just as happy that she didn't recognize anyone else on the ever more popular beach, and, thus, need to socialize.

"What a view!" Lyle exclaimed, for the snow-tipped Maritime Alps seemed to rise out of the impossibly blue sea in front of them. "I can understand why you like it here. And this is a bonus," he added, opening a bottle of champagne. "Having a legal bottle of a very fine vintage in public."

She laughed as he poured her a glass.

"To us," he said, staring at her so sensually that she wanted just to throw herself into his arms and succumb to the desire that radiated from him.

They had a leisurely and companionable afternoon, playing in and around the water with the boys, nibbling at the gourmet feast, not wanting the day to end. Lyle readily accepted an invitation to dine at the villa, and asked Lizzie if she would show him some of the highlights of the area, which she did in the ensuing days, without the children. Sidonie invited the three of them to dine with her at the opulent, palatial Hotel de Paris in Monte Carlo, with a bit of gambling afterwards in the famous casino next door. Her boatman ferried them by sea, so it was enchanting to watch the lights of the perched villages pierce the dark mountains, while the seafront villas and hotels and anchored boats spilled theirs across the calm Mediterranean. Another evening, Sid took them to a party on a friend's yacht, where they danced aboard a regal ship draped with fairy lights. It had a crew of twenty, and Sid would be cruising the Greek Isles with them for a month, but that calm night they sailed to St. Tropez and back.

It was a heady week, and Lizzie constantly had to resist the impulse to invite Lyle into her bed.

Jack left for Paris on Lyle's last day, so that was the only evening they were alone. They had an intimate dinner on the terrace at the villa. Now that there was no threat of interruption, Lizzie was a bit nervous.

Swirling his cognac in the snifter, Lyle said, "This is how I shall imagine you. Sitting in a fragrant garden, poised over the warm sea stretching to jagged mountains and reflecting the lights of distant shores. I wish I could stay here with you."

He looked at her with such longing that she said, "As do I."

He cleared his throat of emotion. "May I come again?"

"As often as you like."

"Shall we dance?"

Lizzie had brought the gramophone out. Lyle put on *If You Were the Only Girl in the World*. Dancing with him was almost a sexual experience, so when he kissed her she felt weak with desire.

"We may never have more than this one night, but will you stay with me?' she whispered.

"Oh God, yes, Lizzie!"

It was an intense and magical night. They hardly slept as they made love and, between-times, mused how they might be forever together. Divorce wasn't much of an option for either of them at the moment. Lyle promised he would visit as often as he could, and they schemed about how they could snatch private moments when she came to Muskoka next summer.

"We've wasted all these years," Lyle lamented.

"No. You mustn't think like that. We've grown. We may not have appreciated each other as much if things had been easy for us. I'm not proud of some of the things I've done or desired, but I know enough now to leave the past behind, to forgive myself, and to make positive changes. To become a better person."

"You're wise as well as irresistible."

"You've given me the reason and courage to be strong and hopeful. Thank you for that."

Lizzie didn't yet know how much she would need that.

•   •   •

"What the hell?" Jack said, not believing his eyes when he walked into Véronique's bedroom. He had arrived a day early in Paris, and thought he'd surprise her. "What the fuck is going on here?"

Étienne sniggered. "Fuck indeed. My little sister enjoys that too much." Both were naked and she was lying in his arms, one shapely leg thrown across his.

"You bastard!" Jack went towards them, ready to haul Étienne out of bed and thrash him.

But Véronique sidled over to Jack, putting a restraining arm on his. "He's right, Jacque. I do like it too much. And the more challenging the conquest, the more it excites me. He was even harder to seduce than you."

Jack couldn't believe what he was hearing.

Étienne smirked as he lit a cigarette and blew out a satisfying stream of smoke. "We have different fathers. Mother was never faithful. So we're not of full blood anyway."

"Now that you are here, we could have fun together – the three of us," Véronique suggested as she draped herself around Jack and ran her hand seductively down to his crotch. "I expect you've never abandoned yourself to such pleasure as we can give you."

He pushed her away roughly. "You disgust me! The pair of you."

"Oooh-là-là, you are suddenly a self-righteous adulterer," she said flippantly, throwing on a silk wrap. "And averse to sex?"

"Only to depravity," he retorted. "I won't be visiting you again, Véronique."

"C'est dommage," she replied with a careless shrug as she lit a cigarette.

"And the less I see of you the better," Jack said to his brother-in-law.

"I think it best if you don't tell Elizabeth," Étienne replied. "It won't change anything and would only upset her. She knows I'm not faithful, and I never promised her that."

"She'd be better off without you."

"Would she? Of course I won't allow Elizabeth to take the children from me. And I think she is too good a mother to leave them behind. And do you not think she enjoys being a Comtesse, meaningless as that is? Did she not trade her wealth for it?"

It was ironic, of course, that Étienne had married Lizzie to tap into Jack's fortune. Jack had slowly come to realize over the years that Étienne cared little for his estate but what profits he could siphon from it for his pleasures – racing expensive cars, betting on horses, gambling in casinos, supporting mistresses. So all of Lizzie's money and what Jack had loaned Étienne had gone into keeping the winery viable.

"And what of your nephews? Should they not have their heritage?"

"I won't give you another penny to keep the winery afloat, Étienne. If you waste their inheritance then I will take the boys into business with me. I expect they will never forgive you for that."

"You forget that we have a very valuable asset, brother-in-law. The truth, which you may not want broadcast."

"Are you threatening me, you bastard?"

"I am merely stating a fact. How much is your reputation worth to you? Or your wife's happiness? Her brothers' good will?"

"Damn you both to hell!" Jack swore before stomping out.

As he walked the night-time streets of Paris and stopped for a double shot of cognac at an outdoor café, he thought of the licentious behaviour for which the city had become notorious. Why should anything surprise him? But he still couldn't shake the image of Véronique and Étienne in bed together, looking so natural and unconcerned, like long-time lovers. They were completely devoid of shame or guilt.

But Jack didn't know what was best for Lizzie. He was sure that if he told her, she would be too disgusted to stay with Étienne. But perhaps she should keep him out her bed. Promiscuous as Étienne and Véronique were, Jack would be surprised if they weren't diseased.

And what about the implied blackmail? He wondered now if they hadn't cooked the whole scheme up between them, Véronique seducing Jack so that she and Étienne had a stranglehold on him. How was he ever going to get out from under that constant threat, which was sure to suck away vast quantities of his hard-earned money? The de Sauveterres obviously had no scruples.

Perhaps Jack should just confess to Chas and Fliss. But he'd hate to lose Chas's friendship and respect as much as he would hate to hurt his sweet wife. This had brutally awakened him to what was truly important in his life.

For a moment he considered that it wouldn't be hard to find a thug to get rid of Étienne, thereby solving not only his problem, but also Lizzie's. But he knew he couldn't live with someone's blood on his hands. And there was still Véronique.

How could he have allowed his perfect world to be threatened by an unprincipled chit of a girl?

•　　　　•　　　　•

Dear Lizzie,

I'm going to be brutally honest with you because we have never had secrets from each other, and you know that I want only the best for you.

I was having an affair with Véronique, which I now deeply regret. Being generally circumspect and striving to build an enviable reputation as well as a fortune, I failed miserably to resist her dangerous charms.

There's no way to say this kindly. I've just discovered that Étienne is also one of her lovers. I'm so sorry, sweetheart.

Lizzie dropped the letter and gasped for breath. Never having been comfortable with Étienne's affairs, she suddenly felt polluted.

You know that I will do all I can to support you, but Étienne swears he won't let you have the children if you leave him. Think about how you want to handle this, and we will talk before I go home. Perhaps you can divide your time between France and Canada. There's no reason why you can't spend each summer at our cottage, and drag it out to six and more months - thereby weaning him from you and the boys, and avoiding your own obligations as a wife. I've been renting the Annex house that Uncle Richard gave us, but will now keep it exclusively for you, so you will have a home base in Toronto as well.

Because he is virtually blackmailing me, I will continue to support the winery, but I will negotiate a deal he won't be able to resist, which will give me control. I had never thought to be a vintner! And now that Ontario looks like it will finally repeal the Temperance Act, there will be a market there for me to tap as well.

Lizzie thought that Jack always managed to dredge something positive out of the dregs of hardship.

And she felt a wonderful freedom to pursue her own happiness, which was no longer tied to France or any lingering loyalty to her husband.

Her first thought was that if she took the boys to Canada next summer and never returned, what could Étienne actually do? But then she realized that he would probably threaten to expose Jack's affair. She would never allow that to happen. If it weren't for Jack's hard work and cleverness, she would still be a maid in someone else's home. If her life wasn't perfect, it was a hell of a lot better than it had been for the first seventeen years, thanks to him.

Jack might be right that she could stay in Canada for long periods of time. Perhaps Étienne would find a much richer heiress and want a divorce. She would be sure to throw some in his path through her own connections. She chuckled at this new mission in her life.

My dearest, darling Lyle,

I am determined to make Toronto my home for part of each year as well, which provides us with so many more opportunities for happiness.... she began the letter.

Part 4: 1934

Chapter 27

"You shouldn't be smoking, Elyse," Charlie warned. She had snatched a few cigarettes from the humidor in the library, and lit one as they sat on the upper deck of the boathouse.

"Why not? You do."

"I'm much older than you, so I'm allowed." He would be nineteen in December, but she was only fourteen. Although you wouldn't know it, Charlie thought. Her stylish, flared shorts exposed her long, attractive legs, and she had noticeable breasts, as well as the sassy, flippant manner of a seasoned flapper. Her dark hair curved provocatively in finger waves to her chin. He had even seen her sneak drinks from the bar.

Rafe was not yet back from his honeymoon, so Elyse was still staying at The Point. She actually spent a lot of time with them or Aunt Fliss, here and in the city. And because she had been a part of his life since she was born, she was like a sister.

With a sultry voice, Elyse sang a few lines from Cole Porter's *Let's Misbehave.*

There's something wild about you child
That's so contagious
Let's be outrageous - let's misbehave!!!

She fluttered her long eyelashes provocatively.

"Very funny."

"Don't be a flat tire, darling," Elyse drawled, throwing back her head and blowing out a long stream of smoke.

She was obsessed with the movies, and imitated Hollywood's leading ladies, trying to cultivate a Greta Garbo-like mystique, and making good use of her soulful green eyes.

"You don't have to be outrageous to get attention," he told her, for she already turned heads. There was something beyond her obvious physical beauty that captivated people.

"I don't try to be. I come by it naturally. After all, my mother is notorious."

He never understood how Aunt Sidonie could have abruptly picked up and left eight years ago, abandonning Elyse, never even writing to her. He knew that Elyse must be deeply hurt, but she seemed indifferent rather than angry or upset. Even a bit boastful at having an unconventional mother who was a renowned hostess among the elite and titled on the Riviera. But then you never could tell what Elyse really felt.

"Do you like your new mother?" Charlie asked.

She shrugged. "Better than the last bitch."

Although he agreed with her, he tried not to be shocked by her swearing – or anything else she said and did – but it seemed wrong for her to be so cynical, and revel in vulgarity.

Rafe had married a gold-digger after his divorce from Sidonie, but wife number two left him when she realized that the stock market crash in '29 nearly bankrupted him.

Jack had seen the warning signs of the market volatility months earlier, and pulled out the majority of his investments in stocks, and put them into yet more real estate, bonds, and gold. So he and those whom he advised or whose money he managed, like Chas and Ria, were only minimally affected by the crash. Rafe, of course, wouldn't listen to Jack, and had been riding high on the euphoric wave of seemingly endless profits - until they evaporated.

So Chas had bailed Rafe out, buying Thornridge, while allowing him to continue living there, along with their mother, and setting up a trust fund for him, which he couldn't gamble away, but which would allow him to live like a gentleman if he was careful. That was forever the issue – keeping Rafe from temptation, ensuring he lived within his means.

His stables were doing well, so Chas encouraged him to devote more time to them. It was on the horse racing circuit that Rafe had met his new bride, whose father also had champion thoroughbreds.

"I don't expect to hang around long anyway," Elyse confided.

"Running off to Hollywood, are you?' Charlie teased.

"Damn right! As soon as I'm old enough. You won't be smirking when I'm more famous than Norma Shearer." Norma was a Canadian who had made it big in the movies, even winning an Oscar, and was one of Elyse's idols. "I'm going to impress Uncle Hugo with our play this summer, and I bet he'll give me a part in one of his Broadway shows in a few years. Aunt Emily was only seventeen when she became a star."

"You don't have a voice like hers."

"But I can dance and act," she countered, for she studied those assiduously, and knew that she sang tolerably well. "I want to get into films anyway, not stage musicals."

Charlie had to admit that she could indeed act. She had coerced cousins to join her in a play she had concocted from scenes in *Alice's Adventures in Wonderland* and *Through the Looking-*

Glass. Ria had agreed that they would invite all their friends to watch the performance later this summer.

Elyse picked up her 8 mm Kodak movie camera and pointed it at him. Ria and Chas had given it to her for her birthday, and she was never without it.

"Do stop with that thing," Charlie protested as she came in for a close-up.

"Do you *want* to go to Oxford?" Elyse asked, ignoring his request.

"Dad says that getting a degree from Oxford will make me a well-rounded person. What I really want to do is fly aeroplanes, but he won't let me. Especially not after Will Barker was killed in that crash a few years ago."

Charlie remembered how exciting it had been whenever the two Billies flew in to visit them here. It had shocked them all when Barker crashed in a test flight of a new aeroplane, allegedly and unbelievably because of pilot error. His impressive military funeral in Toronto had drawn a crowd of 50,000, come to honour a great Canadian hero. Chas was one of the VCs who marched in the mile-long cortege. Other WWI comrades flew overhead and dropped rose petals. It had been a poignant and memorable day.

"But when I'm twenty-one, I can do as I like," Charlie stated. "Enough with the camera, OK?"

"You should come to Hollywood with me," Elyse said as she put it down. "You're much more handsome than Clark Gable or any of the other leading men." She examined him critically. "You actually look quite a bit like Dad and Uncle Chas in the pictures that Granny has from before the war. Are you sure you're adopted?" Her face lit with excitement. "Maybe Aunt Ria and Uncle Chas had you before they were married, which is terribly scandalous, of course, so they pretended that they adopted you!"

"Don't be a goof! I remember my real mother. And Mum and Dad were married before I was born."

Charlie was used to Elyse's melodramas and fantasies. People who didn't know his history sometimes commented on how much he and Drew resembled their father, but he figured they just said that to make conversation, and wondered what they actually noticed when half of Dad's face was scarred. Although now the idea nagged. Did Elyse truly see a likeness? But he forgot about it as Drew and Max's three kids joined them on the deck, and Elyse picked up her Cine-Kodak once more.

As usual, the dog, Zorro, was with them.

Ever since the kidnapping and murder of aviator Charles Lindbergh's infant son, snatched boldly from his crib, two years ago, there was unease among the wealthy. In these harsh Depression days when millions of unemployed men wandered the countryside seeking jobs and begging for food, those who had plenty of money feared that they could become targets of desperate or unscrupulous people. One of the American families on "Millionaires' Row" at Beaumaris had installed secret passageways in the boathouses used by the children, so that they could escape if threatened. The Wyndwood and Thorncliff Island children were no longer allowed to go anywhere by themselves, even out fishing or canoeing, which Charlie thought rather paranoid. Chas and Ria had also decided that three well-trained German Shepherds would guard them. Zorro had particularly attached himself to Drew.

"They should be here soon," eleven-year-old Drew said excitedly. "Look, we made a banner." It read "Welcome Home". "Can you help us tack it up, Charlie?"

Chas had gone to the train station to pick up Sophie and Philip. It had been a year since they had married and left for England, and her family had missed her terribly. The young couple would be staying for the summer, and would have the boathouse to themselves.

When James lost most of his fortune in the crash, it had given Ria great satisfaction to buy lavish Westwynd and the entire north end of Wyndwood, paying her father a generous sum, for which he needed to be grateful, and renting it back to him for a nominal fee. Sophie had been offered Westwynd as a wedding gift, but declined, saying it was too large and might not be well used if she and Philip couldn't come back for lengthy periods each summer. She wanted to stay at The Point with the family. Some time in the future, she and Philip might wish to build a cottage at the Shimmering Sands, if that were permissible. Which, of course, it was.

Charlie was looking forward to going over to England with them at the end of the summer, especially since he could then start investigating his real father's whereabouts. He had missed Sophie perhaps more than anyone, because as a fellow French orphan, she had taken him under her wing the moment they met.

Elyse put the latest hit from Cole Porter on the gramophone. "Come on, Charlie, let's Lindy Hop. Drew can film us," she added, passing him the camera, which he was thrilled to use.

She danced with the skill of a professional, and was determined that Charlie should be a good partner. He had to admit that it was fun. The others joined in as best they could, which occasioned much merriment.

In olden days, a glimpse of stocking
Was looked on as something shocking.
But now, God knows,
Anything goes.
Good authors too who once knew better words
Now only use four-letter words
Writing prose.
Anything goes.

With Sophie arriving, another glorious summer was stretching before them.

• • •

"So what's the mood in Britain?" Chas asked Philip over dinner. Most of the relatives had been invited for a welcome-home party. The children ate earlier and were playing games in the billiard and sitting rooms. Charlie stayed with the adults, of course.

"The economy is rebounding, although the Depression didn't hit us as hard is it has Canada," Philip replied. "But there's plenty of unrest. I expect you heard about our General Strike in May, and we have Oswald Mosley and his fascist Black Shirts stirring up trouble. With Adolph Hitler now in power in Germany, there are some, like Winston Churchill, who are predicting there'll be another war."

"Dear God!" Ria cried. She wasn't the only one thinking about the children who might be old enough to be recruited. Certainly Charlie. And if a war started in a few years from now and lasted as long as the previous one – God forbid! – it could even involve Drew. She was horrified.

Zoë was sure that Ethan would not be considered fit enough because of his heart, and was thankful that her son Jonathan was only seven. But Max's eldest boy was already fourteen, and her brothers Rupert and Miles would probably be the first to go.

Charlie felt a shiver of fear and excitement. He sure as hell didn't want to end up maimed like Dad, but the thought that he might have a chance to join the Royal Canadian Air Force and be a hero appealed to him. It would be a noble excuse for him to fly.

"France seems to be preparing for a German invasion," Jack said. "They're spending billions of francs constructing the Maginot Line."

"It's ominous that Hitler pulled Germany out of the League of Nations last year," Chas said. "Not that the League has had much clout anyway, especially since the U.S. never joined."

"There's concern that the Prince of Wales is rather too fond of Germany and admires Hitler," Philip informed them.

"And what will that mean for Britain when he becomes King?" Freddie mused.

"It's disturbing to hear that Hitler has seized control of the media," Arthur said. "And his storm troopers have rounded up anti-Nazi groups and confined them to concentration camps, along with Jews and gypsies. Which means no freedom of speech, and if you dare to oppose the government, you might even be executed, as a number of dissenters in his own party were just a few weeks ago."

"I can't imagine sending my boys off to war!" Fliss said in distress.

"I had a dream about fireworks exploding over fields oozing blood, and my son wading through them," Phoebe confided. "Strange. I don't have a son."

Edgar tried to hide his shock, but Phoebe noticed and looked at him dissectingly, which he always found disturbing. It was as if she was somehow probing his mind. His father, Albert, had died last year, so he now had sole responsibility for Phoebe, which definitely wasn't easy.

She was having one of her good periods, but still went for occasional "rest and recuperation" at the private Homewood Sanitarium in Guelph, where she had spent a year after Silas's death. Like a posh resort, it was set in extensive, picturesque grounds that included its own farm, and had tennis courts, bowling alleys, and billiard tables. It offered psychoanalysis, hydrotherapy, massage, electro-stimulation, and compassionate care for those suffering from mental issues. Phoebe definitely benefitted from her stays, but her psyche was fragile.

To dispel the gloom that had settled like an unwelcome guest in the room, Ria said, "Let's hope that wise heads will prevail. Now, Sophie, what do you think about our new electric lighting and telephones?"

"They're keen! This chandelier adds a certain *je ne sais quoi* to the dining room."

Chas and Jack had arranged for the utilities to be brought in from the mainland by submarine cables and across the Stepping Stone Islands. Thorncliff and its three neighbouring islands were connected from the north end of Wyndwood. Because of the telephone service, Jack now had an easy way to keep up with his business dealings from the cottage.

"Being tethered to the modern world makes island life less of an escape, though," Philip opined.

"You've obviously never spent much time trying to read by acetylene lights and kerosene lamps," Alice said with a laugh.

"Philip has this romantic, Swiss Family Robinson notion of island life," Sophie said, smiling at her husband.

"Well, it's definitely made things easier, especially for the staff, because we now have modern appliances. Even I could manage in the kitchen," Ria joked. The old icehouse was empty for the first time in fifty-six years, and had, with the addition of windows, been turned into a playhouse for Drew and his young cousins.

"Speaking of modernizing," Sophie said, "You'll be interested to know that Priory Manor now has central heating. Philip's father had it installed especially for me."

"And about time! I told him that the house needed it when *we* lived there, and he accused us of being soft Colonials," Ria said.

"I remember how bloody cold it was," Max said, having stayed there whenever he was on leave.

They laughed, although Chas, with some reserve. It rankled that Lance was Sophie's father-in-law, much as he liked Philip and couldn't fault him. And if there was going to be a war, he sure as hell didn't want her in Britain. The Germans had caused enough destruction last time with Zeppelins and Gotha bombers, but with modern aeroplanes, they could now inflict much more damage. And an invasion of Britain would be easier.

"You might be surprised at what Sophie has already done with the gardens at Priory Manor," Philip said proudly.

"Turning them into a showpiece, if I know my daughter," Chas said with a grin. Growing up in her parents' flower shop, Sophie had early developed a keen interest in horticulture.

"Planting cabbage roses rather than cabbages," Ria quipped. She had loved the tangle of gardens among the Gothic stone ruins of the monastery behind the stately Georgian house, and the five-acre lake overlooked by a summerhouse and fringed with feathery reeds and dripping willows.

"It's funny you should say that, because Clive reminded me of the 'children's victory gardens' that we planted during the war," Sophie said. "He's never forgotten your kindness to him and his family, Mum. Did you know that he's now the head trainer?"

"And an excellent one," Philip added. "I learned more about horses from him than I did in vet school."

"I'm so glad to hear that he's done well, although not at all surprised," Ria said. "Now tell me, how's Cousin Bea?"

"She's pretty well recovered from pneumonia, but I do worry about her," Sophie said. "She suddenly seems old." Sophie had lived with Cousin Bea for part of the war, and thought of her as a grandmother. Beatrice, although now eighty-five, had always been fit and active, and younger than her age.

"We're planning to come over in late autumn to visit, and then we can take Cousin Bea to her villa in Antibes for a few months, and you and Philip and Charlie can join us there for Christmas, or as long as you can stay."

"Oh, Mum, that would be nifty!" Sophie glowed with excitement.

"Now that Dad's not racing anymore, we don't have to be in Florida every winter," Ria said. She and Chas felt that travel formed an important part of their children's education, particularly when it gave them a chance to practice other languages, so they always took along a tutor to ensure that the kids kept up their studies.

"Are you certain there isn't another race on the Riviera that you want to win, Chas?" Esme asked with a grin. "We haven't been there since Adam and Amy were three, and Brooke hasn't been at all," she added, referring to her children. "April in Antibes is divine!"

Chas laughed. "Sorry to disappoint you, Esme, but there's always room for you at Cousin Bea's villa anyway. No, I'm leaving the racing to the youngsters. Besides, it's not actually fun going a hundred miles an hour on the water. The spray feels like glass shards trying to carve off your flesh at the same time as your bones are being rattled apart." Racing had become almost suicidal. One of his former RFC colleagues died a few years ago in a crash while setting a world speed record on Lake Windermere in England.

"And Ellie reminds us that spending a king's ransom on something as frivolous as race boats is unconscionable in these dire times," Ria added.

"I wouldn't expect anything less from her," Zoë said.

"But Ellie's not impressed that half a million people still come to the races," Chas said. "She claims they're just waiting for some rich nob to crash and burn."

They laughed.

"The Boatworks is doing well, though, isn't it, Stephen?" Freddie asked. "I heard that Ditchburn is in trouble again, and may not survive this time."

"Thankfully, our Seawind line is thriving. It's the custom-designed orders that have dropped off," Stephen explained.

"You and Mac were very wise to insist on those stock runabouts," Chas admitted. "They're beautiful and fast, and give the impression of being custom-built. But just because I'm no longer racing doesn't mean that I won't be commissioning more boats. We have to keep trying new designs. *Windrunner X.*"

"You're as bad as a woman who always needs the latest Paris fashions!" Ria accused.

"On the contrary, my darling. We're the ones creating the styles."

They heard the distant ringing of the telephone, and Philip said, "I do find that oddly intrusive here."

"You only want to hear the mosquitoes buzzing around your ears," Sophie teased.

"Not to worry; the telephone exchange closes down at 9:00 and doesn't open again until well after the loons have roused you in the morning," Ria informed her son-in-law with a smile. She was delighted to realize that she essentially had another son, even if it was strange that he was Lance's.

Grayson came into the dining room and said to Jack, "There's a call for you, Mr. Wyndham."

Jack took it in the library. On the other end of the line, the Thorncliff butler said, "I'm sorry to disturb your evening, Sir, but a telegram has just arrived from your sister-in-law in Paris, and I thought it might be important."

"Of course. Perhaps you could read it to me, Foster."

There was a rustling of paper and Foster said, "I'm afraid it's in French, Sir."

"Ah, yes. Spell it out, would you?"

Jack jotted down the words, and hung up the phone with a dozen thoughts whirling through his head. He found Grayson outside in the hallway. "Would you ask my sister to come to the library, Grayson?"

Jack went back in and poured two cognacs from the drinks trolley.

"Jack? What's wrong?" Lizzie asked. "Has something happened to Maman? It isn't Claire, is it?"

He put his hands on her shoulders. "Étienne's been killed in a car crash."

She was stunned. "Oh, thank God!" she breathed as she went into his arms. "I'm finally free!"

So was he, Jack thought. Véronique wouldn't be interested in blackmailing him. Fearful that her beauty was disappearing, she had recently married a wealthy, self-indulgent and somewhat decadent industrialist with homes all over France.

Jack had control of the winery, in any case, and would now look after it for his nephews. With profits no longer being siphoned off by their father, the winery would provide them with a secure future.

And Lizzie could finally marry Lyle, who was divorced from Adele. He and Lizzie had been having a clandestine affair for eight years, and both were heartily sick of the secrecy and not being able to be together all the time. Lizzie spent half of each year in Canada, and Lyle had found business to take him to France annually. He understood her not being able to divorce Étienne because she would lose her boys, but had already built a cottage on Wistful Island in anticipation of sharing it with her.

Her tears might have been seen by some as sorrow, although family and close friends knew what a sham her marriage had become. But she did grieve for her boys, whose father had always appeared to be perfect, when he found time for them. Thankfully, they liked "Uncle" Lyle as much as he did them.

•   •   •

Because Ria considered traditions important, the usual summer balls and activities were still held. Sadly, some friends no longer came to Muskoka, their cottages remaining shuttered these past few years, and a couple had even been sold to those whose fortunes had not tumbled.

But Ria knew that most of her family and friends had much to be grateful for. So the Dominion Day Ball also celebrated Justin Carrington's winning a Liberal seat in the Ontario Legislature in the June election, his party achieving an overwhelming majority after a long Conservative reign. As a result, Justin had sold the *Launston Mills Observer*, which he had inherited, to Arthur and Alice, knowing that his grandfather would have been delighted that the paper was in such competent hands.

Alice was having success with an engaging novel she had written based on Grandfather Keir's stories. Unfortunately, the old gentleman had not lived to see it finished. She and Arthur were happily entrenched in Launston Mills with their two children.

The Spirit Bay Children's Retreat had a waiting list, despite a couple of expansions. Ria and Chas were proud of Thomas Mayhew for graduating top of his class at the Bracebridge high school. They had financed his room and board in the town for five years, there still being no schooling beyond eighth grade available in Port Darling. Now he had won a Thornton scholarship to study medicine at the University of Toronto, maintaining that his ambitions stemmed from years of watching Doctor Ellie at the Retreat.

Pineridge Inn was surviving the downturn in tourism because it attracted the moneyed professionals, thanks to Esme's influence. Zoë and Freddie were happy and remarkably well suited, and had a four-year-old daughter as well as a son. Max was gaining recognition for his haunting symphonies.

Ria tried to ignore the fact that her father wasn't well. Why should she care when they'd never had a good relationship? But it irked her that Helena had grown bitter and reproachful since the '29 crash. Their economies now allowed for only one servant, and they had managed to keep their Toronto home, but Jack had purchased their Palm Beach estate at a rock-bottom price. Helena's constant recriminations - echoed by eighteen-year-old "Princess" Cecilia, who had expected to be an heiress - were taking a toll on James.

At least Ria managed to get Jimmy away from that toxic atmosphere as much as possible, and he loved spending time with her family. If he was mentally a bit simple, he was honest and transparent, and thoroughly likeable. With additional lessons from professionals, he had become an amazing artist. Ria enjoyed going on painting outings with her little brother, and was now learning from him.

So when the children presented Elyse's play to much acclaim from family and friends, life was still good.

•   •   •

"Watch it, kid!" Luke Miller said, brushing Sylvia aside. He and his friends had just finished a round of golf and were coming out of the Country Club bar lounge. At seventeen, he was still too young to drink legally, so the boys had bought cokes and were now going to add their own supply of booze, out on the patio.

"I think I know you," she stated, looking at him curiously.

He stopped and eyed her, but dismissed the gangly twelve-year-old, who was too young to be flirting with him. "I don't think so, kid. You're a Wyndham, aren't you?"

"Sylvia Robbins."

"Jeez! Crazy Phoebe's daughter! I was told to stay away from you."

"Dry up, Miller!" one of Edgar's twins warned as they bracketed Sylvia protectively.

"What? I can't speak the truth around here? You Nazis or something?" Luke asked the twins. His friends laughed. "Everybody knows that Phoebe's off her rocker."

"Just ignore him," Matt said to his cousin.

But she had felt a tangible connection with Luke. Perhaps she knew him in a different dimension. That was how she sensed things about people, and how she could sometimes bend them to her will. She stared at Luke's back now, compelling him to turn around.

He did, looking puzzled. How very strange that she seemed to be gazing into her own eyes.

•   •   •

"Hard to believe it was twenty years ago that Grandmother died and our world suddenly changed," Ria said to Chas. They were, as usual, sitting on the veranda reading the morning mail and newspapers. "That was the day that you told me you were going to join the RFC, and I was so terrified that I might never see you again." She recalled how desperately in love she had been, with that needy, burning, youthful passion that had mellowed over the years into what Chas had once called "the abiding love that requires that second chair on the dock."

As if sensing her thoughts, he reached over to take her hand and kiss it. "I rather fancy that it was because your formidable grandmother left us that the world fell apart," he said.

Ria laughed. "She would love to hear you say that! And according to Phoebe, she probably just did!" Ria looked around, not totally dismissing her cousin's ghostly visions. "I do still wonder how Grandmother could have fallen off the cliff path. But I know that news of the war had upset her, and Ellie said she could have had a dizzy spell or even a mild stroke, which unbalanced her."

"She was a feisty old lady, and I recall that she was much too proud to use a cane, despite her need of one. I trust you won't become that stubborn when we totter over to the Shimmering Sands, and take up where we left off all those years ago," he said, reminding her of their lovemaking.

She chuckled, and gripped his hand tightly. How delicious and daring their trysts had been amidst the fears of Chas going off to war. And how innocent she and Chas had been, nonetheless.

Augusta's dying wish was that Ria would marry Justin Carrington, so Ria really hoped that Grandmother *could* see them now, and realize that Chas was her soul mate, without whom she would never feel complete. Justin, along with his wife, Toni, would forever be among her dearest and staunchest friends.

She recalled that in her final letter, Augusta had also warned Ria about Jack, saying that although she admired him, she didn't trust him. *He was too hungry, and money would always be his first love, for which he would do anything and use everyone to get ahead,* she had written. Grandmother had sadly misjudged him, since it was thanks to Jack's sage advice that most of the Wyndhams had not lost all their money in the '29 Crash. She would surely be proud of him as well. The Thorntons had been Augusta's favourite people, and having two of her grandchildren marry into that family would have delighted her. Jack and Fliss were obviously happy, and he was devoted to their three children.

"Despite everything, we've been lucky," Ria said. "And even if we don't have half-a-dozen children of our own, there's never a shortage of young people around."

"Who all adore their indulgent Aunt Ria, who never acts her age," Chas teased.

"That's because I'm still eighteen inside," she replied with a grin. She felt both older and younger than her thirty-eight years.

"I don't doubt it!" His loving glance warmed and reassured her. "Which is why I'm surprised you're not inside cavorting with the kids."

It was a drizzly morning, so the children were dancing to gramophone records in the sitting room. Rafe and his bride were at the Saratoga Springs races, and Elyse was once again staying at The Point.

A Gershwin tune drifted out to the veranda:
I got rhythm
I got music
I got my girl
Who could ask for anything more?

"I may just do that after I finish reading the mail," Ria said.

"Well, I should respond to some business letters." Chas kissed her cheek before going into the library. En route, he smiled as he heard Sophie say to the others, "Remember when we practiced the Charleston for hours on end on the boathouse deck?"

"I sure do, although Drew was probably too little," Charlie replied. "You two were wicked, but are you too old now?" he razzed Sophie and Philip.

"Watch us!" Sophie retorted with a laugh.

Drew went to the storage cupboard and hauled out a photo album. "Mummy took pictures of us."

He, Charlie, and Elyse sat on the sofa to browse through them.

"Here we are at the cousins' party," Elyse pointed out. "I loved that dress. Aunt Ria bought it in Paris for my birthday."

"Girls! Always thinking about how you look," Charlie ribbed.

Elyse stared at one of the snapshots of Charlie, and then looked hard at Drew. He had Ria's startling turquoise eyes, while Charlie's were a gentler blue. Like Chas's. But, of course, you couldn't see that difference in the black-and-white picture. Elyse raised a skeptical eyebrow to Charlie, reminding him of their conversation earlier this summer.

In the photograph, he was the same age as Drew was now. Charlie examined it more closely. And felt a flash of emotion so intense he couldn't even define it. He grabbed the picture from the black corners that secured it to the page and marched into the library, slamming the door behind him.

"Charlie?" Chas noticed how pale he was, and taut, as if he were in danger of bursting apart.

Charlie threw the photo onto the desk in front of Chas. "Why does Drew look so much like me?"

"Sit down, Charlie."

"No!"

"I was going to tell you before you went off to England."

Charlie's heart was pounding so violently he thought it might leap from his chest.

"I met your mother during the war, when I was in a deep funk and she was lonely, and we had a... relationship."

His legs suddenly too weak to hold him upright, Charlie sank into a chair.

"So you are my son."

The words that Charlie had been longing to hear all his life were tainted and tasted vile. "Your bastard, you mean," he hissed. "Why didn't you marry her?"

"Because I was in love with Mummy Ria, and we were engaged."

"You're the bastard! How could you have just left Maman? And me?" He forced back tears.

"That relationship was never meant to happen."

"And I was just a mistake," Charlie concluded bitterly.

"I provided for you, Charlie, and then we adopted you when we had the opportunity."

"So why did you never tell me?"

"Because you were too young to understand how your life could be ruined if society knew you were actually my bastard. You are now my legitimate son. That's all the world needs to know."

Charlie shook his drooped head as if to dislodge all these bizarre words and thoughts. His eyes glistening, he looked accusingly at Chas. "You're ashamed of me. You don't want to acknowledge me as a true son."

"It's not that simple, Charlie. Reputation is critical in our world. What would you have said to Cecilia's taunts when you were Drew's age? Wouldn't you have been tempted to put her in her place, if you had known?"

"Bastard! Bastard!" Charlie muttered, referring to himself and Chas.

"Remember what I said to you after you ran away? I told you that you were as much my son as Drew. But of course you didn't realize how true those words were."

Charlie looked up with tears trickling down his face. "All my life I've longed to know my father and be with him, and now I just feel... cheated. So many wasted years."

Chas got up and went over to Charlie, gripping his shoulder hard, struggling with his own emotions. "Not wasted, Charlie. We've been together."

"But I didn't KNOW!"

"Does that truly matter? We've been a happy family, haven't we? I love you, son."

Charlie shrugged him off and jumped up from his chair. "No! It's not that easy for me to accept and forgive! I HATE you!"

He stomped out of the room, nearly colliding with Ria.

"Charlie, what's wrong?" she asked.

He brushed her off roughly. "He chose YOU!"

Charlie dashed from the room, and she could hear his footsteps pounding down the hillside staircase to the boathouse. The others in the sitting room were astonished and just gaped at each other. "Jeez, I was right!" Elyse muttered to herself, surprised, and sorry now that she had pointed out the resemblance.

Ria went into the library, where Chas was pouring a large cognac and trying to compose himself.

She knew instantly. "He found out, didn't he?" she said, after she had closed the door behind her.

"It shouldn't have happened this way," Chas replied, running a hand through his hair in agitation. He indicated the snapshot on the desk.

"Bloody hell! I never realized how much Drew resembles him."

"It's not usually that obvious. Just this instant that you captured shows that they are unmistakably brothers."

They heard the roar of an engine. "He's taking a boat out, although he's obviously much too distraught to be on his own right now. We have to do something, Chas!"

"We can't go after him, Ria. He's virtually an adult, and needs time to himself, to work out his anger. To deal with the sense of betrayal. The realization that we've been living with secrets and lies all these years. You were right, Ria. I should have told him that time he ran away. He was still enough of a child to have appreciated and forgiven me."

Ria took him into her arms. He clasped her tightly, saying, "He may rebel, but he won't do anything stupid, my darling."

Perhaps not deliberately, Ria thought, but what if his rage drove him to be reckless. She recalled how she had felt that day she ran away, twenty years ago. There had been moments when she was so unhappy that she really didn't care what became of her.

So she was anxious until she heard the boat return.

The others had been curious, of course, and were told that it was for Charlie to reveal why he was upset, if he chose to.

But he ignored them all and went to his room. Drew followed him, and found him tossing things into the suitcase he had pulled out from under his bed.

"Charlie, what're you doing?" He could sense that something really bad had happened to his brother, and was scared.

"Going away!" Charlie snapped without looking at him.

"But you're not supposed to leave for weeks yet!"

"Buzz off, Drew! I'm busy."

"I don't want you to go, Charlie."

"Get lost!"

"What's eating you, anyway?" Drew said glumly, slumping down on his own bed.

Charlie glared at him, but his vehemence suddenly diminished when he realized that Drew really was his brother. "You know how I've always wanted to fly? Well, now I'm going to."

"But Daddy..."

"I don't care what he says! I'm joining the Air Force. He can't stop me."

Drew brightened. "Will you take me up for a ride?"

"We'll see. Now let me finish packing."

After Drew confided Charlie's plans to Ria, she went up to the boys' room. Steeling herself, she knocked, but didn't wait for an answer.

"I know that you're upset and resentful and want to run away. But you can't just dismiss all the love that we've given you, Charlie. You're an important part of our family."

He didn't look at her, but just kept shoving things into his suitcase.

"I forgave your father for betraying me. War takes a terrible toll on all of us, and sometimes we just muddle through to survive. Try to understand and forgive him, too."

He was a bit shocked by those words, realizing that Chas had cheated on Ria, not on his mother. "I can't."

"Perhaps not this instant, but give it time. Be open to it. And don't do anything rash."

"I'm not. You know I've always wanted to be a pilot. I figure I don't owe it to Dad to do what *he* thinks I should. So I guess I'm my own man now."

"You are, but you will also always be my petit poussin."

He tried to hide his tears.

Ria kissed his cheek. "We cherish you and have always been proud of you. And I know you'll do the right thing."

When she left him, he gave in to his tears. But he was coolly composed when he went downstairs with his luggage.

"If you're determined to leave, I'll drive you to the train station," Chas offered. He wasn't pleased that Charlie was planning to join the RCAF, and hoped that he might be rejected. But he also realized that at this moment, he had no influence on his son's decisions.

"I'd rather you didn't. Stephen's here today, so he can take me."

"Charlie... Let me know if I can help in any way." Chas patted his shoulder.

Charlie refused to look at him as he replied sarcastically, "As Chas Thornton's *son*, I shouldn't have any problem being accepted by the RCAF."

Because she knew him so well, Ria noticed Chas's distress, and pleaded, "Keep in touch, and come home whenever you can." She embraced Charlie, and felt hopeful when he hugged her back, even if not as enthusiastically as usual.

The others accompanied him to the boathouse.

"Do you want to talk?" Sophie asked.

"Not at the moment. I'm sorry I'm not coming to England with you, but I'll write." He hugged her tightly.

Philip shook his hand, "Best of luck, old boy. I hope you like the Air Force as much as Chris does."

When Elyse hugged him, she whispered, "At least they wanted you."

For a moment he saw past her nonchalance to the hurt little girl whose mother had blithely abandoned her and whose father had little time for her.

Damn her for making him feel guilty about his own anger and pain! But he smiled sadly at her, and kissed her cheek. "Look after yourself. Cousin."

"You'll be back, won't you?" she asked hopefully.

He wasn't about to forsake her as well. "You bet."

Watch for more novels by Gabriele Wills at
Mindshadows.com

Online support for the author is greatly appreciated. If you enjoy her novels, visit Mindshadows.com for links to "Like" her on Facebook and other social media.

Comments and questions are always welcome by email at info@mindshadows.com

Author's Notes

The following notes might answer some readers' questions:

- Many of those who survived the Spanish Influenza of 1918 suffered aftereffects, some for the rest of their lives.
- Although Billy Bishop and Will Barker had already formed Bishop-Barker Aeroplanes Limited in 1919, they didn't fly into Muskoka until the summer of 1920.
- Port Darling is based on Port Carling – the name changed to allow for artistic licence. The fictional 1919 fire echoed the "great fire" of 1931.
- There was sometimes conflict between the Ojibwa at the Indian Camp and the villagers. James Bartleman, former Lieutenant-Governor of Ontario, gives a fascinating account of growing up as a "half-breed" in Port Carling in his memoir, *Raisin Wine*.
- Fictional Pineridge Inn is typical of the many struggling farmsteads that evolved to become popular summer resorts. Cleveland's House on Lake Rosseau is one of the very few that have survived to this day.
- Prohibition in Canada was complex, as it was provincially dictated and enforced. Ontario was one of the last provinces to repeal "temperance" laws when, in 1927, strict government control was introduced with the Liquor Control Board of Ontario (LCBO).
- Tuberculosis (TB or consumption) was one of the major causes of death in those days. Before the discovery of antibiotics, the only treatments for TB were as outlined in the novel.
- The Lakeview Sanatorium is based on the Calydor Sanatorium in Gravenhurst. It closed down during the Depression in 1935, when many patients could no longer afford private care. (The larger, government-subsidized Muskoka Sanitarium was nearby.) The site is now a public park, where you can find Claire's secret rock.
- Details of the Prince of Wales's Canadian tour in 1919 are based on his and other accounts. Because he bought a ranch in Alberta, he came to Canada unofficially other years, including 1923, when he travelled incognito as Lord Renfrew.
- Commodore Harry Greening was a true "gentleman" boat racer, whose innovative ideas helped to expand the

boundaries of boat design. Also setting new world records, he was highly respected in the boat racing fraternity.

- There were a few women who raced boats in the 1920s, like the eccentric British heiress, Marion Barbara "Joe" Carstairs, who drove ambulances during WW1, and who tested her racer on Lake Muskoka in the summer of 1929.

- Between the wars, boat racing was a big sport on the Muskoka lakes, as well as internationally. It was not unusual for races like the APBA Gold Cup and the Harmsworth Trophy to have half a million spectators, even during the Depression.

- The Banff Springs Hotel closed for winters until 1968.

- The Commonwealth War Graves Commission cemeteries in France and Belgium are beautifully maintained, and a moving tribute to the vast numbers of dead. The cemetery at Etaples – mentioned in the book - is the largest in France with over 11,000 graves.

- The Muskoka Assembly of the Chautauqua was established on Tobin Island in 1921 by the Reverend Charles S. Applegath. It sought to combine spiritual, educational, and cultural enrichment in a magnificent setting that also encouraged healthy outdoor activities. Applegath was a great promoter of Canadian literature, and by 1928, the Assembly had become known as "Canada's Literary Summer Capital". The Muskoka Chautauqua was revived in 2010, and I was thrilled that my novel, *The Summer Before the Storm*, was chosen for its prestigious Reading List.

- Poet Wilson MacDonald was a frequent visitor at the Muskoka Assembly. That the setting inspired him is evident in the stanzas quoted from his poem "Muskoka" in the introduction to this novel.

- Martin Daventry's plane crash with Billy Bishop is based on a real one, which effectively ended Bishop's flying career at that time.

- The Huckleberry Rock is now a public park, and can be accessed from the Milford Bay Road off Hwy. 118, between Bracebridge and Port Carling.

- The Massasauga rattlesnake is an endangered species, found in only a few areas of Ontario, including parts of Muskoka. The method of dealing with snakebites illustrated in the novel was advocated by several medical texts even as late as the 1950s, but is now considered mostly ineffective, and possibly harmful. Antivenin (or antivenom) was developed for North American rattlesnakes in the late 1920s and is considered the only viable treatment.

- Marijuana was not made illegal in Canada until 1923.
- The Sagamo's popular 100 Mile Cruise began in 1923, not 1922 as portrayed in the novel.
- You can still experience the spirit of the era aboard the R.M.S. Segwun, North America's oldest operating steamship, which sails out of Gravenhurst. While there, be sure to visit the Muskoka Boat and Heritage Centre, which has North America's only in-water exhibit of impressive antique boats that are still in use.
- L.M. Montgomery vacationed at the Roselawn Lodge in Bala in 1922, which inspired her adult novel, *The Blue Castle*. It's well worth a visit to "Bala's Museum with Memories of Lucy Maud Montgomery", and having a tour conducted by the enthusiastic and knowledgeable owners, Jack Hutton and Linda Jackson-Hutton.
- The renowned Homewood Sanitarium in Guelph – to which Phoebe went for treatments for schizophrenia – is now the Homewood Health Centre.
- There was a large ex-pat community in Paris – some 30,000 Americans by 1924 – with many being artists, writers, musicians, and intellectuals. Ernest Hemingway was a reporter for the *Toronto Star* in Paris in the early 1920s.
- Zelda and Scott Fitzgerald rented the Villa St. Louis in Juan-les-Pins, which became the Hotel Belles Rives in 1929, and is still operating as such. It was never the Villa Blackthorn, of course.
- The incidents involving the Fitzgeralds, described in the novel, are based on actual events.
- Sara and Gerald Murphy are credited with making the Riviera a popular summer destination, especially for Americans. Until then, the season was September to April. Ironically, the luxurious Hotel du Cap now closes for the winter months.
- The kidnapping and murder of Charles Lindbergh's infant son in 1932 sent shock waves through the affluent community that hadn't been devastated by the 1929 stock market crash and consequent Depression. An American family on "Millionaires' Row" at Beaumaris did indeed install secret passageways in the boathouses used by the children, so that they could escape if threatened.

- By 1934 there were already signs and fears that another global conflict was imminent. WWII began in 1939, and would have involved the children born before 1926 – thus many of those introduced in the novel.
- The novel set in Launston Mills that Alice wrote might well have been *A Place to Call Home*. Visit mindshadows.com for more info.
- Kit Spencer from my novel, *Moon Hall*, is the granddaughter of Zoë and Freddie.
- Great care was taken to realistically portray the era. For example, although some expressions may sound very modern to our ears, all slang was verified through *The Oxford Dictionary of Slang*. Research materials included hundreds of books and other sources.

For additional information, including reviews, bibliography, and sample chapters of Gabriele's other novels, please visit *Mindshadows.com* or theMuskokaNovels.com

About the Author

Gabriele Wills

Born in Germany, Gabriele emigrated to Canada as a young child. She is a graduate of the University of Toronto, with an Honours B.Sc. and a B.Ed. in the social sciences and English. As an educator, she has taught in secondary, elementary, and private schools, and worked as a literacy coordinator for two newspapers. For ten years she operated a part-time website design business.

Writing, however, is Gabriele's real love. Her passion is to weave compelling stories around meticulously researched historical context in order to bring the past to life.

She grew up in Lindsay, Ontario, enjoyed several years in Ottawa, and currently resides in Guelph. Although she has relished many visits to Muskoka, she also finds inspiration at the family cottage in the Kawartha Lakes.

Other Books by Gabriele Wills:

The Summer Before the Storm
Book 1 of the Muskoka Novels

Muskoka, 1914. It's the Age of Elegance in the summer playground of the affluent and powerful. Amid the island-dotted lakes and pine-scented forests of the Canadian wilderness, the young and carefree amuse themselves with glittering balls and friendly competitions. This summer promises to be different when the ambitious and destitute son of a disowned heir joins his wealthy family at their cottage on Wyndwood Island. Through Jack's introduction into the privileged life of the aristocratic Wyndhams and their social circle, he seeks opportunities and alliances to better himself, including in his schemes, his beautiful and audacious cousin, Victoria.

But their charmed lives begin to unravel with the onset of the Great War, in which many are destined to become part of the "lost generation".

This richly textured tale takes the reader on an unforgettable journey from romantic moonlight cruises to the horrific sinking of the *Lusitania*, from regattas on the water to combat in the skies over France, from extravagant mansions to deadly trenches - from innocence to nationhood.

The Summer Before The Storm, the first of the epic Muskoka Novels, evokes a gracious, bygone era that still resonates in this legendary land of lakes.

The Summer Before The Storm was selected for the esteemed Muskoka Chautauqua Reading List in 2010.

Elusive Dawn
Book 2 of The Muskoka Novels

Elusive Dawn continues to follow the lives, loves, and fortunes of the privileged Wyndham family and their friends. While some revel in the last resplendent days of the season at their Muskoka cottages, others continue to be drawn inexorably into the Great War, going from a world of misty sunrises across a tranquil lake to deadly moonlight bombing raids, festering trenches, and visceral terror.

For Victoria Wyndham, too many things have happened to hope that life would ever return to normal, that innocence could be regained. Caught in a vortex of turbulent events and emotions, she abandons the safety of the sidelines in Britain for the nightmare of France. Her fate as an ambulance driver remains entwined with those of her summer friends, all bound by a sense of duty.

Living in the shadows of fear and danger awakens the urgency to grasp life, to live more immediately, more passionately amid the enormity of unprecedented death. Those who survive this cataclysmic time are forever changed, like Canada itself.

Impeccably researched, beautifully written, *Elusive Dawn* will resonate with the reader long after the final page has been turned.

A Place to Call Home

Set in the turbulent, formative years of Ontario, this compelling saga spans five decades and two generations. Barely surviving a disastrous journey on a cholera-ridden immigrant ship, Rowena O'Shaughnessy and her family settle in the primitive backwoods of Upper Canada in 1832. Her complex relationship with the wealthy and powerful Launston family leads to tragedy, and eventually to redemption.

Their lives are played out against a rich tapestry of events - devastating plagues, doomed rebellions, mob uprisings, religious conflict, and political unrest.

A Place to Call Home is a novel about Canada, and its less civilized pioneer past.

Moon Hall

Two women who live a century apart. Two stories that interweave to form a rich tapestry of intriguing characters, evocative places, and compelling events.

Escaping from a disintegrating relationship in the city, writer Kit Spencer stumbles upon a quintessential Norman Rockwell village in the Ottawa Valley, where she buys an old stone mansion, "Moon Hall". But her illusions about idyllic country life are soon challenged by reality. Juxtaposed is the tragedy of Violet McAllister, the ghost that reputedly haunts Moon Hall, who comes vividly to life through her long-forgotten diary.

Moon Hall is a gripping tale of relationships in crisis, and touches on the full spectrum of human emotions – from raw violence and dark passions to compassion and love.

Music Quoted in *Under the Moon*:

(M = Music, L = Lyrics)

The Alcoholic Blues – 1919 - Albert Von Tilzer (M), Edward Laska (L)
Anything Goes - 1934 – Cole Porter
I Got Rhythm – 1930 - George Gershwin (M), Ira Gershwin (L)
I'll See You In My Dreams – 1924 - Isham Jones (M), Gus Kahn (L)
Jazz Baby – 1919 - Blanche Merrill and M.K. Jerome
Let's Misbehave – 1927 - Cole Porter
My Buddy – 1922 - Walter Donaldson (M), Gus Kahn (L)
A Pretty Girl is Like a Melody – 1919 - Irving Berlin
Toot, Toot, Tootsie, Goo'Bye – 1922 - Gus Kahn, Ernie Erdman, and Dan
　　Russo
Whispering – 1920 - Vincent Rose (M), John Schoenberger and Richard
　　Coburn (L)

Music Mentioned in *Under the Moon*:

Blue Skies – 1926 – Irving Berlin
Blues My Naughty Sweetie Gives to Me – 1919 - N. Swanstone, Charles R.
　　McCarron, and Carey Morgan
By the Beautiful Sea – 1914 - Harry Carroll (M), Harold Atteridge (L)
By the Light of the Silvery Moon – 1909 - Gus Edwards (M), Edward
　　Madden (L)
The Charleston – 1923 - James P. Johnson (M), Cecil Mack (L)
For Me and My Gal – 1917 - George W. Meyer (M), Edgar Leslie and E.
　　Ray Goetz (L)
If You Knew Susie – 1925 - B.G. DeSylva
If You Were the Only Girl in the World – 1916 - Clifford Grey (L), Nat D.
　　Ayer (M)
In the Good Old Summertime – 1902 - George Evans (M), Ren Shields (L)
The Maple Leaf Rag – 1899 – Scott Joplin
The Midnight Trot – 1916 - George Linus Cobb
Moonlight Bay – 1912 - Percy Wenrich (M), Edward Madden (L)
Pretty Baby – 1916 - Tony Jackson and Egbert Van Alstyne (M), Gus
　　Kahn (L)
Ragtime Nightingale – 1914 - Joseph Francis Lamb
Russian Rag – 1918 - George Linus Cobb
Shine on Harvest Moon – 1908 - Nora Bayes-Norworth (M), Jack
　　Norworth (L)
That's a Plenty – 1919 - Lew Pollack (M), Ray Gilbert (L)
The Vamp – 1919 - Byron Gay
You Made Me Love You – 1913 - James V. Monaco (M), Joe McCarthy (L)

Bruce County Public Library
1243 Mackenzie Rd.
Port Elgin ON N0H 2C6

CPSIA information can be obtained at www.ICGtesting.com
Printed in the USA
LVOW131509171012

303239LV00001B/95/P